Praise for Dan Simmons's

THE
FIFTH
HEART

"That somewhere in this tangle Holmes will succeed in solving the mystery of Clover Adams's death seems foregone. That Simmons will take us on some fancy side trips is the reason to read. He delivers a buddy comedy that stands with the best of them, full of arch conversations and delightfully silly supporting characters."

—Susann Cokal, *New York Times Book Review*

"It's a team-up you definitely never would have expected: Sherlock Holmes and Henry James. As strange as that pairing may sound, Simmons makes it work in this Victorian-era murder mystery. He combines the central dynamic of Conan Doyle's original Holmes stories—two opposite personalities working together to solve a crime—with the effusive prose and upper-class pageantry of a James novel....An engrossing literary mash-up." —Christian Holub, *Entertainment Weekly*

"Simmons has essentially written a literary buddy comedy, and the result is his funniest and breeziest novel to date....Even with a body of work as impressive as Simmons has accrued in the past thir' *The Fifth Heart* is one of his most engrossing and addictive k

— *Post*

"Outstanding....Simmons knows the   that expertise in the service of a highly   the beloved sleuth."   *Publishers Weekly*

"Is there a contemporary writer more   me in a multitude of genres—not to mention geographical locales and historical eras—than Dan Simmons?...The combination of Holmes's existential speculations with the complex mechanics of two intertwined investigations adds richness and complexity to what might otherwise have been a standard post-Doyle Sherlock Holmes tale....Simmons's version of Holmes is both instantly recognizable and subtly different....The result is a much more human portrait of the Great Detective than we usually encounter.... Watching this odd pair progress from the suicidal thoughts of the opening pages to a renewed sense of purpose is one of the central pleasures of this beguiling book."   —Bill Sheehan, *Washington Post*

"An amusing yarn featuring the unlikeliest of crime-fighting duos, Sherlock Holmes and Henry James....Simmons does an exemplary job of using the errors and inconsistencies in the Arthur Conan Doyle canon as a springboard for Holmes's metafictional musings on whether he exists or not. James proves a perfect foil for him: worried about appearances, reluctant to engage in any unpleasantness. Their prickly friendship...is what makes *The Fifth Heart* such an unexpected delight."
   —Michael Berry, *San Francisco Chronicle*

"A riveting mixture of historical fact and fiction....The book isn't just for Holmes fans—it's a solidly constructed, beautifully told mystery; a portrait of one of the nineteenth century's most important writers; and an intriguing blend of fact and fantasy. Fans of Simmons's special brand of historical metafiction should seek this one out."   —*Booklist*

"Brisk, funny, and a hell of a good time."   —Adam Morgan, *BookPage*

"A metafictional jeu d'esprit that dares to partner Sherlock Holmes with Henry James....*The Fifth Heart*'s dominant mode is suspense, not self-consciousness, and at its core is a good old-fashioned mystery....At 600 pages, this is a doorstopper to lose yourself in."
   —John O'Connell, *The Guardian*

"A gorgeously realized mystery....Simmons's eye for detail and his carefully constructed plot work so well that it's hard to stop reading."
   —Margaret Cannon, *Globe and Mail*

THE
FIFTH
HEART

THE
FIFTH
HEART

DAN SIMMONS

BACK BAY BOOKS
LITTLE, BROWN AND COMPANY
New York Boston London

This book is dedicated to Richard Curtis,
my invaluable agent and dear friend
and fellow fan of both baseball and Mr. Henry James

Copyright © 2015 by Dan Simmons

Back Bay Books / Little, Brown and Company
Hachette Book Group
1290 Avenue of the Americas, New York, NY 10104
littlebrown.com

Originally published in hardcover by Little, Brown and Company, March 2015
First Back Bay paperback edition, December 2015

Back Bay Books is an imprint of Little, Brown and Company, a division of Hachette Book Group, Inc. The Back Bay Books name and logo are trademarks of Hachette Book Group, Inc.

The publisher is not responsible for websites (or their content) that are not owned by the publisher.

The Hachette Speakers Bureau provides a wide range of authors for speaking events. To find out more, go to hachettespeakersbureau.com or call (866) 376-6591.

Library of Congress Cataloging-in-Publication Data
Simmons, Dan.
    The fifth heart / Dan Simmons. — First edition.
        pages ; cm
ISBN 978-0-316-19882-0 (hc) / 978-0-316-19879-0 (pb)
    1. Holmes, Sherlock—Fiction. 2. Private investigators—England—Fiction.
3. Murder—Investigation—Fiction. I. Title.
PS3569.I47292F54 2015
    813'.54—dc23
                                                        2014021881

10 9 8 7 6 5 4 3 2 1

RRD-C

Printed in the United States of America

PART 1

CHAPTER 1

In the rainy March of 1893, for reasons that no one understands (primarily because no one besides us is aware of this story), the London-based American author Henry James decided to spend his April 15 birthday in Paris and there, on or before his birthday, commit suicide by throwing himself into the Seine at night.

I can tell you that James was deeply depressed that spring, but I can't tell you for a certainty *why* he was so depressed. Of course there had been the death in England, from breast cancer, of his sister Alice a year earlier on March 6, 1892, but Alice had been a professional invalid for decades and had welcomed the diagnosis of cancer. Death, she'd told her brother Henry, was the event which she'd always been anticipating with the greatest enthusiasm. At least in his letters to family and friends, Henry had seemed to support her in her eagerness for an ending, down to describing how lovely her corpse had looked.

Perhaps this unchronicled depression in James was augmented by the problem of his work not selling well over the immediately preceding years: his 1886 novels *The Bostonians* and *The Princess Casamassima,* both influenced by Alice's slow dying and her Boston-marriage relationship with Katharine Loring, had been a major sales disappointment for all concerned, both in America and England. So by 1890 James had turned his quest for riches toward writing for the theater. Although his first melodramatic stage offering, *The American,* had done only moderately well, and that only in the provinces rather than in London, he'd convinced himself that the theater would turn out to be his ultimate pot of writer's gold. But already by early 1893, he was beginning to sense that this hope was both illusion and self-delusion. Just as Hollywood would beckon literary writers to their doom for more than a century to come, the English theater in the 1890's was sucking in men of letters who—like Henry James—really had no clue as to how to write a successful stage production for a popular audience.

Most biographers would understand this sudden, deep depression better if it were early spring of 1895 rather than March of 1893, since his first major London play, *Guy Domville*, two years hence will see him jeered and booed when he foolishly will step onto the stage to take his author's bow. Most of the paying spectators in the hall, as opposed to the many glittering ladies and gentlemen in attendance to whom James sent complimentary tickets, will have never read a novel by Henry James, most will not know he had written novels, and thus they will boo and jeer the play based on its merits alone. And *Guy Domville* will be a bad, bad play.

Even a year from now, after January of 1894 when his friend Constance Fenimore Woolson will throw herself to her death from a high window in Venice (possibly, some shall whisper, because Henry James had not come to stay near or with her in Venice as he'd promised), we know he will have to fight off a terrible depression tinged with real guilt.

By the end of 1909, the elderly James will fall into his deepest-depression yet—one so deep that his older (and dying from a heart condition) brother William will cross the Atlantic to literally hold Henry's hand in London. In those years, Henry James will be mourning the "disastrously low sales" and lack of profit from his 1906–1908 "New York Edition" of his works, an exhausting project to which he'd donated five years of his life rewriting the long novels and providing lengthy introductions to each piece.

But that final depression was sixteen years in our future in this March of 1893. We have no real clue as to why James was so terribly depressed that spring. Nor why he suddenly decided that suicide in Paris was his only answer.

One factor may have been the severe attack of the gout that James had suffered that cold English winter of 1892–93, cutting down on his daily walks and causing him to put on more weight. Or it could have been the simple fact that his upcoming birthday in April was his 50th: a landmark that has brought depression to stronger men than the sensitive Henry James.

We'll never know.

But we do know that the reality of that depression—and his plan for self-annihilation by drowning in the Seine on or before his April 15 birthday—is where this story begins. So, in mid-March, 1893, Henry James (he'd dropped the "Jr." sometime after his father died in 1882) wrote from London to family and friends saying that he was "taking a short leave from the daily duties of composition to celebrate spring and my own mid-century anniversary in sunlit Paris before joining my brother William and his family in Florence later in April". James had no intention of ever going to Florence.

Carrying some of his sister Alice's purloined ashes in a snuffbox, James left his tidied-up apartments in De Vere Gardens, burned some letters from Miss Woolson and from a few younger male friends, took the boat-train to Cherbourg, and arrived in the City of Light the next evening on a day darker and wetter and colder than any he'd suffered that March in chilly London.

There he settled into the Westminster Hotel on the Rue de la Paix where he'd once stayed for a month when he was writing several stories in Paris, including a favorite of his, "The Pupil". But this time, "settled in" was not the correct phrase. He had no intention of spending the weeks there until his birthday. Besides, the fares at the Westminster were too extravagant for his current budget. He did not even unpack his steamer trunk. He did not plan to spend a second night there. Or, he decided on a whim, a second full night anywhere on this earth.

After a wet, cold day walking in the Jardin de Tuileries and a dismal, lonely dinner—given his resolve, he'd made no effort to contact any of his Parisian friends or other acquaintances who might have been passing through Paris—Henry James drank a final glass of wine, tugged on his woolen overcoat, made sure that the sealed snuffbox was still in his pocket, and, with the bronze tip of his still-folded umbrella tapping on wet cobblestones, set off in the drizzle and darkness for his chosen final destination near Pont Neuf. Even at his portly gentleman's gait it was less than a ten-minute walk.

The ultimate man of the written word left no note behind.

CHAPTER 2

The place James had chosen from which to leave this life was on the north side of the river less than sixty yards from the broad, well-lighted bridge of le Pont Neuf, but it was dark there below the bridge, even darker on the promontory along the lowest level of walkways where the black, cold waters of the Seine swirled around the base of moss-darkened stone. Even in the daylight, this promontory was little used. Prostitutes, James knew, sometimes frequented the place at night, but not on a cold and drizzling March night such as this; tonight they stayed close to their hotels in Pigalle or stalked their furtive patrons in the narrow lanes on either side of the glowing Boulevard Saint Germain.

By the time James had umbrella-clacked his way to the narrow esplanade promontory that he'd picked out in the daylight—it had been just as he'd remembered it from earlier trips to Paris—he could no longer see to find his way. Distant street lamps across the Seine were ornamented with ironic halos by the rain. The barges and water taxis were few this night. James found his way down the final steps to the esplanade more by feel than by sight and tapped his way slowly beyond them like a blind man with a cane. Somewhere seemingly very far above, the usually distinctly pronounced sounds of carriage wheels and horses' hooves were muffled and made more distant, almost less real, by the worsening rain and deeply puddled thoroughfares.

James could sense and hear and smell the river's imminence rather than see it in the near-total darkness. Only the rather shocking emptiness of the point of his umbrella suddenly finding a void where pavement should be ahead brought him to a stop at the edge of what he knew to be the short, curved promontory. There were no steps going down to the river here, he knew: only a six- or seven-foot drop to the swirling black waters. The Seine ran fast and deep and wicked here. Now he could take one step forward into emptiness and it would be done.

James removed the small ivory snuffbox from his inner pocket and stood running his fingers across it for a moment. The motion made him remember a squib in *The Times* the previous year that claimed that the Eskimaux of the Arctic made no artwork to view, but shaped certain smooth stones to enjoy by touch during their many months of northern night. This thought made James smile. He felt he had spent enough of his own months in the northern night.

When he'd purloined a few pinches of his sister's ashes the previous year—Katharine Loring waiting just outside the door at the crematorium where she'd come to claim the urn she would take back to Cambridge and the Jameses' corner of the cemetery there—it had been with the sincere plan of spreading them at the place his younger sister had been most happy. But as the months passed, James had realized the impossibility of that idiot's mission. *Where?* He remembered her brittle happiness when they were both much younger and had traveled in Switzerland with their Aunt Kate, a lady as literal as Hamlet's by-the-card Grave Digger. Alice's already pronounced penchant for hysterical illnesses had receded somewhat during those weeks free from her larger family and American home—and his first thought for his fiftieth birthday was to travel to Geneva and spread her ashes where he and she had laughed and matched wits, with poor Aunt Kate understanding none of their ironic wordplay, happily teasing each other and Aunt Kate as they walked the formal gardens and lakeside promenades.

But, in the end, Geneva did not feel right to James. Alice had been play-acting her "recovery" from her destined life of invalidism during that trip, just as he had been play-acting his collusion with her brittle high spirits.

The point of land near Newport, then, where she'd built her little house and lived in apparent health and happiness for a year or so.

No. That had been her early days with Miss Loring and, James felt more grimly in every month that had passed since Alice's death, Miss Katharine P. Loring had had enough time and way with his sister. Not Newport.

So in the end he could think of no place to spread these few pitiful ashes where Alice had truly been happy. Perhaps she had glimpsed happiness, never really seized it, only during those months or years in Newport and then Cambridge, before what she called that "terrible summer" when her oldest brother William and Alice Gibbens were married on July 10, 1878. For years her brother William, her father, her brother Harry, brothers Bob and Wilkie, and an endless succession of visitors to their homes had kept up the joke that William would marry *her*—Alice James. Alice had always acted irritated at the running joke, but now—after her years of self-imposed invalidism and death—Henry James realized that she'd begun to believe in that marriage to William and had been all but destroyed when he married someone else. And someone else named, with cruel irony, Alice.

As she'd once put it to Henry James, that summer of William's marriage had been when she "went down to the deep sea, and the dark waves clouded over her."

So now, this night, this final night, James decided that he would merely hold tight to the snuffbox with its remnants of Alice's tentative existence as he stepped forward and fell into the black water and oblivion. To do this, he knew, he would have to shut his author's imagination down: no wondering in the second it will take to step forward as to whether the water will be freezing cold or whether, as the filthy water of the Seine began to fill his lungs, his atavistic urge for survival would cause him to thrash around, try to swim to the unclimbable mossy stone of the promontory.

No, he had to think of nothing but leaving his pain behind. Empty his mind of everything—always the hardest thing he'd ever tried to do.

James moved one foot forward, beyond the edge.

And suddenly realized that a dark shape he'd taken for a post was really the outline of a man standing not two feet from him. Seeing the dim outline of the soft hat pulled low and the silent figure's aquiline profile half-hidden by the turned-up collar of a traveler's cape-coat, James could now hear the man's soft breathing.

*   *   *

With a stifled gasp, James took two clumsy steps backward and to the side.

"*Pardonnez-moi, Monsieur. Je ne t'ai pas vu là-bas,*" he managed to say. It was the truth. He *hadn't* seen the man standing there.

"You're English," said the tall form. The man's English had a Scandinavian accent. Swedish? Norwegian? James was not sure which.

"Yes." James turned to go back up the steps and away from this spot.

At that moment a rare—for the season—Bateaux Mouches, part water taxi steamer, part tour-boat—passed by, and by the sudden light from the boat's starboard lanterns, James could clearly see the tall man's face.

"Mr. Holmes," he said almost involuntarily. In his surprise he stepped backward toward the river, his left heel went over the edge, and he would have ended up in the water after all if the tall man's right arm hadn't shot out with lightning speed. Long fingers grasped James's coat front in an amazingly firm grip and with one jerk the man pulled Henry James back onto the promontory.

Back to his life.

"What name did you just call me by?" asked the man, still tightly gripping James's coat front. The Scandinavian accent was gone now. The voice was distinctly upper-class British and nothing else.

"I am sorry," stammered James. "I must have been mistaken. I apologize for intruding upon your solitude here." At that second, Henry James not only knew the identity of the tall man—despite blacker hair than when he'd met him four years earlier, fuller hair somehow, now raised to odd spikes rather than slicked back, and a thick mustache that had been lacking four years ago, combined with a nose slightly altered with actor's putty or somesuch—but also knew that the man had been on the verge of throwing himself into the Seine when James had interrupted him with his arrival in the darkness announced by the tap-tap-tap of his ferule.

Henry James felt the fool at that moment, but he was a man on whom nothing was ever lost. Once he'd seen a face and learned its name, he never forgot.

He tried to move away, but the powerful fingers still gripped the front of his coat.

"What name did you call me by?" demanded the man again. His tone was as chill as iron in winter.

"I thought you were a man I'd met named Sherlock Holmes," gasped James, wanting only to get away, wanting only to be back in his bed in the comfortable hotel on the Rue de la Paix.

"Where did we meet?" demanded the man. "Who are you?"

James answered only the second part. "My name is Henry James." In his sudden panic, he'd almost added the long-abandoned "Jr."

"James," said Mr. Sherlock Holmes. "The younger brother of the great psychologist William James. You are the American scribbler who lives in London much of the time."

Even in his intense discomfort of being held and touched by another man, James felt an even stronger resentment at being identified as being the younger brother of the "great" William James. His older brother had not even been known, outside of small, tight Harvard circles, until he'd published his *The Principles of Psychology* three years earlier in 1890. The book, for reasons somewhat lost on Henry, had catapulted William to international fame among intellectuals and other students of the human mind.

"Please be so kind as to release me at once," said James in as stern a tone as he could muster. His outrage at being handled made him forget that Holmes—he was certain it was Sherlock Holmes—had just saved his life. Or perhaps that salvation was another mark against this hawk-nosed Englishman.

"Tell me when we met and I shall," said Holmes, still gripping the front of James's overcoat. "My name is Jan Sigerson. I am a Norwegian explorer of some renown."

"A thousand apologies then, sir," said James, feeling absolutely no apology in his heart. "I am obviously mistaken. For a second here, in the darkness, I thought you to be a gentleman I met four years ago at a tea-party benefit in Chelsea. The party was given by an American lady of my acquaintance, Mrs. T. P. O'Connor. I arrived with Lady Wolseley, you see, along with some other writers and artists of the stage—Mr. Aubrey Beardsley, Mr. Walter Besant... Pearl Craigie, Marie Corelli, Mr. Arthur Conan Doyle, Bernard Shaw, Genevieve Ward. During the tea, I was introduced to Mrs. O'Connor's house guest for the weekend, a certain Sherlock Holmes. I see now that there is... no real resemblance."

Holmes released him. "Yes, I remember now. I was there at Mrs. O'Connor's estate briefly while solving a series of country home jewel thefts. It was the servants, of course. It always is."

James straightened the front of his overcoat, arranged his cravat, firmly planted the tip of his umbrella, and resolved to leave Holmes's presence without another word.

Ascending the dark steps, he realized with a shock that Holmes was walking beside him.

"It's amazing, really," said the tall Englishman in the slight Yorkshire accent James had heard at Mrs. O'Connor's tea party in 1889. "I've used this Sigerson disguise for the past two years and passed close by—in daylight!—personages I've known for years, without their recognizing me. In New Delhi, in broad daylight in a sparsely populated square and for more than ten minutes, I stood next to Chief Inspector Singh, a man with whom I'd spent two months solving a delicate murder in Lahore, and the trained professional never glanced at me twice. Right here in Paris, I have passed by old English acquaintances and asked directions of my old friend Henri-August Lozé, the recently retired Prefect of Police for Paris with whom I'd worked on a dozen cases. With Lozé was the new Prefect de la Somme, Louis Lépine, with whom I have also had a close working relationship. Yet neither man recognized me. And yet you did. In the dark. In the rain. When you had nothing but self-murder on your mind."

"I *beg* your pardon," said James. He stopped out of sheer shock at Holmes's effrontery. They were on the street level now and the rain had subsided a bit. But the numerous street lamps there still held their halos.

"Your secret is safe with me, Mr. James," said Holmes. He was trying to light his pipe despite the damp. When the match finally flared, James could see even more easily that this was the "consulting detective" whom he'd met at Mrs. O'Connor's tea party four years earlier. "You see," continued Holmes, speaking now between puffs on the pipe, "I was there for the same purpose, sir."

James could think of no reply to that. He turned on his heel and headed west along the sidewalk. Holmes caught up to him with two strides of his longer legs.

"We need to go somewhere for a late meal and wine, Mr. James."

"I prefer to be alone, Mr. Holmes. Mr. Sigerson. Whomever you are pretending to be this night."

"Yes, yes, but we need to talk," insisted Holmes. He did not seem angered or perturbed by being found out. Or frustrated that his own suicide-by-Seine had been interrupted by the writer's arrival. Only fascinated that James had seen through his disguise.

"We have absolutely nothing to discuss," snapped James, trying to walk more quickly but only making himself look foolish in a portly way as the tall Englishman easily kept pace.

"We could discuss why you were ending your life with your sister Alice's ashes in a snuffbox clenched so tightly in your right hand," said Holmes.

James came to a full stop. After a moment he managed, "You... can...not...know...such a...thing."

"But I do," said Holmes, still working with his pipe. "And if you join me for a late snack and some good wine, I shall tell you how I know and why I know you will never complete the grim task you assigned yourself tonight, Mr. James. And I know just the clean, well-lighted café where we can talk."

Holmes grasped James's left elbow and the two began walking arm-in-arm up the Avenue de l'Opéra. Henry James was too shocked and astonished—and curious—to resist.

CHAPTER 3

Despite Holmes's promise to lead them to a "well-lighted place," James expected a dimly lighted out-of-the-way café opening onto some back alley. Instead, Holmes had brought him to the Café de la Paix, very near James's hotel and at the intersection of Boulevard des Capucines and Place de l'Opéra in the 9th arrondissement.

The Café de la Paix was one of the largest, brightest, and most vividly decorated establishments in all of Paris, rivaled in its elaborate décor and number of mirrors only by Charles Garnier's Opéra directly across the plaza. The place had been built, James knew, in 1862 to serve guests at the nearby Grand-Hôtel de la Paix and had come into its full fame during the Expo Exhibition of '67. It had been one of the first of Paris's public buildings to be lighted by electricity, but as if the hundreds or thousands of electric bulbs were not enough, bright lanterns with focal prisms still threw beams of light onto the grand mirrors. Henry James had avoided the place over the decades, if for no other reason than it was a common saying in Paris that to dine in the Café de la Paix meant one would eventually run into friends and acquaintances. The place was that popular. And Henry James preferred to choose the times and places that he would "run into" old acquaintances or friends.

Holmes seemed undisturbed by the crowds, the roar of conversation, and scores of eager faces looking up as they entered. James listened as the faux-Norwegian explorer requested his "usual table" from the maître d'—in fluent and properly accented French—and they were led to a small, round table somewhat away from the primary hustle and bustle of the buzzing establishment.

"You come here often enough to have a 'usual table'?" asked James when they were alone. Or as alone as they could be amidst such bustle and noise.

"I have dined here at least three times a week in the two months I've been in Paris," said Holmes. "I've seen dozens of acquaintances, former police partners in my detection business, and clients. None have looked twice at or through my Jan Sigerson disguise."

Before James could respond, the waiter appeared and Holmes had the effrontery to order quickly for the both of them. After designating a rather good champagne, and perhaps due to the late hour, he ordered a huge after-Opera assortment for two: *le lièvreen civet, pâtes crémeuses d'épeautre* accompanied by a *plateau de fromage affinés* and a concurrent platter of *la figue, l'abricot, le pruneau, en marmelade des fruits secs au thé Ceylan* and *biscuit spéculos,* concluding with *mousse légère chocolat.*

James had no appetite. His delicate stomach was upset by the shocks of the past hour. More than that, he did not care for hare—especially jugged hare with the heavy and grainy French wheat-sauce ladled on it—and this night he had no taste whatsoever for the fruit. And after indulging in it far too much when he was a small boy in France, he detested chocolate mousse.

He said nothing.

James was dying to know how Holmes—this cut-rate street-corner magus—"knew" that sister-Alice's ashes were in the snuffbox, but he would die rather than bring up the subject here in this public place. It was true, however, that between the din of chatting, laughing diners and the placement of their table, it would have been terribly hard for anyone to eavesdrop on them. But that was not the issue.

As they sipped the rather good champagne, Holmes said, "Did you read my obituary in *The Times* almost two years ago?"

"Friends brought it to my attention," said James.

"I read it. The paper was three weeks old—I was in Istanbul at the time—but I did get to read it. That and the later interview with poor Watson describing my death at Reichenbach Falls while struggling with the 'Napoleon of Crime', Professor James Moriarty."

Henry James would have preferred to stay silent, but he knew he was expected to fulfill his role as interlocutor.

"How *did* you survive that terrible fall, Mr. Holmes?"

Holmes laughed and brushed crumbs from his bristling black mustache. "There was no fall. There was no struggle. There was no 'Napoleon of Crime'."

"No Professor James Moriarty?" said James.

Holmes chuckled and dabbed at his lips and mustache with the white linen serviette. "None whatsoever, I am afraid. Invented from whole cloth for my own purposes...purposes of disappearance, in this event."

"But Watson has told *The Times* of London that this Professor Moriarty had authored a book—*The Dynamics of an Asteroid,*" persisted James.

"Also invented by me," said Holmes with a smug smile under the Sigerson mustache. "No such book exists. I cited it to Watson only so that he could later give the press—and his own inevitable publication of the events preceding Reichenbach Falls in his only recently released tale 'The Final Problem'—some...what do you authors call it?...verisimilitude. Yes, that's the word. Verisimilitude."

"But might not," said James, "after this detail has been mentioned in the various newspaper accounts of Moriarty and your demise, might not people attempt to find this *Dynamics of an Asteroid* book, even if just out of simple curiosity? If it does not exist, your entire Reichenbach Falls story must collapse."

Holmes laughed this away with a flick of his hand. "Oh, I stressed to Watson, who has in turn stressed to the press, that Moriarty's book was of the most unreadable and difficult advanced mathematics—I believe my exact words to Watson were 'it was a book which ascends to such rarefied heights of pure mathematics that it is said that there was no man in the scientific press capable of criticizing it'. *That* should give pause to the merely curious. I also remember telling Watson that so few copies of Moriarty's famous book—famous within mathematical circles only—were published that copies were extremely rare, perhaps not even findable today."

"So you deliberately lied to your friend about this...this 'Napoleon of Crime'...only so that Dr. Watson would repeat these total fabrications to the press?" said James, hoping that the chill in his tone would get through to Holmes.

"Oh, yes," said Holmes with a slight smile. "Absolutely."

James sat in silence for a while. Finally he said, "But what if Dr. Watson were called to give sworn testimony...perhaps in an inquest into your demise?"

"Oh, any such inquest would have been completed long before this," said Holmes. "It's been almost two years since Reichenbach Falls, after all."

"But still..." began James.

"Watson would not have been perjuring himself in such testimony," interrupted Holmes, showing the slightest hint of irritation now, "because he sincerely believed that Moriarty was, as I explained to him in such detail, the Napoleon of Crime. And Watson believes with equal sincerity that I died with Moriarty at Reichenbach Falls in Switzerland."

James blinked several times despite his best effort to show no reaction to this. "You have no remorse about lying to your best friend? The press has reported that Dr. Watson's wife has died in the interval since your...disappearance. So presumably the poor man is now mourning the loss of both his wife and his best friend."

Holmes helped himself to more fruit. "I did more than lie, Mr. James. I led Watson on a merry chase—pursuing the mythical Moriarty, you understand—across England and Europe, ending at the fabled waterfall from whose waters neither my body, nor Professor Moriarty's, shall ever be recovered."

"That was beastly," said James.

"That was necessary," Holmes said with no anger or emphasis. "I had to disappear completely, you see. Disappear without a trace and in a manner that convinced the multitudes—or at least that small share of the multitudes that has shown interest in my modest adventures—that I was dead. Was there much mourning in London upon news of my demise?"

James blinked at this and was sure it was levity. Sure, that is, until he saw the serious expression on Sherlock Holmes's disguised face.

"Yes," he said at last. "Or so I hear."

Holmes waited. Finally he said, "Watson's telling of the Reichenbach tale, his story called 'The Final Problem', appeared in *The Strand* only three months ago—December of 'ninety-two. But I'm curious about the reaction when the news stories appeared two years ago."

James resisted a sigh. "I don't read *The Strand*," he said. "But I'm told that young men in London, both when the news of your death was first published and then again this winter when Dr. Watson's story appeared, started wearing black armbands."

It was true that James would never read the kind of cheap-romance fiction and casual science-fact and household gossip that appeared in *The Strand*. But his younger friends Edmund Gosse and Jonathan Sturges both did. And both had worn black mourning armbands for months in solemn memory of Holmes's presumed death. James had thought it all ridiculous.

Sherlock Holmes was smiling as he finished the last of his mousse.

Henry James, still terrified that the conversation would turn back to the contents of his snuffbox if Holmes were allowed to guide it, said, "But why carry out such a hoax, sir? Why betray your good friend Dr. Watson and thousands of your loyal readers with such a ruse if there were no grand criminal conspiracy—no Napoleon of Crime—pursuing you? What could be your motive? Sheer perversity?"

Holmes set his spoon down and stared directly at the writer. "I wish it had been something so simple, Mr. James. No, I decided that I had to fake my own death and disappear completely because of discovering through my own ratiocination . . . through the inductive and deductive processes by which I've become the most famous consulting detective in the world . . . a fact so shocking that it not only irrevocably changed my life but led me, as you found me tonight by le Pont Neuf, ready to end it."

"What single fact could possibly . . ." began Henry James and then closed his mouth. It would be the worst of manners and presumptuousness to ask.

Holmes smiled tightly. "I discovered, Mr. James," he said as he leaned closer, "that I was not a real person. I am . . . how would a literary person such as yourself put it? I am, the evidence has proven to me most conclusively, a literary construct. Some ink-stained scribbler's creation. A mere fictional character."

CHAPTER 4

Henry James now knew beyond a doubt that he was dealing with a crazy person. Something had driven this Sherlock Holmes person—if this *was* the Sherlock Holmes he had met four years earlier at Mrs. O'Connor's garden party—to and beyond the raveled edge of rationality.

But the perverted truth was simple and shocking: James was fascinated with Holmes's delusion that he was a fictional character and he wanted to hear more about it. It struck him as a wonderful conceit for a short story someday—perhaps one involving a famous writer who also had descended into believing that he was one of his own characters.

Holmes had ordered cognac—a poor choice, James thought, after the champagne and late evening meal—but both men sipped it now as the writer worked to pose his questions. Suddenly a noisy commotion erupted in the terrace-covered area of the café across the wide dance floor from where they were seated. Dozens of people had gotten to their feet; men were bowing; a few applauded.

"It's the King of Bohemia," said Holmes.

Henry James wondered if he should humor the madman across from him and then decided not to.

"There is no King of Bohemia, Mr. Holmes," he said flatly. "That is the Prince of Wales. I've heard that he dines here from time to time."

Holmes, not sparing another glance at the royal party across the crowded room, sipped his cognac. "You really have *not* read any of Watson's chronicles of me in *The Strand*, have you, Mr. James?"

Before James could reply, Holmes continued, "One of his first published stories of our adventures—if, indeed, John Watson *was* the chronicler or author of these adventures—was titled 'Scandal in Bohemia' and dealt with an indelicate case—a former prima donna of the Imperial Opera of Warsaw using a certain photograph to blackmail, for...romantic indiscretions...a very famous member of a certain royal house. Watson, always discreet, invented the 'King of Bohemia' in his clumsy attempt to disguise the royal gentleman's true identity, which was, of course, our very own Prince of Wales. In truth, the 'scandal' was the second time I had helped the Prince out of a jam. The first time was with a potential scandal dealing with a debt incurred in card games." Holmes smiled above the rim of his cognac glass. "There is, of course, no 'Imperial Opera of Warsaw' either. Watson there was doing his earnest best to disguise the Paris Opéra."

"You are making up for Dr. Watson's attempts at discretion with amazing indiscretion," murmured James.

"I am dead," said Sherlock Holmes. "A dead man has little use for discretion."

James glanced over to where the Prince of Wales was at the center of a laughing, bowing, fawning circle of dandies.

"Since I have neither read nor heard of the story...chronicle...of your 'Scandal in Bohemia' adventure," he said softly, "I must presume that you reclaimed the blackmailing adventuress's incriminating photograph for the Prince."

"I did...and in a most clever manner," said Holmes and laughed out loud. In the noise of the busy restaurant, no one seemed to notice. "And then the woman stole it back from me, leaving a framed portrait of herself in its place."

"You failed, in other words," said James.

"I failed," said Sherlock Holmes. "Completely. Miserably." He took another sip of his cognac. "I've been bested by very few men in my career, Mr. James. Never before or since by a...*woman*."

James noticed that he uttered that final word with a strong tone of contempt.

"Does this have anything to do with your recent revelation that you are not a real person, Mr. Holmes?"

The tall man across the table from James rubbed his chin. "I suppose I should really ask you to address me as 'Sigerson', but tonight I do not care. No, Mr. James, the ancient case of the Prince of Wales and his former paramour—may she rot in peace—has nothing whatsoever to do with the reasons for me realizing that I am not, as you said earlier, 'real'. Would you care to hear those reasons?"

James hesitated only a second or two. "Yes," he said.

* * *

Holmes set his empty glass down and folded his long-fingered hands on the tablecloth. "It began, as so many things in life do, with simple domestic conversations," he began. "Those who have read Dr. Watson's chronicles in *The Strand* are aware—from certain background information he has given—that in eighteen eighty, the good doctor was removed from the Fifth Northumberland Fusiliers, then on duty in India, to the Berkshires Sixty-sixth Foot. On twenty-seven July of that year, Watson was severely wounded during the Battle of Maiwand. For many weeks his life teetered in the balance—the intrusive piece of lead had been a jazail bullet, that kind of heavy slug fired by the long, heavy musket so commonly used by the rebels in Afghanistan—and it had done serious internal damage.

"But Watson lived, despite the heat and flies and primitive regimental medical care available to him," continued Holmes. "In October of eighteen eighty-one, he was dispatched back to England on the troopship *Orontes*."

"I fail to see how this proves or disproves..." began Henry James.

"Patience," said Holmes, holding up one long finger to command silence.

"The wound from the jazail bullet was in Watson's shoulder," said Holmes. "At various times, in Turkish baths and once when we had to strip to swim a river while on one of my...adventures...I saw the ugly scar. But Watson had no other wounds from the wars."

Henry James waited. A waiter came by and Holmes ordered black Turkish coffee for the both of them.

"But five years ago—I remember the date in eighteen eighty-eight," said Holmes, "Watson's spidery shoulder wound from the jazail bullet had suddenly become a bullet wound he was complaining of, even in print, *in his leg.*"

"Could there not have been two such wounds?" asked James. "One in the poor man's shoulder, the other in his leg? Perhaps he received the second wound in London, during the course of one of your adventures."

"A second Afghan *jazail* bullet?" laughed Holmes. "Fired at Watson in *London?* Without my knowledge? It would seem highly unlikely, Mr. James. And added to that improbability are the twin facts that Watson was never wounded, never shot, during any of our adventures he chronicled and...this I find most interesting...the original shoulder wound that I'd seen, a terrible spiderweb of scars and a livid entry wound still visible, simply had disappeared when Watson began talking and writing about his *leg* wound."

"Distinctly odd," said James. He wondered what he should do if this Holmes-Sigerson person, almost certainly an escaped patient from some secured madhouse, should suddenly grow violent.

"And then there is the fact of Dr. Watson's wives," said Holmes.

James merely raised one eyebrow at this non sequitur.

"He has too many of them," said Holmes.

"Dr. Watson is a bigamist then?"

"No, no," laughed Holmes. Their coffee arrived. It was far too bitter for James's taste, but the madman seemed to enjoy it. "They simply come and go—as if they flicker in and out of existence—primarily depending upon what I take to be a fiction-author's need to have Watson living with me at our apartments at two-twenty-one-B Baker Street or not. And their names keep changing almost at random, Mr. James. Now a Constance. Then Mary. Then no name at all. Then Mary again."

"Wives have a way of dying," said James.

"That they do, thank God," said Holmes, nodding in agreement. "But in reality there is usually some warning of that, some illness, and—failing that—some period of mourning for the widower. Watson, bless his heart, simply moves in with me again and our adventures continue apace. Between these mythical wives, I mean."

Henry James cleared his throat but could think of nothing to say.

"Then there is the odd fact of our residence itself," bore on Holmes, taking no clue to stop based on his interlocutor's obvious boredom. "I have lived—Watson and I have lived—at two-twenty-one-B Baker Street since shortly after we met in January of eighteen eighty-one."

"Is there a paradox in that?" asked James.

"When these doubts of mine began and multiplied in the winter and spring of eighteen ninety and eighteen ninety-one," Holmes said very softly, "I went to the office of the City Surveyor and looked at the most recent maps of our neighborhood. As of eighteen ninety-one, a full ten years after we took up residence at two-twenty-one-B, the residences and structures on Baker Street ended at Number Eighty-five."

"Incredible," muttered James.

"But mostly..." continued Holmes as if he'd not heard Henry James speak, "it is the...cloudiness, lack of daily detail, *emptiness*...for me of the periods between my actual cases that most makes me doubt my existence separate from some fictional page. It's as if I'm alive...real...only when investigating a case."

"Could not your...ah...disposition toward indulging in certain drugs account for that?" asked James.

Holmes laughed and set his coffee cup down with a clatter. "You *do* read my adventures in *The Strand* after all!"

"Not at all," said James. "But as I mentioned, some younger friends of mine do. I remember their commenting on your frequent injections of...cocaine, was it not?" James well remembered Edmund Gosse's fascination with Holmes's dependence upon the drug. It had made Henry James suspect that Gosse himself had experimented with injecting it upon occasion.

"Only a seven-per-cent solution," laughed Holmes. "Quite tame by any opium-eater's scale. But since my death on twenty-four April eighteen ninety-one, I have successfully cured myself of that self-indulgence."

"Very good," said James. "How did you manage that?"

"By the replacement use of a much less harmful injected substance called morphine," said Sherlock Holmes. "And in the past weeks, I have discovered an even more miraculous and innocuous replacement—distilled by our German friend who created aspirin, Mr. Bayer himself—a drug so habit- and side-effect-free that both Bayer and those who use it have named it after its heroic qualities."

"Yes?" said James.

"It is called heroin," said Sherlock Holmes, "and I look forward to finding greater...and less expensive...quantities of it in America when you and I go there next week. Morphine has been sold in abundance on the streets of the United States—much more so than in England—since so many tens or hundreds of thousands of wounded soldiers continued to use it after their Civil War thirty years ago. And now this heroic heroin, while not yet released to the general marketplace, is becoming equally abundant there."

James was goggling at the tall man. "We're going to America? *We?*"

"We're leaving for Marseilles and a steamship bound for America early in the morning," said Holmes. "There is a seven-year-old murder there in their capital city that I am duty bound to solve, and it is in your very deep interest—*compelling* interest, my dear James—for you to accompany me. I could not, in good conscience, leave you behind in Paris while you are in this melancholic and possibly still self-destructive state of mind. Besides...you will enjoy this! The game's afoot and we're called to it as certainly and inescapably as your next story or book calls to your creator's soul and writer's pen."

Holmes beckoned for the waiter to bring the bill and paid it while James sat there with his eyes still wide and his mouth hanging unbecomingly open.

CHAPTER 5

In the ten days that followed, while crossing the Atlantic from France to New York and then taking a train to Washington, D.C., Henry James felt as if he were in a dream. No, not so much in a dream—his dreams tended to be specific and colorful and powerful—but, rather, in a fog. A delicious and dangerous and decision-free fog.

They sailed from Marseilles on the older French liner the *Paris*. James thought he remembered being aboard her twelve years before, the last time he'd visited America, when he'd hurried home to Cambridge during the period when first his mother and then his father had been dying. Sherlock Holmes refused to take a more modern English steamship since it would mean a stop somewhere in England on the way—the *Paris* paused only briefly in Dublin—and Holmes would not set foot in England, he said, until he was "fully satisfied". Satisfied as to what, was not further defined at that time, but James had to guess that it related to the subject of the consulting detective's real versus fictional existence.

There had been five amazing conversations—revelations, in truth—during the past ten days before landfall in New York, and James had to sort them out not only by content but by the context of where they had been announced.

The first had been outside his hotel on the Rue de la Paix after their late-evening dining on the night they had met.

"It is, of course, absurd to think that I can—or should wish to—go to America now," James had said, holding his umbrella in both hands like a weapon.

"But you must," said Holmes in calm terms. "My case depends upon it."

" 'Case'?" repeated Henry James. "I thought you had left being a consulting detective behind when you faked your own death almost two years ago."

"Not a bit of it," said Holmes. "Even as Jan Sigerson, I did my bit of detecting in Turkey, India, and elsewhere. But that was for my brother Mycroft, for Whitehall, and for England. Now I find I must take up a private case again. Solve what is almost certainly an apolitical mystery."

James continued to hold his folded umbrella at port arms. The rain had stopped. "Let me guess," he said. "In Dr. Watson's absence, you need me to chronicle your adventures. To be your Boswell."

Sherlock Holmes laughed loudly enough that the sound echoed back from the nearby stone buildings. "No, no, not at all, Mr. James. Nor do I think such a role as Boswell would suit you in any event, but certainly not in writing up the details of a mystery."

James's spine stiffened a bit at that. He considered himself capable of writing any sort of story—as long as neither its topic nor style was beneath his dignity. And he had done a few of those stories for money in his youth.

"What I mean," continued Holmes, "is that while I have not had the pleasure of reading your novels and shorter fiction, Mr. James, many of my more literary acquaintances—including Watson himself—have. And from what they tell me, your rendering of the most exciting adventures you and I might have in America would end up with a beautiful young lady from America as the protagonist, various lords and ladies wandering through, verbal opaqueness followed by descriptive obtuseness, and nothing more exciting being allowed to occur in the tale than a verbal *faux pas* or tea service being late."

James wondered whether he should be—and act—offended, but decided that he was not. All in all, he was amused.

"Then you could have no conceivable need for my presence in this quixotic jaunt to America you seem about to undertake, sir."

"Ah, but I truly do, Mr. James," said Holmes. "I need you for introductions, for information, for American context, for—what did you call it earlier?—for cover, and for companionship. I shall be a stranger in a strange land and to solve this mystery I shall need your help. Do you wish to hear more of the reasons for this?"

James said nothing. His thought had already turned away from suicide in the Seine toward the soft bed in his hotel room a few dozen paces and a lift ride from where he stood in the darkness.

"In March of eighteen ninety-one, almost exactly two years ago," continued Holmes, either unaware of or indifferent to James's very obvious lack of interest, "I had a visit at my bachelor quarters at two-twenty-one-B Baker Street from a prospective client. The distressed gentleman was an American, the topic was murder in the American capital, and his name was Edward Hooper. He showed me three thousand dollars that he was willing to pay me if I came with him to America and solved the mystery of his sister's death. I accepted only one dollar—as my retainer—but it has taken these three years for me to become active in the...mystery."

"No, I do not know nor have I heard of..." began James and then stopped abruptly.

"I believe you knew Mr. Edward Hooper's sister—Marian Hooper Adams," said Holmes.

"Clover," James said so softly that he could hardly hear the two syllables himself. "Clover Adams," said Henry James. "From the time she was a girl, everyone called Marian Hooper 'Clover'. It suited her."

"You knew her well then," pressed Holmes.

"I have been friends with Henry Adams for...many, many years," said James. He wished he could will himself not to speak of any of this, but this night he seemed under some strange compulsion to break confidences he normally would have guarded with his life. "I was also close to Clover Adams—as close as anyone could be to such an intelligent but unpredictable and frequently melancholic woman. I was a guest in their home the last time I was in America in the early eighteen eighties."

"You know the public details of her death then," said Holmes. There was a strange light in the consulting detective's eye, James thought, but it could have been a reflection from one of the gas lights that still illuminated this section of the Rue de la Paix.

"Her death by *suicide*," James said in a sharper tone than he might have intended. "By her own hand. Six...no...some seven-and-a-half years ago now. It is ancient history for all but the most closely bereaved such as her husband Henry and her dear friends—a category which includes me."

"On six December, eighteen eighty-five," Holmes said quietly. "The date is part of the mystery presented to me by her brother, Mr. Edward Hooper."

James started to say that he had never had the pleasure of actually meeting Clover's brother Edward, that Clover and Henry had always referred to him as "Ned", but instead he heard himself snapping words like a whip. "Death by sad *suicide,* Mr. Holmes. Everyone agreed to that. Her husband Henry. My particular mutual friend and neighbor to the Adamses, Mr. John Hay. The doctor. The police. The newspapers. Everyone agreed that she had taken her own life. She was of a melancholic nature, you see. All of us who knew and loved Clover Adams had known that. A tendency toward melancholy—and even self-murder—ran in the Hooper family. And she was in a deep, perhaps irrecoverable mourning for her father who had passed away earlier that year. She had been very close to her father, you see, and nothing that Henry Adams or anyone else could do in the months following Mr. Hooper's death seemed capable of breaking the iron bonds of loss and melancholy that had closed around poor Clover."

James stopped. He was almost panting from the intensity and exertion of his little speech. He felt like a fool for saying so much.

Holmes reached into an interior pocket of his tweed jacket and removed what looked to be a small white card. Despite his spirit of resistance, James unclenched one hand from his umbrella and took the offered card. It looked like a lady's visiting card, although it was done in simple white rather than the colorful cards now in vogue in England and America and was embossed with a subtle white rectangle within the rectangle of the card itself. At the top of the card within that plain border, there were five hearts embossed. Four of the hearts had been colored in, in blue, with what looked to have been hasty strokes of a colored pencil or crayon. The fifth heart was left uncolored—blank.

Henry James knew immediately the more general meaning of what the hearts signified. He had no clue as to what the empty heart or the single line of print below the hearts—a single sentence that looked to have been added by a typewriting machine—might mean.

She was murdered.

"When he visited me asking for help two years ago, Edward Hooper, Clover's brother, said that he had received exactly this card every six December—every anniversary of his sister's death—since the first anniversary of her odd death in eighteen eighty-six," said Holmes. "And I notice, Mr. James, that you instantly recognized the significance of the five embossed hearts on the card. Mr. Hooper told me that the four surviving members of the Five Hearts also annually received such a card. This, he said he knew for a certainty, included Mr. Henry Adams, although Adams had never spoken to the others about it."

"Ned Hooper was not one of the Five Hearts," James said numbly.

Holmes nodded. "No. And he believed that he was the only person who was not one of the Five Hearts who annually received this note. But, of course, he could not be certain of that."

"Clover Adams's death was by her own hand," repeated Henry James. "It is of no one's business except her husband's, and Henry Adams does not speak of that time or that event. He came close to death himself from sheer grief after... her actions."

"What of her brother's suspicions?" asked Holmes.

"They are misplaced," said James. "These... cards... if they are or were actually being sent, are an example only of someone's sick and perverted sense of humor. As I said, melancholy—and perhaps some not-infrequent sense of persecution—runs in the Hooper family. I have not met Mr. Edward Hooper—I always heard him referred to as 'Ned'—but I am sure that he was—and remains—mistaken."

"Mr. Edward Hooper is dead," said Sherlock Holmes.

"Dead?" James could hear how small the single syllable sounded amidst the carriage and pedestrian background bustle of Paris's joyous Rue de la Paix at night.

"He attempted suicide this past December—the day after the December-six anniversary of his sister's so-called suicide—by throwing himself from a third-story window of his home on Beacon Street, in Boston," said Sherlock Holmes. "Although badly injured, he survived and was taken to a Boston asylum. Hooper appeared to be recovering, both mentally and physically, but two weeks ago he came down with pneumonia. The disease carried him off."

"This is terrible," muttered James. "Horrible. Henry did not write me of these events. How is it that you, Mr. Holmes, who say that you have been in the wilderness of the far-flung Empire for these last two years, should be aware of such recent events in America when I am not?"

"Every good Englishman is behind *The Times,*" said Sherlock Holmes.

James blinked either his lack of understanding or his disgust at hearing the ancient joke in this context. Perhaps he meant to signal both.

"I have read my London newspapers even when, as in India, they were weeks out of date," elaborated Holmes. "Here in Paris, they are quite current. And the choice of American newspapers here—including the newspaper from Boston which carried the news of Edward Hooper's suicide attempts and final death by pneumonia—is very extensive indeed."

James took a ragged breath and looked back toward the beckoning lights of his hotel.

Holmes took a half step closer until he gained James's full attention again. "You see why I owe it to Ned Hooper to fulfill my promise of taking up the case of his sister's death."

"There is no 'case'," James said again. "There was only the tragedy of her suicide more than seven years ago. The 'case', as you so melodramatically call it, is closed."

"Do you remember the cause of Mrs. Adams's death?" asked Holmes.

Henry James knew that he should turn away at that point, go into his hotel, and never talk to this madman again. But he did not move.

"At the depths of her melancholy, when she was alone for a few moments one Sunday, Clover drank a potion that was part of her photographic developing chemical apparatus," James said at last rather than continue suffering the silence. "It contained arsenic. Death was instantaneous."

"Death from that type of arsenic, potassium cyanide, is relatively quick but rarely instantaneous," Holmes said calmly, as if he were discussing railroad timetables. "She would have eventually asphyxiated but only after long moments of the most exquisite agony."

James raised his free hand as if he could shield himself from such words and images.

"Who found her body?" persisted Holmes.

"Her husband . . . Henry . . . I am certain," said James, coming very close to stammering. He suddenly felt very confused. Part of his consciousness wished that he had been alone to do what he had planned to do on the sidewalk along the Seine.

"Yes. The police report said it was Henry Adams who discovered her—'on the floor and comatose before the fireplace'," agreed Holmes. "This was at a certain time of the morning on Sunday, six December. Does that time of the day and week bear any significance for you, Mr. James?"

"No. None at all. Other than . . . do you mean because it was the time each Sunday that Clover had for years set aside to write to her father, especially during his illness?"

Holmes did not answer. Instead, he took another half step closer and whispered, "Henry Adams had told friends that he never left his wife alone at that hour, on those Sundays, precisely because he feared that her melancholia would overpower her reason. And yet on that Sunday the sixth of December seven years ago, she was alone. At least for several moments."

"I believe that Henry was on his way out to see his dentist about a tooth that was giving him . . . *are you interrogating me,* Mr. Holmes?"

"Not at all, Mr. James. I'm explaining why your presence during this investigation is of the utmost importance."

"I will not betray a friend, Mr. Holmes."

"Of course not," said the detective. "But would it not be a case of betraying both your friend Henry Adams and your former friend Clover Adams if it were murder and if no one even bothered to look into it?"

"It . . . was . . . not . . . murder," James said for what he vowed to be the last time. "Clover was one of the first—and I would venture to say the preeminent—female American photographers of her era. Her work was ethereal. Other worldly. But that very quality of other-worldliness added to her inherited tendency toward terrible melancholy. On this particular winter day, that tendency must have overwhelmed her and she drank some of the easily accessible chemicals from her photographic laboratory—a mixture which, she must have known, contained arsenic."

"And who gave her those specific developing chemicals?" asked Holmes.

"I assumed she purchased them herself," snapped James. "If you are again hinting of any shade of guilt accruing to my good and honest friend Henry Adams..."

Holmes held up a gloved hand. "Not at all. I happen to know that it was a stranger who provided those chemicals to Mrs. Adams. A brother of a female 'friend', a certain Miss Rebecca Lorne, whose acquaintance Mrs. Adams had made quite accidentally in Washington. That friend, Miss Lorne, was there waiting...according to police reports and newspaper accounts given to me by Ned Hooper two years ago...when Henry Adams returned from his dental errand. Miss Lorne told Adams that she had dropped in to see Mrs. Adams and asked if she was receiving. Mr. Adams said he would run upstairs to see if his wife felt up to seeing a visitor and then he found her body on the floor."

"Again, you seem to be insinuating..." began James, showing the fiercest scowl he could manage. Usually even a much lower-wattage version of that scowl served to silence any presumptuous or personally trespassing interlocutors. Not so this night with Holmes.

"I am insinuating nothing," said Holmes. "I am merely explaining why you and I will be catching the early express train to Marseilles at six quarter seven tomorrow morning and be boarding a steamship to New York by tomorrow night."

"There is no power, means, force, blackmail, inducement, or other method of persuasion—in this lifetime or in any other possible variation of this life—that you could use to persuade me to travel with you tomorrow to Marseilles, much less to America, Mr. Sherlock Holmes," said Henry James.

CHAPTER 6

The two men were alone in a first-class carriage compartment on the express train to Marseilles, which was some comfort to Henry James, and for the first three hours of the trip neither man spoke. James was pretending to read a novel. Holmes was behind *The Times*.

Suddenly, with neither warning nor prelude, Holmes lowered his paper and said, "You had a beard then as well."

James looked up and stared. "I beg your pardon." Eventually, he would get used to Sherlock Holmes's sudden changes of topic or seemingly irrelevant announcements from the blue, but not this day. Not yet.

"Four years ago," said Holmes. "When I was introduced to you at Mrs. T. P. O'Connor's garden party. You wore a full beard then as well."

James said nothing. He'd had that full beard since the Civil War.

"It is partially how I recognized you in the dark along the Seine," said Holmes and returned to his paper.

Finally, seeing a way to irritate his irritating compartment-mate, James did speak. "I would think that the world's most famous consulting detective might rely upon more points of physiognomy for recognition than a man's beard."

Holmes laughed. "Of course! I see the physiognomy of men, not their added facial-hair accouterments. I am, for instance, somewhat of an expert on ears."

"You didn't even remember we had been introduced," said James, ignoring the absurd comment about ears.

"Not true, sir," laughed Holmes. "I remember at the time that when I'd heard the American Mr. James was to be at the garden party, I'd hoped that it would be your brother, the psychologist, with whom I looked forward to discussing several things."

"William hadn't yet published his *Principles of Psychology* in eighteen eighty-eight," groused James. "He was—to all intents and purposes—unknown to the world. How could you have known you wanted to talk to him? Your memory serves you poorly, Mr. Holmes."

"Not a bit of it," chuckled the detective. "Friends in America—friends who shared, in some way, my own peculiar vocation—had sent me copies of your older brother's various papers on psychology, years before his full book appeared. But the primary reason I was distracted upon meeting you at Mrs. O'Connor's garden party, Mr. James, was that at that precise moment I was watching my suspect—the jewel thief—ply his trade. We caught him, as Watson would say, red-handed. Although I admit to having never learned where that silly phrase—'red-handed'—came from."

"A mere servant you said last night," said James, looking back down at the hieroglyphics of the novel on his lap. He was too upset to read, which was a very rare occurrence for Henry James.

"A mere servant, but one in the rather intimate employ of your very own Lady Wolseley," said Holmes.

James almost dropped his book. "One of Lord and Lady Wolseley's servants responsible for jewelry thefts!" he cried. "Impossible. Absurd."

"Not at all," said Holmes. "Lord Wolseley had paid me to solve the series of crimes that were plaguing his friends with such lovely country houses, but he needn't have bothered coming to me. A moderately competent village constable could have solved that simple crime. I knew who it was—or had narrowed the very small category containing the obvious culprit—within hours of taking the case. You see, the thefts had begun in various high English houses in Ireland. All the major English houses, in fact, save for Lord Wolseley's and a few English aristocrats there who were out of favor with Lord and Lady Wolseley."

Henry James wanted to object again—on various obscure personal grounds as well as logical ones—but he could not yet find the words.

THE FIFTH HEART || 35

"The chief thief's name was Germond," continued Holmes. "Robert Jacob Germond. A rather aging corporal who had served as the General's—Lord Wolseley's—batman and even valet on various campaigns and in both the Irish military camps and at Lord Wolseley's estate on that green isle. One has to say that Corporal Germond did not look the role of a jewel thief—he had a long, rather basset-hound face with the accompanying luminous, sad, and sensitive eyes—but one look at the record of thefts within Lord Wolseley's regimental garrisons in Ireland over the years, and then amongst the homes of Lord W.'s friends in Ireland, and then again in England during his and Lady Wolseley's various visits home, and the identity of the mastermind—although I admit that it is far too grand to call him by that title—of this jewel-theft ring was immediately obvious to even the least deductive mind. At the very moment you and I were meeting at the garden party, Mr. James, I was covertly watching Corporal Germond go about his actual thieving. He was very smooth."

James felt himself blushing. He'd come to know several of Lord and Lady Wolseley's primary servants over the years—most of them former military men under the General—but Germond had been assigned as his own personal servant during James's only visit so far to Ireland and Lord Wolseley's estate there. James had felt a strange . . . affinity . . . for the soft-spoken, sad-eyed personal valet.

*　*　*

James was not pleased that he and Holmes had to share a stateroom on the *Paris,* even though it was in first class and adequate to their needs. The booking had been so close to sailing time, Holmes had explained, that only a cancellation of this two-bed single stateroom had been available. "Unless," he had added, "you would have preferred traveling in steerage . . . which, I know from personal experience, has its peculiar charms."

"I do not wish to be traveling on that ship . . . or any ship . . . at all," had been James's rejoinder.

But save for the sleeping hours, the two saw little of each other.

Holmes never went to breakfast, was rarely seen partaking of the rather good *petit déjeuner* in the morning dining area, was never glimpsed at lunch times, and only occasionally filled his assigned seat at the captain's table where, every evening in his black tie and tails, James tried to converse with the French aristocrats, German businessmen, ship's white-bearded captain (who seemed primarily interested in his food at any rate), and the single Englishwoman at the table—an almost-dotty dowager who insisted on calling him "Mr. Jane".

James spent as much of each day at sea as he could either browsing the ship's modest library—none of his works were there, even in translation—or pacing the not-terribly-spacious deck, or listening to the occasional desultory piano recital or small concert arranged for the passengers' amusement.

But twice Henry James had accidentally caught Sherlock Holmes in powerfully personal and embarrassing moments.

The first time he'd surprised Holmes—who showed no surprise or embarrassment either time—had been after breakfast when James was returning to the shared stateroom in order to change his clothes. Holmes was lying, still in his nightshirt, on his bed, some sort of strap wrapped around the upper bicep of his left arm, and was just in the process of removing the needle of a syringe from the soft flesh at his inner elbow joint. On the bedside table—the table they had *shared*, the table on which James set his book when it came time to extinguish the lights—there was a vial of dark liquid that James had to assume was morphine.

Henry James was not unacquainted with the delivery and effects of morphine. He had watched his sister Alice float off on its golden glow, away from all humanity (including her own), for months before her death. Katharine Loring had even been instructed by Alice's physician on how to administer the proper syringe-amount of morphine should no one else be available. James had never been required to give his dying sister the injection, but he had been prepared to. Alice, in her final months the year before, had also received regular sessions of hypnosis, along with the morphia, in the concerted efforts to lessen her seemingly endless pain.

But Sherlock Holmes was in no physical pain that Henry James knew of. He was simply now a morphine addict, after having been a cocaine-injection addict for many years. And he'd already stated that he was eager to find and use this new "heroic" drug of Mr. Bayer's since it was so available in the United States.

Holmes had not been embarrassed—he'd simply looked up at James under heavy eyelids and calmly set away the bottle, syringe, and other apparatus in a small leather case James had already seen him carrying (and assumed to be his shaving kit)—and then smiled sleepily.

Disgusted and making no efforts to hide that reaction, James had turned on his heel and left the room, despite the fact that he had not changed into his deck-walking clothes.

*   *   *

Another painfully intimate moment came when James entered the stateroom after a perfunctory knock late on the fourth night out from Dublin only to find Holmes standing naked in front of the nightstand that held their water basin and small mirror. Again, Holmes showed no appropriate embarrassment and did not hurry to pull on his nightshirt, despite his stateroom-mate's obvious discomfort.

Henry James had seen grown men naked before. He tended to react in complicated ways to the naked male form, but his primary reaction was to think of death.

When Henry James had been a toddler, he'd followed his brother William—older by just a year—everywhere William went. Henry couldn't (and did not wish to) keep up with William during his brother's rough-and-tumble years of outdoor play, but later, when William decided that he would become an artist, Henry decided that he would also become an artist. As many times as he could, he would join William in the drawing and painting classes their father paid for.

One day James entered the Newport drawing studio to find his orphaned cousin Gus Barker posing nude for the life-drawing class. Shocked to his marrow by the beauty of his red-headed cousin—that paleness of skin, the flaccid penis so vulnerable, Gus's nipples so femininely pink against that white skin—James had pretended to an

artist's professional interest only, scowling down at William's and others' drawings as if preparing to seize paper and stroke some lines of
charcoal of his own to capture such an ineffable power of nakedness.
But mostly young Henry James, the incipient writer in him rising
more certainly than any specific sexual consciousness, was fascinated
with his own layered and troubled response to his male cousin's calmly
displayed body.

Young Gus Barker was the first of their close circle of family and
friends to die in the Civil War, cut down by some Confederate sniper's
bullet in Virginia. For decades after that, Henry James could not think
of his first shock of admiring the naked male form without thinking of
that very form—the copper stippling of Gus's pubic hair, the veins on
his muscled forearms, the strange power of his pale thighs—lying and
rotting under the loam in some unknown Virginia field.

After Henry James's youngest brother Wilkie was badly wounded
during the Massachusetts 54th black regiment's ill-planned and disastrous attack on South Carolina's Fort Wagner, he had been in such
terrible condition when he'd been brought home—found among the dying in an open army surgical station in South Carolina and saved purely
by the coincidence of family friend Cabot Russell there looking for his
missing dead son on the battlefield—that they'd had to leave Wilkie on
his filthy stretcher in the hallway entrance by the door for weeks. James
had been with both his father and mother when they'd bathed their
mutilated youngest child, and Wilkie's naked body was a different sort
of revelation for young Henry James, Jr.: a terrible wound in the back
from which the Confederate ball had not yet been removed and a sickening wound to the foot—they'd roughly operated on the boat bringing
Wilkie north to remove that ball—that showed both decay and the early
conditions of gangrene.

The first time Henry had watched his brother naked on the cot, being
turned and touched so gingerly by his mother after Wilkie's filthy-
smelling uniform had been cut off, he had marveled at how absolutely
vulnerable the male human body was to metal, fire, the blade, disease. In
many ways, especially when turned—screaming—onto his stomach so
that they could bathe his back and legs, with both wounds now visible,

Wilkie James looked more like a week-old corpse than like a living man. Than like a brother.

Then there was the other "Holmes" whom James had seen naked. Near the end of the war, James's childhood friend—only two years older than Henry but now aged decades by his war experiences—Oliver Wendell Holmes, Jr., had come to visit James in Boston and then traveled with him to North Conway, where James's cousin Minnie Temple and her sisters had lived. For the first night of that North Conway visit, this other Holmes and young James had been forced to share an absurdly spartan room and single sagging bed—before they found a more suitable rental the next day—and James, already in his pajamas and under the covers, had seen Oliver Wendell Holmes, Jr., standing naked in the lamplight in front of a wash basin and mirror just as Sherlock Holmes was this night somewhere in the tossing North Atlantic on the *Paris.*

The young James had once again marveled at the beauty of the lean and muscled male body when Oliver Wendell Holmes, Jr., had stood there in the lamplight that night, but once again there had been the all-too-visible connection with Death: terrible scars radiating like white spiderwebs across Oliver's back and sides and upper leg. Indeed, that other Holmes—James's Holmes—had also been terribly wounded in the war and was so proud of the fact that he would talk about it, in detail not usually allowed in front of ladies, for decades afterwards. That other Holmes, eventually to be the famous jurist, insisted on keeping his torn and bloody Union uniform, still smelling of gunpowder and blood and filth just as Wilkie's cot and blanket and cut-away uniform had, in his wardrobe for all these decades to follow. He would take it out upon occasion of cigars and conversation with his fellow men of name and fortune and show them the blood long dried-brown and the ragged holes that so paralleled the white-webbed ragged holes James had glimpsed scarring his childhood friend's bare body.

For James, it had been another glimpse not only at the beauty of the naked male form but at the mutilating graffiti of Death trying to claim the mortality of that form.

So, even in his shock, Henry James was not surprised to see in the stateroom's dim lamplight that Mr. Sherlock Holmes—leaner even than

Oliver Wendell Holmes, Jr., had been at an age fifteen years Sherlock's junior—also had scars across his back. These looked as raw as the bullet wounds James had seen in Wilkie's and Oliver's flesh, but those wounds radiated outward like some zealot flagellant's self-inflicted lashes that had cut through skin and flesh.

"Excuse me," James had said, still standing in the open door to the stateroom. "I did not..." He did not know what he "did not" so he stopped there.

Holmes turned and looked at him. There were more white scars on his pale chest. James had time to note that despite the tall man's extreme thinness—his flanks were all but hollowed in the way of some runners and other athletes whom James had seen compete—Mr. Sherlock Holmes, whose flesh in the lamplight glowed almost as white as James's cousin Gus Barker's had been, was a mass of corded muscles which seemed just waiting to be flexed and used in some urgent circumstance.

"Excuse me," James had said again and had gone back out through the door. He stayed in the First Class Lounge that night, smoking and reading some irrelevant magazine, until he was certain that Holmes would be in bed asleep before he himself returned to the stateroom.

* * *

The *Paris,* far behind its own rather unambitious schedule, came into New York Harbor in early evening when part of the city's oldest skyline was backlit by the setting sun. Most of the transatlantic liners James had taken back from Europe over the years, if arriving in New York, did so early in the morning. He realized that this evening arrival was not only more aesthetically pleasing—although James could no longer tolerate the aesthetics of New York City—but also seemed somehow more appropriate to their covert mission.

Holmes had joined him, uninvited, at the railing where James had been watching the scurry of tug boats and flurry of harbor traffic, listening to the hoots and bells and shouts of one of the world's busiest harbors.

"Interesting city, is it not?" asked Holmes.

"Yes," was James's only response. When he'd left New York and America ten years earlier in 1883, he'd vowed never to return. Safely back in Kensington, he had written essays about his American and New York impressions. The city itself—where James had enjoyed years of what he thought was a happy childhood in their home near Washington Square Park—had changed, James observed, beyond all recognition. Between the 1840's and the 1880's, he said, New York had become a city of immigrants and strangers. The civilities and certainties of the semi-rural yet still pleasantly urban Washington Square years had been replaced by these hurtling verticalities, these infusions of strange-smelling, strange-speaking foreigners.

At one point, James had compared the Jews in their ghettoes of the Lower East Side to rats and other vermin—scurrying around the feet of their distracted and outnumbered proper Anglo-Saxon predecessors—but he also admired the fact that these...*immigrants*...put out more daily newspapers in Hebrew than appeared in the city in English; that they had created a series of Yiddish theaters that entertained more people nightly—however boorishly and barbarically—than did the Broadway theaters; that the Jews—and the Italians and other lower orders of immigrants, including most of the Irish—had made such a niche for themselves in the new New York that Henry James was certain that they could never, having attached themselves like limpets to that proud Dream of America shared by so many of its inhabitants, be displaced.

It had made Henry James feel like a stranger in his own land, in his own city, and his essays had returned to that theme again and again and again.

He said nothing of that now as he and Holmes silently watched the final preparations for the old liner to be nudged into its proper berth along the busy docks.

"You will want to know how I knew that night along the Seine that you were carrying your sister Alice's ashes," Holmes said very softly. People were shoving and milling to lean along the long railing now, but there nonetheless seemed to be a bubble of privacy around the two men.

"I want to know nothing of the kind," returned James with equal softness but much more intensity. "Your wild and inaccurate speculations do not interest me in the least, Mr. Holmes."

"I had been there in the dark longer than you," continued Holmes, his eyes on the surrounding ships and fireboats and rowboats and busy mayhem, "and my eyes had much better adapted to the dark than had yours. I saw you remove the small ivory snuffbox several times...hold it in a way that almost might be called prayerful—return it to your inner pocket, then retrieve it again. I knew it was an ivory snuffbox—only ivory gleams that way in such low light—and I also knew at once that you did not take snuff."

"You know nothing of my habits, sir." James's voice could not have been colder nor more dismissive of this uninvited conversation. But because of the crowd behind them, he could not simply turn and walk away. He shifted his gaze away from Holmes instead.

"I do, of course," said Holmes. "A user of snuff, even an occasional user, has telltale nicotine stains on his thumb and second finger. You did not. Also, someone using a snuffbox to retrieve pinches of snuff does not carefully and permanently join the various openings of the box with sealing wax."

"There is no way you could have seen such things in those seconds, in that darkness," said James. His heart was pounding against his ribs.

"I could. I did," said Sherlock Holmes. "And then, as we were leaving, I contrived to light my pipe to confirm my earlier observations. You were not aware of it—holding the snuffbox obviously had become a nervous habit with you, Mr. James, especially in extremis, as it were—but you had removed it briefly several times after we'd walked away from the river. I could see that it was more than a mere talisman for you; it was sacred."

James turned angrily to stare at the intruder and was shocked to see that Holmes had removed the blue lenses that had altered his true eye color. Now Henry James's coldly angry gray-eyed stare met the calm gray-eyed gaze of Sherlock Holmes.

"While I was in India, I'd read in *The Times* of your sister's death in March of eighteen ninety-two and, later, a notice of Miss James's funeral and cremation at Woking and the mention that your sister's companion, Miss Katharine Peabody Loring, would be returning the ashes to Cambridge, America, for interment there at the family plot."

James said nothing. He continued to glare. He was glad he was leaning on a ship's railing because he thought he might be sick.

"I could tell at once that night along the Seine that—with Miss Loring's and your family's knowledge or, more likely, without it—you had appropriated some of your sister's ashes, made them safe in that absurdly expensive ivory snuffbox, and were transporting them...somewhere. But where? Certainly not just to the bottom of the Seine."

James could not remember ever being insulted in quite this intimate fashion before. If he were his brother William, he knew, he would strike this Holmes in the face as brutally and bruisingly as possible. But Henry James was not William; he had never in his life coiled his fist in real expectation of striking another boy or man. He did not do so now. He continued to glare.

"I think perhaps," concluded Holmes, "that you were considering a voyage back to America anyway. Before your melancholy overtook you in Paris, I mean. I believe that earlier thought of a voyage to America is why you finally changed your mind last night about joining me on this mission. Perhaps you thought to scatter your sister's ashes at some spot important...sacred to both of you? It is not, of course, any of my business. But I respect your bereavement, sir, and I shall not raise this subject again. I did so now primarily to acquaint you with some of the simpler methods of my powers of observation and ratiocination."

"I am not impressed, sir," said James when at last he could speak. But he was. Despite himself, he was very impressed.

The old ship was being settled up against the wharf like a matron being led to a groaning buffet. French sailors fore and aft made ready to toss the ropes that would precede the massive cables that would soon pull them tight to America.

"You'll pardon me, Mr. Holmes. I forgot something in the stateroom. I shall meet you when you clear Customs inspection."

Holmes nodded, seemingly lost in his own thoughts. James knew that Holmes—as Jan Sigerson, traveling on what he presumed to be a false

Norwegian passport—would be held up for some time in line while Henry James, expatriate at heart but still traveling on his American passport, would pass through with only the most cursory inspection.

Still, he trundled quickly back to the stateroom in the hopes that the porters they'd given orders to had not yet taken down the bags and steamer trunks. They had not.

James locked the door to the stateroom behind him, unlocked his steamer trunk, removed a mahogany box from a recessed area, and opened it carefully. The interior was custom-lined in velvet with an indentation cut to his prescribed dimensions.

James withdrew the snuffbox from his waistcoat pocket, set it carefully within the mahogany box, locked the box, locked the steamer trunk again, made sure he had his passport and papers ready in his briefcase, and left the stateroom just as the porters arrived to haul away the luggage. They touched their caps as they passed and Henry James nodded in return.

CHAPTER 7

I had planned on describing to you Holmes's and James's one evening, night, and morning in New York City, but I could find no record of where they stayed. I have the records of both of them clearing Customs by 7 p.m. Thursday evening, 23 March, 1893—Holmes under his J. Sigerson Norwegian national's passport, James under his own name—but lost track of them in the hours after that. Based on the dialogue I know they had on the train to Washington the next day, it's possible that they did not dine together that night or even stay in the same hotel. It appears as if they hadn't spoken since Holmes's intrusive "explanation" along the rail of the French steamship *Paris* as they were docking.

I had also assumed that they would have taken one of the Washington, D.C.–bound trains from the conveniently located Grand Central Depot that Friday the 24th of March, but it turns out that Holmes—who had been in charge of all their rushed travel arrangements—had booked them on the Boston–Washington, D.C., express called the *Colonial* or sometimes the *Colonial Express,* a service provided jointly by the Pennsylvania Railroad and New York, New Haven, and Hartford Railroad. But in 1893 the *Colonial* did not yet come into Manhattan or connect to Grand Central Depot—that change would be made after the *Titanic* sank in 1912—and Holmes and James would have had to have arisen early and taken one of several early ferries to Jersey City, there to board the *Colonial* that would take them down the Pennsylvania main line to

Philadelphia, Baltimore, and finally Washington. It was the fastest express available to them on that Friday, but not the most convenient for someone who had spent the night in Manhattan.

I did confirm that Henry James had sent John Hay a hurried cable from Marseilles stating only that he was coming back to America "for private and personal reasons, please tell no one except perhaps Henry A." and gave the date and rough time of his arrival in Washington and told his old friend that he and "a Norwegian explorer whom I have befriended and who is temporarily traveling with me" would find lodging in a Washington hotel. James received, upon arrival in New York, a cable from John Hay saying, in full:

Nonsense. You and your traveling companion must stay with us for the duration of your visit. Clara and I insist. There shall be room and food and wine and conversation enough for all. Adams is currently away traveling but will be thrilled that you have decided to visit your home country again. By great good coincidence, the diplomatic attaché from King Oskar II, King of Sweden and Norway, is scheduled to be our dinner guest on Sunday night. We all look forward to meeting your intrepid explorer friend!

James showed Holmes the cable on their way to the Jersey City terminal and could not resist a grim smile. "A bit of a problem, perhaps?"

"What is that, my dear fellow?" said Holmes as they waited at the front of the ferry.

"Does the disguise of Mr. Jan Sigerson include a native's facility with the Norwegian language?" James asked most pointedly. "Perhaps you had better stay at a Washington hotel, visit Hay and Adams only upon careful occasion, and be indisposed this coming Sunday evening."

"Nonsense," said Holmes and smiled. "It is a great advantage to stay with the Hays. You said that their home was near that of Henry Adams's?"

"Next door and contiguous," said James. "Just like Sweden and Norway."

"There you have it then," said Holmes. "We shall leave the representative of King Oskar the Second of Sweden and Norway to sort things out for himself on Sunday."

* * *

Their rail tickets were nominally "first class" but there was nothing resembling a private compartment. Luckily, the first-class carriage was not crowded this Friday morning and, while sitting across the aisle from each other, Holmes and James could lean forward and converse in private when they wished. James also noticed that while the disgusting American male habit of constant expectoration had not disappeared, there seemed to be somewhat fewer spittoons visible everywhere than there had been in the early 1880's during his last visit and the red runner down the aisle of the first-class carriage was not so spongily porous with liquified tobacco as so many rugs and carpets had been ten years earlier. James had decided in 1883 that he could never again live in—and possibly never again visit—America if it was only because of the universal spitting.

"Tell me about the Five Hearts," said Holmes as they left Philadelphia. For this conversation, the detective had crossed the aisle and was sitting uncomfortably close to James, knee to knee as it were, and was perched on the north-facing seat across from the south-facing writer. Holmes leaned on his northern-European-style walking stick. James wished that he had brought a stick to the compartment, if only to use as a barrier between them.

James set his palms firmly on his knees as if that created a structure separating them further. "In truth," he said, "they referred to their small group not as the Five Hearts but as the Five *of* Hearts."

"Tell me then about the Five *of* Hearts," said Holmes.

"In truth, it was Clover Adams's *salon,*" said James. "A very uniquely American *salon,* I might say."

"How so?"

James paused a second to comprehend exactly what he *had* meant. "It was not, as are so many scores of salons I've known in France and Italy and elsewhere, centered on things or people literary, nor upon artists and art, nor upon that most central trinity of *salons*—money, aristocracy, or notoriety, although the Adamses might not be found wanting in any of the three of those categories."

"Really?" said Holmes. "I thought there was no aristocracy in the United States of America."

James smiled almost pityingly at the younger man. James was turning fifty in a few weeks and Holmes had mentioned that he was currently thirty-eight years old, turning thirty-nine in April, but at this moment Henry James felt very much the wiser, older gentleman. "Every society has its subtle aristocracies, Mr. Holmes . . . er . . . Mr. Sigerson. If not based on birth, then upon wealth. If not upon wealth, then upon power. And so forth."

"Yet isn't Henry Adams a member of the ruling aristocracy in Washington?" asked Holmes.

James frowned before answering. Was the insufferable detective *trying* to be provocative? *Pretending* to be dense? After a few seconds of thought, James decided not. He was simply naïve.

"Henry Adams is a grandson of one American president and the great-grandson of another, both on his paternal side of course, but he has never held any political power of his own. He is rich, yes. He and Clover were at the center of Washington social power in the first half of the eighteen eighties, yes. But while being a member of what French philosophers or Jefferson might have called 'a natural aristocracy', Adams never controlled power, per se. I mean, he started as a Harvard professor, for heaven's sake!"

Holmes nodded. "Let us return to Mrs. Adams. Describe your former friend Clover to me . . . as briefly and succinctly as you can, please."

James felt his infinitely delicate feathers ruffle again at this peremptory command. "You are asking me to reveal personal details of a dear, departed friend of mine and the wife of a friend of mine, sir," he said stiffly. "You must remember that I am, while not English by nationality, a gentleman. And there are things which gentlemen simply cannot do."

Holmes sighed. "Right now, Mr. James, and for the foreseeable future, you are an American gentleman who has agreed to help solve the possible murder—or at least the mystery surrounding someone annually claiming her death to be murder—of a fellow American citizen. In that sense, sir, your responsibilities to your friend as a witness outweigh vague conceptions of gentlemen not discussing their friends. We must both get beyond that if we are to decide whether your friend Clover Adams was murdered or not."

Easy for you to get beyond it, thought James. *You are not a gentleman.*

He sighed aloud. "Very well. What do you wish to know about Clover?"

"Her appearance to begin with."

James felt himself bridle again. "Why should her appearance be a factor, Mr. Ho...Mr. Sigerson? Do you have the theory that someone murdered her because of her looks?"

"It is a simple piece of a complex puzzle," Holmes said quietly. "And somewhere to start. What did Clover Adams look like?"

James paused again. Eventually he said, "Shall we say that Henry Adams did not marry Miss Marian Hooper in June of eighteen seventy-three for her beauty alone. She was...plain-looking, although, as Henry himself once wrote to me years ago, she should 'not quite be called plain'. And she was petite. But Henry Adams, as perhaps you will see, is also a small man by modern standards. But, although it was not unduly sharpened by education, Clover had a lively and intelligent mind." He hesitated again. "And, I must admit, a quick and acerbic tongue. During the five years they lived in Washington before her death, Clover made many enemies—especially amongst social climbers, shunned senators, and their wives."

"So you would categorize this Five of Hearts *salon* at which she was the center as more exclusionary than not?" asked Holmes.

James wished again that he had brought his walking stick into the carriage...to lean on as he thought this time. "Yes, definitely," he replied softly, more to himself it sounded than to the detective sitting across from him. "Henry and Clover Adams—and the other three members of the Five of Hearts—would never invite someone to their inner circle because of that person's power or notoriety. Rather, they invited artists, writers, minor politicians, and such to the dinners held after the five o'clock daily teas of the inner salon of the Five of Hearts based on that person's ability to *amuse* them. I once wrote a story in which I portrayed Clover Adams in the form of a certain Mrs. Bonnycastle and..."

James stopped in mid-breath. He was aghast at his own lack of discretion.

"Go on," said Sherlock Holmes.

James took a breath. Well, he had already crossed the discretionary Rubicon, as it were.

"It was in a story called 'Pandora'," said Henry James. "But you must understand that I never base any of my fictional characters on actual living or deceased persons. They are always...an amalgam...of experience and pure fiction." This was as disingenuous as Henry James could get. All of his important characters—and most of his minor ones—were based exactly and precisely upon living or deceased personages from his own life and experience.

"Of course," purred Holmes, sounding as disingenuous as Henry James felt.

"At any rate, in this short story, I described Mrs. Bonnycastle as a 'lady of infinite mirth' and her *salon* as one which 'left out, on the whole, more than it took in'."

"But you've already told me that the actual Clover Adams was not exactly a lady of infinite mirth," interrupted Holmes. "You've explained that she had been, since childhood, visited by deep and frequent spells of melancholy."

"Yes, yes," James said impatiently. "One omits certain features of a character for a short story. Had Mrs. Bonnycastle been a central character in a *novel*...well, we would have had to explore all sides of her. Even those that seem, upon first glance, to be mutually contradictory."

"Please go on," said Holmes almost contritely. "You were describing your fictional treatment of Clover Ada...of Mrs. Bonnycastle's *salon*."

"I remember writing that the very rare senator or congressman whom they allowed to visit was invariably inspected with...I remember the precise words, Mr. Holmes...'with a mixture of alarm and indulgence'."

Holmes smiled thinly. It looked as if he wanted to ask James whether the writer could remember, verbatim, large tracts from his dozens of books and hundreds of short stories, but he obviously did not want to derail the conversation again. "Go on, please," he said.

"I know," continued James, "that my good friend Henry Adams recognized himself in the story, 'Pandora', when I described *Mr.* Bonnycastle as having once said to his wife, in a fit of unusual broad-mindedness—'Hang it, let us be vulgar and have some fun—let us invite the president!'"

"And did they regularly invite the president?" asked Holmes.

James made an almost impolite noise. "Not that worm James Garfield," said the writer, "although I imagine that Garfield would have galloped barefoot across Lafayette Square to the Adamses' home should he have ever been tendered. But they did, or at least Henry did—I believe for the first time with their architect, Richardson—cross the street to visit the White House once Grover Cleveland came to power in March of eighteen eighty-five. Only a few months before Clover's death."

Holmes raised a single finger. "Pardon me for interrupting again, James. But this is something else about America that confuses me a trifle. It was my understanding—at least in my childhood—that unlike Her Majesty or most other royalty worldwide, American presidents were elected for a limited period of time. Four years was my hazy recollection. Yet President Cleveland was in office when Clover Adams died in eighteen eighty-five and, correct me if I am wrong, he is in office now in the spring of eighteen ninety-three. Have the Americans discovered the benefits of lifetime public service?"

Can any grown Englishman really be so ill-informed? wondered Henry James.

As if reading James's mind, Holmes smiled and said, "During a railway voyage in a recent case set far out on distant moors, one not mentioned—so far at least!—in his published chronicles of our adventures, I had the opportunity to reveal to Dr. Watson that, until he had mentioned it in passing that day, I had no idea that the Earth went around the sun. I may have learned it at one time, I explained to Watson, but—as with all things that do not relate directly to my profession and avocation of detective work—I quickly put it out of my mind. I can, you shall find, be rather singularly focused. So you will have to make allowances for me at times, sir."

"But for a man who brags of being set so firmly behind *The Times...*" James began and stopped. Holmes could not possibly be telling the truth here. And James wanted no argument. Not yet.

"Mr. Grover Cleveland," he began again, "is in the unique position of being the only President of the United States who has served two *non-consecutive* four-year terms. He was in office between March eighteen eighty-five and March of eighteen eighty-nine. After a four-year interval where a certain Benjamin Harrison served in the office, Mr. Cleveland was elected again just last November and was sworn into office again only a few weeks ago."

Holmes nodded briskly. "Thank you. And please return to your description of all five of the Five of Hearts."

James looked around. "I fear that the dining car will be closing for luncheon service soon. Perhaps we could have a late lunch and continue our discussion there?"

CHAPTER 8

James chose trout for lunch; he didn't care that much for trout, but eating it always reminded him that he was "home" in the United States. Actually, nothing outside the window of the moving dining car gave him any sense of being "home". The trees along the rail line here as they moved from New Jersey toward Baltimore were too small, too tightly clustered, and too obviously just stands of new growth where farms had spared a patch of forest. The farmhouses were of wood and often needed new coats of paint. Some of the barns sagged. It was a tapestry of American chaos overlaid on a layer of poverty; England and Italy and France had more than enough poverty, Henry James knew well enough, but it rarely manifested itself as sagging, unpainted, wildly planted *chaos.* In England—in most of James's Europe—the old and poor and rundown were *picturesque,* including the people.

Many years earlier, in an essay on Hawthorne (who had been an early passion of his), James had made the mistake of writing to American readers that American soil and history were a sad, blank slate for any American writer, poet, or artist: New England, he had pointed out, lacked Europe's all-important castles, ancient ruins, Roman roads, abandoned sheepherders' cottages, and defined social classes capable of appreciating art. American artists of any sort, he'd suggested, could never achieve a real mastery of their art by reacting to the vulgar, pressing, profit-centered, and always-pressing *new* the way writers and artists in Europe could react romantically to the *old.*

Certain American reviewers, editors, and even readers had taken him to task for these less-than-praise-filled paragraphs. In their eyes, James knew, America, even without any true history, could do no wrong and the vulgar and ever-shifting "newness" that he hated so profoundly— primarily as an impediment to his and any American writer's art—was an aphrodisiac to their Philistine and America-tuned senses.

James remembered writing, in 1879 or thereabouts, putting down his thoughts on Hawthorne and his contemporaries—"It takes a great deal of history to produce a little literature" and "One might enumerate the items of high civilization, as it exists in other countries, which are absent from the texture of American life, until it should become a wonder to know what was left." Perhaps this is why he had added, in Chapter VI of his Hawthorne book—"It is, I think, an indisputable fact that Americans are, as Americans, the most self-conscious people in the world, and the most addicted to the belief that the other nations of the earth are in a conspiracy to undervalue them."

No, it had not made him popular to American readers and reviewers.

Now James shrugged and set all that ancient emotion away from his thoughts as he finished his trout and sipped the last of his less-than-mediocre white wine.

Holmes had ordered only tea and then let the poor American imitation of his choice sit unsipped in its Pennsylvania and New York, New Haven, and Hartford Railroad–crested cup. James was not certain that he'd seen the detective actually *eat* anything since their dinner in Paris on the evening of March 13, now eleven days in the past, and was beginning to wonder how the gaunt detective stayed alive.

"We were talking about Mrs. Clover Adams," Holmes said so suddenly that it startled James.

"Were we? I thought we had moved on to her husband and other members of the Five of Hearts." James made sure that no one was seated in their half of the emptying dining car or any waiter within earshot before he spoke. And even then he spoke very softly.

"You mentioned that Clover made enemies, partially through excluding people from her salon, but also with her wit... perhaps you said because of her 'sharp tongue'," said Holmes. "Can you give me some examples of her saying or writing specific things that hurt specific people?"

James dabbed at his lips with the linen napkin as he thought about this. Then, in a choice so rare as to be all but unique, he chose to share a story in which *he* had been the butt of the joke.

"The last time I was here in America," he said, "a decade ago, I wrote to Clover before boarding my ship back to England and in that missive I explained to her that I had chosen her to receive my last note from our common country because I considered that she—Clover—how did I put it? 'Because I consider you the incarnation of your native land' is the precise wording, I think. Clover wrote back at once, saying that she considered my gesture 'a most equivocal compliment' and, she continued, 'Am I then vulgar, dreary, and impossible to live with?'"

James looked up at Holmes but the detective showed no response. Finally Holmes said, "So the lady did have wit and a sharp tongue. Do you have another example?"

James quenched a sigh. "What good do such stories do now, sir?"

"Clover Adams was a victim of a murder," said Holmes. "Or at least of someone's cruel hoax that she was murdered. In either case, learning who the lady's enemies were—even enemies created by the sharpness of her own acerbic wit—is the obvious way to approach this case."

"Unless, of course, as was the case in this instance, it was not murder at all but rather a suicide," said James. "In which case your list of suspects in the so-called 'case' is quickly narrowed to one name. Elementary, my dear Mr. Holmes."

"Not always," Holmes said cryptically. "I have investigated obvious suicides that were the result of other people's murderous schemes. But please continue."

James did sigh now. "My other friends in the Five of Hearts had, for years, expressed their admiration, if not outright adoration, of my fiction," he said. "Henry Adams, John Hay, Clarence King, even Clara Hay, were genuinely enthusiastic about my stories and novels. Clover Adams was always…more reserved. At one point, an interlocutor who…shall we say…knew the lady well said that in an argument with her husband and John Hay on the literary merits, or lack of same, of a certain Henry

James, Clover was quoted as saying, 'The problem with Harry's fiction isn't that he doesn't chaw what he bites off, but, rather, that he chaws more than he bites off.'"

"Droll," said Holmes. "And I presume the American colloquial dialect was meant to be part of the humor."

James said nothing.

"I am surprised that someone close to both of you chose to report that particular *bon mot* to you," said Holmes.

James remained silent. It had been told to him in one of the finest of London's clubs by no less than Charles F. Adams, Henry Adams's brother—a man whom Henry James had always found to be vulgar in the extreme. Charles Adams had a cruel sense of humor, so unlike his brother's generosity, and enjoyed—James knew—seeing the edge of that humor embarrass or hurt others. Yet James had no doubt that Clover had said precisely those words; it was her dismissive style and, yes, her Boston Brahmin's use of rude American dialect. It had hurt James's feelings extremely upon the hearing. But he had kept Clover as his friend, and that barb—and others Charles Adams and others had relayed to him—had done nothing significant to lessen his sorrow when James had learned of her death more than seven years earlier.

If Henry James wished to be *truly* indiscreet about Adams's brother Charles, he could have reported the cruel statement by Charles that John Hay had relayed to him as far back as the announcement of Henry Adams's and Clover Hooper's marriage—"Heavens! No! The Hoopers are all as crazy as coots. Clover'll kill herself just like her aunt!" Indeed, Clover's Aunt Carrie had killed herself when she was several months pregnant.

And upon return to Boston after many months of the newlyweds' honeymoon in Egypt and Europe, it was William Dean Howells who had written to James about yet another truly vulgar comment in a letter from Charles Adams to Howells—"To see Henry these days, I have—quite literally!—to tear him from the arms of his new bride! For Henry's always in clover now! (Joke! ha! ha!)" The "ha! ha!" alone would have made James distrust Charles Adams for life.

"Tell me more about Henry Adams," said Holmes.

James found himself shrugging—a gesture he had long ago given up in Europe. It was a sign of how upset even retelling the Clover-anecdote had made him. "What more do you need to know?"

"Far more than we can cover before this railway voyage ends in Washington," said Holmes. "But for now we shall settle for what else Henry Adams was known for at the time of Clover's death other than being descended from two American presidents and being a member of his wife's *salon* of the Five of Hearts."

"If I gave the impression that the Five of Hearts was solely, or even primarily, Clover's *salon,* I was mistaken to do so," James said rather waspishly. "Everyone in it, except perhaps Clara Hay, was a powerful personality. For four of them, save for Clara who tends toward the literal in a pleasant way, their wit and even their sense of humor matched perfectly. They punned without mercy. I once observed in person that when one of the Adamses' terriers came home with a scratched eye, John Hay immediately announced that it was obviously a *cat*aract. Clarence King's instant addition was...a *tom-cat*aract."

Holmes waited.

"Henry Adams was a respected lecturer in medieval history at Harvard University," said James. "He turned from academic circles to become one of America's most respected historians. He and Clover were consummate collectors—Adams continues to be so—and, as you may see if Adams is home and invites us to visit, their home reflects an astounding level of both high and advanced taste in everything from Persian carpets to Ming vases to exquisite works of art, including Constables and Turners, chosen before most art collectors could recognize those estimable gentlemen's names. Their home, designed by the late H. H. Richardson as was the Hays', *is* a work of art."

Holmes nodded as if he were taking mental notes on these most elementary of facts about a shy but world-famous man. "And Mr. John Hay?"

"A very old and rather close friend of mine," said James. "I met Hay through William Howells—a famous editor and also an old friend—years ago and have enjoyed seeing him and his wife Clara many times in England, on the Continent, and in the United States. He is an extraordinary man."

"So far all of these Five of Hearts sound extraordinary," said Holmes. "At least by American standards."

Before James could protest, Holmes went on, "I've read of Hay being referred to as Colonel Hay. Has he a military history?"

James chuckled. "When Hay was only twenty-two years old, he became an assistant to John Nicolay, who was personal secretary to President Abraham Lincoln."

Holmes waited impassively. James waited for some flicker, some sign, of the detective being impressed—or even *interested*—but none came.

"In truth," James continued, "Hay served as co-secretary to Lincoln during the darkest years of the Civil War. But, you see, there was no appropriation for a second secretary. Nor even for an assistant to Mr. Nicolay as secretary. So his friend Nicolay arranged it that he, young John Hay, would receive a salary as an employee of the Department of the Interior, assigned to the White House. When that was challenged by some appropriations committee in eighteen sixty-four, the War Department commissioned Hay as a major—'assistant adjutant general of volunteers', I believe was his full title. A year later he was promoted to lieutenant colonel and, shortly after that, received the rank of full colonel."

"Without ever seeing a battlefield," said Holmes.

"Only the ones he toured with President Lincoln."

"I assume Mr. Hay has shown certain accomplishments—besides accruing wealth and a wife—since then," said Holmes.

James did not especially like the detective's tone. It seemed very...*common*...to the writer. But he decided not to make an issue of it at that moment. The waiters were standing by the walls at the opposite end of the dining carriage, hands solemnly folded across their crotches, waiting for Holmes and him to depart.

"Even by the time John Hay married Clara Stone in eighteen seventy-four—when Hay was thirty-five—he'd held important diplomatic posts in three countries." James didn't add that Hay had groused and complained of manners, language, culture, and government in all three of those important European countries in which he'd served. "Also by eighteen seventy-four," added James, "John had become well known as a poet, then as a distinguished journalist. He was famous for his coverage of the Chicago Fire and of the assassination of President Garfield in eighteen eighty-one and of the trial of the anarchist-assassin Charles Guiteau."

"Interesting," said Holmes. "I confess that I wasn't aware that President Garfield had been assassinated, much less by an anarchist."

James simply did not believe this statement. He chose to say nothing.

"Is Mr. Hay still a journalist?" asked Holmes. The detective had lit his pipe and showed absolutely no concern about the impatient waiters.

"He became editor of Mr. Greeley's famous paper—the *Tribune*—but then returned to government service," said Henry James. "In eighteen eighty, poor President Garfield had asked John to move from the State Department to the White House, to become the president's personal secretary. But Hay declined. He left public service before Garfield was shot. Amongst his other pastimes—or perhaps I should say *amusements*—was writing fiction anonymously. At one time, his friend Henry Adams wrote and anonymously published a novel called *Democracy*. Since then there has been infinite speculation about the author's identity; Clover Adams and Clarence King were both suspects of the *literati*'s fevered detecting at one point, but it was John Hay whom most of the experts were sure was the actual author. One rather suspects that the Five of Hearts enjoyed leading the literary world on their round robin chase."

"*Democracy*," muttered Holmes around his pipe. "Did not that book sell rather well in England some years back?"

"Amazingly well," said James. "In England. In America. In France. In Germany. In Timbuktu, for all I know." He was dismayed to hear an undertone of bitterness in his remarks.

"And Clara Hay?" said Holmes. He removed his watch from his waistcoat and glanced at it.

"A lady's lady," said James. "A delightful hostess. A helpmate to her husband. A generous soul. One of the most important *loci* in the Washington social whirl."

"How would you describe her...physically?" asked Holmes.

James raised an eyebrow at the impertinent question. "A pretty face. An impeccable dresser. Lovely hair. Exquisite complexion. Physically...a bit on the pleasantly solid side."

"Stout?"

"*Solid*," repeated James. "She looked thus when John Hay fell in love with her and married her almost twenty years ago, and time and children have added their solidity."

And eating, thought James with a slight pang of betrayal. He remembered a letter from Hay only a year ago in which his dear friend said that the couple and their son were visiting Chicago where he, Hay, had been very active indeed but where Clara, according to Hay, had stayed at the hotel and... "tucked enthusiastically into every victual the dining room offered." Privately, Henry James thought Clara Hay to be matronly, not terribly intelligent—although she was well-read and wise enough to admire James's novels—sanctimonious in a backwoods American Baptist-minister's-daughter's sort of way (although this was not at all her background, although she *did* come from Ohio), and altogether an unworthy member of the extraordinary Five of Hearts.

He would never tell Sherlock Holmes this.

"Tell me about Clarence King," said Holmes, "and we shall return to our carriage and let these good people tidy up their dining car for the dinner service."

"There is no dinner service on the *Colonial Express*," said James, inwardly pleased to have caught the famous detective out on an error. "We are scheduled to arrive in Washington before the dinner hour."

"Ahhh," said Holmes, blowing a column of smoke from the oversized pipe. "Then you can describe Clarence King at leisure. Oh, I should say that I remember reading about Mr. King's exposure of that western diamond-mine hoax in the late eighteen seventies. Somewhere in Colorado, was it not?"

"It was supposed to be," agreed James. "Clarence King—all five foot six of him—is a truly extraordinary man: geologist, mountain climber, explorer, surveyor, government servant, *aficionado* of fine food and fine wine and fine art. Henry Adams and John Hay always believed—sincerely, one thinks—that of all of the Five of Hearts, Clarence King was the one whose future was least limited... most probable for fame, glory, and high position."

"Did Clover Adams believe that?"

James hesitated for only the briefest of heartbeats. "She thought Clarence something of a rogue. But she loved him more for that, if anything. It was Clarence King who sent the Adamses and the other Hearts both fine Five of Hearts stationery for all of their use and a beautiful Five of Hearts tea set."

"Describe it, please," said Holmes, removing the pipe stem from his mouth.

"I beg your pardon?"

"Please describe the tea set."

Henry James looked out the window at the increasingly summer-like forests and fields flashing by as if he could gain strength from the gaze. It was evening. The last rays of a late-March sunset tinged the trees and telegraph poles.

"The tea set is quite charming, actually," he said at last. "Five cups and saucers, of course. All heart-shaped and a bit undersized."

"All five of the Hearts are—were—small people," said Holmes.

"Why...yes," said James, a bit nonplussed by the observation. Had he supplied that information? He only remembered mentioning Clarence King's height.

"What else can you tell me about the tea set?" asked Holmes.

The man is *mad,* thought Henry James. He said, "The tea tray is beautifully enameled and inset with designs that look like small fruit on branches but are actually each a cluster of five hearts. The sugar and cream bowls also follow the hearts theme. On the teapot, and just below the upper appendage of the tray—which, if I remember correctly, is set off by a large and quite fragile capital 'T'—are painted clocks showing the hour of five o'clock, exactly."

"The hour the Five of Hearts met each day of the work week," said Holmes. "Usually in front of the Adamses' hearth in chairs designed specifically for their diminutive size. Adams and his wife Clover seated opposite one another in tiny—and matching—red-leather chairs."

"Yes," said James, having no idea where Holmes had dredged up that last fact, although it was accurate enough.

Holmes nodded as if satisfied. "Let us return to our rather public first-class carriage," he said.

* * *

Problems with the track somewhere south of Baltimore set the *Colonial Express* far behind schedule. For hours Holmes and James sat in the relatively uncomfortable so-called "first-class" section with nothing to look at out the windows—night had fallen hours earlier—no dinner, and little relief from the tedium save for their reading and an occasional cup of coffee brought by an apologetic steward. Holmes asked no more questions—a rather pathetic show for a detective, James thought—and they sat in silence for the long, humid hours.

At long last the *"Express"* got back under way, but they arrived in the nation's capital many hours late—long after civilized Washingtonians had dined and after many had turned in for the night.

But the Hays' brougham was waiting for them at the station, along with Hay's first footman, Severs, and their trunks and valises were soon loaded outside, and covered with a tarpaulin (a light rain had begun to fall), as James and Holmes climbed into the compartment of the gleaming black Kinross Brougham that Hay had sent for them.

Street lamps were surrounded by soft halos that reminded James of the night some eleven days earlier when he and Holmes had met on the bank of the Seine. With those thoughts came a dire sense of something very much like terror. What was he *doing* introducing this strange and almost certainly deranged man into the inner circle of some of his closest private friends? Holmes's pathetic disguise of "Mr. Jan Sigerson, Norwegian explorer" would be found out, if not on Sunday evening when the Norwegian ambassador was dining at the Hays', then even earlier than that. What would his old friends John and Clara Hay—much less Henry Adams, who *never spoke to anyone* of his late wife or her suicide out of the long resonances of his terrible grief—think of him for deceiving them in this way, for introducing this madman to them?

Henry James was actively sick to his stomach as the brougham rolled through the brick and cobblestoned streets of this least-businesslike of all major American cities. The few shops, restaurants, and public places they passed along the way were closed and dark. Even in the finer neighborhoods here near the Executive Mansion, only a few interior gas or electric lights still burned. The trees in this southern city were fully leafed out and it felt to James as if they were being carried deeper and deeper into a dark tunnel of his own foolish construction.

"I believe the Americans have a saying—'They roll the sidewalks up after dark'," Holmes said at one point and the sound of the tall shadow's voice gave James a start but did not bring him fully back from his broodings. "It certainly seems true of Washington, D.C.," added the detective.

James said nothing.

Then they were next to Lafayette Square—a darkened Executive Mansion was visible through the trees—and turning at the intersection of Sixteenth Street onto H Street. St. John's Church rose whitely on one side of the street and the Hay residence loomed in wet red brick on the other. John Hay was standing in the strange Richardsonian arched-tunnel of an entranceway to greet them.

"Harry, Harry, we're so delighted you came back," boomed Hay, a compact, thin, elegant man with receding hair parted neatly in the middle, dark brows, and a full but triune-shaped mustache-chin-beard that was going white before the rest of his hair. Hay's eyes were alight with intelligence and his voice echoed in the tunnel of an entrance with a sincere welcome.

And then they were in the house proper, coats and hats were smoothly removed by servants while other footmen bustled past and then up a staircase beyond the huge foyer with their bags and trunks, and James had made the treacherous introduction of "Sigerson" without faltering, although his heart pounded at his own deception and his mouth was unnaturally dry.

"Ah, Mr. Sigerson," cried John Hay. "I read about your Tibetan adventures last year in both the English and American papers. It is such a pleasure having you as our guest."

James could see Holmes looking around at the house...the mansion. The foyer was huge and paneled with South American mahogany so perfectly polished that one could almost see one's reflection in the dark wood. Above the mahogany wainscoting the walls were a rich terra-cotta red that matched the red in so many of the Persian carpets and runners set about on the gleaming floors. High above them—St. John's

Cathedral–high—the spaces above the gleaming chandeliers were criss-crossed with massive mahogany rafters. Ahead of them, the grand stairway was wide enough to accommodate a marching band walking ten-abreast if the occasion ever arose.

"Clara sends her deepest regrets for not staying up to greet you," said Hay. "I'm afraid she had to take to her bed early tonight due to one of those rare fierce headaches that have plagued her for so long. She looks forward to meeting both of you at breakfast—unless you prefer to breakfast in your rooms, of course. I know that *you* enjoy taking your breakfast in your room, Harry."

"Alas, a bachelor's old habits," said James. "Especially on the first morning after a somewhat arduous week and a half of constant travel."

"Clara and I shall see you later in the morning then," laughed Hay. "Mr. Sigerson? Would you also like to receive your breakfast in your room?"

"I sincerely look forward to coming down and meeting Mrs. Hay at breakfast," said Holmes in what James now heard as an exaggerated—an obviously false—Scandinavian accent.

"Wonderful!" cried Hay. "Clara and I will press you on all the current gossip surrounding Harry." He smiled toward James to show he was jesting.

"But speaking of dining, gentlemen, I know how late the train was in arriving and also know that the accursed *Colonial Express* offers no dinners during its approach to Washington. You must be starved."

"We lunched rather late..." began Henry James, blushing slightly not at the thought of putting his host out but at the sheer awfulness of what he was doing.

"Nonsense, nonsense," said Hay. "You must be famished. I've had Cook and Benson set out a light repast for you." He put a well-manicured hand on each of their shoulders and led them through the cavernous—but strangely warm—space and into the dining room.

James saw at once that the dining room was larger, more elegant, and certainly furnished with a finer taste than the one he had seen in photographs of the dining room in Mr. Cleveland's White House. In every room they had been in or passed by, James had noticed the elaborately

and beautifully sculpted stone fireplaces. The walls boasted art masterpieces interspersed with ancient tapestries and the occasional framed
light sketch—the signs of high taste combined with a gifted collector's
eclecticism.

The "light repast" consisted of a groaning sideboard loaded with a
freshly baked turkey, half a Virginia ham, salads, steaming vegetables,
and a second buffet gleaming with wines, clarets, whiskeys, waters, and
various liqueurs. The long table had been set and lighted by candelabra
for three at the far end.

"We are all bachelors tonight," laughed Hay. "We shall have to feed
and fend for ourselves."

They did this, of course, by pointing and having Hay's Benson and
two under-butlers fill their plates with their choices.

When they were seated in the circle of candlelight and after Hay had
toasted their safe arrival in America, they set to. James was astonished
to find that despite his nausea during the drive from the huge railway
station, he was indeed famished.

"Harry," said Hay, addressing James, "I'm sorry to tell you that
Adams is not yet returned from some southern lark to Cuba with
Phillips. He was scheduled to return home last week but somewhere
down there he ran into Alexander Agassiz and since then he's thrown
schedules to the wind—quite literally—and has been geologizing on
coral reefs with Agassiz. Evidently they drifted north to further relax
with the Camerons at the Coffin Point retreat on St. Helena. I must say
that Adams is not exactly rushing home to spend time with me or his
other friends here."

"Shall I miss him then?" asked James, shocked to hear some audible
sound of relief in his own voice.

"Oh, no, I think not!" cried Hay with a laugh. "I believe that Adams
will show up in the first week of April . . . just days away now. You can
enjoy the comparative sanity with us until he does arrive."

Hay turned to Sherlock Holmes. "Is your repast edible after the ardors
of your crossing and non-express *Colonial Express* traveling, Mr. Sigerson?"

"Delicious," said Holmes, and James noticed that the detective actually *had* taken a few forkfuls of ham. "Quite perfect, Mr. Hay."

"Good, good," boomed John Hay. "And we shall do everything in our modest powers to make all the rest of your stay with us here in Washington equally as pleasant." Hay turned back to James. "Oh, Harry, another bonus—I've just learned today that Clarence King will be arriving in Washington tomorrow, on the way to or from some Mexican gold mine no doubt, but he's agreed to join us for dinner on Sunday night. That is the night when King Oskar the Second's diplomatic emissary is dining with us. Clarence will be so delighted to see you after all these years."

James looked at Holmes and allowed himself a small but secretly wicked smile. "You are in great luck, Sigerson," he said. "Not only will the ambassador from the King of Sweden and Norway be here on Sunday, but so shall one of the world's most famous and best-informed *explorers*. I am sure that each of them will have many questions to put to you."

Holmes looked up from sipping his wine, smiled thinly, and nodded without comment.

CHAPTER 9

Hay had said that breakfast would be served in the smaller dining room—the one with so many windows looking out into their garden area—at 7:30, so Holmes allowed himself to sleep until 7:00 a.m. He slept well but awoke with joint pains and an incipient sense of panic. Going into the resplendent bathroom that was, amazingly, part of his guest suite, Holmes unfolded a soft leather bag and removed the dark vial and syringe from their leather pockets. After holding the syringe's needle for a moment in alcohol that had come from a small stone bottle in an adjacent pocket, Holmes filled the syringe to the proper level, tapped it to remove any air bubbles, removed a short length of flexible chemist's tubing that was folded into the leather travel "sponge bag", tied it tightly around his upper left arm—increasing the tension by gripping the tubing firmly by his teeth and tugging sharply—and then he injected the morphine into the vein at the crook of his inner arm. There were dark marks and scabs showing many, many earlier injections there.

Holmes sat on the edge of the bathtub until the morphine began to work on his pain and panic. For the first time he noticed that the bathtub-rim and walls surrounding the tub were of a beautiful blue-and-white Delft pattern.

He took his time bathing—marveling at the truly hot water that flowed instantly from the tap after only a slight turn of the silver spigot by Holmes's amazingly prehensile toes and then shaved with his straight razor while looking down from the mirror frequently to throw suspicious glances at what looked to be a secondary and much smaller Delft bathtub permanently set into the floor near the corner of the wash basin. Holmes's incredible deductive powers told him that this must be some bizarre American instrument for bathing one's feet. (At the very least it was far too low to serve as a bidet—a French invention and *toilette*-related custom that Holmes, for all of his interest in staying clean, had always found disgusting.)

Bathed and shaved, Holmes touched up his Sigerson-hair with a darkening agent, made the darkened hair wilder and more vertical with some patented hair crème and attacks from two hairbrushes, ran a mustache comb under Sigerson's nose, and dressed in a bit-too-wooly-thick green tweed suit for his day in the city.

Then Holmes found his way down the huge stairway where a servant immediately led him to the breakfast room.

* * *

Wait a minute.

The reader needs to pardon this interruption as the narrator makes a comment here.

Perhaps it slipped your notice, although I doubt it (since it is dangerous for a narrator ever to underestimate the intelligence and observation powers of readers), but at this point we have shifted point-of-view in the narrative. Up until now I have kept our perceptions focused on what writers and professors call either "a limited third-person point-of-view", the third person in this instance being Mr. Henry James, or at most I have indulged in a *very* limited "limited omniscient point-of-view". In truth, there has been a distinct lack of omniscience throughout this manuscript.

As the narrator in question, I may further alienate you from your suspension of disbelief vis-à-vis the current narration by telling you that I dislike shifting points-of-view in a tale. I find a narrator's presumed ability to hop from mind-to-mind both presumptuous and unrealistic. Worse than that, it is so often simply inelegant.

As literature has descended into mere entertainment via a deliberate vandalism and diminishment of our once-proud language, authors also have begun leaping around between and into their characters' minds *for no other reason than that they can.*

Regarding my shift to Sherlock Holmes's point-of-view, I could give a dozen convincing explanations as to why I make this shift at this time: i.e., Henry James later learned this information and I, as narrator, am somehow receiving the intelligence from him retroactively in time. Neither will Dr. John Watson, M.D., ever hear the details of this 1893 American adventure, so I would be lying to claim the overused doctor as my source of information.

Or perhaps this narrator could say that he has, through the usual arcane means involving opened bank vaults or misplaced trunks found in attics, come across a long-lost manuscript (discovered, perhaps, alongside Holmes's equally lost volumes titled *The Whole Art of Detection?*) which conveniently included encrypted notes from these days in question, notes which somehow allow us to perceive things from the detective's point-of-view for this part of the tale. Surely more apparently miraculous things have happened in real life than this "discovery" of long-lost notes by the beekeeping retired gentleman who lived out the last years of his life in "a small farm upon the [Sussex] downs five miles from Eastbourne."

Alas, no. No encrypted notes from the beekeeper. No discovery of Holmes's promised-but-never-found *The Whole Art of Detection.* To be specific, none of my information comes directly from James or Holmes, nor even from Dr. Watson or his literary agent, Arthur Conan Doyle. At some point I may—or may not—discuss the source of my information about this period and these men, but for now the simple truth and short version are that I know more about most of Holmes's and James's three-month stay in America in 1893 from Sherlock Holmes's point-of-view than James's. I don't know all of his thoughts—I do not have that power over or insight into either character, either *man*—but I do have more information on Holmes's actions during these weeks than I know of anyone else's in this narrative, and, from that, any competent narrator should be able to guess or intuit or deduce or simply imagine many of his thoughts.

But if the reader is not already overly estranged by this temporary shift in our focus, your narrator will do his best to keep the number of points-of-view to two while working diligently to keep those two viewpoints from hopping back and forth like the proverbial grasshopper in the very real skillet.

* * *

The buffet in the sunny breakfast room was smaller than last night's long mahogany sideboard in the dining room, but its groaning nature was comparable. Artfully arranged on delicate china and in silver chafing dishes were the makings for full English breakfasts, light French breakfasts, astounding American breakfasts, and, of course, presumably because Jan Sigerson was supposed to be Norwegian, smoked salmon and slivers of whitefish, a salmon-omelette, pickled herring, and English cucumbers—supposedly a London favorite of visiting Norwegians—mixed in with red and green peppers. John Hay—or, to be more precise, John Hay's cook—had somehow provided Syltetøy, a Norwegian sweet jelly, to go with the morning breads. With the French, Swiss, and American cheeses were Jarlsberg, gouda, Norwegia, Nøkkelost, Pultost, and grunost, a very sweet Norwegian cheese made from goat's milk. (Holmes had tried grunost once and that, he'd decided at once, had been more than enough experience with the cloying goo.)

Sherlock Holmes filled his plate with bits of English, American, and Norwegian breakfasts—although a French croissant and Turkish-strong coffee were his usual breakfast when he was at 221 B Baker Street—and enjoyed his morning conversation with John and Clara Hay.

The 44-year-old Mrs. Hay, Holmes saw at once, had long since passed Henry James's somewhat unkind description of "solid", had—probably in her mid- to late-30s—passed through and beyond the category of "matronly" and was now set firmly in a thickset, multiple-chinned sort of upper-class glory that would probably stay with her until her last years. It did not seem to diminish John Hay's delight in her (Holmes remembered James saying that she was "solid" when Hay fell in love with her and seemed to revel in it) and, in truth, Holmes still saw Clara Hay's beauty in the perfection of her clothing, the gleam of a perfect but modest jewel on one soft finger of her pudgy hand, the coruscations of her perfectly set hair, her near-flawless complexion, and a lustrous quality to her wide, bright eyes that no amount of "tucking into her victuals" would probably ever erase.

Also, Clara Hay was a pleasant, caring person and a wonderful hostess. Holmes—especially in his strange, wild-haired, fiercely mustached Sigerson persona—could tell that almost at once. Her voice was a pleasant contralto and, when Clara Hay was in a position where listening was called for (such as after asking Mr. Sigerson a question), she actually *listened.* Holmes knew how rare this gift was of being patient enough actually to listen and immediately saw why Mrs. John Hay, "Clara" to so many hundreds of her close friends (in that bold American way where people in society actually used each other's Christian names without that English fear that they would be mistaken for a servant), would be the indispensable hostess for a capital city such as Washington.

When Holmes complimented Clara Hay on the beautiful blue-and-green gown she was wearing—and it *was* beautiful, in a dignified and understated way—his hostess did not blush or act like a falsely modest maiden but said, "Yes, it is nice, isn't it, Mr. Sigerson, even if designed only for everyday wear. I appreciate your appreciation of it—a sign of your good taste, I believe. The design is by the Parisian couturier Charles Worth...who was referred to me by our late friend Mrs. Clover Adams." Clara Hay glanced at her husband as if to ask if she could tell more, but if there were some signal sent from the colonel to his lady, Holmes missed it.

"Clover used to say," continued Clara Hay, "that a Worth gown not only filled her soul with happiness but...what was her exact phrase, John."

"Not only filled her soul with happiness but sealed it hermetically," said Hay.

"Ah, yes," said Holmes's hostess, smiling as he did. "Monsieur Worth won Clover Adams's undying loyalty one day in Paris in eighteen eighty-one when the couturier continued to stay with Clover and make last-minute alterations to her gown when both Mrs. Vanderbilt and Mrs.

Astor were waiting in the outer room. That was enough recommendation for me, you see, and I have never regretted turning to Monsieur Worth first when we are shopping in Paris."

"It is a truly stunning dress," said Holmes. "Knowing as little as I do about such things as I am a bachelor, I would still venture to say that Monsieur Worth's particular genius has more than repaid your allegiance." He set down his empty coffee cup and shook his head slightly when the under-butler moved to refill it.

"So what would you like to do today, Mr. Sigerson?" asked John Hay. The more Holmes saw of the diplomat's long, white fingers, the more he was sure that Hay could have been a fine violinist if his musical tastes had turned that way, as Holmes's had, at a young age.

"We can wait for Harry and take a carriage excursion through the city," continued Hay. "Show you the historical sites and monuments, drive through Rock Creek Park, perhaps peek in on Congress in session and have some bean soup there for lunch." Hay laughed easily. "Harry hates sight-seeing of any organized sort, but we shall simply outvote him. That's what democracies are for, after all . . . the tyranny of the less-cultured majority such as myself!"

"Thank you," said Holmes. "But if you and Mrs. Hay do not mind, I would like to spend this first day in Washington as I tend to spend all first days in new cities or locales . . . exploring on foot."

"Very good," Hay said with real enthusiasm. "Would you like us to give you some directions for the major sights?"

Holmes smiled under his Sigerson mustache. "Getting lost is my preferred first step in each of my explorations."

Hay laughed at this.

"If you leave before Harry comes down we shall tell him that you will be back by . . . when?" said Clara Hay. "Shall we plan on you for luncheon, tea, or dinner?"

"Tea, I think," said Holmes. "Do you have it at five p.m.?"

"That is the hour," said John Hay, dabbing at his lips beneath the billowing white mustache with a pure-white linen napkin. "Although there may be other options than tea for us men if you've had an adventurous day exploring."

Fifteen minutes later, James having still not made an appearance, Holmes left the house in his green tweed suit, a walking stick with a silver head in the shape of a barking dog, and a full briefcase clutched in his left hand. He was striding briskly under low gray clouds. The day was rather muggy, much warmer than either Paris or New York had been, and Holmes's/Sigerson's wool suit was too warm for such a spring day, but this did not stop him from walking at a very brisk pace with the effortless, long-legged strides of the indefatigable explorer he was supposed to be.

The briefcase contained a strange change of clothes. In the upper inside pocket of his tweed jacket he carried photographs of three men, one much younger than the other two. In his right trouser pocket, Holmes carried a French-made, spring-opening knife with a 6-inch blade that had a cutting edge so sharp that one could remove all the hairs on one's arm with it without feeling the slightest touch of contact.

* * *

Holmes had two objectives for his day of "exploring" in Washington: the first was a mere local errand that might end up a tad expensive; the second was a longer voyage by foot into areas that would almost certainly be dangerous. He looked forward to the second task.

Now as he ambled along, seemingly oblivious to the threatening weather or even the city around him, he took in—as was his training and habit—almost everything around him.

Holmes saw that no one was following him.

Holmes noticed that while the homes were rather nice here near Lafayette Square and the Executive Mansion—what Americans would come to call the White House—they were mostly of the flat-fronted, old Federalist design with their modest stoops opening directly onto the sidewalks. The exception to this traditional flavor had been the Hays' and Adamses' towering twin piles of red brick in the Richardsonian design. Even as he'd walked away, Holmes had noticed that the bricks of Hay's mansion facing Sixteenth Street had been architect-unique: longer, wider, and deeper than any standard building brick. He hadn't yet taken time to study the front of Henry Adams's house next door on H Street, but he hoped to see that home soon enough.

The trees in bloom along the not-very-wide sidewalks were relatively young and short. Only in the parks had some of the chestnut and elm trees reached their mature height. Washington, D.C., although almost a hundred years old and despite its gleaming-white Roman civic architecture and few great monuments, had the feel of a new and rather sleepy city.

The boulevards were broad but not very busy even in late morning; by London or Paris standards, they were all but empty. On the busier cross-streets, Holmes caught glimpses of small, hooded gigs—what the Americans called "buggies"—as well as fashionable cabriolets and chaises, commercial coaches and canvas-sided "floats" filled with milk churns or stacked marble, the occasional stylish four-in-hand dashing through traffic, some dog carts (usually with young people at the reins), quite a few gleaming black broughams of the quality Hay had sent to the rail station the night before, a plodding assortment of wagons, wagonettes, and vans hauling goods, a few men on horseback, and even a very few gleaming and belching brass and red-leather horseless carriages being guided by men in dusters and goggles at the tillers.

Even though he had to pass the Executive Mansion, Holmes's glance did not linger on the miniature white palace housing President Cleveland. The detective had last been to the White House in November of 1881—during the trial of President Garfield's assassin, the pathetic and more-or-less insane Charles Guiteau. Holmes had been pressed into the service by his older brother Mycroft at Whitehall and by Mycroft's superior in the intelligence services at the time, Sir George Mansfield Smith-Cumming.

In 1881—as now in 1893—the formal British Secret Service had not yet formally come into being (it will be founded in 1909), much less branched into its domestic intelligence service (MI5) and its foreign intelligence service (MI6), but Prime Minister Disraeli had established a "Joint Information and Research Unit" that was actually an oversight and political-liaison committee between the prime minister's office, Whitehall, and the hodge-podge of intelligence services run by the

Army Intelligence Service, Royal Navy Intelligence, and half a dozen other military agencies.

Mycroft Holmes, only 34 years old at the time but already indispensable at Whitehall due to his astounding mathematical ability and reasoning skills, was second-in-command of the Joint Committee (reporting only to the Acting Director at the time of its founding in 1881, Captain Sir George Mansfield Smith-Cumming of the Admiralty's intelligence service). Mycroft was now co-director of the nascent British Secret Service along with William Melville.

Sherlock's brother had been given a basement office at 12 Downing Street for his intelligence duties, but Holmes knew that his massive brother had never visited the fully fitted-out Downing Street office. All Joint Committee and Military Directorate of Intelligence operations were soon directed out of Mycroft's office at Whitehall with his nominal superiors coming *there* for briefings. This was because Mycroft divided his time between Whitehall and his own creation, the Diogenes Club, a private club half a block away from Whitehall and reachable by both formal tunnels and covered walkways. The older Holmes brother had divided his world between these two interior spaces; there was no third. He slept and ate and amused himself at the Diogenes Club. His younger brother had long known that Mycroft was terrified by open spaces. In years yet to come, Mycroft Holmes would be described as "agoraphobic".

The Diogenes Club itself, begun, as mentioned earlier, by Mycroft and half a dozen other very strange London men of means and power who shared a fear of open spaces and strangers, was by far the strangest of all the scores of men's clubs in the city. There were the usual newspapers and meals available, the usual staff of capable servants and silent waiters, a rather good dining room and an excellent and extensive library, comfortable sleeping rooms and even more comfortable deep leather reading chairs in the Upstairs Lounge, but the primary rule—and primary source of comfort for the Diogenes Club members—was that members (and the very few and very rare authorized visitors) could not begin a conversation or speak to anyone, even other charter members, in any place except the sealed-off Strangers Room. Mycroft and the other founding members of the Diogenes Club were not only afraid of strangers and of talking to strangers, they were afraid of clubs.

Sherlock Holmes knew that his brother had many other debilitating phobias. Such was the nature of the de facto director of all of Her Majesty's de facto Secret Service in late March of 1893.

When Sherlock was hastily dispatched to America in 1881 to interview and investigate President Garfield's assassin Guiteau (an assignment especially inconvenient to Holmes, not the least of which reason being that he'd only recently settled into his new digs at 221 B with Watson and was finally receiving his first trickle of private, paying clients), he assumed that the assignment was to be a waste of time due to what the consulting detective then believed was his brother Mycroft's phobia related to anarchists and what Sherlock Holmes saw as his brother's baseless fantasy about an "international conspiracy of anarchists". Consulting Detective Holmes thought it was about as likely that there would be an annual Anarchists' Convention as any real conspiratorial connections between the random madmen.

But while Holmes helped prove that Guiteau had been a lone actor, the continued international anarchist threats, bombings, assassinations, and sometimes elaborate plots turned out to be very real indeed. In 1886 Holmes was back in America, investigating the site of the so-called Chicago "Haymarket Square Massacre". It was Holmes who discovered who had actually killed the seven policemen—papers and legend were suggesting then that the police had shot each other and textbooks today repeat the calumny—and the results of his investigation remain secret to this day. A year later, in 1887 London, it was Sherlock Holmes and two men from a specially formed squad from Scotland Yard who prevented—only in the very nick of time—the assassination of Queen Victoria by the famed big-game hunter and marksman-for-hire Colonel Sebastian Moran and an accomplice. The two had positioned themselves to fire Jebel rifles placed in an advantageous firing position within the closed Royal Aquarium opposite Westminster Abbey just as Her Majesty entered her royal coach on her own Jubilee Day. The accomplice had been captured; the master marksman and ultimate mercenary huntsman Moran had somehow escaped through the maze of tunnels, labyrinths, steam pipes, and workers' service corridors beneath the Royal Aquarium.

* * *

Holmes's first stop as Mr. Jan Sigerson was at the Clarkson Scientific Apparatus and Photographic Materials shop only some ten blocks from the Hays' front door.

As he entered the dimly lit interior, Holmes could not but speculate that this was almost certainly the very shop in which Clover Adams not only had bought her own photographic supplies before her death in 1885, but whoever had supplied her with the poisonous potassium cyanide fixing-solution as a gift might well have also purchased it here.

"May I help you?" asked a pleasant-looking man with sharp-boned but ruddy cheeks and the tiniest-diameter spectacles Holmes had ever seen.

"I am looking for a magic-lantern projector," said Holmes in his slight Norwegian accent.

"Very good, sir. For in-home purposes or larger commercial presentations—say in a music- or science-hall or general auditorium space?"

"To be put to relatively modest in-home use for now," said Holmes, looking around admiringly at the rows of carefully lighted cameras, enlargers, glass-plate slide projectors, developing devices, and rack after rack of chemicals. The place had the quiet aura of a wizard's shop. "Perhaps later," added Holmes, "I will require a more elaborate projection apparatus."

"To purchase today or to rent, sir?"

"To rent," said Holmes. The irony was that he had no fewer than three specialized photographic-plate slide projectors back at 221 B Baker Street. He had used them for years for a wide variety of reasons, not the least of which was to project and compare fingerprints or microscopically enlarged shard-ends of tobacco or cloth. But obviously he hadn't taken the bulky and delicate projectors—or any of his hundreds of carefully labeled glass photographic plates—with him when he'd arranged to "die" along with the mythical Napoleon of Crime at Reichenbach Falls two years earlier.

The clerk, who announced that his name was Charles Macready—youngest brother of the late English actor William Charles Macready—and that it was his shop and a pleasure to wait on the Norwegian gentleman, led Holmes into a curtained alcove near the rear of the store where a cluster of black-metal and gleaming mahogany-and-brass projectors sat on carefully lighted shelves.

Mr. Macready touched a black-metal device. "This is the newest thing—the lamp is electric so no illuminant fuel is required. A seven-foot electrical cord. No smell of paraffin or fear of tipping over or overheating. The mirror above the electrical bulb focuses the light, you see."

Holmes had noted that the Hay house was electrified, but he thought it would be undignified to ask that cords be hung from chandelier sockets. "I won't require electric."

Macready nodded and moved to a more compact black-metal-and-brass device. "Here is a Woodbury and Marcy Sciopticon. It uses a double flat-wick illuminant, fueled by kerosene, and you can control the height of the wicks for maximum light intensity on the images."

"I think not," said Holmes, stroking his chin. "What is that smaller one?"

"A very bright and sturdy little projector manufactured by Ernst Plank at Fabrik Optischer und Mechanischer Waren in Nuremberg," said Mr. Macready. "But it takes small glass plates. What is the size of the slides you wish to show, sir?"

"Three and a half by five inches," said Holmes. "Reduced by half from original plate size."

Macready nodded. "Then I'm afraid the little Ernst Plank model will not suit your needs. It's wonderful for small science-class presentations or home magic-lantern shows, but your presentation sounds more serious, more...panoramic."

"Yes," said Holmes.

"We have double- and triple-lensed projectors for special effects, especially when shown in a larger hall," said the proprietor. "You may know that it allows the projection operator to fade from one image to the next, to overlay two or three images, and thus to give the illusion of movement if the slide images are consecutive in motion. They really act as a sort of motion-picture projector."

Holmes shook his head. "I require only a good, solid, safe magic-lantern projector. What is this one?" Holmes touched the larger model with its boxes of mahogany-and-brass lenses and a rather beautiful red-leather bellows lens extender. The detective knew its worth because he owned one almost identical.

"Ah, yes, a very fine unit, sir," said Macready, setting his blunt hands on the larger machine. "Made by Archer and Sons in Liverpool. It is illuminated using a limelight burner, so one must take special care—it burns very hot. But the images are spectacular . . . in small rooms or large halls. You see that each side has a square-hinged door opening into the illumination chamber as well as a blue-glass circular viewing door with a swivel glass cover. The Japanned metal top cover attaches the tall chimney-cowl *here* . . ."

Macready gently touched an oval aperture. "I have the cowl and chimney in the back, Mr. . . . ."

"Sigerson," said Holmes.

"You see, Mr. Sigerson, how easily the illumination unit slides right out with one easy pull of this brass knob."

"I shall take it," said Holmes.

"How many nights' rental, sir?"

"Just two nights. I shall return it on Monday."

"That works well since the shop is closed on Sundays, sir. So we shall charge for only one night's rental. We would be delighted to have the projectors returned before noon on the workday they are due, if that is convenient for you, Mr. Sigerson."

"Perfectly convenient," said Holmes. He didn't comment on the price when Macready quoted it but counted the dollars out from a rather absurdly thick wad of American bills he carried in his pocket. Holmes pulled the shopkeeper's small pad closer, clicked open his mechanical pencil, wrote, and said, "Can you have it delivered to this address?"

Macready glanced at Holmes's handwriting and said with a tone of even deeper respect, "Colonel Hay's home. Absolutely, sir. It shall be delivered before five p.m. today."

"Oh, and I'll need fuel for it," said Holmes.

"Included in the price, sir. The carrying bottles are foolproof and fireproof and set into their own wooden carrying tray. And may I compliment you on your choice, sir. Archer and Sons is a superb optical manufacturer and this unit works with such brilliance that the viewers almost think they are actually there within the frames of the photographic slide. This projector will serve you well whether you're presenting your slides to a packed house of scientists at the Smithsonian Institution or in the Executive Mansion itself."

Holmes smiled. "Those venues may have to come somewhat later in my schedule, Mr. Macready."

CHAPTER 10

Now Holmes was seeking out the worst slums in Washington, D.C.

He walked west through the southern reaches of one of these slums—Foggy Bottom—a low-lying industrial area hosting the city's gas works, some still-working glass plants amidst the stone and brick remains of their closed brethren, and a diminishing number of odiferous breweries. The air here was thick enough and foul enough to justify the slum's name, some of the industrial miasma clearly visible as a sort of swirling green fog. As with all of Washington, D.C.'s, worst slums, the inhabitants here built their shelters along the long, unpaved alleys. Many of the residents of Foggy Bottom were—or had been at one time—employed in these abandoned breweries and tumbledown manufacturing ruins, but the alleys were still lined with tin shacks and wooden hovels, many of them abandoned but others still housing families (or solitary, sullen men) too poor to move elsewhere. Along with the miasma that hung over Foggy Bottom, there seemed to hover a second fog of vain hopes that industry and living wages would once again return to the disintegrating neighborhoods.

Holmes found what he wanted near the southwest edge of Foggy Bottom: five rotting, peeling, once middle-class homes standing amidst high weeds on an otherwise abandoned block.

He chose his house carefully, walked around the back, and tested the still-intact rear door. It was locked. These homes were almost certainly for sale, although their former owners and current sales agents were living in a fantasy world if they thought anyone would buy them now for purposes of residence.

Using the small jimmy-tools from his folded leather purse, Holmes let himself in and wandered through the chilly rooms where wallpaper, once eagerly chosen with hope in some long-failed domestic future, peeled away from clammy walls like skin from a corpse.

Upstairs he found what he'd sought: a locked closet. Holmes jimmied it open, undid the clasp of his bulging briefcase, and brought out a change of clothes. When he was completely changed, down to his under-linens, Holmes folded his good tweed "Norwegian suit", shirt, shoes, and underclothes into the briefcase, set the briefcase on the high shelf of the otherwise empty closet, and used his tools to lock the warped door once again.

There was no mirror left intact in the old house but it had grown dark enough out under the advancing storm that Holmes could check his appearance in one of the long windows in an empty upstairs room.

He was now a grubby American laborer—down to the thick boots and soiled Irish cap—complete with dirty waistcoat and baggy trousers held up with one suspender. He'd applied make-up to approximate months of grime to his face and hands and nails. Holmes allowed his hair to fall from beneath his foul cap at random, greasy angles and now even his carefully trimmed Norwegian-explorer's mustache had been augmented into an overgrown American's soup-strainer. Even his fancy cane, the outer sheath slid away, was now a rough walking stick with a lump of brass rather than sculpted silver at its head. Unless someone hefted that stick, they wouldn't guess that it had a core of lead poured down its center and a solid lead sphere centered under the wood in the rough knob at the top. He still carried the French gravity blade in the pocket of his working-man's trousers and kept the three photographs tucked securely in his shirt pocket.

Holmes went out of the old house, locked it behind him, and walked south toward the Southwest slums he sought, his stout stick banging against tilted sidewalk pavers and rough cobblestones as he went.

* * *

No trace of either the Norwegian gentleman he was currently passing as or the English gentleman he'd so long passed as was left as he walked the rough, dangerous streets of southwest Washington, D.C. His "disguise" as an unemployed, rum-reeking common American laborer did not feel strange on him. He had been pretending to be an English gentleman all of his adult life and sometimes the pretense grew wearisome indeed.

In the century and more to come from this moment in March of 1893, there will be multiple biographies written about Sherlock Holmes. Most will get his birth year—1854—correct. Most will write about how he and his older brother Mycroft came from landed gentry in Yorkshire. They will tell of his youthful education in a Yorkshire manor and his years at Cambridge. Almost all of these facts—after the year of his birth—will be incorrect.

Everything that future biographers—speculators—of Sherlock Holmes's past assume as true comes from a few words quoted by Dr. John Watson and published in *The Strand* in a tale titled "The Adventure of the Greek Interpreter". The conversation between the doctor and the detective that particular lazy summer-evening had been running in its *"desultory, spasmodic fashion from golf clubs to the causes of the change in the obliquity of the ecliptic"* (note here that if Holmes had really not known that the earth orbited the sun, he hardly could have been chatting about the "obliquity of the ecliptic") when Watson changed the topic to "hereditary aptitudes". *The point under discussion,* Watson reported in his chronicle, *was how far any singular gift in an individual was due to his ancestry, and how far to his own early training.* In today's parlance, it was a discussion about nature versus nurture.

Then Watson went on with his fateful four paragraphs:

"'In your own case,' said I, 'from all that you have told me it seems obvious that your faculty of observation and your peculiar facility for deduction are due to your own training.'

"'To some extent,' he [Holmes] answered thoughtfully. 'My ancestors were country squires, who appear to have led much the same life, as is natural to their class. But, nonetheless, my turn that way is in my veins, and may have come with my grandmother, who was

the sister of Vernet, the French artist. Art in the blood is liable to
take the strangest forms.'

"'But how do you know that it is hereditary?'

"'Because my brother Mycroft possesses it in a larger degree than
I do.'"

This was the only time, in hundreds of thousands of words "chronicled
by Watson", that Holmes will ever mention his ancestors. It was the first
time he ever mentioned the existence of his brother Mycroft, and Watson was duly astonished.

Yet nothing in this short "revelation" to Dr. Watson by Sherlock
Holmes, other than Mycroft's existence, was true in any real sense: not
even the simple fact of his "grandmother, who was the sister of Vernet,
the French artist".

There was, of course, a well-known French artist of the era, Émile
Jean-Horace Vernet (1789–1863), whose specialty was painting scenes of
battle and Orientalist-Arab subjects. Vernet's most-remembered painting in Holmes's and Watson's time (and in ours) was his large canvas
titled *Street Fighting on Rue Soufflot, Paris, June 25, 1848.* If Vernet is remembered for any utterance today it is from the time when a patron
asked him to remove the image of an especially obnoxious general from
one of his battle paintings. "I am a painter of history, sire," Vernet is reported to have said, "and I will not violate the truth."

But Holmes, in his recitation to Watson, certainly violated the truth;
Émile Jean-Horace Vernet had three brothers and one younger sister who
died of typhus when she was 7 years old. She could hardly have been
Sherlock Holmes's grandmother.

William Sherlock Holmes had been born in the Eastside slums of London and had spent the majority of his young years in those slums and
on those rough streets. When the older Holmes summoned his barefoot, ragamuffin group of "street Arabs"—his Baker Street Irregulars,
as he called them—he might as well have been summoning his much-
younger self.

Future biographers will state with certainty, among other "known
facts", that Holmes's father was either an invalided-out cavalry lieu-

tenant named Siger Holmes or a member of the landed gentry named William Scott Holmes. Neither account has an ounce of truth to it. One famous biography of the Great Detective will have Sherlock's father and the Holmes family inheriting a Yorkshire estate called "Mycroft" and will trace the family ownership of that grand estate back to the 1550's.

This is nonsense and wholly manufactured. Holmes's actual family once had partial claim to some acres of land in Yorkshire, but it was a non-producing hardscrabble farm during Queen Elizabeth's reign and had been under the mere hired-management of Sherlock's uncle for only a few years when that man died in 1860, two years after Sherlock's mother—of whom the adult detective had no clear memory—died of consumption in an Eastcheap boarding house.

It's true that the Yorkshire farm once had held some delusions of grandeur. In the sixteenth century the nobleman owner—who was *not* an ancestor of Sherlock Holmes—had begun work on a grand country house there that was to be known as "Ashcroft Manor". But the nobleman had made the mistake of remaining a practicing Catholic when England had been converted, forcibly when necessary, to the Church of England, and by 1610 "Ashcroft Manor" had been burned to ashes and equally vanished were the fortune and hopes of the noble squire who had so briefly owned the land. History reports that the lord cut his own throat; he had no male descendants who lived beyond the age of 11.

In centuries to come, some Yorkshire locals still referred to the ever-dwindling estate—dwindling due to inevitable entailment of Commons and larger and larger sections being sold off to pay debts by the distant relatives who'd assumed ownership of the farm—as "Ashcroft Farm", but by 1800 the appellation had become "Ash Heap Acres" after the chimneys and windowless brick buildings of a profitless lead mine that had been built on the remaining 60 acres in a last-ditch effort by an American cousin to earn some money from the place. Until the lead works closed down in 1838, "Ash Heap Acres" often filled the entire Yorkshire valley with a thick, dark cloud of unhealthy lead-laced smoke.

After the death of Sherlock's uncle Sherrinford in 1860—he had been administering Ash Heap Acres for an absentee Birmingham land-lord—Sherlock's father had bought (at far too high a price) that overmined and overgrown Yorkshire farm and then brought the 13-year-old Mycroft and 6-year-old Sherlock out to the remaining 38 acres of ruined woodland, unyielding fields, grazed-out pastures, and polluted swamp. Mycroft never left his small room while there, but the farm—what was left of it—was an exploratory and play-filled heaven to the young Sherlock. He even had a swaybacked pony to ride during those three golden years in the Yorkshire Dales.

But by early 1863, Sherlock's father, who was both a drunkard and spendthrift and who, in young Sherlock's memory, had spent most of his time at Ash Heap Acres riding the plow horse to nearby Swinton to waste his nights (and many days) in Swaledale's more sordid public houses, had lost ownership of the farm after spending the last of his brother Sherrinford's money. Then in 1863, the father and his two extraordinary but unappreciated sons returned to London and a succession of ever-more-seedy rental homes and boarding houses. For Sherlock, it meant a return to their family life of always fleeing their creditors and his return to the streets.

But Mycroft, turning 16 that year, did not return to London with them. He went to Oxford instead.

Even while "in exile" at Ash Heap Acres in the Yorkshire Dales, their father had used Mycroft's mathematical gifts to have his son pore through racing touts' data sheets and pick future thoroughbred winners sold at Tattersall in London in Hyde Park, and then Holmes, Sr., after cabling cronies in the city, would place bets on those very horses at Alexandra Park's "The Frying Pan" racecourse in the city. What Sherlock had noticed in those years (but their father hadn't) was that Mycroft—seemingly as lazy and listless as he was overweight and brilliant—had been taking money from his father's bets to place his own racing wagers, adding his secret picks through the agency of his father's crony who lived in London and returning his smaller but ever-accruing winnings to a separate account. By 1863, 16-year-old Mycroft Holmes had set aside quite a bit of money. And he knew precisely how he was going to spend it.

Mycroft qualified to enter Oxford at the age of 16, paid his tuition and board with what he called his "Tattersall-Frying Pan Money", and late one night, after waking his younger brother and uncharacteristically shaking hands with young Sherlock (Mycroft hated touching or being touched by other people), took himself off to Oxford. He brought with him only his cardboard suitcase containing a few clothes and a cheese sandwich Sherlock had made for him.

Over the next few years, disowned by his furious father, Mycroft sent Sherlock elaborately encrypted letters in which the older brother described how he reveled in everything that venerable institution had to offer, including the friendship of a certain mathematics professor at Christ Church named Charles Lutwidge Dodgson, soon to be known to the world as Lewis Carroll. Mycroft and Dodgson soon became fast friends, sharing their excitement about mathematics (especially prime numbers), difficult codes, and odd patterns of numbers within such everyday things as railway schedules.

William Sherlock Holmes never met Dodgson; the younger son spent the later years of the 1860's and early 1870's fighting for his survival in the rough streets of London. In the late 1870's, Mycroft Holmes plucked his younger brother out of the streets and paid to send him to Oxford. Sherlock refused to attend a school where his older brother had been such a well-known and admired figure. Mycroft then used the money to send his brother to Sidney Sussex College, Cambridge, where he hoped Sherlock would focus on Natural Sciences. Sherlock enjoyed some of his chemical-laboratory time at Cambridge but hated his instructors and fellow students and soon dropped out—twice.

To get a glimpse of the actual biography of the early years of Sherlock Holmes—a biography that will never be written—one might use as a template a biography of the younger years of James Joyce, with his drunken, often abusive father first renting fine homes in neighborhoods such as Kensington and then, fleeing landlords demanding rent, dragging his sons to ever-dirtier-and-more-cramped rental houses and then to seedy rooms in boarding houses smelling of boiled cabbage. Sherlock had almost no formal education until his brief stint at Cambridge—had never attended a school, public or private, and had only intermittent tutors at home (when his father had "made a score" on the ponies or some other shady venture).

While Holmes's father, during the brief periods he had a few coins and he and his son were not actively fleeing landlords in the night, had the habit of hiring a succession of fairly useless (and soon-to-throw-up-their-hands-in-surrender) tutors for young Sherlock, the senior Holmes did spend real money on excellent instructors in five areas of young Sherlock Holmes's instruction: single-stick combat which Sherlock studied from the age of 7 onwards, boxing (including time spent sparring with several retired but still-famous English champion prizefighters), four years of having a Thai expert teach him the intricacies of Muay Boran martial arts, fencing (the most expensive instruction, the young Holmes sometimes taught by top French fencing experts even when the family could barely afford food), and shooting.

It was as if Sherlock's father envisioned his strange, wild, but often withdrawn and brooding younger son becoming a soldier someday. Sherlock Holmes, of course, even at the age of 8 or 14, had no more interest in ever being a soldier than he had in being the first aeronaut to travel via balloon to the moon.

* * *

It had begun to rain. Holmes carried no umbrella, of course, since his down-at-the-heels-working-class-American disguise would not have included such a thing, so he simply pulled his soiled and ancient Irish cloth cap lower over his brow and kept slogging along as the paved streets finally gave out for good. Streets, as such, had all but disappeared in this part of the Southwest slums and been replaced by countless, hovel-lined alleys consisting of mud and deep ruts and the occasional board thrown down to more easily traverse some important short distance as from a tumbledown tin shack to a three-sided wooden privy.

His contacts in New York had told him that for what he sought he should seek out a former blacksmith shop on what was called Casey's Alley, but of course there were no street signs here in the slums, no corner policeman from whom to ask directions (not that he would have given them to the unemployed-bounder likes of Holmes), and when Holmes asked directions of some raggedy children playing at torturing a rat, they responded by throwing horse apples at his head.

Before he found the abandoned blacksmith shop and the men he sought, Holmes came across the sort of abandoned commercial building he'd hoped to find amidst these shacks and empty factories. He stepped up onto the structure's disintegrating wooden sidewalk, kicked open the warped front door, and looked inside.

It had been a cheap railroad-man's hotel at one point in the past—the tracks, rusted over now, ran next to it in the high weeds—but now it was home to only pigeons and four-legged vermin. Not even the poorest families from the nearby slums sought shelter here. The reason was fascinating to Holmes—in the large sitting room just off what had once served as a small reception lobby, the ceiling had collapsed in a strange way that had created a rough circle almost ten feet across. It was a four-story building and what made that collapsed ceiling interesting to Holmes was that, peering carefully up through the aperture, he could see similar round cavities on what Americans counted as the second, third, and fourth stories. Staring upward, Holmes's face grew wetter from a constant drizzle dropping through a gap in the old hotel's rooftop some fifty feet above.

What could have weighed so much that it tore such a vertical path through a ceiling and three floors and a rooftop? Granting that the rain and rot had been far advanced when the event occurred, not even the heaviest of beds or metal safes or player pianos could carve out such destruction through a thick roof and three such reinforced layers of flooring.

There was no clue on the ground floor where Holmes stood save for a purplish-red discoloration that had ruined the splintered floorboards in a fifteen-foot-wide asterisk. It was as if twenty or so absurdly obese men had clustered tightly together on the fourth floor and fallen through three floors before splattering to their death here in the wide sitting room just off the lobby.

The man who had billed himself as the World's First Consulting Detective—despite scores of private detectives also working in London at the time—did not put much faith in this primary hypothesis of the Case of the Falling Fat Men.

But the hotel would serve. The banister and railings were fallen away on much of the central staircase, but the stairs themselves might hold.

* * *

Two muddy blocks further on he found three walls and a canvas sheet, the remains of what had once been a blacksmith shop. Besides the old sign hanging slack from one hook, there was a rusted anvil lying in the alley mud. Clues enough for the World's First and Foremost Consulting Detective. Holmes stepped up onto a wooden platform hardly less muddy than the alley below and moved the canvas aside with the knob of his lead-cored walking stick.

Smoking and sorting through what appeared to be piles of trash tossed onto a low table were three of the roughest-looking scoundrels Sherlock Holmes had ever encountered in the daylight. Two of them—they looked like idiot brothers—had arms so long and expressions (behind their red stubble) so primitive that they might have stepped out of a Stone Age Troglodyte diorama in the British Natural History Museum. The third man smelled so strongly of body odor that the stench seemed to shove Holmes physically back against the filthy canvas wall. The tall man had a sheath on the belt around his sagging, patched trousers and in that sheath was a Bowie knife the length of some Afghani and Zulu short swords Holmes had seen.

"What the fuck do you want?" said the taller man with the knife. He put a grimy hand on the heavy hilt.

"Someone told me that you could come up with the amount of morphine I need," said Holmes in his best Philadelphia-American accent. Holmes had first seen the United States when he toured in the 1870's with Percy Alexander's acting troupe—nineteen cities in seven months—and he had taken care at the time to acquire as many regional dialects as he might need in the future.

"And heroin," added Holmes. "I want heroin. If you don't have the morphine, I'll take the heroin."

The tall man looked at Holmes's worn work boots and patched clothing, smirked, and said, "Who's to tell us you ain't a bluecoat without the fuckin' coat?"

"I'm not a copper," said Holmes.

"Take your shirt off," said the man with the knife. "Roll up your sleeve."

Shaking slightly, Holmes removed his jacket, rough waistcoat, and workman's wool shirt and rolled up his torn and dirty undershirt. All three of the men leaned forward to look at the constellation of scabs and scars on his inner arm.

"He slams regular on *somethin',*" said the second Troglodyte, his hairy face hovering close to Holmes's bare arm.

"Shut up, Finn," said the tall man.

"Then who says you got the fucking money?" said the other Troglodyte.

"Shut up, Finn," snapped the man with the Bowie knife. Evidently, since they were obviously brothers, calling both of the Troglodytes by the same name saved time.

Before the closer Finn backed away, Holmes caught a glimpse of a crudely tattooed-in-blue-ink ST on his right wrist. This told Holmes that he was in the right place, at least according to his connections in Hell's Kitchen in New York. He wanted to make contact with someone in the Washington gang known as the Southwest Toughs. It looked as though he had.

That tall man pointed at Holmes. "This ain't Chinatown. Not even a hospital nearby to get supplies from. Mr. Bayer's schmeck comes pure but it costs more hereabouts. You got what it takes to get it?"

"I have money," whined Holmes in the desperate tones of an addict. He pulled out a thick wad of American bills.

"I guess you do, pal," said the tall man with his fingers tapping idly on the hilt of the knife. "Finn, both of you, go get Mr. Culpepper and Mr. J. *Now.*"

Holmes saw a not-unfamiliar light come into their eyes then, although the man with the knife at least tried to conceal his gleam. They were going to kill him for the cash.

CHAPTER 11

With the Finns gone, there were only the three of them in the canvas-walled blacksmith shop—Holmes, the tall man with the big knife, and the tall man's body odor. Holmes stayed silent, the man with the knife stared at him without speaking, and the stench spoke for itself.

Less than ten minutes later, the Finns returned with two well-dressed men. One was tall, thin, and silent, with the slightest trace of thin mustache above perfectly formed lips. He had very dark hair and the kind of pale-to-translucent skin that meant even by this time in the early afternoon, he could have used a second shave of the day, although everything else about the man was impeccable. There was not the slightest hint of mud on his polished shoes or white spats. This tall, thin, silent man was dressed well enough that he could have joined Wall Street executives or—closer to home—Washington's annual Easter Parade on K Street without looking out of place.

The other, shorter and heavier fellow, while expensively dressed, showed too many vulgar aspects not to stand out amongst real gentlemen. He sported a gold tooth that matched the gold-colored threads in his elaborate waistcoat. Visible above the waistcoat, most of it tucked into his impossibly clean trousers given the mud of Casey's Alley, was the butt of a double-action pistol. A new, brown-felt homburg was perched above his greased-back black hair. He was smiling.

"Good God, Murtrick," gasped the shorter, heavier newcomer with the pistol. "It's powerful rank in here. It's almost April...haven't you taken your annual bath yet?" He waved the Finns out of the little shop and Holmes could hear the brothers' boots squelching in the mud outside.

The tall thin man leaned back against a counter, only after dusting it with his handkerchief, and watched the proceedings in continued silence.

The vulgarly dressed man extended a rough hand. "Howard Culpepper," he said in a rich baritone.

Holmes shook hands with him. If this was Culpepper, then the younger, silent man must be "Mr. J"—obviously the most important of the five thieves. The man Culpepper had called Murtrick never quit tapping at the hilt of his huge knife. Holmes felt in luck that his first real contact in Washington was this Culpepper fellow; based on his flashy dress and confident attitude, he might possibly be high enough up in the city's criminal organization to answer Holmes's questions. If given the proper incentive. He doubted very much if Mr. J would be so foolish as to give names—or *any* useful information for that matter.

"And your name, sir?" asked Culpepper.

"Henry Baskers," said Holmes.

"Well, Mr. Baskers, I apologize, if your host has not, for the olfactory unpleasantness currently haunting our temporary place of business," said Culpepper. "You've seen the local neighborhood, sir. Water has to be carried down here by hand all the way from Four-and-a-Half Street. There's not so much as a single public pump in all of this Southwest quarter." He squinted at Murtrick. "But that is little excuse, *since civilization demands a price.*"

Murtrick never took his eyes off Holmes, who had nothing to say to all of this. He allowed himself to show several subtle signs of nervousness without overplaying his role. Mr. "Baskers" would have purchased illicit drugs in unsavory places before this.

From time to time, Holmes allowed his nervous gaze to flick to Mr. J as if he were one gentleman appealing for help from another, but the tall man leaned against the counter with a withdrawn silence bordering on complete indifference. It was as if he weren't there.

But Culpepper rubbed his palms together. "To business then, sir. My

confederates tell me that you wish to purchase a modest amount of morphine and...how shall I put it?...a more significant amount of Mr.
Bayer's new heroic pharmaceutical."

"Yes," said Holmes. He repeated the amount of each he was ready to
purchase.

"You're aware, Mr. Baskers," said Culpepper, "that Bayer has not yet
fully released this miraculous heroin for general sale either in Europe or
the United States. Soon it will be on every grocery store's shelf, but right
now it is undergoing — what do they call it? — trials in select hospitals,
including Dr. Reed's clinic."

Holmes nodded impatiently. He allowed his gaze to remain riveted
on the three bottles of heroin salts Culpepper was holding between the
fingers of his right hand like a magician preparing to do a trick. Each
label read FRIEDIR BAYER & CO., ELBERFELD, 40 STONE ST., NEW YORK.

In truth, Holmes was also noting the make and model of the pistol
set in Culpepper's tight waistband. It was familiar to the detective since
not only was it British-made but had been standard issue for the British
military until it had been replaced by the Enfield pistol in 1880. It was
the .442-caliber Beaumont-Adams revolver that had become so famous
in England's war with the Zulus — this model almost certainly modified,
as so many had been that had seen action in America's Civil War, to take
center-fire cartridges. This pistol had sported the first modern double-
action system. Holmes knew that many American officers and cavalry in
their Civil War had preferred it to the American military Colt due to the
Beaumont-Adams's superior trigger-cocking speed and more rapid rate
of fire in close action. He wondered idly if Culpepper had been an officer
in that war, now almost 30 years in the past, and if he kept this pistol for
reasons of sentimentality. Based on the gray in the man's sideburns and
the obvious use of hair-darkening materials elsewhere under that homburg — perhaps the same patent goop Holmes was using in his Sigerson
disguise — Culpepper could easily be in his late fifties or early sixties.

Holmes assumed that Mr. J was also armed, but almost certainly with
a much smaller and more sensible pistol to carry in a city.

"The morphine will cost you only twenty dollars," said Culpepper,
holding the two smaller vials in his left hand. That was twice what

Holmes would pay for it near one of the hospitals or in the Negro sections of town just a dozen alleys from here.

As if reading Holmes's thoughts, Culpepper chuckled and said, "Yes, yes, you could get if for less in niggertown, Mr. Baskers, but God knows what our darky friends might have mixed into it. And as for the heroin...no, you have come to the one and only supplier in your nation's capital, sir. You will find it nowhere else."

Holmes knew that this wasn't true either, but he said, "How much for the three bottles of salts?"

"One hundred and fifty dollars, sir," said Culpepper. Even Murtrick glanced over at the well-dressed man in surprise. This was more than four times the street price Holmes would have paid for an equal amount of the drug in New York.

He wrestled visibly with the shock of the price, allowing only the slightest hint of the serious addict's always-losing war between absolute need and mere money to show on his face.

"Oh, what the heck," laughed Culpepper. "We'll throw both morphines in as part of the price. A better deal you'll get nowhere east of the Mississippi, Mr. Baskers."

Holmes swallowed hard and nodded. "All right." He watched both men's eyes glint as he counted a hundred and fifty dollars from his absurd wad of American bills. He was carrying more than eight hundred dollars with him—every bit of what he'd brought from France and converted to dollars in New York.

When the transaction was completed and the morphine and heroin bottles nestled most carefully in Holmes's various jacket pockets, Culpepper asked in a casual tone, "Will we be having the pleasure of your future business, Mr. Baskers? I can give you the address of one of my...ah...less fragrant and more convenient places of business."

This was it. If Holmes told them that he was going to be a regular customer, they might let him live. At these extortionate prices for heroin alone, they could have his remaining $650 in a few months without resorting to violence. Over a year or two, he would be worth a true fortune to them.

"No," said Holmes. "I'm leaving tomorrow for San Francisco. I'm from Philadelphia and didn't know if the heroin was in use out there yet and so...I thought..."

"We understand," grinned Culpepper. He gave Murtrick the briefest of glances. "Have a safe trip, Mr. Baskers."

Mr. J did not even turn his head to watch as Holmes left the former blacksmith shop.

CHAPTER 12

They'd sent one of the Finns to follow him up Casey's Alley. Following a man surreptitiously up such a narrow venue, crowded as its sides were with a contiguous wall of shacks and tumbledown ruins, would have been difficult enough when the dirt street was dry; with the mud, it was impossible.

Holmes squelched northward, never looking back, assured that this Finn was merely keeping him in sight while the other three men — or possibly more by now — were moving up an adjacent north-south alley. When Holmes stopped, this Finn would get the word to the others in less than a minute.

Culpepper and Murtrick would be betting that this addict's need was so great that he could not wait to get back to his hotel, but would seek out a private place along the way in which to inject his newly acquired heroin. They would also be banking that Holmes — "Mr. Baskers" — would do this before he left the slums of the Southwest quarter.

Holmes would not disappoint them.

* * *

He left the door of the abandoned hotel ajar behind him. The giant stain in the floor of the large room off the lobby remained just as disturbing as at first encounter and the three stories of cratered floorboards beginning with that room's ceiling just as shocking. The cold spring rain had settled into a heavy drizzle and it continued to fall through the shattered rooftop more than three stories above.

Perhaps a meteor or comet struck the hotel, was the ironic thought that came from the most reasoned and deductive mind in England. Holmes was in great physical pain. The morphine he'd injected that morning had been the last of his store, had been far too little for the pain that had accrued over the past week, and pain continued to distract him despite his years of disciplining himself to ignore it. A gunshot wound, something less than mortal, would have distracted him less than this ferocious full-body ache that came from too long of an interval between applications of his ameliorative.

He climbed the stairs slowly, testing each one carefully before committing his weight. The wood was soaked and rotten but had once been a sound and noble wood and only a few steps had to be avoided completely. The railing was continuous for the length of its long, curving climb, but so many balusters had fallen away that nowhere was the banister solid enough to hold a person's weight should he or she be pressed against it. Between what the Americans called the second and third stories, there was almost no banister at all.

He turned into the dripping, wallpaper-curling corridor on the fourth floor and threw his shoulder against the warped door of his chosen room.

This was it. There was a rotting floor intact for only eighteen inches or more before the huge cavity began. Holmes could see lathing and shards of ancient carpet that had been left in the interstices between joists when the impossible weight had crashed down for forty feet. There was space enough only on the right side of the crater to edge around the hole in this unfurnished room, and the constant drizzle from above—lit by the dim sunlight coming through gray clouds—gave an eerie and unreal illumination to the bare walls and remnant of floor and ceiling. Holmes had hoped that there'd be room enough against the wall opposite the doorway for him and there was—just. Four feet or so of downward-sloping floor there before the hole began.

If Culpepper wanted to kill him, all he had to do was open the door, aim, and fire—their target would be fewer than twenty feet away.

But the odds of "Mr. Baskers" falling forward after being shot by a .442-caliber ball were almost 100% and it was Holmes's mortal wager that Culpepper and Murtrick—or whatever their real names were—wanted the bottles of morphine and heroin intact after their other thievery was finished.

Holmes squeezed against the wall opposite the mild waterfall and empty space separating him across the room from the door he'd closed behind him and then slid down that wall, hoping the sloping floor would hold his weight. It did, although it groaned in protest. He got out one of the bottles and his leather syringe kit.

In France and during the crossing, Holmes had pondered the wisdom of arming himself with a pistol. He'd had one in India but France had been so peaceful—even the time he'd spent with the experimental chemists in Montpelier where he'd decided to wean himself off morphine by shifting to this newer, safer drug—that he'd had no need of a firearm there. His last chance to pick one up had been his one night in New York, but he'd been so busy there getting information about possible contacts in Washington that he hadn't had time to go pistol-shopping. In truth, the thought had never entered his mind while he was there.

Sitting with his knees apart and one shoe bracing the bottle on the floorboards should it roll toward the terrible crater, Holmes set out his various apparatuses and smiled.

In Watson's many written "Adventures..." and "Cases...", most of which he kept in his older medical satchel on the shelf in his room and which the public had not yet heard of or read, Watson almost always portrayed himself as the one who brought a pistol to the adventure when a pistol was needed. In truth, despite the hundreds of hours of shooting instruction by his father and many more hours of lonely practice since, Holmes did indeed dislike firearms of any sort. But he smiled again at the memory of Watson always describing his own pistol only as "my old [or "trusty"] service revolver", but his medical friend had learned enough about writing from Conan Doyle to know that readers were bored by details.

Holmes lived (and would probably die someday) for details. He'd noticed the first time Watson had ever armed himself for one of their mutual adventures that the "service revolver" was an Adams six-shot caliber .450 breechloader with a 6-inch barrel; standard issue for the British Army during the second Afghan war in which Watson had received his suspiciously mobile Jezail bullet. Dr. Watson's weapon was not so different, in size and capability, from the Beaumont-Adams pistol that Culpepper had been showing off from his belted waistband. Holmes had noticed that the dandy had worn both braces—"suspenders" his Mr. Baskers would call them here in America—*and* a thick belt. Mr. Culpepper was a cautious man. Just how cautious, thought Holmes, they would all soon see.

Perhaps all five of them are carrying pistols by now, was Holmes's last thought before he heard the front door of the hotel being forced open three stories below.

But no—Holmes felt certain, to his deep disappointment, that Mr. J had not joined this expedition. He'd certainly returned to report the interaction to his own superior.

Which meant that he would have to leave at least one of the four men tracking him alive. But not necessarily Culpepper.

Holmes's materials were set before him on the leather cloth. He'd preloaded his syringe with saltwater and now he brought out a bottle cap taken from a bottle of Hires Root Beer he'd purchased earlier in the morning, after renting his magic-lantern projector. Holmes had tossed away the bottle and its contents—hideous stuff, "root beer"; he wondered how Americans could buy and guzzle three million bottles of it a year. Now he filled the bottle cap with the heroin salts and then squeezed out enough water to liquify the salts.

From another pouch in his unrolled leather bag, Holmes extracted the bit of chemical tubing he'd used that morning to tie off his arm. He did so again, tapping at the veins on the inside of his elbow and then, from his waistcoat pocket, brought forth perhaps the most unique device he owned—a prototype cigarette lighter presented to Holmes in 1891, just months before his self-disappearance, by a satisfied client: a scientist by the name of Carl Auer von Welsbach. The patenting of a flint-like substance called ferrocerium allowed the von Welsbach lighter to be small, simple, and safe, in comparison to the bulky, complex, and extremely dangerous Döbereiner flame-makers of decades past. He held the blue flame from von Welsbach's gift under the bottle cap.

The von Welsbach lighter had saved Holmes's life numerous times in the Himalayas; now he asked it only to work quickly so he could heat the heroin-crystal-saltwater mixture before the audible footsteps on the stairway reached his floor.

Holmes took a small pellet of cotton he'd been carrying in his shirt pocket next to the three photographs and dropped the cotton wad onto the Hires bottle cap he was using for a cooker. The cotton acted as a filter, blocking the inevitable undissolved clumps of heroin salts that would clog the syringe and stop his heart.

The footsteps were climbing above the second-story landing.

Holmes lifted the filled syringe, tapped it, squirted a tiny bit to be sure there were no air bubbles, and leaned over to inject the contents into his vein.

It sounded like only four men, not five, climbing to the fourth floor. They were trying to climb quietly, but not too quietly. They obviously weren't overly concerned as to whether meek Mr. Baskers heard them or not. What could he do if he did?

Holmes wanted time for the heroin to take effect. He tugged the tubing off, emptied and disassembled the syringe, and put the bottles, bottle cap, and precious von Welsbach cigarette lighter back in their proper places.

The heroin hit his system almost at once.

First came the glowing warmth filling his heart, chest, torso, limbs, and then brain. Then came the fading of all pain—especially the pain of his question of existence or non-existence—and then came the sense of rising on the crest of a curling wave.

The footsteps stopped outside the door of his room. Holmes vaguely heard whispering. He ignored it.

Rising rapidly on that silent wave, he could see and sense his own life better now. He could make out the lacunae, the ellipses, the terrible gaps between his so-called cases, his so-called adventures, his so-called life as a famous consulting detective. Those days or weeks or sometimes months between the cases that Watson had been feverishly chronicling were not a memory of life; they were a glimpse of rough sketches with faces not drawn in, backgrounds not sketched, days not filled. Holmes remembered screeching his bow on his expensive violin. He remembered injecting cocaine. He remembered sleeping long afternoons and fooling around in his locked room with his chemistry set like a child, bubbling things, burning things. He remembered the ghost of Mrs. Hudson carrying trays into the common room, carrying trays out. There were a few times when Mrs. Hudson—still looking and sounding like "Mrs. Hudson" in Holmes's memory—had been inexplicably referred to as "Mrs. Turner" in Watson's chronicles. All that was a blur now. None of it had any sense of solidity or the simple taste of the real.

The warped door was shoved open. The Finns came in, almost tiptoeing, like cartoon characters from *Comic Cuts, Ally Sloper's Half Holiday,* or *Illustrated Chips,* all guilty favorites of Dr. Watson. Holmes ignored them; he had no time left but he also had no choices left. He had to see what the drug would allow him to see before he could pay attention to his would-be murderers.

Holmes's consciousness had expanded until he came up against the horizontal iron bars of his cage. The bars were not solid. Sections of different lengths floated in the gray air—no, not air, some gelatinous aether—in front of him, but no two horizontal blocks were far enough apart that he could press his head or shoulders between them. Holmes realized that the floating horizontal elements of his cage were distinct words, giant words, separate words like slugs of type set into a gelatinous void of a medium, but the huge words and sentences were written backward from his point-of-view. Holmes grabbed at two of the longer floating words—the metal was so cold it burned his hands—and he stared through the imprisoning word-bars with the expression of a madman or a castaway seeing his first ship in years receding from view.

Holmes looks at you. He sees the blurred outlines of the room or space behind you. He strains to make out your face.

"He's slammed," said one of the Finns.

"He's all shot up. He ain't even half here," said the other Finn.

"Shut up," snapped Murtrick.

All four men were inside the open door now, the Finns and Murtrick having worked their way carefully around to their right, Holmes's left. But Culpepper stayed in the doorway. Braces *and* belt, Holmes remembered through the glow and wondrous, fearless terror of the heroin. If Culpepper remained a truly cautious man for the next two minutes, Mr. Sherlock Holmes of London would soon be a corpse.

Holmes had tucked away his leather foldaway and was on his knees as if praying to the drizzle falling vertically in front of him. Somewhere above the hole in the ceiling the sun had grown brighter; the waterfall was now made of skeins of liquid gold. Holmes's walking stick was propped against the wall behind him and to the right. It would be most awkward for him to try to reach it and would take too long to try. The three men creeping up on him noted this. Holmes's eyes were not focused on anything, but he vaguely noticed that Murtrick had removed the Bowie knife from its sheath. Culpepper had removed the revolver from his waistband. The Finns now raised their Paleolithic clubs.

Then Culpepper stepped into the room and wedged shut the door behind him. Most probably it was just old habit—seeking some privacy for a murder. Holmes had instinctively hoped for such a habit to be there, but he had not been certain. He had not been certain. Now he seemed to take no notice.

Now all four men were moving carefully around the perimeter of the terrible hole in the floor, keeping as close to the west wall of the empty room as possible. The Finns kept glancing down into the cavity with something like terror in their little Troglodyte eyes.

Holmes decided that it would have to be one of the Finns who should survive and carry back the details of this encounter to Mr. J and his superiors.

"Don't cluster too close when you get him," whispered Culpepper, following them but staying several paces back, then stopping completely at the west side of the hole while watching the other three advance. "The floor might not hold you there if you cluster up. We need the bottles intact."

No one said anything but the three men opened more distance between themselves. The Finns shouldered their short clubs with nails driven through the working ends. Murtrick had his knife and was moving in an experienced knife-fighter's crouch. Culpepper held his pistol loosely down at his side, every inch the vision of the accomplished duelist anticipating another easy victory. The Beaumont-Adams revolver's hammer was cocked.

Holmes had not turned his head to watch their final approach. His eyes were vacant, the drug obviously in full control. There was a single drop of blood on the inside of his still-bare left arm.

The Finns attacked with Murtrick close behind.

Holmes—so cool behind his buffer that he watched with the most disinterested attention imaginable—whirled, away from the attacking men, as if attempting a retreat into the dead-end corner where the crater came all the way to the east wall, but the whirl was no half-turn away. He twirled almost completely around and came up out of his crouch with his walking stick in his hand.

The Finns shouted a single primal scream and raised their clubs.

Decades of single-stick practice guided Holmes's two-second blur of six blows: two lateral swings to break their right arms; two vertical swings to club their underjaws and drop them to their knees; two fluidly vicious downward swings—one to crush the larger Finn's skull, a lesser blow to knock the slightly shorter Finn down, but to leave him semiconscious.

Murtrick had made the mistake of staring at the blur of violence and leaping blood, but now he leaped closer, crouched lower, swung the deadly blade to the right, to the left. He jumped over the dead Finns: one motionless on its face, a river of blood flowing from his ears, the other twitching on his back, moaning as he cradled his aching head and bleeding scalp with both hands.

Holmes took a step backward, not because he feared Murtrick's blade or needed the room but because he was sending a subliminal message to Culpepper to join the fray. *Come closer.* The dandy did take two steps closer but still stayed well out of club range. His pistol was raised but the man was obviously waiting for Murtrick to do his job. "The heroin bottles!" he screamed at his stinking friend. "Don't break them!"

The Bowie knife was its own blur. Holmes was fast enough with his stick to have batted it across the room in the quarter of a second when

Murtrick tossed it from hand to hand—the man was obviously as ambidextrous at ripping his enemies open from sternum to crotch as he was filthy—but Holmes had use for the knife stuck in the floor here, not lost down the golden waterfall hole or sticking from an unreachable wall or door across the room. He risked more by waiting for Murtrick to sweep the blade a final time and then lunge forward in a ballet-beautiful single motion. Only in Spain and once in Calcutta had Holmes seen knife-fighters perform that brilliantly. It was precisely the kind of super-fast knife move, Holmes knew, that almost always left the expert knife-wielder's opponent's bowels hanging out and then dropping to the floor with that ultimately final, squishy sound that the horrified and dying victim lived long enough to see and hear. The length of a Bowie knife only made that full *hari-kari* more likely, but the *weight* of Mr. Bowie's famous blade and hilt did slow the killing move by that necessary fraction of a second on which Holmes counted.

Holmes arched his body while balancing on his heels, the tip of the Bowie knife took a button off his waistcoat, and then he slammed his weighted stick down on Murtrick's right hand—the knife dropped and embedded its point in the floor exactly where Holmes had wished it—and then, without pausing in its complex arc, the stick swung up and caught Murtrick in the side of the head.

Dazed, Murtrick wobbled toward the drop, started to go over.

Holmes grabbed the man, then pulled him toward his own chest with what felt like an infinitely powerful heroin-assisted left hand, keeping his stick in his right hand between them. Holmes brought his face so close to Murtrick's it seemed as if he was going to kiss the semi-conscious thug, then Holmes lowered his face to the man's chest, making himself smaller as he pushed both of them forward around the perimeter of the crater.

The four cracks from the .442 Beaumont-Adams revolver seemed to reach Holmes hours after the impacts had shattered the back of Murtrick's skull, lodged in the man's spine, blown his left shoulder into bone fragments, and passed through his body—that final ball passing between Holmes's right arm and his torso.

It was a five-shot pistol, but Holmes had pushed the upright corpse up and into Culpepper by this point and the fifth shot blew wet plaster out of the rotted ceiling. Holmes dropped Murtrick's corpse, unhurriedly clubbed the empty gun out of Culpepper's hand, and dragged him back to where he had injected the heroin, both men doing rather dainty dances over the three fallen bodies. The rotted and tilting floor sagged under their weight, but Holmes needed Culpepper near the knife embedded hilt-up in those groaning floorboards.

He swung Culpepper around and shoved him toward the edge of the hole, stopping his fall only with his left hand grasping the older man's jacket collar. Culpepper teetered and whimpered. Holmes suddenly smelled urine.

Holmes tossed away his club and reached into his shirt pocket to retrieve the three photographs there. Still holding Culpepper at a steep angle over the drop, he thrust the first photograph—the one of the older, heavier, dark-eyed, mustached man—in front of the murderer's face.

"Do you know this man?" barked Holmes. "Have you ever seen him?"

"No." Culpepper's baritone was now a soprano's quaver.

"Make sure," said Holmes. "I don't know which of the Southwest Toughs' bosses you report to—Dillon, Meyer, Shelton—but it would have been at their headquarters, maybe in their office. Or perhaps this man and your boss dining together."

"I've never seen him!" screeched the dangling man. Every time Culpepper tried to bring his arms back to grab at Holmes, the detective let him tilt a little more over the drop. Culpepper quit trying to grab and let his pudgy hands and arms flap like a pigeon's broken wings.

Holmes pocketed that photo and brought forth the photograph of the much younger man. In profile—thin lips, long, straight nose, hair combed back, eyes as light as a reptile's. The image terrified Holmes even in the perfectly disinterested state the heroin had granted him.

Culpepper's hesitation told Holmes what he needed to know. "Tell me. Now!" he said and let the big man tilt a few more inches forward. Holmes's left arm and hand were growing tired; he knew he'd almost dropped Culpepper three stories by accident right then. That would never do. But he couldn't change hands. Not yet. "Tell me *now!*" he bellowed.

"I think I saw this fellow...maybe...once. Dear Jesus, don't drop me!" Holmes pulled him a few inches closer.

"A couple of years ago," babbled Culpepper. "Maybe three. At Shelton's office on Pennsylvania Avenue."

"What was his name?"

"I just saw him, from a distance," quavered Culpepper. "I swear to God. If I knew anything more about him I'd tell you. I swear to God. *Please* don't push me! *Please* don't drop me. I'll change my life. I swear to Jesus Christ."

"And *this* man?" demanded Holmes, showing the third photograph. The oldest of the three in the photographs—one of a shockingly pale and cadaverous-looking, hollow-cheeked, and balding man. But the sharpness of features does not create sympathy in the viewer; this face is one of a predator, not of a victim or prey. One's first impression is of an almost disturbingly large shelf and dome of white forehead looming above deep-set eyes magnified by old-fashioned pince-nez spectacles. The sense of the older man being an intellectual created by the oversized forehead and glimpse of old-fashioned collar, ribbon tie, frock coat, and pince-nez is immediately counteracted by the sharp and strong jut of the older man's chin, from which various and strong—and somehow angry-looking—cords of wrinkle and muscle rise to the sharp cheekbones and to both sides of the vulpine blade of a nose. It is a predatory face made even more raptor-like by the hunched shoulders rising like a vulture's black feathers on either side of the grub-white blade of a face.

"Never seen him..." gasped Culpepper. "I'm slipping! I'm slipping! Oh, Jesus..."

"Perhaps you've heard his name," said Holmes, feeling the strength in his restraining hand beginning to fade. "Moriarty. Professor James Moriarty."

"No! Never!" cried Culpepper, and Holmes could see in his eyes that he was lying. *Perfect.*

Holmes shot a brief glance at the surviving Finn, still slumped against the wall and holding his bleeding head. He'd ceased moaning and had seen and heard everything well enough. But there was no fight left in him. Blood from the scalp wound had soaked his fingers, wrists, and sleeves.

Holmes put away the photos and pulled Culpepper back from the edge. He didn't believe he'd get any more. What had he learned? That Lucan might or might not have been in Washington two or more years ago. That Culpepper had definitely *heard* of Professor Moriarty but almost certainly hadn't seen him.

Holmes released his grip on the stocky man and looked at the floor. Blood had pooled completely around the dead Finn's head. Murtrick's body lay across the dead man's legs, his bullet-shattered head no longer recognizable as something that had once been human. The surviving Finn had managed to scrunch back further from his dead brother and boss. The bleeding Finn's eyes were as big as saucers staring at Holmes through his carmine-stained fingers.

All this for the information that Lucan might *have been in Washington and in touch with the Toughs a few years ago? And that the criminal organization here simply* knows *of Moriarty?* He was assailed by a sudden sadness, amplified to something like grief by the fading of the first-freedom of the heroin.

He should have left all this drama aside and simply coldcocked and kidnapped Mr. J and interrogated *him.* He was the only one Holmes had encountered this afternoon who might know if they'd done business with Lucan.

Holmes sighed and turned his back on Culpepper as if to retrieve his dropped club.

The Bowie knife had been sticking hilt-up only inches from Culpepper's right boot. The big man tugged the blade out with a grunt and leaned forward to strike.

Holmes leaned away from him, his head almost to the moldy wall, his right elbow on the floor, and kicked his left leg straight, his foot flat as he'd been trained in his youth, the leverage in that leg of his suddenly uncoiled body carrying enough energy to have kicked in a locked and barred door.

Culpepper actually flew upward and backward so that Holmes caught a glimpse of the soles of his shoes looking like two exclamation marks hanging in mid-air before Culpepper screamed and the drizzle, no longer golden, seemed to carry him down into the center of the ten-foot-wide hole in the floor.

Holmes paused in the room only long enough to pick up the fallen Beaumont-Adams revolver. It was an old weapon, but not unattractive. Wiping it off with his handkerchief, he disassembled it and dropped the pieces down the wide hole.

The living, still-bleeding Finn tried to push himself further back, literally into the wall, as Holmes passed him with his heavy club swinging idly by his side. The detective could only trust that the surviving Finn had just enough intelligence—and not such a serious concussion—that he could reliably report these proceedings to Mr. J and his other bosses.

Holmes had told Watson more than once that when he, Sherlock Holmes, retired, he was going to write his opus—*The Whole Art of Detection.* But the book he should really write, Holmes knew, was *How to Get Away with a Murder.* Rule No. 8 would be—*Never take away anything of the victim's. Nothing at all.*

He closed the door behind him, the surviving Finn still shaking in fear as if he thought Holmes would come back around the hole with its rainbow waterfall to finish the job, and then Holmes was stepping carefully down the stairway. It had borne more weight than it was used to this rainy March day. Holmes did stop in the large room off the lobby. A second broad stain had joined the first. Somehow Culpepper had contrived to land directly on the top of his head. His homburg was not the better for it, and the sharp, bloody-white base of the heavy man's spine had been pushed out through his buttocks.

Holmes rolled the body over, taking care to keep even his disguised-as-poor-American-bloke's clothes free from stain, and retrieved his $150. He would have use for it in the coming weeks.

It was Saturday, March 25. Holmes expected Henry James to come to his senses soon and return to England or France, but he knew that he himself might have to stay in America at least until the official opening on the first of May. President Cleveland was scheduled to push the button that let the fountains jet high, the battleship to fire, and the chorus to unleash the "Hallelujah Chorus". Holmes would have to stay here in

America that unbearable time unless, of course, circumstances of his own doing—including this encounter—or a telegram from his older brother released him from such long and tiresome obligations.

'Tis a consummation devoutly to be wished, thought Holmes, remembering that evening in 1874 when the 20-year-old Sherlock Holmes, understudy to the lead under a different name entirely, had replaced the suddenly-taken-ill bright new acting star in the firmament and troupe-director Henry Irving for one glorious night not as Rosenkrantz, not as faithful Horatio ("Yes, m'lord," "No, m'lord" for two and a half aching hours), but as Hamlet. The ovation had been standing. The reviews in *The Times* had been sterling. Irving had fired him from the troupe the next day.

Holmes left the mold- and blood-coppery-smelling old hotel and walked up Casey's Alley until his feet found pavement again.

His briefcase and other clothes were where he had placed them in the abandoned house in Foggy Bottom. Holmes took care folding away his American clothes and getting into his Norwegian gentleman's too-heavy tweeds. It took him a minute to get the black cover and silver barking-dog's head secured in place over the cruder wooden walking stick he'd had to wash along the way.

Holmes peered into a glass pane that threw back his reflection. He'd made sure his hands were clean but now he saw three tiny rosettes of blood line up like crimson snowflakes along his left cheekbone. Wetting his handkerchief in a puddle near a broken window, he dabbed the spots away. Then he tossed away the un-monogrammed handkerchief.

Leaving the house with the confidence of an absentee owner after an inspection, Holmes headed back through Foggy Bottom and into the lovely Federalist-style-lined streets closer to the downtown and the Executive Mansion. His walk now was the wide and confident stride of a famous explorer. His fancy stick now clacked on perfectly laid bricks.

*   *   *

Holmes had plenty of time to bathe and change before five o'clock tea time.

When they all met in the smaller parlor, Holmes thought that Henry James looked especially bleak, as if he had been brooding away the day. But it was obvious that James hadn't yet revealed anything about Holmes's identity to John or Clara Hay; Holmes could see and hear that in his host and hostess's joyous welcomes and easy behavior during the energetic conversation at tea.

"Did you find our quiet city as exciting as your explorations in Asia?" asked Clara Hay.

"Just as stimulating, in its own unique way," replied Jan Sigerson, his Norwegian accent faint but present.

A few hours later, they had roast beef for dinner. It seemed to be a specialty of the Hays' cook—or perhaps they had made it in honor of Henry James, whom they obviously considered more English than American now.

Holmes chose his slices very rare.

CHAPTER 13

The weekend turned out to be one of the most painful in Henry James's memory.

James's depression had deepened during the long sleepless night, but with the increase of melancholy had come an increase in clarity; he'd decided sometime before the day began growing gray at his windows that as soon as Holmes left the Hays' home that Saturday, he would talk to John Hay and make a full confession about his sin (and he fully considered it a sin, against friendship, against all discretion) of bringing this stranger in disguise into the embrace of one of his closest circles of friends. James could not imagine any way that the Hays and Henry Adams and Clarence King would ever forgive him, and the writer was prepared to skulk away at once, taking the mid-day train back to New York there to seek passage back to England. He knew that other fast friends of the Hays and Adamses—including James's old friend William Dean Howells—would be as equally outraged at his unspeakable behavior. He would accept all their anger and disapprobation; the alternative was to continue this vile charade and James saw now that he could not do that.

He'd hoped to speak to John Hay alone just after breakfast, but business took Hay out of the house, "Jan Sigerson" had left for his walk, and Henry James found himself alone with Clara Hay all morning and into the afternoon. As pleasant as Clara had always been to Henry James, he could not bring himself to reveal the truth to her.

So they chatted about mutual friends, about the weather in England

and on the Continent this time of year versus the early spring of Washington, about various artists they knew—including Daniel Chester French, Augustus Saint-Gaudens, and John Singer Sargent—and then about writers again. After the luncheon dishes were removed, they discussed Turgenev's work and Mr. Emerson's essays (which James did not much admire) and others until Clara Hay finally laughed and said, "You've seen John's library, of course, but you should really see my bookshelves of shameful pleasures, Harry."

James raised an eyebrow. "Shameful pleasures?"

"Yes, you know...books I enjoy tremendously that John and Henry Adams and Howells and others simply think I should not stoop to read. But I enjoy them! Perhaps you can offer me some dispensation. Come along."

She led him up the wide staircase and down the right hallway toward their master bedrooms. For a horrified instant, James thought that this woman with whom he was alone in the house (save for six or eight servants) was going to lead him into her bed-sitting-room, but she stopped in the hall outside. The bookcase there was of polished mahogany and was at least twelve-feet long.

"Yellow-backed books!" he exclaimed.

"Yes. I can't resist picking them up at the railway stations when I'm traveling in England," said Clara Hay and set the fingers of both hands against her reddening cheeks. "Have you ever succumbed to the temptation, Harry?"

He smiled with what he hoped looked like friendly benevolence. "Of course, my dear woman. The yellow-backed books are designed to while away a boring railway trip. I see you have Collins's *The Moonstone* and *The Woman in White* there amongst your other sensationalist novels."

Still blushing, Clara said, "Oh, yes. How I enjoy Wilkie Collins's books. And how sorry I was when he passed away four years ago. I *do* read serious books as well, you know."

"If I remember correctly, you were amongst the first of the Five of Hearts to discover *my* work," said James, removing a few of the volumes from the bookcase of third- and second-rate H. Rider Haggard–style "adventure romances" and glancing at titles before setting them back. Not all of the books here—not even a majority—were actually yellow-backed British novels that invariably dealt with bigamy, illegitimacy, murder, blackmail, and the like, but all were "sensationalist novels".

"Oh, long before Clover's the Five of Hearts began meeting, Harry! John and I were each reading your work when we met."

"What is this?" asked James removing a crisp new volume with a light tan binding. On the spine it read *The Adventures of Sherlock Holmes* and lower on the spine and below that, boxed, *The Strand Library*.

"I became addicted to Mr. Conan Doyle's stories when John and I spent three months in London two years ago," said Clara. "But they don't sell *The Strand Magazine* here so when I heard that they were releasing that collection of the *Strand*'s Sherlock Holmes stories here last month—a dozen stories in all—I purchased it immediately."

"Last month, you say," murmured James, leafing through the indifferently bound book. There were illustrations. "It appeared in February?"

"Yes."

"May I borrow this, Clara?" asked Henry James, slapping the book shut and lifting it. "My gout is acting up and I could use some amusing light reading to take my mind off it."

"Of course!" said Clara Hay, blushing again. "Just do not tell John what *kind* of book I've lent to such an illustrious author. I would never hear the end of it." The two stood in the hallway smiling at one another like two conspirators.

*   *   *

With his gout as an excuse—and it *was* acting up, causing his left foot to ache something terribly—James spent the rest of the afternoon in his room. A girl came in to build up the fire, and James sat close to it, his aching foot up on an overstuffed footstool, as a light rain began to tap and streak the windows.

Edmund Gosse and his other younger friends who enjoyed and recommended Henry Rider Haggard's jungle adventures and the supposedly true Sherlock Holmes tales in *The Strand,* or the longer Holmes pieces in *Beeton's Christmas Annual,* hadn't told James much detail about the Conan Doyle tales—other than it was their perception that Doyle was the literary agent and editor, a sort of collaborator, for Dr. John H. Watson's true tales of the reclusive (but evidently very busy) London detective.

James had attempted to read precisely one H. Rider Haggard romance, but when he came to a graphic scene whereby the white hunter blew his black native bearer's brains out rather than allow his man to be tortured, James had set aside the book—and all thoughts of reading future Haggard—for good. Glimpses of life on the streets of London were difficult enough to reconcile with a graceful, dignified life; James wanted to encounter no more lovingly detailed descriptions of skulls exploding and brain matter flying free.

The Holmes stories he had never been even slightly curious about.

Thinking back now to Mrs. O'Connor's and Lady Wolseley's benefit garden party where he had been introduced to Sherlock Holmes four years earlier, James could remember that A. Conan Doyle had been on the guest list—several popular but not very highly thought of authors had been a part of the charity effort—but he couldn't remember being introduced to Conan Doyle or talking with him. He had no memory of any Dr. John H. Watson being present at the affair.

Shifting his swollen and slippered foot so that it would be more comfortable, nodding his thanks to the footman who'd brought him his tea with lemon, James settled back and began reading the twelve stories in *The Adventures of Sherlock Holmes.*

* * *

James recognized his traveling companion through Dr. Watson's—or perhaps Conan Doyle's—descriptions: the lean physique, oversized pale forehead, gaunt cheeks, hawklike nose, expressive eyebrows, and intense gray-eyed gaze—although the illustrator for *The Strand* stories, a certain Sidney Paget, showed a man much better looking and even more the gentleman than the real Holmes. Of course, James realized, he'd not yet fully seen the real Sherlock Holmes, dressed fully as himself and behaving fully like himself.

If there *were* a real Sherlock Holmes.

In the first story, "A Scandal in Bohemia", James was shocked to encounter "the King of Bohemia"—whom Holmes had clearly identified as the Prince of Wales while the two were late-dining at Café de la Paix a mere twelve days earlier. James thought the quality of prose something less than merely serviceable and the plot ridiculous. Holmes's machinations to retrieve the "incriminating photograph" for the Prince of Wales were contrived and absurd and—in the end—unsuccessful. A mere female adventuress had outsmarted him at every turn. If this tale were true, why would Holmes—whose income seems to flow only through these private clients—ever allow Dr. Watson to work with Conan Doyle to publish the details of such a singular failure?

Even more interesting to Henry James was the sense, sometimes emerging from between the lines or a sardonic comment, that Holmes—at least the *character* of Holmes as shown in this odd tale—holds the "King of Bohemia"—England's actual Prince of Wales—in something like cold contempt. At the end of the tale, Holmes seems to be glad that he had been beaten and that "Irene Adler" had retained the incriminating photograph. (James also noticed that Watson—or Conan Doyle—had referred to the adventuress as "the late Irene Adler.")

"The Red-Headed League" was more amusing but Henry James found the detective's "startling deductions" in the tale merely silly. Nowhere in either of these stories had the author, whoever he really was, attempted to get into the minds or motivations of any of the characters. Watson insisted on viewing his flatmate at 221 B Baker Street with awe no matter the level of idiocy Holmes was perpetuating.

Proofreading errors were rampant. The red-headed character named Wilson started work—simply sitting in a room for four hours a day and copying pages from the *Encyclopaedia Britannica*—on April 29, 1890. After 8 weeks' work and 32 pounds paid for his labors, Wilson shows up promptly at the empty room (save for table and chair where he sits to copy) and finds a note pinned to the door—

THE RED-HEADED LEAGUE
IS
DISSOLVED
Oct. 9, 1890.

But—and James did this calculation in his head—the 8 weeks and 32 pounds would have brought Wilson (and the story) only to June 23, not October 9. And Wilson would have been owed an extra 58 pounds, 10 shillings, and 2 pence were it actually October 9.

The author also has "Wilson" mentioning that he was moving into the "*B's*" in the encyclopedia at the time the Red-Headed League was dissolved and he lost his silly job. Holmes had noticed the recent 1889 Ninth Edition of the encyclopedia in a hallway bookcase, and Henry James rang for a manservant to fetch the first volume of the *Britannica*. After actually counting the words on an "average" page in the first section, James hobbled over to the room's small writing desk, retrieved some foolscap and a pencil, and figured that the character of "Jabez Wilson" had copied some 6,419,616 words in eight weeks' work...and that while copying for only four hours a day! With a little division on his foolscap, James averaged this to a rate of some 33,435 words per hour or a little over 557 words per minute. Extraordinary!

Ridiculous! The author, whether Watson or Conan Doyle, literally had not done his arithmetic.

On another page of the same story, the careless writer has Holmes, Watson, a constable, and others suffering a "long drive" through "an endless labyrinth of gas-lit streets", even though their objective would have been only a short walk from where the party had started.

In another part of the story, Henry James could not stop himself from laughing out loud. Holmes has announced that the mystery facing him was a "three-pipe problem" and then drew his legs up into his chair and—using a disreputable black-clay pipe that James had seen the detective smoke while on their trip here—supposedly smoked three pipes of shag tobacco in fifty minutes. James knew that one shag of such rough tobacco in an hour would almost certainly ruin any man's throat and nose membranes; three shags would probably kill a man.

In "The Boscombe Valley Mystery", the Holmes character is his usual arrogant, condescending self to Watson—a man older and certainly more experienced in life and war than the so-called "consulting detective"—but he also continues to prove that he has no right to act that way. At the first news of a murder in the mythical "Boscombe Valley" near the very-real city of Ross in Herefordshire, Holmes has Watson join him in a pall-mall earliest-train-possible rush to the city and crime scene. But once Holmes arrives in Ross, he inexplicably takes two days off in the hotel there before venturing out to the outdoor crime scene where a man had died by having his skull caved in. Holmes even emphasizes the absolute importance of inspecting that crime scene "before it rains and all evidence is washed away", but then is satisfied that the weather shall remain "No wind and not a cloud in the sky" by consulting a barometer which reports the pressure at 29.

Now Henry James was no meteorologist and to the best of his recollection he had never used a barometer reading as a plot point in any of his stories or novels, but he had spent enough time with farmers—both back in New England and in England and France—and with sea captains during his various crossings of the Atlantic to know that a reading of "29" does not insure good weather; indeed, if, with that reading, a serious rainstorm had not arrived, it was certainly on the way.

After a day lost not viewing the crime scene, Holmes again refers to the barometer reading of 29 as "promising fine weather" and proceeds to waste another day that should have been close to typhoon weather.

Holmes then solves the mystery largely due to inferring that the murdered man's seemingly incomprehensible last words to his (accused-of-murder) son—"A rat"—actually must mean "Ballarat" in Australia. Therefore the murderer had to be from Ballarat. But even granted the identity of the murderer as Australian and Henry James's personal lack of knowledge of the continent, one flip open of the first volume of the *Encyclopaedia Britannica* showed James that there were several other Australian towns and regions that ended with "arat", including "Ararat".

James's dismay at the lack of proofreading—as well as the carelessness of the writing itself—was not diminished in the story called "The Man with the Twisted Lip" when Dr. John Watson's wife, visited in the night by a distraught and veiled lady whom she soon sees to be a certain acquaintance known to her as "Kate Whitney", says—"It was very sweet of you to come. Now, you must have some wine and water, and sit here comfortably and tell us all about it. Or should you rather that I sent James off to bed?"

James? thought Henry James in growing contempt. The gentleman in question, unless Mrs. Watson had a lover hiding under the table, had to be her husband, *John* Watson. *Doesn't this author even bother to proofread his work?*

In the same story, Holmes reveals the true identity of a "filthy prisoner" by rubbing his face lightly with a large, wet sponge he's been thoughtful enough to bring to the prison, thus removing—according to the author of the tale—layers of actor's greasepaint. Henry James, who had spent much of the previous eighteen months traveling around England with an acting troupe putting on his first play, *The American,* knew from simple observation that Holmes's "wet sponge" would have just mottled and muddled an actor's disguise: all of the actors and actresses James had watched removing their make-up first had to carefully apply a layer of cold cream before beginning to remove theatrical make-up.

And so it went, story after story, idiocy after idiocy.

James set aside the collection only when a footman came up to announce that everyone was meeting in the parlor for tea or drinks before dinner. He did not have to feign his limp when going down, and at John Hay's concerned questioning, James admitted that his gout—about which he'd written Hay the previous December—was indeed acting up.

The dinner, although so limited in number it was essentially *diner en famille,* was roast beef for which James had little appetite this particular evening. John Hay was expansive, happy and perfect as their host, Clara was kind and sure that everyone was involved in the conversation, "Jan Sigerson" described his pleasure at seeing the gleaming white Capitol and other such wonders—including what James considered the wedding-cake baroque-on-baroque monstrosity of the State Department just down the street, where Hay had worked for so many years—and James was quiet, save for nods of attention and various smiles of appreciation. The others must have put his quietness down to his gout, although it was more or less characteristic of Henry James at any table.

In truth, James was carefully observing this Sherlock Holmes/Jan Sigerson person. Yes, it had been he—James—who had recognized Holmes in the almost absolute darkness along the Seine, for despite the actor's putty on the nose, added hair, and other make-up (none of which would come off with a simple pass of a wet sponge), the hawk-look of that lean face remained. But James was beginning to have a different feeling about both Holmes and about his own plan to talk to John Hay privately after dinner and there—with endless apologies—expose the hoax and humbug he'd brought to the Hays' household.

No... tomorrow would serve. James saw how it would be better to wait until the *real* explorer and mountain-climber Clarence King exposed Holmes for the fraud he was. Or, failing that, the certainty of the Norwegian emissary tripping up Holmes's clumsy and shallow disguise. Then James could act as shocked and deceived as everyone else at the table. It would be embarrassing, yes, but it wouldn't necessarily put Henry James beyond the pale with these old friends. Holmes would be banished, James would apologize to John and Clara for his own unforgivable naïveté in believing the man, he would leave almost immediately to sail to England, and that would be that.

Hay invited the men into his library for brandy and cigars, but after quickly finishing his drink there, James pled gout again and went back upstairs, leaving his host and "Sigerson" energetically discussing the European gold situation, the recent slaughter of thousands of Arabs by Congo cannibals, and the possible injustice of canal-builder de Lesseps's imprisonment for fraud.

CHAPTER 14

James read into the night. The authorial and plot idiocies continued
to accrue. But here and there, James did see elements of the *Sherlock
Holmes character* which reminded him of the man he'd met thirteen
days earlier and with whom he'd dined that night. And he began to
understand, dimly, the attraction of these "adventures" to educated
friends of his such as Edmund Gosse. The heart of *The Adventures
of Sherlock Holmes* lay not in the clumsy "adventures"—which never
struck James as that adventurous—but rather in the friendship between Holmes and Watson, their breakfasts together, the foggy days
shared indoors by the crackling fire, and Mrs. Hudson coming and
going with her food trays and messages from the world. Holmes and
Watson lived in a *Boys' Adventure* universe and, like Peter Pan, and despite Watson's rather confused mentions of being married, neither of
them ever grew up.

In "The Adventure of the Noble Bachelor"—which, like so many of
the other Holmesian "adventures", was no adventure at all, but just a
vulgar domestic misunderstanding in the flimsy guise of a mystery—a
certain "Lord Robert St. Simon" of high-birth visits 221 B Baker Street
to seek advice and Holmes is instantly rude to him. Besides botching
the title and crying "Good-day, Lord St. Simon" rather than the proper
"Lord Robert" or "Lord Robert St. Simon", Holmes immediately insults
his guest and client.

Henry James had to stop himself at the last minute from marking the following passage in Clara's book with pencil or pen. Lord Robert, who has been left at the altar by an American bride, is speaking:

"'A most painful matter to me, as you most readily imagine, Mr. Holmes. I have been cut to the quick. I understand that you already managed several delicate cases of this sort, sir, though I presume that they were hardly from the same class of society.'

"'No, I am descending.'

"'I beg pardon?'

"'My last client of the sort was a king.'

"'Oh, really! I had no idea. And which king?'

"'The King of Scandinavia.'

"'What! Had he lost his wife?'

"'You can understand,' said Holmes suavely, 'that I extend to the affairs of my other clients the same secrecy which I promise to you in yours.'"

What utter bombast, thought James. Any gentleman with a shred of discretion might have mentioned similar *details* in another case, but would never be so indiscreet as to mention the *name* of another client—especially not a royal one.

It was all a reverse snobbery that James had heard from Holmes—or at least from the man downstairs who might be pretending to be Sherlock Holmes in the same penumbra of insanity that led him to *pretend* that he was Holmes pretending to be explorer Jan Sigerson—and it led, along with so many other clues both in these "adventures" and in James's time with the detective, to one conclusion: Sherlock Holmes was no gentleman. He was simply someone gifted in disguises who had been play-acting for years at being a gentleman—cultivating the casual dress, bored air, and upper-class educated accents of a true gentleman, but never showing the soul of one.

*   *   *

The last story in *The Adventures of Sherlock Holmes*—read with the window open because of a growing warmth in the air and with moths batting at the lamp—made the usually staid Henry James stifle his laughter with his hand over his mouth. It would not do to have the Hays' servants—or perhaps the other guest down the hall—hear gout-ridden Henry James laughing aloud after midnight.

The final story in the collection was "The Adventure of the Copper Beeches" and it was a fitting finale, since it included all of the authorial sloppiness, logical idiocies, and Holmesian blunders that made the other stories all but unreadable. Here they were gathered into a primary mass of one sensationalist writer's execrable laziness.

The story starts with an attractive but far-too-familiar young lady—a stranger to Holmes and Watson but one acting as if she were already an intimate of the detective—a certain Violet Hunter, appearing one morning and demanding the Great Detective's advice on an earth-shattering matter: should she take a well-paying job as governess for the son of an immensely fat man named Jephro Rucastle.

Mr. Rucastle's interview with her was "odd" because he declared himself and his wife as "faddy" and said her employment would require her to wear a certain dress "Or to sit here, or sit there, that would not be offensive to you?"

Miss Hunter declares herself shocked to hear of the idea of her wearing certain clothing—although all domestic servants and many governesses of the era were required to do so—and the warnings of orders "to sit here, or sit there" were foolish for Rucastle to mention if he had dark intentions; the lord and lady of households routinely ordered their domestics and governesses around.

Then Mr. Rucastle informed Violet Hunter that she would have to cut her lovely and luxuriant hair short. At this outrageous condition, Miss Hunter turned down the job offer but kept thinking about the high salary and after a few days came close to changing her mind. Then a letter arrived from Rucastle, still insisting on the cut-hair and wearing of certain clothes as a condition, but raising her proposed salary to thirty pounds a quarter: a fortune for a governess, especially one with the admittedly limited education and experience of Miss Violet Hunter.

"'That is the letter which I have just received, Mr. Holmes, and my mind is made up that I will accept it.'"

"Then what in Hades are you doing wasting this detective's time in asking for advice *if you've already decided?*" softly hissed Henry James in the moth-circling night.

With the certainty of the machineries of plotting thudding and racketing along, drowning all logic and careful introspection, the telegram "which we eventually received came late one night"...

> Please be at the "Black Swan" Hotel at Winchester at midnight
> Tomorrow. Do come! I am at my wit's end.
> Hunter

This wasn't a telegram; it was a royal summons. So naturally Holmes and Watson are thundering toward Winchester in a morning train. In this sequence, the interesting part, from what James's brother William would have called "a psychological perspective", was this rather amazing outburst from Holmes as he looks at the peaceful English countryside beyond London and comments upon the bucolic homes and cottages:

"'...I look at them, and the only thought which comes to me is a feeling of their isolation, and of the impunity with which crime may be committed there.'

"'Good Heavens!' I cried. 'Who would associate crime with these dear old homesteads?'

"'They always fill me with a certain horror. It is my belief, Watson, founded upon my experience, that the lowest and vilest alleys in London do not present a more dreadful record of sin than does the smiling and beautiful countryside.'

"'You horrify me!'

"'But the reason is very obvious. The pressure of public opinion can do in the town what the law cannot accomplish. There is no lane so vile that the scream of a tortured child, or the thud of a drunkard's blow, does not beget sympathy and indignation among the neighbours, and then the whole machinery of justice is ever so close that a word of complaint can set it doing, and there is but a step between the crime and the dock. But look at these lovely houses, each in its own fields, filled for the most part with poor ignorant folk who know little of the law. Think of the deeds of hellish cruelty, the hidden wickedness which go on, year in, year out, in such places, and none the wiser...'"

Henry James had lived in England long enough to know that this was pure twaddle. There were certainly instances of crime and domestic brutality in any picturesque village or cottage, but none of the wanton crime, neglect, and lack of law that Holmes here states—absurdly—would be so quickly reported and corrected, with punishment invariably handed out, in the slums and tenements of London. Indeed, the cruelty of Henry James's favorite city was known to all of its urban inhabitants.

What struck Henry James in this silly outburst of the literary Sherlock Holmes was twofold:

First, it was not an English attitude about the city versus country. In fact, it was decidedly "un-English". French, perhaps, Russian, possibly, but never English.

Second, James could all but hear his brother William's strong voice saying—"This is a sort of confession from the man's own background, Harry. A psychological plea for help and understanding. Something very dark and painful happened to this man in the country sometime in his past—a countryside he was not used to, being a former city slum-dweller perhaps—and his subconscious now loathes and fears the very idea of bucolic quiet and those stretches of peaceful darkness between the country homes and cottages. It would be very interesting to explore the basis for this man's deep fears."

*   *   *

Henry James occasionally lectured on great writers, but should he ever give a symposium on Ludicrous Writing, he would use as his text the rest of "The Adventure of the Copper Beeches":

Miss Hunter—her hair now cropped short in a way that reminded James, with a pang, of his teenaged cousin, now deceased, Minnie Temple posing as Hamlet for them after a serious illness had caused her hair to be roughly shorn—meets Holmes and Watson at the Black Swan Hotel (evidently she is a governess who has no problem leaving her young charge, the Rucastles' only child—a son, Edward, described only as having "a huge and oversized head" and of being "evil"—at any time of the day or night).

Indeed, other than her ascertaining that the odd-looking boy is evil, there is no mention of Miss Hunter's governess duties or interactions with the boy. The Rucastles have informed Violet Hunter that their daughter—who looked very much like Violet Hunter—had died of "brain fever" (which was the reason for the daughter's shortened hair), and now Hunter informs a solicitous Holmes and Watson that she has been made to sit in front of a bow window (with her back to the window, of course) in the dead daughter's dress and laugh aloud at Mr. Rucastle's endless trove of amusing anecdotes. When Violet secreted a small mirror into her handkerchief to look out the window behind her, she saw a young man standing at the fence to the property, staring intently at her back. But the humorless Mrs. Rucastle noticed the mirror, exclaimed that there was an intruder on the property, and demanded that Violet wave him away before they immediately lowered the blinds. Miss Hunter then easily unlocks a "locked drawer" in a chest of drawers in her room and finds a coil of hair that has precisely the color and texture of her own when it had been long.

As established forever in such gothic tales as *Jane Eyre,* there was the inevitable locked room—in fact, an entire locked wing—which Miss Violet Hunter was told to avoid. Naturally, she soon finds a key (inevitably, conveniently) left in the lock there and explores the empty, dusty wing...empty save for one room which is also locked, with the iron headboard from a bed used as bars across it. She does not have time to go inside.

Mr. Rucastle almost immediately learns of her transgression and threatens to feed her to the large mastiff, called Carlo, that he orders the single manservant, named Toller, to loose from the kennel to prowl the grounds at night. Toller, it seems, has drunk himself into oblivion that very afternoon. Holmes immediately announces that she must lock Mrs. Toller in the cellar that evening and that he and Dr. Watson, carrying his trusty service revolver, will be at Copper Beeches at seven p.m.

Holmes has stated that it is obvious that Mr. Rucastle has imprisoned his still-living daughter—Judy—in the locked room for some nefarious reason, probably about an inheritance he wants to control, and the three adventurers have soon broken through the locks and bedstead grille and flung open the door, only to find...

"It was empty. There was no furniture save a little pallet bed, a small table, and a basketful of linen. The skylight above was open, and the prisoner gone.

"'There has been some villainy here,' said Holmes; 'this beauty has guessed Miss Hunter's intentions, and has carried his victim off.'

"'But how?'

"'Through the skylight. We shall soon see how he managed it.' He swung himself up onto the roof. 'Ah, yes,' he cried, 'Here's the end of a long light ladder against the eaves. That is how he did it.'

"'But it is impossible,' said Miss Hunter. 'The ladder was not there when the Rucastles went away.'

"'He has come back and done it. I tell you that he is a clever and dangerous man...'"

Here Henry James cannot resist the soft laughter that overcame him. "A clever and dangerous man..." who for some reason found it necessary to bring a tall ladder to his own home, cross the roof, and drop through a skylight to retrieve a young woman from a room to which he had the keys and could easily unlock and walk in—and take his daughter out the normal way should he need to—any time he chose. This was typical of Holmes's "deductions" and—James thought—it was typically asinine.

The end of the story was almost apologetically *pro forma:* Rucastle appears: "You villain!" cries Holmes. "Where is your daughter?" Then Rucastle rushes out to free Carlo, the giant mastiff, who we know from

Mr. Toller's two days of reported drunkenness—has not been fed for two days. Our trio hears "the baying of a hound"—another authorial idiocy, James notes tiredly. Although Henry James prefers small dogs, lap dogs suitable for parlors, such as dachshunds, he's been around all breeds of dogs enough at other people's country homes to know that mastiffs—which are usually quite gentle around people—are incapable of "baying". Growling, perhaps. Roaring from the chest when threatened, perhaps. But baying, never. That ability to "bay" belongs to the "hounds" group of canines—and a mastiff is not a hound.

At any rate, Carlo chews out Mr. Rucastle's throat, Dr. Watson with his trusty service revolver "blew its brains out" (but too late, alas!), and a suddenly helpful Mrs. Toller explains the entire plot, the need for Rucastle to fake his daughter Judy's death (for inheritance reasons!) and hide her away in the locked wing, and the whole pantomime of Violet Hunter being made to impersonate Judy so that the daughter's persistent fiancé (a "Mr. Fowler" whom Violet Hunter glimpsed in her mirror) will give up, accept Judy's death, and go away.

In one final paragraph all the loose ends are tied and tidied up—we never meet Judy or Mr. Fowler, but hear from the narrator that they were married and that the lucky groom is now "the holder of a Government appointment in the Island of Mauritius", and that Miss Violet Hunter has gone on (perhaps with the help of Sherlock Holmes?) to be "the head of a private school at Walsatt". (A rather good job for a young woman with no real references who admitted in the story that she had as skills "only a little music, a tiny bit of French and German".)

Henry James, setting the finished book on his bedside table, again has to press his knuckles against his lips lest an audible laugh escape.

The writer—Dr. John H. "James" Watson? Arthur Conan Doyle? A bizarre blend of the two hacks?—has forgotten all about the son, Edward. The boy with the "oversized head" and reported penchant for evil. It's obvious that all of the characters, including his former governess, Miss Hunter, had also forgotten that Edward was supposed to exist. With the happy ending of Mr. Rucastle having his throat torn out by a hungry and impossibly baying mastiff, Edward just seems to have vanished. *Poof!*

Lying in the warm darkness, James thinks of a future story about a governess that he's contemplated writing from time to time: his story, should he ever write it, would be from the governess's mentally clouded point-of-view and would deal with a palpable—although imagined—evil that seems to threaten the child or children in the remote country house. James sees it as a ghost story without any certain ghost and knows it will require the lightest and subtlest of touches to make the increasingly nervous reader begin to wonder if the governess is insane... or evil...or if it is the children who are evil. Or perhaps there is a ghost (or ghosts, James hasn't decided), despite all the psychological suggestions to the contrary.

His brother William would almost certainly like such a "psychological" tale.

All James knows for certain is that the tale will require all of his hard-earned skills and the most delicate of authorial brushstrokes to help the reader slowly become aware of the multiple levels of honesty, lying, guilt, and innocence—not even to mention survival—even while keeping the story explicit enough to chill the reader to goosebumps. But everywhere and always he will have to leave the reader in deep doubt about what has "really" happened and which of the events are only in the increasingly unstable governess's mind.

Smiling slightly from the pathetic absurdities of the "Copper Beeches" and thinking ever so gently of ghosts and of the human mind in murky conflict with itself, Henry James falls asleep in the warm Washington night.

CHAPTER 15

Sunday was quiet in the sprawling Hays household—at least until Henry James cornered Sherlock Holmes.

Clara Hay had gone to church after informing everyone that she would be doing some charity volunteer work for hours after the church service proper. John Hay had hosted his two guests at breakfast but then disappeared into his beautiful study for hours of his own sort of literary or historical devotion. The huge home was quiet except for the reassuring sound of horses' hooves and buggy wheels on the street outside and the occasional nunlike hushed rustle of servants moving efficiently to and fro within the light-filled, mahogany-scented mansion.

It was late morning when Henry James knocked on "Jan Sigerson's" guest room door. Holmes, smoking cheap shag tobacco in his disreputable black clay pipe, let the writer in and beckoned to an extra chair near the window where he'd been reading. James was carrying a book of his own but he carefully kept the cover and spine hidden while the two men took their seats.

"Clarence King will be here in a few hours," said James.

"Yes," said Holmes. "I'm very much looking forward to meeting him."

"I think you should not." Henry James's soft voice could be firm to the point of hardness when he willed it to be. He willed it so now.

"I beg your pardon?" Holmes batted the ashes from the old pipe into a crystalline ashtray on a side table.

"I think you should not put the household through this farce," said James. "John Hay may be busy in his study until tea time. I propose that you pack your bags and leave while you can."

"And why would I do that?" Holmes asked softly. "Henry Adams won't even be back until sometime next week. I've hardly begun the investigation into his wife's death."

"That's all humbug," snapped James. "Clover Adams suffered from a melancholic disposition. She fell to a low after her father's death and never recovered. Melancholy ran in her family, as her brother Ned's suicide attests. Turning it into a mystery is humbug."

Holmes looked as if he were interested in what the writer was saying. "Then what about the annual 'She was murdered' notes sent to..."

"More humbug," Henry James said firmly. "I shall not allow you to re-open old griefs in such a way. I have no idea why I've gone along with your insanities this long. But no matter. It must end. Today. You pack and leave and I shall think of something to tell the Hays and Clarence King and the others. I myself shall leave early tomorrow."

"So you no longer think me capable of solving this mystery?" asked Holmes, repacking and relighting his pipe.

"I no longer think that you are Sherlock Holmes." *There,* thought James. *I've said it.*

The other man looked up from his pipe with obvious surprise and an even greater expression of interest. "James, it was *you* who identified *me* from memory—despite my Sigerson disguise—near le Pont Neuf."

"I was mistaken. Or perhaps I had met you at Mrs. O'Connor's garden party four years ago, but you were in disguise then as well."

"In disguise as..."

"As Sherlock Holmes. A fictional character."

"Oh hoh!" cried the man whom James had known as Holmes. "So now you agree with me that Sherlock Holmes does not really exist! What changed your mind, James?"

"This." The writer held out the tan edition of *The Adventures of Sherlock Holmes.*

"May I?" asked the man with the pipe. He took the book gently in his long, strong fingers and began to flip through it. "I was vaguely aware that the American edition of Watson's collected *Strand* stories was coming out this year, but I had no idea it would be published here so early."

"Last month," said James and wished that he hadn't spoken.

"The illustrations by Sidney Paget are rather good, aren't they?" asked the other man. His tone held mild amusement.

"If they purport to be of you," said James, "they flatter you."

"Oh, absolutely!" cried Holmes. He removed the pipe from between his teeth as he laughed. "But, you see, I've never met Mr. Sidney Paget. Nor have I allowed a photograph to be taken of me. Paget uses his brother as a model for his 'Sherlock Holmes'—or so I am told. His brother is an even more well-known illustrator and Watson informed me that the *Strand* people had meant to hire *him* rather than his brother Sidney, but the letter went to the wrong Paget."

James stared blankly at Holmes—at the man whom he still thought of as Holmes—until finally he could stand the silence no longer. The smoke from the shag tobacco made him cough before he could get a sentence out. "I now believe, sir, that you are some person... some *deranged* person... pretending to be the fictional character Sherlock Holmes who, in turn, is pretending to be a fictional explorer named Jan Sigerson."

"Oh, I *say!*" cried Holmes, removing his pipe again and smiling most broadly. "Very good, James. Very good indeed. That hypothesis makes much more sense than my own... that is, that I simply don't exist outside these little"—he held up the book—"fictions."

"So you admit it," said Henry James. He felt a strange and not very pleasant but quite persistent invisible weight press against his chest.

"Admit that I am deranged? I can hardly defend myself against that accusation. Admit that I am someone other than the possibly—quite probably—fictional character Sherlock Holmes? Alas, I cannot confess to that, sir. I am either the *real* Sherlock Holmes or the fictional simulacrum of same. Those are my sad choices at the moment."

James felt something like panic pluck at him. The other man was deranged. And he might well be *dangerous*—a physical threat to James even at this moment.

"Oh, I think not dangerous," said Holmes, puffing away again. "Not to you, at least, Mr. James."

It was as if he'd plucked the author's thoughts out of the air.

"What did you think of Watson's...stories?" asked Holmes, closing the book and setting it on the table next to James.

"They're absurd."

Holmes laughed again. "Yes, they are, aren't they? Poor Watson works so hard to bring the rough notes of his chronicles up to Conan Doyle's literary standards, but I doubt if either man understands how the reality of my cases could ever really be translated into any work of art. You see, James, the better cases already *are* works of art—without the melodrama and fictional trappings."

"So you admit that these stories are inferior literary efforts," managed James. "Mere overwrought...romances."

Holmes winced at the last word but sounded amiable enough as he said, "Absolutely, my dear chap." He opened the book again. "I see that Watson included the tale he called 'The Copper Beeches'. Shall we just take that as an example of literary failure?"

"I already have taken it as such," said James.

"As well you should," said Holmes, prodding the stem of his pipe in James's direction. "I ask you...does it make any sense whatsoever that this..." He had to fan through pages and glance down at the story. "That this Violet Hunter person should come to our apartment and take up our time, Watson's and mine, asking advice on whether she take some dreary governess position in the country? No matter how odd her employer's requirements might have been, I mean. And does it make sense that I would waste my time listening to such a plea for advice...unnecessary advice, since you may have noticed that the baggage had already made up her mind about taking the position."

"Total nonsense," said James. He felt a sense of oddness verging on vertigo that he was agreeing with Holmes. Or vice versa.

"This 'Violet Hunter'—that wasn't the wench's real name, of course—was not my client."

"No?" James would have called back the syllable if he'd been able to.

"No. Our client—the person in need of help who showed up on this cold day in early March of eighteen eighty-six—was the 'Mr. Fowler' to whom Watson refers, but who is never directly introduced to the reader."

"Mr. Fowler?" repeated James, despite himself. "The imprisoned Alice Rucastle's fiancé? The man in the mirror? The one whom Dr. Watson informs us ends up marrying the liberated Miss Rucastle and moves with her to Mauritius?"

Holmes grinned around the pipe in a way that looked almost evil. "Precisely," he said. "Although 'Mr. Fowler'—I shall call him Peter since that was the gentleman's real first name—did not, as it turned out, marry the liberated and enriched Miss Alice Rucastle and...how did Watson put it?" He flipped pages. "Oh, yes...become 'the holder of a Government appointment in the Island of Mauritius.'"

"Is any of this relevant or of any importance whatsoever to your fraudulent representation of yourself as Sherlock Holmes?" asked James.

"Only if you wish to understand the wide gap between this...fictional...Sherlock Holmes's *life* and his reported *adventures,*" said Holmes.

"I see no purpose to discussing either," said Henry James.

Holmes nodded in agreement but removed the pipe and began speaking in slow, low tones.

"Peter...Fowler...came to see Dr. Watson and me in March of eighteen eighty-eight. His problem was a domestic one, yes, but one which I thought at the time might serve my need to some true detection. In the end, you see, James, 'Mr. Fowler'—who was a very nice London gentleman, by the by—did not marry Miss Alice Rucastle and live happily ever after. The truth of the matter...the sort of truth that Watson so frequently works so hard to avoid...was that his former fiancée, Alice Rucastle, tore Fowler's throat out with her teeth. She murdered him."

"Good God," breathed James.

"Mr. Fowler came to me because he'd been happily engaged to Alice Rucastle...Watson's clumsy choice of a name, of course...until what Fowler had referred to as his fiancée's 'pleasant if frequent flightiness' had turned into a severe brain fever...whatever 'brain fever' might actually be. Watson, like most medicos in our benighted era, swears by 'brain fever', but not one doctor in a thousand can describe its cause or cure."

"But Miss Rucastle...whatever her real name might be...did have it?" asked James. His weakness for hearing bizarre stories was almost the equal of his penchant for writing them.

"She had it...but her infant younger brother, Edward, was the one who died from it," said Holmes.

"Edward," repeated James. He remembered the moths circling the lamp late the night before as he approached sleep and the end of the collection of tales. "The little boy with evil behavior and the oversized head. The object of Miss Violet Hunter's efforts of instruction as a governess."

Holmes laughed again. "Miss Violet Hunter was not hired as a governess. Baby Edward had been murdered by the time Mr. and Mrs. Rucastle hired her...and they hired her only to impersonate their imprisoned daughter Alice."

"Wait," said Henry James, holding up one well-manicured hand. "You're saying that Violet Hunter, by any other name, knew from the start that she had no duty except to impersonate the imprisoned daughter of the Rucastles? Mr. Fowler's fiancée?"

"That's precisely what I am saying, James." Holmes stared out the window at leaf-shadows on St. John's across the street. "'Violet Hunter' was nothing more than a woman of the streets...in company, she could not have impersonated even so lowly a lady as a governess. Mr. 'Jephro Rucastle'—who, by the by, was no villain as Watson re-created it but who also was soon to die violently—made it clear to the London wench from the first that she would be paid thirty pounds a month—not a quarter as Watson's re-telling has it—thirty pounds a month just to cut her hair as Alice's had been cut during her terrible illness, to wear Alice's blue dress, to sit in the window where Peter Fowler could, from behind her and from a distance, see her laughing and evidently recovered from her madness."

"Her *madness?*" gasped James.

"Oh, yes. I forgot to put that little fact in sequence, didn't I? This is why Watson says that I must never write up my own adventures. When Alice's father—Alice was her real Christian name, by the way—when her father realized that she would never regain her sanity, he wrote to Peter Fowler in a poor imitation of his daughter's hand to break off their engagement. But Fowler never believed that the letter was from Alice."

"Alice Rucastle was mad?"

"As a hatter," said Holmes with absolutely no tone of sympathy in his voice. "It had manifested itself in sly and then secret but serious ways for years, but during the winter of her engagement to Peter Fowler—a marriage which her parents did not know of and would never have allowed since the insanity was hereditary—the worsening illness led first to the fits, then to the seizures, and finally to the violent behavior that the Rucastles reported to Fowler and the world as 'brain fever'."

"But surely Mr. Fowler would have understood," said James. He tried to imagine writing this tale himself, but failed. It was too sensationalist. Too much the fever-dream territory of a contemporary Wilkie Collins.

"Understood that in her violent madness Alice Rucastle had murdered and partially eaten her two-year-old younger brother Edward?" Holmes asked blandly. "I rather doubt it."

"Good Lord," gasped James. "But you knew of this...abomination?"

"From the beginning," said Holmes, no longer smiling. "Far from being a villain seeking an inheritance or whatever twaddle Watson added to distort the tale, the so-called Jephro Rucastle—his real name Jethrow Dawkins—was such an indulgent and loving father that he could not abide the thought of his daughter Alice—the murderer of his only son, the heir of the family name and title—being locked away in a bedlam. Thus the locked wing, the barred door."

"But if Miss Violet Hunter did not discover these things...if she already knew about Alice's madness, the reason for the locked wing and room..."

"It was Peter Fowler, not the harlot Violet Hunter, who insisted on luring the Rucastles into town that March night in eighteen eighty-six," Holmes said grimly. "He sent us a telegram stating his intentions of 'saving' his beloved Alice. I sent him an immediate telegram in return, ordering him not to go anywhere near Hodgkyss Hall—he never received the telegram since he had already left his hotel in Wells—and Watson and I rushed out to Wookey Hole as fast as we could..."

"Wookey Hole?" chimed James.

"Yes, of course. Close by the famous caves near Wells in Somerset. 'Fowler' was staying in the Wookey Hole Hotel in Wells. Watson's fictionalized 'Rucastles' were actually the well-known Dawkins family. Alice's father was Jethrow Dawkins, Lord Hodgkyss of Hodgkyss Hall, first cousin to the Vicar of Wookey and so-called 'Hero of the Transvaal' in the eighteen eighty-one Boer Rebellion."

"Even I, a mere American, have heard of the Witch of Wookey Hole," said James. His voice sounded strange to his own ears. He could not quite believe what he had just said. Henry James, Jr.—like his father Henry James, Sr., and his older brother William—had always had a weakness for ghost stories.

"The Witch of Wookey Hole is a limestone stalagmite that's been scaring tourists since the sixteen hundreds," Holmes said in the flattest of tones. "Alice Dawkins was the real-life Monster of Wookey Hole. And only seven years ago."

Henry James squinted at Holmes. "You said that Peter Fowler was murdered. It was written that Mr. Rucastle—and this Dawkins, Lord Hodgkyss, 'died violently'. There's a lot of yet-unexplained mayhem there."

"We arrived only minutes too late, Watson and I," Holmes said in a barely audible voice. "Fowler had brought a tall ladder, risked the dangerous traverse across ancient slate tiles in the darkness, and let himself down through the small skylight in Alice's locked room. She must have sat on the bed in silence and let him unlock her manacles, padlocks, and chains while he whispered endearments. Then she used her teeth and uncut nails to slash his throat. She was eating his heart when Dawkins, her father, rushed in. The 'Violet Hunter' hired harlot was close on Dawkins's heels, and, by pure coincidence, wearing Alice's blue dress that evening."

James sat, staring and waiting. Despite the fact that all this had to be pure invention, he found that he had trouble breathing.

"Mr. Dawkins, Lord Hodgkyss, had brought a pistol with him," continued Holmes in the same flat tones. "He had told me in an interview the week before that he was sure he could never use it on his daughter, no matter what new unspeakable actions she might undertake. He was correct. As Watson and I ran down the dusty hallway and shouted at him, Dawkins raised the pistol to his temple and blew his own brains out."

"And Miss Violet Hunter?" asked James. "The non-governess governess?"

"Mad," said Sherlock Holmes. "She began screaming at the sight of what was transpiring in Alice Dawkins's room and continues to scream to this day, although her asylum care is paid for by Lady Hodgkyss."

James smiled to show that he was not a total rube. "Rube"—the word came from when a traveling circus had come to the outskirts of Newport when he was young. James hadn't thought of that word for years; he'd never used it in a story.

"And what about Carlo?" he asked softly.

"Carlo?" said Holmes.

"In 'The Adventure of the Copper Beeches', Watson writes about Carlo, the giant baying mastiff that prowled the yard at night and that tore out Mr. Rucastle's throat in the end."

Holmes smiled thinly. "'Baying mastiff'. Watson never has been able to tell his Hound Group from his Herding Dogs . . . Watson just doesn't know dogs. There *was* a mastiff at Hodgkyss Hall. His name was Barney, he was fifteen years old, and if he'd encountered a burglar in the night, Barney would have rolled over to have his belly rubbed. The only infamy Barney ever committed, according to Jethrow Dawkins when Watson and I spoke to him three days before he died, was when he playfully chewed up one of Lady Hodgkyss's stuffed animals."

"But Watson wrote in 'The Adventure of the Copper Beeches' that he had to take his service revolver and—I quote—blow the creature's brains out after it had killed Mr. Rucastle," said James in a strained voice.

"It was Mr. Dawkins's revolver, and I used it," said Holmes. "Alice Dawkins was preoccupied with devouring her father when I took the fallen revolver and blew her brains out."

The two men sat in silence for several minutes.

Finally Sherlock Holmes—or the man pretending to be the imaginary Sherlock Holmes—said, "I believe I understand why Watson felt he had to write about the Wookey Hole Affair . . . the so-called 'Adventure of the Copper Beeches'. It haunted him. Bothered his sleep. It's in Dr. Watson's nature to try to rearrange things into simpler stories of right and wrong. But if I were he, I would have left the entire Wookey Hole business alone."

Henry James looked the other man in the eye and said, "You realize, of course, that everything that you've told me here sounds absolutely insane."

"Absolutely," said Holmes. The detective checked his watch. "John Hay said that a light lunch would be set out in the conservatory dining area at noon and for us to go ahead even if he were still busy. Would you care to join me, Mr. James?"

"I'll wait until tea with Clarence King and dinner with the Norwegian emissary, Mr. Holmes," said James. He said nothing else before going back to his room to lie down on the perfectly white bedspread.

CHAPTER 16

Clarence King arrived promptly upon the chime of 5 p.m. A portly 51-year-old now and long past his once athletic, mountain-climbing physical prime, King appeared at the Hays' threshold wearing a large beret and a well-worn green velvet corduroy suit complete with knee breeches and high wool socks.

"Your old European traveling suit!" cried John Hay, fervently using both hands to shake King's. "Are you going abroad again?"

"Not unless one counts Mexico as 'abroad'," laughed King in a voice Henry James found as velvety as the absurd traveling suit—and just as well-worn. "I found myself traveling through Washington with no other clothes available and knew that my oldest friends would understand this velveteen invasion. Consider it a tardy celebration of St. Patrick's Day."

"You could have worn your old cowboy britches and chaps and been dressed perfectly for this home, Clarence," said Hay, who had already made the dinner less formal by decreeing it only black tie rather than white tie, even with a Norwegian emissary and his wife and daughter attending.

King whipped off the oversized beret and handed it to the waiting servant. James noticed that Clarence King's hairline had receded considerably since the writer had seen him last, leaving only the graying hint of what had once been long golden locks. King still wore a beard clipped closely in the U. S. Grant manner that had long since gone out of style for younger men. Combined with the velvet-corduroy suit, thought

James, the beard and added weight made the explorer look not a little like paintings of Henry VIII. Then again, realized James, some had almost certainly made the same comment about *him*.

James and Holmes stood and watched Clara Hay hug and kiss their old family friend with an almost girlish enthusiasm that struck both men as very un-Clara-Hayish.

"Clara, my dear!" cried King. "You remain the truest and brightest ray of sunshine in this old man's too-clouded life. You have, as you know"—and here King shot an almost boyishly mischievous glance at John Hay—"ruined for me all other members of your sex. I must now remain a bachelor for all my few remaining days, looking forward only to cremation since that alone guarantees to be a new experience."

"Ohhh!" cried Clara Hay and slapped King on his green-velvet-corduroy sleeve.

"Harry, by God!" cried King, shaking Henry James's hand with great animation. "Adams has so far won the race to baldness amongst our band, but I see that you and I are finally giving old Henry a run for his money. What brings you out of the London fog and back to the States, my friend?"

"First and foremost," James said softly, retrieving his hand and resisting the urge to rub circulation back into it, "this chance to see old friends. May I introduce a traveling companion and fellow guest...Mr. Jan Sigerson? Mr. Sigerson, I present to you the original and inimitable Clarence King. Mr. King, Mr. Sigerson."

King shook hands but then took a step back in the huge foyer as if needing to give Holmes a second inspection. "Sigerson? *Jan Sigerson?* The Norwegian explorer? The fellow who just a couple of years ago penetrated deeper into the Himalayas than any white man has been known to go? *That* Jan Sigerson?"

Holmes bowed modestly.

"By God, sir," boomed King, "it is a pleasure and honor to meet you. I have a thousand questions for you regarding the Himalayan Mountains and the Forbidden Land you managed to penetrate. While I misspent my youth clambering up this continent's molehills, you, sir, have gone to *real* mountains."

"Only to their most modest passes, Mr. King," said Holmes in his Norwegian accent. His dark mustache seemed thicker this evening and James actively wondered if he'd touched it up somehow. "And even then on the backs of ponies."

"Come into the parlor, King," cried John Hay, obviously delighted to see his friend. But there was something else that James was picking up from their host...embarrassment at the way their friend was dressed? Some unfinished and probably unnameable business between the two? Money borrowing, perhaps? As portly and ruddy as King appeared upon first glance, a closer inspection suggested that he had recently passed through an illness...perhaps a serious one.

"It is tea time!" exclaimed Clara Hay.

Clarence King smiled almost sadly. "Ah, those were the days, Clara. John leaving the State Department early—choosing to leave the nation to unintended wars and misdirection rather than miss our five o'clock tea. And Adams poking his pale dome out of his study precisely at five—nothing else would have separated him from his lamprey-like attachment to his moldy green books. And Clover...Clover laughing and leading us into the fireplace room where the little red-leather chairs awaited."

King seemed to notice the effect his eulogy was having on the company and immediately lightened his tone and expression. "Actually, John, I was hoping that we might substitute some of your sherry for tea this one afternoon."

"And so we shall," said Hay, putting his arm around King and leading the way into the fireplace-dominated parlor. "And so we shall."

* * *

Sitting sipping his tea—they had poured sherry, but he would have it after the tea—Henry James was reminded of how small all five of the Five of Hearts had been. Clarence King, at five foot six, had been the tallest of all of them.

After some friendly chatter—Hay probing as to whether King was off that week for a diamond mine in the Andes or a gold mine in the Alaskan Rockies (to which Clarence King had replied only, "Neither! A silver mine in Mexico!")—King asked Holmes a few questions about the Himalayan peaks. Holmes seemed to answer, albeit vaguely, but then the two men began discussing exploration in earnest. James waited for the inevitable revelation that Sherlock Holmes could not tell the difference between a Himalayan peak and a Herefordshire hillside.

"I read your book," 'Jan Sigerson' said almost diffidently to King. "*Mountaineering in the Sierra Nevada*. I enjoyed it immensely."

"That old tome," laughed King. "It's more than twenty years out of date. And half the chapters are about my Early Pleistocene period around the summer and fall of eighteen sixty-four. But tell me, Mr. Sigerson...did you enjoy the section where I described conquering Mount Whitney?"

Sherlock Holmes only smiled.

John Hay said, "Now, Clarence..."

"I used two chapters to describe clambering up Mount Tyndall," boomed King. "Half the book to describe hiking all over other peaks around Yosemite. But only two subordinate clauses to describe my triumph atop the mighty Mount Whitney."

"Not all peaks are ascendable upon one's first attempt," Holmes said softly.

King laughed and nodded. To Henry James he said, "Here were my two subordinate clauses in toto, Harry—and I quote: '*After trying hard to climb Mt. Whitney without success, and having returned to the plains...*'"

King was the only one in the room laughing, but that did not seem to inhibit his mirth. James watched him closely, seeing the deeper bitterness that had settled into the old friend of his old friends—no, more a damp rising from within than something settling from without, as Dickens used to describe the damp rising from tombs under an old church until it chilled the entire congregation.

"Young, fit, outfitted, motivated to greatness," said King, "and not only could I not get within four hundred feet of that summit on the first attempt, but when I finally returned and climbed it, *it was the wrong mountain*. Somehow, in the exertion of the climbing, I'd managed to misplace an entire mountain...all fourteen thousand five hundred feet of it."

"But you did return again and make the summit," John Hay said softly.

"Yes," said King, "but only after other white men had joined the Indians who'd made the summit before I did. And I named the mountain!"

"And you have one named for you," said Holmes. "Mount Clarence King...northwest of Mount Whitney in the Sierra Nevada range, I believe."

"Our exploration group was keen on naming mountains after one another," said King, holding out his sherry glass so the silent but everpresent male servant could refill it. "It's called 'Mount Clarence King' because there was already a peak in the Yosemite named after a preacher called Thomas Starr King. My hill is twelve thousand nine hundred and five feet tall. Somehow I always manage to be the runt of the litter. How high was that pass you crossed to get into Tibet from Sikkim, Mr. Sigerson?"

"Jelep La?" said Holmes. "Thirteen thousand nine hundred and ninety-nine feet at the pass's summit."

"Admit it now," said King. "Weren't you a tiny bit tempted to pile up a little rock cairn, just a foot or so tall? Then you could have said you summited a 'fourteener'. Fourteeners are highly thought of in the American West."

Without waiting for an answer, King began to question Sigerson/Holmes about climbing; it was almost a staccato interrogation. Holmes answered each question promptly and succinctly, evidently understanding the terms well enough. Sometimes he posed counter questions that made Clarence King laugh and say that he'd been burrowing into and under mountains the last two decades or so, not climbing them. James could only note the arcane terms that were filling the air: belay, being on belay, going *off* belay, debating the best new forms of belay, rappelling, rappel ropes, anchors high and anchors low, stemming and counterforce, manteling, methods of chimneying, fist-jamming, using one's bootlaces for Prusik knots when dangling from a rope after a fall from an overhang...James understood none of it, but Holmes made it sound as if *he* understood it all.

Finally Clarence King sighed. "Well, I leave the mountains to you younger generation of climbers. My days on belay—or being belayed—are finished, I fear."

Rather than let this set the tone again, John Hay said to King, "I'm sure Adams will be damnably sorry he missed you."

"As well he should be," muttered King, holding his glass out for another refill of sherry.

"You should tell our other guest of how you met Henry Adams," said Hay.

Clarence King seemed to ponder a minute on whether it would be worth anyone's time to hear the story, but then he drank down his sherry and turned to Holmes. "You've not met Adams yet, is that right, sir?"

"I've not yet had the pleasure of making his acquaintance."

King grunted. "Way back in eighteen sixty-seven, not being able to find honest work—and not especially wanting to—I convinced Congress to create a Survey of the Fortieth Parallel and to put me in charge of it. In eighteen seventy-three I was headed from Cheyenne, Wyoming, to Long's Peak in Colorado Territory to meet up with one of my partners, a certain Arnold Hague...Do you happen to know about Long's Peak, Mr. Sigerson?"

"No," said Holmes.

"It's one of those much-loved Colorado fourteeners...fourteen thousand and ninety-three feet, I seem to remember...named after Lieutenant Long of Zebulon Pike's expedition and it happens to be at the easternmost bend in the spine of the Rocky Mountains in all of North America. Which is all irrelevant to my story..."

James smiled. He'd almost forgotten how Clarence King had the born raconteur's ability to let his tales meander like a mountain stream without making his audiences impatient. James had often pondered why that gift rarely translated from verbal storytelling to the written page.

"Anyway, I'd only reached the valley of Estes Park by the time the sun had set that night when I was trying to get to Long's Peak, so I got the loan of one of the little shacks there in which I could spend the night.

"Well, the shack had a bed but no stove and the night was cold. I was shivering under every blanket I'd brought with me when I heard this sound from outside and I carry a lantern out and there's...Mr. Henry

Adams on muleback. I'm not sure which one looked more relieved to have found a human habitation...Adams or his mule.

"At any rate, Henry had just finished his first year as an assistant professor of history at Harvard and had recently become interested in geology after writing an article about the British geologist Charles Lyell for the *North American Review.* A friend had suggested to Adams that he come out west for the summer to see the work of our survey party, so he had. I guess Henry figured that there had to be some geology involved in so much surveying. Adams actually knew Arnold Hague from Boston and had been hanging around his camp on Long's Peak when Henry decided that he'd board a mule and do some fishing. Naturally he got lost, but Adams had the good sense to give the mule her head...if there's one sure way to find cooking and civilization, it's by giving a hungry mule its head. So he ended up at my little cabin in Estes Park at about ten o'clock at night."

Here Clarence King grinned and James could see that John and Clara Hay were smiling in anticipation of the finale of the explorer's little story.

"I'd actually briefly crossed paths with Henry before that night," continued King. "Once in Washington and again in Cheyenne the week before this. But I didn't think I knew him well enough for the giant bear hug he gave me when he got down off that mule and came into the light of that cabin. Henry had grown hungry and, I imagine, a mite anxious. Anyway, Estes Park is high up and it was a cold night for August, it can snow in August up there, so after sharing some cold beans, we crawled fully dressed into that bed—the only one the cabin had to offer naturally—and talked almost 'til dawn. We've been fast friends ever since."

"Adams will be so sorry he missed you," said John Hay.

"Yessirree, but I have to get to that silver mine in Mexico or head back to the high Sierras and find gold if I'm ever going to add a Constable to my Turners."

John Hay smiled at Holmes. "Harry knows this story, but it's worth repeating. Some years ago Clarence was in England buying art—amongst other things—and Ruskin had two wonderful Turners for sale. When he asked King which one he wanted, Clarence bought both, saying 'One good Turner deserves another.'"

King smiled wanly. "In those years I was buying twin Turners. These days I am forced by penury to come to my best friends' formal dinner party in a faded velvet-corduroy traveling suit."

"*Corde du roi,*" murmured Henry James. "The corded-cloth of a king. And such a beautiful wale."

"Those were Captain Ahab's last words before Moby Dick sank the *Pequod* out from under him," said King.

When Holmes raised one eyebrow in query, John Hay said, "It was a novel that came out more than four decades ago and wasn't really noticed by most readers and reviewers, but Clover had recommended it and all of us in the Five of Hearts loved it and referred to it frequently. It's about Ahab, a whaler sea captain who becomes obsessed with a white whale that took his leg years earlier."

"Ahab's policy toward his white whale has become my attitude toward life in general these days," said Clarence King.

"Which policy is that?" asked Henry James.

"'...to the last I grapple with thee; from hell's heart I stab at thee; for hate's sake I spit my last breath at thee'," recited King, leavening the ferocity of the statement with a boy's sweet smile.

Clara Hay, who had slipped out of the parlor a few minutes earlier, returned with her hands clasped together. Her smile was radiant. "Emissary Helmer Halvorsen Vollebæk, Mrs. Vollebæk, and their daughter have arrived. It's a bit crowded and warm in here, so I thought we might take our drinks into the conservatory. Cook assures me that dinner will be ready in less than an hour."

CHAPTER 17

Henry James had known an elderly duchess who may have been the cruelest person he'd ever met. When she returned for the London Season after months in Venice, her habit upon arriving at her townhome was to throw an initial dinner party that might have been designed by the Borgias. James had been invited to one of these autos-da-fé to fill out the complement of bachelors at the table (and perhaps, as part of his role, to serve as observer of the rites of cruel sacrifice to be explored that night) and, although he'd long since been forewarned of the duchess's venom, he had attended out of sheer curiosity. The turn of the social screw at the dinner party he had attended included inviting five couples who—although none of them rising to the duchess's social circle and not socially acquainted with one another—were comprised of four of the women having illicit affairs with no fewer than five of the men present. In addition were the brace of bachelors—Henry James foremost amongst them in both age and social ranking—and five unmarried young ladies, each of whom (the duchess well knew) were (or had been) involved in disastrous liaisons with some of the single or married men.

In no case was the spouse aware of the connections with others at the table.

That dinner had been fairly leaking with tensions, but Henry James found himself far more tense at this cozy dinner on Sunday, March 26, 1893, where the Hays—perhaps the least cruel couple James had ever known—were happily hosting their old friend Harry, Mr. Sigerson, Clarence King, and the Norwegian emissary and his wife and daughter.

The emissary, Mr. Helmer Halvorsen Vollebæk, was not the ambassador to the United States from the Kingdom of Scandinavia only because King Oskar II of Scandinavia preferred to have two emissaries in Washington at all times—one from Sweden and one from Norway, titularly united under Oskar II but still proud of separate origins—and currently the Swedish emissary was the official Scandinavian Ambassador. In two years, it would be Mr. Vollebæk's turn.

James judged Vollebæk's age at around 60, but his wife, Linnea, if James had heard correctly during introductions, must have been at least 20 years younger. Their daughter Oda, who was also present, was in her late adolescence and was reputed to be the most sought-after debutante on Embassy Row. They all spoke English flawlessly.

James was disappointed—or perhaps relieved, it was hard for him to record his emotions at the moment—when "Sigerson" was introduced to Mr. Vollebæk, and the two men clicked heels and bowed at the same moment, but exchanged greetings in English.

The early courses were passed in easy conversation. John and Clara Hay were experts at involving everyone at a table in conversation. The only element even approaching politics was the Vollebæks' united enthusiasm at the pageantry of Grover Cleveland's inauguration a few weeks earlier and their eagerness to look in on the Columbian Exposition—Chicago's World's Fair—in May before they returned to Norway for the summer. Miss Vollebæk appeared to have given her attention only to the many inaugural balls around the city that night and weekend of March 4.

"Oda is of the age now where every ball is an opportunity to meet eligible young men," said Mrs. Linnea Vollebæk in her soft Scandinavian accent.

"Mother!" cried Oda, blushing fiercely.

"Well, it is true, is it not?" laughed her father. Emissary Vollebæk dabbed at his lips with the napkin. "My baby girl will soon be finding herself a husband."

While Oda blushed more deeply, Clara Hay smiled and said, "Why, we have two of America's most eligible bachelors at this table, Your Excellency."

When Mr. Vollebæk raised an eyebrow in polite interrogation, Clara went on, "Mr. James and Mr. King have long been considered prize catches for the young lady who finally lands one or the other."

"Is this true, Mr. James? Mr. King?" asked Mrs. Vollebæk in a tone that actually sounded interested. "Are you both still eligible bachelors?"

Henry James hated this. He always hated it when he was teased about this at someone's table. He'd been irritated by it for decades, but at least he knew his response by heart.

Smiling softly and bowing his head ever so slightly as if he were being knighted by the Queen, James said, "Alas! I am on the cusp of turning fifty years old and at that age an old bachelor may no longer be called 'eligible', but, rather, 'confirmed'. It appears all but certain now that the only marriage I shall enjoy in this lifetime is to my art." When he saw a flicker of confusion in Mrs. Vollebæk's lovely eyes, he added, "To my writing, that is, since I am only a poor scribbler and currently a playwright."

"Mr. James, as I believe I mentioned to you, my darlings," said Mr. Vollebæk, "is one of the greatest of all living American writers."

James bowed his head again in response to the compliment, but smiled and said, "Based on sales of my work in recent years, my publisher—alas again, even my readership—might well disagree with you, sir. But I thank you for the generous words."

"And how about you, Mr. King?" teased Mrs. Linnea Vollebæk as she leaned forward over the table the better to see the geologist/explorer. The emissary's wife was still young enough to be attractive when she teased in a coquettish manner. "Are you wed to your profession?"

Clarence King raised his glass of wine to the lady. "Not in the least, ma'am. My problem is that I keep being introduced to the loveliest young ladies in New York, Boston, and Washington—including, of course, now to your truly beautiful daughter Oda . . ."

King raised the glass higher and then drank from it while poor Miss Vollebæk began blushing wildly again. "But, as our friend Harry puts it so well, alas!" continued King. "All of America's and England's . . . and

Norway's...finest beauties are so wonderfully *pale,* while some strange inclination in my make-up has made the dusky ladies of the South Seas the avatar and pinnacle of feminine beauty for me."

John Hay began to laugh at this and most people at the table joined him.

"Have you been to the South Seas, Mr. King?" asked Mrs. Vollebæk.

"Alas, no," said King with a mischievous smile. He was obviously enjoying tweaking at James for using the lady-poet's word. "But Henry Adams and John La Farge spent a couple of years traveling from island to island in the Pacific, sending me long letters describing the beauty of the dusky ladies there." He finished his wine. "Darn their mangy hides."

John Hay nodded to a servant, and everyone's wine glasses were refilled in an instant. "Clarence has been to Cuba and the Caribbean," said Hay.

"And to Mexico and Central America and points south of there, but...alas..." He bowed his head in a caricature of defeat.

"To Mr. King finding his dusky beauty," said little Oda as she raised her refilled glass, and after everyone laughed long and heartily at the young lady's pluck, they toasted King.

The primary courses were arriving. James found himself agitated with impatience and his appetite depressed as he waited for the inevitable unveiling of "Jan Sigerson" as a humbug. He also realized that he was motioning for his own wine glass to be refilled more than was his usual practice at dinner.

Suddenly the focus turned to Clarence King again, and the men—and even Clara Hay—were taking turns trying to explain the 1872 Great Diamond Hoax (and King's role as hero in it) to the female Vollebæks. Mr. Vollebæk required no tutorial since it turned out that his uncle had been in New York at the time and had been eager to be an investor in the "miraculous diamond mountain" somewhere in western Colorado. King's first role had been in finding the mesa-shaped mountain and proving that it was all a hoax; the diamonds, rubies, and other gems found there were real enough, at least $30,000 worth, but they were low grade and purchased in London by the men "seeding" them, just as others had blasted real gold into played-out gold mines in Cripple

Creek and elsewhere, to make millions from their $30,000 investment. Clarence King had saved Helmer Halvorsen Vollebæk's Uncle Halvard—and scores of American millionaires and eager would-be investors—from losing their trousers in the hoax.

"But had not Mr. Tiffany of New York certified that the diamonds and other gems found on the mountain were worth huge fortunes?" asked Mrs. Vollebæk.

"He did indeed," said King. "But it turned out—as I knew even while Mr. Tiffany was certifying them being worth millions—that the jeweler and his associates had no real experience with uncut diamonds."

"When you found the mountain, Mr. King," queried Miss Vollebæk in her delightfully accented tones, "what...how do Americans say it?...what 'tipped you off' that the stones had been planted there?"

King laughed so richly that others joined in for no reason. "My dear young lady," he said at last. "We arrived at the so-called Diamond Peak on an early November day so cold that our whiskey had frozen in its bottles. We got off our mules on a bare, iron-stained strand of coarse sandstone rock about a hundred feet long and we could not put our boot soles down without dislodging a diamond or other precious stone.

"At first we ran around like children at Christmas, seeking out gems and diamonds as fast as we could, but then my scientific training took over. I noticed that we never found the valuable stones at any place where the earth had not been disturbed. We were finding rubies in anthills, for instance, but only in anthills that had two holes—one where the ants came and went and another, smaller break in the crust on the opposite side. I immediately understood that someone had been pushing the rubies in with a stick.

"Diamonds, rubies, and other valuable gems are never found together in such profusion, Miss Vollebæk. And to prove this to the men in San Francisco and elsewhere who were so eager to buy shares in the fraudulent mining corporation the hoaxers had set up, my friends and I spent two days digging a trench three feet long and ten feet deep down in a gulch where—if this was truly a 'Diamond Peak'—hundreds of diamonds should have been found beneath the surface. Instead...nothing."

John Hay held his glass of wine in both hands. "And so young

Clarence King was awake three more days and nights hurrying back to San Francisco not only to prevent the investors from losing millions, but to stop speculators from scoring big by selling short on the stock." Hay lifted the glass. "To an honest man!"

"To an honest man!" said everyone save for Clarence King and lifted their glasses to him. King's blush was visible even through his deep tan.

"Now," said His Excellency Emissary Vollebæk when the main course had been served and a temporary hush had fallen over the table, "I would beg everyone's apology for my rudeness, but I would like to address my fellow countryman, Mr. Sigerson, in our native language for a moment or two."

"By all means!" cried Hay.

Henry James set his own glass down and found that his hand was shaking.

*   *   *

Mr. Vollebæk leaned across the table toward Sigerson/Holmes and unleashed a rapid-fire volley of rather melodious Norwegian. "Sigerson" looked as if he were about to speak but then said nothing. Vollebæk followed up with another paragraph.

Sherlock Holmes still remained silent.

James realized that his heart was pounding as if it wanted to escape his ribcage. In seconds it would be revealed that the man he had brought into the family circle of his dear friends the Hays was an imposter and it would be equally obvious that *James had known that "Sigerson" was an imposter.*

Or would it be so obvious? James looked at the suspended moment as if it were a scene in one of his novels or short stories. How should "his character" respond to the coming revelation—a hoax much more damaging to those at this table than King's long-ago Great Diamond Hoax? James could feign the shock and surprise and anger that the others here—especially John and Clara—would actually be feeling.

But then Holmes might very well reveal everything—James's complicity from the beginning—and James would have to choose between calling the uncloaked "Sigerson" a liar...pistols at dawn at 20 paces!...or simply apologizing profusely with whatever dignity might remain, announce that he would leave Washington that very evening, and leave the table after bowing in apology to everyone there.

James felt sick to his stomach. He was sure that Holmes would explain their ruse in terms of solving the "mystery" of Clover Adams's suicide and he knew that this would send another seismic tremor of shock through the Hays. (Which would be nothing to the level of shock and betrayal that Henry Adams would feel next week when he arrived home to hear this terrible story from his neighbors and intimate friends. Henry James had not forgotten that Clover's death was so traumatic to Adams that his historian friend had never once mentioned the day or details of her death in the more than seven years since the event.)

James felt actively dizzy as the nausea and excess of wine mixed to make the table and all the silent, waiting people around it seem to rise and fall before him. He set both his palms flat against the white linen, pressing down hard to try to stop the vertigo.

Then Holmes/Sigerson began to speak.

* * *

It *sounded* like Norwegian to James. And while Holmes started speaking slowly, the trickle of what-sounded-like-Norwegian soon turned into a torrent. When Holmes paused, Mr. Vollebæk asked a fast question in even-more-rapid Norwegian and "Sigerson" replied at the same rate—a long few paragraphs in a language that Henry James refused to believe that Sherlock Holmes had picked up in a quick study session or two.

James looked at the two Vollebæk women, but mother and daughter's faces showed interest, not astonishment or disbelief of any sort.

Emissary Vollebæk apparently posed another question. The Norwegian explorer—Sherlock Holmes—laughed and responded for half a moment in the quick, fluid language of Jan Sigerson's supposed homeland.

As a writer, Henry James often—more frequently than not if truth be told—felt somewhat detached from events and conversations occurring around him. Even as he worked at being a man on whom nothing was lost, the world often seemed more like a template for fiction than something that should be indulged in for its own sake. But this Sunday evening in March, James felt as if he had completely floated out of his body and were hovering over the table, a ghost watching the still-living chatting in an indecipherable language. Or perhaps like a spectator at a play—the way he felt while watching the touring acting groups in England rehearse or actually act the lines from his first effort, *The American*. Detached, critical, unconvinced, but strangely enchanted.

Except that now he felt convinced and horrified.

Emissary Helmer Halvorsen Vollebæk turned to the Hays, King, and James, and said, "Again I apologize for the rudeness of us speaking our native language and thank you for your patience and kind indulgence. But speaking to Mr. Sigerson has convinced me of something I only guessed at before hearing him speak . . . things are not completely as has been represented regarding Mr. Sigerson."

James felt his breath catch in his throat. So Holmes's attempt at Norwegian *had been* deficient. How could it not be? An Englishman can't fool a Norwegian into believing that he, the Englishman, is a native Scandinavian. James had simply been disoriented by Holmes's wholethroated attempt.

" . . . we had read and heard that Mr. Sigerson was a Norwegian explorer," continued Helmer Halvorsen Vollebæk in an apologetic tone. "But after speaking with him for only these few minutes, my family and I realize that Mr. Sigerson is almost certainly the preeminent explorer from our nation at the present time. The London and American papers spoke of Mr. Sigerson's . . . ah . . . penetration of certain mountain ranges in India, but we had no idea of how unique and spectacular his explorations into Tibet in the past two years truly were. Also, Mr. Sigerson is from Løiten, my own tiny hometown in Hedmark County—fewer than one hundred people live there—and Mr. Sigerson grew up knowing my cousin Knut who still lives there."

Holmes said something brief in Norwegian.

Mr. Vollebæk laughed. "Oh, yes, and my Aunt Oda after whom our daughter was named."

"Incredible coincidence," said John Hay.

"I always say, 'It's a small world'," said Clara Hay.

James felt that he might be having a heart attack. His chest felt so constricted that he had to *will* himself to breathe in and out.

"I asked Mr. Sigerson about his surname," continued Vollebæk, "since 'Sigerson' is not a common Norwegian name—or at least not a common spelling of it. As I expected and as Mr. Sigerson explained, his family name had been Sigurdson but his grandfather had married a German lady—they had lived a few years in England—and the spelling had been changed for convenience' sake during that time and never changed back."

Henry James's mind was churning. Obviously "Jan Sigerson"—or "Sigurdson"—was not the English consulting detective impersonating a Norwegian explorer; rather, Jan Sigerson/Sigurdson was a *real* Norwegian, a *real* explorer, who—for reasons probably not sane—was pretending to be the most likely fictional English personage known as Sherlock Holmes.

Then to whom was I introduced three years ago at Mrs. O'Connor's benefit party with Lady Wolseley?

The most logical guess—the *only* logical guess—was that it was Jan Sigerson playing out his fantasy of being the written-about detective.

But the Sherlock Holmes stories had not yet begun being published in The Strand *in 1889.*

True, thought James, but he was vaguely aware of Gosse or one of his Holmes-fanatical friends mentioning that the first Holmes novel or novella (he was not sure which)—*A Study in Scarlet*—had appeared as early as 1887, to be followed by—what was the title?—*The Sign of the Five? The Sign of the Four?*—something like that—in *Lippincott's Magazine* 1889. Gosse had said that the book version had come out the following year. Only after these initial forays into print did Sherlock Holmes begin to appear regularly in *The Strand Magazine*. A demented Jan Sigurdson/Sigerson would have heard much talk, both in England and on the Continent, about the London detective.

James later vaguely remembered something baked being brought for dessert, but whether he'd eaten a slice of cake or pie or baked Alaska, he later had no memory.

* * *

The men gathered in John Hay's impressive study. Clara Hay and the Vollebæk ladies had conferred and decided that they were not that interested in images of cold, high places. Hay, King, Sigerson, Emissary Vollebæk, and James were served their brandy in the study. Servants had already set up a screen and Sigerson's rented magic-lantern projector—all polished wood and brass—and had fueled and primed it. The men took their seats in various deep leather chairs or couches. James was so rattled that he drank off half his snifter of brandy without agitating it or inhaling the fumes in preparation.

The silent servants drew the blinds and let themselves out. Sigerson ignited the projector lamp and a rectangle of bright light illuminated the square screen that covered one wall of books.

"I only brought a few of my glass slides," said Jan Sigerson. "There are few crimes more heinous than boring one's audience."

"Bored by images of the Himalayan peaks and Tibet?!" cried Clarence King. "I hardly think so!"

"Clara will be sorry she missed this and may ask for an encore," said Hay.

"I will be most happy to provide it," said Sigerson with a short, quick, northern-European bow. "This first image is of our approach to the Himalayas in northern Sikkim." An image filled the screen.

"Dear God," cried King. "Are those tiny specks beyond the moraine there men and mules?"

"Men and mules and Tibetan ponies, yes," said Sigerson.

"It gives one perspective on how truly astounding the Himalayan Range is," said Mr. Vollebæk.

"They make the Alps and the American Rocky Mountains look like molehills," said King.

"Here is the Jelep La that we mentioned earlier," said Sigerson. "*La,* of course, means 'pass' in Tibetan." An image changed to a line of small ponies and heavily bundled men—no more than two dozen—crossing boulder-fields amidst near vertical snow slopes on either side. "It seemed formidable at the time but was no more than fourteen thousand feet at its summit."

The slide changed. The room was filled with the smell of the projector's limelight fuel.

"This is Tang La," said Sigerson. "The last real gateway before the Forbidden Kingdom of Tibet. Tang La, which means 'Clear Pass', was a bit more of a challenge since it is exposed to snow avalanches, even in the autumn when my small party attempted it, and its high point above fifteen thousand feet saw severe blizzards. You can see that both we and the ponies were liberally caked with ice."

These photographs were not taken by "Sigerson", thought James. *He's come into their possession somehow and passes them off as his own, but one always sees the Europeans and Tibetans from a distance. One can never make out the so-called Sigerson.*

The next photograph was a close-up of Sigerson in padded clothing—mustache and eyebrows caked with ice—sitting astride one of the ponies. Behind him, out of focus but solid, was the trail down the pass to a high valley rimmed with countless giant peaks.

"The Tibetan pony is a tough little creature," said Sigerson, "but with emphasis on 'little' as much as on 'tough'. As you can see, my boots constantly dragged on the ground. If the pony attempted to take me somewhere I did not want to go, I would simply stand up and let the pony run out from under me. At other times, if I did not want the pony to go somewhere it wanted to go, I would grab that uncomfortable-looking Tibetan wooden saddle and lift the pony off its hooves until we agreed on a direction."

The next photographic slide showed palm trees, tropical plants in giant pots, and Sigerson standing with a much younger blond man on a terrace of some sort. Women in saris stood in the background.

"Sven Hedin!" cried Mr. Helmer Halvorsen Vollebæk.

"Yes, I'm sorry," said Sigerson. "This slide is out of sequence. I asked an acquaintance to take this photo in Bombay when I stopped there to see Sven Anders Hedin."

"May we inquire who Mr. Sven Anders Hedin is?" asked Clarence King, rising to pour himself more brandy from a decanter on a side table.

"Oh, Mr. Hedin is one of Norway's most promising young explorers and alpinists," replied Mr. Vollebæk. "He is only twenty-eight yet already he has shown glimpses of his great accomplishments to come."

"In Bombay, Sven told me that he decided to become an explorer when he was fifteen years old," said Sigerson, stepping back from the heat rising from the projector's chimney. "He witnessed the triumphant return of our nation's great Arctic explorer Adolf Erik Nordenskiöld and then and there decided his future profession."

"I am surprised that young Hedin did not cross the passes into Nepal with you, Mr. Sigerson," said Clarence King.

Sigerson nodded. "Hedin was seriously ill with recurring malaria when I visited him in Bombay," he said softly. "But this autumn he should be embarked upon his first great quest—a multi-year exploration of Central Asia."

The large glass slide rasped in its mechanism, and the image on the screen changed. Most of the men in the room gasped.

"The Potala...the temple-residence of the Dalai Lama in Lhasa in the heart of Tibet," said Sigerson.

Henry James, who had also gasped at the photo, tried to take in the impossible *scale* of the palace. Were those saffron-colored specks at the bottom of the golden staircase actually human beings?

As if reading his thoughts, Sigerson said, "Yes, the scale of the Potala is hard to fathom...especially since the rest of Lhasa is so pathetic: sagging mud-and-timber homes, endless narrow alleyways filled with dog carcasses and unspeakable refuse. But rising above all that...*this.* To give you a sense of its scale, all of Britain's Parliament would fit along the lower third of the Potala, with Big Ben rising only to the high point of the staircase. The temples and lamas' residences are all higher than that in the structure."

"I don't see how you did it, Mr. Sigerson," Clarence King said flatly. "I just don't understand how you did it."

"Did what, Mr. King?"

"Got into Tibet...all the way to Lhasa. Scores of Europeans have tried it. None have succeeded. Surely you couldn't have disguised yourself as a Tibetan pilgrim as so many of our explorers have...down to shaving one's head and wearing saffron rags. The Tibetan authorities always find them out. And you're *far* too tall to pass yourself off as a Tibetan."

Sigerson smiled. "I did not disguise myself in any way. I simply told the sheriffs, warlords, soldiers, and palace police whom I met that I was a pilgrim."

"And did your fellow travelers over the high passes also get to Lhasa?" asked John Hay.

"No. They were all turned back near the border."

"I don't understand," King said a final time.

"We Norwegians are a persistent race," offered emissary Mr. Vollebæk.

The last slide filled the screen. It was taken from a distance but showed Sigerson sitting on a low boulder in a courtyard talking to a young boy in a saffron robe. The brown-skinned lad's head was shaved save for a single topknot, and his back was to the camera.

"The thirteenth Dalai Lama," said Sigerson. "He was sixteen years old when I was allowed multiple audiences with him in the winter of eighteen ninety-one, 'ninety-two. The audiences were a double honor since His Holiness was in seclusion away from the Potala, receiving intense and rigorous instruction for the role he was soon to assume."

"I've read that most of the young Dalai Lamas don't live long enough to assume temporal power," said John Hay.

"This is true," said Sigerson. "The ninth through twelfth Dalai Lamas all died young, many presumed to have been murdered by their acting regents, all of whom have a tendency to cling to power. This young man's predecessor, the twelfth Dalai Lama, died after his regent arranged for his bedroom ceiling to collapse on him while he slept."

"Mother of God," whispered King.

"One of the few religious concepts that Tibetan Buddhists do not recognize in some form," Sigerson said without any obvious irony.

"May we ask what you discussed with the thirteenth Dalai Lama?" Hay asked diffidently.

"The nature of reality," said Jan Sigerson/Sigurdson.

* * *

The Vollebæk family was the first to depart. Handshakes and announcements that it had been a wonderful evening filled the huge mahogany-walled foyer.

When Clarence King asked a servant to fetch his cape, hat, and walking stick, Sigerson surprised James—and the others it seemed—by saying, "Could I please speak to you gentlemen in Mr. Hay's study for one minute?"

The study was still overheated and smelling of limelight, although servants had already removed the screen and bulky projector.

"I have to go soon," grumped King. "I have to travel to New York tomorrow before heading to Mexico and..."

"This will take only a second, gentlemen," said Sigerson, presuming the liberty of closing the door of Hay's study behind him.

"I need to talk to all of you tomorrow at ten a.m.," said Sigerson in a voice that James had not heard from him yet. If it was not a tone of absolute command, it was very close to it. "Mr. Hay, may I presume upon your good graces a final time to allow the meeting here in your study?"

"I...well...on Monday I must...well, yes. If it's a brief meeting."

"It will be brief," said Sigerson.

"Not possible," said Clarence King. "I have the noon train to New York to meet and several..."

"Mr. King," Sigerson said softly, "I would not ask you to come back unless it were of extreme importance. One might say it is a matter of life and death. And it involves your friend Mr. Henry Adams."

Hay and King looked at each other, and James could almost imagine the near-telepathy at work between the old friends.

"Damn it, man," barked King, "don't make a mystery out of it if it's something that involves Adams. Tell us now why you have us gathered here."

"I'm sorry but it must be tomorrow morning here at ten o'clock," said Sigerson. "I understand that Mrs. Hay will be out of the house for most of the day so we will not be disturbed. Do I have your solemn promises that you will be here?"

"I also have plans to..." began Henry James and then stopped when he saw the hawk-like intensity of Sigerson's glance at him. The Norwegian was quite obviously mad as a hatter and it seemed safer for James to play along with the others present than to become the sole object of the madman's attention.

John Hay, Henry James, and Clarence King promised to be there. King did not sound happy.

"Thank you," said Jan Sigerson and opened the door to the study as if releasing them all from his control, but only for the time being.

CHAPTER 18

They assembled in Hay's study promptly at 10 a.m. and took the same seats they'd occupied the night before: John Hay behind his broad desk; Clarence King and Henry James in leather wingback chairs set on both sides of the desk and still turned toward the wall of books where the screen had been. King was grumbling. Hay looked embarrassed that this was happening in his home. The internationally renowned wordsmith Henry James kept his mouth shut.

At ten minutes after ten, King said, "What the hell? That impertinent Norwegian orders us...*orders* us...to be at his beck and call at ten a.m. and then *he* doesn't show up? I've boxed men's ears for less."

"Benson told me that Sigerson left the house very early this morning. Very early," said Hay. "And Benson said that he was carrying his portmanteau."

"Have you counted the silver?" said King.

James concentrated on not speaking. He'd gone to Sigerson's room at eight that morning only to find the room empty. His first impulse had been also to pack and flee, but then he realized that the imposter's absence might give him a way to make things right with John and Clara—perhaps even with King if the Norwegian lunatic did not reappear.

At quarter after ten, all three men stood.

"I see no need..." began Hay.

"If he thinks..." began King.

James was straightening his waistcoat and trying to get his thoughts in proper alignment.

A stranger stepped into the room and closed the door behind him.

It took even Henry James, who'd met the man in this form only a few years before, to see that it was Sherlock Holmes. The Sigerson make-up had disguised the Englishman more than James had given it credit for. Holmes was now in a proper British suit. His hair was now brown, not black, and receding much more dramatically than had Sigerson's spiky top. With the mustache and make-up around the nose and eyes removed, this version of Sigerson/Holmes looked even leaner, a face that seemed all sharp cheekbones, deep shadows, hawk nose, strong chin, and those piercing eyes.

"Be seated, gentlemen," said Holmes. His upper-class British accent had returned. "And thank you for coming."

"Who..." began John Hay.

"Who do you..." said Clarence King.

Holmes closed the door behind him and motioned with palms out for them to sit. "Everyone here but Mr. James—who has some hint of the truth—knew me the last few days as Jan Sigerson. My true name is Sherlock Holmes. I am a consulting detective. Until two years ago, I lived in London. I went to Nepal in eighteen ninety-one and have now come to Washington in service of Her Majesty's Government and in the vital interest of the government of the United States of America."

There was babble and outrage. Clarence King shouted until servants came knocking at the door inquiring as to whether everything was all right. Hay sent them away. Only James had remained seated. For a few moments he felt anaesthetized, totally immobilized, and during those moments he was convinced that either he had died in Paris, in the Seine, that Sunday night, or the deep melancholy that had driven him to France and the Seine two weeks earlier had driven him quite mad. Madness was the only *logical* explanation for what he was experiencing now.

But is it my *madness or this Sigerson/Holmes's?*

Holmes waited until the outcry died down and at least John Hay sat back in his chair. Clarence King still stood and paced, his hands clenched into fists, his usually amiable expression now frozen into a frightening scowl.

"In the spring of eighteen ninety-one, Edward Hooper—you all knew him as 'Ned'—hired me to look into the circumstances of his sister's death in eighteen eighty-five and the fact that every year on the anniversary of her death, he—and each of you—has received one of *these*." Holmes removed from his tweed jacket not one but six of the She-was-murdered typed cards and handed the short stack to John Hay, whose expression of surprise almost instantly changed to one of shock.

"Ned is dead," snapped Clarence King. "A suicide like his sister seven years before him."

"I know that Ned Hooper is dead," said Holmes. "I do not yet know—none of us here know—if either his death or his sister Clover's was so simple as suicide."

"Everyone...everyone...agreed that Clover's death was suicide," snapped King, taking an aggressive step toward Holmes, who watched the shorter but stouter man with what seemed to be complete calm. Holmes removed his black clay pipe and with a "May I?" to Hay, who nodded distractedly, fussed with lighting it. At least, based on the scent when it was lit, the tobacco was not that cheapest of shags he'd used near James a few times on the ship and train.

"Clover took potassium cyanide when she was alone in her house," continued King, who waved away the stack of cards when Hay tried to pass them to him. "Ned Hooper tried twice to kill himself—once by throwing himself in front of a trolley—and finally threw himself from a high window of the sanitorium...some called it an asylum...to which he'd been referred."

"But no one we know of saw either Mrs. Adams's death by potassium cyanide or her brother Ned's actual throwing himself from the window," said Holmes between slow puffs that seemed to be further antagonizing King.

"You don't need to *see* the snow falling to know it's snowed if you go to sleep outside in the mountains on dry grass and wake up under a coating of new snow," growled King.

"Very good," said Holmes. "I applaud the use of inductive logic.

However, in this case, we have a brother and sister dead supposedly by their own hand, but in neither case need it be suicide. Mrs. Clover Adams became quite good friends with a Miss Rebecca Lorne in the year before she died. Is this not true?"

"What?" snapped King.

"She did," said John Hay. "I met Miss Lorne on several occasions. A pleasant lady."

"And this was the lady who was waiting outside Mr. Adams's former home when he came home to find his wife dead upstairs, is this not correct?" said Holmes. He relit the pipe.

"So what?" said Hay, sounding angry himself now. "Miss Lorne visited Clover almost every day in those last months. She was waiting outside when Adams was about to go to his appointment that morning. Or perhaps when he came back for something, I forget which. At any rate, Miss Lorne did not find the body... poor Henry did."

"And Miss Lorne moved away from Washington a month or so after Clover Adams's death?" Holmes's voice was soft but persistent.

"Yes... to Baltimore," said Hay. "Where she married a Mr. Bell some months later... by the summer of eighteen eighty-six, I believe. Henry still corresponded with her in the years after Clover's death. Perhaps he still does from time to time."

"I doubt it very much," said Holmes. "I believe the woman you knew as Miss Rebecca Lorne was murdered shortly after she left Washington. Perhaps before."

"You're mad," said Clarence King.

"Wait a minute," said Hay. "Let's discuss this... performance of the past few days and last night in which you claimed to be an explorer named Jan Sigerson. What on earth was that about?"

"A necessary ruse," said Holmes. There was a third leather chair empty, one facing Hay's desk, and he sat in it. "Those who have been hunting me knew that I would come to honor Ned Hooper's request."

"Those who have been *hunting* you..." said Hay.

"Damned slow about getting here," said King. "You say Hooper—you have no right to call him 'Ned', whoever you are—asked you to come help him with this cards-thing in the spring of 'ninety-one, yet here you are showing up in the spring of 'ninety-three, months after Ned killed himself. Good thing you're not a fireman or policeman."

"I am a policeman in a manner of speaking," Holmes said quietly. He had sprawled into the deep chair with one leg thrown carelessly over the other.

Henry James finally found his voice. He deliberately spoke to Hay and King, not to the man sitting opposite him. "Last night we received, from Mr. Vollebæk and his family, near-conclusive proof that this man, in make-up or not, is the Norwegian explorer Jan Sigerson. We heard the Norwegian language spoken fluently between them. We heard His Excellency Mr. Vollebæk speak of Norwegian friends he and Sigerson had in common. We then saw the slides of Sigerson's expedition into Tibet, including the photograph from Bombay of Sigerson with the younger explorer Sven Anders Hedin—known to all three of the Vollebæks. It seems to me that the only sane conclusion we can draw here is that this man has long been pretending to be the English detective Sherlock Holmes. Perhaps the high-altitude in the Himalayas affected his mind . . ."

Holmes removed the pipe from his mouth and chuckled. "My dear James, do you accept the legerdemain of a theatrical magician with as much eager credulity as you did my bona fides for being Jan Sigerson?"

James felt himself flushing with anger and embarrassment but he forced his voice to remain calm, reasonable, and civilized. "There was no reason for Mr. Vollebæk and his wife and daughter to perjure themselves with . . ."

"There was one excellent good reason, my dear James," said Holmes, standing again and prodding the air with the stem of his pipe. "As soon as I learned that I'd be dining with the Vollebæks on Sunday, the twenty-sixth, I cabled King Oskar the Second of Scandinavia and asked him to have his Norwegian emissary support my story and disguise. You see, I still have use for explorer Sigerson. Mr. Vollebæk is giving interviews to reporters from the *Washington Post* and a writer from the *Washington Critic* even as we speak, telling all about his delightful evening with his fellow countryman Sigerson at the home of Mr. John Hay . . ."

"So you get the King of Scandinavia to do your bidding with a cable?" said Clarence King, who'd decided to sit down in the chair Holmes had just vacated. "Including having one of the most respected diplomats in Washington and his wife and daughter lie to two people so respected as John Hay and Henry James? And you expect us to *believe* that?"

"Believe what you will," Holmes said carelessly. He'd crossed to a window and opened the slats of the louvered wooden shutters and was peering out onto the street.

"The dialogue in Norwegian..." said Henry James.

"Was far from fluent on my part," said Holmes, half turning from the window so that his rather distinctive silhouette was visible against the light. "My greatest fear was that the daughter, young Oda—despite being coached by her father to go along with the fiction that I was Norwegian—would blurt out a criticism of my pathetic Norwegian, most of which I picked up while spending time with His Majesty King Oskar the Second in London for two months in eighteen eighty-eight, and again for nine weeks in the winter-spring of eighteen ninety-one, shortly before my 'death' at Reichenbach Falls."

"You must have handled a *very* delicate domestic problem," King said sarcastically, "to put European royalty so deeply into your debt."

"I did, actually," said Holmes. "But that is not the reason that His Majesty the King of Scandinavia ordered his emissary to lie during a social occasion. Rather, King Oskar the Second well knows the reasons both for my mission to Tibet and my mission here in Washington. He knows the enemies we face...and they are his enemies as well, gentlemen. Should these people have their way, His Majesty is on a long and distinguished list of targets who will be murdered in the next few months or years."

Clarence King sighed and steepled his fingers. "'These people...' Now we have the conspiracy talk and the paranoia. Are there no traits of madness you will not trot out for our distraction, Mr....Whoever You Are?"

Holmes laughed almost boyishly at King's comment. Without answering, he fished in his inside jacket pocket and removed what looked to be four photographs. Setting two of them back in his pocket, he handed the first of the two remaining photos to King. "Would you hand that around to Mr. Hay and Mr. James? Thank you."

James waited. When the photograph finally came his way he saw that it was almost certainly blown up in size since the subject was in two-thirds profile against a grainy and blurry background of a crowded street. The photo was of a dark-complexioned man with black hair brushed straight back, a carefully trimmed mustache that looked rather military in origin, and fiercely angled eyebrows. The man looked to be in his late forties or early fifties, but only a tendency toward jowls betrayed his age.

"That is Colonel Sebastian Moran, a veteran of the Indian Army and formerly of the First Bangalore Pioneers. He was mentioned in various dispatches during the different Afghan wars, received a medal for killing nine Afghans in a hand-to-hand fight in Kabul, and was considered by many to be the finest hunter and rifle marksman in Asia...perhaps in the world. His full name is John Sebastian 'Tiger Jack' Moran, although very few people know that."

"Colonel Sebastian Moran..." muttered Clarence King when James handed the photograph back to him. "By God, I read his books! *Heavy Game of the Western Himalayas* and *Three Months in the Jungle.* Hunting memoirs...and cracking good tales!"

Holmes, now standing with his back to the window, nodded. "He published both of those in the early eighteen eighties. He gave his publisher his birth date as being eighteen forty, but in truth it was eighteen thirty-four. Colonel Moran will be sixty years old next February."

"He certainly does not look that old in the photograph," said John Hay. "When was the photo taken?"

"A year and a half ago. In Calcutta," said Holmes. "You see, Colonel Moran followed me to India from Switzerland in order to assassinate me. He was paid quite a large amount of money for my assassination...assassination is the Colonel's major source of income, just ahead of guiding fat, rich gentlemen-hunters to where they can kill dangerous animals and far ahead of his less taxing profession of separating fat, rich gentlemen from their money at various card tables."

"Hired to kill you..." sighed King. "And now comes the paranoia."

"Oh, yes," said Holmes. "Colonel Moran tried twice...once in Calcutta, again in Darjeeling...but was unsuccessful in both attempts. Then, having spent almost all of the money paid to him for the botched job and not wanting to wait for me to re-emerge from Tibet, the good colonel returned to London. For one of the world's greatest hunters, Moran has surprisingly little patience."

"I fail to see what any of this has anything to do with..." began John Hay.

"Imagine my surprise then, when I came back to Sikkim from Tibet over the high passes, to be shot three times by a high-velocity rifle fired from almost a mile from my position."

The room fell thickly silent. James could hear a servant's shoes against carpet on the main staircase and a carriage passing outside.

"Shot three times by a high-velocity rifle," said Clarence King at last. "Then you are...must be...quite dead. So we have been dealing not only with a liar and imposter but with a ghost." King checked his watch. "And my time here is almost up. I must..." He looked up, saw what Holmes was doing, and fell silent—aghast.

Holmes had removed his jacket and waistcoat and collar and cravat and was in the process of unbuttoning his shirt.

John Hay stood. "My dear sir..."

"This will take only a few seconds," said Holmes. He was wearing no undershirt. He folded his shirt carefully across the back of the closest chair, turned sideways to the window, and opened the louvered shutters.

For the second time—and even more clearly now—Henry James saw the two terrible round wounds on Holmes's upper right back near the shoulder blade—"entrance wounds" he believed they were called when caused by bullets—and the livid spiderweb tracery of scars radiating from them. There was a third pattern of white scars just above the man's right hip.

Holmes turned around so that the light fell on his chest and belly and right side.

There was another cratered round scar—the "exit wound" James had heard it called—on Holmes's upper right chest and below and to the left of it a few inches, a more complicated and ghastly scar, not circular, with even more scars radiating from it. Just above his right hip was the pattern of exit scars of the third wound.

Holmes's long, white fingers touched each of the wounds starting with the highest just under his collarbone. "As I said, the assassin fired from almost a mile away and struck me three times, ratcheting the bolt-action of his powerful rifle and firing three times in less than two seconds. This third wound . . ." He touched the latticework of scars above his hip. "Struck me as I was falling." He moved his fingers, which were as steady as a surgeon's, back up to the terrible white web of scarring of the second wound. "The second round did not pass through me and my savior—and surgeon in this instance—had to dig it out. She started from the back and then realized that it was closer to the surface in the front, under my chest muscles. It was a long process and she had no anaesthetic."

"*She?*" Clarence King said in a strangely dulled voice.

"My savior and surgeon?" said Holmes, calmly putting his shirt back on. "She is an English missionary named Annie Royle Taylor who had just made an attempt to travel to Lhasa—*her* Saviour had spoken to her in a dream and said that her destiny was to carry Christ's word to Lhasa, the Dalai Lama, and to all of the Forbidden Kingdom. So Miss Annie Taylor had shaved her head and dressed herself in Tibetan males' clothing, but she was discovered far from Lhasa, turned back, and escorted back to the border by Tibetan guards. My own Tibetan helpers, assigned to me by His Holiness the Dalai Lama to escort me over the newly opened passes, had just bidden me farewell on the south side of the final pass and were heading their ponies homeward north again when they heard the three shots and were kind enough to return to where they'd last seen me. I was unconscious and bleeding badly. My Tibetan friends brought me to the nearby border trading post of Yatung. There was no doctor there, but the Tibetans and Sikkimese had grudgingly allowed Miss Taylor to take up residence nearby as she waited for her next covert attempt to enter Tibet. Perhaps the locals allowed her to stay there because her first name, 'Annie', sounds very much like the Tibetan word for 'nun'—and so this missionary, who'd studied medicine and had occasion to practice it in the slums of London and again in China—staunched the bleeding, dug the second bullet out of me, and arranged blood transfusions that saved my life."

"Incredible," whispered John Hay.

"Yes, isn't it," agreed Holmes.

"How do we know that those supposed scars aren't just more make-up?" demanded Clarence King.

Holmes had buttoned up his waistcoat and was in the act of sliding on his jacket when he paused. "Would you like to set your fingers into the wounds?" he asked softly. "You can, especially in the surgical incisions. Almost up to the knuckle of your index finger. Here, I shall remove my shirt again..."

"No!" cried King, waving for Holmes to stop the unbuttoning.

"So you are saying that Colonel Sebastian Moran did wait through the winter and tried to assassinate you as you came down out of Tibet in the spring of eighteen ninety-two," said Hay.

"Not at all," said Holmes, shooting his cuffs. "This man is the one who shot me three times from so far away. He's perhaps the only marksman in the world who could have pulled off that shot and he's long since displaced Colonel Sebastian Moran as the world's deadliest assassin." He'd set the second photograph in his outside jacket pocket, but now he handed it to be circulated in their small circle.

When it came to James, he was surprised to see a blurred photo of a much younger man than Moran—very short hair in a widow's peak, sharp cheekbones, ears close set to his head, eyes that appeared all black in the image.

"You're looking at the only known photograph—taken on a busy Indian street by a British Secret Service agent in New Delhi who was murdered the day after he sent that photograph to his superiors in Whitehall—of Colonel Sebastian Moran's son. It's a poor image, but the only photograph police and intelligence services have of this young man. He was illegitimate of course—Colonel Moran left a brace of bastards in his wake across India, Africa, Europe, and England—but this child was sired to a young adventuress in Warsaw. Surprisingly, Moran took the boy from his mother at a young age and raised him himself, dragging the boy around the world with him and using the lad as a sort of gun-carrier and general assistant in his Asian and other long hunting expeditions and...I am sure...on more private missions of paid assassination. The boy learned quickly. His first name is Lucan. He has in recent years, as

I said, replaced his father as the most accomplished assassin the modern world has had the misfortune to know, but, totally unlike his father, he *never* kills for money. Lucan kills for his fanatical political beliefs. In this case his goal and god is...Anarchy.

"In that sense, never assassinating his enemies for pay, he is as much unlike his father, Colonel Moran, as any man on earth could be. But they both ended up serving the same master in Sikkim along the border of Tibet...the international group of anarchists who first paid Colonel Moran to follow me to India in eighteen ninety-one and then dispatched Lucan early the following year after his father had failed."

"Anarchists," muttered Clarence King. "Now comes the conspiracy."

"A very real conspiracy, I'm afraid," said Holmes. "I was also skeptical about the international threat of anarchists when I came to America in September of eighteen eighty-one to investigate your President Garfield's assassination—and, indeed, there was no direct conspiracy involved there. But I later became certain that Colonel Moran had been the assassin in the pay of the anarchist terrorists at Chicago's so-called Haymarket Square riots in eighteen eighty-six. The rifle shots that killed three of the four dead civilians and four of the seven dead policemen were fired, I proved to the American police and authorities beyond any doubt, from a rooftop half a block from the square. Colonel Moran and one henchman, not Lucan, used the same modern Lebel rifles that the colonel left behind in his attempt to assassinate Her Majesty in London the following year."

"I've never read any of this anywhere," said Hay.

"And you shan't," said Holmes. "At least until the Anarchist threat against England, Europe, and the United States is dealt with."

"It seems a rather haphazard and random threat, Mr. Holmes," said Hay.

James thought, *Does John now believe that this is Sherlock Holmes with whom we're dealing?*

"Not haphazard or random at all, in their scheming," said Holmes. "They have a list of presidents and royalty whom they plan to assassinate. In eighteen eighty-seven, as I said, they hired Moran to assassinate Her Majesty, Queen Victoria, at her own Golden Jubilee. Moran came far too close to succeeding. He did leave his new Lebel rifles—the first to use smokeless ammunition—behind in London, and using certain techniques I've refined over the years, I was able to ascertain that it was one of the same rifles used at Haymarket Square.

"The anarchists' list remains. They currently plan to have your President Cleveland assassinated on May first, Opening Day of the World's Columbian Exposition in Chicago. I need to stay here in America long enough to stop that."

"Moran...senior or junior?" asked King.

"What?" said Holmes.

"You said that Moran had tried to kill Queen Victoria six years ago," said King. "Colonel Moran, senior, or young Lucan Moran?"

"Oh, the only 'Moran' we're dealing with is Colonel Moran...the father," said Holmes. "He never gave his son Lucan his name."

"May I see that second photograph again?" asked John Hay.

Holmes, who'd received it from King after it had gone around the circle of three men, carried it over and set it on the leather desktop in front of Hay.

"I know this man," whispered Hay. "He was Rebecca Lorne's...Clover Adams's good friend Rebecca Lorne's...young cousin, Clifton Richards. Also a photographer. Clover enjoyed talking to the young man about their shared art."

"He bought her the new developing chemicals she used," said Holmes, not asking a question. "Including the potassium cyanide solution."

"Yes...yes...I believe you are correct," said Hay in a pinched voice.

"I am," said Holmes. He removed a third image from his jacket pocket and set it on the desk in front of Hay. James and King both stood and moved to Hay's side to peer down at the photo.

It was obviously a professionally taken photograph, the kind done up for celebrities, and the woman was as beautifully dressed and attractive as any celebrity in any photograph James had ever seen—her dark hair raised in an artful sculpture, her large, dark eyes dancing with subtle lighting, her full lips at the level of her beautiful hands that were raised to grasp the handle of the parasol that shaded her.

"Why, that's Rebecca Lorne, Clover's good friend during the last year of her life," said Hay. "She's younger here than when I knew her in the months before Clover's death, but I'm certain it's the same woman. Very attractive."

"Yes," said King. "I also met her then...this Rebecca. I remember that Clover first saw her from her window at the Adamses' former house, the house where Clover died, the Little White House at sixteen-oh-seven H Street just down the block. Clover saw her walking alone in Lafayette Square daily for some weeks before she finally went down to introduce herself. After that they were fast friends, even during Clover's long period of melancholy."

"And, strangely," said Sherlock Holmes, "Mrs. Adams's melancholy only grew worse despite the best efforts of her new friend Miss Lorne—and her young cousin Clifton—to cheer her up."

Henry James had never seen this woman before, but then, he'd only heard about the delightful Rebecca Lorne in letters.

"I remember Adams saying that Clover had photographed her friend Rebecca several times," said Hay, touching the borders of the lovely woman's photograph.

"Ned Hooper told me that two years ago," Holmes said very quietly.

"And she photographed Clif...Rebecca's cousin...as well," said Clarence King. "I saw work prints of photographs Clover had taken of the young man when they were all on a picnic in Rock Creek Park. She said that he should have been a good photographic subject but she mustn't have clicked the shutter probably because his head was almost always blurred in movement despite her admonitions for her subjects to be still."

"Almost certainly a deliberate movement to blur his own features," murmured Holmes.

"But I believe that one or two images of the cousin came out," said King. "They just were not up to Clover's high standards."

"And Adams still has those photographs?" asked Holmes. "Of the cousin as well as Miss Lorne?"

"I'm sure he does," said John Hay. "All labeled now and set away in archives."

"But he'll never let you see them," said Clarence King. "Adams can't speak about Clover, much less about her death, and he would never show her photographs to anyone. Not even the ones she'd shared in public of her father or of Henry or of Richardson, their architect."

"That's why I need to get into Adams's house next door—with the servants out of the way—before Mr. Adams returns home in the coming week," said Holmes. "If Clover Adams achieved a clear photograph of Rebecca Lorne's nice young cousin Clifton, it will be only the second photograph the Secret Service or police services around the world will have of the anarchists' chief assassin. Colonel Moran's bastard son and brilliant protégé, Lucan."

"If Clifton was this...Lucan," said Hay, his perfectly manicured fingers still surrounding the photograph on his desktop, "then who was Rebecca Lorne?"

"Lucan's mother, whom he murdered shortly after I believe they worked together to arrange the death of Clover Adams," said Holmes.

He took the photograph from Hay and carefully set it away in his jacket. "This is an earlier photograph—I've had it for years, gentlemen—of Lucan's mother, the late American-born opera diva and actress and successful blackmailer named Irene Adler."

CHAPTER 19

Holmes was following his man on the afternoon train from Washington to New York City.

The detective this afternoon was the perfect image of a poorly paid, mid-level bureaucrat or office worker: his dark suit was presentable, but only just; his shoes were shined but down at the heel; his homburg was brushed, but showing its age; his battered old briefcase was over-stuffed with folders, papers, and pens. This particular bureaucrat was red-headed, with a mop of unruly curls escaping from the homburg on every side and red cheek-whiskers—what the Americans had called "sideburns" ever since a Civil War general named Burnside had made them popular—coming almost to the corner of his mouth. Prominent, yellowed, and somewhat carious teeth gave the clerk a rabbity look (and Holmes knew that people tended to look away, or at least not look carefully, at faces where prominent and poorly cared for teeth were on display). His cheeks were red not with a flush but with what seemed to be a permanent—and unhealthy looking—reddish-pink rash.

Another reason not to stare too closely.

This bureaucrat or clerk was reading the mid-day Washington paper and every time Holmes's prey looked back from where he was sitting near the front of this railway carriage, all the man would have seen was the raised paper.

Holmes really did not want to spend this afternoon of March 27—the same Monday on which he'd spent part of the morning revealing his identity to John Hay and Clarence King—tailing this man to New York, but he realized that it might be now or never. There was a complex spiderweb woven around the death of Clover Adams, and Holmes knew that before he could penetrate it, he would have to follow several of the strands—at least those of Clover's closest friends near the time of her death—to wherever they might lead.

This one might well lead nowhere and Holmes would rather have been spending his afternoon organizing the years of typewritten envelopes and correspondences that Hay had promised him. He also had to break into Henry Adams's mansion next door to the Hays. This would have to wait until after dark tomorrow night, Tuesday. Clara Hay had told him that Adams's servants, who'd been permitted a few days of holiday this extended weekend during Mr. Adams's extended absence, would be returning on Wednesday afternoon, the 29th of April, to begin the process of opening up and airing out the house in preparation for their master's return on Friday, the first day of May.

So it was now or possibly never concerning following his man, and Holmes peered over the top of his raised newspaper and watched the broad back and head of short-cropped blond hair. It was quite possible that his quarry might bolt out of the carriage at one of the many stops on this line to New York and Holmes must be prepared to follow him at a second's notice. And to do so while looking casual about it.

After almost two full years away, Holmes missed London. He missed his rooms at 221 B Baker Street and he missed Mrs. Hudson—and even Watson—but mostly he missed the city. At one point, to prepare for his future profession as Consulting Detective, Holmes had spent a year driving a London hansom cab. He rather flattered himself that he knew every street, boulevard, thoroughfare, and alley in the City. More than that, Holmes had set his goal to memorize every business and manufactory and warehouse and noble townhouse in the City—a Herculean task, made even more impossible by the fact that, since the 1870's, Old London was being torn down, torn up, and rebuilt in a crazed hurry like no other city on earth. Business establishments that may have stayed at the same address for a century and a half were suddenly out of business or moved to much lesser surroundings because of the hurtling cost of rent as the "trendier" neighborhoods in the city were fruitful and multiplied.

Most importantly, Holmes knew the trains and times in general in England and specifically in London. He and Watson had each worn out their respective *Bradshaw's*. Mycroft Holmes—to the detective's chagrin, since his portly brother never really went anywhere—had memorized the national *Bradshaw's Guide* and could give any timetable for any railway at any time of the day or night for any connections.

Sherlock Holmes felt that Mycroft's little trick rather amounted to showing off.

But at least in England, Holmes always had his yellow-covered *Bradshaw's* in his pocket or portmanteau. Here in America, he'd found nothing comparable to the great *Bradshaw's Guide*...only untrustworthy timetables for this specific railway company or that one. He could only hope that this train actually *was* going to New York City.

While they rumbled north, Holmes thought about Henry Adams, the late Clover Adams, Clarence King, John Hay, and Clara Hay. They all held secrets relevant to Holmes's investigation, even Clover Adams. The dead, Holmes knew, hug their secrets tightly in the grave, but not as tightly as the living.

He was aware that Henry James had known Clover Adams a long time, even before she had married Henry Adams. And Holmes had met few men in his life and career who hugged their secrets closer than did Henry James. But he already knew the secret-of-secrets that James would die to protect.

They hadn't discussed it, of course, but both Sherlock Holmes the detective and Henry James the writer were celibate. Holmes had given up any plans for a romantic or a sexual life so that he could devote one hundred percent of his time and vital energies to his career. If pressed, James would—Holmes knew—claim the same; and he'd already written that now, as an "old bachelor", he should never marry because he was already married to his art.

But Holmes knew that there was more to the story. There had been many attractive young women and men on the ship coming over from

France—the men and women often walking the promenade deck arm-in-arm, men with men, women with women.

The detective didn't know whether James played whist or poker or bridge or any other card game where concealment was a great part of the game, but he knew that James's impassive countenance would be an asset in such a competition. He showed little reaction, even to surprising statements or revelations. But once, unaware that Holmes was even looking his way, Henry James's gaze had paused for no more than a second on two loud, laughing, carefree young American men, walking arm-in-arm along the deck in the way American men do so freely, and Holmes caught the complex flicker of reactions in James's gaze: envy, wistfulness, longing, and—again—that vague hunger. The hunger had not seemed primarily sexual in nature to Holmes's trained eye but it was most certainly an emotional reaction.

Holmes didn't care about this fact, only that it was James's deepest secret—that and some hidden shame about his health and back pains and relationship to his older brother William—and what made Holmes care even less was that it could not have any direct bearing on either the serious business that had brought the detective to America or on this odd little case of Clover Adams's death.

* * *

After far too many suburban stops, the train from Washington finally pulled into New York's Grand Central Depot at the junction of 42nd Street and Park Avenue. This three-story Victorian pile was not the new six-story "Grand Central Station" that both Holmes and James would see after the turn of the century, much less the "Grand Central Terminal" that would stand at the same spot from 1913 on for a century into the future.

This "Grand Central Depot", Holmes could see, was a hodge-podge wedding-cake of a place with dark portals opening for more rails that would allow a few horse-drawn trains to continue toward downtown Manhattan and oversized signs for the NEW YORK AND HARLEM, NEW YORK AND NEW HAVEN, and NEW YORK AND HUDSON RIVER lines.

Holmes's man, obviously familiar with the maze of connections here, hurried out of the stopped carriage, up flights of stairs, across a crowded open space, and outside, where he ran to catch a horse-drawn trolley headed down Park Avenue. There was nothing Holmes could do but run even harder—a solid sprint with his side whiskers flying and one hand holding his homburg in place—and leap onto the trolley at the last second.

If his prey looked back, he would be most obvious. But Holmes could see that the man he was following had already settled into a seat far forward on the trolley and was paying no attention to anything but the newspaper he'd opened in front of him.

Holmes knew that his man belonged to several rather elite (for Americans) clubs, including two where he kept a room—the Union Club at 69th Street and Park Avenue and the Century Club at 42 East 15th Street. The man also had a permanent room at the Brunswick Hotel at Madison Square at Fifth Avenue and 25th Street.

Holmes knew that the Union Club was not the immediate destination, because his target stayed on the slow trolley as the horses took it further south on Park Avenue. The Union Club's 69th St. and Park Avenue address obviously would mean that Holmes's man would have gone north from Grand Central Terminus at 42nd Street. The same applied to his quarry's rooms at the Century Club, since that elite institution had recently moved to 7 West 43rd Street, which would also have required a turn north from the terminal.

If the man he was following was heading toward the Brunswick Hotel—where Holmes knew he kept a permanent room—he should get off the trolley no further south than 25th Street, since the Brunswick was two blocks east where Fifth Avenue crossed 25th St.

But the man, hunched over slightly and seeming lost in the afternoon edition of the New York paper he'd picked up at Grand Central, stayed on the trolley past both the 25th and then 23rd Street stops. So the destination wasn't the Union Club, the Century Club, or his much-frequented Brunswick Hotel.

At Union Square, the trolley took the slight jog to avoid the transition from Park Avenue to Broadway and followed 4th Avenue for five blocks to Lafayette Street. Holmes's man showed no interest in getting off anywhere along these blocks just above and below Canal Street. When Lafayette Street merged with Centre Street, and City Hall came within view, the man stood on the running board to hop off the trolley. Holmes let the horses plod on another half block before he also jumped off and doubled back through the throng of pedestrians, keeping his target's head and shoulders in view at all times.

Holmes immediately saw their destination and was a little surprised. He'd imagined that if they were going to cross the East River, his quarry would take one of the ferries. The fact that they weren't going to a ferry landing pleased Holmes; he'd been in New York City several times since the Brooklyn Bridge was finished a decade earlier in 1883, but he'd never had reason or opportunity to cross it before. As with Henry James a week and a half earlier, a ferry had always seemed a more reasonable way to make the switch of railway connections from Manhattan to Staten Island or Brooklyn.

He watched his man pay his toll at the ornamental iron tollbooth and climb the broad iron stairway to the waiting platform. Half a dozen heads behind him in the queue, Holmes paid his nickel and joined the crowd on the platform. The train cars crossing the bridge followed their course in the center of the span with the pedestrian walkway above it and the roadbeds for carriages and other conveyances running along on either side, and Holmes knew that the trains made no stops on the bridge. Thus he felt perfectly comfortable taking a seat and relaxing in the rear of the car his man had entered, his back to his quarry. He could see reflections of the front of the car in nearby windows, but it would be difficult — not to mention senseless — for his target to jump from one of the train cars in mid-span.

Holmes noted for future reference — although he doubted he'd ever have a case concerning the Brooklyn Bridge railway cars — that the cars were very much like the newest and most luxurious cars on New York's elevated trains: double-sliding doors opening from open platforms decorated with elaborately worked wrought-iron, comfortable rows of seats, and large windows.

New Yorkers and Brooklynites had long since grown accustomed to the fact that the cars had no engines pulling or pushing them, but the occasional tourist exclaimed when their car began moving smoothly away from the station, seemingly under its own power. Holmes knew that down under the rails there was an ever-moving steel traction cable that the cars hooked onto for motivation. Holmes knew that San Francisco had a much more elaborate web of cable cars and that the grades were much steeper there. Still, one could feel this Brooklyn Bridge car climbing up the visible grade of the suspended roadways and superstructure.

Sherlock Holmes was not a man who usually went out of his way to be impressed either by works of nature or works of man. The latter he found largely irrelevant to his work except for the layouts of interior murder scenes and the like; the former he always considered ephemeral in terms of the expanse of time and mankind's tiny part in it. Holmes had studied his Darwin when he was a boy and it had left him not only with the feeling that he and everyone he might know had their place in the world, and then would know it no more, in a blink of an eye, but even the Pyramids and other "great works" were as ephemeral as a castle of sand on the beach at Brighton.

So cathedrals and great buildings of any age did not move Sherlock Holmes to any level of emotion—with the few exceptions such as London Bridge or Big Ben, the latter heard more often than seen through the City's deadly fogs. They were touchstones of the city he worked in and, in his own rigidly controlled way, loved.

But now, looking up, Holmes had to admit that the stone towers of the Brooklyn Bridge—they were just passing under the first one set out in the river—were impressive indeed. For many decades, the tallest structure in New York City had been the spire of Trinity Church at 284 feet. Just three years earlier, New York's World Building, at the corner of Park Row and Franklin Street, became the tallest structure in the city at 309 feet. And while this stone arch in the tower that the train was presently passing through was only 117 feet and the height of the towers only 159 feet above the roadways and rail tracks, 276 and a half feet above the river itself, the sheer stone-Gothic *strength* of the towers impressed the unimpressionable Holmes to some degree.

Holmes knew that remembering such precise numbers was just a waste of his precious mental attic space—remembering the heights of the arches and towers and roadway of this bridge would almost certainly never help him in a case—but he'd encountered the information during one of his many sleepless nights spent reading one of the twenty-five volumes of his newer, 1889, 9th Edition of the *Encyclopaedia Britannica.* Watson had called that purchase a foolish waste of money since Holmes already owned the 6th and 8th Editions, but Holmes treasured his 9th Edition. Unfortunately—and although his brother Mycroft was the one with the amazing mathematical abilities—once Sherlock Holmes was exposed to facts in the form of numbers, he found it all but impossible to forget them.

This seemingly miraculous bridge supported by cables descending from two stone towers that rose 276 feet above the river.

America, he thought, and not for the first time, *is a nation with huge dreams and not infrequently the ability to realize them.*

Meanwhile, the car descended the grade beyond the second tower and slowed as it approached the Brooklyn terminal, even more of an elaborate and painted iron structure than on the New York side, with a gentle release of the ingenious "Paine's grip" device freeing them from the cable. Holmes knew about Colonel W. H. Paine's gripping-releasing device only because he'd been hired in the mid-1880's by one of Paine's executives to look into a patent infringement of the grip, then in use only in San Francisco, by a would-be cable-car company in Paris.

Holmes followed his man down onto the street and then to a short series of horse-drawn trolley rides, finally walking half a block behind the man as he strolled southeast down a rough cobblestoned extension of Flatbush Avenue. His target never looked back over his shoulder or paused at a window front to check in the reflection to see if he was being followed.

Brooklyn, Holmes vaguely knew, had once been—save for Irish and Negro areas along the river to the north—a wealthy and self-satisfied city of wide, leaf-shaded avenues and many stately homes. The neighborhood they were in now, not that far from where they had demolished so many old structures to allow for the approaches to the Bridge, was far from stately. An apparently self-respecting three-story home, its trim and siding brightly painted in the most popular current colors of rose or aqua or mint green or sunset orange, might have on either side of it a rundown old structure whose inhabitants had abandoned all efforts at repair or upkeep.

It was at one of the nicer homes on Hudson Street that Holmes's man bounded up the four front steps, unlocked the front door, shouted something that Holmes could not quite hear from his place more than half a block away, and was immediately engulfed in hugs from two little girls and a woman with a babe in arms.

The girls and babe and woman were Negroes—the woman especially ebony in color. The two girls in clean, white shifts were lighter shades of tan in complexion but had kinky hair carefully brushed, braided, and tied up in fresh ribbons. There was no doubt that this was an affectionate homecoming. This surprised Holmes a bit. The man Holmes had been tailing all day was white.

* * *

"Yeah, they got three children. The two older ones are girls," said Mrs. Banes, the woman with a missing front tooth.

"The littlest one, the baby's a boy. They had a boy before, he was their first, but he died," said Mrs. Youngfeld, an older woman with gray hair. It was her house across the street on Hudson. "They named the first boy, the one who died, LeRoy."

Le roi, thought Holmes. *The king.*

Holmes had lost the excessive facial hair, wig, and prominent front teeth, and parted his own hair in the middle with a generous use of hair crème. He now wore thick but frameless spectacles. There were seven pencils visible in his left jacket pocket. From his briefcase he had produced an oversized ledger filled with what looked to be official forms.

It was late and several homes on Hudson Street had not responded to his knocking—a white man knocking in what was obviously a colored neighborhood—but Mrs. Youngfeld and her visitor and good friend from down the street, Mrs. Banes, had peeked through the sidelights and decided that the prissy-looking Holmes was not a threatening character.

They'd had no interest when Holmes had explained that his name was Mr. Williams and he was taking a "local census" so that the Brooklyn Benevolent Neighborhood Association could upgrade local parks and facilities, but when he'd brought out the two dollars he'd pay each of them in return for their brief time answering a few questions about their neighbors, they warmed to him.

"And the family's name is Todd?" said Holmes, pursing his lips and fussing with the complex form of boxes and printed lines on the leaves of paper in his ledger.

"That's right," said Mrs. Youngfeld. "James and Ada Todd. You want the children's names too?"

"I don't believe that will be necessary," said Holmes. "But you say there are the two girls and one baby boy in the household."

"Another baby on the way," said Mrs. Banes. "Ada told me that their old house there is getting too small for them."

"Would you happen to know their ages? Approximate ages will suffice." Holmes was speaking with a slight whistling lisp through his permanently pursed lips. He was a government bureaucrat who *liked* being a government bureaucrat. (A charge he'd once, in pique, leveled at his brother Mycroft, who had responded at once in his slow, unexcitable drawl—"But, Brother, I do not *work* for the British Government. At times I *am* the British Government.")

"Mr. Todd, he about fifty-one, fifty-two. Ada's going to be thirty-two this coming April nine," said Mrs. Youngfeld.

Holmes made no comment on the disparity of ages. He'd seen that with his own eyes in the failing light of evening.

"And would you have any idea of when they were married?" asked Holmes, pursing and whistling ever so slightly. Just another line to fill. Just another box to check.

"What's it matter to the Benevolent Whatever of Brooklyn *when* a legally married couple got married?" demanded Mrs. Banes. Her hands were now fists and her fists were on her bony hips.

"September twenty-two, eighteen eighty-eight," said Mrs. Youngfeld.

Mrs. Banes turned a wide-eyed stare on her friend. "Ella, how...do...you...know...*that?* The exact date that Ada got hitched? I can't even remember my own anniversary."

"I remember numbers and dates," said Mrs. Youngfeld. "Totty, your anniversary is on December fourteen...not that it matters since Henry run off four years ago."

Mrs. Banes looked away and stomped her foot.

"Ada told me that she and James got married over in New York at her aunt's place on West Twenty-fourth Street," Mrs. Youngfeld continued to Holmes, who scribbled quickly to keep up. "She said they brought a colored Methodist minister down from a church on Eighty-fifth Street to do the ceremony. They had an organ brought in to play and a cake with white icing."

Mrs. Banes stared daggers at her friend but said nothing.

"Almost done here," said Holmes. "Mr. James Todd's occupation...he is employed by the gas works?"

"No, you got that wrong!" laughed Mrs. Banes. "Ada's man James is a railroad porter, 'riginally from Baltimore. A *head* porter. He works for the New York Central Railroad, but...poor Ada...the railroad keeps sending him all over the place: Pennsylvania, Michigan, Ohio, Illinois, Massachusetts...even up into some places in Canada."

"Ontario and Quebec," said Mrs. Youngfeld.

"*Wherever* they send him, he's gone a whole bunch of the time," said Mrs. Banes, clearly exasperated at her friend and neighbor's vast store of information. "Ada's home alone, expecting again, alone all by her own self with the two girls and the baby boy to take care of most of the time. That man may make good money as a chief porter, but he's not home two days out of fifty."

"I shan't take up any more of your time, ladies," said Holmes, putting away his ledger and adjusting his glasses on his nose. "You've been most helpful. Your census information on the Todds and other neighbors may well enable the Brooklyn Benevolent Neighborhood Association to fund a fine playground near here."

"The childrens got plenty of empty lots 'round here to play in," said Mrs. Banes. "What we really could use is a nice, clean, respectable *saloon* like the ones that used to be up on Flatbush Avenue before the Bridge squashed everything."

"Oh, hush up, Totty," said Mrs. Youngfeld. Looking Holmes in the eye, she said, "She doesn't mean that, Mr. Williams."

Holmes nodded, raised his hat, backed down to the sidewalk level, made as if to turn away, but then turned back to the two women. "You'll forgive me if this question is insensitive...it is supposed to be part of the neighborhood census, but I rarely have to ask it..."

The two ladies waited.

"Coincidentally, I have had the occasion to *see* Mr. James Todd without having the pleasure of actually making his acquaintance," Holmes said softly, showing visible signs of embarrassment. "The gentleman has blue eyes, blond hair—not much left, but definitely blond—and a very fair complexion..."

Mrs. Banes laughed heartily. "So he fooled you, too," she said, the missing tooth even more visible in an otherwise perfect wide expanse of white teeth.

"Fooled..." began Holmes.

"James Todd is passing," said Mrs. Youngfeld. She also sounded embarrassed. "He told Ada that he's been passing since he was a boy."

"Oh, yes," said Mrs. Banes, still laughing. "James Todd, he *good* at passing."

"Passing?" said Holmes. "You mean, passing as..."

"White," said Mrs. Youngfeld. "James Todd doesn't look black, but his wife Ada told us a dozen times that his grandpa and mama were field slaves down in Carolina. Lots of 'scegenation going on with those field slaves and lots of children of those 'scegenations trying to pass up here. Though not many *looks* as white as James Todd."

"At least he kept to his own kind in marryin'," said Mrs. Banes.

Holmes tipped his hat a final time. "Thank you again, ladies."

* * *

On the late-night train back to Washington, Holmes realized he was very tired. Tomorrow would be busy because he would have the mystery of who sent the annual She-was-murdered cards solved by afternoon and he would have to break into Henry Adams's mansion after dark—always a delicate proposition in such a swanky and well-policed area as the Hays and Adamses had chosen to live in.

He knew one of the original Five of Hearts secrets now—Mr. Clarence King, "America's most eligible bachelor" according to his friend John Hay and an editorial writer in *Century Magazine,* had been married to a colored woman named Ada Copeland since September, 1888. There seemed no doubt—at least to his neighbors—that the two girls, living baby boy, deceased baby boy named LeRoy, and baby on the way were all his. And Holmes himself had noticed how light-skinned the baby and one of the girls had been, especially when compared to their attractive ebony mother.

Uncovering one such secret of the Five of Hearts was a start, Holmes knew, but there remained secrets he would have to ferret out of John and Clara Hay's lives, of Henry Adams, and even of the late Clover Adams.

Every man or woman alive, Holmes knew, had secrets. Most, like Clarence King—deliberately misleading his closest friends with his boisterous talk of being attracted only to "swarthy South Sea Island beauties"—had secrets within secrets.

A few, like Henry James and Holmes himself, had secrets within secrets within secrets.

One of Holmes's small secrets had asserted itself before he left Brooklyn. It had been too many hours since that early morning's injection of the heroic drug, and before Holmes took a ferry across the river back to Grand Central Terminus, he found an empty shed in Brooklyn in which he could cook-up his little solution of heroin and inject it with some privacy. He'd been in pain, both physical and psychological, for the entire afternoon, and the relief in the moment after the injection was heaven-sent.

Now Holmes closed his eyes and literally nodded off as the train rushed south through the night.

CHAPTER 20

"My dear Harry," cried John Hay, "you simply cannot desert me now!"

"Not deserting, surely," said Henry James. "Merely drawing a polite boundary to my intrusion, despite your and Clara's generous and obviously boundary-less hospitality. You remember that you helped find a room for me to rent near here in eighteen eighty-three when I was here last and visiting the Adamses."

"But that's quite different!" said Hay. Both men were standing in Hay's study this Tuesday morning. Hay had informed James that the servants had reported "Mr. Sigerson"—hat brim low and collars high—coming in and retiring to his room not long before dawn.

"We have Holmes and his mysteries now," continued Hay. "This is all simply too fascinating to face alone. You *must* share this excitement with us."

"I apologize again for bringing the detective here in disguise and under false pretenses..." began James.

"Nonsense," cried Hay, waving away the apology with his long, elegant fingers. "It's a profoundly exciting experience and one that I wouldn't have missed for the world. Look at what he's had my secretaries doing all yesterday afternoon and this morning."

James looked at the boxes of envelopes and cards which covered every desk and table surface in the study.

"Surely you are not going to allow this...stranger...to read your personal and business correspondence," said James. He was unable to keep his sense of shock out of his voice.

Hay laughed. "Of course not, my dear Harry. These are envelopes and cards with typed addresses only, although he will be comparing the first line or so of some harmless correspondence to the ominous cards all of us in the Five of Hearts receive annually. All these addresses and notes have been typewritten, you see. Holmes told me yesterday morning that, and I believe I quote him correctly—'A typewriter has really quite as much individuality as a man's handwriting'."

James made a noncommittal sound.

"So you really must stay," repeated Hay. "I need your advice and ready counsel, old friend. It will be a very sensitive thing when Adams gets home."

"It will indeed," said James. "You have no intention of..."

"Of telling him that the English detective Sherlock Holmes is investigating Clover's suicide?" finished Hay. "Certainly not. You know as well as I that Henry will never agree to discuss that terrible December day. Adams would be outraged and appalled at the very *idea* of a detective poking around amidst the burned rubble of his painful memories."

"We can only hope," said James, "that what Adams does not know doesn't end up somehow hurting him anyway. Lies and omissions have a way of getting out, especially among close friends."

Hay frowned at this in silence for a long moment but finally said, "The real question is whether to tell Clara about all this. By odd coincidence, she's a great collector of the published tales of our new friend's so-called adventures."

"Tell Clara about *what?*" asked Clara Hay from the door that had been quietly opened while the two men had been so loudly debating.

*   *   *

Leaving his room locked, James took his umbrella—despite the fact that the skies were perfectly blue this warming Tuesday in March—and set off on what Hay had told him was a walk of about two miles to the U.S. Capitol and its Library of Congress. Hay had added that if Harry wanted to see the beautiful new Thomas Jefferson Building currently under construction to house the enlarged Library in a few years, he might add a block or so to his walk to view the rising front façade facing 2nd Street N.E.

James felt bad telling his friend Hay that he simply wanted to get in some exercise and a spot of sight-seeing when, in truth, he had a much more sinister reason for visiting the Library of Congress installed in the Capitol Building.

The previous afternoon, Henry James had done what was almost certainly the least-gentlemanly act of his adult life.

The maids were cleaning "Mr. Sigerson's" room when James went upstairs that afternoon. They were carrying out sheets and fetching new ones while airing out the room of a visible miasma of pipe smoke and they'd left the door ajar.

James had paused and peered in. Holmes had bustled out earlier, working to hide his appearance with a derby pulled low and a macintosh collar tugged high, but almost certainly had been in some disguise. There was no telling when he might return. His room, the bedding being dealt with first by the maids, was a mess—clothes flung on the floor, books strewn everywhere, ashes spilled on the Hays' expensive bedside tables and sitting-area tables, maps of Washington and New York lying open on the floor atop discarded socks and shoes. A messy young boy intent upon outraging his parents with his slovenliness could hardly have done worse.

But there, hung over the back of a chair not three feet inside the room, was the jacket that Holmes had been wearing yesterday morning when he'd spoken to Hay, King, and James in Hay's study.

Glancing guiltily over his shoulder, seeing no one but realizing that he would have only a few seconds in which to spy and pry, James stepped quickly into the room and felt in the inside breast pocket of that jacket. Holmes had taken out four photographs at the beginning of his talk and eventually shown them three of them—Colonel Sebastian Moran, the blurred image of young Lucan Adler, and an old photograph of the woman he said was Irene Adler before she pretended to be Clover Adams's friend Rebecca Lorne.

The fourth photograph, he'd never shown them.

James did not expect to find anything, so he was surprised when he pulled out the small pack of four photos and a telegram flimsy. Three of the images were indeed the ones shared with the other men on Monday, but the fourth photograph—quite formal, the man wearing a long-tailed black suit and old-fashioned high collars, the single image obviously snipped with scissors from a larger photograph—was of a man in his forties or fifties, clean-shaven and strangely hollow-cheeked, his penetrating gaze peering out from under a commanding (and balding at the top) brow. A few loose strands of both dark and graying hair hung down over the man's oddly lupine ears.

There was something professorial in the man's dress and slightly hunched manner, but also something predatory in the way the sharp-featured face protruded forward with the black shoulders rising behind it. As formal as the man's pose was, James thought he could see a strange glimpse of the man's tongue caught in the act of flicking out over just-visible small, disturbingly sharp teeth.

The telegram was addressed to Sherlock Holmes to be picked up in a nearby Washington Western Union office, had the previous day's date on it, and was brief:

CONFIRMED THAT MORIARTY HAS ADVANCED NETWORKS WORKING IN FRANCE GERMANY ITALY AND GREECE STOP ALSO NETWORKS FUNDING AND SUPPORTING CRIMINALS AND ANARCHISTS IN WASHINGTON NEW YORK BALTIMORE AND CHICAGO STOP PROCEED WITH CAUTION STOP MYCROFT

James set the four photos and folded telegram back in the jacket pocket and hurried out into the hall just as one of the maids carrying fresh linens turned the corner.

She stepped aside to let James pass toward his own room and the author detected no recognition of his quick trespass in her properly downturned eyes.

* * *

James crossed the small park and walked east on Pennsylvania Avenue, occasionally glancing without much interest through the iron fence across the north lawn of the Executive Mansion on its open acres of grass. At the corner he turned south on 15th St. N.W. and walked a little more than four blocks that way before he turned southeast onto a more southerly extension of Pennsylvania Avenue N.W.

After a brisk mile on Pennsylvania Avenue, James had to wait a moment before he could cross between carriages and heavy horse-drawn carts to follow Constitution Avenue a little more than a half mile due east. He'd decided to get a glimpse of the new Thomas Jefferson Building, if only to tell Hay later that he had.

Three blocks walking south on 2nd Street brought him to the construction site—three stories of the imposing new home for the Library had risen, but the shell was still hollow and the façades festooned with cranes, ropes, nautical-looking arrangements of block and tackle, and wood-and-iron lattices making rigid the empty areas between the high pillars up on that third-story level. The entire city block surrounding the rising structure was littered with numbered blocks of granite, pallets of lumber protected from the weather with rubber-canvas wrappings, loaded carts, workmen, and even more cranes, pulleys, and cables.

James could have continued walking south and then back to the Capitol via Independence Avenue, but he chose to turn around, retrace his steps to East Capitol Street, and pass through a muddy expanse of nothingness which might have been unkempt gardens—making sure to stay on the narrow paved path—before climbing the stairs to the east entrance of the nation's Capitol.

* * *

That morning when James and Hay had been overheard by Clara, the author expected either a row or for his friend John to lie, but neither occurred. Hay confessed everything to his wife. Instead of being outraged at being misled, Clara Hay had been delighted that their guest "Jan Sigerson" was actually the detective Sherlock Holmes in disguise. James guessed that Hay had revealed all this to his wife because he was uncertain about when Holmes himself might appear before Clara and the servants sans the Sigerson disguise.

"Oh, he's a master of disguise!" Clara had gushed, clapping her hands together as if in prayer. "What an honor to have the World's First and Foremost Consulting Detective as a guest here in our home. I cannot wait to tell Marie and Ellen and . . ."

"You must tell no one, my dear," interrupted Hay, holding one finger up in stern admonition. "Mr. Holmes is here in disguise on what I take to be a very serious mission indeed, and one in which his life may be in danger if the news of his presence in America were to become known. This is a good part of the reason that Harry has asked us to keep his visit with Holmes confidential as well."

"Oh, yes, of course . . . I understand . . . but *after* the adventure is over," said Clara Hay, her steepled fingers moving to her lips as if sealing them for the time being. She was still smiling broadly. "I must bring down the January issue of *Harper's Weekly* with the shocking story 'The Cardboard Box' in it! Oh, and the February *Harper's* with the 'Yellow Face' tale in it. We must ask Mr. Holmes's opinion on Dr. Watson's chronicling of these adventures!"

Hay took his wife's hands in his own. "Clara, darling, we must not make our guest feel self-conscious. Mr. Holmes is not the author of these . . . published adventures . . . you must remember. There might be elements of exaggeration or other possibly embarrassing parts to the tales that Mr. Holmes may feel uncomfortable about."

"Of course, of course," said Clara. But she was still smiling. And James was sure, as he hurried upstairs to fetch his umbrella so he could leave before Holmes awoke, that the copies of *Harper's Weekly* would make their way downstairs and into Holmes's sphere of attention before the day was out.

*   *   *

When James had told Hay that "I might drop in at the Library of Congress" to browse a bit, Hay had insisted on writing "a little note of introduction". James hadn't thought that a note of introduction would be needed to use what he understood was a public library, but he'd tucked the note in his jacket pocket and not thought about it until stopped by some minor librarians just inside the door of the cluttered Library part of the Capitol Building.

Naturally, Hay being Hay, the "note of introduction" was to the Librarian of Congress, a certain Ainsworth Rand Spofford. The lowly librarians at the entrance desk had leaped out of their seats upon reading the note from Hay, fluttered like startled pigeons, and then the chief amongst these lowly workers personally led Henry James up two flights of stairs to the Librarian of Congress's office.

Spofford himself was a thin, sickly looking old fellow with a scraggly gray beard and long, lank hair that fell away from a part that was more bald pate than part. His face was dominated by a nose that James thought might be up to chiseling stone over at the Library's new site.

The Librarian came around his huge desk to shake James by the hand, although it was more a limp offering of a dead, white, boneless thing than a handshake. "Welcome, Mr. James, welcome indeed. The Library of Congress is honored to have you visit us. How can we be of service today?"

James was, for the instant, a bit nonplussed. He'd imagined his research here as being anonymous, invisible.

"Looking in on our collection of your own wonderful novels and collections perhaps?" prompted Ainsworth Rand Spofford. He was still standing next to James and seemed to be feeling out of his element when not sitting behind his huge desk.

"Oh, gracious, no, no," demurred James. "Just a few minutes of . . . research . . . one might generously call it."

"Of course!" cried Spofford, rubbing his bony hands together as if the two men had just consummated a major business deal. The Librarian touched an elaborate gadget on his desk, and a second later a hidden door in a wall of books to one side opened and a tall, thin lady entered silently.

"This is Miss Miller, my chief librarian assistant," said Spofford. "Our honored guest today, Miss Miller, the famous American writer Henry James."

Since Miss Miller had stopped three yards away, too far for even an American gender-egalitarian handshake, the famous American writer Henry James bowed slightly.

Miss Miller, James saw, was a newspaper cartoonist's caricature of a librarian. Tall, thin to the point of visible boniness, hair done up in an unattractive bun, dressed in an ugly brown cotton shift with what looked to be a man's shirt buttoned beneath it, tiny Benjamin Franklin bifocals perched on the end of her long nose, and with a name tag on the slight bump of what could be her left breast under the burlap-looking fabric of her shift. D. MILLER.

D. Miller, thought James. *Please, God, no.*

"Miss Miller's first name is Daisy, so the two of you should be well-acquainted," said Librarian Ainsworth Rand Spofford with a graveled bark that must have been some form of laughter.

Miss Miller blushed mightily. James looked down at his shoes, which had picked up some unsightly dust during his walk from the construction site.

"Mr. James would like to conduct some research, Miss Miller," Spofford was saying. "If you need any additional help, Mr. James, please call upon me at once..." And the limp hand was offered again.

James touched the relic and followed Miss Miller out through the door in the bookcase.

The mere librarian...no capital "L" with her...led him through a warren of book-cluttered small offices and then out into a narrow, three-story-high corridor which James, with a sense of shock, realized was the Library of Congress itself. Or part of it. Books not only filled every available shelf but were stacked on the main floor, behind the iron railings on each mezzanine, and on each available table, desk, and surface.

Miss Miller caught his shocked gaze.

"When Librarian Spofford assumed his post in eighteen sixty-four, appointed by President Lincoln himself," she said in a surprisingly sensual voice, "the Library of Congress had fewer than sixty thousand volumes, much of the collection based upon Thomas Jefferson's original gift of his

private library. Now we have almost four hundred thousand...passing
the Boston Public Library as the richest library-source in America...and
Librarian Spofford fully intends for the Library to have one million volumes by the time we move to the new Thomas Jefferson Building in
three years."

"Commendable," James heard himself murmur as they moved down
the crowded corridor, dodging piles of books. "Most commendable.
Wonderful."

They paused at a junction of corridors. More heaps of books visible everywhere below the narrow, vaulted corridor ceiling three stories above.

"How may I help you, Mr. James?"

"Ah...I was thinking..." stammered the famous author. "That is, I
wondered if you might have a copy of a rather obscure book of physics or
mathematics titled *The Dynamics of an Asteroid?*"

Miss Miller laughed softly and her laugh was as pleasant and melodious as her superior's had been grating. "Professor Moriarty's book! Of
course, we have it, though you are right, Mr. James...it is very rare. But
Librarian Spofford has continued the Library's original goal of advancing
its collection of science and mathematical references."

James put both hands on his umbrella handle and nodded, trying to
hide how startled he'd been by her quick recognition of the volume's author.

"It's good you asked for assistance, sir," said Miss Miller. "For we've
had to put *The Dynamics of an Asteroid* on a restricted viewing basis."

"Really? For such an obscure and technical title? Why is that, Miss
Miller?"

"Why, after the Reuters News Agency story two years ago—as well
as the story *The New York Times* reprinted from the London *Times*—of
Professor James Moriarty's disappearance at Reichenbach Falls with the
English detective Sherlock Holmes, we've had far too many requests by
common visitors to the Library to see this valuable book. We were afraid
that without supervision, someone would pilfer it for novelty value if
nothing else."

"Ahhh," said James.

"This way, Mr. James." Miss Miller led him toward a staircase with only a narrow aisle on the iron steps between more unruly stacks of books.

* * *

The next two hours were an odd education for Henry James.

He would have never found Professor James Moriarty's works or any references to him had he been left to his own devices, as he'd planned so furtively to be, but Miss Miller tracked down everything the United States Library of Congress had on the now famous—or infamous—professor.

The first two books she brought him were the much-mentioned *The Dynamics of an Asteroid*—two hundred and nine pages of impenetrable equations with very few words, just as advertised—and then a thinner book, the 68-page *A Treatise on the Binomial Theorem.* The latter had been published way back in 1871, the same year, according to a brief note in the back, that James Nolan Moriarty received his twin degrees, in mathematics and applied physics, from University College, Dublin. The book had been released by a small Dublin publishing house which James had never heard of and was dedicated to Carl Gottfried Neumann, a professor at the University of Leipzig.

James had never heard of Professor Neumann, but Miss Miller assured him that he was an important figure, mentioned frequently in German and other foreign journals of mathematics, and even brought him Neumann's book *Das Dirichtlet'sche Prinzip in seiner Anwendung auf die Reimann'schen Flächen* to prove it.

James might have paused to wonder why a student at Trinity College in Dublin was so advanced that he dedicated his first book of mathematical theory to a professor in Leipzig, but instead he explained to Miss Miller that he was primarily interested in biographical information about Professor Moriarty—and any photographs of the professor, if those were handy.

He could see the curiosity in her eyes, but Miss Miller was far too much the professional to inquire *Are you thinking of writing a book about the man who killed Sherlock Holmes?* She hurried off to find more references in various science sections of the maze of stacks, shelves, and locked rooms that was the Library of Congress.

In less than an hour, James had every reference the Library had on the man Sherlock Holmes, in print, had called the Napoleon of Crime and, in person, had insisted was a figment of his imagination.

Even dates and places of birth did not agree. One *Who's Who in European Mathematics* from 1884 stated that Professor James Moriarty—no middle name given—author of the *Treatise on the Binomial Theorem,* had been born in Dublin in 1846. A reference book for the University College, Dublin, which showed a Professor James N. Moriarty as being a professor of mathematics there from 1872 until 1878, gave the man's year of birth as 1849 and the place of birth as Greystones, which Miss Miller helped James look up in an atlas of Ireland and which turned out to be a small village between Dublin and Wicklow.

So if Moriarty were alive today, if he hadn't died in 1891 at Reichenbach Falls, how old would he be—47 or 44?

The next shock for James was when he found the copyright date of *The Dynamics of an Asteroid,* published by an imprint he'd never heard of in London—1890. Even if Moriarty had been born at the later date given, he would have been 41 years old in the year the book was published. Old, from the little that Henry James understood, for a mathematician's first major publication. Some don at Oxford had once told James, in passing, that mathematicians such as Charles Dodgson, known to the world as Lewis Carroll, usually published their best work when they were younger than thirty.

Thumbing through the literal hieroglyphics—to James—of the mathematical equations of *The Dynamics of an Asteroid,* he found himself muttering aloud, "If I only had the vaguest idea of what this volume is about..."

"I've heard some of the visiting scientists discuss it," said Miss Miller, thinking that he had addressed her with the question. "It seems that the asteroid in question creates what is known to astronomers and mathematicians as a Three-Body-Problem. Take any two celestial bodies, and their gravitational attraction, tidal effect on the other, tumbling, three-dimensional orientations, and so forth can be plotted with both modern and classical mathematical techniques. But add a third body...evidently then the tumbling, orientation, and even trajectory of an asteroid becomes all but incalculable. Professor James Moriarty's great renown in this book came, if I understand the scientists and mathematicians correctly, from pointing out what cannot be calculated."

"Very interesting," said James, although her summary of others' analysis was useless to him. After a moment he spoke again, "So it appears that there is no chance of finding a photograph of Professor Moriarty."

"Please come with me, Mr. James." Miss Miller—James tried not to think of her unfortunate first name—marched ahead of him with elbows pumping, a soldier going off to war.

They had to climb into what had to be the dusty attic of the Capitol (although not under the great dome as far as James could tell) and Miss Miller had to unlock three more doors before they came to a room filled with thousands of carefully filed journals.

"Mathematics...European...conferences..." muttered Miss Miller to herself, gesturing behind her back for James to take the only seat available in the room. A low chair at what seemed to be a student's desk in the center of the impossibly cluttered room. James was certain that he would have nightmares about this Library for years to come.

"Here!" she cried at last and brought a German journal with a title too long and umlauted and Fraktured for James to bother trying to decipher. She opened to page thirty-six and stabbed her finger down at a line of eight middle-aged men standing in a line facing the camera. The caption, in German, beneath the photograph said "Conference on Advanced Mathematics and Astronomical Physics, University of Leipzig, July, 1892."

The names were listed under each man, but James didn't need to read them. He saw Moriarty at once, on the far right—the same balding head, straggling dark hair, reptilian forward thrusting of his neck, and hint of tongue showing between the thin, pale lips. It was precisely the photograph that he'd illicitly taken from Holmes's jacket and peeked at that very morning. Holmes must have torn it out of a copy of this very journal.

"Professor James N. Moriarty, London." No university affiliation given. But the date of the conference—July, 1892. More than a full year after Holmes and the newspaper accounts recorded Moriarty as dying at Reichenbach Falls in May of 1891!

Satisfied that he would find out no more about this particular Lazarus at the Library of Congress, James went through the motions of taking a few notes and assured the apologetic Miss Miller that no, no, despite the apparent paucity of information available, she had been of inestimable help to him. *Inestimable.*

He stood and turned to go then but could not even find his way through the attic to the stairs. Miss Miller inquired as to which exit from the Capitol he wished to use.

"The main...front...entrance, I believe," said James.

"Wonderful," said the helpful Miss Miller. "You'll get some glimpses of the actual Capitol."

She was his Aeneas down several flights of stairs, around endless stacks of books that would have stopped him in his tracks, through the long, high, cluttered corridors, and then out into the formal marble vaults and under the majestic dome of the United States Capitol Building itself. Henry James was impressed not by the colossal Roman size of the structure, but by its almost Grecian white purity. And the early afternoon light shining down onto the marble floors was lovely.

Out under the high portico and with the grand columns framing a view back toward the Executive Mansion less than a mile away, James turned to the librarian. "Once again, Miss Miller, I must thank you most sincerely for your inestimable help on my little research errand."

He tipped his hat and started to descend but stopped and turned back when Miss Miller called his name.

"Mr. James, I..." She was wringing her hands and blushing. "I may not get another chance, so I hope you will not think it impertinent of me if I take this opportunity to thank you so much for writing what I consider such a lovely and wise novel about a woman's *mind.*"

Daisy Miller? thought James. *The poor lady has so much to learn about life.* He'd certainly had when he wrote that popular but shallow confection so many years earlier.

"Thank you, Miss Miller," he said smoothly. "But the eponymous title pales in comparison to its namesake's true beauty and wisdom."

"Eponymous..." repeated Miss Daisy Miller and then blushed an even deeper crimson. "No, Mr. James...I did not mean your novel *Daisy Miller*. That was adequate as an...entertainment. No, I was referring to your wonderful *The Portrait of a Lady.*"

"Ahhh, so kind," murmured James through his beard and tipped his hat again and bowed slightly and then turned to umbrella-tap his way down the wide, white stone steps. *Adequate as an entertainment?* Who did this homely prune of a spinster think she was?

* * *

It was already mid-afternoon. Not ready to return to the Hays' home, James hunted for a place near the Capitol where he might have a light luncheon. He'd imagined a bistro or charcuterie, but managed to find only a delicatessen sort of place—obviously the kind of establishment attuned to the needs of busy government workers and clerks with only a brief break time for their luncheons—that served only rude sandwiches and tepid coffee. But it had empty tables outside at this after-luncheon hour and he was glad to sit in the shade and sip his coffee and think about the import of what he'd seen and learned in the Library of Congress.

Until this afternoon, James had been determined to say good-bye to the Hays, preferably before Henry Adams returned home later in this week, and to return to London on his own. Whatever wave of despair had driven him to Paris and the bank of the Seine at night had passed over, dissipated, and he only wanted to extricate himself from this sticky web of disguises and assumed identities that this Holmes-person, whoever he really was, had entangled him in.

But now, knowing beyond a doubt that Holmes—by whatever name—had lied to him about inventing Professor James Moriarty just so that he could "die" with him at Reichenbach Falls, and after seeing the photograph of the real Moriarty both from Holmes's jacket pocket and the European journal covering mathematicians and astronomy physicists, James felt a grim new determination to stay with his friends, the Hays and Henry Adams, until this "Sherlock Holmes" was completely exposed as the fraud and humbug he was.

Reinvigorated by this new resolve, James took the scenic route back to Lafayette Square and John and Clara's front door.

Hay, in a state of some excitement, rushed down the stairs to escort him up to the study the minute a servant had let him in.

"He's just now revealing it," Hay said. "He wouldn't until you returned, Harry."

"Reveal..." said James. He felt the shadow of dread that came over him every time this Holmes-person "revealed" anything.

Hay's study was a mess—typewritten cards and envelopes turned out of their boxes and files and strewn everywhere. James was surprised to see Clara there along with her husband and Holmes not wearing his Sigerson disguise.

"Clara," said James, somewhat bewildered, "you are a part of this..."

"Oh, yes, yes!" cried Clara Hay, the respectable Washington society matron, while squeezing his hand like a school girl with one hand while fluttering two copies of *Harper's Weekly* with her other hand. "And Mr. Holmes has given me his impressions of both 'Silver Blaze' and 'The Yellow Face' and..."

"Silence!" shouted John Hay. The diplomat renowned for his unflappability was beside himself with excitement. "We're just about to hear, for the first time, the results of the typewriter font comparisons."

Sherlock Holmes obviously had the spotlight and he reveled in it, holding up the original She-was-murdered cards along with various envelopes and typed notes.

"I have the typewriter behind these annual anonymous cards, if not the man," said Holmes, showing the aspects of the typefaces that matched up "beyond any doubt".

"For heaven's sake!" cried John Hay. "Who is it, man?"

Holmes peered up from examining the font on different notes under a hand lens. "Who," he asked, holding up matching typewritten fonts, "is this...Samuel Clemens?"

CHAPTER 21

Holmes waited restlessly for the Hay household to go to sleep. He smoked pipe after pipe in his room, cracking the door occasionally to listen. Still, the last shufflings and whispers of the servants continued long after both the Hays and Henry James had gone to their respective bedrooms.

Finally it was silent. Opening wide the window of his room—a window that looked out upon the dark backyard of the large house here at the junction of H Street and Sixteenth Street—Holmes took his heavy shoulder-bag of burglary tools and slipped out of the room and down the stairway. He wore a black sweater under a soft black jacket, workman's black trousers, and black shoes with crepe soles Holmes had ordered made specially for him by Charles F. Stead & Company, a tannery in the north of England. He tip-toed through the kitchen, opened the door without a noise, slipped out, and used one of his breaking-and-entering tools to lock the door behind him.

The Hays' backyard, mostly garden, faced the Adamses' backyard and shared a tall brick wall separating the two. Holmes tossed a rope with a small grapple, tested it, then climbed the wall and dropped to the other side in ten silent seconds. The garden here was little more than a gesture and the back of the Adamses' property was dominated by a stable designed by the same architect who had done both homes—but an empty stable this night.

As Henry James had told him, Henry Hobson Richardson had designed and built both the Adams and Hay houses at roughly the same time, but the designs were different. Holmes had spent a long tea with Clara Hay this Tuesday afternoon showing more than a polite interest in the layout of both grand homes. Now he moved toward the Adams house with the floor plan in his mind.

Henry Adams no longer kept a dog. The house was dark save for a few gas pilot lamps burning. The stables were a tall, dark mass behind him. Holmes had made note that all of the first-floor windows of the Adams house were covered with wrought-iron grilles.

The kitchen rear door was the best place to enter and Holmes knew that the easiest way to do that would be to cut a circle of glass from a pane—the iron grille there would be no hindrance to his instrument—but this would leave a sign of his illegal entrance. Holmes placed a soft cloth on the ground outside that door and went to one knee. He could manage the door lock in less than a minute, but the kitchen door had been bolted at two places from the inside before the last servants had left for the night. He would have to dismantle the entire lock, reach in with a rigid piece of wire he could bend to his purposes, pull back those bolts, get in, and then reconstruct the entire lock in its proper place. It would take the better part of an hour, but since he did not plan to leave via this same kitchen door, it would only have to be done once.

Holmes glanced at the stars. It was not yet one a.m. He had time.

Once inside the kitchen, Holmes squatted for several minutes of absolute silence—controlling his breathing so that even he could not hear it—and did nothing but listen to the house. He'd heard both John and Clara Hay mention that Adams's people were off at play for these final three days before they would regather and regroup to prepare the house for Henry Adams's return on Friday, and Holmes's instincts told him that the huge house was indeed empty.

He lit a hand lamp no larger than his palm and closed the upper and lower louvers so that it cast the dimmest of lights and that only straight ahead in a narrow beam. In a few minutes he'd reassembled the entire lock and doorknob apparatus, locked and bolted the back door from the inside again, and was stealing silently up the narrow steps of the servants' rear staircase.

Although both houses had been designed in the so-called Romanesque style, Adams's home had a different feeling on the inside and different proportions on the outside. Holmes had noted to James the profusion of towers, turrets, gables, and huge chimneys on the Hays' home; the Adamses' abode—dwelt in only by the widower and his staff now, of course—was simpler, more modern-looking from the outside, set off architecturally only by the twin white arches of its entrance.

Both homes were four stories tall, but the Adams house had a flat front. One of these rooms on the second floor was Henry Adams's private study and Holmes found the locked door to it in no time. Next to the study, door also locked, was a room that had been Clover Adams's combination darkroom and small photographic workshop and which now—according to Clara Hay—had been converted to archives for the dead woman's carefully inventoried photographs.

The simple lock took Holmes less than a minute and then he was in the windowless inner archives room, re-lighting his louvered hand lamp and looking at the drawer upon drawer of photographic prints and plates.

He trusted in Henry Adams's famous neatness and efficiency and was not disappointed. It had been Adams who had inventoried and archived most of Clover's photographic images after her suicide in December of 1885. It took Holmes only a few minutes to find both the inventory journal—most of it typed out, some still in Henry Adams's neat hand—and then the key to the specially constructed archival file cabinets.

Vol. 7—p. 24—#50.23—"R. Lorne, Feb., 1884", the caption in Clover's tighter script—"Rebecca Lorne, standing, in Roman costume".

Holmes found and removed the photo and crouched low to prevent any escape of light as he played the beam of his hand-lantern over it.

The woman's pose was awkward, the "Roman costume" amateurly made, and her face was turned two-thirds away from the camera. But there was no doubt at all that "Rebecca Lorne" was the woman Sherlock Holmes had known as Irene Adler. He set this photograph back in place.

Vol. 7—p. 9—#50.9—"R. Lorne", no date given, caption in Clover's hand—"Rebecca Lorne with banjo". And also in Clover Adams's hand—*"Very good"*.

Holmes turned the narrow beam on the image. It *was* a very good photograph of Irene Adler/Rebecca Lorne. The woman was older than Holmes remembered, but Adler was still quite attractive. Clover Adams had posed the woman in the corner of a room near a window, holding her banjo as if she were playing it. Holmes had seen that banjo before. Lorne's/Adler's face was turned toward the window and tilted slightly forward, catching the soft light. Clover had used a wide-angle lens—Holmes guessed it to be the Dallmeyer lens, new to photography about the time Clover died—and had achieved an image poised somewhere between a portrait and capturing an instant of everyday life.

Vol. 7—p. 10—#50.10—"R.H., Feb. 8, 1884", date and the identical caption to the first photo Holmes had seen, also written in Clover's hand—"Rebecca Lorne, standing, in Roman costume". Again the face was turned mostly away from the camera. Holmes set it back.

Vol. 9—p. 17—#50.106—"Old Sweet Springs, Virginia, June, 1885, Rebecca Lorne, her cousin Clif Richards, H.A."—"On piazza of house".—The writing was all in Henry Adams's careful hand.

Holmes removed his small magnifying glass and studied the image. Rebecca Lorne was looking at the camera with only the upper part of her face hidden by her bonnet, but her "cousin Clifton Richards" had lowered his head so that the brim of his hat hid all of his face. The form of the man was athletic-enough looking to be Lucan Adler, but one would never be sure. He put the photograph back in its archival setting.

Vol. 9—p. 21—#50.108—"Old Sweet"—captions written in Henry Adams's hand—"View of house with people on piazza". Again, part of "Rebecca Lorne's" face was visible, but the man, still Clifton Richards from the clothing and hat, had turned his face full away.

Holmes swore under his breath. There was only one more photograph in this series.

Vol. 9—p. 23—#50.109—"Old Sweet Springs, June, 1885, Rebecca Lorne and Cousin"—all in Henry Adams's careful script—"Standing in meadow with house in background".

Clover had obviously taken this photograph with no warning to her subjects. The two figures stood in high grass that rose almost to their waists. "Rebecca Lorne's" head and shoulders were a blur as she turned her head to hear something spoken by the man standing next to her and slightly behind her.

The man's face—unaware that Clover was taking a photo—was in perfect focus. It was the single finest and clearest image of young Lucan Adler ever captured in a photograph.

Holmes's heart was pounding. There were two identical prints in the archival sleeve. Holmes removed one of them, checked with his narrow-beam lantern to make sure that the face was as clear as in the top print, and put that photograph in his inner pocket above his heart. He set the other image back in the proper file and closed and locked the long archival drawers.

He was just leaving the room when he heard voices downstairs.

*　*　*

"…rousting me out of bed in the middle of the night…" a man was saying in an angry voice.

"Not his fault the weather turned rough on the Atlantic…" another man, an older man, was saying.

"…home two days early with no warning…" groused a third and younger man.

"Have to change the linens in the master bedroom, air everything out, check the towels and…" a woman was saying to another woman who kept interrupting with complaints about the late hour.

"The cable didn't say what time in the morning Mr. Adams will be arriving," came the older man's deep voice again. "Let us have everything ready tonight and have everyone back and ready for inspection at seven in the morning. I've ordered Martin to deliver messages to the rest of the staff."

"Damn," whispered Holmes without actually saying the word aloud. He shut off his tiny lantern and tip-toed toward the rear staircase.

The servants—almost certainly the head butler and two other male under-butlers, the housekeeper and at least two of her staff—were coming up the main staircase. Obviously Henry Adams was returning several days early and his diligent staff was making sure everything would be ready for him in the morning.

"Damn," Holmes mouthed again and slipped up the narrow servants' staircase to the rear of the high third floor. With no carpet, the ancient wooden stairs creaked under his weight.

"Hear that?" one of the under-butlers cried from downstairs.

"If it's a burglar, he's going to get an unwelcome surprise," came the head butler's deep voice.

"Shall I send for the police?" asked the head housekeeper.

"No," said the head butler. "William, Charles, get two pokers from the fireplace. Bring one for me. Come with me, William, and we'll check the back rooms and rear staircase."

Most of the third floor was given over to servants' rooms. Holmes had to feel his way in the dark until he found the final staircase—almost steep enough to qualify as a ladder—and as the men stomped and climbed to the second and then third floor below him, calling to one another as they checked rooms, Holmes tip-toed up to the attic. The door to the attic was locked and it took him precious minutes, working in the near absolute darkness, to use his burglar wires and tools to pick that lock. He stepped into the musty attic.

The men had checked all the rooms on the second floor and were converging on the third floor beneath him. Holmes had to risk a light as he shined his lantern in the attic packed with old steamer trunks, a dressmaker's form rising in front of him like a headless corpse, more suitcases, an empty birdcage. He tip-toed away from the door even as the voices grew louder below him and someone started climbing the steep stairway to the attic. Holmes had been playing his narrow beam across the steeply sloped ceiling until he found the inevitable trap door to the roof.

Luckily it was directly above two tall trunks that he clambered up like a ladder. He put his back into lifting the trap door and hoped that the crashing footfalls below would drown out the slight noise it made as it creaked up on hinges.

Then Holmes was outside on the steep and slippery rooftop.

The trap door had opened onto the back side of the sloping roof that faced the backyards and the stables. Giving silent thanks for H. H. Richardson's elaborate care with the quality of the building—thick floorboards that had not transmitted his crepe-soled steps, this triple-thick roof with sturdy tiles—Holmes moved quickly toward the taller pitches and chimneys and gables of John Hay's home.

From H Street and the front of the Adamses' house, the two grand brick homes looked to be contiguous, but in reality Richardson had separated the east wall of Adams's house from the west wall of the Hays' house by a gap of about eighteen inches. Holmes prepared to jump that gap—a narrow black abyss that fell more than fifty feet to the street level—with the full knowledge that the Hays' roof was slightly higher than the Adamses' roof he was jumping from.

Hearing noises at the trap door far behind him, Holmes shut down his imagination and leaped. He slid back down the steep, gabled surface, slipping toward the sheer drop-off to blackness, but stopped his descent by spread-eagling his body and using his toes and fingers and his body's friction against the tiles.

Men were emerging from the trap door in the Adamses' roof.

Holmes slid two feet to his right. The main chimney handling a dozen outlets to Adams's many fireplaces on the east side of his huge house was at this east edge of Adams's rooftop and it was easily twenty feet tall. Holmes kept it between himself and the trap door in order to hide himself from the view of the men emerging onto the Adamses' roof as he scrambled up the much steeper roofline of the north-south gable on the Hays' home. He rolled over the ridgeline of that gable and ducked low just as the head butler and his two assistants reached the east end of the Adamses' roofline and shined their bright lantern along the empty west slopes of the Hays' gables. Part of the tall, triangular façade that faced H Street and Lafayette Square and the White House hid Holmes from view of anyone out there in the night.

When Adams's servants had convinced themselves that no burglar was on their rooftop, they carefully—holding hands at one point—made their way back to and down through the trap door into Adams's attic.

Moving on tip-toe again, only occasionally using his fingertips on the terrible steep rooftop, Holmes went up to the ridgeline and then north along it to where the Hays' rooftop gabled up to its highest point, the highest ridgeline almost seventy feet above the sidewalk level.

Rather than two massive chimney structures—one west, one

east—as on the Adamses' home, the Hays' rooftop sprouted six varying brick chimneys.

Holmes allowed himself to slide down the steep upper roof until he'd planted his rubber-crepe soles against a tall, thin chimney only about a third of the way up on the northwest roofline. He rested there a minute, panting softly, and listened to the lonely clop-clop of a single carriage going down Sixteenth Street.

Someone was moving horses into the Adamses' stables. Holmes had no idea where they'd been stabled during Henry Adams's weeks of traveling, but here were grooms or stable boys returning them to their stalls at two a.m. Various lanterns and at least one glaring electric light illuminated the stable yards, garden, and the entire west rooftop and west side of the chimney behind which Holmes was hiding. He checked his watch and sighed softly.

This had not been his first or second plan for egress from the presumably empty Adams home and return to his own room. But at least he'd *made* a Plan C. While the grooms got the horses settled below, trying to keep their work as quiet as possible, Holmes removed the thick loop of rope from his burglar bag.

It would be embarrassing if he'd not estimated the length of the rope properly. Embarrassing and—from this height—most probably fatal.

Eventually the Adamses' horses were back in their stalls, the lanterns extinguished, and even the glow of light onto the backyard from Adams's kitchen had grown dark, although Holmes guessed that the butlers, housekeeper, and the few other servants there so late tonight were in their rooms sleeping.

Holmes checked his watch again with the briefest flicker of his hand lantern.

Almost four a.m. The Hays' domestics would be rising soon to start their interminable days.

Holmes tapped the photo secure over his heart, secured the lantern in his burglar bag, and then made sure the bag was clasped shut and its strap secured over his head and shoulder. There were two coils of rope, one short and one long and heavy. Years ago, he'd learned the basic art of rappelling in the Alps. Now he looped the shorter strand of rope around the fireplace, tied it off securely with double fisherman knots backed up by overhand knots, and ran his longer rope through this anchor sling at mid-point. Running the double rope between his legs, just under his backside, and out to his right hand in what his first Alpine climbing guide had called the *dulfersitz.*

Firmly holding the doubled line of rope that led to the anchor strap around the chimney in his left hand and the dangling longer strand of doubled rope that made his uncomfortable *dulfersitz,* he carefully let himself down the steep gable to the west edge of the long drop to the Hays' backyard.

That morning—the previous morning, he realized now—and again that afternoon, he'd walked to the rear and sides of the Hays' backyard, nominally to smoke his pipe and think but actually to look up and measure the alignment of this thinnest of the six chimneys directly above his second-floor (by American reckoning) room. Now he had to trust to his estimated measurement even while trusting again that no servant, wandering the halls after midnight, had felt a draft in the hallway and been brazen enough to go into his guest room and shut and latch the window he'd left open. Someday, some repairman on the roof would find his anchor sling, but that was of no concern to Holmes this night. Leaning far back, almost to the horizontal, letting the rappel rope shuffle through his left hand as he wrapped the other length of rope around his right wrist, Holmes walked himself down the side of John Hay's huge brick home, hopping the four feet over the dark window on the third floor that Holmes had ascertained earlier to be an empty servant's bedroom currently being used for storage.

Eventually he was at the second-story window and he bounced far over the upper glass pane—not wanting to have to explain how his own bedroom window was broken in the night—and, after tapping his crepe soles on the lower windowsill, swung himself far enough into his own room to grab the headboard of the heavy brass bed and steady himself.

First setting the photograph of Irene Adler and Lucan Adler carefully on his bedside table, Holmes went back to the open window and pulled the long length of rappel rope down, taking care that it did not strike a lower window when it dangled. Then he pulled it up, coiled it carefully, and set it back in his black burglar bag. The well-tied short length of anchor rope would remain up there.

The night air was cool and he left the window open until the sheen of perspiration he'd worked up in all the climbing, jumping, and rappelling dried off.

Then Holmes took off his burglar clothes—folding them away neatly—washed himself at the basin, got into his nightclothes, and set his watch to tap its small rod against the open cover at nine a.m. He and Henry James were leaving for New York City on the 10:42 a.m. train.

Holmes had left his palm-torch out on the table next to his bed and before falling asleep he activated it and played its narrow beam one last time on the photo marked by Henry Adams as "Old Sweet Springs, June, 1885, Rebecca Lorne and Cousin—Standing in meadow with house in background."

Staring most intensely at the young man's face, Holmes thought at him—*Why did you kill your mother?*

CHAPTER 22

So I had stopped by the office of the *Century* on a whim after our ship docked and was sitting there on their horsehair sofa reading over some early galleys for my new book, *Pudd'nhead Wilson,*" said Clemens, "and what do I discover but that some pragmatical son of a bitch had been mucking about with my punctuation. *My* punctuation, gentlemen! The punctuation which I had so carefully thought out and laboriously perfected! I sat there seeing more of this vandalism until my hot fury turned itself loose and I had a comment for every publisher, editor, secretary, and errand boy in the *Century*'s office. I found as I shouted that the fury had turned itself into a volcano and the words I was using...well, they were not suited to any Sunday school."

"So what happened to the edited copy?" asked Howells.

Clemens lowered his head and peered out from under his bushy eyebrows. "It was explained to me, as one would explain the lower multiplication tables to a drooling idiot, that the culprit proofreader was peerless, imported from no less than Oxford University, and that his word around the *Century* was considered, and I quote, 'sacred, final, and immutable'."

Howells was smiling openly. James showed a hint of a smile and had lowered his chin to his bosom. Holmes sat with his head cocked at a slight angle of polite anticipation.

"So did you have a chat with this just-down-from-Oxford don whose copyedits are 'sacred, final, and immutable'?" asked Howells, who obviously had played straight man to Clemens many times before this.

They were between courses and Clemens was puffing away at a cigar, his brow was furrowed, his bushy eyebrows almost coming together in his anger, his chin firmly set, and upper body imitating that of a bull ready to charge the toreador. He removed the cigar from beneath a full mustache that was turning white.

"I did," said Clemens. "I confronted him in the publisher's office, using the poor man as a witness should an actual homicide occur. I was a volcano. And such an angry volcano that not a single poor wretch in the *Century*'s offices escaped without being scorched. The publisher and his Oxford proofreader were Pompeii and Herculaneum to my Vesuvius."

"What did you say to your punctuation culprit?" Henry James asked in soft tones.

Clemens shifted his fierce stare to the other writer.

"I told both men that I didn't care a fig leaf in Hell if the Oxford Marvel was an Archangel imported directly from heaven, he still could not puke his ignorant impudence over *my* punctuation. I said I wouldn't allow it for a moment. I said I couldn't stand or sit in the same room, in the *presence* of a single proofreader sheet where that brainless blatherskite had left his chicken-manured tracks. By this time, both Herculaneum and Pompeii had backed up all the way to the windows and I had a hunch they were ready to throw themselves out those twelve-story-high portals. So I literally buttonholed the Archangel before he attempted to fly and explained that all this...stuff...must be set up again and my punctuation restored exactly as I had typed it. Then I promised to return there tomorrow, that is today, precisely at noon to read the deodorized proof."

Howells was laughing loudly now. James was smiling as broadly as Holmes had ever seen him. Holmes allowed himself a thin smile.

When the laughter at the table subsided—nearby diners looking over at the table and then murmuring amongst themselves, obviously the curly-haired author now burying his teeth into the Cuban cigar—Howells said, "When did you leave Europe, Sam? And from which port?"

"From Genoa," said Clemens. "On the steamship *Lahn.* Got in, as I said, yesterday morning."

"That was a very rapid crossing," said James.

"The captain said that he knew of a short cut," said Clemens, exhaling rich smoke. "And—by dander—so he did!"

Howells, usually a serious man, Henry James knew, was still laughing and still eager to play the straight man.

"A short cut across the North Atlantic," laughed Howells. "Can you tell us what secret route your captain of the *Lahn* took?"

Clemens leaned back in his chair and crossed his arms. "I fear that I cannot. A small group of perspicacious passengers—with me as their leader, of course—plotted to steal an officer's sextant and thus learn our latitude and longitude."

"Did you carry out your plot?" asked Holmes.

"Indeed we did, sir," answered Clemens. "We simply forgot that none of us knew how to use the device. So after several hours of messing with the clumsy thing, we had succeeded only in pinpointing our precise location either in central Africa or, equally improbable, Saskatchewan."

Howells was howling now, but Clemens never relinquished his bushy-browed scowl.

"There were no clues as to the nature or direction of this trans-Atlantic short cut?" asked James, allowing himself a quick glance at Holmes when he said the word "clues".

"None," said Clemens. "None, I should say, save for the time my fellow passengers and I noticed penguins dancing and frolicking in the ice floes that the *Lahn* was bullying her way through."

"Penguins!" cried Howells and laughed all the harder. Henry James suddenly understood that the serious and often melancholy author, deadly serious editor, and mature citizen who was William Dean Howells used Samuel Clemens's presence as an excuse to become a boy again.

"Naturally we assumed that the penguins were the ship's waiters and doormen, still in their formal attire," said Clemens, "allowed out by the captain for a short period to frolic on the ice."

"No!" cried Howells with tears running down his cheeks. The loud negative seemed more related to an earnest request that Clemens give him a moment to catch his breath.

"Alas, the knowledge of their penguintude was too late," Clemens said in a remorseful tone. "I had given generous tips to three of them. At least one of them had the decency to hide his face under his upper flipper, or wing, or whatever that thing is called."

Howells continued to laugh.

The waiters were bringing their main courses.

*　*　*

On the previous day, Tuesday, March 28, when Holmes had announced to the small group in John Hay's study that the typewriter that had produced the She-was-murdered cards over the past seven years was the same machine that had typed addresses and cards to the Hays from someone named Samuel Clemens, the room had erupted in babble and surprise. It was Hay who explained that Samuel Clemens was the real name for the famous author who wrote under the nom de plume of Mark Twain.

"I must interview him at once," Holmes had said. "Either Hay or James shall accompany me."

"I fear that will not be possible," said Henry James. "I've read over the past few years in the London papers that Mr. Twain...Mr. Clemens...has been, *en famille,* on an extensive tour of Europe—Germany, Switzerland, Italy—since eighteen ninety-one, I believe. Something to do with debts, persistent American creditors, and the strength of the dollar on the Continent. The last I read, Clemens and his family had moved on from Florence and to Bad Neuheim, with Mr. Clemens occasionally taking the baths for his rheumatism."

Holmes looked crestfallen until John Hay said brightly, "Actually, we're in luck. I received a letter from Sam...from Mr. Clemens...only two weeks ago in which he said he'd be sailing from Italy on the twenty-second of this month, bound for New York, to carry out several business meetings. I believe he was eventually going to Chicago, to meet with someone there and to get a preview of the Columbian Exposition, before returning to Europe six weeks from now."

"He'll be in New York?" Holmes asked.

"He should be there—or on the point of arriving there—even as we speak," said Hay.

"We must leave at once," said the detective.

Clara Hay gave her husband a sharp glance and Hay held up his hands. "Alas, I'm too busy this week—socially and otherwise—to take time out for a trip to New York. But I'm sure Harry would enjoy accompanying you. I don't believe that he and Clemens have met yet. And Harry...Sam wrote me that he planned to dine with Howells as soon after he reached New York as he could. Perhaps you could join them."

"Who is Howells?" asked Sherlock Holmes.

"William Dean Howells," said Hay. "He's an old friend of Harry's as well as of Sam's, an author of some renown in his own right, but also a well-known critic. Howells was fiction editor of *The Atlantic Monthly* from 'seventy-one to 'eighty-one—helping not only to publish friends such as Harry and Sam, but to promote them—and wrote a column for *Harper's Weekly* until 'eighty-two."

"Good," said Holmes. "James can introduce me when the three old literary colleagues are chatting and we can ease our way into the Clover Adams business. If you shall be so kind as to cable Howells of our arrival, we shall leave today for New York."

"But..." said James but could come up with no reason for his not going other than his not wanting to do so.

"Clemens might well have taken the typewriter to Europe with him," said Hay.

"Not important," Holmes had said. "The important thing is for Clemens to tell us who had access to his typewriter between December six, eighteen eighty-five, and December six, eighteen eighty-six."

"But that..." began Clara Hay and then stopped. "I see. If the cards were all typed at the same time, you think it must have been between Clover's death and the first anniversary of her death...the first time we all received the typewritten cards."

"Surely you're not considering Samuel Clemens...Mark Twain...as a suspect!" said John Hay.

"Only his typewriter," replied Holmes. "And before we go any further, we must know who had access to it after Clover Adams's death."

"Someone could have typed those cards *before* her death," said Clara Hay.

Holmes had smiled thinly at his hostess. "Perhaps. But that person would also have been her murderer. All the more reason to speak to this Twain-Clemens person as soon as possible." Turning to Henry James, Holmes cried, "Quick, James. Pack some things in your Gladstone bag and let's be off. The game is afoot!"

* * *

"What brings you back to the States, Sam?" Howells was asking.

"Business," growled the man between bites of his prime rib. "All business. Money, debt, and business. Business, debt, and money. Last night I had dinner with Andrew Carnegie."

James, who paid little attention to millionaires or their comings and goings, was still impressed.

"How did that dinner go?" asked Howells.

"Just dandy," said Clemens. "Carnegie wanted to talk to me about yachting, about the price of gold, about the British royal family, about libraries, about my family's experience living in Europe the past few years, about Swiss tutors, and especially—at great length I might say—about his harebrained scheme for the United States to absorb Canada, Ireland, and all of Great Britain into a single American Commonwealth. I, on the other hand, wanted to talk about him lending me some money...or I should say, investing some capital in marvelous and foolproof ventures."

"I trust your conversations were productive," said James.

Clemens's brows came down. "I explained to Carnegie my own investments in Kaolatype, in various other sure-to-be-hits inventions and games, in my publishing house, and especially in Mr. Paige's typesetting machine, which, by itself, to date, for only the Paige typesetter investment, I have poured something like one hundred and ninety thousand dollars into without ever seeing the godda...without seeing the blasted thing work properly for more than two minutes at a time."

"What did Mr. Carnegie say to these investment possibilities?" asked Howells.

"He leaned forward and whispered to me his secret of getting and staying rich," Clemens said in a low, conspiratorial tone of voice.

The three other men at the table, even Holmes, also leaned forward conspiratorially to hear the secret from no less an expert than Andrew Carnegie.

"Carnegie said," whispered Clemens, "and I quote him exactly... 'M'boy, put all your eggs in one basket, *and watch that basket.*'"

While Howells and James laughed and Holmes allowed himself a smile, Sam Clemens continued to scowl. "He was serious," Clemens growled into the laughter.

"Perhaps the Paige typesetter is your basket," said Howells.

Clemens grunted. "If it is, it's a basket without a bottom or handles."

"Why don't you just...how do you Americans put it?...cut your losses and get out?" asked Holmes.

"I've invested too much," growled Clemens. "As a businessman, I give the word 'fool' a bad name. Livy says so. My muscular Christian minister friend Joe Twichell says so. All my friends who are not earlobe-deep in debt say so. But I still hope this Paige machine will be the avenue to my own fortune and to my family's security. The thing not only sets type brilliantly, you see, it automatically justifies...something that no typesetting device on the planet can do. The good news is that forty or fifty of Paige's miracle typesetters are in the process of being produced and *The Chicago Tribune* is going to give one a trial by fire. Before this trip is over, I plan to make the eight-hundred-mile trip to Chicago to talk to Paige. My goal was to dissolve our partnership during that conversation..."

"But James Paige can be very convincing in person," suggested Howells.

"Convincing!" cried Clemens loud enough that a few other diners looked toward his table. "Why, every time I arrange it so that Paige's doomsday moment is nigh, the termination of my investment irrevocable, and my lawsuits against the man shatteringly inevitable, the inventor pitches another bravura performance that would put Edwin Booth to shame—tears, earnest promises, heartfelt assurances, injured dignity, a list of facts and figures that would put a certified accountant into a coma, and all while showing a woeful, profoundly hurt expression that would put a basset hound with hemorrhoids to shame. Why, James Paige could persuade a fish to come out and take a walk with him. No matter how much resolve and determination I stockpile ahead of time for the encounter, whenever I am with Paige I believe him. I can't help it. Livy says that the man is a mesmerist, not an inventor. I say that he is one of the most daring and majestic liars ever to bilk a hard-earned fortune out of a hard-working author. One ends up giving him another fifteen or twenty or fifty thousand dollars just for the quality of his performance."

There was an uncomfortable silence broken only by the change of plates by the waiters and then Howells cleared his throat.

Holmes had heard of William Dean Howells, had even read one of his novels, and found little unusual in the writer-editor-critic's appearance: stolid form, short-cut hair thinning on the front and top to the extent that Howells combed a few curly strands forward, a full mustache turning white, an intelligent gaze, and a soft voice.

"Do you know, for me this is a most important—one might almost say 'historical'—evening," said Howells.

"Why is that?" asked Clemens. "Because of the overpriced mediocrity of this somewhat decrepit claret?"

Howells ignored that comment. "Tonight two of my most famous authors, and two of my oldest and dearest of friends, are dining with me. I was beginning to think it would never come about."

"I've read," said Henry James, "that Mark Twain and I are as opposite, in all things literary, as the North and South Poles."

"I have never understood that bromide," said Clemens. "Certainly from what we know of the Arctic and what they are now calling the Antarctic, the poles must be far more alike than different. So saying that we are Howells's poles would mean that we're both cold, barren, impossibly distant, impossible to reach, and dangerous to travelers."

"However that may be," said James, determined not to be sidetracked by Sam Clemens's nonsense, "you, Howells, especially during your years at *The Atlantic Monthly,* have managed to make literary successes of both of us."

"Nonsense," said Howells, flicking away the tribute with his well-manicured fingers. "You both were destined for literary immortality. It was simply my honor to publish and write essays about your work."

"You often didn't sign the critical essays of praise that you printed in your own magazine even while our books were being serialized there, Howells," laughed Clemens, obviously, in James's estimate, feeling the wine. "I appreciated it, as I'm sure did Mr. James, but if there were an Editors' Board of Ethics and Review..."

"You know, Mr. Clemens," interrupted James before the joke could hatch into a full insult, "I actually met you—or at least shook hands with you—once before this."

"Upon what occasion?" asked Clemens. They were now on the post-dinner wine-and-cigars course and James could see that Mark Twain was enjoying both vices as he worked to focus his eyes a little better on James.

"December fifteen, eighteen seventy-four," said James. "There was a grand dinner in the Parker House in Boston to celebrate *The Atlantic's* first year under its new owners. You were there, Mr. Howells..." James turned toward his host and nodded.

"And so were many other well-known authors—now published in *The Atlantic*—as well as editors, various dons from Harvard and Princeton, architects, clergymen—although not the Reverend Henry Ward Beecher that evening..."

"Ah," said Clemens. "That was in the early days of the Elizabeth Tilton scandal, was it not? Alas, poor Beecher...I knew him, Horatio...his sister Harriet was my neighbor at Nook Farm in Hartford. Poor Henry Ward had all those ladies in love with him—or at least with his preaching voice—and then most of the leading suffragettes turned against him like harpies during the scandals: Elizabeth Cady Stanton, Victoria Woodhull, even his other sister, Isabella Beecher Hooker. They all wanted his hide."

"But his other sister, your neighbor in Hartford, Harriet stuck by him, did she not?" said Howells.

"She did," said Clemens. "Until the end. And since it's been six years this month since Reverend Beecher died of that sudden stroke, I raise a glass to him and to all poor men who are punished so by harridans and harpies for such venial sins."

All four men solemnly drank their toast to Beecher and his adultery.

The other tables there in the restaurant of the hotel were empty. The waiters were standing, visibly waiting, their gloved hands folded over their crotches. James knew that the evening was over and that he had to speak now or lose the opportunity.

"Mr. Clemens," he said. "Howells mentioned that you were traveling up to Hartford tomorrow."

"Yes," said Clemens. "A necessity. Money, debt, and business. Just for the day though. I'll be returning to Dr. Rice's tomorrow evening."

James knew that Clemens was currently the house guest of Dr. Clarence C. Rice, an ear-and-throat specialist who included amongst his famous clients Miss Lillian Russell, the aging actor—referred to earlier by Clemens—Edwin Booth, and Enrico Caruso.

"We wondered if Mr. Sherlock Holmes and I might travel to Hartford with you," said James. "And perhaps convince you to stop by your home there on Farmington Avenue."

Clemens stared as if he'd been asked to swallow a snake.

"Would you happen to know if your typewriter is still at your Hartford house?" Holmes asked quickly.

Clemens turned his head to look at the detective. "My typewriter?"

"We mentioned earlier that certain cards typed on that machine have been coming to Henry Adams, John and Clara Hays, and Clarence King for the years since Clover Adams's death. It might help me in my investigation if I were to see the actual machine."

"Your investigation?" repeated Clemens. He leaned closer to Holmes. "I have been polite so far this evening, but I do have to ask...are you *really* Sherlock Holmes? The 221 B Baker Street Sherlock Holmes? The 'Come, Watson, the game's afoot!' Sherlock Holmes?"

"I am," said Holmes.

"Well then you...and James, and you, too, Howells, if you're not doing anything important...are welcome to travel up to Hartford with me tomorrow, and perhaps we'll be able to get into the house if I cable ahead—it's being leased, you know—but first, Mr. Holmes, you must answer a most pressing question that has been haunting me all through this evening's fine meal and frivolity."

"I shall if I am able," said Holmes.

Clemens leaned even closer to the detective. "The question is simply this, sir...are you real, or are you a fictional character?"

"That is one of the things I am attempting to determine in this case of Clover Adams and the Five of Hearts," said Holmes.

Clemens looked at him and said no more.

Howells gestured for the bill, they paid, and—since James and Holmes were staying overnight at this hotel, the Hotel Glenham on Broadway—the two men walked Clemens and Howells to the cabs waiting at the curb.

"Come, Howells," said Clemens, "we'll take this one and I'll drop you on the way to Dr. Rice's place."

"But it is out of the way..." protested Howells.

"In the cab, sir," said Clemens. "It would be unseemly for two gentlemen of our age and station to be arrested for wrestling on the curb at this hour of the night." He turned his dangerous gaze on James and Holmes. "It's a fool's errand you're on, gentlemen, but this Great Fool always welcomes other fools for company. I'll meet you all tomorrow at Grand Central Station at nine a.m."

CHAPTER 23

William Dean Howells accompanied them to Hartford that Thursday—Holmes was not sure why, since he assumed Howells had a full business day in New York—and the dreary passing countryside was surpassed only by the dreariness of the conversation. In that one railway trip, Sherlock Holmes learned more about the business of writing and publishing than he could ever use.

Clemens and the usually reticent James had been agreeing vocally while Howells mostly listened and Holmes tried to catch a nap.

"Publishing is changing rapidly, and not for the best," Clemens was saying.

"I agree," said James.

"The magazines want a new type of story, if they want stories at all," said Clemens.

"I heartily agree," said James. "My number of short story sales has dropped off abysmally. A writer of short fiction can no longer make a living."

"And subscription novels—once my livelihood and the bread and butter of my own publishing house—are disappearing."

"Too true, Mr. Clemens."

"So where in blazes are we to find our wages?" demanded Clemens between puffs on his Havana cigar. "Even serialized novels are disappearing from the magazines."

"Very difficult to place, very difficult," murmured James.

"Henry," said Howells, his tired eyes coming alive. "Do you remember about nine years ago—I *think* it was early in 'eighty-four—when my *The Rise of Silas Lapham* was being serialized in the *Century* at the same time as your *The Bostonians*?"

"I was deeply honored that my modest early effort was sharing space with your masterpiece," said James. William Dean Howells nodded his appreciation for the compliment.

Holmes noticed a very subtle, quite hidden, but still—to him—noticeable expression come over Henry James's face. The look, gone before it could be seen for a certainty, reminded Holmes of a proper little girl who was going to say or do something mischievous.

"Mr. Clemens," said James, "did you by any chance ever happen to read *The Bostonians*?"

A strange, embarrassed look came over the confident Clemens. "Ah...no, sir...Mr. James, I've not yet had that pleasure."

"I ask," said James very softly, with more than a hint of a smile, "because an English friend mentioned to me that he'd been at a banquet in Boston around that time—eighteen eighty-four, I believe—during which you said from the podium, and I think I am quoting you properly, 'I would rather be damned to John Bunyan's heaven than to read *The Bostonians*.'"

Holmes was astounded at Henry James's bold frontal attack on Clemens. Holmes had only known James for a short time, but everything he had observed in the writer's demeanor—*everything*—suggested that James would avoid controversy at almost any price, and if forced to react would do so by the most subtle suggestion and most shaded ironical nuance. Yet here he was coming at Clemens like Admiral Nelson at the French or Spanish fleets—straight at 'em.

Also astounded, it was obvious, was Samuel Clemens/Mark Twain. The other writer's face, so animated by dramatic scowls or controlled expressions of exaggerated surprise or joy in every other exchange Holmes had seen, now bore a look as blank and open and pathetically embarrassed as any 11-year-old boy caught with his hand in the cookie jar.

"I...he...I..." stammered Clemens, his cheeks and nose looking as though they might burst any second from exploding capillaries, "it doesn't . . . I certainly did not mean . . . *podiums* . . . *banquets!*" The last two words were launched in a tone of disgust emphasized by Clemens waving his hand as if wafting away a noxious odor. Clemens worked to light a new cigar, bending to focus all his energy on the business, even though he had two-thirds of one still burning in the ashtray.

Holmes could see by William Dean Howells's paled and absolutely frozen face that he had been the one to carry original word of the insult to James almost a decade ago.

James let a few more delicious seconds of this heavily weighted silence pass before he said, "But, sir, many readers—including this one after sufficient time had passed—fully agreed with you on the faults of *The Bostonians.* And I fully and heartily agree with you, sir, that it would be the worst sort of Hell to be damned to John Bunyan's heaven."

*   *   *

For a while the silence ruled. Clemens held his cigar, James and Howells smoked their cigarettes, and Holmes puffed away at his pipe. The four men peered at each other through a strained but collegial blue haze.

"Henry," said Howells after clearing his throat, "you have diversified, as the businessmen say, into the theater, have you not?"

James nodded modestly. "Three years ago, at Mr. Edward Compton's request, I adapted my novel *The American* into a play. The novel was not entirely suited to dramatization, but writing and revising the play gave me much needed theatrical experience."

"Did it reach the stage?" asked Clemens.

"Yes," said James. "And with some success. Both in the provinces and eventually in London. The next drama I write will be done exclusively for the theater and will not be an adaptation. In some ways, to be candid, I feel that I have finally found my true form. I find dramatical writing, with its emphasis *on the scene,* much more interesting than the novel or short fiction, do you not?"

Clemens grunted. "I adapted my book *The Gilded Age* into a play, known by most folks as *Colonel Sellers* because of the strength of the main character, played by John T. Raymond. Do you know Raymond, Mr. James?"

"I've not met him or seen any of his plays," said James.

"He was a perfect Colonel Sellers," said Clemens. "This was during the Grant presidency, and President Grant attended one of the New York performances and friends of mine told me that one could hear the president laughing all the way to the rear balcony rows."

"It was a comedy then?" said James.

"In part," said Clemens. "Certainly John T. Raymond made it so. I would have appreciated it if he had played his famous turnip-eating scene more in the spirit of the pure pathos of poverty which I'd intended rather than the broad comedy Raymond made of it. But I cannot complain. *Colonel Sellers* netted ten thousand dollars in its first three months and I imagine that it will make me seventy-five or a hundred thousand dollars before it, or I, or both of us together, die of old age."

There was another silence then amongst the four men as the vulgarity of someone stating how much money he'd made from a job was left to drift away slowly with the cigar, cigarette, and pipe smoke. Holmes looked at Samuel Clemens with his most analytical gaze. Much of Holmes's job depended upon reading people as much as reading clues. Coming to a decision on the quality of a person or the veracity of his statements or the solidity of his personality led to more revelations in detective work than did the inspection of footprints or types of cigarette ash left behind. Clemens, Holmes saw, used vulgarity as a device—not only to shock his audience (and everyone around him was, always, his audience), but to move beyond that shock at obvious vulgarity to some (hoped-for) higher level of humor or farce.

Or at least to Clemens it would seem a higher level.

As if reading Holmes's thoughts, Clemens removed the cigar from his mouth and leaned forward into the circle of men facing each other. "What about you, Mr. James? What do you think of seeking one's fortune by writing for mere actors?"

James smiled. "I have friends who would say that such money is tainted."

"By Jove, it *is* tainted!" cried Clemens in a loud voice while slapping his knee. All of the boy's embarrassment and guilt was gone now, replaced by a boy's enthusiasm. "The kind of wealth being made these days by writing for the stage by, say, that Irishman Oscar Wilde is *twice* tainted!"

"Twice tainted?" echoed Henry James.

"Twice tainted," repeated Clemens. "Tain't yours, and certainly tain't mine."

* * *

Hartford was a dreary one-business town—insurance companies on every other dreary corner and no civic architecture of any significance—but by the time the brougham carrying the four men to Nook Farm turned onto Farmington Avenue, Holmes and James could see the beauty of Mark Twain's old neighborhood.

The houses were large but distinct from one another, obviously designed by architects with their particular clients' dreams and desires in mind. Each lot covered several acres and, while a house might put an iron fence around some of the front yard to separate it from the paved and gently curving avenue, the larger properties themselves tended to blend together in forest and glade with no proprietary fencing.

"See that gazebo?" said Clemens, pointing into the trees between two fine homes. "Harriet Beecher Stowe and I shared the expense of building that since it sits right on the invisible line between our properties. She and I would meet there often on a warm summer day or brisk autumn morning to swap yarns and discuss the inevitable decline of Western Civilization."

"Is she still living?" asked Holmes. *Uncle Tom's Cabin* had run on the stage in London literally for decades since his boyhood.

"Oh, yes," said Clemens. "Almost eighty-two now, I believe, and still as gracious and cussed as ever. The little woman, as President Lincoln said upon first meeting her, whose book started the great war."

Their brougham paused to let two builders' wagons slowly pass and since they were still gazing at the gazebo amidst the trees, Clemens went on, "Some nights when I couldn't sleep, I'd steal out to sit on the railing in the gazebo and smoke and admire the stars or moonlight. Often I'd find Mrs. Stowe already there. We'd talk 'til almost dawn, two happy insomniacs."

"One must wonder," said Henry James, "what two writers of such major accomplishment and diverse talents would discuss in the starlight or moonlight. The nature of evil? The past and future of the black race in America? Thoughts on literature or dramaturgy?"

"Mostly," said Clemens, taking the cigar from his mouth, "we talked about our aches and pains. Especially before *Mr.* Stowe died in 'eighty-six. She'd tell me hers; I'd tell 'er mine."

Holmes saw Howells smile at this. Obviously some Sam Clemens story was imminent while they waited for the dray wagons to rumble past.

"I remember one night," said Clemens between blue puffs, "when she listed her aches and pains, sure that they must signify imminent mortality...the darling lady was almost as hypochondriacal as I was...when I was amazed to hear that her problems exactly matched a recent list of my own...and a list of pains and symptoms of which I had just been cured!"

Holmes folded his arms. The dray wagons were past and now their brougham turned onto a paved lane that curved up a gentle hill.

"I told her..." continued Clemens. "I told her...'Harriet,' I said...'my doctor just cured me of precisely those ailments. Precisely!' 'What medicine did he prescribe?' asked little Mrs. Stowe. 'Why, no medicines at all!' says I. 'My doctor just told me to take a two-month sabbatical from my habits of heavy drinking, constant smoking, and exploding into wild bouts of profanity in irregular but frequent intervals.' I told her, 'Harriet, you give up cussin', drinkin', and smokin' for a couple of months and you'll be right as rain.'"

Clemens peered at them through the smoke, making sure that they were still absorbed in his tale.

"'Mr. Clemens!' cried she. 'I have never partaken of any of those terrible behaviors.' 'Never?' says I, and I can tell you, gentlemen, I was shocked. 'Never,' says Harriet Beecher Stowe, gathering her shawl around her because the night was nippy. 'Well then, my dear lady,' I broke it to her with infinite sadness, 'there is no hope for you. You are a balloon going down and you have no ballast to cast overboard. *You have neglected your vices.*'"

The brougham stopped at the crest of a rise and there was Samuel Clemens's former home. Although he still owned it, he explained, for the last two years he and Livy had leased it to a certain John Day and his wife Alice, the daughter of Isabella Hooker, for a much-needed two hundred dollars a month. Clemens said that he'd cabled ahead and John and Alice would be out this afternoon; the house was theirs for the time-being.

Stepping out of the carriage, Holmes looked at the house. The sunlight created a rich mixture of shade and colors on three stories of salmon-colored bricks. The steeply pitched gables along with five balconies gave the large home a bit of a castle look. Its main window was on a two-story tower and overlooked the porte cochère over the driveway.

Clemens saw where the detective was gazing. "Some have written or said that I wanted that bit to resemble a riverboat's pilot house," he said, stubbing his last cigar out on the curb. "But I didn't. That wasn't the plan at all. It's just, as they say, a happy coincidence."

Clemens fetched a key from a flower pot on the front porch, unlocked the door, and swept it open for them to enter.

A few yards down the hallway they could peer into the main rooms and Holmes knew that it was a home dedicated to good taste and quality items. Sherlock Holmes's bachelor bedroom and sitting room at 221 B Baker Street might be a toss-about mess—*was* a toss-about mess when Mrs. Hudson wasn't interfering—with everything thrown and dropped rather than folded and placed, but Holmes knew attractive domestic order when he saw it. He was seeing it now.

"Nineteen rooms, seven bathrooms," Clemens was saying as if he were a real estate man intent upon selling the house to them. "All the bathrooms with flush toilets, which was a curiosity in its day. Speaking tubes so that anyone can talk to anyone from any floor. In this parlor—enter, gentlemen—you see Hartford's first telephone in its particular little niche there. Since I was one of the first to install the infernal device, there were precious few other telephonic interlocutors I might talk to.

"Here's the drawing room...the stencil designs on the walls were from Lockwood de Forest."

"A partner in the firm begun by Mr. Tiffany," added Howells.

"This little solar conservatory area was where my girls would put on their plays," said Clemens, gesturing to an area filled with plants. "You see how the drapes can be drawn across here like a theater curtain." Clemens paused and then seemed to look at the room and peer into the adjoining rooms for the first time.

"This is...strange," he said in a choked voice. "For the first year or so we were abroad, Livy and I had all the furniture, carpets, vases, beds, knick-knacks in storage, but when John and Alice leased the place, rather than have the young couple furnish such a large house, we got everything out of storage for them...for a small additional fee. But..."

Clemens walked into the library and returned to the drawing room. Above the broad, carved mantel in front of them was a window looking out onto the yard from above the fireplace. Clemens patted it. "This was my idea. Few things are cozier than sitting inside on a winter day with one's family, watching the snow fall just above the crackling fire." He touched little carvings and vases set along the mantel and atop the bookcases on either side.

"John and Alice have placed everything *just* as we had it," he said in that strange voice. "Every vase and carpet that Livy and I had purchased on our early travels. Every beloved-by-the-children carving and knick-knack." He touched one of the carved pieces on the mantel. "You see, every Saturday, Susy and Jean and Clara would demand stories about various ornaments and paintings that stood on these top shelves and on this mantelpiece. At one end of the procession, you see, was a framed oil painting of a cat's head; at the other end was a head of a beautiful young girl, life size, called *Emmeline,* an impressionist watercolor. Between the one picture and the other there were twelve or fifteen of the bric-a-brac things...oh, and also an oil painting by Elihu Vedder, the *Young Medusa.* So my little girls required me to construct a romance—always impromptu—not a moment's preparation permitted—and into that romance I had to get all that bric-a-brac and the three pictures. I had to start always with the cat and finish with *Emmeline.* I was never allowed the refreshment of a change, end for end. It was not permissible to introduce a bric-a-brac ornament into the story out of its place in the procession. These bric-a-bracs were never allowed a peaceful day, a re-poseful day, a restful Sabbath. In their lives there was no Sabbath. In their lives there was no peace. They knew no existence but a monotonous career of violence and bloodshed. In the course of time the bric-a-brac and the pictures showed wear. It was because they had had so many and such violent adventures in their romantic careers."

"Good practice for a writer," chuckled Howells.

"The stories often included a circus," said Clemens. He hadn't seemed to have heard Howells. He didn't seem to remember that the other men were in the room with him.

"The girls truly loved stories about a circus and so I usually wove a circus into..."

Clemens seemed stunned. He took a few staggering steps and collapsed more than sat in a flowery chair.

"Sam?" said Howells.

"I'm all right," said Clemens, shielding his eyes with his hand as if hiding tears. "It's just that... it is only, you see, that everything is in its proper place."

The others stood without knowing what to say.

"I promised Livy that even though I had to see old Hartford friends about investing in some of my endeavors, I would not get close enough to the Farmington Avenue house even to see its high chimney. But as soon as I entered the front door here I was seized with a furious desire to have my entire family in this house again... and right away... and never go outside the grounds of here and Nook Farm anymore forever. Certainly never again to Europe."

Clemens lowered his hand and looked around him as if in a dream.

"Everything in its place. Everything that Livy and I so treasured and shopped for and debated purchasing and celebrated in what now feels like our youth. When the girls were babies or toddlers or wee ones."

He turned and looked directly into the eyes of Howells, then James, and finally Holmes.

"How ugly, tasteless, repulsive are all the domestic interiors I have ever seen in Europe, gentlemen. Compare that baroque awfulness with the perfect taste of this ground floor, with its delicious dream of harmonious color and its all-pervading spirit of peace and serenity and deep, deep contentment. This is simply nothing more than the loveliest home that ever was."

"It *is* beautiful, Sam," said Howells.

It was as if Clemens hadn't heard him speak. "Somehow, through some dark, malevolent enchantment, I had wholly forgotten our home's olden aspect," he said softly, speaking to himself. "This...*this*..." Clemens simultaneously slapped his palms on the arms of his chair and brought his polished shoes down hard on the floor, although he meant to signify neither in its isolation. "This place, to me, gentlemen, is bewitchingly bright and splendid and homelike and natural and it seems at this moment as if I have just burst awake out of a long and hellish dream. It is, gentlemen, as if I have never been away and that I will turn my head..."

He did so toward the stairway.

"...and see my dearest Livy drifting down out of those dainty upper regions with the little children tagging after her." He looked at them each in turn again. "But I feel in my heart that it is not to be. That it is *never* to be."

No one spoke after this.

Clemens passed his hands over his eyes again and stood abruptly. "Enough of this nonsense," he said, voice harsh. "Let us get up to the billiards room on the third floor where I kept my typewriter...that instrument of the Devil around which Mr. Holmes's murder investigation pivots so ingeniously."

CHAPTER 24

James and Howells were trailing behind Clemens and Holmes and on the second-story landing, Howells touched James's sleeve to bring him to a stop.

"That was Sam and Livy's bedroom," whispered Howells, pointing to a door at the far end of the hall as Clemens and Holmes climbed out of sight to the third floor. "In Italy they'd bought this amazingly large bed with such an intricately carved headboard that Sam and Livy always put their pillows at the footboard end so, Sam would say, that staggeringly expensive headboard would be the last thing they'd see at night and the first thing they'd see in the morning. John and Alice Day provided their own bed, so Sam and Livy's carved wonder is still in storage."

James nodded, but Howells's soft grip on his forearm continued.

Using his free hand to point to another door far down the hallway, Howells whispered, "That was always my room when I visited. Many's the time that I would awake to some stealthy sound at one, two, even three o'clock in the morning only to peer out and see Sam in his night-shirt carrying a billiards cue . . . walking the halls in search of a playmate as it were."

"Did you accommodate him?" whispered James.

"Almost always," said Howells with a soft chuckle. "Almost always."

Clemens's voice suddenly roared down the stairway—"Are you two coming up, or are you busy ransacking through drawers down there in search of treasure? I need someone to play billiards with. The World's

Foremost Consulting Detective doesn't know how to play the game and refuses to be taught!"

*   *   *

Henry James made mental notes of the American writer's billiards room. The inward-sloping walls—this room was at the top of the tallest tower rising from the home—had been painted a light red that bordered on pink. The room was dominated by the five-foot-by-ten-foot billiards table, and James noticed that it was one of the more recently designed pocket-billiards tables with the six holes and external pockets of gold cloth and tassels at each corner and halfway down each long side. The billiards pockets gave a sense of Christmas-stocking celebration to the room, and the sloping ceilings made it feel like what it was—a playroom in a high attic.

The floor was completely carpeted over with a Persian rug that boasted patches of more (and brighter) red amongst its intricate designs. A brick fireplace on the far wall was offset from the center of the table and room and James could imagine how cozy this small, high room could be in the winter or on a chilly and stormy summer night. Next to the fireplace was a rough-hewn and open-faced storage cabinet rising about five feet high. There were still a few stacks of papers and books in it.

A few feet beyond the far end of the billiards table was a table with an oil lamp on it, but actual lighting at night would be provided by the four large, upward-opening gas lamps suspended low over the table on a four-spoke brass chandelier. Beyond both the billiards table and writing table was a door opening out to one of the balconies; sunlight poured in through the fan light over that door, through the tall lights on either side of it, and through smaller square windows low to the floor.

There was no door on the wall to James's left as he entered, but the tall, fan-light-topped windows there were of stained glass with its central design showing crossed pool cues, a smoldering cigar between the cues, and a foam-topped glass mug of beer above the center of the crossed cues.

"My family crest," said Clemens, who had already lighted a fresh cigar and was pacing back and forth between the fireplace and the billiards table, a cue stick in his hand. "Shakespeare's family crest boasted only a sort of sickly looking pen against what Ben Jonson called a mustardy background. Mine is better, I think."

James noticed that the theme of crossed cue sticks was also repeated on the painted ceiling. In the far left corner, in front of one of the low, square windows, was a smaller table with the typewriter and what looked to be some lead typesetting slugs on it. Holmes was already there.

"May I put this machine on that table and try it out?" asked Holmes.

Clemens just flicked a fast glance to his left. "By all means." He removed the cigar and stared at Howells and James. "Now, Mr. James, would you join me in a fast game of pocket billiards to decide who is the Anglo-American Literary Billiards Champion of the World?"

"Alas," demurred James, "I do not play. Have never played. I would never risk vandalizing that perfect field of green baize by attempting to learn to play today."

"No?" said Clemens, audibly disappointed. "Are you sure, sir? In all of its many versions, billiards is most amusing and satisfactory you see, and when I play badly and lose my temper it shall almost certainly amuse you. Unless, of course, you are one of those blue-light Methodist preacher sorts who find oaths, epithets, blasphemies, and inventive obscenities objectionable."

James held his hand up, palm out, and seemed to underline his rejection by taking a step backward. He noticed the mismatched furniture in the room: a few more small tables, wicker chairs, rocking chairs, and a couple of what he thought of as Wild West Saloon Chairs. He chose one of the few upholstered chairs to his left and sat.

"Very well," exhaled Clemens with a cloud of smoke. "Howells, old foe, dear friend, fine foil, it is just you and me…again."

Howells went around to choose a cue stick from where they were propped against the wall to the left of the fireplace.

"Please observe," said Sherlock Holmes, "that the blank, white card I am placing in the typewriter is identical in size, texture, and cotton content to the one received by Henry Adams, the Hays, and Clarence King every December on the anniversary of Clover Adams's death. Ned

Hooper also received one each year before his untimely death this last December."

"How do you know it's the same cotton content and all that?" asked Clemens.

"I took the liberty of analyzing the card under my microscope and with some portable chemical apparatus I'd brought to Washington with me," said the detective.

Holmes centered the card and typed a few words. For a moment, everyone gathered behind him.

                    She was murdered.

The detective had set out six of the cards received by the Hays and one on loan from Clarence King and now he set the new card flush below each of the old ones.

"You see," said Holmes, "this chip in the 'a', this tendency in each card for the 'r' to be above the bottom alignment, the shape and increasing murkiness within the closed loop of the 'd', and the common opacity within the angles of the 'w'."

No one said anything. Now that his attention had been brought to the small imperfections, James could see them as a product of this machine. He also noticed that each small problem was more distinct on the card Holmes had just typed.

Holmes seemed to read his mind. "Use has somewhat exaggerated these nicks and alignment problems," said the detective. "Since the original seven cards we have here look exactly the same, I would deduce that they were all typed at the same time, necessarily at least seven years ago since the Hays, King, and presumably Mr. Adams all received their first card on six December eighteen eighty-six."

Clemens thrust out his fists, wrists close together as if awaiting hand manacles. "I confess. I will go peacefully."

Holmes twitched an impatient shadow of a smile. "I presume, Mr. Clemens, that it would not have been difficult, say during the daytime, for one of your house guests to come into your billiards room and spend a few minutes typing a few dozen cards?"

"Certainly it's possible," said Clemens, putting the cigar between his teeth and striding back to the billiards table. "Even at night, no one save for me would have noticed the sound of typing and been curious."

James cleared his throat. "You had no need for your typewriting machine while you have been in England and Europe the last few years?" he asked.

"Obviously not," said Clemens, leaning forward over the edge of the table and positioning his cue in that odd but graceful sprawl of arms and elbows. "The last few years in Europe, I have written longhand once again and—in the few instances I wanted a typed version of any of my manuscripts—I hired a stenographer who provided the machine along with his or her note-taking skills."

"Could I impose upon you, Mr. Clemens," said Holmes, "to provide me with the names and last-known addresses of all the servants who worked for you here in eighteen eighty-six?"

"The list will be somewhere here in the house," grumbled Clemens. "I shall find it for you before we leave today. May we resume our game now?"

"By all means," said Holmes.

Clemens smashed the white ball into a random cluster of waiting balls. Three of those he'd struck with his ball or which had been struck in ricochet went into three of the pockets. Clemens straightened up and put chalk on the end of his cue as Howells frowned and leaned over the table.

"In billiards, that's called nigger luck," said Clemens.

"Did you keep a guest book from eighteen eighty-five until you began your travels?" asked Holmes.

"Yes," said Clemens. "I don't believe we packed them away and John and Alice Day keep their own guest book. There's a drawer in that table at which you're sitting, Mr. Holmes—yes, just lift up that tablecloth a bit..."

Holmes removed four leather-bound 8 x 12 journals or ledgers.

"May I..." began the detective.

Clemens nodded.

Howells struck the white ball and it caromed off two other balls and two of the side cushions before being the only ball to go in a pocket. "Heck and spit and damnation," muttered the former editor.

"I'll rack them up properly and we'll start again," Clemens said to Howells. "I don't know why I've come to enjoy pocket billiards more than the carom billiards that stole so much of my youthful time, energy, and fortune. Most of the tables in England and Europe don't even *have* pockets."

While Clemens retrieved the white ball and shoved the others toward the point on the table where a wooden triangle waited, Holmes said, "Mr. Clemens, you and your family had many hundreds of visitors . . . per year it looks like."

"Yes, well . . . ." said Clemens and just trailed off in whatever he was going to say. "I have nothing to hide, Mr. Holmes. I am serene in knowing that I have stealthily excised the pages on which Madame Lafarge and Her Writhing Pack of Belly-Dancing Virgins have written their names and left their comments on the visit."

Holmes looked up from the four books filled with their hundreds of scrawls. "Perhaps, if it might be possible . . ."

"Yes, yes," said Clemens. "Those four guest books cover eighteen eighty-five until we all sailed in June of eighteen ninety-one. All the names of all our overnight guests are there. Take the books with you, but make sure that Hay returns them to me in pristine condition. For I am certain, you see, that someday my biographers will have much need to refer to those guest books after they're done with the immediate task of blotting the spot where I leave off."

"Thank you," muttered Holmes, "but I won't need to borrow the guest books. Merely memorize the December 'eighty-five pages and all of the eighteen eighty-six." Holmes began flipping through the pages of names and comments, running his finger down each page.

"You can *memorize* those hundreds of signatures and comments merely by looking at them once?" asked Clemens. His tone sounded dubious to James's ear.

Holmes's finger paused and he looked up at the others. "Unfortunately, my memory has been like this since I was a small boy. If I see something, I can call it back at any time. It is more of a curse than gift."

"But it must be wonderfully handy in your line of work," said Howells.

"At times, quite so," said Holmes. "But it took me years to learn how to deliberately forget things which were of no use to me."

"Remind me never to play poker with you, Mr. Holmes," said Sam Clemens.

But Holmes had immersed himself in the 1886 guest book again, his finger rapidly sliding down page after page.

Clemens shrugged and gestured toward Howells, who leaned forward, got the white ball in his sights, and rocketed it into the triangle of clustered spheres. Balls rolled and caromed everywhere. One went in. Howells continued—sinking a second, then third before failing to get any in a hole on his fourth attempt.

"I presume we are playing eight ball, Sam," Howells said.

"Ah hah!" said Clemens, flicking ash into a waiting bowl. "Assumptions are dangerous, Howells! In truth we're shooting straight pool—fifteen points wins."

"What can you tell me about billiards technique based on what I have seen so far?" asked Henry James as Clemens lined up his next shot.

"Well," said Clemens, "from observing both Howells and me, you can see that if your ball glides along in the intense and immediate vicinity of the object ball, and a score seems exquisitely imminent, you must lift one leg; then one shoulder; then squirm your body around in sympathy with the direction of the moving ball; and at the instant when the ball seems on the point of colliding, you must throw up both your arms violently. Your cue will probably break a chandelier and then catch fire from the exposed gas jet, as Howells has demonstrated here in this very room so many times, but no matter; you have done what you could to help the final score."

* * *

The game proceeded, Clemens evidently winning, when suddenly Holmes finished scanning the thick guest book, slammed it shut, and said, "You had Rebecca Lorne and her cousin as guests in February of 'eighty-six!"

"Lorne? Lorne?" said Clemens, his head snapping up with its lion's mane of white hair. "Oh, yes, I remember the woman and her shy cousin…what was his name? Carlton? No…Clifton. 'Clif' with one 'f' as Miss Lorne called him. I couldn't have told you that it was in February of 'eighty-six, not so soon after Clover Adams's suicide."

"How did you know them?" asked Holmes.

"Oh, I'd met Miss Lorne the previous summer…no, early autumn, just after Congress had convened…while I was staying with Hay and Adams for a few days as I lobbied before a congressional committee for my copyrights. She was spending quite a bit of time with Mrs. Adams…with Clover…as I recall. Henry Adams was beside himself with worry about Clover's unhappiness…it's why I shifted my visit from his home to Hay's…and it seemed as if Rebecca Lorne was the only friend who visited her on a regular basis during that dark time."

"But how did she and her cousin Clifton end up spending a night with you here in Hartford two months after Clover's death?" asked Holmes. "Had you struck up a separate friendship or habit of correspondence with Miss Lorne and her cousin?"

"Heavens no!" said Clemens. "As I remember, the two simply dropped by one Sunday to pay their respects. A Sunday in the middle of the month as I recall."

"The fourteenth of February," said Holmes, whose gray-eyed stare was so intense that it might have frightened Clemens if the humorist-writer hadn't been staring into space as he tried to remember Rebecca Lorne and her visit.

"That's right," said Clemens. "But you must remember, Detective, that this was more than seven years ago. Miss Lorne and her cousin Clifton stopped by to pay their respects since they, or at least Rebecca Lorne, were aware that I'd known Clover Adams for years and they ended up having to spend the night because of a terrible snowstorm that swept in that afternoon. I remember that Livy insisted they stay with us rather than try to get to the train station. I believe they were going to Boston at the time…not just visiting, as I recall, but in the process of moving there from Washington."

Clemens leaned on his cue stick, getting blue rosin on his cuff, and fixed Holmes with a stare almost as intense as the gaze the detective had shown only a moment earlier. "Why this interest in Miss Lorne, Mr. Holmes? Is she a...suspect...in this investigation of yours?"

"She is an unknown factor, Mr. Clemens," said Holmes, not shrinking from the writer's formidable gaze. "Mrs. Adams...Clover...had known Rebecca Lorne for only a year, yet they seemed the most intimate of friends in the weeks and months before Mrs. Adams's apparent suicide."

"*Apparent* suicide?" barked Clemens. "How could it be anything *but* suicide, Mr. Holmes? Henry Adams himself found her body, still warm after drinking the cyanide from her photographic developing potions."

"With Miss Rebecca Lorne waiting outside the house," said Holmes. "Miss Lorne may have been the last person to see Clover Adams alive."

"You are misinformed, Mr. Holmes," barked Clemens, his face growing dark above the white mustache. "I have it from Henry Adams himself that he encountered Miss Lorne waiting *outside* their house at sixteen-oh-seven H Street because she had come to visit Clover but had been waiting to go up because no one answered the bell."

Holmes nodded. "You have it from Henry Adams himself that the woman who called herself Rebecca Lorne said that she had been waiting outside when no one answered the bell. But there remains the possibility that Miss Lorne had visited Clover Adams during the few minutes that Henry Adams was gone and was coming out of the home at sixteen-oh-seven H Street rather than waiting outside it."

"Preposterous," cried Clemens.

"Possibly," said Holmes.

"And what do you mean by saying 'the woman who called herself Rebecca Lorne', sir? Who else might she be?"

"Indeed," said Holmes.

James had been watching this exchange with the utmost interest and now he looked to Holmes to give his theory about Lorne being the woman Holmes had known as Irene Adler.

Instead, Holmes asked the humorist, "During Miss Lorne's brief visit here in Hartford or during your earlier encounters with her in Washington, did she give you the sense of having *ever* been familiar with theatrical life?"

"Theatrical life," repeated Clemens, lighting a new cigar. "I don't know what you...wait. Wait. Now that you mention it, I remember telling Livy after their visit—'This woman has been on the stage'. Yes, by God, I remember now."

"Did she say as much?" asked Holmes.

"No, no, not in the least," laughed Clemens. "But once when her cousin Clifton took the wrong chair at dinner—next to her, not what couples or guests do at another's table—she'd said, 'You've missed your mark.' And another time, we were playing billiards that evening—Mrs. Lorne, or whoever she might be, was deucedly good at the game—turned to her cousin as he was ready to take a shot and she said, 'Break a leg'. Now, as far as I know, those terms are little known outside the theater."

"Do you actually think that Rebecca Lorne might have been upstairs with Clover Adams when she...when the poison was taken?" asked William Dean Howells, the billiards cue still in his hand. It had been so long since Howells had said anything that all heads turned toward him.

"It's possible," said Holmes. "It is more likely that the woman taking the name Rebecca Lorne had been posted outside to make noise should Henry Adams return early...which he did."

James blinked. He'd not heard this part of Holmes's surmising before and it made a terrible dark sense.

"Make noise..." said Clemens, clearly not seeing the implications.

"So that the man she called her cousin Clifton would not be interrupted in whatever he was doing upstairs with Clover," said Holmes.

"But Adams went straight upstairs," said Howells, his face white with horror. "He saw only Clover's body on the floor."

"Even though the Adamses' old house was much smaller than Henry Adams's current home, it also had a rear servants' staircase," said Holmes. "I inquired."

Sam Clemens exhaled blue smoke. "So he could have come quietly down that rear stairs while poor Adams went up the main stairs," he rasped. "And out the back door, no doubt." Clemens turned to Holmes. "Do you know the true identity of this 'cousin Clifton'?"

"I do," Holmes said softly and with not the least tone of triumph or superiority. "There was no record of Clifton Richards in Washington or Boston save for the six months previous to Clover's death, when this 'Clifton' worked in the photographic supplies department in the Department of State. It was he who provided the new developing solution—with the cyanide—to Clover Adams. He resigned—and disappeared—in January of 'eighty-six, just a few weeks after Mrs. Adams's death. His true identity—absolutely confirmed by me only yesterday—is that of Lucan Adler, an international anarchist and deadly assassin."

"My God!" cried Clemens, sending the billiards cue crashing onto the green baize table. "Livy and I hosted a murderess and murderer. We could have been poisoned at our own table. Stabbed in the night. Smothered to death in our own bed!"

Holmes smiled thinly. "Possible, but not probable. It was not you they were after but, rather, Clover Adams. They closed their circle around her for months."

"But why?" asked Clemens. "Clover offended some members of the Washington establishment, but certainly no one disliked her to the point of wanting to *kill* her."

"That is what I am looking into," said Holmes. "At this moment, I fear that a former actress and adventuress named Irene Adler and her son Lucan Adler arranged Mrs. Adams's death primarily in order to bring *me* to the States."

The other three men could only stare at the detective. Finally James said, "Bring you here to America in December of 'eighty-five or the winter of 'eighty-six, you mean?"

"No," said Holmes. "To bring me here after Ned Hooper brought me the evidence of the She-was-murdered cards. To bring me here *now.*"

For a moment no one said anything. Then Clemens took Howells's cue, set it against the wall with his own, and said, "Come with me please, gentlemen."

* * *

James had assumed that Clemens was going to show them out of the house—the brougham and driver were still waiting in the driveway—but instead their host led them out onto a covered second-story porch. It was a wide porch with a wonderful view, and seven rocking chairs waited there in the shade.

"Please be seated, gentlemen," said Clemens. "You may choose any rocker save for this one." He had his hands on the back of a mustard-yellow rocker with well-dented cushions. "And God bless John and Alice Day for keeping everything here where it should be."

When they were all seated, Howells and James lit cigarettes. Holmes worked to get his pipe drawing properly. Clemens found yet another cigar in a pocket, bit off the end, spit the shred over the railing, and lit the cigar with a satisfied grunt. James had smoked cigars but he did not pretend to be an aficionado of the many brands. He only knew from the smoke that Clemens's cigar was a cheap cigar.

Clemens caught his gaze. "I used to smoke cigarettes as you do, Mr. James. But Olivia told me that it was a dirty habit and certainly no benefit to my health. So, on the principle that the only way to break one bad habit was by replacing it with an even worse habit, I began smoking cigars."

Howells guffawed at this, although he must have heard it many times before.

"But I do follow Livy's admonitions to moderation, Mr. James," continued Clemens. "I rarely smoke more than one cigar at a time."

"Have you ever tried to break the habit, Mr. Clemens?" asked Holmes.

James immediately thought of Holmes's syringe and his addiction to whatever he was daily injecting into himself. Holmes also smoked constantly, varying between cigarettes and his pipes. Was Holmes really curious about whether Twain had found a way to break his addiction to tobacco?

"Oh, of course," laughed Clemens. "It's easy to quit smoking. I've done it hundreds of times."

James saw Howells smile and Holmes nod recognition of the tiny clench. They were, James knew, bits and pieces of prepared and rehearsed lines that had flowed from the podium and over footlights many times, but James was not offended by being turned into yet another audience. Clemens seemed to require an audience at all times.

But for several moments Clemens fell silent and no one else spoke. The only sound was the unsynchronized creaking of their four rocking chairs and ambient bird sounds and leaves stirring in the wind. James wondered if the great elms and chestnut trees and maples might be further along in their stately process of leafing out than usual for the end of March. The smaller dogwoods were in their glory. Henry James remembered winter surrendering its sovereignty in Cambridge with frigid and snowy rearguard actions deep into April in some late springs, including the year a decade ago when his parents died and he had stayed behind to sort out insurance and moneys owed and moneys promised. He remembered how he and Alice James—the *other* Alice James, William's wife—had begged William by letter not to return home from his sabbatical in England. His presence would have only made the confusion—of money going to Wilkie and others, of Henry forsaking his own share of their father's modest fortune by signing it over to their sister Alice, of Aunt Kate's and sister Alice's part in all this—hopeless. William had stayed in England and Europe, but not without threatening a hundred times that he would board the next ship U.S.-bound.

That had been a sad but deeply satisfying few months for Henry James. For once he was undoubtedly and indisputably in charge of the family—its finances, its security, its future with both parents now gone—and he had liked the feeling. He had liked being free and separate from the shadow of the all-powerful older brother William.

The wind rustled leaves again and James enjoyed the view from this high porch. He could see the white gazebo, needing paint now, where Clemens had spent starry nights talking with Harriet Beecher Stowe. Or so he had said. James had read that the old lady, in her 80's, was almost an invalid now. And no longer interested in life or ideas since her husband had died.

James remembered reading the novel—*Uncle Tom's Cabin, or Life Among the Lowly*—only a year or two after it had been published in 1852. Henry James, Jr., was only 10 years old but he had instantly seen the crude melodrama of the novel as the propaganda broadside it was meant to be, filled with stereotypes and unartistic exaggerations: not drawn from life. But he had also sensed the flame of fury and indignation that had driven the author and—even then at 10 years of age—Henry James had known for a certainty that he would never write anything or paint anything or create anything from any similar boundless passion. His work, he knew even before he had known what direction his work in life might take him, would all be *minded*—carefully thought out and planned, deliberate, well-chewed.

Samuel Clemens turned his rocker so that he could look directly at James and said, "I had dinner in Florence with your brother just a few months ago."

"Indeed?" James said politely, his heart sinking. Of course William had written to him about the encounter. Of course William had thought it significant, primarily due to sharing his wisdom with this rustic who had so presumptuously dismissed his younger brother Harry's book *The Bostonians.* But in the end, James remembered, after many Italian courses and several bottles of wine, William had come away deeply impressed with this Mark Twain/Samuel Clemens dual personality.

"We talked until very late—until the waiters were making noise with brooms and coughing discreetly to let us know it was far past the Florentine restaurant's closing time," said Clemens. "And for the last two hours, I did little more than listen to your brother."

I am sure that is the case, thought Henry James. *Thus it is with me, his wife, and most of his interlocutors.*

"I was in something like awe," said Clemens. He turned toward the other two men in their rockers. "You both know of Mr. William James's amazing book *Principles of Psychology?*"

Holmes merely nodded but Howells said in mock anger, "*Know* of it? Sam, I not only penned one of the earliest positive reviews of the book but I was the first to *recommend it to you.* I purchased a second copy of it myself and mailed it to you with an admonition to read it despite your aversion to 'dry' books, if I recall correctly. And I *do* ... recall correctly."

"It's an amazing book," continued Clemens as if Howells had not spoken. "But in our conversation in Florence, William James elaborated even further than his seminal book does on the definitions of—and differences between—'I' and 'me'."

Oh, my, thought James, trying to calm his thoughts by looking out toward the distant gazebo once again.

"Mr. Holmes," cried Clemens, leaning toward the thin man in his black suit and long black scarf despite the warmth of the day. "Do you enjoy being a detective?"

"It is what I do," said Holmes after the briefest of pauses.

Clemens nodded as if the answer satisfied him deeply. "The published stories of your adventures are becoming very popular both here and, as I understand it, in England."

Holmes said nothing to this.

"Are you satisfied with the way Dr. Watson and Mr. Doyle present your adventures?" pressed Clemens.

"I've never had the pleasure of making Mr. Doyle's acquaintance," Holmes said softly. "As for Watson's writing — many is the time I've told him that his little romances based on my cases mistakenly emphasize drama, and sometimes, I admit, melodrama, rather than the cold, sure science of deduction that he could have shared with interested and intelligent readers."

Holmes leaned forward on his walking cane. "Furthermore," he said, "both Watson and his editor and agent, Mr. Doyle, have a deep fear of mentioning any well-known public names — or even private ones, or even the accurate place or time — in the published tales. More often than not it leads to a great confusion in the tales themselves. The published versions hardly ever match the original notes in my case files."

"But you enjoy being a detective?" Clemens asked again.

"It is what I do," repeated Holmes.

Clemens laughed and slapped his knee. "By God, I am going to write a book called *Tom Sawyer, Detective.* Between my beloved literary character and your profession, sir, we shall sell a million copies."

Holmes said nothing to this.

"Enjoy your pipe and cigarettes, gentlemen," cried Clemens. "For I am now going to explain Mr. William James's brilliant definitions of the quite different 'I' and 'me' in all of us and should show Mr. Holmes why he might be correct in thinking that he does not exist!"

CHAPTER 25

Our friend Henry James's brother William sees the 'I' in each of us as the active agent, the first-person doer, as it were—that part of our consciousness or being which sets our goals and initiates our actions in quest of those goals, whether the goals be getting closer to a pretty girl or being seen as the best writer of our generation," said Clemens between deep draws on his cigar. "Does anyone here disagree with such a definition?"

No one spoke for a moment and James returned his attention to the sound of the breeze in the nearby trees. Then Holmes said, "This seems somewhat self-evident, perhaps to the point of being obvious."

"Quite so!" cried Clemens. "Then perhaps you will also agree with Mr. William James's definition of 'Me' as being the third-person object of self-reflection...reflecting on one's own traits, as in *'Am I a friendly person?'* or pondering our own beliefs, as in *'Do I really believe in an all-powerful God?'* or *'Do I really like chocolate?'* as well as querying our states...*'Am I angry that Clemens is wasting my time like this?'* and so on."

"What does this have to do with the question of whether Mr. Holmes exists or not?" asked Howells.

Clemens put a hand on his old friend's knee. "Be patient, Howells. Be patient." Clemens removed his hand and clasped both hands over his stomach while he began to rock again. Then he removed the cigar and flicked ash on the wooden floor of the porch. "Our friend Henry James's brother William explained to me that these two parts of each of us, the self as known—the 'Me'—and the self-as-knower—the 'I'—are in constant interplay, sometimes actively competing with one another."

"How can this be?" asked Holmes. "A man's deepest self, his soul as it were, cannot be divided against itself."

"Can it not be?" said Clemens. "Are we not, each of us in our deepest selves, divided against ourselves? The 'Me' asks *Am I not a kind man?*' and hopes it to be so, even while our 'I' commits selfish or thoughtless actions which hurt our spouses, our children, our closest friends. Have you not encountered, Mr. Holmes, rogues who committed the worst of actions—murder even—yet insist they are good people, decent people, and that their heinous crimes were mere temporary aberrations, done, as it were, against their will?"

"I have," said Holmes after a moment. "But I fail to see how this has anything to do with the question of whether I am real or a fictional construct, existing only within the confines of some author's imagination."

Clemens nodded and flicked ash. "Our little bark is heavily loaded, but we trust that it will reach shore by and by, Mr. Holmes. The 'I' in us acts; the 'Me' in us weighs those actions as we reassure ourselves that we are really fine fellows after all. And since the 'Me' becomes what your brother called our 'empirical selves'—the ones people see and know—it becomes the one the world knows." He exhaled a small cloud of smoke and pulled a folded slip of paper from his vest pocket.

No one spoke as Clemens unfolded the page and held it at arm's length to read. "As your brother writes, Mr. James—'I am often confronted by the necessity of standing by one of my empirical selves and relinquishing the rest. Not that I would not, if I could, be both handsome and fat and well-dressed, and a great athlete, and make a million a year, be a wit, a bon-vivant, and a lady-killer, as well as a philosopher, a philanthropist, statesman, warrior, and African explorer, as well as a 'tone-poet' and saint. But the thing is simply impossible. The millionaire's work would run counter to the saint's; the bon-vivant and the philanthropist would trip each other up; the philosopher and the lady-killer could not well keep house in the same tenement of clay. Such different characters may conceivably at the outset of life be alike, possibly to a man. To make any one of them actual, the rest must more or less be suppressed. So the seeker of his truest, deepest self must review the list carefully, and pick out the one on which to stake his salvation. All the other selves thereupon become unreal, but the fortunes of this self are real. Its failures are real failures, its triumphs are real triumphs, carrying shame and gladness with them.'"

There was a long silence—common to groups who have just had a long passage read to them—and then Howells said plaintively, "Sam, how on *earth* did you just *happen* to have that page at hand to read?"

Clemens grinned. He looked at Henry James. "I tore it out of this man's brother's book, *Principles of Psychology,* in my library not ten minutes ago."

"For shame," said Howells.

"It is better to break the spine of a man than of a book," murmured James.

"Oh, its spine is intact," said Clemens. "But I confess to the crime of ripping a page out of the guts of William's beautiful book. Page...ah..." He peered at both sides of the page. "Pages three hundred and nine and three hundred ten."

"Unforgivable," said Howells.

"I shall do my best to repair it," said Clemens. "I am, you know, in the book-binding business myself." He turned to Sherlock Holmes. "Did that passage not reassure you that even though you are a fictional character, your failures would be your own, your triumphs would be your own?"

"It did *not,*" said Holmes. "If I am some hack author's pawn, then neither my triumphs nor failures can I call my own."

Clemens sighed.

Howells said, "That's all very well for this theoretical 'Me' that is, at any given moment, the sum of all behaviors, decisions, and possessions. But what about the 'I.' Where is it all this time?"

When no one spoke, James cleared his throat and said, "The 'I' knows all past thoughts and appropriates them—but outside of time, as it were—since the 'I' itself is a thought from moment to moment, each different from that of the last moment, but appropriative of the latter, together with all that the latter called its own."

The other three men were staring at James as if he'd broken wind. Howells ground out his cigarette underfoot. Holmes was holding his pipe in his lap.

"You see," continued James, knowing that he should say no more, "William's logic is that since the stream of thought in each of us is constantly changing, there is no reason to suppose some fixed entity beyond the stream itself. No soul. No central spirit. No ego, as such. Rather, there are pulses of consciousness—thoughts which are unified in and of themselves—involving among other things the immediate awareness of the body. And William thinks that these thoughts...as sovereign 'I's...can remember and appropriate prior thoughts to the stream. But the 'I' is always in motion, always in flux—part of a greater stream of consciousness, one might say."

Sam Clemens tossed his stub of a cigar over the porch railing. "Yep. That's pretty much what Mr. William James and I thrashed out in Florence—at least by the time the espresso had come."

"You explored *all this* with my loquacious brother over the course of a mere dinner?" asked James.

"Never in your life!" cried Clemens. "It was over a long *Italian* dinner, then brandy and coffee, and dessert and cheese, and then more brandy and then the espresso. The World was created in less time. Or at least its peninsulas and fjords were."

"But you are speaking of identity, Sam, not of reality of existence," said Howells.

"Are they not the same thing?" asked Clemens. "My little dog knows me, therefore I am myself. Identity, good sirs!"

"My little dog knows me, therefore I am?" James asked drily. "*This* was the depth and breadth of my brother's philosophy?"

"Not quite," said Clemens. "Your brother William explained to me that in its widest sense, a man's Self is the sum total of all that he can call his: not only his body and its ailments and his psychic powers, such as they are, but also his clothes and his wife and children, his ancestors and friends, his competitors and sworn enemies, his reputation and works, his lands and horses and yacht and bank account."

"I have no yacht," Howells said softly. *"Non navigare, ideo non esse."*

James and Holmes both surprised themselves by laughing. Howells did not sail, therefore he was *not*.

"Ego navigare, ergo sum," said Holmes. "Except that I don't. Sail, that is."

Now even Sam Clemens joined in the laughter.

Suddenly Howells cried "Look!" and pointed.

A deer bolted across the shade-dappled lawn behind Harriet Beecher Stowe's home. It disappeared into shrubs to the north, and the men on the porch remained quiet. James was wondering whether he should suggest that they go; he and Holmes had a long train ride ahead of them.

Clemens spoke and his voice had a strange, strained, changed, distant tone to it. "Just before I sailed from Genoa last week," he said softly, no longer rocking, "my daughter Susy celebrated her twenty-first birthday. It bothered me for some reason—in more ways than having a father's daughter grow up and thus never again be his little girl, which is bothersome enough, God knows.

"My own birthday was last November—I turned fifty-seven years old—and I remember thinking, I think it to this day, that I wished it were seventeen or ninety-seven, any age but fifty-seven."

When no one else said anything, James found himself thinking of his own fiftieth birthday—less than two weeks away now—and how he had long vowed that he would be recognized as Master in his field by the time he was fifty. Instead, he could barely get a new short story published. He was attempting to start over as a writer—at age fifty!—to make his fortune in writing for the stage. His enthusiasm for that self-transformation had waned a little more each day since he had left Paris and steamed to America.

He knew that Howells was 56 years old. Clemens, as he complained, was soon to turn 58 years old. Holmes was the relative youngster in the group, only 39.

"People wonder why I've traveled back to the United States so much—and why I shall continue to do so, no matter how long our European exile lasts," Clemens was saying, "so when they ask, 'Why do you go so much, Mr. Twain?' I say to them . . . 'Well, I go partly for my health, partly to familiarize myself with the road.' But mostly I go, gentlemen, primarily to convince the 'Me' in me that I truly exist, that there is something more to Mr. Samuel Clemens than his clothes and his wife and his children..."

All four of them had ceased rocking now and three of the men were looking at the white-haired humorist.

"You see, I dreamed that I was born and grew up and was a pilot on the Mississippi, gentlemen," said Clemens, his voice little more than a whisper. "I dreamed that I was a miner and journalist in Nevada and a pilgrim in the good ship *Quaker City* and wrote a very popular book about those travels abroad and that I had a wife and children, yes, and went with them to live in a villa just outside of Florence...and this dream goes on and on and on, and sometimes it seems so real that I almost believe it *is* real. But there is no way to tell...*no way to tell,* Mr. Holmes, Mr. James, my dear Howells...for if one applied tests, then they would be part of the dream, too, and so would simply aid in the deceit. I wish I knew...I wish I knew..." Clemens looked down and, for a terrible moment, James thought he might be weeping.

"Knew what, Sam?" asked Howells.

Clemens looked up at them and his eyes were dry. Distant, with a tired and haunted look, but dry. "I wish I knew whether it all was a dream or real," he said.

"Livy is real," said Howells. "You have that indisputable point of reality to cling to when the black dog and blue devils try to pull you down."

"Livy...Olivia," said Clemens and nodded. "I wrote, not long ago, about Adam and Eve...about how Adam had no name for this new creature taken from his rib and how he became bewildered by all these new events over which he had no control. He resented her, you see. She was an intrusion on the placid perfection of his life alone in the Garden.

"But after years passed, I had Adam change his mind. 'I see that I was mistaken about Eve in the beginning,' he says. 'For it is better to live *outside* the Garden with her than *inside* it without her.'"

James thought that Clemens was finished with his long digression, but the humorist cleared his throat and said, "When Eve finally dies, after centuries with Adam, I have Adam carve her headstone on wood and on that slab of wood he has carved—'Where she was, *there* was Paradise'."

Clemens looked around with an expression of embarrassment. "Well, we are discussing Mr. Holmes's reality and identity, gentlemen. Mr. Holmes..."

He looked directly at the detective.

"Mr. Holmes, you will have an identity as long as there are deerstalker caps and magnifying glasses in the world." Clemens pantomimed holding the handle of a magnifying glass.

Howells chuckled.

"Oh, dear God," moaned Holmes. He folded his hands into fists and set his fists on his knees.

"The artist for *The Strand,* the artist who draws versions of me," said Holmes, "is named Sidney Paget. I have never had the dubious pleasure of making his acquaintance and he, in turn, has never set eyes on me. I have never allowed my photograph or a photogravure to appear in any newspaper, no matter how major the crime might have been or how clever the apprehension of the criminals. Paget has only the vaguest idea, through Watson's stories, of what I look like or how I dress.

"Since *The Strand* had originally intended Sidney's older brother Walter to be the illustrator of the stories, perhaps Walter Paget's only consolation is that his younger brother uses him as his model for me. That is, for the detective Sherlock Holmes as illustrated in *The Strand.*"

Holmes struck his walking stick hard against the wooden floor of the balcony. "I do own a soft, two-flapped cap like that but hardly wear it constantly as the Paget illustrations would have it. And yes, I *do,* upon occasion, travel in a wool, caped traveling overcoat, but so do thousands of other English gentlemen when leaving the city. And here is the magnifying glass I use to examine dust, ash, particles, fibers, and other minute clues..." Holmes reached in his jacket pocket and pulled out a tiny magnifying lens with no handle; it was black rimmed and thick, the sort of glass one would use to magnify tiny details on a large map.

Clemens and Howells were laughing at Holmes's outburst, and James could not help it, he also chuckled.

"Well," said Clemens as Holmes sat silent, leaning on his stick, "I only wish I had a trademark like your deerstalker hat, caped coat, and magnifying glass, Mr. Holmes. God knows I do love being known and recognized. Providence and Presbyterians please forgive me, I live for recognition and for my own insignificant little bit of fame. Life is short enough, is my belief, without passing through it unnoticed by the multitudes. If you hadn't become known for your deerstalker cap, Mr. Holmes, perhaps I would be wearing one myself. I do so enjoy standing out in a crowd."

"Go about a German or American city in a deerstalker," said Howells, "and you will stand out in an asylum."

James chuckled again. Sherlock Holmes said, "Wear white."

"I beg your pardon?" said Clemens. He was preparing a new cigar.

"Wear a white suit...but with your regular black shoes," said Holmes.

"I wear white suits from time to time every summer," said Clemens, puffing the cigar to a glow. "A lovely, comfortable white-linen suit. And, yes, *with* my regular black shoes, which is a mortal sin and unspeakable *faux pas* at Newport and at several clubs to which I have been invited. But, alas, I am only one white suit amidst thousands as the temperatures soar and the season of white suits rolls round."

"Wear them in the winter," said Holmes. "Year-round."

"Year-round?" repeated Clemens, looking to Howells who only smiled and shrugged. "They *will* put me in an asylum if I start doing that."

"With your notoriety...fame I should say..." said Holmes, "and with your mane of white hair, it will be seen as an attractive eccentricity, a whim of a great and amusing man. You will stand out in every crowd, at least from September to May. The white suit shall become, one could say, your signature in society. Behold, Mark Twain cometh."

Clemens laughed along with the rest of them, but there was a calculating look in his eye.

Henry James, allowing himself to get into the mood of the moment—which was very rare for him—said, "If anyone asks why you wear white linen suits all winter, Mr. Clemens, tell them that cleanliness is paramount for you and that you have become aware that men's black suits merely hide the dirt and soot. How many weeks or months—or years—go between cleanings of those dark suits? No, sir...you will not be part of that suspiciously dark crowd. Cleanliness is next to Godliness, you can say, and Mark Twain is next to his white linen suit."

This time Clemens threw his head back and roared with the others.

*   *   *

Howells stayed in Hartford with Clemens as the humorist made his afternoon round of visits and had dinner with old Connecticut friends who might just have money to invest or loan. James and Holmes took the afternoon train back to New York where they would catch the evening train to Washington.

"Henry Adams will be home in a very few days," said James after they had made the connection in New York. "I'm a trifle curious how you will present yourself to him...the intrepid Norwegian explorer Jan Sigerson or the consulting London detective Sherlock Holmes. Of course, you and John Hay have three or four days to decide the better course."

Holmes was reading a small guide to Chicago that he had picked up at a Grand Central Station kiosk, but now he looked up at James sitting across from him. "I'm afraid Hay and I have no more time to discuss such things. Mr. Adams is returning today—almost certainly before you and I arrive at Mr. Hay's home."

James blinked rapidly. "But John Hay said...the servants said...everyone said." He calmed himself and leaned on his stick. "Are you sure of this, Mr. Holmes?"

"I am, Mr. James."

"So will you be introduced to Adams as Sherlock Holmes or as Mr. Sigerson?" asked James.

"With luck, by tomorrow morning we'll have shifted quarters to those nearby rooms to let about which Mr. Hay talked to you. You are certain they will be satisfactory?"

"They were in 'eighty-three when I was here last and Clover Adams arranged for me to stay there," said James. "Light, clean rooms—and Hay says that we shall each have a corner bed-sitting-room of our own."

Holmes nodded. "The privacy will help in my investigations."

James looked out at the countryside passing by, the small white houses and red barns and newly plowed fields and small remaining bits of forest enriched by the warm light of the setting sun and the long shadows. When he turned back, he said, "I take it you would rather meet Henry Adams as yourself—as Holmes."

"It would simplify much," said Holmes and they rode in silence for half an hour or so.

"Mr. James," said Holmes at last, "since we may not have the opportunity for a private conversation for some time to come, allow me to say Mr. Clemens's reprise of your brother William's theory of self—of 'I' and 'Me'—was of the greatest interest to me."

James nodded his appreciation and stifled a sigh. He'd been in his older brother's shadow for fifty years now and, while he loved William dearly—part of James still wanted to follow William around and be in his presence constantly as he did when he was a small boy—he would, at age fifty, appreciate stepping into the sunshine of praise for his own work, his own achievements, his own life.

"I mention it," continued Holmes, "because I see the same analysis of the polyphonicdialogic of multiple selves and most especially of the spiritual core, the 'I' caught up constantly in the flow of thoughts and events—what your brother so brilliantly labeled as 'the stream of consciousness'—in your writing, sir. That is, in your stories and novels and characters. It is astounding to me that two brothers, usually separated by an ocean, could so masterfully come to the same impression and explanation of human consciousness—your brother from the scientific side and you, even more powerfully, from the literary."

For the first time in years, Henry James found himself speechless. Finally he managed to say—"Thank you, sir. You have read my work?" He heard the odd tone in his own voice in that query.

"I've read and enjoyed your work for years," said Sherlock Holmes. "For reasons that may be all too obvious, I found your *The Princess Casamassima* a wonderful examination of how the working classes in England and America turn to anarchy...and thus to terrorism."

James again nodded modestly toward his interlocutor. The author had been inordinately fond of his *The Princess Casamassima*. For one thing, the novel was a far cry from *Daisy Miller* and his many stories about young American women encountering Europe, but the critical response to the book had been muted and mixed.

As if reading his mind again, Holmes said, "I happened to read one review in *The Times* that criticized the book—and you—for placing so much of the social interaction on Sundays." Holmes shook his head and smiled. "That reviewer, and perhaps too many of our upper classes, simply don't realize that for the foreign working class you were describing, Sunday afternoons are the only time they *have* for any sort of social activity."

"Exactly," said James, who had actually researched his novel about the foreign-born working classes more diligently than any other work he'd written. "Thank you for realizing that."

"The prison so aptly described in your book was Millbank Prison," said Holmes. "I saw you there—inside the prison—early on a December morning in eighteen eighty-four. You were being led by one of the surlier day wardens, he took you to the women's wing probably conjecturing that it might seem less oppressive to a renowned author's sensibilities, but the warden with a small lamp was so far ahead of you that you seemed alone, squeezing up the metal stairs from cell ward to cell ward with your shoulders brushing cold stone."

"Yes!" cried James, amazed. "But I saw no other gentlemen during my visit. Not even Millbank's warden with whom I had corresponded, through the kind offices of a friend in Whitehall, to receive permission for the visit. There was only that surly, as you say, and infinitely uncommunicative guard. Where were you, sir? In the process, perhaps, of delivering some fiend you and Dr. Watson had just caught?"

"I was a prisoner," said Holmes. "I saw you through the tiny Judas hole in my cell's door—the guards were often too lazy to close it—before you climbed the steps to the women's ward."

"A *prisoner?*" gasped James. He knew his features were aghast, reflecting the shock he felt.

"I was there for a little more than two months in disguise—if a prison uniform, welts from beatings, and severe malnutrition from the slop Millbank served out can be called a disguise—and my plan was to get close to another inmate whom I was sure was a killer of young women, but I admit, Mr. James, that it crossed my mind more than once that if something were to happen to both Inspector Lestrade and the warden, I might be in Millbank to this day."

"Who was the killer?" asked James in a soft voice.

"An Oxford-educated barrister named Montague Druitt," said Holmes, his eyes veiled as he seemed to be looking backward in time. "Druitt was also a schoolmaster with a record of occasional insanities and was found one Sunday outside the school where he taught. He was covered in blood. Inside the school was the dead and vivisected body of a certain Mary O'Brian, one of his students. Druitt was found guilty by a lower court but was in Millbank Prison only a few more days than I was. He had friends in high places, especially among the Inns of Court, and a second trial declared him innocent—they accepted his explanation that he had dropped by the school on a Sunday to pick up his books so that he could prepare his Monday lessons, found Miss O'Brian dead there, and, in his distress, held her body in his arms—thus explaining the copious amounts of blood on him.

"No knife was found on Mr. Druitt's person or in the vicinity of the crime, so the courts let him go. He was a gentleman, you see," said Holmes. "But I saw Miss O'Brian's body before it was moved. She had been dismembered, sir. Her body had been eviscerated and was in pieces—each piece slashed and stabbed until she was turned almost inside out. Even the most compassionate gentleman would not have cradled that dissectionist's work."

"So you think he was guilty?" asked James.

"After he was released, I found the knife where he dropped it down a nearby sewer," said Holmes. "It actually had his initials inscribed on it. And I was in the same terrible cell with him for seven weeks. He never fully confessed to the crime, Watson...I'm terribly sorry, Mr. James...but, in the privacy of that dark, dank cell along the Thames, Druitt smirked enough to me about no one ever solving the crime that, in my professional opinion, he all but bragged of committing it."

"Surely Scotland Yard must have arrested him again after you showed them the knife and told them of his demeanor?" said James.

"Scotland Yard misses much, Mr. James—including this knife in their searches just after the crime. Including the family history of Druitt's bouts of madness. But Scotland Yard does not want to advertise the things and criminals they miss."

"That's terrible," said James, looking at Holmes in a new and strange light. "What happened to Mr. Montague Druitt?"

"After his release from Millbank, he returned to an ever more successful career as a barrister," said Holmes. "When the so-called Jack the Ripper murders in the East End captured the press's attention in 'eighty-eight, I joined Mr. Anderson of the CID in looking at many suspects. There were other murders of women through that period, but I was certain that the Ripper's victims were only five—the poor ladies Chapman, Stride, Nichols, Eddowes, and a certain Mary Kelly, who had known Miss O'Brian who had been murdered in eighteen eighty-three. The man whom I became convinced was behind all the so-called Jack the Ripper murders was Mr. Montague Druitt."

"But Jack the Ripper was never caught!" said James.

"No, but the body of Montague Druitt was fished out of the Thames on December thirty-first of eighteen eighty-eight," said Holmes. "The police ruled it a suicide."

"Was it . . . a suicide?" asked Henry James.

"No," said Holmes. His gray eyes now looked so cold to James that he would have described them as inhuman, reptilian. But a reptile that was both satisfied and deeply sad.

Suddenly Henry James felt his body grow cold and a strange and unpleasant prickling flowed down his arms, the back of his neck, and along his spine.

Eventually James said, "I thank you again for your comments about my *Princess Casamassima*. It pleases me that someone as thorough with detail as yourself approves of its research."

Holmes smiled. "You remember the location of the Hotel Glenham where we met Mr. Clemens last night for dinner?"

"Of course," said James. "Nine ninety-five Broadway."

"Well, Mr. James," said Holmes. "Within ten blocks of that hotel were more than thirty beer halls, union halls, lecture halls, and even churches where anarchists meet every week. For your American anarchists are primarily socialists, you see, and your American socialists are primarily German... moderately recent German immigrants, to be precise."

"I would never have guessed that, sir," said Henry James. "Of course, many of the workers in my *Princess Casamassima* were German, but that was due to the prevailing feeling... the stereotype in England, as it were..."

"The German neighborhoods in the Lower East Side of New York are the nexus for ninety-eight percent of anarchist sentiment and activity in America," continued Holmes, as if James had not even spoken. "I found it located primarily in the Tenth, Eleventh, and Seventeenth Wards. Germans refer to this part of New York as *Kleindeutschland*—'Little Germany', as I am sure I don't have to translate for you. This area is bounded by Fourteenth Street on the north, Third Avenue and the Bowery on the west, Division Street on the south, and the East River on the east. It has been *Kleindeutschland* since the Civil War."

"Certainly, sir," protested James, "you are not saying that all German immigrants in New York are anarchists."

Holmes was still smiling. "Of course not," he said softly. "But I am saying that a surprisingly large number of your German immigrants have brought socialism with them from Europe, and at the core of the most fanatical socialism lie the embers and sparks of today's anarchism and terror."

"I find this hard to believe," said James.

"Between eighteen sixty-one and eighteen seventy," continued Holmes, "some zero-point-three percent of your immigrants were from Austria and Hungary, fewer than eight thousand people. Between eighteen eighty-one and eighteen ninety, more than six-point-seven percent of your immigrants are Germans or Austrians, almost seven percent of your total. Some eighty-two thousand people, most of whom chose to reside in the most crowded sections of New York or Brooklyn and not move west. And the ratio is rising dramatically. Demographers working in my brother Mycroft's department at Whitehall predict—rather confidently, I feel—that a full sixteen percent of your immigrant population will be German by the year nineteen hundred, almost six hundred thousand German men and women and children, and by nineteen ten, lower-class Germans should be almost twenty-five percent of your total immigration, numbering more than two million."

"But certainly there are German immigrants who are hard working, God-fearing...I mean, you mention only a few German beer halls..." stammered James.

"There are more than two hundred German beer halls associated with the anarchist movement in New York City right now, just in eighteen ninety-three," said Holmes. "Many of these are what they call *Lokalfrage*—secure places—where they can speak freely or hold socialist meetings where they can openly discuss anarchist plans."

Holmes leaned forward, his weight on his walking stick.

"And yes, your German immigrants are very hard working, Mr. James—I can tell you that by working alongside them under the most inhuman of conditions in factories in New York. But the majority of them resist learning the English language. And the literate among them—and literacy is high in the German community, as you doubtlessly know—have read and absorbed their European communist-anarchist philosophers such as Bakunin and recently have moved on to the more violent communist-anarchist leaders such as Peter Kropotkin, Errico Malatesta, and Élisée Reclus. Your German immigrants have brought with them not only their capacity for hard work six long days a week, but their hatred of the upper classes and their interest in anarchy and...for a minority, but still for too many of them...a willingness to turn to the bombings, uprisings, and the assassinations of all-out anarchy."

Holmes patted his cane absently, as if his own recitation upset him.

"Socialists—and anarchists—also use these beer-house *Lokalfrage* as clubhouses for trade-union locals, singing societies, and German mutual-aid organizations. But the anarchists, including the most virulent kind, Mr. James, also meet there, store weapons there, make their plans for assassinations there. And we could have walked to a dozen of these *Lokalfrage* from the Glenham Hotel last night."

James desperately needed to change the subject. Many of his characters in *The Princess Casamassima* had been German immigrant workers, but Henry James actually knew no such Germans, no industrial workers. The Germans he did know were teachers, professors, artists, and literary men in Germany itself. He said, "But the man you are seeking...this Lucan Adler...he is not German."

"No," said Holmes in a strange tone. "Lucan Adler is not German."

Knowing he should stay silent and let this disturbing conversation die, he still spoke. "This search for the person behind Clover Adams's death—the search for Lucan Adler, Mr. Sebastian Moran's bastard son, is terribly personal to you, is it not, Mr. Holmes?"

Holmes stared at him with those cold gray eyes and nodded ever so slightly.

"It must be because of the wounds," said James. "Those terrible gunshot wounds inflicted upon you by Lucan Adler."

Incredibly, inexplicably, Sherlock Holmes smiled. He flung his long black scarf around his neck in the flamboyant manner James had become accustomed to, while cocking his head back, chin jutting strongly beneath that odd, almost lighthearted, smile.

"Not at all," said Holmes. "The wounds are a price of my profession. But it's true I seek out Lucan Adler for a deeper reason than an attempt to save untold public figures from the world's most terrible anarchical assassin. You see, Mr. James, Sebastian Moran took the small child Lucan away from Irene Adler, claiming him and raising him as his bastard even though he never gave the boy his last name. He trained Lucan in every dark art of murder that he knew, and young Lucan, no older than twenty-one years of age, learned even more on his own, surpassing Moran as both a marksman and an assassin."

Holmes looked directly into James's eyes, the detective's fathomless gaze meeting James's frightened but deeply curious and unblinking gray gaze in return.

"Trust me that I have more reasons for finding Lucan Adler than I can share at this time," said Holmes. "He needs to be put to death. But I hope to speak with him first."

PART 2

1

The Damned Cross in the Stonework

Henry Adams awoke in his own bed in his Lafayette Square mansion and for a moment he was disoriented. The air seemed too cool. The bed too familiar. The morning light too soft. And the floor was not moving.

Adams had enjoyed his last two months of lounging in Havana with a friend, then spending a fortnight at Senator Don Cameron's place at Coffin Point on St. Helena Island, and—most of all—he'd enjoyed "geologizing on the coral reefs" with the zoologist Alexander Agassiz, son of the famous geologist Louis Agassiz, on Agassiz's comfortable yacht *Wild Duck*.

But now he was home—a place he'd mostly preferred not to be in the seven years since his wife's suicide—and after his bath he found his clothes laid out for him by his own valet rather than by one of Don Cameron's people.

Having been so emotionally solitary in the past seven years, Adams had expected to feel some sense of relief when his shay—he'd been met at the station, as requested, only by his driver—had pulled up in front of his home on H Street next to the Hays' similar mansion fronting on Sixteenth Street, if for no other reason than his constant daily socializing, first with Phillips in Havana, then with the Camerons, then with Agassiz, and finally with the Camerons yet again, would be at an end.

But instead he'd felt a wall of depression wash over him as he approached the familiar arches of his front door.

Clover hadn't died in this house, of course, or he'd never have returned to it. They'd been planning to move in on New Year's Day 1886 after the two years of elaborate work inside and out was finished but Clover had drunk her developing-chemicals poison on December six.

But the damned cross she'd insisted on, without his approval, was there above the elaborately scrolled stonework above the arches.

He and Clover had been at Beverly Farms that July when the cross—the damned cross—had been added to the façade of the stonework. Henry had asked his friend from the State Department Library, Ted Dwight, to oversee that important bit of stonework and engraving and he'd written to Dwight—"If you see workmen carving a Christian emblem, remonstrate with them like a father."

The place between the windows above the main pillars needed something decorative, insisted their architect, H. H. Richardson, so Henry had suggested to Clover that a peacock be carved there since—to his way of thinking—the entire new mansion complete with its beautiful art, furniture, and contents was a way of showing off for a Washington society he and Clover had snubbed at the best of times. Richardson had argued for a lion, roaring and rampant. Perhaps, Henry Adams thought, because the huge architect had been forced to put up with so many of Henry's roars and complaints over the course of building this impressive mausoleum for the living.

But it turned out that, secretly (from Henry's point-of-view), Clover had ordered an elaborate stone cross to be carved into the brick space there between the windows. By the time Adams at Beverly Farms had heard the news of the cross, the stonework was a done deed. It had bothered him deeply. Neither he nor Clover were religious in any way. They'd often made light fun of their less-than-pious Washington acquaintances who'd managed to work Christian symbols into the stonework or interior carvings of their expensive new homes.

When Ted Dwight had written to inform him that the cross had been added by artisans under Richardson's supervision at Mrs. Adams's insistence, Henry had written what he hoped had been a lighthearted-sounding letter in which he said—"Your account of the cross and the carving fills my heart with sadness and steeps my lips with cocaine." And he'd added, "Never fear, Ted, we shall plaster over it with cement soon enough."

But of course, they never had. So he'd also written to Dwight—"It's a done thing, a *fait accompli* in stone, so I can neither revolt nor complain, though the whole thing seems to me bad art and bad taste. I have protested in vain and must henceforth hold my tongue." But he'd also asked Ted not to tell anyone else about the cross yet, since "Washingtonians chatter so much that one is forced to deny them food for gossip."

Goodness knows that Clover had provided them all with years of food for gossip within six months of that cross going up—she a December suicide, lying dead on the carpet of their living room at the Little White House at 1607 H Street.

The cross, rising between two arches, was a backdrop for a carved medallion showing off a slightly indefinable winged beast. Certainly not Pegasus. Not quite a griffon, nor a dragon—though Adams had wished it might have been. Whatever Clover had in mind when she ordered Richardson to add that design remained a mystery to this day, but even in the summer and autumn of that fateful 1885, Henry had written to friends that the "d——d cross and its winged creature was prophetic of the future" and that they filled him "with terror."

They still did. He had no idea, save for his peripatetic absence at the mansion being more common than his solitary presence in the past seven years, why he hadn't gotten rid of the cross and winged monstrosity after Clover's death.

To Adams, that entire horrible year had been filled with omens. That spring of 1885, when the minister was trying to impress upon Clover—with the utmost care, sympathy, and gentleness—that her father was indeed dying, Adams had heard her say, "No, no, no...everything seems unreal. I hardly know what we are saying or why we are here. And if it seems so unreal, it must be. Or at least *I* must be."

And during that hot, miserable, endless, and pointless summer at Beverly Farms while Richardson was obeying Clover's secret orders to carve that abomination into the front of their staggeringly expensive new home, Adams had—upon more than one occasion—heard his wife cry out to her sister, "Ellen, I am not real. Oh, make me real. For God's sake, make me real. You...all of *you*...are real. Make me real as well."

As Adams breakfasted alone that morning—he had frequently breakfasted, had lunch, and dined alone for the past seven years as long as he was in this house and not traveling—he thought of the damned cross on the wall and of that sick, hot summer at Beverly Farms and of Clover's growing melancholia and...yes...insanity.

Then he put all of that firmly out of his mind and went into his study to go over his pile of recent unforwarded and shamefully unanswered correspondence.

*   *   *

It was late morning when his head butler knocked softly, entered, and said, "Mr. Holmes is here to see you, sir."

"Holmes!" cried Adams. "Good heavens." He put down his pen, buttoned his jacket, and hurried out to the foyer where Holmes had just handed his hat and coat to the second butler.

"My dear Holmes!" cried Adams, stepping forward to shake his friend's hand with the special holding-the-elbow-with-his-left-hand handshake that he reserved for old friends with whom he really wasn't that close. "I had no idea you were in town," continued Adams. "Please come in! Can you stay for luncheon?"

"I can stay for only a minute," said Holmes. "I need to catch my train back to Boston in an hour. But I would happily sit in your study with you for a few moments and would heartily welcome a cup of coffee."

Adams gave orders for the coffee to be brewed fresh and led Holmes to his study. At five-foot-six, Henry Brooks Adams had never felt tall—even among the shorter Americans of the nineteenth century—but he always felt especially short next to Oliver Wendell Holmes, Jr. Holmes was still "Jr.", even at age fifty-two, because his famous father was still alive. He'd not yet struck off the mildly subordinating appellation as Henry James had a decade earlier upon the death of *his* father. But with Oliver Wendell Holmes, Jr., even the "Junior" seemed to add to his appropriate grandeur.

Even while standing in the foyer with Holmes, Adams had realized that his old acquaintance was becoming *more* handsome in his fifties—tall, erect, the high collar trying to hide his one flaw (a neck that some said was too long), with his perfectly curved mustache only beginning to go gray and his perfectly parted hair contrasting boldly with Henry Adams's bald pate. (And not only bald, Adams knew, but still peeling from the various sunburns he'd suffered on St. Helena and on Agassiz's yacht, despite constantly wearing yachting caps and straw hats.)

As the steaming coffee came, Adams realized that even though he was only fifty-five, three years older than Holmes, it was his destiny to continue to grow balder and fatter and, yes, shorter, while Holmes would almost certainly keep his erect, tall, parade-ground-proud posture into his nineties and would probably reach the apogee of his male beauty in his eighties.

"What brings you to Washington, Wendell?" asked Adams. "Down to see Chief Justice Fuller perhaps?"

"Yes, Justice Fuller and President Cleveland," said Holmes, carefully sipping his coffee. He did not offer to explain why he would be seeing the president, and Adams pointedly did not ask.

Holmes had been serving as an associate justice on the Massachusetts Supreme Court since 1883 and most astute observers Adams knew expected him to be Chief Justice of that state before long. Others would lay odds that before another decade was out, Holmes would be on the U.S. Supreme Court, although Adams had his private doubts about that.

"Well, how is Mrs. Holmes?" asked Adams. "Well, I hope."

"Fanny is quite well, thank you." It had been John Hay who had once commented privately to Adams about the slightly dismissive tone that always was present when Wendell mentioned his wife. Hay and Adams were in silent agreement that if ever there were a purely companionate marriage, the Holmeses' was such.

Holmes set down his cup and saucer on a trivet the butler had placed on the top of a low bookcase next to his chair. "I stopped by to ask you about these rumors," said Holmes in his old, somewhat abrupt manner.

"Rumors?" Adams felt his heart race when he knew he shouldn't be alarmed. Lizzie Cameron would never reveal the contents of their personal letters—especially not Adams's last and most personal letter to her, from Scotland to Paris, just a couple of months earlier. Still, his pulse pounded with anxiety.

"About the Hays' visitors," said Holmes.

Adams let his eyebrows rise. "I wasn't aware that John and Clara had any visitors of special note, but, then, I've been traveling awhile now."

"So Hay told me when I stopped by next door a few minutes ago," said Holmes. "But your service staff must be buzzing about the visitors... mine certainly are."

"Your servants in *Boston* are buzzing about the Hays' visitors?" Adams cried with a smile.

"Of course not, but I've been here in Washington several days now and I always bring my personal valet and cook along."

Adams folded his hands under his chin and smiled openly. "I've not had time to hear my servants whispering. By all means, Holmes, tell me the gossip."

Holmes made a flicking motion with his hand—Adams noticing the long, tapering, perfectly manicured fingers—and said, "It's certain that Henry James is back. He was staying with the Hays for the past week or so... I just missed him, evidently. He's taken up lodgings nearby. At Mrs. Stevens's place, I believe."

"Clover arranged for Harry to stay there ten years ago, the last time he was here," said Adams in a low voice.

Holmes nodded impatiently. "I stopped by Mrs. Stevens's place before coming back here, but both James and his fellow lodger—the Hays' other guest this past week and more—were out."

"I wonder what Harry came back for," mused Adams. Just before Henry James had left America in 1883 after his parents' deaths and all the problems created by his father's will and properties in Albany, Adams had heard him swear that that would be his last visit to America. His home now was in England and Europe, their old friend had said.

"Whatever brought him back, he's trying to keep the visit confidential," said Holmes.

Adams steepled his fingers and tapped his bearded chin. "Why would Harry want to do that? Unless... but William is in good health and away with his family to Italy or Switzerland or somewhere the last I heard, and I believe there were no complications last year with Harry's sister Alice's will. Miss Loring brought the poor girl's ashes home last year to be interred in the family plot in Cambridge."

"Perhaps the confidentiality relates to James's companion—or, rather, companions—on this trip," Holmes said softly, leaning forward over the desk. "Two men. Both rather strange, from what I hear."

Adams allowed his steepled fingers to tap his lips. If Wendell's gossip was about some physical liaison that Harry finally allowed to occur with some other man—on his encounters with Harry in England and the Continent, Adams had sensed the almost-perfectly-hidden infatuation that James felt toward some of his younger male artist friends—Adams most assuredly did not want to hear about it. He hoped that his expression and posture, while seemingly neutral, conveyed this message to the often too-blunt and sometimes indiscreet Wendell.

"Who are these traveling companions?" Adams asked with no great show of curiosity. "Certainly they must be above reproach if Harry is introducing them to the Hays." Rumors of Oscar Wilde's private behavior crossed his mind but he smiled away such an absurd thought about Henry James. Harry, while loving gossip as much as the rest of their male epistolary circle, was perhaps the most essentially private person Adams had ever known.

"Certainly, certainly," Holmes was muttering. "But one of the guests—Hay says that he left some days ago—was supposedly the Norwegian, or perhaps it was Swede, Jan Sigerson you may have read about in the past year or two. An explorer of some sort."

Adams dropped his small hands to his lap. "Sigerson...Sigerson...yes, I vaguely recall the name. Norwegian, I believe. He was in the news briefly a year or two ago for climbing some mountain or finding some pass in the Himalayas, wasn't it? Or spending some time in Tibet perhaps. That *is* unusual." Adams was speaking as a veteran world traveler. After Clover's death, he'd wandered around the South Seas for almost a year with the artist John La Farge. It had been a telegram from Paris...from Lizzie Cameron...that had brought him rushing back around the planet like a fool.

Adams set that out of his mind.

"Yes, I remember something about a Jan Sigerson," he said again. "So the explorer has come to America with Harry. Odd, but I fail to see any reason for Harry to keep his presence in America secret from old friends, unless Mr. Sigerson desperately wishes to avoid publicity, and Harry was waiting for him to depart before notifying the rest of us."

"It's Hay's second guest, also James's traveling companion, that has the servants buzzing," said Holmes, who brought out his watch from where it was set in his vest pocket next to his Phi Beta Kappa key and checked the time. It was a short ride to the train station from Adams's home and Henry had noticed that Holmes had his cab waiting.

"Do you want me to guess the second gentleman's name?" asked Adams with another friendly smile.

"You wouldn't in a hundred years," said Associate Justice Holmes with heavy, measured tones. "It is Sherlock Holmes."

Adams laughed heartily, actually slapping his knees under the desk.

"You laugh," observed Holmes. Adams's old acquaintance—they had known each other for more than thirty years—had never been known for his sense of humor, certainly not in the way John Hay and Clarence King might have been, but since he had taken up his black robes of the Massachusetts court, he seemed especially humorless to Adams.

"But isn't Sherlock Holmes a fictional character," said Adams, not really making it a question. "A creation of Arthur Conan Doyle? Did Harry bring Mr. Doyle on a visit to Washington?"

"No, he brought Sherlock Holmes," repeated Holmes. "I almost got John Hay to admit it, although he seemed bound to confidence. Not only have his servants been whispering about the London detective being a guest in the house, but Clara Hay, after making her friends take an absolute oath of secrecy, has told about a hundred of those friends of Sherlock Holmes's days in the house."

"Perhaps an English relative of yours?" asked Adams, his mischievous smile back.

"Certainly not that I know of," said Holmes, who was looking at his watch again. "I must go if I'm to get my luggage sorted out at the station before boarding."

But before he stood, Adams said, "Was this Sherlock Holmes the second lodger at Mrs. Stevens's home that you attempted to see along with Harry this morning?"

"Yes," said Holmes, already moving with much longer strides with Henry toward the foyer, where the head butler, Addison, stood waiting with the justice's coat, hat, and cane.

"What would you like me to do?" Adams said softly as the two men stood in the open doorway. The late-March morning air was still chill. "Watch out my window and send you a report on whether this Sherlock Holmes looks fictional or not?"

"You still do not dine out all that much, do you, Henry?" Holmes asked bluntly.

"Not really," said Adams. In the seven years since Clover's death, he'd come to be known as a recluse and now the invitations—save from Clarence King when he was in town or John Hay next door, old members of the Five of Hearts—no longer came in. "You know how it is in this town," Adams heard himself saying. "If you accept someone's dinner invitation, then the favor must be returned. I dine here now usually with the occasional fellow old widower or young bachelor."

"Well, you'll be invited by Hay to dine Sunday evening with a young widower whom we both know well and, since this Mr. Sherlock Holmes is reputed to be one of the other guests, I had hoped you'd write me about *that*."

"A young widower whom we both know well..." began Adams as he walked Holmes outside under the arches and that damned cross. "You don't mean..."

"I *do* mean," said Holmes, almost crossly to Adams's sensitive ear. "The Boy."

"The Boy...oh, dear me," was all that Adams could muster.

He waved to Holmes's carriage—knowing full well that Wendell never looked back—until it disappeared around the corner.

"The Boy," muttered Adams, feeling that he had made a great mistake in coming home several days sooner than he'd originally planned. "Oh dear me."

2

Seven Inches Below Floor Level and Sinking

Holmes much preferred their new living areas in Mrs. Stevens's home to being a guest at the home of John and Clara Hay. It was true that even here at this boarding house, Henry James was still residing in the same *house* as Holmes, but the door to James's bed-sitting-room was down a long hallway and they no longer had to see each other constantly or to share each meal. But first and foremost in importance was his freedom—the second story had its own outside door and wooden staircase and each tenant received a key to that door. Holmes was free now to come and go whenever he pleased—and in whatever guise he chose—without scrutiny by Henry James or the Hays' servants.

This morning he was in no disguise; he wore his London-tailored suit, waistcoat, top hat and gloves, long black scarf, and was carrying his cane sheathing a three-sided razor-sharp 30-inch sword.

Across Lafayette Square, Holmes hailed a hansom cab and told the driver to take him to the Metropolitan Police Department Headquarters at the corner of Fifth and Louisiana. Once there he had the driver park across the street from the old rundown precinct house.

Holmes didn't have to wait more than ten minutes before the Major and Superintendent of the Metropolitan Police, William C. Moore, came down the steps, glanced irritably at his watch, and hailed a cab. Holmes ordered his driver to follow that cab, even though he knew where it was headed.

Holmes had never met Major and Superintendent Moore but he'd studied photographs of him and there was no mistaking that white, General Robert E. Lee–type beard. And he knew that the irritability he'd glimpsed ran deep this morning since the major and superintendent was not accustomed to being summoned *anywhere* by *anyone,* much less to the unimportant Maltby Building by order of someone in the mere State Department.

Holmes's cab drew to the curb at the corner of New Jersey Street and Constitution Avenue just as Moore had alighted and almost bumped into the former Major and Superintendent of the Metropolitan Police, William G. Brock. Where Moore's beard looked full, white, and happily plumped, former Major and Superintendent Brock's beard was a straggly gray that matched his haggard appearance.

"What are you doing here..." began Moore.

"I might ask the same of you, sir," snapped Brock.

The two men disliked one another intensely. More to the point, Holmes did know former Major and Superintendent Brock by sight and vice versa. Brock had reason—or thought he did—to hate Holmes even more than he detested the current Major and Superintendent of Police.

Holmes waited until the two men, still grumbling and demanding answers from one another, went into the building before he stepped out of his cab and paid the driver.

Holmes had asked John Hay about the Maltby Building the previous week, mentioning only that he'd passed by the odd-looking building, and Hay had laughed and explained that the lift inside was treacherous because the Maltby Building, a five-story apartment building purchased twenty years earlier to provide overflow space for Senate offices, had been built on the site of an old stable by its New York developer. Essentially, "as is true of so many things in Washington," Hay had said, the building had been built on sand. The massive elevator had begun sinking into the sand, dragging the entire building down with it, and now to enter the lift one had to step up or down some seven inches. "What's more," added Hay with an additional laugh, "those offices still remaining in the Maltby Building are freezing in the winter, literally intolerable in the summer, and cramped at all times."

Perfect, Holmes had thought and had cabled his brother Mycroft to have Whitehall "summon" Major and Superintendents Moore and Brock and the others to the Office of Steamboat Inspection on the fourth floor of that building. The Supervising Inspector General of Steamboat Inspection was a certain James A. Dismont, who had been warned by the State Department of this morning's invasion but had not been told the reason for the gathering. Now when Dismont's flustered clerk, a certain Andrew McWilliams, according to the sign on his desk, led Holmes into the Inspector General's crowded office, it was also entry into a din of outraged voices—led by William C. Moore's.

Holmes rapped his cane soundly on the wooden floor four times and all heads turned in his direction.

"Gentlemen," said Holmes, using his most commanding tone, "I am Mr. Sherlock Holmes and it is at my request—relayed through Whitehall, your president, and your State Department—that we are all gathered here this morning. Mr. Dismont"—Holmes nodded at the confused Inspector General of Steamboat Inspection—"we shall need the use of your office for only about forty-five minutes and we invite you and your clerk, Mr. McWilliams, to leave the building and enjoy the lovely spring day for the next hour."

Dismont puffed his cheeks as if ready to argue but then looked at the faces of the important men in his office, nodded curtly, and left, closing the door softly behind him. Holmes made sure that the Inspector General and his secretary were gone from the outer office and then turned back to those same apoplectic faces ready to explode at him. He held up one gloved finger.

"Stop!" he said. "Before any remonstrations or demands are made, please understand that this meeting was approved by Her Majesty Queen Victoria and President Cleveland and arranged by our Whitehall and your State Department . . . precisely for reasons of privacy."

"My office at police headquarters would have been perfectly private!" thundered Major and Superintendent of Police Moore through his white whiskers.

"No, Major and Superintendent Moore, it would not have been," Holmes answered softly. "For not only is the entrance to your police headquarters at Fifth and Louisiana being observed by scouts . . . touts, you might call them...on the payroll of this city's criminal gangs, but there are members of your staff and police department also on that payroll."

"That is...*outrageous!*" roared Moore.

"As outrageous as the charges by Mr. Holmes, more than ten years ago, that my detectives were corrupt!" rasped former Major and Superintendent Brock. "I lost my position in eighteen eighty-three due to such rumor mongering."

Holmes nodded. "That was unfortunate," he said softly. "I was invited to America to look into the assassination of your President Garfield... more specifically, to see if the assassin Charles Guiteau was connected to the anarchist conspiracy that had later attempted to murder Queen Victoria. My investigations showed that Charles Guiteau acted alone and out of motives concocted only in his insane mind. But those same investigations showed the active corruption of many members of your Detective Bureau—including taking money from known anarchist conspirators."

Brock turned his back on Holmes and went to the window to look out.

Before Moore could roar again, Holmes said, "Let me introduce the three other gentlemen whom President Cleveland wanted to be here today."

Holmes nodded toward a short, handsome man standing near Brock and the window. The gentleman's mustache was waxed and curved in the French fashion, his dark hair was slicked close to his skull, but any sense of dandyism was immediately dismissed by his square jaw, firm mouth, and powerful gaze.

"Mr. William Rockhill, if I'm not mistaken," said Holmes. "Executive Secretary to the Third Assistant Secretary of State and our liaison with the State Department and various European governments, should the need arise to communicate with these governments."

Rockhill bowed toward Sherlock Holmes. "*Un plaisir de vous rencontrer,* Monsieur Holmes." He bowed to the other men. "Mr. Vice-President. Gentlemen."

Holmes gestured toward a tall, silent man with his white hair parted in the middle, the only man in the room other than Holmes who was clean-shaven. "You are Mr. Drummond, I presume?"

The tall man bowed slightly. "Andrew L. Drummond, at your service."

"Mr. Drummond is currently Chief of the Secret Service Division of the Department of the Treasury," said Holmes.

Drummond nodded his head again. His bright blue eyes seemed to show some slight amusement.

"What in blazes do the State Department or Treasury Department have to do with anything?" roared Major and Superintendent Moore. "And for that matter, sir"—the Major and Superintendent raised his cane in Holmes's direction—"who the blazes *are you* and by what authority do you summon the Chief of the Metropolitan Police Department?"

Before Holmes could answer, the sixth and final man in the room, the only one not yet introduced, a quiet, balding, mustached man in his early sixties standing in the shadows of a corner, said softly, "I will answer that, Major and Superintendent Moore. I am Vice-President Adlai E. Stevenson. Mr. Sherlock Holmes, England's most renowned and respected consulting detective, was asked to call today's meeting on the authority of President Cleveland, who has asked that everyone here might give their full cooperation on an issue of the gravest national importance."

"Mr. Vice-President..." stammered Major and Superintendent Moore and fell silent. Holmes knew from Hay and others that Vice-President Adlai Stevenson, elevated from assistant postmaster to vice-president by a whim of Cleveland's party at the 1892 Democratic Convention, could walk into almost any party or assembly in Washington and not be recognized. (Nor will Holmes be surprised, four years hence, late in 1897, when he will read a small item in *The Times* of London—"When asked whether President Cleveland had ever asked his opinion on any matter, Vice-President Adlai E. Stevenson responded—'Not yet. But there are still several weeks remaining in my term.'")

"The issue in front of us, gentlemen," said Holmes, noting that even former Major and Superintendent Brock had turned his attention back from the window, "is the anarchists' plans to assassinate Her Majesty Queen Victoria, and the monarchs, emperors, and elected leaders of at least twelve other nations, beginning with the assassination of President Grover Cleveland on or before this May first."

*　　*　　*

It was Vice-President Stevenson who took charge of moderating the outbreak of gabble into a series of questions and answers with a calm Sherlock Holmes at the swirling conversation's locus.

Secret Service Chief Drummond: How reliable is this intelligence regarding President Cleveland, Mr. Holmes?

Sherlock Holmes: Very reliable, sir.

Secret Service Chief Drummond: Are there any specifics to this warning or is it the usual vague threat?

Sherlock Holmes: The most specific threat to date suggests that President Cleveland will be assassinated on May first...the socialist International Workers' Holiday since the Haymarket Square incident...most probably while he is officially declaring open the Columbian World Exposition in Chicago.

State Department Sec. Rockhill: Is this supposed to be another Haymarket Square operation, Mr. Holmes? Mobs? Bombs thrown? Rampant shooting at police as well as at the president?

Sherlock Holmes: That is always possible...but our intelligence suggests that it is more likely to be the work of one or two master assassins hired by the anarchists.

Secret Service Chief Drummond: Do we have the identity of those hired assassins?

Sherlock Holmes: We do. Here are photographs of the two men. The older man is probably well known to you...Colonel Sebastian Moran. The younger man is the more able assassin...twenty-year-old Lucan Adler...and this photographic plate is the first official photograph of Adler. Please be careful with the glass. Can you make close-up copies from that plate, Chief Drummond?

Secret Service Chief Drummond: Of course. (Holding Clover

Adams's photographic plate up to the light while the other men craned to catch a glimpse of the face.) Why...this Adler is only a boy."

Sherlock Holmes: That photograph was taken almost seven years ago, gentlemen. Lucan Adler was thirteen years old...a boy, as you say. But even at age thirteen, he was a remarkable hunter and marksman with a rifle and already trained as an assassin by his guardian, Colonel Sebastian Moran.

Former Metropolitan Police Major and Superintendent Brock: Who took this photograph of Lucan Adler?

Sherlock Holmes: I'm afraid I cannot reveal that information at this time. But I assure you that the young man in the photograph is indeed Lucan Adler and that his face, while more angular and more cruel, still looks much the same today.

Secret Service Chief Drummond: How do you know his current appearance, Mr. Holmes?

Sherlock Holmes: I've encountered him in recent years.

Former Metropolitan Police Major and Superintendent Brock: *(Laughing derisively.)* What? The famous Sherlock Holmes "encountered" our assassin and the fellow is not in custody? How can this be? Are the faculties of the famous detective slipping some with age, sir?

Sherlock Holmes: Lucan Adler stalked *me,* Mr. Brock. And two years ago he put three rifle bullets into me and through me from extremely long range. My survival was pure chance with some aid from the fact that the bullets were steel-jacketed—in the way of military ammunition—so they passed through me rather than tumbled. Had they been ordinary rounds, the softer bullets would have taken out my lungs, heart, and spine.

(A long silence ensues.)

Metropolitan Police Major and Superintendent Moore: On whose evidence...on what basis...are we to believe in this grand anarchists' conspiracy? The May one date for the attack on President Cleveland? All of it?

Sherlock Holmes: On the basis, sir, of specific intelligence obtained by Her Majesty's Secret Service. The information has been corroborated by the new Prefect of Police of Paris, Monsieur Louis Jean-Baptiste

Lépine, and by Inspector Hanaud of the French Sûreté, as well as through other intelligence gathered by the Belgian and French Secret Services. And, finally, gentlemen, we act based on additional information obtained through my own investigations in the seven years since I provided evidence to the Chicago police regarding the Haymarket Square Massacre.

Former Metropolitan Police Major and Superintendent Brock: The general opinion in the United States now, Mr. Holmes, is that the Haymarket Trial was a one-sided farce, headed by an unfair judge and overzealous prosecutors. The general opinion now, Mr. Holmes, is that the five hanged men were martyrs to the workers' movement—martyrs for the eight-hour workday.

Sherlock Holmes: If what you say is true, Mr. Brock, then the general opinion in the United States is an ass.

Metropolitan Police Major and Superintendent Moore: It seems certain, Mr. Holmes, that Illinois's new governor, Mr. Altgeld, is going to pardon the three convicted Haymarket men who were given a fifteen-year sentence rather than death . . . Schwab, Fielden, and Neebe. A pardon with full amnesty. As Mr. Brock said, people are now of the opinion that the entire Haymarket Trial was a farce—unfair—and that Fischer, Lingg, Parsons, Spies, and Engel were unfairly executed.

Sherlock Holmes: Only four of the guilty men were hanged, sir . . . Engel, Spies, Parsons, and Fischer. Lingg, the bomb-maker, took his own life by biting into a blasting cap that he'd hidden in his cell. It blew his face off. Yet it still took him some hours to die.

Former Metropolitan Police Major and Superintendent Brock: Yet Governor Altgeld and many, many other people are saying now, seven years later, that these men were heroes of the working class.

Sherlock Holmes: These eight men were murderers and conspirators to murder. I proved this to the satisfaction of the Chicago police and to the courts. Not the least by breaking their code in the anarchist paper the *Arbeiter-Zeitung* . . . a code which coordinated the making of the bombs, the arming of the anarchists, and their ambush of the police that May Day at Haymarket Square.

Secret Service Chief Drummond: But no one ever caught the man who was said to have actually thrown the bomb . . . Schnaubelt.

Sherlock Holmes: Rudolph Schnaubelt.

Secret Service Chief Drummond: Yes. Schnaubelt just disappeared. Vanished. Probably forever.

Sherlock Holmes: Not forever, Chief Drummond. I found Rudolph Schnaubelt in France five years ago this May.

(The room again fills with gabble until Vice-President Stevenson raises his hand. When silence descends, the vice-president opens his palm to the Major and Superintendent of the Metropolitan Police Force.)

Metropolitan Police Major and Superintendent Moore: I heard nothing about Schnaubelt's apprehension.

Sherlock Holmes: I am afraid that Mr. Schnaubelt died before he could be taken into proper custody. He threw himself through a glass window and drowned in the fast-running Swiss river below. But not before he admitted to—boasted of, I should say—his part in the conspiracy *and* his act of throwing the bomb at the police from the Chicago alley opening onto Haymarket Square on May fourth, eighteen eighty-six.

Former Metropolitan Police Major and Superintendent Brock: So, Mr. Holmes, we have only your word of Rudolph Schnaubelt's... confession.

Sherlock Holmes: My word and the word of two rather extraordinary law-enforcement officers who were with me when Schnaubelt made his boasts and then tried to escape.

Secret Service Chief Drummond: Can you tell us the names of these men, Mr. Holmes?

Sherlock Holmes: Certainly. The first fellow detective present was Inspector Lépine of whom I spoke earlier, and the second police officer there to hear Schnaubelt's confession—and to help us pull his dead body from the river—was a young and very promising new member of the Brussels police force, an inspector junior-grade by the name of Hercule Poirot. But enough of old cases. What are you gentlemen going to do in the next four weeks—or less—to save the life of President Grover Cleveland?

* * *

Holmes stepped out of the circle and set his back against a bookcase filled with steamboat boiler regulations and specifications.

Vice-President Stevenson stepped forward and faced the other men in the room. "The president," said Stevenson, "has directed that this group—and anyone else we might find it necessary to invite—meet biweekly on this problem of executive protection. I believe Sunday mornings, ten until noon, shall suffice."

"Sundays!" cried Brock. "Now I am to give up my Sundays and attending divine services with my family because of this…shadow of a phantasm of a threat? Besides, I no longer have any official capacity in law enforcement. There is no reason for me to be here."

"The president wished you to be part of this first assembly," Vice-President Stevenson said softly.

"For what possible reason?" demanded the haggard former major and superintendent of police.

"Your Bureau of Detectives was deeply corrupt when you resigned," said Sherlock Holmes. "You left, many of them remained and are in positions of higher authority today. Detectives on the payroll of the gangs or anarchists could be fatal to our plans. Your expertise in that area is required. In other words, sir, the President of the United States has commanded you to be what I believe American criminals call… a rat."

Brock made blustering noises but had nothing discernible to say.

"Fine, let us move on," said Stevenson, as if some minor motion had been passed in the Senate. "Major and Superintendent Moore, please explain to us your department's role in protecting the president."

The major and superintendent cleared his throat. "The Metropolitan Police provide security for the president when he makes public appearances in Washington City."

"Do your officers accompany the president to and from these public venues?" asked Stevenson.

"No, Mr. Vice-President."

The pale, round face with its faded mustache looked around the room. "Who does travel in the city with the president?"

Silence.

"Who protects the president when he is in the Executive Mansion?" asked Stevenson.

"The White House Police," said Major and Superintendent Moore.

"Is that a unit under your jurisdiction, Major and Superintendent Moore?"

"Not directly, Mr. Vice-President." Moore again cleared his throat. "We train the recruits and send them to that unit, but the White House Police Force has its own autonomy."

"Who is in charge of the White House Police Force?" asked Stevenson.

"Sergeant O'Neil, sir," answered Major and Superintendent Moore.

"*Sergeant* O'Neil?"

"Yes, sir."

"How many police officers are under your supervision in the entire Metropolitan Police Department, Major and Superintendent Moore?"

"Two hundred, Mr. Vice-President."

"Not counting the White House Police."

"No, sir."

"And how many officers are assigned to the White House Police?"

"There were three until this spring, Mr. Vice-President," said Major and Superintendent Moore. "But the number and intensity of the death threats that President Cleveland has been receiving has caused that unit to raise its numbers to twenty-seven."

"Working on three shifts around the clock, one presumes."

"More or less, Mr. Vice-President."

"So at any given time, the president has about nine rookie police officers guarding his life."

"Yes, sir," said Moore, who was beginning to sound aggrieved. "But that is by far the most any American president has had guarding him, with the exception of President Lincoln who sometimes had an escort of federal cavalry or infantry billeted on the White House grounds."

"But not that night at Ford's Theatre," said Vice-President Stevenson.

"No, sir," said Moore. "The soldier usually assigned to sit outside the president's booth at the theater was not present that evening."

"When President Cleveland goes to Chicago on May first to open the Columbian World Exposition in front of a crowd of a hundred thousand or more people, how many of your Metropolitan Police or the White House Police...or the army, for that matter...will accompany the president?" asked Stevenson.

There was silence as the men looked at one another.

Finally Major and Superintendent Moore said, "None, Mr. Vice-President. When the chief executive travels to other cities, his protection is the responsibility of the police force of that city."

Stevenson looked at Major and Superintendent Moore for a long, strangely tense moment. Stevenson's gaze remained as soft as his voice, but there was some electrical charge in the air. The vice-president turned his gaze toward the tall Secret Service Chief.

"Mr. Drummond," said Stevenson, "I understand that your department has had some experience in recent months in guarding the president."

"A small amount, sir," said Drummond. "We have well-trained and -armed agents, as you know, and from time to time in the past few weeks, the White House Police have asked us to provide some additional protection for President Cleveland."

"At the White House or when he leaves it?" asked the vice-president.

"When he leaves it to speak or make any public appearance, sir," said Drummond.

"That is the role of the Metropolitan Police Department, *sir,*" snapped Major and Superintendent Moore. It was obvious that this was the first the major and superintendent was hearing about the Secret Service poaching on the Police Department's prerogatives.

Drummond nodded. "Yes, Major and Superintendent, we know. But during events such as the president's address to the large crowds at City Park last Christmas, your department had only three uniformed officers there to guard the president. At the request of the White House Police—presumably because of specific threats received—we sent six of our armed agents in plain clothes."

"Unnecessary," snapped Major and Superintendent Moore.

Ignoring the Metropolitan Police Major and Superintendent, Vice-

President Stevenson said, "Chief Drummond, has not the Secret Service Department of the Treasury also experimented in accompanying the president during his travels in the city?"

"Oh, yes!" cried former Major and Superintendent Brock, braying a laugh. "Six men in a carriage rumbling after the president's coach, trying to keep up, getting lost on K Street! What a farce that was! The entire population of Washington, D.C., was amused by the folly."

Drummond bowed his head. "Agents following the president's carriage in a separate coach has not proved effective, Mr. Vice-President. And President Cleveland and his advisors understandably do not want agents in the presidential coach with them."

Vice-President Stevenson folded his arms. "Chief Drummond, if Congress were to assign full-time protective duties to the Secret Service—full-time both here in Washington and wherever and whenever the president travels—how long would it be before your agency could assume those duties?"

Drummond blinked. "We would have to hire and train more agents, Mr. Vice-President. Currently we simply do not have enough for full-time protection duties for the president even here in Washington. And these agents would have to be trained…bodyguard duties require special skills beyond the usual police officer's purview."

"Nonsense," said Moore.

Drummond turned his cold gaze onto the major and superintendent. "Are Metropolitan Police officers trained to throw themselves in front of the person they are assigned to protect?" he asked in a low, firm voice. "To take the bullet meant for that official?"

"Of course not," barked Moore. "The very idea is absurd. Police seize the suspect or foil the aim of the would-be assassin before any shot can be fired. They're not trained in suicide."

"Effective executive protection agents from the Secret Service will have to be trained in exactly such tactics," Drummond said flatly. "Stop the assassin if possible. Take the assassin's bullet in protection of the president if necessary."

Moore turned away to look out the window.

"How long, Mr. Drummond?" repeated the vice-president.

"By the beginning of the new year, Mr. Vice-President, for full, round-the-clock, traveling anywhere with the president, executive protection. We shall have to open new bureaus in various American cities. Train some agents in the full panoply of advance security work."

Stevenson nodded almost sadly, as if he had expected that date. "But you can provide some ad hoc protection in the meantime? When called upon?"

"Yes, sir," said Drummond.

"Arrange to have at least eight of your agents travel with President Cleveland to Chicago in May," said the vice-president.

"Yes, sir."

"If I may make a suggestion, gentlemen," said Sherlock Holmes.

Everyone looked at the consulting detective, who was taking his ease sitting on one corner of the empty desk.

"I would suggest, Chief Drummond, that when you choose those agents who will most closely accompany the president, that they be chosen in part for their height and thickness of torso."

"The public won't be able to see the president!" cried former Major and Superintendent Brock.

"That is precisely the idea," said Holmes. "It is a shame, however, that this tall phalanx of bodyguards cannot surround the president when he is greeting dignitaries or speaking to the crowds. Still, the closer they can press, the safer the president will be."

Drummond nodded and made a note. "We have such large and tall men amongst our best agents," he said softly. "I shall see that they shall be closest to the president when he is walking somewhere or standing alone."

"Preposterous," said former Major and Superintendent Brock.

Ignoring Brock and nodding slightly to Holmes, Vice-President Adlai E. Stevenson said, "And so we shall continue having meetings here on Sunday, gentlemen, until the details of this transfer of executive protection responsibilities are worked out." Again he glanced at Holmes and then at Brock and Washington's current police Major and Superintendent, Moore. "Although not everyone here today may be required in all future meetings."

"What shall we call this committee, sir?" asked Rockhill from the State Department.

Stevenson smiled slightly. "Since it is the Office of Steamboat Inspection Department's Supervising Inspector General Dismont, I suggest we refer to our little group as the Steamboat Inspection Committee. Any objections?"

No one spoke.

Before the men began moving toward the doorway, Vice-President Stevenson said, "A final question, gentlemen. Who is in charge of liaison with the Chicago police for the president's security at the Columbian Exposition on May first?"

The silence was embarrassing.

"I can do that, sir," Drummond said at last.

"I shall as well," said Major and Superintendent Moore. "I had always intended to send a telegram or two."

Sherlock Holmes moved away from where he lounged against the bookcase. "I shall be going to Chicago next week to make arrangements," he said while tugging his kid gloves tighter. "I would be pleased to work with Chief Drummond and his Secret Service on such liaison with the Chicago P.D."

The six men took turns riding the lift down in pairs. Holmes rode down with the vice-president. At the bottom, the two men had to take care in stepping up the seven inches the heavy elevator had sunk below the level of the first floor.

The Supervising Inspector General of Steamboat Inspection and his secretary were standing in the lobby, their faces red with indignation.

"Thank you, Mr. Dismont," said the vice-president to the flustered Steamboat Inspector General. "I will be in touch regarding any future weekend needs for your office."

"This is ridiculous," muttered Dismont as he and his secretary jumped the seven inches down into the elevator to ride back up to their offices and while Holmes held the front door for the vice-president.

Outside on the sidewalk, Stevenson turned to the detective. "Is it, Mr. Holmes?"

"Is what, sir?"

"Is our whole effort . . . no, is this entire talk of attempted assassination by anarchists . . . ridiculous? Are we all *being* ridiculous?"

"We'll know soon enough, Mr. Vice-President." Holmes touched the handle of his walking stick to the brim of his top hat and turned away up Constitution Avenue.

3

Tombstones for Teeth and Tame Cats

On Saturday morning, Henry James received a hand-delivered message from John Hay asking if James could drop by that afternoon—anytime that afternoon—for a talk that would take no more than a few minutes.

James did stop by the mansion commanding the corner of H and 16th Streets, taking care to time his stop late enough after lunch and early enough before tea time so as not to put Hay to any obligation.

James had barely given his hat and coat and cane to Benson when Hay hurried from his study to shake James's hand, thank him for coming, and lead him into the parlor.

"I've always admired the two kinds of stone you and Clara chose for this room," said James, settling into the deep leather chair to which Hay had gestured.

"Do you?" asked Hay, looking around idly as if he'd not looked at the stone—or the parlor—for some time. "The African marble is called Aurora Pompadour, I seem to recall, and the rest is Mexican onyx."

"My favorite combination of stone in your lovely home may be the yellow fireplace in the library with its reddish or pink hearth," said James.

"Oh, yes...that hearthstone was damnable hard to find. Everything was either too red or too pink or too...something. As it was, we decided on that very subdued reddish porphyry...'Boisé d'Orient' I think they called it. Would you care for something to drink, Harry?"

"No...thank you. This is a restful pause in the middle of my constitutional. Walking allows my mind to wander back to work. I've been pondering a new play, but nothing clear enough to talk about yet." James had hurried that last phrase in, to make sure they would not be discussing his work.

"Then I'm doubly sorry for intruding on your Saturday afternoon," said Hay. "But I thought a fair warning was due to you."

"Warning?"

"And an apology," said Hay. "You and Mr. Holmes should be receiving an invitation to a tiny dinner party for tomorrow evening, nothing elaborate, just Adams and a few friends here at the old fort. Half the sincere apology is for such short notice."

"And the second half?" murmured James.

"You asked for discretion when you arrived—your presence not to be advertised, that is—but that was almost two weeks ago, Harry. You know how word gets around in this small town in spite of all our efforts."

"Of course," said James. "And I am delighted to hear that Adams is back and I look forward to seeing him."

"He says that he never dines out," Hay said, still seeming somewhat distracted. "But you know as well as I that that's all hogwash. Henry has fewer full-fledged dinner parties next door, but he's as social as ever. He simply wants to *appear* the recluse."

"I possess some kindred feeling there," said James. "May I ask who else will be attending besides Adams? King's not back in town, is he?"

"Not that I'm aware of," said Hay. "I sent a cable to his Union Club in New York but haven't received a reply. He's probably a mile underground in Mexico by now, up to his earlobes in gold nuggets or diamonds."

James waited.

"The rest of the party will be made up of the usual suspects," continued Hay. James remembered all too well going to a mediocre play—little more than a comic-romance melodrama, really—in London with the Hays and how for days afterward John had kept repeating that (to James) eminently forgettable line—"The party will be made up of all the usual suspects." Knowing the rather tight Washington social circles the Adamses, Hays, et al. had always moved within, James caught at least a glimmer of the humor Hays found in "all the usual suspects".

"Don and Lizzie are coming," said Hay. "And Lodge and Nannie, of course. And Adams...the whole thing is a sort of welcome-home thing for Adams. And...oh, yes...when you inquired about the children last week, I told you that Alice, Helen, Clarence, and Del were all away at school, but Del has the weekend off from St. Paul's Academy and Helen will also be joining us."

"Wonderful," said James, who loathed having children—even nearly grown children—at a dinner party. "It's been far too long since I've seen them. You said in a recent letter that Del has had quite the growth spurt?"

Seventeen-year-old Adelbert—"Del"—Hay had always struck Henry James (and probably his father John Hay, as well) as a rather slow, dull, uninteresting boy. But James hadn't seen any of the four children since the Hay family's last *en masse* descent upon London at least five years ago.

"Amazing growth spurt," laughed Hay. "Del's over six feet tall now and weighs more than two hundred pounds. And he's become quite the athlete at St. Paul's. He's going to Yale in the autumn and plans to go out for football. *Football,* Harry. American football, where one rarely uses one's feet."

"Football?" James said blankly. The name, in an American context, rang only the faintest of bells. "But not what we call soccer?"

"No, an entirely new game," said Hay. "Evidently it was invented—or, rather, adapted from European football and rugby, mostly rugby, I think, and its rules laid down—a dozen or so years ago by a Yale undergraduate at the time, a certain Walter Camp, who became general athletic director and...head football coach...whatever that means. Football is all the rage at Ivy League colleges now, Harry. It seems that Harvard and Yale have been in a deadly annual football competition for some years. Last year, a Harvard chess master named Lorin Deland introduced a devastating new play or maneuver or move or...something...called 'the Flying Wedge'—no clue as to what that means—but Yale still managed to win, six to zero. Del can't wait to play under Walter Camp's tutelage."

"And Helen will also be here tomorrow night?" said James. He would have stabbed himself in both eyes with a dull knife if that is what it would have taken to get off the subject of sports. "She must be . . . eighteen?"

"Yes," said Hay. "And she's very dedicated these days to writing poetry and even some short fiction. Don't let her corner you, Harry."

"In London last, she was a lovely and invigorating interlocutor at age thirteen," said James. "I can only imagine how pleasant it would be now to be 'cornered' by her to pursue the discussion of all things literary."

"Adams needs to meet Sherlock Holmes," said Hay, his voice suddenly serious. "That's the primary reason for this gathering . . . not that Adams wouldn't have arranged to see *you* at the earliest possible opportunity, Harry. He was distraught at having missed your first week here. But I wasn't sure what to tell him about . . . the whole Holmes thing. Do you think it will be Sherlock Holmes or Jan Sigerson who will appear tomorrow night?"

"To whom did you address the invitation?" asked James.

"To Mr. Holmes."

"Then I wager that it will be Mr. Holmes who appears."

"Oh . . . I almost forgot," said Hay as he walked James through the foyer to the door. "We've also invited . . . as Adams and Wendell always call him . . . the Boy."

"The Boy," mused James. "Oh, you mean . . . oh! Oh, my. Oh, dear. I keep forgetting that he's in Washington these days."

"I made him promise to be on his best behavior," said Hay.

James's smile was three parts irony to two parts anticipation. "We shall see. We shall see."

*   *   *

Sherlock Holmes had been invited as "Mr. Sherlock Holmes" to the 8 p.m. Hays' Sunday dinner gathering so he arrived as Mr. Sherlock Holmes. His second and third steamer trunks had caught up to him via the British Embassy in Washington, so he wore the latest London fashion in white tie and black tails, soft pumps so highly polished that they could be used as a signaling mirror in an emergency (but not the overly flexible Capezio black jazz oxfords so popular with the younger set for a long night of dancing), a crimson-lined black cape, the silkiest of silk, six-and-a-half-inch-tall top hat, a formal vest with lapels and scooped front, a brilliantly white formal shirt with a stand-up rather than wing collar, and — since it was a dinner, not a ball — no white gloves.

The other men were dressed similarly — no sign of the less formal (and, to Holmes, definitely déclassé) new "tuxedo jacket" — and, upon their introduction by Hay, Holmes had to award Henry Adams the laurels for oldest, most worn, and by far most beautiful jacket of the evening, although Henry Cabot Lodge's shining new threads must have cost five times the price of Adams's time-worn perfection. The only man there that night who did not look to have been born into his clothes was Hay's heavily muscled and bull-necked teenaged son, Del, who seemed to be bursting out of his formalwear even as they all watched.

The ladies, with only a few missed cues, were also upholding the highest standards of modern French-American design.

The group had only a few minutes for introductions and polite conversation before they were called into the dining room.

Holmes had to admit to a feeling of admiration. He'd dined with the Prince of Wales, the King of Scandinavia, and more elite and sophisticated hosts in England, France, and around the world, but he couldn't remember a more beautiful room, chandelier, or table. Realizing that this dining room might comfortably seat fifty at a State Department banquet, Holmes marveled at how Clara Hay had arranged it to perfection for the twelve of them — four women and eight men.

The dinner was lopsided in terms of gender, but Clara and John Hay had made up for that in careful placement of their guests and beautiful but low centerpieces that hid no one's face from anyone else. After they found their seats — there seemed to be a white-tie-and-tails servant behind every chair to help them with the extreme effort of scooting in or scooting out — Holmes took a minute to appreciate the seating arrangements.

At the head of the table was not John Hay, as one would expect in the man's own home, but Henry Adams. The placement emphasized

the "Welcome home, Henry" aspect of the dinner, but Holmes also suspected that the chair provided to Adams had a little higher seat, a little
extra cushion, and thus put the short, bald man at eye height with everyone else.

Down the right side of the table—Holmes's side—was first the
newly sworn-in Massachusetts Senator Henry Cabot Lodge (perfectly
groomed down to his perfectly cropped beard and mustache, but cold of
eye—*very* cold of eye), then the stolid but animated Clara Hay (whose
gown of royal-blue silk blended with satin and a design of garnet-colored
peacock feathers with sleeves and trim of garnet-colored silk-satin and
velvet would have been absolutely breathtakingly original if it hadn't
been featured in that March's issue of *Harper's Bazaar*), and then Pennsylvania Senator James Donald Cameron (whose dark eyes seemed as
sadly drooping as his thick mustache), then Sherlock—who found himself sitting directly across the table from Henry James and who knew at
once that this was no accident, since at mid-table both of them could
then field questions from both ends of the table—and to Sherlock's
left, young "Del" Hay smiling and ham-fisted but obviously comfortable
with formal dining in such elite company as Henry Adams, Senator J.
Donald Cameron, author Henry James, and the ice-eyed congressman-
billionaire only this month turned U.S. Senator Henry Cabot Lodge.

At the end of the table to Holmes's left was seated the other "special
guest" of the evening, Civil Service Commissioner Theodore Roosevelt.
Other than hearing from Henry James that Adams and Hay and Clarence
King and the late Clover Adams had sometimes referred to young Roosevelt whom they'd known for many years as "the Boy", Holmes knew
little about the man.

But Holmes was interested in what he saw. Merely in the act of helping young Helen Julia Hay, to his left, into her seat and then taking
his own chair and beaming down both sides of the table, Theodore
Roosevelt radiated aggression. With small eyes squinting out from behind pince-nez, a military-trimmed mustache, and rows of teeth that
seemed strangely aligned top and bottom, a horse's teeth, a fierce stal-
lion's pre-breeding grimace, and a powerful, coiled, compact body that
made athlete Del Hay's tall form seem to shrink by comparison, the

grinning Theodore Roosevelt seemed prepared to attack everyone at the table.

Or eat them whole, thought Holmes.

John Hay's 18-year-old daughter Helen Julia sitting to the Roosevelt-creature's left was, to Holmes's always objective eye for such things, one of those rare beautiful female creatures who actually lived up to the image of the new "Gibson Girl"—long, white neck, her hair swept back close to that perfect head until it rolled most naturally into a gay Gibson Girl puff, her soft chiffon dress emphasizing the modern ideal of a woman as tall and slender yet with ample bosom and hips, all while giving off a sense of high intelligence mixed with an athlete's glow.

Then across the table from Holmes was Henry James, his balding dome seeming to give off an extra beneficial glow in the candlelight. Holmes could see in an instant that James was in his native element, even at an extraordinary table such as this at which sat two senators, a man who was a grandson and great-grandson of Presidents of the United States, several of the wealthiest men in America, no fewer than four famous historians, three of the most beautiful women Holmes had seen in years, and an energetic young cannibal flashing his tombstone-sized teeth.

The Hays obviously had given James the gift of beauty on either side—Helen Julia Hay to his right and Nannie Lodge to his left.

Nannie Lodge sitting between Henry James and John Hay was lovely in the usual Gilded Age ways—slim, fair, wasp-waisted, with lovely hands and a sweet disposition—but the most outstanding aspect of the 43-year-old aging beauty were her eyes...eyes which Holmes's friend Watson would have immediately described as "bewitching" and which Margaret Chanler described in writing as "the color of the sky when stars begin to twinkle."

No such poetic phrases entered Holmes's mind on Sunday, April 2, 1893, as he paused a second to study those eyes—Nannie was turned to her left toward John Hay and was not aware of the detective's brief but intense appraisal—so he filed away the odd, soft intensity of Mrs. Cabot Lodge's eye color and was reminded of it years later only when his new friend, the painter John Singer Sargent, lamented never having had the chance to paint Nannie Lodge, saying, "I had such an unqualified regard for her that the odds were in favor of my succeeding in getting something of that kindness and intelligence of her expression and the unforgettable blue of her eyes."

Perhaps.

Beyond Nannie Lodge and the smiling, laughing John Hay, at the corner of the table near Mr. Adams, was the true beauty at the table—Lizzie Cameron.

The doleful-looking Senator Cameron's wife was, according to Henry James's whisper as they walked to the Hays' home that evening, the loveliest and most-sought-after woman in all of Washington society. In his cool, distant way, Sherlock Holmes saw why at once. Lizzie Cameron's dress was simultaneously the simplest and most daring of any of the perfectly dressed women's at the table. Her shoulders were bare and white. Her arms were long, perfectly white, and ended in long-fingered hands that looked as though they'd been designed by God to caress men's faces and hair. She had a long neck unadorned by jewelry or cloth bands and a sharply oval face. Lizzie's hair this night was gathered up on both sides and rose in a bun in the back but looked impossibly natural.

She did not smile much, Holmes had already noted, and yet with those arching brows, deep, dark eyes, and perfectly shaped mouth, Elizabeth Sherman Cameron was that rarest object of her sex—a woman whose entire beauty could shine through when she was not smiling or even when she looked actively severe.

In the few minutes they'd been seated, Holmes had seen enough of the almost imperceptible glances, nearly invisible reactions to tell him that Henry Adams, at age 55 some 22 years older than Lizzie Cameron, was in love with her; that their host John Hay, without ever looking directly at his table partner to the left, said with his entire body's balance and tension that he was madly in love with Lizzie Cameron.

Henry James, Holmes could see (and would have predicted), admired Lizzie's beauty the way a cat might admire a bowl of milk it had no intention of sipping from. Henry Cabot Lodge took his wife's friend's beauty as a given of their station in life, young Del Hay had known Lizzie Cameron for most of his life and was obviously looking at her as one of his parents' friends, and Theodore Roosevelt bestowed his giant, menacing grin upon her with a happily married man's innocent benevolence. Senator James "Don" Cameron—who would be 60 in two months—looked as miserable as if he'd been actively cuckolded by all the scores and hundreds of men who had dreamt of achieving that blissful goal with the beautiful Lizzie Cameron.

Holmes felt—knew—that Lizzie Cameron teased, teased, tempted, and teased, but did not actually bestow her favors. Not on poor Adams who, Holmes would soon learn, had rushed 10,000 miles around the world from the South Seas to come to Lizzie's beckoning telegram from Paris only to be shunned by her once he'd arrived. Not on poor John Hay, who—Holmes sensed at once—had yet to declare his physical love for the lady but who, after his inevitable rebuff, would join Henry Adams and a mist-shrouded legion of gray others who had been relegated to the role of "tame cat" in Lizzie Cameron's life.

And Holmes also felt—knew—that Lizzie Cameron was a dangerous and treacherous person. Certainly, Holmes exempting himself and since neither Professor Moriarty nor Lucan Adler appeared to be present this evening, the most dangerous and treacherous person in the room.

The oysters arrived and the dinner officially began.

4

A Shocking Shortage of Canvasbacks

While guests had been milling prior to this dinner, Henry James had stepped into the kitchen to say hello to Hay's chef for this meal, a man named Charles Ranhofer who had served, for a while, as the personal chef for William Waldorf Astor—the richest man in America until he moved to England in 1891. Chef Ranhofer was preparing to publish a cookbook, which ran to more than 1,000 pages, called *The Epicurean.* It would sell more copies worldwide than any novel Henry James ever published.

James had first met Ranhofer when he was a guest at Lansdowne House, Astor's rented London mansion, and often heard of the chef's reputation at Delmonico's restaurant on Fifth Avenue.

This evening, the famous chef was too busy filling Hay's oversized kitchen and extended staff with commands, orders, and ultimatums to pause to chat, so James simply wished him well...but not before he caught a glimpse of Charles's menu for the evening—

Menu

Huîtres en coquille Ruedesheimer

Potage tortue verte Amontillado

Caviare sur canapé Médoc

Homard à la Maryland Royal Charter

Ris de veau aux champignons

Selle de mouton

Pommes parisiennes Haricots verts

Suprème de volaille

Pâté de foie-gras, Bellevue {Illegible}

Sorbet à la romaine

Cigarettes

Teal duck, celery mayonnaise   Clos de Vougeot

Fromage Duque Port Wine

Glacée à la napolitaine Château Lafite

Old Reserve Madeira

The "cigarettes" had been crossed out, which James wholly approved of, especially in mixed company, but also because it had become déclassé in most upper-class English and Continental meals to include smoking as a formal menu item.

* * *

The oysters were followed by soup, a light dish which James paid little attention to because of the conversation with the beautiful women on each side of him, then a fish course.

The first ten minutes of conversation were mostly taken up by questions—almost exclusively from the ladies at the table—to Sherlock Holmes. Was he really a consulting detective? What did a consulting detective do? Were his adventures as exciting as they read in *The Strand* and *Harper's Weekly*?

"I can't answer that last question, I fear," said Holmes in his clipped, formal but friendly English accent. "It's only been the last year or two that these so-called chronicles of my cases have been published by Dr. Watson, and I honestly haven't had the time or opportunity to read any of them."

"But they're based on truth?" asked Helen Julia Hay.

"Quite possibly," said Holmes. "But my friend Dr. Watson—and his editor and agent Mr. Doyle—are pledged to entertain the reader. And, in my experience, the hard truth and entertainment rarely co-exist peacefully."

"But what about Silver Blaze?" asked Clara, her voice small but determined. "That case was true, was it not?"

"Who or what is Silver Blaze?" asked Holmes.

Clara grew a little flustered but managed—"The case...the name of the race horse that was stolen...that ran away...the story in last month's *Harper's Weekly*."

"I confess that I've never heard of an English race horse named Silver Blaze, Mrs. Hay," said Holmes.

"You see, Clara," said John Hay. "I told you it was fiction. I lose a fortune at the track when I'm in England, and I'd never heard of a colt named 'Silver Blaze' either."

Holmes smiled at that. "I did have a minor case involving a horse named Seabreeze in eighteen eighty-eight—he won the Oaks and St. Leger in that year—but his 'disappearance' amounted to little more than his wandering away one night. The neighboring farmer found him and I worked to the limits of my detecting ability to follow clear hoofprints in the mud to the neighboring farmer's home."

The group chuckled but Clara persisted. "So the trainer *wasn't* found dead?" she asked.

"He was, actually," said Holmes. "But it was a mere accident. The

306 || DAN SIMMONS

poor lad was taking Seabreeze for his evening walk, evidently had noticed some possible problem with the colt's right rear hoof, had knelt
behind the filly—never a good idea at the best of times—and lit a
match in the failing light even before raising the hoof for inspection.
Seabreeze kicked once, purely out of instinct, and the poor fellow's head
was..." Holmes glanced around the shining table at the shining faces.
"That is, he died instantly of a head injury. But no foul play."

"Silver Blaze was a colt in the story anyway," said Clara Hay. "Not a
filly."

Everyone laughed with her.

Guided by both Hay's and Henry Adams's hosting expertise, the
attention soon moved away from Holmes, and localized conversations
quickly began to include entire ends of the table and then everyone.
Twelve diners was close to the perfect number for intimate and audible
table conversation, especially with such reticent conversationalists in the
group as Henry Cabot Lodge, Don Cameron, and smiling, attentive, polite, but mostly quiet Del Hay.

James was reminded that Adams and Hay—and the late
Clover—were neither too educated nor too proud to pun.

"Our poor Vito Pom Pom came home with an injured eye today," said
Nannie Lodge, speaking loudly to be heard by Helen Julia Hay on the
other side of James so that everyone at the table heard her.

There was no lag in response.

"How dreadful," said Henry Adams. "Now, I forget, Nannie...is Vito
Pom Pom one of the servants or a relative?"

"*Henry,*" sighed Mrs. Lodge. "You know perfectly well that Vito Pom
Pom is our beloved Pomeranian."

"*Your* beloved Pomeranian, my dear," murmured Henry Cabot Lodge
in disapproving bass tones that caused the crystal chandelier to tremble.

"How strange," said John Hay. "And I had thought the new immigration acts had all but shut off the flow of Pomeranian refugees into this
country. Tragic, tragic."

Nannie Lodge frowned prettily at Hay sitting on her left.

"My diagnosis is that Vito Pom Pom is most likely suffering from a
*cat*aract," said Henry Adams.

"Most likely a *tom-cat*aract," added Hay.

Those who allowed themselves to chuckle at such things—a group which certainly did not include Senator Lodge nor Senator Cameron, and to which Del Hay wasn't sure to join or not—chuckled.

"It could have been much worse," Henry James said softly. "Our friend Vito might have been completely *cur*tailed."

There was the briefest of pauses and then more chuckles. Lizzie Cameron laughed out loud—a fresh, gay, unselfconscious laugh.

Then, with the happy irrelevance of youth, Helen Julia Hay said to the table at large—"Is everyone looking forward to going to the Chicago World's Fair this summer? I know I am! Everything I've read about the White City says it's perfectly marvelous!"

"It's not precisely a World's Fair, my dear," said her father. "Chicago is hosting the World's Columbian *Exposition,* commemorating the four hundredth anniversary of Columbus's discovery of America."

"But the Exposition is opening in eighteen ninety-*three,*" said Del.

Henry James opened his palms. "Columbus missed finding America by...what?...some two thousand miles between here and Trinidad?"

"Two thousand one hundred and seventy-three miles from where we sit right now," said Henry Adams.

"So Columbus missed discovering America by two thousand one hundred and seventy-three miles," continued James. "The Exposition missed the anniversary of this non-discovery by only one year. Our aim is improving."

Hay turned to Adams. "You're sure about that extra one hundred and seventy-three miles?"

"Quite certain," said Adams with a small, mischievous, and rather charming smile.

"Did you know that when Columbus landed on Trinidad, the island was occupied by both Carib- and Arawak-speaking groups?" said Helen, her tone not one of satisfaction at knowing such trivia but, rather, of anticipation.

"What does one call a resident of Trinidad?" asked Lizzie Cameron. "A Trinidadian?" She'd used the short vowel sound for the "a".

"'Dadians' for short," said John Hay.

"Miss Hay was correct about the natives speaking only Carib and Arawak," said Theodore Roosevelt, his voice seeming to boom even when he spoke in low tones. "But that was only after the Pomeranian invasion of the island in fourteen thirty-nine A.D."

They were on their fourth of nine wines to go with this dinner and the laughter was flowing more easily now.

"Vito Pom Pom understands only Arawak?" said Nannie Lodge. "How distressing."

"Probably why that little hairball of a rat-dog can't learn the simplest of commands," grunted Senator Henry Cabot Lodge.

Nannie wiggled her lacquered fingertips at her husband.

"But *I* don't want to miss the Fair and the White City and Mr. Ferris's Wheel and Mr. Cody's Wild West Show and . . . everything," cried Helen Julia Hay in a voice that suddenly sounded 10 years younger than her 18 years.

"There's no reason you should have to," said Senator Don Cameron. "None of us is leaving for Europe until July. The Exposition opens on May first. Sometime in May, I'll lay on a few private railroad cars and we'll all go together for a few days. Are you game, Adams?"

Henry Adams grumbled but looked at Lizzie Cameron and then nodded his assent.

"Hay?"

"Absolutely. We're with you, Don."

"Mr. Holmes, will you join us?" asked Cameron. "We'll park the cars right at the entrance to the Fair and there will be sleeping rooms for everyone."

"Thank you for the invitation," said Holmes with a nod. "I may have to be at the Exposition earlier than that. We shall see."

Helen Julia Hay didn't actually clap her hands, but she folded them like a little girl preparing to pray. Her smile, thought James, truly earned that tired descriptor of "radiant".

In a departure from usual dining protocol, the remove, what Henry James knew as the *relevé,* this evening a saddle of mutton sliced very thin and set on a warm plate with a little gravy, was carved in the dining room by Chef Ranhofer and served between the two entrees. Servants glided in and refilled everyone's champagne glass.

"I say," said Senator Don Cameron, "this is smashing-good champagne. I seem to recognize it and then I don't. What is it, John?"

"Royal Charter," said Hay.

"I thought only Delmonico's was allowed to lay in Royal Charter!" boomed Roosevelt.

"It is," said Hay. "It does."

"Well, I'd rather spend the whole summer at the Chicago Exposition than in boring old Europe, boring old Switzerland," said Helen.

"I believe we'll be in Zermatt and Lucerne this summer with the Camerons and the Lodges and Mr. Adams for only a few weeks," said Clara Hay. "The July and August months of the Fair will just have to get along without us."

"Best thing," said Adams. "I went to the Bicentennial in 'seventy-six and, other than the warning that the telephone was about to invade our homes, the whole affair was overblown and useless. More boring than Switzerland, Helen."

"Except for the part where they scalped Custer," said John Hay. "*That* was entertaining."

"John!" said Clara.

Hay folded his hands meekly in his lap and looked chastened.

"Buffalo Bill and his Wild West Show *will* be at the Chicago Exposition," said Roosevelt. "I hear that they may re-enact the Custer debacle with Sitting Bull acting his part. Sounds like great fun."

"Wasn't Crazy Horse with Sitting Bull when they ambushed Custer?" asked Del.

"Yes, yes," boomed Roosevelt, turning his entire upper body so that everyone could be the recipient of his grin. "But we killed Crazy Horse in 'seventy-seven."

"You have a history of the Wild West coming out soon, don't you, Mr. Roosevelt?" said Lizzie Cameron.

Roosevelt nodded but also ducked his massive head almost shyly. "I do. It's called *The Winning of the West* and Volumes One and Two should be published this summer. But even though I've spent years working on it, I hesitate to mention my scribbling in the company of the great historians at this table."

It was true, thought James. Henry Adams was perhaps the most honored living American historian and his volumes on the Jefferson administrations were masterpieces of their kind. John Hay's book about his former boss, Abraham Lincoln, written in collaboration with his old friend John Nicolay, had sold well in both America and Europe and was considered *the* reference book on Lincoln's presidency. Henry Cabot Lodge's ancestors had not only known George Washington on a first-name basis, but Lodge had just finished a magisterial history of Washington. Young Roosevelt, although obviously a dynamo of energy and intellectual accomplishment, had much to be modest about in this evening's company of fellow historians.

Or in politics for that matter, thought James.

Suddenly Don Cameron piped up and his voice was surprisingly strong. James had almost forgotten that the Husband with the Doleful Countenance was also a U.S. Senator. "You have nothing to fear from me, Commissioner Roosevelt. I've not written a history of anything or anybody. Nor shall I. I prefer to *read* histories and biographies in the quiet of my study."

"But you have so much you could write about, Don," said John Hay. "You were Secretary of War under President Grant during the Great Sioux Wars, yes?"

Cameron nodded.

"It's an interesting age we live in," said Adams. "In a few years... or at least it seems like only a few years to an Ancient such as myself... we've gone from watching the Indians wipe out Custer's entire troop and terrorizing the western territories to paying to watch Sitting Bull play-acting himself in Mr. Cody's Wild West Show. A massacre with no blood. A battle with no death."

"Mr. Roosevelt," said Nannie Lodge, "you have a ranch out west somewhere... or you *did* have one. Have you ever had to shoot at an Indian?"

James looked carefully at the young man. He knew that Roosevelt had bought and moved to that ranch when his beloved first wife, Alice, had died in February of 1884 just after giving birth to a daughter. As with Adams and Clover, Roosevelt had never mentioned his wife Alice again in public. Shortly after her death, Roosevelt had left his new daughter—named Alice—to be raised by his sister while he moved out to the Badlands of Dakota Territory to begin life anew as a rancher and cowboy.

Roosevelt gave Nannie an even larger grin than he'd shown so far, something Henry James would have not thought possible.

"Mrs. Lodge, I've shot at Indians, White desperadoes, drunken Mexicans, sober Mexicans, grizzly bears, wolves, scorpions, rattlesnakes, and a hundred more varieties of God's most miserable creatures. And I tend to hit what I shoot at."

"Do you think Indians are among God's more miserable creatures, Mr. Roosevelt?" asked Lizzie Cameron.

The bright candlelight reflected from the chandelier's crystal prisms made Roosevelt's pince-nez gleam like two round beacons of light as he turned his gaze toward Lizzie.

"As your husband knew well when he was Secretary of War, Mrs. Cameron," said Roosevelt, his grin never quite disappearing, "the most ultimately righteous of all wars is a war with savages...though it's true that such a war is apt to be also the most terrible and inhuman. The rude, fierce settlers who drove the savages from our western lands with Remington rifles and Bowie knives have laid all of civilized mankind under a debt to them."

"So you think there's no place for the various Indian nations in our national future?" asked John Hay, his voice soft but intense.

"American and Indian, Boer and Zulu, Cossack and Tartar, New Zealander and Maori," barked Roosevelt. "In each case the White victor, horrible though many of his deeds had to be, has laid deep the foundations for the future greatness of a mighty people. It is of incalculable importance that America, Australia, and Siberia should pass out of the hands of their red, black, and yellow aboriginal owners, and become the heritage of the dominant world races."

Chef Ranhofer had wheeled in his *pièce de résistance* for the evening—a rich and elaborate meat pie made from sliced goose-liver terrine and cooked truffles that were glazed in aspic and arranged in layers in a raised pastry shell that had been baked in an intricate mold in the shape of a nautilus—and now the servants were cutting the pie and setting the warmed plates in place, but no one but Roosevelt began eating even after everyone was served and an obviously piqued chef had retired to the kitchen. Everyone was waiting for Roosevelt's next words.

Between large and voracious bites, he continued. "You see," he said, glancing up from the steaming goose-liver pie to Lizzie Cameron, "as my modest volumes of *The Winning of the West* will show in detail, hard-earned White supremacy over the savages and savage lands of this continent has given birth to a new race of mankind...the American Race."

Henry Adams cleared his throat. "My British publisher has sent me an advance manuscript copy of Charles H. Pearson's new book—I believe it will be published early next year—titled *National Life and Character.* Oh, have you heard of Mr. Pearson by any chance, Mr. Holmes? Or met him perhaps?"

"Yes, I've heard of him," said Holmes. "I've not met him. I believe he only recently retired from Parliament."

"Quite so," said Adams. He was fumbling in his jacket and waistcoat pockets. "I'd copied down one of his...for possible reviewing purposes...just at...oh, here it is." He removed a folded piece of paper, flattened it next to his untouched but still-steaming meat pie, leaned forward so the intense candlelight from the chandelier glowed on his bald pate, and said, "Mr. Pearson's fear for the coming new century...and for the near future here and in Europe as well...was put this way."

Adams's reading voice was smooth and assured.

"'The day will come, and perhaps is not far distant, when the European observer will look round to see the globe girdled with a continuous zone of the black and yellow races, no longer too weak for aggression or under tutelage, but independent, or practically so, in government, monopolising the trade of their own regions, and circumscribing the industry of the Europeans; when Chinamen and the natives of Hindostan, the states of Central and South America, by that time predominantly Indian...are represented by fleets in the European seas, invited to international conferences and welcomed as allies in quarrels of the civilized world. The citizens of these countries will then be taken up into the social relations of the white races, will throng the English turf or the salons of Paris, and will be admitted to inter-marriage. It is idle to say

that if all this should come to pass our pride of place will not be hu-
miliated...We shall wake to find ourselves elbowed and hustled, and
perhaps even thrust aside by peoples whom we looked down upon as
servile and thought of as bound always to minister to our needs. The
solitary consolation will be that the changes have been inevitable.'"

Adams folded up the paper and his tiny spectacles and looked down
the length of the table to see young Theodore Roosevelt still grinning at
him.

"You don't agree, Mr. Roosevelt?" asked Adams.

"Pearson's speaking primarily about the Black and Yellow races," said
Roosevelt. "By the time they will have the capability of threatening us
militarily or in trade, the descendants of the Negro and today's China-
man may be as intellectual as the Athenian. The American Race...and
the English as well, of course...shall simply then be dealing with another civilized nation of non-Aryan blood, precisely as we now deal with
Magyar, Finn, and Basque. This is as it should be, since White Europeans and Americans were never designed by their Creator to live and
propagate permanently in the hot regions of Africa, South America,
and India. It's only here on our continent—and the White Russians on
theirs, the White Australians on theirs—that we must essentially eliminate savages and their cultures so that the American Race shall rule in
its own home."

"Perhaps you'd like to review Mr. Pearson's book," said Adams.

"I would!" said Roosevelt with an even broader grin.

"I'll ask his publisher to send you an advance copy."

"In the meantime, I heartily recommend the pie," said Clara Hay.
"The truffles are especially tasty and I hope that everyone had a chance
to notice their artful arrangement by Chef Ranhofer. And after the pie,
we shall have some sorbet and then...then...the teal duck, I believe."

"*Teal?*" said Henry Cabot Lodge. "Not canvasback?"

"Evidently canvasback are all but impossible to procure these days,"
said John Hay. "Possibly due to lack of their favored wild celery, or the
disappearance of their wetlands, or some say due to overhunting."

"It's most likely a deliberate shortage," said Henry Adams. "A ploy to
raise the price of canvasback in the restaurants and butcher shops. Did

you know that almost two-thirds of the decent restaurants in New York are owned, directly or indirectly, by Jews?"

No one paused in their eating save for Del Hay, who said, "Really?"

"It's the truth," said Adams. "Creating a canvasback shortage to drive up the price of the duck is precisely what those people—the Jews—are so clever at doing."

There was another moment of silence.

"Well," said Henry Cabot Lodge turning to his left to look at the obviously distraught Clara Hay, "teal is every bit as tasty as canvasback and I don't believe anything could surpass tonight's *pâté de foie-gras, Bellevue* that amazing goose-liver terrine. My compliments not only to the chef but to our lovely hostess."

Clara smiled and blushed. Servants cleared glasses of Steinberger Cabernet that had accompanied the *foie-gras* and filled everyone's new and larger glasses with Clos de Vougeot. The conversation at the table moved on.

* * *

It was almost two and a half hours since dinner had commenced and if everything simply ended now—if everyone had gone home immediately after the *fromage* course—several lives would have had different futures. But the *glacée à la napolitaine* had revived sagging spirits and the closing wines of the evening (before brandy in the library for the men, of course)—the Château Lafite and Old Reserve Madeira—were especially fine, although Del Hay looked as if he had drunk enough wine for the evening as early as the Duque Port with the *fromage* or even the Clos de Vougeot that had come with the teal pie. The eighth and ninth wines of the evening made Del grow quiet, perhaps even a little morose, but it loosened the already glib tongues of the majority of the people at the table. Only Sherlock Holmes and Senator Cameron were saying almost nothing; Henry Cabot Lodge had told a funny story with the *fromage* and was still in a talkative mood.

Suddenly Helen raised her wine glass. "We've toasted other things, but we haven't toasted Uncle Harry returning to the United States!"

"Hear, hear!" cried John Hay, and everyone drank to Henry James's return.

"I hope and trust that Mr. James will be staying in America this time," said Theodore Roosevelt. The younger man's eyes were bright but James had noticed all through the meal how very little wine the Civil Service Commissioner had drunk.

James smiled his appreciation at the comment, but said, "Alas, I must soon return to my modest little flat in London at De Vere Gardens. I scribble for a living and ever more rarely can find time to enjoy delightful nights out such as tonight. A true delight, Clara. John."

Clara Hay flushed pink and smiled and her husband nodded.

"No, I mean it," said Roosevelt. "This new American Race needs its writers. America needs its expatriate writers to come home and to write about America. Don't you agree, Mr. Holmes?"

Holmes, who had been listening in silence for so long, showing no reaction other than a polite smile, merely nodded recognition of Roosevelt's misplaced question. Perhaps Roosevelt hadn't noticed that he was English.

"But Uncle Harry *does* write about Americans," protested Helen.

"So much so that my publishers and literary agent all but despair," said James with a smile.

"Did you read *The Portrait of a Lady*?" Helen asked Roosevelt. "It is an amazing word-portrait of an American woman."

"And published more than a decade ago, about the last time Mr. James was here in the United States," said Roosevelt. "I say again—America needs its writers to come home from Europe or other decadent and comfortable hiding places and to re-learn America and its people."

Hay leaned forward as if to intervene, but James, smiling, said, "I would wager, Mr. Roosevelt, that you did not write every word of *The Winning of the West* while you were *in* the West. Your notes and memories and research certainly prepared you to continue writing that valuable tome when you were in New York or Washington or, I would assume, even aboard a steamship bound for somewhere far away."

"Of course," said Roosevelt and pumped his fist in an odd gesture for dismissal. "But I had lived in the West. Hunted game in the West. Tracked and captured bad men and faced down murderous Indians in the West. I was *in* the West and *of* the West before I began writing the first page of my book about the West."

"And I was *in* America and *of* America for many years before I went to Europe to write about many topics, but often about Americans encountering Europe," James said softly.

"But you left thirty years ago, sir, and have returned only for visits . . ." ground on Roosevelt's high, insistent voice.

"For more than visits, I'm afraid," James said sadly.

"You were of age to join the army during the Civil War but you never did," said Roosevelt with an oddly triumphant tone, a chess master moving his knight to a threatening position.

Henry James's usually cool gray eyes flashed heat. "My younger brothers Wilkie and Bob were both wounded in that war, sir. Wilkie served under Colonel Shaw in the Fifty-fourth Massachusetts Regiment, mostly colored soldiers, and was terribly wounded during the attack on Fort Wagner. Terribly wounded, Mr. Roosevelt . . . he was found, by pure chance, amongst the heap of dying soldiers by our family friend William Russell, who had gone hunting for his own son — Cabot, who died at Fort Wagner — and Wilkie was not expected to live and for many weeks he had to be left on the filthy cot they brought him home on, just inside our front door. My brother Wilkie suffered the pains and disabling effects of those wounds until his death ten years ago in November of eighteen eighty-three. I knew the Civil War, Mr. Roosevelt. You were . . . what? . . . eight years old when the War ended?"

"Seven," said Roosevelt.

"So many served and suffered in so many ways," said John Hay. "The Civil War was a nightmare from which an entire nation — an entire people — could not awake."

James turned to his left to look at Hay. He found the comment interesting, coming from a man who had just made a fortune co-authoring a book about Lincoln and who had been at the center of that terrible vortex of war at the age of twenty-two then for more than four years.

"I do not worry about a dearth of American writers," said Henry Adams. "Look at this table. Almost everyone here writes for publication or aspires to and soon will...yes, I'm looking at you, dear Helen."

Hay's daughter blushed prettily.

"*I* do not write nor aspire to," said Clara Hay.

"You wrote a cookbook, my dear," said John Hay.

"My point," continued young Roosevelt, who simply would not be deterred, "was that America, emerging into the world's limelight as it is, simply cannot accept or tolerate the kind of undersized man of letters—all present company excepted, of course—who flees his country because, with all his delicate, effeminate sensitiveness, he finds that he cannot play a man's part among men, and so goes where he will be sheltered from the winds that harden stouter souls."

There was an audible intake of breath around the table. John Hay closed his eyes for a second, touched his forehead with his long white fingers, and was about to say something when James silenced him by raising two fingers of his left hand.

"Mr. Roosevelt," said James, his piercing gaze never leaving the younger man's double-barreled steel-spectacled stare, "first of all, I believe that the preferred word is 'sensitivity', not 'sensitiveness'. Secondly, I have to believe that the Civil Service Commission must be a truly ferocious habitat indeed to house and feed such lions as yourself. My respect for government bureaucrats has just risen exponentially."

Roosevelt opened his mouth to respond but Henry James continued in the same smooth purr as before.

"But, alas, the value of your roars this evening, my dear sir, is impaired for any possible intelligent precept by both the truly wonderful incoherence of their observations and the puerility of their oversimplifications."

Lizzie, Nannie, and Helen laughed. Del looked in a sort of wondrous, concerned confusion from Roosevelt to James and back again. John Hay steepled his fingers, his lips thin and white. Clara Hay looked from face to face in confusion as her beautiful dinner party was shredded like a regimental banner under heavy musket fire.

"Your sentences, Mr. James," said Roosevelt through his huge, gritted

318 | DAN SIMMONS

teeth, "are as incomprehensible and unparsable in person as they are on the page."

Henry James smiled in an almost beatific manner. "On that issue, my older brother William agrees with you, Mr. Commissioner."

"So we're definitely all going to the Chicago Columbian Exposition in May?" asked Helen.

"I can't wait to see Daniel Chester French's Statue of the Republic goddess—sixty-five feet high, I understand—right in the center of the White City and lagoons," said Lizzie Cameron.

"I admit to being eager to see Saint-Gaudens's statue of Diana, goddess of the hunt, perched, I hear, at the very top of McKim, Mead and White's agricultural hall," said Nannie Lodge.

James looked to his left. As far as he knew, Henry Adams had never mentioned Clover or her death, but would he discuss Augustus Saint-Gaudens's already famous statue overlooking her grave in Rock Creek Cemetery? Or would the mention of the sculpture bring on a long Adams silence?

Adams looked at James and, as if reading his old friend's mind, he said, "Harry, you've never seen Saint-Gaudens's sculpture at Clover's grave in Rock Creek Cemetery, have you?"

"No, Henry. I haven't been back since it was completed."

"Then we must go together to look at it tomorrow," said Adams. "Would you like to come with us, Mr. Holmes?"

"Very much."

"It's settled then," said Adams, as if he were unaware of the Lodges, Camerons, and Hays staring at him in something like shock. "I'll come for you at Mrs. Stevens's in my open carriage around ten a.m."

"Good," said James, for once not knowing what else to say. He had not the slightest clue as to why Henry Adams would suddenly be willing to take two people, one of them a stranger, to see his wife's grave and mourning sculpture.

John Hay rose. "Why don't the ladies retire to the parlor while we gentlemen retreat to the library for brandy and cigars or cigarettes?"

"I second the motion," said Senator Lodge. Everyone stood.

Roosevelt's fierce gaze had never left James's bearded face. "Overstuffed mass of emasculated inanity," he murmured under his breath as servants pulled back chairs and the beautifully dressed men and women began to move in opposite directions.

James turned back toward Roosevelt, smiling slightly, and remained fixed as John Hay whispered something in the author's ear. Henry James spoke in low tones but loud enough for Holmes to hear from across the table and presumably Roosevelt at the end of the table. "...perhaps expecting something more than this mere monstrous embodiment of unprecedented and resounding noise."

The four women bustled out of the dining room. The eight men headed toward the library at a more leisurely pace. Only Sherlock Holmes was smiling as they left the dining room.

5

Kwannon, Peace, Silence or Grief

Monday morning, April 3, was the beginning of what promised to be an almost perfect spring day. The air was cool and fresh after night-time showers but the warming sun promised temperatures in the low seventies. Every street showed trees leafing in, cherry and dogwood blossoms, and flowerbeds coming into color.

James and Holmes were waiting outside Mrs. Stevens's home when Adams showed up in his beautiful old open carriage pulled by two large, perfectly groomed horses. A footman jumped down from the box and held the half-door as Holmes and James stepped in and sat opposite Adams, who had both hands resting on his walking cane. He was smiling. "I'm so glad you were both free to do this with me today." To the driver, he said, "Back around Lafayette Square, please, Simon."

Holmes exchanged a glance with James. Lafayette Square was only a few blocks away. Was Adams taking them back to his home—or Hay's—for some reason?

No. When they reached Lafayette Square, the driver kept going, the clop-clop of their horses' massive hooves echoing back from the buildings surrounding the wooded and open space. The grass in the square looked very green today. Holmes glanced at the equestrian statue of Andrew Jackson in the center of the square.

Adams saw the direction of the detective's gaze and said, "My wife, Clover, always referred to that statue as 'Jackson on his rocking horse'. She wasn't far from the truth . . . it was the first bronze statue ever cast in America and the first equestrian statue to have a horse rearing back on its hind legs. Alas, the sculptor, a certain Clark Mills, had never seen an equestrian statue before and I fear that this shows in the finished product."

Holmes smiled but was aware of a quick look from Henry James. It was well known that Henry Adams never—ever—spoke of his dead wife, yet he just had.

"Actually," continued Adams, "I asked Simon to bring us back this way before we head out to Rock Creek Park and the cemetery because I didn't know whether Hay had told you the history of some of these homes facing the square, Mr. Holmes. The events here might be interesting to someone from your profession."

"No," said Holmes. "No one's mentioned the other homes besides yours and Mr. Hay's."

"This narrow house here..." said Adams, pointing with his cane, but subtly, the point of the cane never rising above the height of the carriage door. "It was rented by General George McClellan during the Civil War. John Hay tells the interesting story of one night when President Lincoln—with twenty-three-year-old Hay in tow—went over to confer with the general...Little Bonaparte, he liked to be called...but McClellan was out. Lincoln and Hay sat down in the parlor to wait. Almost an hour later, the diminutive General—diminutive in stature only, I assure you, since McClellan felt that he should be Dictator and had the habit of referring to Lincoln as the 'Original Gorilla'—came in, saw Lincoln waiting, and went up the stairs. About half an hour passed, according to Hay, and Lincoln finally asked a servant when General McClellan might be coming back down. 'Oh, the General's gone to bed, sir,' reported the servant."

"Incredible," said Henry James.

Adams smiled. "That's what Hay said to President Lincoln as they were walking back to the White House in the dark and rain. He suggested that Lincoln—that no President of the United States—should tolerate such insolence. Mr. Lincoln's response to John was—'I would hold the man's reins if he can win this war for us.'"

"Fascinating," said Holmes, "although I'm not sure I see the connection to my profession."

"True," said Adams. "But here . . ." The cane pointed to another house just a few doors down. "Here lived Colonel Henry Rathbone who was stabbed by John Wilkes Booth at Ford's Theatre on the same night that the president was assassinated there." Adams paused and looked at Holmes. "I thought that might interest you, Mr. Holmes, since you seem especially interested in assassinations."

"Did the colonel survive?" asked Holmes.

"Yes, yes . . . yes, he did. Colonel Rathbone wrestled with Booth after the actor had shot the president in the back of the head, but Booth had come equipped with a dagger as well as his pistol and the assassin slashed Rathbone cruelly in the arm and head before he—Booth—leaped to the stage and shouted his melodramatic '*Sic semper tyrannis*'."

"Didn't I read somewhere about Colonel Rathbone blaming himself for not stopping Booth?" said James.

"Precisely," said Adams. "His wounds healed, but his agony at not preventing the assassination weighed heavily on poor Rathbone. A decade ago, when he was serving as U.S. consul in Germany, the colonel killed his wife Clara—both shooting and stabbing her multiple times—and would have killed their three children if someone hadn't arrived in time to stop him. He told the police that he was innocent, that the real murderer was hiding, along with others, behind the pictures on the walls."

"Where is he now?" asked Holmes.

"In an asylum for the insane in Hildesheim, Germany," said Adams. The black cane pointed again. "This brick house was the home of Secretary of State William Seward and, on the night of Lincoln's assassination, Seward was attacked in his bed by his own would-be assassin, a mentally deficient giant of a man named Louis Paine, who got into the house—at almost the same moment the president was being shot at Ford's Theatre—by saying that he was bringing medicine for the patient and had to deliver it in person."

"Patient?" said Holmes.

"Seward had recently been in a serious carriage accident, and among his other injuries was a broken jaw that was set in a metal splint. Paine stabbed Seward's son and then leaped like a demon on poor bed-bound

Seward, stabbing him with a huge knife, stabbing repeatedly in the face, neck, chest, and arm ... and kept stabbing at him even after Seward had fallen down in the narrow gap between his bed and the wall. But it seems that the metal jaw splint, the plaster casts, and the thickness of the bandages saved Seward's life that night."

"His son?" said Holmes.

"He also survived, but with terrible scars," said Adams. "They hanged Paine, of course ... with the other conspirators. Now you see that tree there ..."

Adams allowed his cane to rest on the carriage door as they approached a tree set into its little circle of dirt along the sidewalk. "Right there is where Congressman Daniel Sickles—notorious for being a rake, a gambler, and a liar even above the usual level of congressional mendacity—shot and murdered young Philip Barton Key, the son of Francis Scott Key, the fellow who gave us the 'Star-Spangled Banner', in February of eighteen fifty-nine. Sickles had married, after seducing, a rather exotic fifteen-year-old lady named Teresa Bagioli and their five years of marriage were ... shall we say 'explosive'? Even though Sickles was carrying on multiple liaisons with other women at the time—he took a known prostitute named Fanny White with him to England and introduced her to Queen Victoria, all this while poor Teresa was pregnant—when he learned that Key was his wife's lover, he intercepted the poor man ... there, right *there* at that tree ... and shot him multiple times."

"I know of this case," said Holmes. "Sickles was found not guilty due to ... what did they call it? ... a temporary insanity brought on by his wife's unfaithfulness. I noted it in my files because it was the first time, in any English-speaking country, as far as I know, that 'temporary madness' served as a reason for acquittal in a murder trial."

Adams nodded. "Sickles hired the best lawyers in this city of lawyers, including Edwin Stanton, Lincoln's future Secretary of War, and a certain James T. Brady, who came up through Tammany Hall as Sickles did."

"Wasn't Sickles injured during the war?" asked James, who seemed to be enjoying this rather unusual sight-seeing tour.

"Yes, he lost a leg at Gettysburg," said Adams. "But that didn't stop

Sickles from rushing back to Washington the day after his injury and amputation, July fourth, so that he could be the first man, outside of the president's military telegraphers, to tell the story of the battle. It seems he had made a mess of things as a brigadier general and wanted to get his side of the story out first...which he did. Sickles was a great friend of Mrs. Lincoln and spent much time visiting her. You can visit the leg if you wish."

"Visit the leg?" said Sherlock Holmes.

"Yes, when they amputated it at the army's surgical tent that same afternoon of July second, eighteen sixty-three, Sickles insisted that they keep his leg and he had a little coffin-shaped box made for it. He gave it as a gift to the Army Medical Museum—just a few blocks from here—where it's been on display in a glass case to this day, along with a small cannonball that Sickles insisted was the size of the one that shattered his leg. Dan Sickles makes annual pilgrimages every July to visit his leg...often he's in the company of attractive young women. Stop the carriage please, Simon."

The carriage stopped again and Adams pointed to an attractive brick home facing the square—it could be called a mansion—and said, "This is the house—Benjamin Tayloe's house in eighteen fifty-nine—to which they carried the mortally wounded Philip Barton Key. He died on the living room floor and they say that his bloodstain is still soaked into the wood under the beautiful Persian carpet there now. Both the Tayloes and the current residents swear that Key's ghost still haunts the house to this day."

"Who are the current residents?" asked Holmes.

"Senator Don Cameron and his wife Lizzie bought the house in eighteen eighty-six," said Henry Adams. He touched the driver's back with his cane. "Drive on to Rock Creek Cemetery, Simon."

*   *   *

Adams had said that it was about five miles from Lafayette Square to the cemetery and he and Henry James chatted most of the way: middle-aged men's gossip, inquiring after mutual friends and various artists or writers. The sun was quite warm now, the pace slow, the clop-clop of the huge horses' hooves almost metronomic, and Holmes pulled down the brim of his hat not only to shade his eyes but to think in peace.

He was amazed at Henry James's calmness in the face of last night's savage attack during dinner by Theodore Roosevelt. In the previous century, or the earlier decades of this century, words like "effeminate" and "emasculated" would have required the principals to meet at dawn, seconds standing by, pistols loaded and ready. Holmes had been astonished that James had stayed for brandy and cigars; he would have guessed that the writer would have excused himself early to walk back to Mrs. Stevens's boarding house alone. But it was young Roosevelt, obviously ill at ease in Hay's library after behaving so poorly during dinner, who was the first to say good night and leave. Holmes did so not long after that—it must have been around midnight—and was astonished again that James still stayed to talk.

Holmes had to keep reminding himself that James, Hay, and Adams were old friends. Still, it was hard for the detective to imagine how *any* friendship could survive such public insults—or why James showed such calmness and restraint in the company of two of those friends who not only had invited the insulting party to dinner, but who had said nothing to defend James.

Their carriage continued up 14th Street N.W., jogged east onto Harvard Street for a few blocks, then left again onto Sherman Avenue and then northwest on New Hampshire Avenue. Holmes allowed the lassitude that sometimes came with his morning injection of heroin to spread until he balanced there on the edge of sleep, his mind working at a furious rate despite the somnolence creeping over him. He knew that he would have to solve the riddle of Clover Adams and the sender of the annual cards in the next week or so, since he had to be in Chicago before the middle of April. He had exactly four weeks until the Columbian Exposition was to open on May 1 with President Cleveland still scheduled to throw the opening switch that would light electric lights, activate some device to pull the covering off Saint-Gaudens's huge statue, and start all the hundreds if not thousands of pieces of machinery at the Fair.

And cables from Mycroft continued to say that the anarchists' hired assassin, Lucan Adler, would be there to kill the president.

Holmes realized that Adams had said something to him. "I'm sorry," he said, sitting up straighter and pushing up the brim of his silk top hat. "I was half-dozing and didn't hear you."

"I was just pointing out that rooftop and cupola ahead there on the right," said Adams. "It was the Soldiers' Home where President and Mrs. Lincoln used to go for a little cool air and relaxation during the summers of the Civil War."

"Of course," said Adams, "in the three decades since the War, Washington has sprawled out and around the Soldiers' Home, Rock Creek Park, and Rock Creek Cemetery not far ahead. It was all countryside when Mr. and Mrs. Lincoln used to come here to escape the heat."

"And did Mr. Hay come with the president?" asked Holmes.

Adams chuckled. "Very rarely. Lincoln left John and Nicolay in the sweltering White House to catch up on paperwork. Hay was especially good at forging Mr. Lincoln's signature and he wrote many of the letters supposedly from President Lincoln himself. You'd be surprised at how many of Lincoln's more famous letters were actually written by young John Hay."

Holmes made that seal-barking noise that often passed for a laugh with him. "The Gettysburg Address, perhaps?" he said. "Rumor has it that it was scribbled on the back of an envelope."

"Not that particular document, I think," said Adams, possibly smiling as much at the unusual form and force of Holmes's laugh as at the idea of Hay writing the Address.

Henry James, who had covered his bald pate with a straw hat, said, "You must have been very bored last night, Mr. Holmes, at all that talk of Red Indians, as you English call them."

"Not really. I've long had an interest in the various tribes and nations of Indians on this continent."

"Have you ever had a chance to see an Indian in person? In the flesh, so to speak?" asked Adams. "Perhaps when Buffalo Bill Cody's Wild West Show visited London?"

"In slightly more interesting circumstances than that," said Holmes. "In fact, I was taught by some Oglala Sioux how to speak a modest bit of the Lakota language." He was sorry that he'd said anything almost as soon as the words were out.

"Really?" said Henry James with unfeigned curiosity. "Could you tell how this came about?"

Silently cursing himself for revealing too much, Holmes weighed whether he could avoid telling the story altogether but decided he could not.

"When I was in my early twenties," he said as the carriage rolled on, "I was stagestruck and wanted to be an actor. A troupe I was with—one with mostly a Shakespearean repertoire—came to America for an eighteen-month tour, and I came with them.

"We performed in Denver and in more crowded Colorado Territory gold towns such as Cripple Creek and Central City when the director of our troupe decided that, before heading to San Francisco, we should perform in Deadwood, Dakota Territory, since that was 'just next door' in the Black Hills. Of course, 'just next door' amounted to five days of travel in a convoy of no fewer than six stagecoaches to accommodate our people and props. Twice we all had to get out to swim swollen rivers that were in our way. They floated the stagecoaches across.

"At any rate, we arrived in Deadwood on June twenty-ninth, eighteen seventy-six..."

"Four days after they massacred Custer," said Adams.

"Exactly. There were no roads open going east, west, north, or south—and the railroad hadn't yet come to the Black Hills—so our troupe was stuck in Deadwood for five weeks. We gave performances five evenings a week and a matinee on Saturday, but I soon started riding down out of the hills in the morning to spend my time with a small band of Oglala Sioux that was camping near Bear Butte, a tall hill out on the plains that was sacred to them."

"One would think that the American cavalry would have rounded up those Sioux...or worse," said Henry James.

Holmes nodded. "This band of Sioux were mostly women, children, and old men. In fact, the old men were mostly medicine men—what the Sioux called *wičasa wakan*—who'd come to Bear Butte weeks before Custer would be rubbed out at the Little Big Horn, what they called the Greasy Grass, in order to speak to a sort of immortal medicine man, a myth surely, named Robert Sweet Medicine. Supposedly this Robert Sweet Medicine lived in a cave somewhere on Bear Butte. But yes, even though the band was harmless enough to start with, the local cavalry stationed at Belle Fourche had taken all of the old men's weapons. The band of about fifty Sioux was dependent upon the cavalry providing beef and they were starving, emaciated."

"But one or more of them took time to teach you some of their language," said Adams.

"Yes. And I would bring food to them every time I visited. The adults would immediately give it to the children."

"I'm curious," said James. "What did you learn from the cowboys, drunks, mule skinners, buffalo hunters, Indian fighters, bandits, cavalry deserters, and gold miners during your troupe's five weeks in Deadwood?"

Holmes smiled thinly. "That they much prefer *Hamlet* or *Macbeth* over *As You Like It*. But by far their favorite was *Titus Andronicus*."

The carriage turned right off the broad and dusty New Hampshire Avenue onto Allison Street. The stone and wrought-iron welcoming arch of Rock Creek Cemetery was just ahead.

* * *

As the carriage rolled through the green landscape, moving into tree shadow and then out again, Adams explained that the 86 acres of Rock Creek Cemetery had been planned in the "rural garden style" so popular not long before the Civil War. Interest in classical Greek and Roman cemeteries had led to modern cemeteries such as this being laid out to serve both as a final resting place and as a public park. People would bring their children to picnic and hike in Rock Creek Cemetery on Sundays, according to Adams.

"Clover was a dedicated equestrian," said Adams, "and we rode in this park many times. I'm sure that we must have ridden directly over the ground in which she now lies buried." Adams looked away and fell silent after that.

They passed no other carriages or pedestrians. Holmes knew that the cemetery must have a small army of gardeners to keep the acres of grass so neatly clipped, the beautiful flowerbeds weeded and watered, but they saw no one working. Halfway around a long, sweeping curve where the cemetery road ran between two grassy areas festooned with trees and headstones, the carriage stopped.

"If you'll follow me, gentlemen," said Henry Adams.

* * *

There were swatches of open grass separating sections with headstones so one did not have the feeling of walking upon graves, but Adams led them to an asphalted path that meandered under some trees and then crossed more open spaces. The visible headstones were all tastefully done. Holmes realized that Adams was leading them to what looked like a solid green wall of high hedge intermixed with densely planted holly trees, or some deciduous American version of holly which almost certainly stayed green all year round.

Adams led them around to the side where a granite column about ten feet tall rose on a two-tiered stone base. The leaves from the closely planted trees overlaid part of the column in creeping frondescence.

"This is the important side of the monument," said Adams, touching a carved emblem of two overlapping rings set into the granite. Each ring was about twelve inches across, both were inscribed with faint leaves like laurel rings, and Holmes saw that they were entwined. There was the faintest of depressions in the granite around each ring.

Without stopping, Adams led them around the side of the leafy square. The trees rose in a solid green wall about twenty feet high, opening to a narrow gap amidst the greenery.

"Watch your step," said Adams as he entered the break in the trees. It was good advice since, although there was gravel underfoot, that gravel was bisected by a cement ridge that separated the planting areas.

The three men stepped through the leafy doorway, stepped up and onto a higher level of stone edge and gravel base, and stopped in their tracks.

"Good heavens," said Henry James.

Sherlock Holmes, who had little interest in funerary objects or sculptures from any era, nonetheless felt the breath leave his chest.

They were standing on a raised hexagon twenty-some feet across. On three sides rose a stone bench—the stone not made of the granite of the monument across from it—and the arms at the end of each bench were in the form of griffon's wings with carved stone talons seizing a ball at the base.

But the focus of the hexagon was the monument and sculpture opposite the three benches.

Upon a raised granite base and set back against the high granite block, capped in classical style, was the larger-than-life bronze figure of a man or woman in a robe. The robe rose over the figure's head like a cowl and other than the face in shadow, only a bare right arm and hand were visible.

Holmes stepped closer and so did Henry James.

"Henry," said James, "you sent me photographs, but I had no idea..."

"No, photographs do not do it justice," said Adams. "Lizzie Cameron sent me photos when I was in the South Seas, but it was not until I saw the monument in person a year ago this February that I realized its power. Many is the time in the past two years that I've sat and watched and listened, without being watched or listened to, as people encounter this piece for the first time. Their comments run the gamut from interesting to cruelly puerile."

The visible parts of the human form in the massive bronze sculpture were androgynous. The raised forearm was strong, the fingers folded under the cheek and chin, but the figure might have been either male or female. There was a Pre-Raphaelite perfection to the firm descent of the cheek, the solid chin, and the straight line of the nose, but it was the eyes—almost but not quite closed in contemplation, the eyelids lowered as if in sorrow—that brought the figure out of any era or school of art, classical or otherwise.

"It's as if his...or her...face beneath that cowl is lost in a cave of thought," said James.

"When John La Farge and I returned from Japan in eighteen eighty-six, we all but buried Saint-Gaudens in photographs and images of Buddhas, trying to inspire him," Adams said softly. "During my long wanderings in the South Seas, I would refer to the sculpture—not yet created by Saint-Gaudens—as 'my Buddha', but this is no Buddha."

It's true, thought Holmes. The Buddhas he'd seen in the Far East gave off a sense of calm and repose; this figure conveyed to the viewer the deepest possible sense of loss, absence, thought, pain, and even sorrow—all the emotions that the Buddha and those who followed him to enlightenment had left behind.

Holmes made a mental note that the massive robed figure was seated on an indistinct bench or boulder which lay against the upright granite block. The figure's feet—invisible beneath the shadows of robe—rested upon a large, flat stone some three feet across, the stone in turn on the horizontal hearthstone of granite coming out from the vertical block.

As one moved to the left or right, the figure's eyes—as cowled as the sculpture's head—seemed to follow the viewer. The folds of the robe lay heavy between the bronze sculpture's covered knees, which were already slightly shiny from the touch of human hands.

"Does the piece have a name?" asked Holmes, still moving to the left and right and sensing the shadowed eyes following him.

Adams sat on the bench opposite the form. He folded one leg over the other. "I want to call it 'The Peace of God'," he said. "But that isn't quite right, is it? There is something beyond peace—or short of it—in this sculpture. My artist friend La Farge calls it 'Kwannon' after the counterpart we saw in Japan to the Chinese Kuan Yin. Petrarch would say: '*Siccome eternal vita è veder Dio.*' I would think that a real artist—or deep soul—would be very careful to give it no name that the public could turn into a limitation of its nature."

"The benches?" asked James, turning to look in Adams's direction.

"Oh, Stanford White designed the benches and plantings, and obviously fell even further from my wish for the Oriental than did Saint-Gaudens. White's workers had the site covered by a tent for more than a month in the winter of 'ninety. But the griffon wings...not exactly in the Sakyamuni tradition that La Farge and I had in mind when we returned from Japan. Although this sculpture is, I think, the *ultimate* Saint-Gaudens—the most anyone could ask for or receive from this great artist's core of being."

Turning back to look again at the sculpture, James said, "Does Saint-Gaudens have a name for it?"

"Several," said Adams. "His favorite—the last time I heard anyone ask—is *The Mystery of the Hereafter*—but he knows that is not adequate. Saint-Gaudens's native language is stone, not words."

" 'I am the doubter and the doubt'," said James.

"Yes," said Adams.

"I don't recognize the reference," said Holmes.

"The poem 'Brahma' by Emerson," said Henry James and recited:

> *If the red slayer think he slays,*
> *Or if the slain think he is slain,*
> *They know not well the subtle ways*
> *I keep, and pass, and turn again.*

> *Far or forgot to me is near,*
> *Shadow and sunlight are the same,*
> *The vanished gods to me appear,*
> *And one to me are shame and fame.*

> *They reckon ill who leave me out;*
> *When me they fly, I am the wings;*
> *I am the doubter and the doubt,*
> *And I the hymn the Brahmin sings.*

> *The strong gods pine for my abode,*
> *And pine in vain the sacred Seven;*
> *But thou, meek lover of the good!*
> *Find me, and turn thy back on heaven.*

Holmes nodded.

"When I was in India, trying to meditate beneath the sacred bo tree . . . which was as small as a twig now in modern times," said Adams,

"I wrote my own poem in which I attempted to summarize the truly transcendental moment. I failed even worse than Emerson had."

"Tell us the poem, please, Henry," said James.

Adams started to shake his head but spread his arms wide on the back of the bench and said softly:

> *Life, Time, Space, Thought, the world, the Universe*
> *End where they first begin, in one sole Thought*
> *Of Purity in Silence.*

Then, startling both James and Holmes, Adams laughed quite loudly. "Pardon me," he said after a moment. "But the Emerson poem reminds me of something that Clover wrote to her father in the winter of . . . eighteen eighty, I think it was. I believe I can quote it correctly—*A high old-fashioned snowstorm here: the attempts at sleighing numerous and humorous. 'If the red sleigher thinks he sleighs,' Ralph Waldo Emerson would point him to the Brighton Road for the genuine article.*"

Holmes and James laughed softly at this. James caught Holmes's eye and said, "I think I'm going to take a stroll out there amongst the headstones. I shall return in a few minutes."

When James had edged his way out through the small opening in the greenery, Adams stood and said, "Good. Mr. Holmes, you and I must now speak in earnest."

*   *   *

"I know why you're here, Holmes," said Adams. "Why you came to Washington. Why you dragged poor Harry with you."

"Hay told you," said Holmes. He leaned forward, both hands on his stick, as Adams remained seated.

"No. He hasn't . . . yet. But he will. John could never allow me to look or play the fool for long. We're more than friends, Holmes. We're like brothers."

Holmes nodded, wondering just how much Adams knew or suspected.

"But I knew at once that you'd come to solve the so-called 'mystery' of the cards we surviving Hearts receive on the anniversary of Clover's death," said Adams. "So . . . have you?"

"Solved it?"

"Yes." The syllable snapped in the languid afternoon air like the tip of a whip.

"No," said Holmes. "I do know that the cards were typed on Samuel Clemens's typewriter. I looked at a list of the Clemenses' guests from Christmas eighteen eighty-five through December 'eighty-six . . . the time during which the cards were typed."

"And have you narrowed the list down?"

Holmes opened his hands palms outward even as the heel of one hand kept pressure on his cane. "Rebecca Lorne and her cousin Clifton spent a night there that year. So did Ned Hooper. So did all of the remaining Hearts save for Clarence King. So did *you*, Mr. Adams."

Adams nodded tersely. "You actually suspect Rebecca Lorne?"

Holmes removed a photograph from his jacket pocket and stepped forward to hand it to Adams. It was part of a program for a Polish opera, and the diva whose photograph was on the front was the British singer and actress Irene Adler.

"It could be the same woman," said Adams. "It's hard to tell with the dramatic make-up and hairdo. Miss Lorne always dressed herself plainly."

"It is the same woman," said Holmes.

"What if it is?" said Adams. "That solves nothing."

"How did you know my reason for being here if Hay or James did not tell you?" said Holmes. "Ned Hooper, I presume."

Adams smiled, handed the photo back, and crossed his arms. "I loved Ned Hooper and was crushed when we learned of his death this past December. Before that, Ned came to me almost every year, in private, begging me to bring the authorities into the so-called mystery of the December-six cards. Two years ago on New Year's Day he promised . . . threatened . . . to go to London to hire the famous detective Sherlock Holmes if I did nothing."

"What did you say to him then?"

"I seem to remember saying that I thought the famous detective Sherlock Holmes was fictional," said Adams.

Holmes nodded. The two men remained silent for a long moment. Somewhere outside their leafed-in space, a distant carriage clopped along one of the cemetery's long, curving lanes.

"My beloved wife took her own life, Mr. Holmes," Adams said at last, his voice low. "This is why I have not spoken of her or written about her except to the most intimate of my friends these past seven years."

"Yet today you were speaking freely," said Holmes.

"That is because today I am going to ask you to relent in this useless quest, return to England, and leave me and my memories alone, Mr. Holmes," said Adams. Each word was as sharp as a round fired from a Gatling gun.

"I owe something to my client, sir," said Holmes.

Adams laughed, but it was a sad sound. "I did love Ned Hooper, Mr. Holmes. But the same strand of madness ran through Ned that ran through Clover, her father, and so many members of the Hooper family. It was no one's fault. But Ned was as destined as poor Clover to take his own life. Your 'client', Mr. Holmes, suffered from multiple strands of insanity. Would you continue in your efforts when you know that any false clue or misplaced fact you might pick up in this 'mystery' would hurt me as surely as forcing me to swallow shards of broken glass?"

"My intention is not to hurt you, Mr. Adams. Nor anyone else, save for anyone who might be behind these..."

"*Damn* your intentions!" interrupted Adams. "Don't you understand yet? It was Ned Hooper who typed those cards when he was visiting Clemens in eighteen eighty-six. It was Ned who managed to sneak the cards into all of the Five of Hearts' mail on December the sixth each year."

"Did he admit that to you?" asked Holmes, who had long considered that possibility. It was the presence of Irene and Lucan Adler in the last months of Clover Adams's life that had convinced him otherwise.

"No, not in so many words," said Adams. "But Ned was unbalanced, fragile, ready to crack or break at any shock...and his sister's suicide was just that shock that caused the break to be final. Clover's death was *meaningless,* Mr. Holmes—logical only to her and to her own pain and despair—and Ned could never accept that someone so important to him would disappear for no reason."

"Perhaps," said Holmes. "But in this instance, Ned's fears seem founded more on malicious fact than innocent madness. The true identities of Rebecca Lorne and her cousin Clifton argue for..."

"I have a proposal for you, Mr. Holmes," interrupted Adams.

Holmes waited.

"We've all heard what a master of deduction you are, Mr. Holmes...what a master detective. But none of us, not even Harry, I'm sure, have yet seen the slightest indication that you can solve *anything* with your so-called deductive powers."

"What must I do to prove myself?" asked Holmes.

"Solve the mystery I've set for you," said Adams.

"The mystery of the December-six cards..."

"No!" cried Adams. "The mystery that *I* have set for you. Solve it by five p.m. tomorrow, and you may stay—I will even cooperate with you in your investigation. Fail to solve it, and you must, on your word as a gentleman, agree to leave this town, leave this nation, and leave the so-called 'mystery' of my wife's death alone forever. Agreed?"

"Shall you tell me the nature of the mystery you've given me?"

"No," said Adams, his voice flat. "If you're the marvel of observation and deduction that your...fictional stories...say you are, you'll be able to find the mystery and solve it by tomorrow afternoon. If you *are* not, if you *can*not, then you must say good-bye and leave me alone."

Holmes lifted his cane and tapped it on his right shoulder for a moment. Finally he said, "I cannot return to London until other work of mine is finished, but I will agree to leaving Washington and to dropping the case of your wife's death."

Adams again nodded tersely. "Discover the mystery and solve it by five o'clock tomorrow afternoon or leave Washington and leave me alone. We are agreed."

The two men remained silent for several moments, looking at each other but seeing little, when Henry James came back through the foliage and startled both of them.

"Did I miss something?" said James.

6

A Blind Man Could Have Seen It

Henry James was very curious.

It was obvious when he returned to the hedged-in area in front of Clover's monument that something had happened between Sherlock Holmes and Henry Adams, but neither man would say what had occurred... or admit that anything had, for that matter. But Holmes and Adams were also silent during the entire ride back, Adams saying only "So long for now, my friends" as his carriage dropped Holmes and James off at Mrs. Stevens's boarding house.

When pressed there at their temporary lodgings, Holmes still would say no more. When James asked the detective if he'd like to go out for an early dinner together that evening, Holmes said only, "Thank you, but I may not eat dinner tonight." And then he'd gone into his room.

James spent the rest of the afternoon and early evening sitting in the window seat in his own room, smoking, looking at pages of a novel without being able to concentrate on them, and keeping watch out the window that looked out above the front entrance and short walkway to the house.

When Holmes emerged at last, about an hour before darkness would fall, dressed in a too-heavy tweed wool traveling coat with cape and matching-wool soft cap with ribbon tie-up earflaps and carrying a small canvas bag, James grabbed his own cane and top hat and hurried down to follow the detective. Holmes was certainly dressed like a gentleman, but James thought that the canvas bag made him look like some plumber or craftsman coming home from work.

Assuming that Holmes would spot him sooner or later, James was willing to bluster it out by saying that he was only out for a little evening constitutional of his own. But Holmes did not look back over his shoulder or appear to notice James striding along a half block behind and across the street.

First Holmes went three blocks and stepped into a telegraph office. James stepped into the shadows of a closed haberdasher's front entrance and looked at ties through one of the windows, all the while watching the reflection and waiting for Holmes to emerge, which he did after only a few minutes.

Holmes walked quickly, whistling as he walked, occasionally twirling his cane, and within a few minutes was nearing the intersection of 12th Street N.W. and Pennsylvania Avenue where the old Kirkwood House hotel was in its last months before being torn down. James waited for a break in the busy carriage and occasional auto traffic to make his way across Pennsylvania Avenue, and when he reached the safety of the opposite sidewalk, Holmes had simply disappeared. James continued up the street, but more slowly, wondering if Holmes had stepped into one of these commercial buildings. The shadows were growing longer, the sun very close to setting, when James crossed a narrow alley only to have Holmes step out and block his way. James saw the sharp steel of Holmes's sword-cane for an instant before the detective pushed the sword back in its sheath and clicked the silver cane-head tight.

"James," said Holmes and laughed softly. "I thought it was a bit early for Lucan Adler."

James blinked at this. Was Holmes expecting the anarchist-assassin to be stalking him? Was that one of the reasons Holmes had acceded to attending the Hays' dinner party the previous evening...to widen the news that Sherlock Holmes was in Washington so that his enemies could attack him?

Stepping out of the alley, Holmes whistled and gestured to get the attention of one of the cabbies on his box on one of the several hansom cabs lined up at the curb outside the Kirkwood House hotel.

Once they were settled in, Holmes gave the driver directions to go two blocks west and then to turn right.

"Are we going somewhere?" asked James, realizing even as he spoke how absurd the question was. Of course, they might be going back to Mrs. Stevens's—although west was the wrong direction for that.

"I need to think and I often find that a long hansom ride is conducive to serious thinking," said Holmes. "Haven't you also found this to be true, Mr. James?"

James made a noncommittal sound. In truth, he couldn't remember ever having done any deep creative thinking while in a cab. In a railway carriage when traveling alone, yes, and—first and foremost—when in the bath or when taking a morning walk, but not in a cab. James made little note of which direction they were heading as Holmes called up directions—"Right here, driver", "Left, driver", "Straight along here until I tell you, driver."

"Do you have some compelling reason to think about something?" asked James. "Or something new that we should both be thinking about?"

He knew that he was taking a risk asking the question so directly—a risk of rebuff or active embarrassment—but James was very curious and had been since he'd returned to the Saint-Gaudens memorial and found Adams and Holmes sitting there in such distracted silence.

"Yes," said Holmes, "but it could be very personal...to Adams, to your other friends here...so are you certain you want to hear about it?"

James did not have to think about this for long. "I'm certain."

* * *

Holmes succinctly described his graveyard conversation and agreement with Henry Adams.

"But you don't even know what the mystery *is?*" asked James, feeling both shocked at Holmes's decision and relieved that the detective soon would be leaving his friends alone.

"No idea," said Holmes.

"Did you interrogate Adams about it...receive even a clue?"

"No," said Holmes. "You know Henry Adams, Mr. James—and I do not, other than what Ned and you have said about him and impressions he made upon me last night at dinner and today—do you think he is being honest about there being a mystery?"

James thought about that for a while as the hansom clopped along, the cabbie receiving another "Turn right here, driver" order from Holmes. The passing scenery looked like so much of Washington—glimpses of fine homes, then rare commercial blocks, then empty fields, then more trees and homes.

"Yes," James said at last. "Adams can be...*playful* is the word that comes to mind...especially when he is with Hay and Clarence King or Sam Clemens...and he guards his privacy as zealously as a dragon guards his gold, but if there were no mystery whatsoever, he would never have come up with this absurd...game. He would have just insisted you leave him and his friends alone."

Holmes, who had been passing his black gloves through his other hand over and over, nodded distractedly. "You don't have a clue as to what the mystery might be, do you, James?"

"Beyond the one you came here for—the death of his wife seven years ago—I do not," said James. "But, then, for the past decade, my contact with Adams has been either epistolary or when he is visiting London or when we see each other somewhere on the Continent."

"I'm convinced that this mystery he speaks of lies here, now," said Holmes. "Not some conundrum he brushed up against in London or elsewhere."

"Do you have a guess as to what the mystery might be?" said James.

Holmes slapped his gloves against his open palm, frowned, and said sharply, "I *never* guess, James. Never."

"Then, have you ever had a case like this before?" asked James.

"How do you mean, sir?"

"I mean a case where to solve a mystery you must first figure out if and where there *is* a mystery."

"In roundabout ways," said Holmes. "Often I'm asked to consult on something little more than a curiosity—why a father might ask his grown daughter to change bedrooms after she's heard something in the night, that sort of thing—and only then discover that the curiosity is wrapped in a true mystery. But I've never been given the task of searching out a mystery, pulling it from the background of the entire world, as it were, before having only twenty-four hours…" He glanced out at the long shadows and fading sunlight. "Less now…in which to solve it. Stop here, driver." Holmes thumped the box above them with his cane.

Outside in the last of the evening light, James looked around but did not recognize the place.

"Here's an incentive to wait for us for as long as it takes us to return," Holmes was saying to the driver, giving the man what James thought was an absurd number of gold coins. The driver grinned and touched his beaver top hat.

"Come, James," said Holmes and began walking briskly down the tree-lined side street running off the main avenue they'd come up.

It was only when he saw the arched entrance twenty yards or so ahead to the left of the street that he realized they had returned to Rock Creek Cemetery.

* * *

"Do you expect to find your mystery to solve here?" asked James as they walked along the paved lane that curved through the huge cemetery.

"Not necessarily," said Holmes. "But if we want to walk while we think about this problem, this is certainly a contemplative place in which to stroll."

"It will soon be a *dark* contemplative place," said James.

It was true. The sun sat on the western horizon, a red orb perfectly balanced on the horizon glimpsed through the trees and various head-stones and monuments. The trees in the cemetery had thrown out ever-lengthening shadows until those shadows had touched and coa-lesced into growing patches of darkness. It would soon be too dark to read the inscriptions on the headstones that were giving off their last warm glows of sunlight for this day.

"I brought a dark lantern should we need it," said Holmes, jiggling the canvas bag he was carrying. He busied himself with lighting his pipe. Normally, Henry James enjoyed the smell of burning pipe tobacco, but Holmes's choice of tobaccos was so cheap and so strong that now

James changed places as they walked abreast so that he would be upwind of it.

"James, do you remember any mysteries being embedded in Mr. Adams's conversation at dinner last night?"

"I'm afraid that due to Mr. Roosevelt's extended and repeated efforts to be boorish, much of the dinner's conversation was lost on me," said James.

Holmes stopped walking and gave the writer a sharp glance through the pall of pipe smoke. "*Nothing* is ever lost on you, James. You know it and I know it."

James said nothing and they resumed their walk. The sun had disappeared and much of the three-dimensionality of their surroundings disappeared in the pleasant twilight. Trees, monuments, lower headstones, and grassy knolls all took on a flatter aspect without their glow and shadows to set them off.

"There was the mystery of the canvasback ducks," said James. "But Clara Hay brought up that subject when she explained we were having teal, and it was her husband who said that the disappearance of canvasbacks in the restaurants and shops was a bit of a mystery."

"And Henry Adams solved that mystery," said Holmes. "The Jews were behind the disappearance... just as they are behind *so many* nefarious plots."

Holmes's tone was not lost on James and he started to speak to explain his friend, to say that Adams was usually a most liberal person but had this blind spot when it came to the Jews.

Holmes interrupted the apologia with a swing of his cane. "It's no matter, James. Many Englishmen share this reflexive mistrust and hatred of Jews, but in this country, of course, it is overshadowed by the Americans' treatment of more than eight million Negroes as something less than citizens or full human beings."

James almost said *Not here in the North* but remembered that they were in Washington, D.C., and that had never really been part of the North. He had a sudden and almost overpowering memory of a beautiful spring day in 1863 — May 23 — when James had deliberately chosen not to go watch his brother Wilkie parading down Beacon Street with his regiment, the famous black 54th Massachusetts Regiment then under the command of the young (and, of course, white) Colonel Shaw. Henry James had been wasting his time at Harvard, paying almost no attention to his courses in law and using his time to read fiction, but on that day when classes were canceled so that all the young Harvard men could go cheer on the departing Massachusetts regiments, James had stayed in his rented room and read. Later, he found out that his older brother William—also at Harvard—had done the same. James was certain that William could no more explain why he hadn't joined family, friends, and strangers in seeing the regiment off than young "Harry" could.

For a moment, James felt guilt at using the wounding of his brothers Wilkie and Bob in his retort to Theodore Roosevelt the previous night. Wilkie's wounds had been so terrible, his agony so great while lying for day after day on the moldy and bloody cot set near the front door where they had carried him in, and Wilkie's courage so profound in later returning to active duty with his regiment, that the experience had changed something in the writer forever. He rebuked himself now for using Wilkie's suffering as part of his argument.

But he also knew that if he had that May 23, 1863, to do over again, he still would not go to Beacon Street to watch Wilkie's regiment parade, in all their radiant and masculine health and high spirits and bannered glory, to the train station on their way to war.

James was brought out of his reverie by the sharp report of Holmes striking the metal end of his cane on the lane. "We have to assume that—if Adams is playing fairly, as you say he probably is—his so-called mystery has to do with something he was talking to us about today rather than at the dinner party."

"That seems likely," said James, feeling suddenly weary. "But you remember that I missed several minutes of your conversation at Clover's monument when I went for a walk."

"Yes," said Holmes and swerved them off the lane and onto the grass.

James saw the dense trees of the enclosure for Clover's memorial ahead and said, "You think the monument may be a clue?"

"I think that there is a bench there on which I can sit and smoke while we think," said Holmes.

They approached the back side of the monument in silence. Just as they got to the granite block, Holmes said, "Odd...Adams said to both of us that *this* was the important side of the monument." He touched the granite block gently with his stick.

"Not odd at all," said James. "As powerful as Saint-Gaudens's sculpture is, it's the entwined wedding rings on this side of the monument"—he had to reach on tip-toe to touch the large double rings—"that symbolizes their years of marriage, which is what this memorial piece is all about."

"Yes, certainly," said Holmes, resting his cane on his shoulder and squinting at the now-shadowed block of stone. James thought that the detective did not sound totally convinced.

Holmes led them around and through the narrow gap through the trees and hedges. The interior area bounded by the hexagon, benches, slab, and sculpture was quite dark. Holmes sat on a bench directly opposite the sculpture, set his heavy canvas bag down on the bench, laid his cane beside it, and crossed his legs while he relit his pipe.

"What did I miss when I left you two alone here this afternoon?" asked James.

Between puffs, Holmes said, "I showed him the picture of the actress and diva Irene Adler, who—I am convinced—played the part of Clover's friend Rebecca Lorne in the months before Clover's death. Adams said that he could not be sure it was the same woman. He asked me to drop this inquiry. I said that I had a debt to my client, which led to Adams cursing me and..."

"He cursed you?" said James, not even attempting to keep the shock and amazement out of his voice. This was not the character or behavior of the Henry Adams he had known all these years.

"He cursed me," repeated Holmes, "and then explained that while he had loved Clover's brother Ned, that madness ran through the Hooper family. He essentially suggested that I was on a mission designed by a madman and said flatly that it had been Ned who'd typed the cards and distributed them to the Five of Hearts every December six..."

"Did he have proof of that?" asked James. He'd considered that possibility and it certainly made sense...more sense than any other hypothesis.

"He did not," said Holmes. "It was just his belief."

"Was there more?"

Holmes opened his hands. James thought of white doves taking flight in the gloom. "Not really. Then he challenged me to find and solve this 'mystery' and you returned."

"It doesn't sound as if..."

"Silence please!" snapped Holmes. At first flush, James was certain that Holmes had heard someone approaching their enclosure and the writer prepared himself to come face to face with Henry Adams again. But no one came through the thin portal amongst the leaves and James realized that Holmes was requesting silence so that he could think.

James looked at the sculpture across from them and although it was impossible—the top of the bronze piece was lower than the top of the line of trees or the granite slab behind it—the cowled figure seemed to glow with more light than the rest of the dark enclosure.

Holmes sat smoking and thinking for at least twenty minutes. James did not mind the calm, although the settling darkness was mildly disconcerting. He was startled when Holmes finally spoke in a loud voice—"'Many is the time in the past two years that I've sat and watched and listened, without being watched or listened to, as people encounter this piece for the first time—their comments run the gamut from interesting to cruelly puerile.'"

"What?" cried James. "I thought that today was the first time you'd seen this monument!"

"It is," said Holmes. "It was. Those were Adams's words this afternoon—to both of us."

"Yes," said James, casting his powerful memory back like a searchlight. "Those were his precise words."

"'I've sat and watched and listened, without being watched or listened to'," Holmes again quoted Adams. In the gloom, Holmes opened his arms to take in all three of the benches that formed one half of the hexagon. "Where could he sit and listen without being seen in return, James?"

"I took him to mean that he stole glances at other people's reactions to the monument when they were not paying attention to him," said James. "And that he overheard their comments."

"That is how I interpreted the words," said Holmes, standing, "but you know even better than I that Henry Adams is not careless with language. He used those words deliberately—*I've sat and watched and listened, without being watched or listened to.* He has a place around here where he can eavesdrop without being observed in return."

"Certainly not here at the benches," said James.

"No, it must be outside this space," said Holmes. "Do you remember a bench outside this enclosure, close enough to hear voices and to see anyone sitting on these benches?"

"I didn't notice one during my stroll today," said James, "but of course I wasn't looking for benches. I was thinking."

"Let's find out," said Holmes. "We can both go look."

"It will be too dark in here for us to make out any shape from outside," said James.

Holmes knocked the last of his ashes out of his pipe and set it away in a pocket of his caped coat. "Precisely," he said. "This shall be our surrogate person." He pulled the dark lantern from his bag, set it on the winged arm at the left end of the bench, lit it, and pulled the shutter back. The lantern threw its beam of light toward the only entrance through the trees. Leaving the bag and lantern behind, Holmes led the way back outside.

Outside, it was much less dark. The spring twilight still filled the sky with faint gray, although one or two of the brighter stars were making an appearance. It was almost, not quite, light enough to read by.

"What's to have kept Adams from sitting on the grass anywhere here?" asked James, gesturing toward the various rises and dips in the turf.

"Can you see your friend Adams sitting on the grass in a cemetery?" laughed Holmes.

James shook his head. "A bench or monument then. And it has to be on this side because this is the only path through the trees wide enough to allow a view inside or out."

Holmes pointed his cane to the right as he walked to the left. They spread out, studying the monuments and looking for a bench.

After a couple of minutes, James cried out, "This is flat. One could sit on it." Holmes walked over to join him. Above them, bats and swallows were carving the evening sky into arcs.

"This headstone is high enough and broad enough to make a comfortable perch," said James, patting it.

"Then why don't you sit on it?"

James frowned at the detective's tone. "I cannot. It is, after all, a headstone."

"Exactly right," said Holmes, "and we have to assume that Adams does the majority of his looking and listening here in the daylight."

"Hay has told me that Adams comes so often to this cemetery that he's referred to it as his real home," said James.

Holmes nodded, distracted. "The view of people standing or sitting within the enclosure would not be good from here," he said.

James looked. The detective was correct. Only a fringe of the lantern's glow could be seen through the narrow break in the trees and virtually all of the hexagon area was totally out of sight.

"And it must be sixty paces from the hexagon in front of the sculpture with the trees adding another buffer," continued Holmes. "Too far to overhear people speaking in normal tones."

"Where then..." began James.

"The trees and hedge!" said Holmes, almost loping back to the ever-darkening enclosure.

They walked the outer perimeter together. "I take it that we're hunting for what we Americans call a 'duck blind'," whispered James. He wasn't sure why he had whispered.

"Yes," replied Holmes. "Some concealed blind in the foliage here." He poked away with his cane. "In England, a 'blind' is what we call a legitimate business that conceals some criminal enterprise."

"If we find this so-called duck blind," said James, "we still will not have answered the more important question."

"What's that?" asked Holmes, feeling into foliage with his bare hand as well as with his cane.

"Whether we're hunting canvasback ducks or teals."

They did the rest of the careful search without speaking. It was no use—the trees were only trees, the hedges real hedges. There was no place of concealment unless one bodily forced his way into the shrubbery and James knew Adams well enough to know that would never happen.

They returned to the lantern and Holmes shuttered it again, allowing their night vision to return, but instead of leaving or sitting on the bench again, he stood there several minutes obviously lost in thought. Waiting for him again, James wondered idly if Holmes's friend and chronicler, Dr. Watson, spent much of his time waiting for Holmes to come out of his deep-thought fugues.

"Of course!" exclaimed Holmes, snapping his fingers. "I've been an absolute fool. A blind man could have seen it!" He lifted the lantern, unmasked it, and carried it to the sculpture, holding it first on one side and then the other, first close then further away.

James stayed where he was. He'd found Saint-Gaudens's brooding statue disconcerting enough in the daylight; by lantern light it was downright frightening.

"Come," said Holmes, striding quickly and returning to pick up the bag and shutter-down the lantern's beam until it was a narrow glow.

"Are we going home now?" asked James.

"No," said Holmes. "We're going to Henry Adams's duck blind."

7

The Constant Red Glow in the Darkness

It was the intertwined marriage rings, of course.

For several minutes both Holmes and James had reached up to feel around the sunken edges of the granite rings with Holmes muttering much of the time—"This is the important side of the monument"—"The monument was covered with a tent for a month and a half"—"Who needs to protect a granite slab from the weather?"—"Adams did everything but draw me a map and leave real arrows on the grass showing me the way."

On the first three tactile explorations, Holmes's fingers found nothing. But then he felt the slight niche, the smallest of indentations, at the bottom of the ten-inch-wide right ring.

"Stand back," he said to James and retrieved a burglar's tool from his bag: a very short crowbar with a chisel's narrow end to it. It fit. There was a corresponding snap from behind the granite and the two rings swiveled to almost right angles from the monument. Holmes pushed on one of them. A panel in the granite swiveled, opening into absolute darkness.

"Good Lord!" cried James as he took a quick two steps backward as if he feared being swallowed up by that black aperture.

Before stepping in, Holmes played the narrow beam from the dark lantern into that darkness and it was good that he had. About fourteen feet inside, the floor ended and a square hole in the floor—showing a ladder on the right side and just big enough for a man—dropped into blackness. Straight ahead, on the far side of that hole, was a strange cushioned seat one could reach by walking carefully along granite ledges on either side. The far side of the interior of the granite monument was irregular, a series of bronze protrusions and indentations.

"The statue's hollow," said Holmes, his voice showing no surprise because he'd realized all this while sitting out on the bench. He put the tool back in his bag, held the bag and his walking stick in one hand and the lantern ahead of him in the other, stepped in, moved to the ladder side along the narrow strip of granite, then played the lantern beam back over the entrance. "Take care when you step in, James."

"I'm not going in there," said the writer. He'd kept his distance from the monument when the panel had swiveled open.

"All right," said Holmes, "but go back to the carriage waiting for us on New Hampshire Avenue. I shan't be long in here." He started to swing shut the panel.

"Wait!" said James. "I *am* coming in." The portly writer stepped in with great care and balanced on the granite ledge on the left side of the hole. Holmes played the lantern beam over the inside of the portal. "I need to make sure there's a release mechanism on the inside that does not require a key so that we don't get...ahh, here it is." Holmes worked the mechanism to his satisfaction and then swung the swiveling panel shut until it clicked.

They were entombed.

"The ladder first," said Holmes and aimed the beam down the iron ladder driven into the granite. It had a railing and rungs and went down about eight feet. Nothing else was visible at the bottom until he realized that the wall on the statue side of the bottom of the short shaft was actually a black curtain.

"Would you please hold the lantern with that beam playing just so until I get to the bottom?" asked Holmes.

"No!" cried James. "I mean...you can't. We must not! This is...all this...down there...it's too terrible!" The last was said in a dying whisper since this place seemed to call for whispering.

Holmes looked at his companion's face in the reflected lantern light and knew exactly what James was thinking lay beyond that black velvet curtain: a glass coffin with Clover Adams's rotting remains in it. *What would she look like after seven years?* Unfortunately, Holmes knew all too well what a body dead seven years looked like. He whispered, "No, no, I think not, James. Your friend Adams is strange, perhaps even mad by some standards, but there's a method to this madness. I am convinced that we will find nothing terrible or gruesome down there."

He handed the lantern to James, set his bag and stick on the cushioned chair that was suspended along the far wall by a round iron post that was secured in the interior of the sculpture.

"Down just a bit," said Holmes and, when James tipped the dark lantern forward, he clambered down several rungs. "I'll take it now." The tall man's white fingers reached for the metal handle atop the lantern.

At the bottom, Holmes paused a moment and played the light on all sides. It was a narrow shaft, hardly broader than his shoulders, and it would have been problematic for anyone who suffered from claustrophobic panics. Holmes smiled, thinking that he must look like some archaeologist entering a newly discovered tomb in Egypt or Babylon or Troy.

But there were no hieroglyphics on these three granite walls, nor switches or niches or clues. Only the ladder and this black curtain.

Raising the lantern and opening the shutter a little wider, Holmes pushed the curtain aside and stepped forward, making sure that there was granite beneath his feet before taking his steps.

"What do you see?" James's voice came down the shaft in a harsh, urgent whisper.

"Just a moment," said Holmes.

The room was a rectangular prism about six feet wide and eight feet long that had been laid under the footing for the monument sculpture and the paved and graveled hexagon above. Holmes estimated that there were probably two feet of solid concrete or even granite above his head. Then soil.

Carved into the granite to his left was a long niche about shoulder high. It was filled with books. To his immediate right there was a granite column extending from the wall, also about shoulder height. On it was a small lantern. Holmes was tempted to light it with his prototype cigarette lighter — the resident lantern's light would be better than the beam from his dark lantern—but he wanted to be sure to leave no signs of his having been here.

The rest of the granite wall to his right was carved into a larger niche, rising only some three feet from the floor, and on the upper surface of that niche was a narrow bed cushion with two pillows set at the far end. The whole bed was only about six feet long and Holmes would have had to curl his legs up if he'd lain on it. He did not. The bed was made up neatly and Holmes touched the blanket and sheets: warm, not cold or moldy-feeling. They must be changed regularly.

Holmes would wager money that these were the only times in his 55 years of life that Henry Brooks Adams had ever made his own bed.

There was a second narrow granite column at the far end and a second small lantern on it. Tucked by that lantern was a book. Holmes picked it up—it was leather bound—and played the lantern's beam over it.

The Light of Asia: The Teacher of Nirvana and the Law by Sir Edwin Arnold. It had caused a slight stir in America and England when it was released in 1879, but Holmes had read only part of it before impatiently setting it aside. He thought Arnold's writing was insufferably prolix. Still, he remembered the review in *The Times* of London, written by the noted Japanologist Lafcadio Hearn, when the 1883 edition came out: "After all, Buddhism in some esoteric form may prove the religion of the future... What are the heavens of all Christian fancies after all but Nirvana—the extinction of individuality in the eternal."

Indeed, thought Holmes.

After carefully setting the book back in place above the pillows by the second lantern, Holmes stepped back through the curtain into the short vertical shaft. "Come down, James."

"I cannot," came the whisper in return.

"You really should," said Holmes. "Otherwise you shall spend a lifetime wondering if I was telling the truth. Trust me that there is nothing disturbing here."

There came down a sound like stifled hysterical laughter. In an urgent whisper, James said, "Everything about this moment is disturbing, Holmes. We have invaded the deepest part of a good man's privacy, intruding into his mourning and perhaps into his madness. Our behavior is criminal. Unspeakable."

"Agreed," said Holmes. "But it's done. Come down and look and then we'll finish our business here."

"Hold the lantern higher," Henry James whispered and ponderously started down the iron ladder.

* * *

Five minutes later they were both up in the aboveground part of the monument again. The chair with its padded seat was broad enough for both of them to perch on it if each steadied himself with a leg outstretched to the granite ledge on one side.

"There's no view through the eyes," whispered James. It was true. They were able to make out the inverted features of the sculpture's face now with the aid of the lantern beam, but although the eyes had seemed empty of bronze from casual inspection outside the piece, now they could see two oval slugs of metal—not bronze—covering those openings. Holmes had seen those non-bronze insets within the otherwise open, downcast eyes when he'd held the lantern up to inspect the sculpture.

"Look for a lever," whispered Holmes. "These plugs are attached to...ahh!"

The lever mechanism was on James's left side.

"Put your hand on it, but don't open it yet," said Holmes, his mouth close to James's ear. "Let me turn out the lantern first and let our eyes adapt to the darkness for a moment."

It was disconcerting for Holmes to spend that moment pressed so close to another man. He could feel James inching away, putting most of his weight on his left foot so as to avoid touching.

"Now," whispered Holmes.

The shutters over the eyes made almost no noise as the metal rod above them rose and they lifted the eye plugs out of place.

Their angle of vision was good—the androgynous sculpture's head was angled forward and the face partially sheltered by the cowl, but the eye openings were larger than life-size and, with Holmes taking the right eye and James the left, they could see the entire hexagon before them, the benches, and the stars above the enclosure of trees. The space was empty.

After a moment, they both sat back. The view was still good.

"This is how Adams sees and hears people's reactions without being observed in turn," whispered James.

Holmes nodded.

"I'm not sure that..." began James but silenced himself when Holmes firmly gripped his upper arm.

Someone had entered the shrub-bounded enclosure outside.

Both Holmes and James leaned forward, instinctively not putting their eyes too close to the oval openings to be sure that starlight did not cause a gleam.

Holmes could not make out any detail save for the shadows of trousered legs—definitely not a woman in a dress—but the man seemed to be very tall and very thin. This impression was confirmed when he sat on the bench directly opposite the sculpture, for his shoulders were higher than the very high back of the bench—higher even than Holmes's had been when he'd sat there.

James leaned over to whisper directly into Holmes's ear. "It's not Adams!"

Holmes shushed him by squeezing harder. The scrape of the man's boots or shoes against the gravel had been so audible that Holmes suspected the enclosure acted as a sort of hearing gallery, amplifying sound. He suspected that Adams had directed Stanford White to achieve that effect—thus the oddly high back of the benches and the triangle of stone. Holmes worried that any noise from within the sculpture might as easily be carried out to the open area.

James intuited the message and leaned forward again.

For several minutes the man did nothing. As Holmes's eyes adapted even further to the moonless night, he could see the man's long arms spread to either side on the back of the bench—the same posture that Holmes had assumed earlier.

After a few minutes of this silent staring match, the man's arms came down, Holmes could make out pale hands touching pockets of a jacket or waistcoat, clearly heard the scrape of a match, and the man leaned forward to light a cigarette.

That flare of a match should have revealed the man's face, but Holmes saw only a glow with an arc of blackness cut out of it. He realized at once that the man was wearing a broad-brimmed hat of some sort and the brim had occluded any view of his face.

Had that been an accident or coldly deliberate? Sherlock Holmes never guessed, but his hunch at the moment was that it was the latter.

He and James sat there, uncomfortably perched on the same chair, hardly daring to breathe while the man smoked his cigarette.

A single red glow in the darkness. No features visible. Only the dot of red in the darkness.

The man eventually finished that cigarette, there was a half-seen movement of pale hands, and he lit another one. Again the downturned brim of a hat concealed any features that might have been caught in the brief flare of the match.

He's playing with us, thought Holmes.

He hadn't expected Lucan Adler to find him so soon, but Holmes realized that he might have underestimated the speed of gossip about his presence, gossip spreading outward not only from the Hays and their servants and the Cabot Lodges and Camerons and Roosevelt, but from Clemens and William Dean Howells as well. Lucan was the ultimate predator and Holmes realized, with a tightening in his chest not unlike fear, that he had given that predator-assassin more than enough time to find him.

Then why am I alive? thought Holmes. He realized that, without thinking about it, he'd slid his right hand into his traveling coat's pocket.

Instead of the reassuring handgrip of a pistol—he still had not taken time to buy one here in Washington—his fingers found the short, flexible grip of the cosh—Americans called it a "blackjack"—that he'd brought with him. The tough leather of the working end of the cosh was filled with sand and it was guaranteed, when used properly, to bring even the largest opponent to his knees if not facedown on the ground.

In his trouser pocket, he had his folding penknife with its four-inch blade. In his burglary bag, the short crowbar he'd used to open the monument was the closest thing to a weapon.

The great Sherlock Holmes, thought Holmes with hot irony overriding the stab of panic he'd felt a few seconds earlier. *Brings a penknife and a cosh to a gunfight.*

He had never wanted to confront Lucan Adler with Henry James at his side. But now, he felt almost certain, he had. He was almost as certain that Lucan knew that Holmes and someone else were in the monument looking at him.

The red glow was extinguished. Holmes tensed, gripping the handle of his cosh. At least if Lucan entered the monument—Holmes had little doubt that the anarchist assassin had watched James and him enter it—there would be so little room that Lucan's marksmanship with a rifle or pistol would be largely negated.

A perfect space, especially with the open shaft that Lucan might not know was there, for a fight with a knife or cosh, thought Holmes.

But with Henry James in the middle of it.

A third match flared. Again the taunt with the head downward, the large brim of a hat concealing the face. Again the steady glow of the cigarette's end in the deep darkness of the monument's enclosure.

They had sat there for more than half an hour, Holmes estimated, staring at the unknown man who was staring at them. Or at least at the sculpture, which would be only a dark shape in the night. Holmes was almost certain that it wasn't Henry Adams out there—even if he were wrong about the man's height, would Adams ever wear a hat like that?—and every minute that passed made him more certain that it was Lucan Adler, playing with James and him the way a cat plays with a mouse in the minutes before biting its head off.

Holmes's legs were cramping in the uncomfortable posture, but worse than that was the rising pain from his three bullet wounds. The one in the lower right of his back was the worst. Holmes realized that in the intensity of his brooding on Adams's mystery that afternoon and evening, he'd forgotten to take his second injection of heroin. Its absence seemed to make the wounds ache more.

Ten minutes, he gauged, into the third glowing red dot, and Holmes set his mouth almost against James's ear—he could smell the expensive pomade in his hair—and whispered, "Stay here . . . I'm going out there."

He could feel rather than actually see James shaking his head no, but Holmes gripped him tightly on the upper arm again, repeating his instruction to stay where he was.

Perhaps Lucan didn't actually see us enter the monument after all, thought Holmes. *If he did not, then James has a chance to survive even if Lucan kills me.*

Stepping silently on the right-side granite strip, Holmes found the lantern by feel and lifted it in his left hand. He would have to light it again outside, then shutter it quickly. *But a bright beam of light shone in Lucan's face might . . .*

He did not finish the thought because he did not really believe it would.

Taking one last glance to make sure that the figure and cigarette glow were still there, Holmes gingerly stepped over his burglary bag, found the opening mechanism by touch, and clicked it open. The click was a small noise, but it sounded as loud as a rifle shot to Holmes's anxious ears.

The air that rushed in was cold and Holmes realized how overheated the small space had become during the time that he and James had been in there, emanating body heat.

Once outside, Holmes took the risk of pushing the panel shut—another intolerable click—to give James that tiny chance of survival if this was Lucan Adler waiting.

He knelt, fished his mechanical lighter from his trouser pocket in one swift movement, and lighted the dark lantern. He'd already fully shuttered the front, so the only light had been the flare of his lighter—but that had seemed interminable and visible to anyone in the cemetery.

He'd looked away as he flicked the lighter and lit the lantern, not wanting to lose his night vision, but he still had to stand there half a moment and blink before he could fully see again. Holding the lantern forward in his left hand, the fingers of that hand ready to open the shutter all the way in one fast movement, Holmes pulled out the cosh and carried it by his side.

Holmes walked stealthily around the right corner of the enclosure, toward the side where the cleft in the trees allowed access. No light escaped from that opening. Holmes was taking care where he put his feet but did not want to walk too slowly. Surprise, after all, and perhaps a sudden shaft of light in Lucan's eyes, were almost certainly Holmes's only hope for surviving the next few minutes.

He got to the opening in the trees and stopped, finally leaning forward to put only his head forward in a fast peek around the edge. Even that movement, he knew, would be target enough for a master assassin with a pistol ready. Holmes knew that even though clouds had occluded the stars, it was still lighter outside the enclosure than within, and his head would be in silhouette.

No shot. No sound.

Holmes looked again, eyes straining, but could not make out the flowing cigarette or the form of the man on the bench. It was simply too dark in that enclosure now. He realized that when the clouds had come in sometime in the last forty-five minutes, he and James had been watching the red glow of the cigarette rather than the dark outline of the man in the blackness.

No further reason to wait, thought Holmes. Raising the lantern high, seeing nothing but darkness ahead in and beyond the entrance cleft, Holmes strode quickly forward, the sound of his brushing branches as loud as an avalanche in his ears.

The instant he was through the cleft in the trees his fingers swept open the shutter on the lantern, his right arm flexing as he hefted the cosh.

The place on the bench where the man had been sitting was empty.

Where had he moved? Anywhere in the enclosure would afford him a perfect shot.

Holmes considered slamming shut the lantern's shutter—Lucan's sharpshooter advantages eliminated, just two men in blackness, feeling for each other, and Holmes had the knife and the cosh—but he found he was too impatient for whatever the showdown would bring to follow that saner tactic.

He moved quickly, in erratic patterns, holding the lantern away from his body, aiming the beam this way and then that way. The benches were empty. The graveled hexagon in front of the sculpture was empty. The area around the granite and bronze monument was empty.

Behind the benches. It would have been Holmes's first choice for a hiding place if he were waiting to shoot a man here.

Holmes leaped up onto the bench and then over the high back, going to a quick crouch on the back side of the bench closest to the opening in the trees, lantern beam illuminating the narrow corridor ahead of him between the stone bench and the trees.

Empty.

Rushing forward, still in a crouch so that his head was below the level of the back of the stone bench, he reached the first corner and set the lantern on the ground, its aimed beam shooting to the left.

No shot. No sound.

Holmes looked around, saw this second corridor of space empty, saw no new breaks in the wall of foliage to his right, and he hurried to the last turn, not bothering to pause before he swept around it. He was ready to dash down the lantern in a second if he couldn't get close enough to blind his opponent with it.

Nothing.

Holmes came out into the opening and checked all the walls of foliage. Someone *could* have forced his way through the tree branches and hedges and out into the opening, but Holmes certainly would have heard him do so as he approached.

Satisfied that no one else was in the enclosure, he held the lantern high again and walked toward the bronze sculpture on its two-level base. He approached it obliquely, visualizing Henry James dead, his body dropped into the vertical shaft, and Lucan's young hunter's eyes at one of the eyehole openings and a pistol pressed against the other opening. The eyes were large enough to pass a bullet from a revolver.

His cape-coat brushed against foliage as he crept toward the seated, brooding, still-powerful sculpture. The combination of darkness and harsh lantern light brought out the draped folds in the robe, the shadows under the cowl, the straight nose and solid chin, the up-raised and folded-in right arm with its fingers disappearing under bronze cheek and chin.

"James?" Holmes had used a normal, conversational voice and the loudness of it in the thick night made him jump.

No response.

Louder—"James?"

"I'm here," came the oddly muffled reply from the statue's head.

Holmes imagined the portly writer under duress, the muzzle of a pistol pressed under his double chin. For that matter, he hadn't been certain that the muffled voice belonged to Henry James.

"What was the name of that novel of yours that I said I liked?" said Holmes, still standing close to the right side of the monument so that he could not be seen or targeted from inside the sculpture.

"What?" The echoing voice sounded more like James this time. An obviously irritated James.

Holmes repeated his question.

"*The Princess Casamassima,*" came the anger-tinged reply. "But what on earth does that have to do with anything?"

Holmes smiled and stepped out in front of the cowled figure. He could not help but glance over his shoulder every few seconds. "Where is he?" he asked the statue.

"I don't have the vaguest idea, Holmes." Holmes could hear the voice better from this new vantage point and it was definitely James's, although muffled by the bronze. "Just after you stepped out, the cigarette glow disappeared. I didn't see the man move...did not see him go out through the entrance. He just...disappeared."

"All right," said Holmes. "I missed him then. Could you please bring my bag when you come out?"

"It's too dark," said James through one of the eyeholes. "I can't see where to put my feet. The shaft...can't find the lock mechanism...I'll try, but..."

"No, on second thought, it's better that I come fetch you," said Holmes. "Sit tight for just another moment and I'll bring the lantern."

But instead of going outside and to the rear of the monument, Holmes went straight across the hexagon, dropped to one knee, and began examining the graveled ground near the bench. Then he took several minutes to move the lantern close to the ground near all three benches. Then he stepped around behind the bench and did the same careful examination. He was checking the ground in the open space of the hexagon when the statue made another muffled noise.

Holmes walked over to it and held the lantern high. "What was that, James?"

"What in *God's name* are you doing!" demanded the androgynous face of deepest mourning.

"Looking for the cigarettes and/or ashes," said Holmes. "We watched Lucan—this figure in the dark—smoke at least three cigarettes to their end—we could both smell the tobacco smoke in the darkness—but there's not a single ash or remnant of a dead cigarette anywhere. He must have dropped the ashes from the cigarettes into his palm and put the ashes and the cigarette butts in his pocket. Don't you find that odd behavior for an innocent person, James?"

"*Damn* the cigarette ashes," said the shadow-sharpened bronze face. "Come get me out of here, Holmes. I've needed to relieve myself for more than an hour now."

* * *

The hansom and its cabbie were not there when they reached New Hampshire Avenue.

"That blackguard!" cried James, referring to the driver. "That cursed driver took your money but left anyway."

"We've been a long time," said Holmes. He'd done the entire walk from the monument with his shoulders hunched until they ached, waiting for the impact of the pistol or rifle shot whose sound he would not hear. They stayed tensed out in the open of the lightly traveled avenue. There were no street lights or house lights here.

"Maybe our smoking friend took it," said James. "What do we do now?"

"It's only a little less than four miles back to Mrs. Stevens's place, so we walk," said Holmes, knowing that despite his best efforts to relax, his body would be expecting the impact of a bullet every step of the way.

And for every hour and minute of the days and nights to come until this whole matter was resolved.

Some minutes later, they came to a single gas lamp on a post in the lawn of a darkened house. The light drew a yellow oval on the macadam of the road and illuminated both of them as James stopped for a second.

This is the perfect spot, thought Holmes. Lucan in the darkness behind the house or in the blackness under the trees to either side. His target—or perhaps targets, if Lucan was in an especially bloody mood—frozen like a deer in the beam of an illegal hunting lantern.

"I somehow contrived to lose my watch," said James. "What time is it?"

Holmes could only hope that the author hadn't lost the watch *inside* the monument. Tomorrow morning, Holmes was going to let Henry Adams know that *he* had figured out the little mystery, been to and inside the most expensive duck blind in history, but he didn't want Adams to know about his friend James's participation.

Now he set down his heavy canvas burglar bag, lifted his watch out of his waistcoat pocket by its chain, and held it so that James could see in the light.

"Quarter past midnight," said Holmes. James merely nodded, lifted the bag for Holmes, and began walking again.

Past midnight, thought Holmes as he caught up to the other man, macadam crunching under their soles. It was now Tuesday—the fourth of April—Sherlock Holmes's birthday.

He had just turned 39 years old.

8

Wiggins Two Arrived Safely New York Today

The morning after the absurd and disturbing melodrama in Rock Creek Cemetery, Henry James awoke with the immediate and determined resolution to do *something*. He just could not decide what. Return immediately to England. Go to Henry Adams with a confession and abject apologies for invading his most hidden privacy? (No, no...the thought of that bed in that sarcophagus of stone under the ground on the subterranean level close to Clover's buried remains not only still gave James goosebumps, but made him slightly nauseous. He could never bring it up with Adams, nor hint in any way that he knew about the secret world inside Clover's sculpture and monument stone. Nor tell John Hay. Never.)

As James bathed and trimmed his short beard and dressed that rainy Tuesday morning—wishing for the hundredth time that he had the Smiths, his mediocre cook and her less-than-mediocre tippler husband of a manservant, with him from De Vere Gardens—he decided to tell Mrs. Stevens's slow-witted daughter that he would again take his breakfast in the privacy of his room. He was in the hall looking for her when the last man he wanted to see—Mr. Sherlock Holmes, looking damp and red-cheeked and in the process of shrugging off his waterproof macintosh—was preparing to knock him up.

"Just the man I wanted to see!" cried Holmes, as good-naturedly as if they hadn't invaded a good man's mind and most sacred secret the night before. "Come down to Mrs. Stevens's breakfast room and we'll talk over a good breakfast."

"I was going to have mine in my room," James replied in a cool tone.

Holmes didn't seem to perceive the frost in the air. "Nonsense. There's much we have to talk about and very little time in which to do it, James. No, now come on down to the breakfast room like a good fellow."

"I have no intention of discussing any part or aspect of last night's... events," said James.

Holmes actually smiled. "Good. Neither do I. This is more important news. I'll see you down in the breakfast room."

And Holmes turned with one of his sudden, almost spastic (although strangely graceful), moves and bounded down the stairway, shedding rain from the macintosh folded over his arm as he went.

James paused at the head of the stairs. Should he snub Holmes now and set their relationship on the new and definitely colder and more formal level to which it needed to be adjusted? Or should he suffer hearing this "more important news"?

In the end, James's hunger for breakfast won out over the higher moral arguments. He went downstairs.

*　*　*

"I have moved out of Mrs. Stevens's comfortable abode," said Holmes, eating his bean and egg and sausage and fried-toast English-style breakfast which he'd charmed Mrs. Stevens into making for him each morning.

For some reason, James was stunned. "When?" he said.

"This morning."

"Why?" asked James a second before he realized that he did not want to know the answer and that it was none of his business anyway.

"Things have become too dangerous," answered Holmes, almost gulping his coffee. Usually, James had noticed, the detective was indifferent to food, but there were times—such as this morning—where he seemed to be stoking a steam engine with fuel more than merely eating.

"Whoever that man was smoking his cigarettes at the monument last night, odds are that he was someone who had followed us there with an intention to do me harm... in short, to kill me," said Holmes, eating his eggs with gusto. "My continuing to reside here would put you, Mrs. Stevens, her daughter, and everyone else around me in some danger."

"But you're not sure that the man last night was... an assassin," said James, almost stumbling over that last melodramatic word.

"No. Nowhere near certain," agreed Holmes. "But for the time being, I should take no chances with my friends' well-being."

Something about that phrase—"my friends"—made James feel warm inside. And he hated himself for feeling that way. He certainly had not included this Sherlock Holmes person in his rigidly vetted and constantly reviewed list of friends, and for Holmes to suggest that their association had reached that plane was pure presumption.

Yet James still felt the warm glow.

Holmes finished eating and lit a cigarette. The detective never ate the yolk of his fried egg and this was one reason that James dreaded having breakfast with the man; invariably, when finished with his cigarette, he would stub it out in the runny yolk, leaving the butt end sticking up like some artillery shell that had failed to detonate. The repulsive habit always bothered Henry James and this morning, he knew, it would actively nauseate him.

"I'm not very hungry this morning," lied James, pushing his own plate forward and preparing to leave. "I wish you luck in your new habitations..."

"Wait, sir. Wait," said Holmes, actually putting his long violinist's fingers on James's lower sleeve as if ready to physically restrain him if the author attempted to rise and leave. "There's more I need to tell you."

James waited but with growing anxiety as the cigarette Holmes was smoking burned itself shorter and the runny yellow-orange egg yolk sat there amidst the debris of the eaten breakfast like a leaking bull's-eye. He was waiting because he wanted to know where Holmes would be... if this was indeed the last of their absurd adventure together.

"Are you going to tell me where you've moved?" said James, shocked at his own rude bluntness.

"No, it would be better for everyone if you didn't know, James."

Say nothing, James commanded himself. Several times in the last few days, he'd already stepped out of the character of "Henry James, Author" that he'd created over almost fifty years. Time to come back to himself again. The watcher, not the initiator. The wary listener, not the yammering fool. Still, he heard himself saying—"Will you be leaving Washington then? I'm asking just in case Hay or Adams or...someone...might need to know."

"If you need to get in touch with me," said Holmes, "send a note to this establishment." Holmes clicked open his retracting mechanical pencil and wrote quickly on the back of one of his own business cards.

James looked at the address. It was a cigar shop on Constitution Avenue.

"You're residing at a cigar store?" James couldn't help saying.

Holmes made that abrupt, almost barking sound that served him as a laugh. "Not at all, my dear James. But the proprietor there will forward any message sent to me by dispatching a boy either to my new place of residence or to send a cable. For some reason known only to Americans, the cigar shop is open twenty-four hours a day, so feel free to contact me at any time."

James nodded, slipped Holmes's card into his wallet, set the wallet back in his jacket, and was about to rise again when Mrs. Stevens appeared in the doorway with a young boy in tow.

"He has a message for you, Mr. James." She paused, perhaps reading James's expression, and added, "I know the lad. His name is Thomas. He carries messages between some of the best homes and families around Lafayette Park. If you wish to send a reply message, I'm sure it will be safe and secure in his keeping—and unread until it reaches its source."

James nodded, interpreting her final comment to mean that young Thomas couldn't read. He beckoned the boy forward.

Unfolding the paper, he saw that it was on John Hay's private stationery.

Dear Harry—
    Should you like to drop around today just after tea-time—say 5:15 or

so—I would be pleased to discuss a most important (and perhaps urgent) topic with you. I look forward to seeing you then.

Your Obedient Servant,
John Hay
    P.S.—Please do not inform Mr. Holmes of your visit. This is very important.—JH

Mrs. Stevens had thoughtfully brought a small stationery pad should James wish to respond. He did. Shielding his writing from Holmes's view, he accepted Hay's invitation and said that he would be there promptly at 5:15 p.m.—a rather specific time, James thought, but then John Hay was a man who'd devoted his life to specifics since he'd been secretary to President Abraham Lincoln.

James handed the note and a coin to the boy, saying, "Deliver this into the hand of the person who sent this message, son."

Thomas might not be able to read, but there was intelligence in his eye as he nodded.

"Oh, you don't need to pay the boy, Mr. James," Mrs. Stevens was saying. "I'm sure the person who sent the message already did that."

"Nonetheless," said James and waved Thomas away on his errand.

At that moment two other lads were shown in by Mrs. Stevens's daughter, who looked confused at the sudden invasion of messengers. One was a boy about Thomas's age although less-well dressed, the other a young man in his late teens who was wearing the livery of a Western Union delivery boy.

"Message for Mr. Holmes," said the ragged lad.

"Telegram for Mr. Holmes," said the older boy.

James still thought and felt as if he were on the verge of leaving, but stayed seated out of sheer curiosity. With Holmes moved away—God knows where—he might not see the detective again. All of the tantalizing events of the past couple of weeks might forever remain a mystery.

Holmes stubbed his cigarette out right in the center of the egg yolk and James looked away to control his rising nausea.

Holmes quickly read his telegram, set the flimsy on the table next to his napkin, said, "No reply" to the Western Union lad who touched his cap and left, and then waved forward the other boy with the private message. This he read quickly, clutched the pad that James had used for his own reply, and said, "I shall be back in one minute, James. I'll only walk our young Mercury here to the door as I scribble a reply."

Mrs. Stevens and her daughter had already left. The telegram boy was gone. Alone, James could clearly hear the footsteps of Holmes and the second messenger on the parquet floor of the foyer beyond the parlor, and then the squeak of the front door hinges as they stepped out onto the porch. The obscene cigarette butt still rose from the center of the bleeding yolk.

Beside it lay the telegram Holmes had forgotten near his napkin.

No, thought James. *Absolutely not.*

He stood as if heading for the stairway up to his room, turned right instead of left, and opened the top fold of the telegram with his left hand.

WIGGINS TWO ARRIVED SAFELY NEW YORK TODAY STOP BE INFORMED THAT SCOTLAND YARD AND INTELLIGENCE AGENCIES HERE AND IN FRANCE REPORT THAT MORIARTY'S NETWORKS HAVE BEEN ACTIVATED IN PARIS, BERLIN, PRAGUE, ROME, BRUSSELS, ATHENS, LONDON, BIRMINGHAM, NEW YORK CITY, CHICAGO AND WASHINGTON, D.C. STOP NO CONFIRMATION OF LUCAN ADLER'S WHEREABOUTS DURING PAST FIVE WEEKS STOP TAKE GREAT CARE
       MYCROFT

James quickly let the top fold of the telegram drop into place and he walked to the stairway on the opposite side of the room as he heard Holmes's usual brisk steps on the parquet and then on the boards and braided rug in the parlor. He was standing on the first step with one foot raised to the second step when Holmes bustled back in. Holmes noticed the telegram, folded it, and set it in his hacking jacket's pocket with the other message without showing any signs of concern at it being read.

"So, you're heading back up to your room now," said Holmes.

"Egad, Holmes," said Henry James, feeling a need to put this imitation gentleman in his place. "Your powers of deduction...how *do* you do it?"

Instead of showing anger or embarrassment, Holmes merely made that semi-bark of a laugh again, raised his walking stick—the one with the sword in it, James knew—and said, "Well, then, it's cheerio for the time being, although I fully trust that our paths shall cross again before too much time goes by."

"I'm thinking of sailing for England very soon," said James. He wasn't sure why he said it, since he'd not made up his mind about any such thing. He absently touched his waistcoat pocket where the ivory snuffbox containing his sister Alice's ashes was as firmly embedded as a tumor.

"Ah, well, then perhaps we shan't see each other again," Holmes said, almost lightly, almost *merrily,* thought James with an inward glower. "Ta-ta," said Holmes and turned his back and walked briskly out of the room and to the front door, whistling some cheap music-hall tune that sounded vaguely familiar to James. Something he'd heard at the Old Mo on Drury Lane.

James realized that he had been standing there for almost a full minute after he'd heard the front door slam shut, one foot still raised to the second step, standing like a statue of a man turned to stone by the Gorgon's stare. Worse than that, he realized that he was waiting for Holmes to come back to say that he'd changed his mind, he wasn't moving out after all.

Mrs. Stevens came into the breakfast room to clear the dishes, saw James standing there frozen on the stairway with the odd look on his face, and she was clearly startled. "Is everything all right, Mr. James? Do you need something?"

"Everything is fine, Mrs. Stevens. I was just heading up to my room to do some writing. A good day to you, madam."

"And a good day to you, Mr. James." She craned her neck to watch him climb the steep steps as if she'd been hired by Holmes...or Mycroft...or Moriarty...or Lucan Adler...to spy on him.

* * *

James started to knock at the Hays' front door—that is, raised his knuckled fist to knock, but decided to push the new-fangled electrical doorbell button instead—promptly at 5:15 p.m.

It had been a hard morning and afternoon. He had tried to write—working with pencil and pad on the new play he'd promised the popular actor-manager George Alexander—but while Mrs. Stevens's boarding house was a relatively pleasant place, it was still a boarding house. Noises, loud conversations with workmen and the dull-witted daughter, the sounds of two men looking at and loudly appraising Holmes's now-vacant bed-sitting-room, even Mrs. Stevens humming as she ironed in the little room off the kitchen or, when his window was open, when she was hanging wash on the clothesline below after the rain had stopped, all had conspired to distract the strangely anxious and irritable Henry James. A hundred times that afternoon he had unconsciously touched the hard bulge of the ivory snuffbox in his waistcoat pocket and wondered what he would do next. Go straight back to England? Go to the family burial plots in Cambridge outside of Boston and finally carry out his self-appointed duty of burying the last of his sister's ashes there? Go to join William and his family in Florence or Geneva or wherever they were off to at the moment? He could talk to William—sometimes. Well, rarely. In truth, almost never.

In the meantime, he was happy to have this invitation from John Hay. James felt like a man who, in leaning over a ship's railing to get a better view of something below, has fallen overboard. This invitation had felt like a life ring, complete with attached line to pull him in, tossed to him with happy, expert aim.

Benson answered the bell and, after silently directing a footman to take James's wet coat, top hat, and walking cane, led the writer directly to Hay's now-familiar study. Upon looking up from a formidable stack of papers to see James standing in his doorway after being announced, John sprang to his feet, was around the desk in a minute, and used one hand to shake James's while clasping the author firmly on the shoulder with his other hand. It came close to being a hug—which, of course, would have horrified and appalled Henry James—but now it made him feel that glow of good feeling that he'd been certain he had lost.

"I am *so* happy to see you, Harry," said Hay as he escorted James to the comfortable chair just opposite Hay's across the broad desk. Hay had kept in literal contact, holding James by the elbow as he walked the few paces to the chair. When James had taken his seat, Hay perched on the corner of his desk—amazingly spry for a man who would turn 55 in October, was James's thought (and not his first on that subject about Hay)—and cried, "Well, it's quarter past the old Five of Hearts' tea time, always precisely at five y'know, but we can have tea anyway—Clover's ghost would not object although we may hear a disembodied rap or two from the table there—or perhaps some really good whisky instead."

James hesitated. It was far too early for such a strong drink for him, he rarely touched whisky anyway, but this rainy afternoon, with the fire crackling and popping in John Hay's study's fireplace, he found the idea of a strong drink attractive—almost compelling.

"Is this an honest Scotch whisky, with no 'e' in the word?" asked James. "Or one of your American sour-mash whiskeys with the 'e' inserted?"

Hay laughed. "Oh, Scotch whisky, I assure you, Harry. I'd never offend your Anglicized sensibilities with either sour mash or a sneaky, unwanted 'e'." Hay gestured to Benson who seemed more to dissolve in thin air than step away.

"I have a twelve-year-old single-malt Cardhu from Speyside, matured in oak casks, that I find better than most twenty-one-year-old single-malt whiskeys," continued Hay, going around the desk to take his place in the high-backed and leather-tufted chair there. "Its only drawback is that one can purchase it only at Speyside, so I must either travel there each time I'm in England or constantly be paying a man to travel to Speyside, purchase it, pack it, and ship it."

"I look forward to tasting it," said James, knowing that he'd sipped 12-year-old Cardhu single malts with Paul Joukowsky and even in Lady Wolseley's salon, the latter thanks to the tastes of her husband, Field Marshal Viscount Wolseley, the inspiration for the "very model of a modern major general" in Gilbert and Sullivan's operetta *The Pirates of Penzance.*

Even before Hay began speaking again, Benson was back with a silver tray holding the decanter of Cardhu, crystal whisky glasses, a spritzer of soda water, a pitcher of regular water, and a short stack of leather coasters with John Hay's crest on them. When Benson turned toward the writer and raised one eyebrow, James said, "Neat please."

"The usual dash of water for me, Benson," said Hay.

When they had their whisky glasses and Benson had left, silently closing the study door behind him, each man raised his glass—the desk was too broad for any clinking of crystal—and Hay said, *"Amicus absentibus."*

James was surprised by the toast—to which absent friends, exactly, would they be drinking?—but he nodded and drank some of the amber whisky. It was excellent. James knew enough about judging whiskies to know that the palate on this one was smooth and well-balanced, the finish bringing out some lingering, sweet smoke in the aftertaste, but never overpowering. Never "showing off" as so many single malts had the tendency to do.

James nodded again, this time acknowledging the quality of the whisky, all the while thinking—*Which absent friend or friends?*

"Harry, I won't beat about the bush," said Hay leaning forward and cradling his Scotch glass with both hands above the papers on his desk. "Clara and I are hoping that you might consider moving back in with us for as long as you stay in Washington."

Is this related to last night? James's heart was pounding painfully—all the men in the James family had bad hearts that would get them someday—so he drank a bit more of the Cardhu to give him time to think. No, he couldn't believe that Holmes would have told anyone about James's presence in the cemetery and in Clover's tomb-sculpture interior. He'd promised that he wouldn't. *What is a promise to a man who is not really a gentleman?*

"Why, John?" he said softly. "Surely I spent enough time here as your guest that you must welcome the quiet household after our disruption."

"You were here with Holmes," said Hay, "or here when Holmes was impersonating that Norwegian explorer, Jan Sigerson, which was enjoyable in its own way. But Clara and I felt that we never really had a chance to talk to you."

James set his chin on his chest in a posture that would, half a century later, come to be called "Churchillian".

"Unless," continued Hay, leaning far back in his chair now and drinking the whisky almost hurriedly, as if enjoying its fragrance weren't part of the process of enjoying it, "unless you plan to leave the city soon. To Cambridge? Perhaps then on to England? Paris?"

"No, I have no immediate plans to leave." James realized that he'd decided that even as he spoke the words. "But my room at Mrs. Stevens's is quite adequate."

Hay grinned beneath his carefully trimmed whiskers. "Adequate for a bachelor junior congressman, perhaps, Harry, but certainly not for a writer. You *are* doing some writing, aren't you?"

Too little, too little, thought James. But then, the plan had been to commit suicide in Paris and part of the attractiveness of that plan had been to end all the deadlines, to get his agent and stage producers and publishers and everyone else with their baby beaks wide open and waiting to be fed to — how did the Americans put it? — then *get off his neck.*

"Some very modest attempts at my next play," said James, his tone as doleful as his countenance. "Little more than notes."

Hay grinned again. "I trust that your room was comfortable when you and Holmes were staying here, but we have a much larger suite of guest rooms at the far end of the wing opposite to the one where you stayed before. We didn't place you there during your last stay because it's inconveniently far from the main stairway, but if you'd honor us with another visit, that suite will be yours — bedroom and much larger sitting room, both with fireplaces, of course, the sitting room with its own rather pleasant library. The colored tiles around the large bathtub are somewhat brighter than those in your former bathroom, but the wash basins are marble, the taps are silver, and I can promise you that the water will be hot as well as cold."

James took a breath, trying to frame his refusal in the politest way possible. In truth, it was the proximity to Henry Adams — the man whose secrecy he'd so callously invaded — that was preventing him from saying yes.

"And as nice as Mrs. Stevens's little place is," continued Hay, the whisky gone from his glass, "I don't believe that she can provide you with as excellent a manservant as we can."

"Manservant," James repeated, feeling strangely numb all over. *Is this the way a character in a novel feels when the author is manipulating him or her in a way contrary to their nature or to common sense?* He wished he could ask Holmes that question and actually patted the jacket pocket where his purse held the detective's card with the name and address of the cigar store where James could get in contact with him.

"Yes, and not just any manservant," said Hay, leaning further over the desk now, "but Gregory, one of our longest serving and most trusted employees."

James remembered a tall, white-haired man on Hay's staff being referred to as Gregory. The servant had emanated dignity and quiet efficiency. "Is Gregory his first or last name?" asked James.

"Last," said Hay. "I believe his Christian name is Terrance. Gregory is not only the perfect man to stoke up your fires and lay out your clothes in the morning, but he gives the best and closest neck-shaves of any man on the staff."

"I really have a powerful reluctance to being in your and Clara's way once again..." began James.

Hay held his hands up, palms forward, and then moved them quickly in opposite directions as if opening a door or brushing something aside.

"This shan't be like your first visit where you were a guest with a guest's... well, one might call them obligations: coming down to dinner with us, making small talk, joining me for luncheon, and so forth. No, the guest suite would be yours—it's on the northeast corner and there will be some light traffic noise coming through the windows there, but it's very soft noise—our boy Del lived in those rooms for a while but went back to his own before going back to school. He thought the suite was *too* quiet. *Too* large."

Perhaps the rooms in the suite are haunted, thought James. He smiled as he realized that he wouldn't be averse to a few ectoplasmic visitations. Perhaps his sister Alice could advise him as to what to do with her ashes that he'd pilfered.

"... and daily service from the maids, of course, but only when you're out," Hay was going on. "And you can have all your meals and tea breaks in your room if you like...Gregory will be your guard at the gate as well as your valet. And of course you shall have your own key to the front door so you can come and go whenever you want without disturbing anyone."

"I confess that I have found myself a trifle lonely at Mrs. Stevens's place," said James, already surrendering himself to the invitation. He could rest. He could write.

"No wonder you do...especially with Mr. Holmes leaving so abruptly," said Hay. The statesman did not seem to notice the minor levitation of James's eyebrows. "You agree then, Harry?"

James nodded.

"Wonderful!" cried Hay. "I'll have some of the lads go over now in the wagon to fetch your steamer trunk and other luggage."

A minute later, they were standing just inside the open door, watching the spring rain fall and enjoying the scent of the rain on new grass and fresh leaves when Hay's brougham was brought around for James—the manservant Gregory was up on the box next to the driver and sheltering under a red umbrella—and then came the good-natured stablemen, wool and leather caps beaded with raindrops, driving the flatbed wagon for his luggage.

James said, "John, how did you know that Holmes had moved out? It happened only this morning."

Hay grinned and clapped the author on his right shoulder, opening an umbrella at the same time to escort James into the brougham. "Harry, Harry...one must never underestimate the speed with which even the smallest news travels in Washington City. Especially around Lafayette Park. Your landlady's daughter, slow as the poor girl is, gave all the details of Holmes to our footman, at the morning outdoor market probably before either of us was up and dressed."

James settled into the sweet-smelling leather of the covered brougham. Hay folded the umbrella and tapped the box with the wooden handle.

"See you soon, Harry!"

James rode in silence for the few blocks. The daughter telling the footman about Holmes's early departure, who then mentioned it to other servants who were then overheard by Clara or John, made all the sense in the world.

But Henry James did not believe it.

9

We Get Lots of Cyclists Buying Lemon Squeezers

All in all, Sherlock Holmes had enjoyed an enjoyably productive birthday morning. At home—or at what he still thought of as home in his former digs on Baker Street in London—he'd often sleep in until eleven a.m. or later during those dull periods between cases. And then he'd often have breakfast and return to bed. Of course, the mixture of cocaine he injected during those dull times added to the lethargy—something this new heroic drug he was injecting himself with in the States didn't seem to do—but then he was always especially alert when he was on a case.

This particular morning of April 4, he'd wakened at dawn and gone out to find himself a new place to live—the same old Kirkwood House hotel at the corner of 12th Street N.W. and Pennsylvania Avenue that he and James had passed the night before. Rumors still persisted that the old hotel would be torn down almost any month, but the place had a comfortable lived-in quality that Holmes approved of: expensive drapes but faded from sunlight, marvelously well-made chairs showing wear that even antimacassars could not hide, a combination of attentive service mixed with the discretion of knowing when to leave its guests to their own devices. Holmes understood why the more successful traveling salesmen were still loyal to the place.

He hired three reliable men—vouched for by the manager of the Kirkwood House since one of the men was the manager's son—and their wagon to fetch his packed bags and steamer trunks from Mrs. Stevens's boarding house without making a fuss.

Then, with the shops just opening, Holmes had bought himself a pistol. He'd noticed the generous number of gun shops around Washington and entered the one closest to the Kirkwood House a minute after the store opened. There was a vast array of pistols under glass, some of them evidently designed for cowboy desperadoes, and more hanging on the wall. The air smelled rather pleasantly of steel and gun oil.

"May I help you, sir?" the mustached clerk asked.

"Do you have any new lemon squeezers for sale?" said Holmes.

"Yes, sir, absolutely, sir. Which barrel length—two inches or three?"

"Three."

"Yes, better accuracy with the three-inch barrel, sir," said the clerk as he opened the glass case and removed the weapon.

Yes, with the three-inch barrel I might be able to hit the wall of a barn if I were inside the barn firing from close range, thought Holmes. *Maybe.*

"Any caliber you prefer, sir?"

"Thirty-eight S and W caliber," said Holmes.

"It also comes in thirty-two, sir. A bit less expensive and a tad lighter."

"The thirty-eight, please," Holmes said firmly.

The clerk ceremoniously displayed the small pistol—and it *was* smaller than the vast majority of the revolvers in the store—and snapped the cylinder open to show his client that the weapon was unloaded, then handed it to Holmes.

Holmes noticed that .38 S&W cartridges would be a tight fit in the chambers and then he snapped shut the cylinder and held the weapon at arm's length, aiming at the brick wall at the back of the store.

"One squeezes the grip as well as the trigger," said the clerk.

"Yes," said Holmes. He dry-fired the pistol twice. Not a good practice, overall, but necessary to get used to a new revolver.

"You like the hammerless lemon squeezers then, sir? You a bicyclist by any chance?"

"Exactly," said Holmes. "Wouldn't do to snag a hammer and have the pistol go off in my trouser pocket, now would it?"

"No, sir. We get lots of cyclists buying lemon squeezers. Most popular. These pistols are guaranteed not to fire if one takes a fall while cycling." The clerk paused and cleared his throat. "Are you a bicycle fanatic then, sir?"

"Quite so," said Holmes. "Absolutely mad about it."

"Not too many customers from England, though...not to be overly personal or anything, sir." The clerk's cheeks reddened as he realized he'd overstepped his bounds with a gentleman.

"Not at all," said Holmes with a smile. "One needs a pistol here to keep up on the target shooting with one's American friends, what?"

"Of course, sir."

"The absence of a hammer feels strange," said Holmes. "Does the weapon jam or misfire very often?"

"No, sir. Not the Smith and Wesson brand. As reliable a double action as they make. Looks strange, I agree, but it's the best weapon you can carry concealed when you don't have large pockets. And even then, hammers and the larger sights can snag on cloth in pockets and such, can't they?"

"Indeed," said Holmes. "How much for this pistol?"

"Five dollars, sir."

"That seems a bit steep."

"I throw in two boxes of cartridges with the lemon squeezer, sir."

"Done," said Holmes.

"Shall I box it and wrap it up, sir?"

"No," Holmes had said. "I'll carry it on me."

* * *

And Holmes was carrying the seemingly hammerless S&W, loaded save for one empty chamber, in one oversized outer pocket of his tweed suit and the two boxes of cartridges in the opposite oversized pocket, a short time later when he called on John Hay. The former diplomat was just sitting down to breakfast when Holmes was shown in and the detective assured him that his visit wouldn't take more than two minutes and he'd be happy to have some coffee while Hay ate.

As succinctly as possible—and never mentioning the previous night's adventure in Rock Creek Cemetery or the ominous figure smoking his cigarettes in the dark—Holmes explained that he was moving out of Mrs. Stevens's boarding house, a necessity, alas, and that he was concerned for Mr. James's safety.

"Certainly James has no enemies in Washington!" cried Hays.

"I would doubt that Mr. James has enemies anywhere," said Holmes. "But *I* have enemies. And it has come to my attention that they may know of my presence in Washington...even my current address at Mrs. Stevens's establishment."

Hay looked concerned and dabbed a linen napkin at his sharp beard and perfectly trimmed mustache. "But certainly they wouldn't...an innocent such as Harry..."

"It is a long shot, as you Americans say," said Holmes. "A remote possibility. But these particular people are beyond all laws of reason and decency. I would not sleep well imagining them showing up at Mrs. Stevens's home and coming across Mr. James..."

Hay looked sharply at the detective. "Would my family be in danger if Harry stayed here?"

"Not in the least."

"How can you be so sure, sir?" Hay's pleasant demeanor had disappeared for a moment into the sharp cross-examining tones of a prosecutor.

"These...people...may not recognize the extent of Henry James's literary fame," said Holmes, "but I am certain that they know *your* reputation, Mr. Hay, and would do nothing associated with you or your family...or your guest...that would bring publicity down on their heads."

"Then I'll ask Harry to drop by today and insist...*insist,* I tell you...that he stay with us again," said Hay. Holmes loved the tone of a man who could make up his mind in a few seconds.

"Could you ask him to drop by at about five-fifteen?" said Holmes.

"Yes, if you wish." Hay squinted slightly at the detective. "Is there a special reason for that time?"

"Just that I don't wish to bump into Mr. James once I've moved out of Mrs. Stevens's pleasant home and I may be in this area earlier in the day."

"I shall specify five-fifteen," said Hay and started to rise as Holmes stood.

"No, please, don't get up, and thank you for this favor," said Holmes.

"If I need to get in touch with you..." began Hay.

Holmes handed him one of his cards with the cigar store address handwritten on the back. "This establishment is open around the clock for some inexplicable reason," he said. "And they promise to get any message to me as quickly as they can."

Holmes and Hay had shaken hands and then the detective hurried down the street to catch Henry James before he had his breakfast brought to his room.

10

A Small Bouquet of White Violets

Holmes knocked on Henry Adams's front door at five p.m., precisely the time he'd suggested in his early-morning note and to which Adams had agreed in his return note that morning.

The door was opened at once and Holmes was confronted with the dour face of an elderly butler; he now knew all of the Hays' family servants by face and name, but he hadn't been formally introduced to Henry Adams's home or staff.

The butler said nothing, closed the door behind the detective, nodded his head to indicate that Holmes should follow, and led him directly up a staircase Holmes had seen only in the darkness of his burgling night. At the upstairs study, the grim-faced butler waited only for Adams to nod from his place behind a full but not cluttered desk before he closed the door behind Holmes. There had been no announcement, no greeting, not even a "Please follow me, sir" from the side-whiskered old retainer, but perhaps Adams had directed his man not to speak to Holmes. At any rate, Holmes did not feel slighted. He looked around the book-lined study with some interest. It was a scholar's study and illuminated not only by desk and table lamps but by large windows, some leaded with ornate stained glass, others clear. Through the clear windows, Holmes looked directly across the street at the president's Executive Mansion.

Adams neither rose nor spoke, so Holmes took the initiative of walking across the room to the desk, setting his top hat, gloves, and walking stick on one chair, and sitting on the other one that was opposite Adams across the desk.

"You have put me in an impossible position, Mr. Sherlock Holmes," the bald scholar said softly—but not so softly that Holmes missed the substrate of anger and frustration in Adams's tone.

Rather than disagree or comment in any way, Holmes merely nodded.

"I made my...mystery...far too simple, didn't I?" said Adams. "Too many clues."

"Actually, just enough clues," said Holmes. "And not all of them deliberate."

"Your note this morning said only that you had solved the mystery and looked out at the world from a mourner's eyes. I presume that means you..."

"Went in the monument?" finished Holmes. "Yes."

Henry Adams looked down at the papers on his desk and for a moment the man's face—even the flesh of his mostly bare scalp—went so terribly pale that Holmes was concerned that the older man was having a heart attack or stroke. But then Adams looked up, sat up straighter.

"Well, then," Adams said in an only slightly shaky voice, "you know the greatest secret in my life, Mr. Holmes. I was foolish enough and overconfident enough to give a man...like you...far too simple clues to the secret and now you know." Adams's body twitched suddenly as if he'd been jolted by an electric current. "You didn't tell James, did you?"

"I've spoken neither to Henry James nor to anyone else about this matter last night or this morning," said Holmes, feeling the lawyerly dodge of his words almost stick in his craw.

Adams nodded. "For that I can be thankful." The scholar sighed and folded his hands on his desk. "And now what, Mr. Holmes? Do we discuss the concept of money changing hands?"

Holmes could have acted outraged—was tempted to do so—but did not.

"I accept fees for my services as an investigator, Mr. Adams," he said coolly. "Not payment as a blackmailer."

Adams's expression still had not changed. "Then what are your...fees as an investigator...in this instance, Mr. Holmes?"

"One dollar," said Holmes. "And already paid—two years ago—by your wife's late brother, Edward."

"Ned," said Adams with a strange, almost pained tone to his voice.

Holmes nodded again.

Suddenly Adams seemed to shake himself out of a haze. "I apologize," he said, half rising and reaching for a velvet pull rope on the wall. "I haven't asked you if you would like a cup of tea . . . or coffee . . . or a glass of whisky?"

"Nothing, thank you."

Adams almost collapsed back into his chair. "You are," he said very softly, "probably the only man alive who knows what a monster I am."

"Mourner," said Holmes. "Not monster. Never monster. A mourner of someone truly loved who has found a unique way to see others mourning his lost love."

Adams almost laughed. "If you heard some of the comments . . . saw some of their clowning at first encountering Saint-Gaudens's sculpture. Heard them guessing at the price of the monument or criticizing its solemnity, or its lack of religious purpose, or its lack of joy in the hope and sure certainty of eternal redemption. We are a strange and inexplicable species, Mr. Holmes."

"Indeed."

"What do you want, sir?" asked Henry Adams.

"I want . . . need . . . to discover the truth of your wife Clover's death more than seven years ago," said Holmes.

"She drank potassium cyanide and died almost instantaneously," Adams said briskly. "There is really nothing else to discuss, much less uncover."

Holmes sighed and leaned forward so that his hands were also folded on Adams's broad desk. "I apologize for my bluntness, Mr. Adams. And there will be more such bluntness before we are finished. But it is not out of cruelty I make these comments or ask these questions, but out of a need for clarity."

Adams had sat further back in his chair but met Holmes's sharp, gray gaze with a steady one of his own.

"Mrs. Adams's death would have hardly been—near instantaneous,"

Holmes said in soft but solid tones. "I have published monographs on more than three hundred poisonous substances and combinations of such—their symptoms, their lethality rated on a scale of one hundred, their odor, their efficacy. Potassium cyanide, in any dose large enough to kill Mrs. Adams, would have burned her tongue and throat. Then this particular poison cuts off the body's ability to process oxygen—in essence, asphyxiating the victim. But Mrs. Adams would have choked and gasped for air, perhaps ripping off her collar or bodice in an attempt to breathe, for some terrible moments. She would have thrashed about and fallen to the floor, where the poison would have assured more min-utes of violent convulsions. Then..."

"Enough!" cried Henry Adams, slapping his palm so violently against the top of his desk that the noise sounded like a rifle shot in the room.

Almost instantly, the door was flung open and the aged head butler half-entered. "Sir...are you all right? I heard..."

Adams was still looking down but nodded and said through a thick voice, "Quite all right, Hobson. You needn't wait outside any longer."

"Yes, sir." The door was closed silently and Holmes could hear what he'd noticed the lack of earlier—the butler's footsteps receding down the hall and then down the staircase.

Holmes returned his attention to Adams and felt the intensity of the older man's gaze. If looks were knives, this one would have decapitated and gutted Holmes.

"Why do you tell me these things?" rasped Adams.

Holmes pointed to one of the hundreds of leather-bound volumes on the wall of books behind Adams. "Sedford's *Poisons and Their Effects,* Ninth Edition. You know all these details, Mr. Adams. You have re-searched this poison as carefully as you've researched Thomas Jefferson's administrations. You wanted the truth, no matter how hard it was to bear. So do I."

"Yes, all right." The scholar took a deep breath. "The parlor where I found Clover's body looked as if three sailors had been fighting in it—drapes torn, tables overturned, lamps smashed, pillows slashed by her nails, crystal objects flung down from the mantel. And Clover's face...it was monstrous in its frozen terror and distortion, Mr. Holmes."

Holmes nodded. After allowing a moment of silence, he said, "You lied to the police and newspapers, Mr. Adams."

Adams's head and shoulders snapped backwards. Dim afternoon sunlight glinted on his bald head and clenched fists. For a second or two while studying Adams's expression, Holmes was reminded of the *ki* demon masks he'd seen in a Noh play in Kyoto.

But Adams said nothing. Holmes watched the scholar's clenched right hand drop just above the drawer there and wondered if Henry Adams kept a pistol in that drawer. Holmes's new lemon squeezer—loaded—was in the right-front pocket of his tweed jacket.

"You told the police and the papers that you had left your wife alone that Sunday morning because you had to visit your dentist," said Holmes. "That wasn't true."

Adams's small body actually rocked to and fro slightly as if in response to his mental struggle. Finally he said, "No, that wasn't true."

"Why did you leave that morning, Mr. Adams?"

"Clover and I had quarreled. Violently." And then, as if realizing the legal import of that word, he said quickly, "For Clover and me it was 'violently'—although voices were barely raised. We weren't a couple who shouts. Ever."

"But you argued."

"Yes."

"Over what?" said Holmes.

"Clover had been distraught—close to despair—and that morning she was in tears, almost hysterics, because Sunday at that hour had always been the time she wrote to her father. Her father who was now dead."

"You argued about her emotions or about her writing a letter?" said Holmes.

"I insisted she begin a new Sunday routine," said Adams. "Write a letter to her sister Ellen. Make Sundays a day for something other than melancholy and mourning after those many months."

"She did write that letter, or a fragment of it, to her sister after you left," said Holmes. "She told her sister that, and I believe I quote—'*Henry has been more patient and loving than words can express*' and, in the final uncompleted paragraph, *'Henry has been—and is—beyond all words tenderer and better than all of you even.'* Why do you think she would write such a note just after the two of you had quarreled and you'd stalked out, Mr. Adams?"

Adams looked like a writer forced to watch his entire life's work burned page by page in a fire. "I don't know, Mr. Holmes. No more than I know how you got the precise wording of Clover's letter to Ellen."

"The police made a copy," Holmes said, making a gesture with his bare right hand as if batting away something trivial and not worth discussing. He cleared his throat. "It sounds as if," continued Holmes, "Mrs. Adams was writing a form of suicide note to her sister making sure that you were not in any way to blame."

Adams only shook his head, whether in negation or confusion, Holmes couldn't tell.

"Earlier in the letter to her sister," said Holmes, "Mrs. Adams wrote, and again I believe I can cite it fully from memory—*'If I had one single point of character or goodness, I would stand on that and grow back to life.'* But then the letter ends. Why did you turn around and go home so quickly, Mr. Adams? After only ten minutes or so of walking? I know you had no appointment with your dentist that morning."

Adams lifted a fountain pen from the table top and held it in both hands as if he were going to snap it. "I became . . . alarmed," he said at last. "Concerned. I realized that it had been a bastardly thing to do . . . leaving Clover alone in the house on a morning when she was hurting so much."

"And upon returning to your home then at sixteen-oh-seven H Street—just down the street," said Holmes. "You told the police that you found Miss Rebecca Lorne waiting outside the front door. You said that she asked your opinion on whether she should go up and visit Clover that day."

Adams said nothing. His usually almost frighteningly intelligent eyes seemed to have a haze over them—*A translucent caul of memory,* thought Holmes.

"Why did you lie about that as well, Mr. Adams?" said Holmes.

Adams blinked. "Who said that I lied."

"I did. You encountered Rebecca Lorne coming out the front door of your house on H Street. She was weeping—as hysterical as Mrs. Adams had been a short time earlier. She had trouble telling you what she had found when she went up to visit Mrs. Adams, didn't she, Mr. Adams?"

"Yes. I had to take her into the foyer so that no one could see her hysterics...it took me a full minute or two to get her calmed down to the point where Miss Lorne could tell me what she'd discovered upstairs."

"How did she get in?" asked Holmes, leaning forward again.

"What?"

"I'm sure you locked the door behind you when you left to work off your anger in your walk," said Holmes. "How did Rebecca Lorne gain entry to your home?"

"Oh, Clover had had an extra key made up for Rebecca a month or two earlier," Adams answered almost distractedly. "We'd hoped to go to New York for some shopping—a vain hope, as it turned out—and Clover had given Miss Lorne the key so that she could drop in to check on the servants and see that the plants were properly watered."

"Rebecca Lorne discovered Mrs. Adams's body in the wreckage that had been the parlor, not you," said Holmes. He did not phrase it as a question and Adams did not answer other than to nod ever so slightly.

Eventually Adams spoke in hollowed-out tones, the voice of a man who has passed through Hell and who knows he must go there again. "In those last months, it was only Rebecca Lorne who seemed to give Clover any surcease of her sorrow over her father's death. Clover had stopped seeing most of her usual friends. It's not quite fair to say that she and Miss Lorne were inseparable during those last late-summer and autumn months, but there's no one whom Clover looked forward to seeing more than Miss Lorne."

"Hadn't the two of them paid a call on Mrs. Cameron—Lizzie Cameron—the previous evening?" asked Holmes.

Adams blinked rapidly once again. "Yes, they had. Lizzie had been very ill with...the influenza, I believe. Clover visited her and Miss Lorne accompanied her. They brought flowers and a book."

Holmes removed the untitled publicity photograph of Irene Adler from his upper jacket pocket and handed it across to Henry Adams. "Is this a picture of Rebecca Lorne?"

Adams moved the photograph back and forth to bring it into proper focus. "Well...yes, it appears to be Miss Lorne. Her dress here is more... 'showy' is perhaps the right word...and she looks a little younger than when I last saw her, but this appears to be Rebecca."

Holmes took the photo back. "This is a program advertisement for a certain Irene Adler—American born but European trained."

"Trained in what?" said Adams.

"Opera, acting on the stage, and blackmail," said Holmes. "Most specially that last skill."

"I don't believe it."

"You remember her cousin, a certain Clifton Richards?"

"Of course," said Adams. "He worked in the photographic section of the State Department." Adams paused and the haze came over his eyes again. "He's the one who brought Clover the new developing solution that contained the potassium cyanide."

"His real name is Lucan," said Holmes. "Possibly Lucan Adler. Probably Irene Adler's son."

Adams shook his head again.

"You didn't see or talk to Lucan—this Cousin Clifton—on the day you met Rebecca Lorne coming out of your house...the day Clover died?"

"No."

"So he might have been in the house and exited via the back stairs when you ran up the front stairs, and he may have slipped out the back way into the alley," said Holmes.

"An extraordinary and outrageous supposition," said Henry Adams. "We have no evidence that her cousin Clifton was with her in my home on that terrible day."

"No," said Holmes, "but we know beyond a doubt that 'Clifton Richards' was Adler the assassin. And without questioning Irene Adler—your so-called Rebecca Lorne—we simply cannot know the truth of that day. And there was an obituary for Irene Adler in the March eighteen eighty-six London *Times*."

Adams shook his head again, but with a negative hand gesture this time, a physical pushing away of Holmes's words or their import. "No, no . . . this Irene Adler cannot have been the same woman that I knew so well in the year before Clover's death. I've written letters to Miss Lorne, it's been *Mrs.* Braxton, of Boston, over the years. And she has always responded."

"Recently?" said Holmes, his ears metaphorically perking up like a hunting hound's.

"Her last letter to me was last autumn, I believe," said Adams. "So you see that your late actress person cannot be Mrs. Rebecca Lorne Braxton of Boston."

"And her handwriting has stayed the same?" said Holmes.

"Yes, of course," said Adams. "But I shall show you the letters. You may make your own judgment. Mrs. Braxton has never sent me a typewritten missive such as those accursed annual cards you are so clumsily and invasively investigating."

"When was Miss Lorne married?"

"About two years after my wife's death," said Adams. "Miss Lorne had moved to Boston in January of eighteen eighty-six, only a month after . . . after. She sent me a note of her marriage in August of eighteen eighty-eight. I know only that her husband is somewhat older than she and that he makes a living in the sea trade with India."

"May I see these letters? Hers to you, I mean. Not yours to her."

Holmes expected an argument, possibly harsh words, but Adams must have been expecting the request; he pulled a small bundle of envelopes, tied in a pink bow, from the main drawer of his desk.

"Read them, Mr. Holmes. Take them with you as long as you promise to return them. You shall find nothing in Rebecca Lorne Braxton's letters to me—or in my short notes to her, for that matter, should the lady allow you to read them someday—but normal conversation between an aging widower and his wife's friend, a friend, like the husband, still deep in mourning after seven years." Adams's tone was flat, almost businesslike.

Holmes accepted the bundle of letters in silence.

"Another thing . . . another *mystery,* if you will, Mr. Holmes," said Adams.

Holmes held the letters in his lap and waited.

"Every year on December six," said Adams. "The anniversary of Clover's death. I have found, or Hay and my other friends have found when I was traveling in the South Seas, a small bouquet of white violets, Clover's favorite flower, set on my wife's grave in Rock Creek Cemetery. I am certain that they have been set there every December six by Rebecca Lorne."

"How can you know this?" asked Holmes. "Did she admit to this?"

"No, I have never mentioned it to her in our occasional correspondence," said Adams. "I simply know. I have not written to thank her yet, but someday I shall."

"But you said that Miss Lorne...Mrs. Braxton now...has lived in Boston these seven years."

"Yes."

"Mr. Adams...you really believe that Rebecca Lorne Braxton makes the long trip to Washington every December six, never to contact you, but only to leave this bouquet of white violets on your wife's grave?"

"I do, Mr. Holmes. She has never spoken of it in her letters, but I am certain that particular act of kindness is hers. It matches the personality of the woman I knew in eighteen eighty-five. Rebecca Lorne was and is a kind person, Mr. Holmes. She was my wife's *friend*. To even think that she was in any way involved with or, God forbid, responsible for my wife's death—Clover's death by melancholy, as I often think of it—is more than a grave error in judgment, Mr. Holmes. It is investigative malpractice. And it is also a callous act of slander."

"Thank you for your time, Mr. Adams," said Holmes, standing and retrieving his hat, gloves, and stick. Adams remained seated.

"Are you leaving Washington soon?" asked the scholar.

"I will be doing some traveling in relation to this investigation and...another...but I can be reached through that cigar store address at any time," said Holmes.

"I will have no more to say on this matter," said Adams. "I would appreciate you returning the letters before you begin your travels. You may give them to Hobson when the time comes. There is no further reason for us to meet or speak."

Holmes nodded. "I'll find my own way out, Mr. Adams. I thank you for your time and cooperation." He patted the small bundle of letters in his chest pocket.

But Henry Adams had returned his gaze to the papers on his desk and did not look up.

Holmes paused in the open doorway, sensing but not seeing Hobson hovering somewhere out of sight down the hallway. "One last question, Mr. Adams."

Adams raised his head. There was no sigh, frown, or rolling of the eyes and, once again, Holmes admired the historian's self-discipline.

"Your windows there, the clear ones," said Holmes, "offer an astonishingly good view of the president's house, especially of that one set of windows."

Adams said nothing. He did not turn his head to look at the windows Holmes was pointing toward, nor did he have to. Adams had worked in this study and had that view since 1886.

"Do you happen to know, Mr. Adams, which room in the White House those windows serve and—as odd as my query sounds—whether President Cleveland often frequents that room?"

"I can only tell you that when Mrs. Adams and I visited the president's house during his first term that room was the office and receiving room for the president's sister, Miss Rose Elizabeth Cleveland, who served as the de facto First Lady of the land until eighteen eighty-six when Mr. Cleveland entered into marriage. I believe that ceremony was the only marriage service ever held on the grounds for a chief executive in the history of the White House. When Mr. Cleveland returned to office and resumed his occupancy there only last month, it is my understanding that his sister did not return to Washington with him. I believe she has become the administrator of some little collegiate institution in Indiana...Lafayette, Indiana, to be precise. She has published often on what they now call *feministe* issues—that is, women's rights. I've read that she took part in the First International Women's Conference in Paris last year. So, no, I have no idea what the room behind those windows is used for at the present time. Only that the president's sister will not be there."

Holmes smiled at the historian's completeness—if not civil tone—in answering such a silly question, nodded his thanks, and closed the door behind him.

As he hurried to the waiting hansom before Henry James—visiting next door—might glimpse him, Holmes knew that the interview had given up at least one possibly relevant fact: Henry Adams's study was the perfect location for a Lucan-Adler-type assassin with a rifle.

11

The Wheel of Time

For the first day or two after Henry James returned to the Hays' home as an artist whose privacy had to be respected at all times, the writer was relieved and as happy as he'd been since before the turn of the year. His guest suite at the far end of what Americans called the second story was large, comfortable, and private. If James chose to join John and Clara Hay for a meal, his hosts were delighted to have him. If he preferred absolute privacy—which he did for those first days—the servant assigned to him, Gregory, would bring up a menu before each meal and James would choose his own breakfast, lunch, or dinner, with no reference to what his hosts were having.

In those first few days, James celebrated Holmes's complete absence much in the way he'd quietly celebrated the disappearance of the worst pains of gout that had so hobbled him around Christmas and the New Year in London. There were no more cigarettes stubbed into egg yolks; no more inane conversations about conspiracies and assassinations; no more late-night outings to cemeteries or creeping into memorial sculptures with secret passages. James felt liberated. He was free now, with Holmes gone, free to rest or write or just walk and think. Or to book passage on the next steamship to England if he so wished. Things could not have turned out better.

Then why, he wondered on April 7, the Friday of that first week at the Hays', did he feel as deeply listless and actively melancholy as he had in March when he'd decided to go to Paris to drown himself in the Seine?

Lying in bed that night, the literary contents of his portmanteau poured out onto the blanket beside him, James looked through his notebooks. His markets for short stories seemed to have dried up and publishers in both England and America had mostly moved away from the long, serialized tale that had — in the spirit of Dickens — kept James busy writing for so many years. His last two novels, *The Reverberator* and *The Tragic Muse,* the latter released three years ago in 1890, had sold poorly. As did his story collection published in that same year, *The Aspern Papers.*

He had three books scheduled to be published later this year: *Picture and Text* in June, his essays on art; *Essays in London* to appear later in the summer, essentially a compilation of his tributes to his many friends who had died recently; finally his collection of stories *The Private Life and Other Tales.*

But none of these were major novels. And his essays and short-story collections had never brought in much money or notice.

It was clear that the literary world had passed Henry James by. Or perhaps, he mused, he had somehow wandered away from *it.* Thus his resolution last year, the resolution that had come before his resolution to kill himself, to begin a new and far more financially (and, in its way, socially) rewarding career of writing for the theater.

His first play, *The American,* adapted rather loosely from his novel by the same name (so loosely that he'd first titled the play *The Californian*), had a run of seventy nights in London and more weeks before and after in the provinces. James had enjoyed the process — reading the four-act play to the actors as a French author-director would, watching them rehearsing it, bringing them chicken and soups and other nourishing lunches during their long rehearsal days. Encouraging them. Bantering with them. *Participating.* Being accepted. Laughing with others and making them laugh with his droll wit — some of it in new lines written for the play as it evolved and changed.

How different all that had been from his decades of disciplined isolation while writing his scores of stories and overflowing shelf of novels. But all that labor to what purpose? He made enough money to rent the lovely, light-filled apartments at 364 De Vere Gardens — his home since 1886. But even there he was restless. He'd deliberately given up most of the evening and weekend London social life he'd enjoyed so much in past years in order to spend more time writing. Dedicate one-self to one's work was his new mantra, and to do that one had to stop accepting dinner invitations five nights of the week, endless invitations to join the rich bourgeoisie whom he was invited to amuse at their country houses and Irish estates with his ample supply of small talk, wit, and gossip.

But while he had loved working in isolation, his work was no longer earning him what it should, either in dollars and pounds or in fame.

Oh, not that he'd ever striven after riches or fame! No! The Art had always come first. Always. But he *had* long imagined that before age 50 his work would have allowed him financial freedom enough to... To what? Perhaps to buy himself an English country house by the sea. Just a cottage, of course, a tidy little seasonal home in addition to his flat at De Vere Gardens. A cozy country place at which he would host liter-ary friends and his brother William and his family when they came to England. A place where he could host his younger male friends—Paul Bourget, say, or Edmund Gosse. With privacy.

In the end, after all his work, the theatrical group had totally rewrit-ten James's "gloomy"—their word—third act to turn *The American* into a not-very-successful comedy.

Although the Prince of Wales had come to see *The American* in Lon-don and that had prompted the producer to attempt a "second opening" of the shortened and rewritten play at its fiftieth performance, James once again helping to fill the expensive seats and boxes with the au-thor's literary and high-society friends, audiences remained lackluster until James finally had to agree with the critics. The play into which he and his sister Alice had poured so much of their optimism had been a failure on many levels. He'd frantically abandoned his literary roots, he knew, to achieve a "well-made play" and that eager pander-ing had turned his serious novel into an absurdly paced melodrama on stage. The highly literate drama critic A. B. Walkley had written of the non-stop busyness of his script—"What, Mr. James? All this 'be-tween dinner and the suburban trains?'" James was sure it had also been

Walkley in an anonymous review who'd said that James had offered the public little other than "a stage American, with the local color laid on with a trowel, a strong accent, a fearful and wonderful coat, and a recurrent catch-word."

Edward Compton, the producer and lead actor, indeed had mastered the American dialect to a fault—in his later viewings of his play, James clearly heard the caricature of American English he'd penned—and the catchword phrase James had given him (after Compton told him that such catchwords were important for characters on stage) had been *"That's what I want t'see"*—which, by James's last viewing of the crippled, hobbled, emasculated play, seemed to be every third line for Compton's American character.

As for the giant chocolate-colored coat, Compton had coveted the garment during rehearsals and provincial openings. "Gives the audience a sense of this American's real nature," the actor-producer had said after the first out-of-London auditions. But, James could see now, it had been an absurd wardrobe choice. One critic wondered in print if all Americans skinned buffalos to wear their entire hairy hide as a coat. Another compared Compton's giant brown buttons to chocolate-covered cupcakes.

The best thing written by critics about his American leading lady, Miss Elizabeth Robins, was that her acting was "a tad less somnambulistic" in some of the later stagings. In the earlier performances, critics had called her acting—essentially of an inert woman, a listener, an observer—"bordering on the hysterical if not the outright deranged." The poor actress, James had seen, had been totally miscast in his role for a basically passive and passionless woman, had tried the full spectrum, from deranged, to hysterical, then as somnambulistic as if she'd been drugged with laudanum, and now back to the "tad less somnambulistic". After her recent successes in playing Hedda and Nora in Ibsen's strangely popular plays, this critical pillorying of her "Claire" character in *The American* made her weep after every performance.

James had felt like weeping with her.

An anonymous critic for the *Era* had summed up Henry James's first theatrical contribution thusly: "We are as anxious as the critics of the newest school to hail the advent on our stage of literary men, but it is on condition that they bring their literature with them."

This—the truth of this statement—had hurt James more than he would ever admit. He remembered writing to Henrietta Reubell in 1890, in the early days of his long struggle with *The American*—"I have written a big (and awfully good) four-act play by which I hope to make my fortune."

Well, it had been *big*. But in the end James had to admit that it had not been "awfully good". In many ways it had been merely awful.

He remembered writing to his friend Robert Louis Stevenson, now on a distant island in the South Pacific—"My zeal in the affair is only matched by my indifference" but in the same letter enthusing "I find the form opens out before me as if it were a kingdom to conquer". Yet by the end of the same contradictory letter he was telling Stevenson—"A kingdom, yes, but my standards—by *our* standards, my absent but never-distant friend—a paltry kingdom of ignorant brutes for managers and dense *cabotins* of actors."

And more recently, when he was down with gout before deciding to go to Paris, he'd written to Stevenson:

Don't be hard on me—simplifying and chastening necessity has laid its brutal hand on me and I have had to try to make somehow or the other the money I don't make by literature. My books don't sell, and it looks as if my plays might. Therefore I am going with a brazen front to write half a dozen.

On this Friday evening in April of 1893, only a week and day from his 50th birthday, James realized that he never had come to grips with what writing for the theater really entailed. Yet in his portmanteau here at the Hays' home, he had carried with him to America three completed stage comedies, a drama written specifically for one actress who had aged beyond the role he'd created solely for her, extensive notes on five other possible plays, and the first three sketched-in acts of a serious drama he thought he might call *Guy Domville*.

In one of his earlier notes was a list of possible names for the eponymous character in this play about the lone scion of a wealthy family being called back from a monastery to choose between Holy Orders and continuing his family's name through marriage and children. James also had the original notes he'd made years earlier in Venice after hearing an anecdote about the apprentice monk who had been forced to renounce either his family's continuance or his holy vows. At the time he'd thought it might develop into a short story and had given it the tentative title "The Hero":

> Situation of that once-upon-a-time member of an old Venetian family (I forget which), who had become a monk, & who was taken almost forcibly out of his convent & brought back into the world in order to keep the family from becoming extinct... —it was absolutely necessary for him to marry.

James had long ago abandoned *The Hero* as the title of the play version of this tale, had added several extra dramatic—perhaps melodramatic—layers to the basic decision the hero had to make, and decided that amongst all these possible names for his hero, names filling two full pages in one of the thin notebooks he'd brought with him, he had liked "Domville" the best. It had taken him longer to come up with the eponymous leading character's first name—at one time he'd toyed with "Boy" just because he liked the sound of it—but for the last few months it had solidified into "Guy". *Guy Domville.* Obviously this was no longer a play set in Venice.

But would the male—and very masculine—protagonist's heroic act consist of consenting to a loveless marriage (a marriage into which a villain with the villainous name of Devenish was trying to ensnare Guy Domville) or would his character resist this temptation and renounce life, love, family, and any future for his noble family's name by returning to Holy Orders and cold celibacy?

Lying there in John Hay's guest room in the near-darkness, the small pool of light from his bedside lamp illuminating only his pale hands and the small pile of his notebooks, James imagined that the double-renunciation at the end of the play would bring tears to sensitive souls in the audience. He could imagine his elaborately dressed actor saying loudly—"I'm the last, my lord, of the Domvilles!" Everyone in the theater would either weep or be struck into awed silence.

But would they?

James felt like weeping. He wished Sherlock Holmes would return.

*   *   *

On the next day, Saturday morning, precisely one week before his dreaded birthday, having just finished breakfast—Gregory had whisked the tray away with his usual silent efficiency when James had rung the little bell—and dressed in his finely tailored brown pinstripe suit and waistcoat, Henry James sat in the spring sunlight at the table near the open window of his wonderful guest suite and wrote the following:

> Among the delays, the disappointments, the *déboires* of the horrid theatric trade nothing is so soothing as to remember that literature sits patient at my door, and that I have only to lift the latch to let in the exquisite little form that is, after all, nearest to my heart and with which I am so far from having done. I let it in, the old brave hours come back; I live them over again—I add another little block to the small literary monument that it has been given to me to erect.

James paused and looked at what he had just written. It was hogwash. Sentimental hogwash. He had committed himself to making his fortune writing for the theater and there was no little latch he could lift that would let his cozy—and financially unrewarding—literary efforts come tip-toeing back in.

And what was this self-serving babble about building a "small literary monument" for himself, block by block? Flaubert had answered that conceit rather concisely with his comment—"Books are made not like children but like pyramids and they're just as useless. And they stay in the desert. Jackals piss at their foot and the bourgeois climb up on them."

Henry James would soon turn fifty and while he'd sown his literary wild oats with both abandon and determined discipline, at this dark moment he doubted very much if any of his literary children would outlive him. At least by not much more than a few years at best.

Even his attempts to get his peers—or at least his younger literature-oriented male friends—to call him "Master"—Maître—had failed. If they did so, at his actual urgings, they made it into something like a joke. No, there was no "literary monument" out there for him or of him, no monument built "block by block" by his patient workmanship. And for the temporary "monuments" he'd labored so hard to construct, the critic-jackals were indeed pissing on them, the tiresome bourgeois—especially in America—clambering over his blocks and scratching their initials in his oh-so-carefully-cut stones with nails and knives.

Just last year he'd written a story he'd very much liked titled "The Wheel of Time". In it his main character, yet another reflection of himself as seen through a glass darkly, thinks much about his distant youth while musing on his forty-ninth birthday. About youth...

He regretted it, he missed it, he tried to beckon it back; but the differences in London made him feel that it had gone forever. There might perhaps be some compensation in being fifty, some turn of the dim telescope, some view from the brow of the hill; it was a round, gross, stupid number, which probably would make one pompous, make one think one's self venerable. Meanwhile, at any rate, it was odious to be forty-nine.

But with that round, odious number of 50 now bearing down on him like a freight train in the night—just as impervious, just as terrifying, just as unavoidable—he would pay anything to remain forty-nine forever or, if that was not possible, at least for another few un-passing years.

James realized to his horror that he was close to tears. Maybe that young, pink American pig named Teddy Roosevelt had been right; perhaps he *was* effeminate in his thoughts and writings.

* * *

James was aching to write someone a letter. But he couldn't, shouldn't... this trip to America was to remain a secret from his friends and epistolary interlocutors.

More hogwash. He was a man of letters in more than the literary sense. Henry James wrote a letter to someone, usually multiple letters to multiple someones, every day of his life. In a real sense, writing and receiving letters was the way he kept in touch with life.

At the moment he felt an overwhelming need to write a letter to Constance Fenimore Woolson about what had happened to him over the past few weeks. He knew that Fenimore had turned fifty-three last month in March—he'd written her a clever letter offering his elliptical birthday wishes—so she might understand his feelings about turning fifty. To his recollection, they'd never discussed the topic of aging. Fenimore—an American writer like James, in self-exile in Europe for decades—was the focus of the closest thing to a romantic relationship with a woman that James had ever felt or allowed.

Of course, he really had no romantic notions about Fenimore, certainly no sensual or sexual ones—the thought of an unclad woman's body appealed to him only in a very few classical paintings and sculptures. It was the nude male form that moved James in some deep, solid, but uncertain way—ever since that day he walked into his brother William's Newport art group's life-drawing class and saw their cousin Gus standing there naked as the model. But at one point, for weeks when both of them were staying in Fenimore's rented chalet of Bellosguardo high above Venice, Fenimore in her rooms upstairs and James comfortably in his apartment on the lowest floor, he'd had *some* sense of what it might be like to live with a woman.

To be married.

Of course Fenimore was so masculine in so many ways—fiercely independent, achingly but muscularly ambitious as a writer and poet in her own right, willing to break off even the most delightful conversation with James while sitting on the wide terrace of the Villa Brichieri near Bellosguardo watching a sunset in order to get back to her writing—but she was also a woman with a woman's mysteries. It had taken James months after Fenimore had left her leased home in Oxford before he realized that she'd come there—to the winter darkness of England which depressed her so, she needed sunlight or her moods would plummet— to be near him while his sister Alice was dying.

Near *him*. He'd taken her melancholic presence for granted while it was there for so many months. Only when she left Oxford, in something like exasperation if not outright anger, did he notice her by her absence.

Fenimore could be cast in fiction as an amusing eccentric, made more amusing by her hearing problem that she would not acknowledge and which made real conversation all the more difficult, especially in a salon or crowded public place. But James knew that she was no more eccentric than he. Almost certainly less so. At least Fenimore, as far as he knew, was holding no secret at the core of her being.

He had realized the previous year, just as Fenimore was leaving for Switzerland and then Italy again while showing more asperity toward him than ever before, not only that she'd moved to Oxford for all that time to be near him to offer her support during the last months of his sister's life but that, with Alice now gone, perhaps she had expected more attention from James.

They'd often agreed to meet in European cities and even English towns, rigorously staying in separate hotels, but meeting for walks and dinners together and tours of art galleries or the occasional concert, which Fenimore enjoyed in spite of her hearing problem. Could she possibly have expected more than this?

Could it be possible that she was in love with him?

James had assiduously avoided being seen with her when mutual friends were about. They met in out-of-the-way towns, dined in hotels and restaurants which were nice enough but in which James was close to certain he'd never find any of his friends. He was not ashamed of or embarrassed by her, per se, since Constance Fenimore Woolson was one of the more interesting and sophisticated American writers he knew in Europe. He was, he acknowledged now, simply terrified that a third party would think what sister Alice had, on more than one occasion, written flippantly to William or someone else in his family—"Oh, Harry. He's off flirting with Fenimore Woolson on the Continent."

He allowed his dying sister to make such jokes. Having anyone else he knew do so, even—especially—his brother William, would devastate him.

But he had lived with Fenimore in Bellosguardo, lived with her after a fashion and by her terms, comfortable in their strangely similar and formal fellow-bachelors-devoted-to-their-work way, and those weeks had changed him somehow. Mostly, it had made Henry James realize how terribly, terribly lonely he was.

A year ago, in May of 1892, just a month after his forty-ninth birthday, James had visited Fenimore while she was packing to leave Oxford and then gone straight home to write a passage in his unfolding story "The Wheel of Time". In his story, the 49-year-old main character Maurice Glanvil had, in his twenties, rejected the plain-looking but secretly charming lady friend Fanny Knocker, only to meet her again on the Continent decades later. Maurice's wife had died, leaving him with few memories of actual love and a rather plain-looking daughter.

When 49-year-old Maurice meets Fanny again, now the widowed Mrs. Tregent, he sees to his astonishment that she has grown into that rare sort of beauty which reaches its apex only in middle age. And she has had a son—a strikingly handsome and dashing son just a little bit older than Maurice's rather plain and ordinary daughter.

In the story, Fanny's son repeats Maurice's earlier betrayal of young Fanny Knocker by rejecting his daughter's hopes of marriage despite both his and Mrs. Tregent's efforts to make the match. Maurice's daughter was simply too plain for the handsome youth.

But the real shock of the story occurs when Maurice learns that he—Maurice—had been the secret passion in Fanny Knocker Tregent's life for all these years. A love undeclared. Unrealized. But central to her life.

That day in May a year ago, after visiting the strangely irritated and rapidly departing Fenimore, James had gone straight home and written this scene where Maurice is meditating on this unknown passion, a discovery that makes "his pleasure almost as great as his wonder".

She had striven, she had accepted, she had conformed; but she had thought of him every day of her life. She had taken up duties and performed them, she had banished every weakness and practiced every virtue; but the still hidden flame had never been quenched. His image had interposed, his reality had remained, and she had never denied herself the sweetness of hoping that she would see him again and that she would know him. She had never raised a little finger for it, but fortune had answered her prayer. Women were capable of these mysteries of sentiment, these intensities of fidelity, and there were moments in which Maurice Glanvil's heart beat strangely before a vision really so sublime. He seemed to understand now by what miracle Fanny Knocker had been beautified—the miracle of heroic docilities and accepted pangs and vanquished egotisms. It had never come in a night, but it had come by living for others. She was living for others still; it was impossible for him to see anything else at last than that she was living for him. The time of passion was over, but the time of service was long.

He had written that scene—published that story—all while smugly and secretly (even to himself) knowing that he was writing about Constance Fenimore Woolson's long unstated passion for *him*. He hadn't fully admitted the power of that connection even to himself last year, but he saw it now.

And he also saw, with his gorge rising in horror, that he might have been writing that passage about *himself*. About his unacknowledged, never recognized need—not for love, not for passion, never for desire, but still basic and compelling *need*—for Fenimore to be in his life, to be in his life to relieve his terrible burden of loneliness, to encompass him with her almost masculine understanding and yet persistently feminine presence.

Dear God, thought Henry James on this Saturday morning a week before his fiftieth birthday, *I have to get out of here, away from here.*

He would go to Boston to leave Alice's ashes in the marble urn on her grave where Miss Loring had set to rest the majority of Alice's cremated remains. Then he would go home. Home to England.

One thing was now certain: with Sherlock Holmes gone from his

life, the question Holmes had raised as to whether he was real or
a fictional character—thus making Henry James an adjunct fictional
character if he were merely being used in a work of fiction as Holmes's
Dr. Watson–like assistant made to marvel at Holmes's powers of
deduction—was moot. With Holmes gone, doing whatever he was doing wherever he was doing it, Henry James had returned to being just
a living, breathing human being. Albeit a powerfully gifted and tal-
ented one.

* * *

There was a rapid knock at his door, James said "Enter" without thinking, and Clara Hay fairly danced into the room.

"You must see this, Harry, you simply must!" she cried, as giddy as a
girl. She caught his left hand in both of hers and all but lifted him bodily up and out of his chair.

She led the amazed author to the door. "No need for your coat, Harry.
It's as warm as a summer's day outside. And it's only a few steps. You
simply *must* see this! It's too wonderful to miss."

"See what?" managed James as they hurried down the broad central
staircase toward where Benson held the front door open for them.

"The Flying Vernettis!"

* * *

The crowd had gathered on the green grass of Lafayette Square Park
and were looking up at what Clara reminded him was the Camerons'
huge house. James saw Lizzie Cameron near the front of the crowd (but
not her husband, Don, of course—he would be at work), shading her
eyes with her hand so that she could see better. James noticed other
high-society neighbors, mostly matrons, of the Hays' and Adamses'
and Camerons' neighborhood gathered near the east side of the park
while more common folk, including some street workers still with their
brooms, stood back a bit. Some of the society women—James saw young
Helen Hay—were using opera glasses the better to see.

But everyone was looking upward. Clara pointed. James shielded his own eyes and tried to find what they were all gawking at.

There. Along the highest roofline of the huge, steeply roofed house, a man and a boy were walking with exaggerated high steps, crossing the dangerous distance between one cluster of chimney pots and another. The man had a sort of quiver strapped to his back and from that vessel rose various brushes and strangely apportioned brooms.

"Chimney sweeps?" said James, astonished that Clara had dragged him out into the hot sunlight for mere chimney sweeps.

"Watch!" cried Clara Hay.

James saw that there might be some tension in watching the man and boy move carefully along that high, narrow roof beam, since they were almost sixty feet up and the Camerons' roof was far too steep to stop their fall if either one slipped.

Suddenly James and the crowd gasped as the boy did a forward cart-wheel on the narrow ridge and the man, letting the quiver dangle by its strap so the brushes would not fall, did a handstand behind the boy, his hands on the slippery slate slabs on either side of the apex.

The two were odd-looking creatures. Both man and boy—he might have been eleven or twelve, no older—were rail thin and dressed in black sweeps' clothing that seemed several sizes too small for each of them. That was a deliberate effect, James noticed, since the socks and shirts protruding from the cuffs were red-and-black striped for the skinny man and green-and-black striped for the boy.

The strangeness was enhanced by the fact that the grown chimney sweep had orange hair spiked up into a column, rather like a Mohawk Indian's vertical queue, while the boy's spiky hair, stabbing out in all directions, had been dyed a bright, Kendal green. The man's face had been painted white—a skull—and the eyes were lost to sight in black paint. The boy's face was painted all white save for the narrow-est strip of red on his thin lips. The effect—at least for James—was disturbing.

Suddenly the almost emaciated-looking boy took the quiver of brushes from the scarecrow man and crouched low as the skull-man leaned forward over the boy, tumbling in a perfect somersault along the three-inch-wide ridgeline, and then immediately got to his feet and bent over as the boy jumped up onto his back.

The crowd let out a gasp and low moan and some in the front stepped into those behind them, as if seeking to get out of range for when the man and boy fell.

James felt a sense of unreality fall over him like a cloak as he watched the red-and-black-striped man—his long, white fingers looking truly skeletal—remove the covers to the triple-chimney at the end of the ridgeline. Fingers moving in a blur, working together, orange-haired-man and green-haired-boy used a loose bit of rope to tie those coverings tight at the base of the chimney.

Then the skeletal man—his black shoes looked almost like ballet slippers—leaped straight into the air until his legs were far apart, the shoe-slippers on opposite sides of the four-foot-wide triple chimney.

The crowd gasped again, like a single organism, James thought (he had gasped as well, although not out loud), when the boy simply threw himself into the air sixty feet above the ground, his arms ahead of him like a diver leaping from a cliff into the sea. But there was no water be-low the boy, only a six-story drop to hard soil, grass, and stone walks.

The tall sweep with orange hair caught the boy in mid-air and held him, the boy's terribly thin arms still stretched straight forward, his legs rigid behind him, until suddenly the scarecrow adult swung the skinny lad until his arms and head were pointing straight down into the narrow chimney aperture. It was only then that James noticed that the adult sweep and boy sweep were attached at the waist with two strangely knotted ropes, rather like two Alpine climbers roped together on the Matterhorn.

The skull-faced tall sweep let the boy's torso and legs slide between his long, stick-white fingers until all of the boy save for his lower legs and feet had disappeared down the impossibly narrow chimney. The grown sweep let go of the boy's ankles and the crowd moaned in unison again until they saw that the skull-faced adult sweep now had both ropes in his hands. The man began lowering the rope, first letting it slide through one hand, then through the other, and all the while he was leaning further back from the vertical on the narrow chimney pot ridge, letting the boy's slight weight balance him as he continued backward until it seemed impossible that he might ever pull himself upright again.

James turned away.

"Amazing, isn't it?" asked Clara Hay. "Exhilarating!"

"Extraordinary," managed James, not wanting to hurt his hostess's feelings. Those few seconds of watching had given him a sense of vertigo followed by nausea. *What an insane species we are,* was his only coherent thought.

"They call themselves the Flying Vernettis," continued Clara, obviously not noticing James's sudden paleness. "Father and son, Lizzie Cameron thinks. They have been doing their chimney-cleaning this week for only a few of the finest houses, for the finest families, and Lizzie has been impatient all week for them to get to her house."

"Extraordinary," James said again, not turning his gaze back to the spectacle as the crowd gasped and groaned again at some new impossibility.

"Lizzie says that they're ever so efficient," continued Clara, speaking to James but looking back the other way. "They close every room off before clearing and cleaning the chimneys—and heaven knows some of these older houses need such a clean sweep—and she says they lay newspaper across everything in the closed-off rooms before the actual dusting."

"Extraordinary," said James. He focused his gaze on the White House across the street to the south. "I believe I shall take a brief walk," he continued. "I shall see you later this afternoon or evening, Clara."

Clara did not respond. Her hands clasped tightly together as if in prayer, her mouth open, she was totally absorbed in whatever death-defying absurdities were occurring high above her on Lizzie Cameron's rooftop.

* * *

Later, even many years later, Henry James could never quite explain, even to himself, exactly why he chose to do all the things he did in the hours that followed. *If,* he would invariably add to this particular mental query, *it was truly I who chose to do those things.* It was more the behavior, he felt, of a poorly drawn character in a sensationalist Wilkie Collins or H. Rider Haggard novel.

Luckily he'd brought his silk top hat and walking cane despite Clara's tugging and urgings when leaving the house, so he did not have to go back to the Hays' home. James turned east on Pennsylvania Avenue and walked briskly, refusing to turn his head as the crowd on Lafayette Square Park gasped or oohed or aahed.

The Flying Vernettis was precisely the kind of idiotic American showmanship and bread-and-circus nonsense that had kept James in England and Europe all these years. A chimney sweep risking his son's life, if indeed the boy *were* his son and not some orphan the sweep had picked up from an orphanage and trained, to perform idiot acrobatics sixty feet in the air for the approval of the likes of the Camerons and Lodges and Hays and the dour Henry Adams. James would not have been surprised if President Grover Cleveland and his wife weren't on the front lawn of the Executive Mansion and gawking as broadly as the social elite in Lafayette Park.

America was a nation that refused to grow up. It was a perpetual baby, a vast, pink, fleshy toddler, now in possession of some terrible weapons it did not know how to hold properly, much less use properly.

James hailed a hansom cab and told the driver to take him to the closest steamship company.

At the rather lavish steamship headquarters, James ordered the cab to wait while he went inside and paid for reservations from New York to London on the North German Lloyd Line's new greyhound steamship the *Spree,* sailing at 7:30 p.m. from New York the following Tuesday, April 11. He would spend his birthday at sea.

It was true, James knew, that this German ship hadn't quite matched the eastward crossing records of say the *City of New York* (5 days, 23 hours, and 14 minutes) or the *City of Paris* (5 days, 23 hours, and 50 minutes), but James knew the *Spree* to be lavishly comfortable. He also knew that the American and British steamship companies measured their eastward crossings between Sandy Hook Lightship and Roche's Point, the entrance to Queenstown Harbor; the North German Lloyd Line and the Hamburg-American measured the trips between Sandy Hook Lightship and the Needles, near Southampton.

He would not be in a hurry once he was on the open sea, and he looked forward to a majority of the passengers speaking German, so he would not constantly have to be drawn into conversations (although he was fluent in German).

Satisfied that he would be sailing to England in three days, James went out to his waiting cab and told the cabbie his next destination.

At the railway station, James made reservations for (and paid for) a first-class ticket to New York City, leaving Washington tomorrow—Sunday—afternoon. He also purchased continuing tickets to leave for Boston on Monday morning, returning to New York early on Tuesday afternoon, allowing plenty of time before the *Spree's* evening departure.

He then had the cab take him to a telegraph office where he wired reservations for Sunday night at the upscale New York hotel where he'd stayed when he'd arrived in New York, then another reservation for one night in a familiar hotel in Boston. He'd made up his mind that he would not be looking up old friends there and William and his entire family were in Europe. With some discipline, James thought, on his way to the cemetery to deposit Alice's ashes at her grave, he might avoid walking past the old house in Cambridge where the whole family, Aunt Kate and all, had lived. He also did not want to see brother William's huge home at 95 Irving Street in Cambridge. He would plan his walk to and from the cemetery accordingly.

But thinking about his older brother, James wrote out a telegram to be sent both to Florence and Lucerne—William should be moving his family from Italy to Switzerland about now, according to the schedule he'd sent James weeks ago—but James knew that his brother moved his family around while on schedule much as their father had: with no respect for schedules whatsoever.

The telegram may have caused the telegraphist to glance at James with curious eyes but even that made the author smile:

WILLIAM—I AM CURRENTLY IN AMERICA WITH A MAN WHO EITHER BELIEVES HE IS THE DETECTIVE SHERLOCK HOLMES, OR WHO <u>IS</u> SHERLOCK HOLMES

AND THEREFORE BELIEVES THAT HE IS A FICTIONAL
CHARACTER STOP CAN YOU ADVISE? STOP MESSAGES
WILL BE FORWARDED TO ME FROM JOHN HAY'S HOME
IN WASHINGTON—HARRY

That should confuse his always superior-behaving older brother.

Finally, on a whim, James asked if he could pay one of the Western
Union lads to deliver a handwritten note within the city—they said
he could for only fifteen cents, and they would provide paper and the
envelope—so James put the address of the cigar store through which
Holmes had said he could be contacted at any time on the envelope,
took the white sheet of paper, and started writing, got through "I am
leaving Washington tomorrow, Sunday" and stopped. He could think
of nothing else pertinent to say. Nor was anything beyond this any of
Holmes's business. He quickly signed his name (for some odd reason,
almost adding the "Jr." that he hadn't used for more than a decade),
added "To Mr. S. Holmes—Personal" on the envelope above the cigar
store's address, paid the Western Union people for the use of their lad
and tipped the lad himself ten cents.

Having made all these arrangements, James had the hansom drop him
on Constitution Avenue a few blocks northeast of Lafayette Square so
that, with luck, he could walk back to the Hays' home without encountering the crowds still admiring the Flying Vernettis' dangerous aerial
gyrations. All that energy wasted and death or injury invited only to
clean a chimney or two. Absurd.

He was walking south when he came to an intersection and froze in
his tracks. For an instant he stood in shock, not quite certain, and then
he *was* certain.

Professor James Moriarty—tall white forehead, lank hair over the
ears, old-fashioned collar, swallow-tail black coat, and spidery white
hands—was walking quickly down the sidewalk on the opposite side of
the adjoining street, headed southwest, away from the direction James
was walking.

It is none of my business, James thought fiercely. *He's only an aging mathematics and astral physics professor, you already knew he was alive from the*

photo in the science magazines at the Library of Congress, <u>and it is none of my business.</u>

James mentally repeated this three times, like a mantra, but then he turned right and began following Professor Moriarty from a discreet distance, taking care to stay back and remain on his side of the street.

12

A Rat. A Fucking Rat.

Henry James had never "tailed" anyone before, but he soon found that it was a relatively simple affair. All he had to do, he discovered, was to stay a half block or more behind Professor Moriarty and on the opposite side of the street, hurry a bit to keep him in sight when the professor turned left or right onto some new street, and step back into the shadows of a storefront the few times the professor stopped. It helped that Moriarty never looked over his shoulder or — for that matter — paused to look to his left or right as he walked briskly toward whatever destination he obviously had firmly in mind. Whenever James got close enough to hear the regular tap-tap-tap of the tip of the professor's silver-headed cane on the pavement, he knew he was following too closely and would fall back thirty yards or so.

After twenty or thirty minutes of this clever following, James realized that he no longer had the slightest idea of where in Washington City he might be. He distinctly remembered walking west toward the afternoon sun at one point, and then following the briskly pacing Moriarty left — south — then west and south again more than one time, but he had no clue what neighborhood he was in. It didn't help that street signs and even street lamps had disappeared blocks and blocks ago and it was with something of a shock that James looked down and realized that there had been no sidewalk under his feet for some time now.

From stately homes and quaint shops, he'd followed Moriarty into an area of crumbling brick warehouses and the occasional sagging hovel.

Even the width of the street had narrowed until he was following the professor down filthy lanes that should more properly be called alleys than streets. There was a strange, unpleasant-smelling green fog that hung low over the rooftops. Odd for Washington, D.C., James knew, but nothing compared to London's thick fogs. He wondered if he'd followed Moriarty into that part of town that John Hay had called "Foggy Bottom".

But, strangely—and helpful for his anonymity—there were more people and traffic about in these muddy alleys than had been the case in the nicer parts of town. James realized that most of the people walking here walked in groups and that they were almost all men. Once or twice he noticed a slovenly dressed woman, one obviously and loudly intoxicated, rushing to get out of the way of the striding men and rumbling dray wagons filling the center of the street, but most of the pedestrians were men dressed in working-class rags or large, intimidating "swells" wearing mud-tinged suits that were far too boldly striped and waistcoats of appallingly bright colors.

Still Moriarty walked on without looking left or right. The crowds— mobs, really—of rough men parted for him as if the professor were some unholy Moses and the ruffians mere dark waves on the Red Sea.

Realizing that his clothes and cane and very mannerisms "stuck out" in this part of town, Henry James stopped on the dirt path that passed for a sidewalk and seriously considered turning around and getting back to a decent part of town as quickly as he could.

How? Which way? And what if someone stops me?

As these thoughts sent a chill through him, James noticed three men deliberately approach Professor Moriarty. None of them shook hands—nor offered to—but even from almost a block distant, James could tell that the four men recognized each other. Or rather, that the three large ruffians—poorly dressed from greasy homburgs to their expensive but muddy boots with oddly pointed toecaps—knew Professor Moriarty. The men were big—big-shouldered, big-armed, big-bellied—but Moriarty towered over all three of them. With his skull-like face, protuberant forehead, and bald dome covered with only a few combed-over dark strands, the professor stood out like a well-dressed cadaver looking down at would-be body snatchers.

They exchanged a few words and turned left down a street. Feeling the stares of the clusters of rudely dressed men near him, James made up his mind to stay in the chase and hurried to turn the corner.

Dead end. The street was short and empty of anyone save for Moriarty and his new friends and it ended at a massive warehouse with no windows.

James stepped back around the corner and out of sight mere seconds before one of the men looked over his shoulder at the empty cul-de-sac of mud and brick.

When James dared peek again, two of the men had shoved open a heavy wooden sliding door. The rumble of a large group—whether of men or animals, James could not tell—came through the open door, but then Moriarty followed the first two in, the third man glancing back again but not before James once more dodged out of sight, and then the massive door was rolled shut. There was a regular-sized door—man-door, as it were—about a dozen steps to the right of the sliding door, but it was solid wood and James had no idea if it opened into the same area that Moriarty had entered. It was probably locked.

James stood at the corner and . . . dithered. That was the only word for it, he realized, *dithered.*

What could he do?

He could get out of this dismal neighborhood—or perhaps he could, he'd not noted all the turns and changes of direction that had gotten him *in* this area of town—and find some trustworthy lad to carry a second message to Holmes via that cigar shop.

But certainly that wouldn't be in time for Holmes to arrive before whatever business was detaining Professor Moriarty in the warehouse would be concluded. And Henry James didn't believe he had the nerve to continue. Besides, Holmes had lied to him and stated flatly that Professor James Moriarty, the presumed criminal mastermind, did not exist; that he had been a figment of Sherlock Holmes's imagination, dreamed up solely to expedite the ruse of Holmes's falsified death and subsequent disappearance from the world.

Well, that wasn't true. James had seen him in the 1892 photograph of mathematicians present at the Conference on Advanced Mathematics and Astronomical Physics, University of Leipzig, and now he'd seen him in person.

But what to do?

He could retreat from this neighborhood and find a policeman. But what crime had Moriarty committed? All James had seen was the professor walking down a public street—or alley now, as the case might be—and everything James knew about the man was that he was a legitimate English mathematician and physicist. The police might put *him,* James, in jail for inciting a false complaint.

The obvious and sane choice was for him to turn away now and walk—briskly—out of this dangerous neighborhood (James had the sense that walking north and east would at least get him out of this Foggy Bottom area) and return to the Hays' comfortable home and forget all about Professor James Moriarty for the time being. Should he ever bump into Sherlock Holmes again, he'd share this amusing little story of actually having crossed paths with the real Moriarty in Washington City.

Yes, that was the only sane and safe thing for him to do.

James took two deep breaths and walked down the cul-de-sac toward the warehouse, silently hoping with every pace that the heavy sliding doors wouldn't open as he approached. What if Moriarty and the three ruffians stepped out just as he reached the door? One could hardly claim to be lost when one has deliberately walked the better part of a city block down a dead-end alley.

The sliding door did not open.

James stepped to the right of it and stopped in front of the solid wood door. Setting his hand on the iron knob, he prayed that it would be locked. It should be locked. It seemed more like an office door than a door to the open, noisy space Moriarty and the thugs had stepped into. When he ascertained that it was locked, James could turn about, leave at a brisk but dignified pace, and know that he'd done everything in his power to find out what Moriarty had been up to.

The door was unlocked.

James opened it further, tensed to turn and flee if he made a noise or if he saw anyone.

It was completely dark inside. The slit of gray light showed only a narrow staircase rising steeply straight ahead. There was a thick film of dust on the steps, so the stairway must not have been regularly used.

James stepped in and let his eyes adjust to the darkness as best they could.

The narrow stairway rose with what seemed an alarming steepness between two dark, moldering walls. The upper part of the steep staircase was invisible in the darkness—it could be missing for all James could tell from here—but once his eyes had adapted, he realized that there was the faintest glow from a gas lamp on the wall at the top of these stairs.

He began tip-toeing up, trying not to make even the slightest sound, dreading the inevitable squeak and creak of the old steps, but he soon realized that at this rate, the climb to the top would take him ten minutes or more. Besides, the steps were solid. They did not squeak or creak. Perhaps the dust helped muffle his steps.

James walked normally—mostly normally, he realized, since he was still putting most of the weight on the toes of his shoes—and when the staircase was at its darkest, he put his hands flat on the walls on either side. There was no railing. He felt each step gingerly with the toe of his right foot before putting any weight on it. Then he was moving into the tepid oval of light from the gas lamp above.

Nothing. Just a narrow landing with the flickering light. No doors or windows of any sort. James looked to his left and realized that a second and equally steep flight of stairs rose high to another dim light.

All in all, there were four such long, steep flights of stairs and three dusty, poorly lit landings before he reached the top. Here there was a door to his right. The top half was glass and the glass was glazed. James looked down; his were the only footsteps in the dust here. He tried the cracked-porcelain doorknob.

The door was locked. James used all the strength he could muster, even putting his shoulder to the door, but it remained locked. He knew that he could use his walking stick to break the glass and gain entry that way, but he did not entertain that thought for more than a second. The sound of smashing glass might bring Professor Moriarty's entire mob down on him.

He'd turned and was about to start his steep descent back into the darkness when he noticed something on the left wall, the wall opposite the door. Or rather, he *heard* something from there.

It was the indistinct murmuring as from a loud crowd—perhaps an audience before the beginning of a play. But even the murmurs and half-heard words were coarse. If it was an audience, the play would be a bawdy cockney melodrama.

There was a rectangle in the wooden wall. James crouched low and saw the large wooden flanges near the top corners. He swiveled them to a horizontal position and the rectangular aperture fell back into his hands. The noise was quite audible now and there was light coming up through what seemed to be a floor. James pressed the trap door shut, secured it with a single flange, walked to the gas lamp, and turned the gas off.

Just enough light came through the frosted glass of the doorway across the landing to allow James to find the trap door and its flanges again. Loosening it with exaggerated care, he lowered it to the floor and thrust his head and shoulders into the aperture.

There was no floor, he soon saw, only large, broad beams—the one in front of him at least twenty inches wide—extending out over a great drop. The broad beams were stationed about fifteen feet apart and five or six feet below these major support beams were smaller rafters, mere two-by-four pieces of lumber set narrow-side up. Some sort of cage wire, the kind James associated with chicken coops, was attached to these smaller rafters. Attached to that wire near the walls here was a false floor of some sort of flimsy cardboard or canvas. There was something white, like snow, covering most of this canvas in small heaps and dunes. He was, he realized, in the high attic space of the huge warehouse that Moriarty and the other men had entered.

But about ten feet out, directly ahead of him, the false floor ended and light and noise rose up from below. James heard a deep voice trying to shout the crowd into some sort of attention.

If he were to see anything, James would have to crawl further out on the beam. He set his walking stick in the corner of the landing and be-gan crawling on his hands and knees.

His plan had been to stop before he was over the open drop, but he realized he couldn't see well from that position, so he lowered himself to the broad beam and kept crawling until only his knees remained in the darkness behind him.

Far below him was a huge space with sawdust on the wooden floor. He must be at least sixty feet above the mobs of men down there, perhaps seventy feet. For a second he clung to the beam with knees and his fingernails, letting a surge of vertigo pass, but there was little chance of his being seen by anyone down there. The space below was brightly illuminated by electric arc lamps in metal shades, but the lamps hung down from the lower rafters on long steel rods. Anything above them would be just a dark blur to the men in the light.

James lay flat, tried to control his breathing, and attempted to make sense of what he was seeing.

There were more than a hundred men sitting on barrels and crates in several distinct groups. To James, they all looked like purse-snatchers and highway thieves, but they clustered in definite groups—tribes—and one group of about thirty men looked more like simple working men. He realized that this group was speaking mostly in German. The other ruffians were bellowing in gutter American English.

All of the groups were facing a raised platform. James saw an abandoned metal scale at the back of this platform, realized that the "snow" he'd seen in the canvas below the rafters further back had been chicken feathers, and decided that the warehouse had once been the final stopping place for thousands of chickens to be processed. That also explained some of the stench that he'd ascribed to the unwashed mobs of men below.

There were two men on the raised platform. Professor James Moriarty was at the rear of the ad hoc stage, sitting in a high-backed chair. The other man, cigar in mouth and a derby cocked at a ruffian's angle on his squarish head, was the one shouting for silence and attention.

Finally the mobs of men quieted down and focused their attention on the speaker.

"Well, all the important gangs are here and no one's killed anyone yet," shouted the thickset man on the platform. "That's *something*, at least. We've already shown progress."

No one laughed. Someone in the batch of German-speaking working men was translating for the others.

"Culpepper ain't here," shouted someone in the mob.

"Culpepper's dead!" shouted someone else. "Somebody dropped 'im thirty or forty feet onto that fat head of 'is."

This did bring laughter. The man on the platform waved them into silence again. "Well, while Culpepper's people work out who's going to take his place, we'll go ahead with our project here and give that gang the word later."

"*What* project?" shouted a fat man near the front. "All we heard was big talk about lots and lots of boodle and not one fucking specific."

Before the man on the platform could speak again, a man in the front row of the German-speaking group cried, "Why are we brought here with these...*criminals?*"

The other hundred or so men now roared with laughter, some hooting "these...*criminals*" back at the German. Several others snicked open their seemingly ubiquitous gravity-blade knives.

The man standing waved them into some sort of order again. "As you'll hear in a minute, we need the anarchists for..."

"Socialists!" cried the German working man who'd just spoken.

"These socialist anarchists," corrected the man on the platform, "for our plan. They're necessary. Professor James Moriarty will explain."

The big man nodded to Moriarty and took his own seat on the platform as the professor slowly stood and took measured steps toward the front of the platform.

"Gentlemen," began Moriarty, and something about his sunken-eyed skeletal presence brought a deeper silence onto the entire room full of men, "none of you has ever seen me before, but you all know my name. In the last two and a half years, my planning has made more money for each of your...organizations...than you've ever made before."

There came a low rumble that James realized was one of agreement and approval.

Moriarty held up two fingers. Silence came down like a curtain.

"In the next month," continued the professor, his voice soft but carrying to every corner of the huge space, "you and I shall make more money...more of a true fortune...than has ever been realized in the long history of criminal endeavor."

The silence extended. Finally a shrill, doubting voice shouted, "How?"

"Precisely at noon on the first of May," said Moriarty, "the President of the United States is going to push a button that shall start every electrical device at the Chicago Columbian Exposition. A hundred thousand people may be watching him. One second after he does that, President Cleveland will be assassinated—shot by a high-velocity rifle wielded by the world's greatest assassin."

Somehow the silence deepened.

"In the next fifteen minutes," continued Moriarty, "the Vice-President of the United States as well as its Secretary of State and Attorney General will also be assassinated. Their demise is expertly planned and guaranteed. Within the next hour, the mayors and chiefs of police of Chicago, Washington, New York, Baltimore, Philadelphia, Boston, Cincinnati, and more than eight capital cities in Europe will also be assassinated."

"How does that earn us one single damned penny?" shouted someone at the back of one of the clusters.

Moriarty smiled. Even from his angle so high above, Henry James could see that terrible smile and it made him shake and cling harder to his beam.

"Our anarchist...socialist...friends across this country and Europe," continued Moriarty, holding a hand out toward the German-speaking working men, "will, upon a precise signal, descend upon the police forces in Chicago, Washington, Boston, London, Berlin...all the cities I have mentioned and more. The police will be ambushed at predetermined places and times. Our anarchist friends will be better armed than ever before—with rifles as well as pistols, large quantities of dynamite as well as grenades—and the timing shall be as precise as I described. This one hour on the first of May, starting with the public execution of the chief executive of the United States of America, will make Haymarket Square look like the tiny, insignificant rehearsal it was."

Suddenly James had a terrible urge to sneeze. The chicken feathers behind him on the canvas, others littering the beams above and beside him. He squeezed his nose shut and prayed.

"Where do we..." asked one man from the crowd below, his voice low, almost disbelieving.

"Where do you come in?" Moriarty finished for him. Again that cadaver's smile. Above his squeezing hand, James could see men in the front rows seem to flinch away from the professor.

"When the heads of these serpents of oppressive governments are severed," said Moriarty. "Cut off..." he repeated for the least intelligent among his audience. "With mayors and police chiefs and federal officials murdered, there will be nationwide chaos. And amidst that chaos, you do what you do best...you loot. You plunder." He paused and his tongue licked out like a snake's. "But not randomly. And not with the usual failure of aforethought. No, you will be looting the finest homes in New York and Chicago and Washington and Boston and all the other cities. The fattest banks. The richest federal and state gold depositories. You will be looting according to a plan I have drawn up and will soon share with you...a plan that is foolproof."

Random talking turned into a roar of approval and excitement.

"It'll be like the fucking New York draft riots only with no fucking army coming in to shut it down," shouted one man.

James remembered the draft riots in 1863. Not long after Gettysburg. When the army draft was started in New York City—it had been volunteers up to that time—the street gangs and mobs, mostly Irish, had risen up in civil insurrection that had gone on for days. The homes of some of New York's richest families had been invaded, women raped, money and paintings and furniture stolen. Entire blocks had been burned down. One Irish gang, for the fun of it, had burned down an orphanage for black children, killing several of them.

"It shall be the New York draft riots times one thousand," said Moriarty over the noise. "And you are correct...this time there will be no U.S. Army sent from battlefields to save the beleaguered and outgunned local police and militia. The spoils shall be...yours."

He turned and went back to his seat.

Suddenly, over the roar of excitement, a man with a shotgun leaped out of his seat and pointed with his free hand upwards, directly toward where Henry James lay cringing and trying to make himself smaller on his beam.

"A rat!" screamed the man, his tone almost delirious. "A fucking rat!"

Before James could even think of scuttling backward, the man raised his shotgun, aimed it directly at James from sixty feet or so below, and fired. Five or six other men with shotguns leaped to their feet and also fired directly at James.

13

"I'll Have Lucan Adler Kill Any Man Who Speaks to the Police"

Henry Adams and John Hay both had telephones in their homes. Hay used his all the time, especially related to the consulting he was doing for the State Department. Adams disliked using his, but did so most frequently to call John Hay, who lived in the mansion adjacent to his. Essentially they were just talking through two walls and—due to all the telephonic static and cackling and crossed lines—it would probably have been easier to open windows and shout at one another.

"You're trying to back out of this evening's dinner, aren't you, Henry," said Hay after listening to Adams for a minute or so. It was already Saturday afternoon.

"Well...I didn't feel that I offered much at your last gathering," said Adams. "People in perennially low moods should not be allowed to appear at persistently gay high-society gatherings."

"That would rule out about ninety-three percent of us," laughed Hay.

"And would improve the quality of conversation exponentially," said Adams.

"True, Henry, true. But do come tonight. It's simple fare and stag."

"What happened to all the lovely ladies, including your daughter Helen?" asked Adams.

"Nannie Lodge, Helen, Clara, and Edith Roosevelt—who's in town only briefly with her husband—are all pouring coffee at the huge DAR Gala Fundraiser for Our Civil War Veterans," said Hay.

"Where's that being held this year?"

"In the Capitol Rotunda," said Hay.

"They'll either freeze or swelter," said Adams.

"Probably both."

"Is Lizzie Cameron cutting cake for the geezers as well?"

"No, she's going to the opera tonight," said Hay.

"With Don?"

Hay laughed. "When was the last time Lizzie was chaperoned to the opera or to any other cultural event by her husband *Don?*"

"Who then?" asked Adams.

"Her cousin—whatshisname. The old venerable who bored the brass off the andirons at the Vanderbilts' big do last November."

"You mentioned Edith Roosevelt, which suggests that the Boy will be one of the stags in attendance tonight," said Adams. "Are you really going to put Harry and Teedie in the same pit again so soon?"

"The Boy hates it when we call him by his childhood name of 'Teedie'," said Hay.

"He hates it when we call him 'the Boy', too, but he loves us more than he hates it. Are you really going to put Harry and Teddy at the same table again, Hay?"

"Teddy's terribly remorseful about what he said and about being boorish at our last dinner gathering," said Hay.

It was Adams's turn to laugh. "I've never seen Theodore Roosevelt remorseful to anyone over anything he said, did, stabbed, or shot."

"True," said Hay. "But upon reflection, probably Edith's, he realized that words like 'effeminate' and 'coward' weren't appropriate when directed at one of America's finest men of letters."

"It would have been more fun fifty years ago," said Adams. "Or even thirty. We would be past the process of selecting seconds by now and they probably would have chosen the dueling ground and oiled and charged the pistols."

"Harry seems more like a rapier man to me," said Hay. "And he would have gotten to choose the weapons."

"Rapier wit," said Henry Adams. "None sharper or more pointed."

"But Teddy truly *is* sorry and has begged for a chance to show that he can behave," said Hay. "He wants you witness to his good behavior."

"I was a witness the last time he showed it," said Adams. "That was in 'seventy-three or 'seventy-four, I believe."

"Seriously, Henry. This is just us men tonight. We'll argue politics— politely, of course—scratch when and where we want to, belch ditto, talk like sailors, drink like sailors, and toast the missing fairer sex until Benson and my other men have to carry us to our respective beds. I've invited Dr. Granger because...well, you know."

Adams knew. Dr. Elias Granger was older than most of them, in his mid-sixties now, and had been in deep mourning ever since he'd lost his wife four years ago. With just men, Granger could relax and exercise the happiness which had been his hallmark right up to his wife's death. In mixed company, he rarely spoke when the ladies were present any longer, as if doing so might hurt his dead wife's feelings. Adams, seven years a widower now, thought he understood. If it hadn't been for Lizzie Cameron and, to a lesser extent, Nannie Cabot Lodge, he probably wouldn't be accepting dinner invitations either—at least those with the fairer sex present. As it was, he not only attended such mixed dinners now but had resumed hosting his famous "breakfasts"—held closer to the noon hour than morning—which included Lizzie, Nannie, and other local delights.

"Sounds very nice and I like old Granger," said Adams, "but..."

"Before you get beyond 'but'," interrupted John Hay, "I forgot to tell you that Clarence King will be there. With his proverbial bells on, he said, and, knowing Clarence, possibly with real ones."

"King!" cried Adams. "I thought he had headed off for Mexico or Chile or Patagonia or one of those swarthy-lady places he prefers."

"I thought so too, Henry, but he's back in town...briefly, as I under-stand it...and would love to dine with us."

"Who else will be there tonight?" asked Adams.

"Teddy and James, of course, King, Rudyard Kipling taking time out from his Cosmos Club..."

"I'd come just to hear Kipling tell a tale," said Adams, "but every time Teddy's there and tale-telling, Rudyard just curls his legs up under him like a teenaged girl and listens all night, mesmerized."

"A great story-teller recognizes a great story-teller," said Hay. "Cameron can't make it but Cabot Lodge will be there again..."

"While his wife pours coffee and cuts cake under the Great Dome," said Adams.

"Exactly. And about Harry...did I tell you that he's staying with us again? As long as he'll be in Washington, I believe."

"No," Adams said, his voice low. "You didn't tell me that."

"Well, he is," said Hay. "And tonight should be a rather more unbuttoned social evening than our last dinner turned out to be."

"Harry James unbuttoned," muttered Adams. "Now there's an image that refuses to coalesce in the focal lens of my inner eye." Adams waited a few seconds and had to clear his throat before speaking again. "Will...Mr. Holmes be there again?"

Either not picking up on Adams's tone or ignoring it, Hay said, "Oh, no. Holmes has disappeared. Definitely left town was the last I heard, possibly gone back to England. Either way, he shan't be at our table tonight and I'm glad of it."

"Why?" asked Adams.

"Because my daughter Helen has become besotted by the man," barked Hay. "She asked me the other day how much a detective earns and if such an income might support a married couple in the comfort to which she's accustomed. She also wondered if great detectives were regularly knighted by Queen Victoria."

"Good Lord," said Adams. "She certainly didn't phrase it all that way."

"She might as well have," said Hay. "Oh, Saint-Gaudens will be there tonight, but he says he must leave early, before brandy and cigars—some senator's wife he's chiseling in granite."

"She poses at night?"

"Whenever the senator is out of town," said Hay.

"Kipling, our dear Clarence King, Saint-Gaudens, Cabot Lodge without Nannie—he rarely speaks at the table when Nannie's there but can be rather witty when it's just other men—and then, of course, a chance at a front row seat for the second round between the Boy and Harry," said Adams. "I can't pass this up. I'll be there tonight."

"With bells on?"

"I do have a jester cap I can bring and possibly convince myself to wear after we open the fourth bottle," said Adams.

"Save that jester's cap for young Theodore...just in case," said Hay.

The two were still chuckling when they hung up their telephones.

* * *

The roar of the shotgun blast, though fifty feet below him, was deafening to James. Chicken feathers flew into the air on both sides below him where the canvas covered the thinner rafters. His own higher, thicker beam shook as some sort of shot rattled against its bottom and sides. Cringing into the narrowest straight line the portly James could manage, he still felt a shot—almost certainly bird shot—rip at his left sleeve and stipple his left forearm with pinpricks. He clamped his jaws tight so that he would not cry out.

"You missed him!" shouted one of the gangsters below. "Look out...let me..." Two shots in rapid succession, each with the sharper, clearer report of a rifle rather than a shotgun blast. James felt at least one of the bullets slam into his beam some six or eight feet in front of him. The entire beam shuddered as if it were a tree taking the first, hard swing of an ax.

"Got it!" shouted the man who'd yelled immediately before the rifle shots. The mob roared.

James dared a peek down the left side of his beam.

Most of the men, save for the anarchists, were out of their chairs now, milling in a circle, slapping each other on the back and laughing, the rigid separation of neighborhood gangs forgotten. A man with a rifle was holding up a large gray rat—quite dead—by the tail and turning in a circle to receive the plaudits of his criminal cohorts.

"SILENCE!" Moriarty's voice was so loud and commanding that Henry James almost lost his balance and rolled off his beam. The mobs fell silent at once.

"Grogan will visit each of your leaders in the next week with precise instructions on where you'll muster on May one, what armaments you'll bring and which will be provided for you, exactly where the killing zones for the police will be, your precise positions for the ambushes, and information on where the anar...excuse, me...socialists will have already begun their bombing. We're finished for tonight. But leave in small groups to get back to your own gang areas and beer halls. We don't want the cops picking any of you up tonight, much less arresting clusters of you. And I'll have Lucan Adler kill any man who speaks to the police—even if that man is being held in protective custody at police headquarters."

That seemed to sober the mob into true silence. The man with the rifle tossed away the dead rat. The groups began filing out of the main front and back sliding doors of the old warehouse.

James leaned over to peek again at Moriarty, but the derby-hatted hoodlum named Grogan was the only one still standing on the platform. Moriarty had disappeared.

*   *   *

James continued lying on his side on the high beam until his muscles and bones were in such pain that he thought he might scream. He lay there as the last of the anarchists and gang members walked boldly out into the darkness beyond the sliding doors; he stayed there until the man they'd called Grogan had shut off the lights and been the last to leave. And still he lay there, his left arm hurting, for another hour or more, listening to the scurrying of rats in the rafters near him.

He was sure he would hear heavy footsteps coming up the stairway at any second. He'd pulled the panel up behind him using the peg set on the inside for that purpose but he was sure that anyone coming up the steps would turn the gas lamp back on, see the unlatched top corners of the trap door, and open it behind him.

Eventually he could stand the pain and darkness no longer. James got to his hands and knees, feeling dizzy and not trusting his balance in the darkness, and backed up along his beam until his heels contacted the trap door. He tapped it open with the least force and sound he could manage.

Then he was out on the death-black upper landing and all but unable to stand. He had to pull himself up with his hands on the wall above the trap door until he stood weakly there, still leaning on the wall, his knees and back hurting far more than the lacerations on his right arm under what he could feel as the torn sleeve of his jacket and shirt.

There was no light coming through the frosted glass of the office door on the opposite side of the absurdly narrow landing. Could he possibly have been lying on that beam long enough for it to grow dark outside? He started to raise the strength of the single weak gas lamp on the wall but then thought better of it. If someone was waiting on the dark staircase below, the resumption of light on his landing would make him a perfect target.

He found his hat and walking cane where he'd left them on the floor of the landing.

Remembering how steep and narrow the staircase was, James descended carefully in the darkness, taking each step with care, his arms extended so that he could touch the peeling wall on either side of the staircase, his cane finding each step in the darkness.

At each flickering landing, he expected to encounter someone waiting for him. No one was there. Still, when he reached the bottom of the last flight and was standing at the door through which he'd entered, it took him a minute or two to work up courage to open the door. A terrible thought made him grab the wall again for support: *What if they've locked this door? Locked me in?*

They hadn't. He stepped out into twilight. The cul-de-sac was empty except for himself, standing there so incongruously, so *obviously*.

It was about sixty normal paces to the end of the dead-end alley and the beginning of the unpaved street but it felt like half a mile to the aching writer.

He turned right on the unnamed street, trying to remember a general direction back to the civilized parts of town. There were other people on the street—all men as far as he could tell—but most were clustered near the few lighted saloons. James stayed near the dark buildings across the street from these lighted buildings, walking where the sidewalk would be if the muddy lane had been a real street. At least there was less horse manure on the sides.

As he walked, James questioned himself about his reactions during his time clinging to a beam high above thieves, robbers, rapists, arsonists, and Professor James Moriarty in that old chicken warehouse. He had been frightened, to be sure—especially when the man had yelled "Rat!" and the shotgun blast had rattled all around him—but along with the fear had been something unexpected and rather new to Henry James—simple excitement? A sense of thrill? A strange, inexplicable joy at the wild strangeness of it all?

He wondered if his pounding heart and excited sense of everything slowing down during those tensest moments he'd spent above the mob, the moments when he thought he'd been discovered, the rifle shots, if he had been sharing something he thought he would never have the opportunity to experience after having avoided service in the Civil War. Had his brother Wilkie thrilled to such danger in the minutes or hours before receiving his terrible wounds? How else to explain Wilkie's eagerness to return to his unit months after suffering such undignified, suppurating, and impossibly painful injuries?

And his brother Bob, who had said he'd "enjoyed" life in the army during the war. Could James's experience that afternoon connect in any way to the simple joy of action that his brothers had written about? James thought of his cousin Gus—that beautiful pale, red-head's naked body in the afternoon light on the day James had walked in on the life-drawing class—had Gus felt such a thrill of danger and the joy of risk in the months of service before being killed by a sniper, his body never recovered? Had Gus heard the sound of the shot that had taken his young life? The veterans insisted that one never did—never heard the fatal shot since science had shown that the ball or bullet was traveling faster than sound itself—but James remembered hearing the loud rifle shot just before the beam he was lying on reverberated like a struck bell. It had been...thrilling.

He walked for what seemed like hours as the last of the light left the skies. His sense of direction all but gone now, James headed for lights reflected from lowering clouds. That way lay street lamps. That way, whichever way it was, must be toward civilization.

Several times men broke off from some group and crossed the street toward him and each time James thought—*This shall be it*—but no one accosted him. No one even addressed him except for a bizarrely made-up lady of the night—what the Americans called a "crib doxie," he felt certain, whose place of business was one of the canvas-covered stalls in a reeking alley—whose chalk-white and crimson-rouged face opened to show yellow teeth when she called "Looking for a good time, are you, Mr. Gentleman, sir?"

James nodded toward the apparition and quickly crossed the street.

He had finally reached a cobblestone street—trolley tracks in the center!—with gas lamps at each corner and allowed himself a sigh of satisfaction. There would be street signs here. The slums were behind him.

And just at that moment, three men stepped out of an alley and blocked his way.

"Lost, pal?" asked the tallest one, bearded and filthy. The second man was equally as tall but heavier and had short whiskers rather than a beard. James glimpsed a gold tooth when the light from the corner street lamp briefly touched the first man's face. Both tall men wore wide-rimmed hats that were soiled with sweat and grime and looked to have been gnawed upon by rats. The third man blocking James's way could hardly be called a man yet: a boy of sixteen or seventeen, almost as tall as his two mates but infinitely thinner. The boy's face was mostly nose and with his hair hanging greasily over his eyes and his oversized teeth catching the light, James thought of the rat the gang members had shot off the rafters.

"Let me pass, please," said James and stepped straight toward the bearded man with the gold tooth.

That man stepped aside but the second big man moved to block James's way. The three stepped closer, encircling him. James looked over their shoulders but could see no police officers, no pedestrians, no decent folk he might call out to.

"Nice spats," said the ruffians' leader. And then he hawked and spit, quite deliberately, a gob of brown tobacco onto James's left foot.

The second man touched James's torn right sleeve. "You're bleedin', pal. Better come with us so we's can bandage you up right."

James tried to step to his left, into the street, but the boy and the first man blocked his way again. They stepped forward aggressively and

James realized that he was giving way, backing toward the darkness of the alley from whence they'd stepped. He stopped.

The leader stepped so close that James could smell the whiskey and garlic on his breath when the tall man ran his ragged fingers over James's jacket and waistcoat front. "Fucking spats, fucking top hat, fucking silver-headed walking stick," the bearded leader said, "but no fucking watch in your vest. Where is it?"

"I...I lost it," said James.

"Careless sod, ain't you?" said the second man. "But I bet you didn't lose your fucking billfold, did you, Mr. Spats?"

James drew himself to his full height, his right hand gripping the cane tightly even though he knew they would be on him before he could lift it in his own defense.

He felt something sharp touch his belly and looked down to see that the youngest man had set a knife point there.

"James!" cried a familiar voice from just across the street.

James and the three thieves turned their heads at the same instant. James had to suppress a giggle—possibly a hysterical one—since the two men he least imagined running into were now hurrying across the empty street toward him. It had been Theodore Roosevelt who had called out and with him, in a finer suit than James had last seen him in, was Clarence King.

As the two men trotted up to the sidewalk, the bearded thief—well over six feet in height—looked at the five-foot-eight Roosevelt and King, two inches shorter than Roosevelt, and said, "I bet you a bottle that *they* got watches."

"Not for fucking long," said his equally tall, brawny, and filthy partner.

14

As Good as the Boston Beaneaters

The youngest thug pulled the blade back from James's belly and held the knife down at his side as Roosevelt and King stepped up to the group.

"James!" said Roosevelt again, ignoring the three hoodlums and showing his huge, perfect-toothed grin beneath his gold pince-nez. His blue eyes were very bright, as if in joyous anticipation of something. "How fortunate to bump into you! King and I were hoping to find you...we're headed over to Hay's home for dinner."

Clarence King's hazel eyes were much colder than Roosevelt's blue gaze. While Roosevelt had no walking stick with him, King was carrying the elaborate one that James had first seen at Hay's home: the top was of some burnished stone naturally curved almost like a bird's beak.

The two tallest thugs exchanged glances and the bearded leader nodded. James assumed that they'd just silently agreed to rob and beat—and possibly kill—all three of the "swells" they'd just encountered on the edge of Night Town. James didn't know if these three thugs had been at Moriarty's meeting or not...and realized it didn't matter. He'd tried to warn his friends away with not-so-subtle shoving motions of his hands when they were across the street, but now it was too late. The six men were clustered in a rather tight circle here at the entrance to the dark alley.

"Good evening, gentlemen," young Roosevelt said to the thugs, still smiling that impossible white smile. "Thank you for escorting our friend this far. We shall walk with him from here."

The two tallest men shifted to their right, blocking any easy retreat for King or Roosevelt. The scrawny young man closest to Henry James had his blade raised and visible again.

The leader flicked his grimy fingertips up and then down Roosevelt's waistcoated thick torso. "There's a good watch at the end of that chain, ain't there, four-eyes?" he said, showing his brown teeth.

"Of course there is," young Roosevelt said coldly.

"And a billfold in your pocket, too, ain't there?" added the bearded man.

Theodore's grin somehow grew broader. "Yes," he said softly. "And it's going to stay there. You three go about your business now and no one will get hurt."

The two largest thugs began laughing at this and the youngest one joined in with his unpleasant cackle.

The leader reached forward. The second man produced a short-bladed knife almost identical to the one the youngest thug was again holding against the curve of Henry James's belly.

"Do not touch me," said Roosevelt to the bearded thug. The tall man in the hat must have had twenty pounds and six inches of height to his advantage.

"What're you going to do when I *do* touch you, four-eyes?" The broad, filthy hands were poised in front of Theodore's thick torso and gleaming watch chain.

In fairly fluent German—which James could follow—Roosevelt said, "I shall kick you in the balls, make your teeth eat my knee, and then head butt your paltry brains out."

James noticed that young Theodore hadn't been sure of the German word for "butt" and had just used *Kopfbütten* as an approximate. He'd also used the informal *du* form which an adult would use with an intimate, a child, or an animal. His intention there was clear when he'd used the *fressen* form of "to eat"—dogs and other animals *fressen*—rather than the human *essen*. Theodore carefully removed his pince-nez by its ribbon, set the glasses in an inner vest pocket, and patted the pocket. His smile was thin now with his huge teeth no longer gleaming.

The tall leader laughed and said, "We got a couple of midget Dutchmen here, boys. Let's beat the shit out of them."

The two tall men stepped forward. Roosevelt and King took three hasty steps backward, as if they were preparing to run. The leader widened his stride to cut Theodore off.

Roosevelt opened his arms wide, leaned backward with that massive torso, and kicked the tall man between the legs with the kind of full-force, wound-up, full-legged kick that Henry James had only seen on rugby fields. The polished toe of Theodore's small, expensive boot all but disappeared in the leader's vulnerable crotch. The impact was so great that James saw the leader-thug's feet actually leave the ground.

The big man fell to his knees and started to crumple, his hat falling forward as his head came down. He was using both hands to hold his testicles and the moan that came out of him did not sound human.

As the man's face arched down, Theodore's right knee came up more rapidly than it had in the kick. James heard teeth snap and the man's huge nose break.

The thug's upper torso rocked back—his face smeared with blood—his eyes closed but now on the same level as Teddy Roosevelt's blue gaze. Roosevelt grabbed the thug by the shoulders, jerked him toward himself, and smashed that great, square, Roosevelt forehead against the leader's face and temples so hard it sounded like an ax smashing against thin wood.

The leader went down on his back and did not stir.

The other big thug had not been watching idly. He had his knife out jabbing forward and swinging from left to right even as his long arms went wide as if to encircle Clarence King before stabbing.

King had hefted his heavy cane to his shoulder and now he swung it like a baseball bat. Henry James had never played baseball as a child, but his brother William had...and loved it. And during the last two weeks, James had suffered John Hay's enthusiasm for the sport, so when King made his powerful swing, James guessed that it was more like one of the batters from the Boston Beaneaters—expected to win the pennant this year—than a hitter from the perennially last-place Washington Senators.

The beaked stone at the head of the cane caught the advancing thug full in the face. James saw and heard the cheekbone snap, the nose break, and both he and the youngest thug next to him actually had to jump back to avoid the geyser of blood and teeth that came their direction. The big man dropped his knife and fell to all fours.

Five-foot-six Clarence King had grown a belly but the decades of mountain climbing and mine digging had turned his thighs and arms to powerful engines. He kicked the man in the backside so hard that the thug skidded forward on his ruined face on the alley cinders, his arms and hands trailing palms up.

The boy, who was left-handed, swung away from James and swung his arm back to stab Clarence King in the side.

Henry James had written William just before Christmas that he'd been putting on far too much weight, that he was going forth belly-first into the world these days and it did not please him. He'd told William how he'd hired a fencing coach for three two-hour workouts a week, but also how—while James very much enjoyed the exercise—it hadn't taken an ounce off his weight.

Now James raised his own walking stick and brought it down on the boy's wrist as if he were driving a tent peg with a mallet. Surprisingly, his aim was perfect—he heard the head of the cane make loud contact with the scrawny young thug's wrist bone and the knife dropped to the alley cinders.

The young thug shouted in pain but he was very, very fast. He dropped to one knee to retrieve the knife before James could even get his cane raised again.

King stepped forward and planted his polished but heavy boot on the knife blade. The young thug tugged but the blade snapped off at the hilt.

"Trade knife," said Roosevelt from where he stood astride the fallen leader. "They give them away to the Indians by the gross out in the Badlands. Not worth a damn."

King had shifted his cane to his left hand and suddenly, from a coat pocket, he pulled out a jackknife which he flicked open with a snap of his wrist. The blade was enormous for a folding knife—at least seven inches long, James thought, and tapered to a terrifying point.

King set that sharpened point a millimeter under the young thug's left eye, pushing strongly enough to draw blood and a terrified gasp from the would-be highwayman. James half-expected King to pop the boy's eye out like a street vender scooping out ice cream on a hot summer night.

"There's a lesson here, boy," hissed King. "If you're coming to a knife fight, bring a *knife.* Otherwise you'll end up with a Heidelberg scar."

King flicked the blade right across the young thug's cheek and blood geysered.

The boy screamed, clasped both hands to his opened cheek to hold to-gether the bloody flaps now exposing his molars, stood, and ran off into the night.

James could only stare at the two men unconscious on the ground as the sound of the boy's pounding boots dwindled down the dark alleyway. He jumped slightly when someone touched his elbow, but it was only Roosevelt. "That move of yours was rather neat, Mr. James."

"Very neat, I thought," said King, cleaning off the stone head of his cane in the dirt and cinders.

"Your right sleeve is ripped and bloody," said young Theodore. "Did that young brat do that?"

"No," said James, astounded at how steady his voice sounded, "I . . . fell when getting off a trolley a short while ago. Just tore it up a bit on the gravel."

King and Roosevelt exchanged a glance, but said nothing. They stepped away from the two forms on the ground, one moaning and weep-ing, the other still unconscious.

King twirled his newly cleaned cane. "We really were headed for Hay's place for dinner. Would you care to accompany us, Mr. James?"

"I would, Mr. King," said the writer.

Two blocks further—where the street lights were closer together, shops were open, the street was evenly paved, and the true sidewalks be-gan again—they saw a cab passing that was large enough for the three of them and Roosevelt hailed it with a whistle that made the horse jump.

15

The Panic of '93

Most of the dinner guests had not yet arrived when Roosevelt, King, and James knocked on the door, but Hay immediately took in Harry's dishabille and told his head butler Benson and another servant named Napier to help Mr. James up to his room. Dr. Granger, who'd arrived early just so that he could have a whiskey and quiet conversation with his old friend Hay, looked at James's sleeve and said, "I'd best come up to your room with you and have a look at that."

"It's nothing," said James.

"I'll just get my bag from John's man," said the doctor.

Roosevelt, wearing his pince-nez again, grinned and said, "Dr. Granger brings his medical bag to social occasions?"

"Dr. Granger brings his medical bag everywhere he goes," said Clarence King.

Upstairs, James kicked off his spats first, and when Napier swept them up and said "I'll have these cleaned immediately, sir," James snapped, "No, burn them." He would always see the contemptuous tobacco stain on the one spat no matter how clean it might be.

"Come into the bathroom where it's bright," ordered Dr. Granger. "Imagine, a guest room with its own bathroom, running water, and electric lights. Will wonders never cease?"

The sumptuous bathroom was as bright and sterile as a surgical operating room and, when James had removed his sodden and torn shirt and thrown it in a corner, Dr. Granger looked at the lacerated forearm and said, "How did you say you injured your arm?"

"Jumping off a trolley a bit too soon and falling on cinders," James said, having to avert his gaze even as he spoke.

Granger's blue eyes could sometimes be as playful as Teddy Roosevelt's and he only gave James a glance before saying, "All right, but this particular bit of street or alley appears to have been paved with bird shot."

Napier had brought a small, curved white pan and Dr. Granger used some sort of tong-like instrument to remove the shotgun pellets one by one, each clanking as the round bit of shot dropped into the pan making James blush yet again. Dr. Granger removed twelve of the pellets and put iodine — or something equally as painful — over the extraction cuts and other lacerations where there had been no shot.

"None touched muscle," said Dr. Granger. "Most barely penetrated the skin. If I didn't know better, I'd swear you'd been in a slight hunting accident, suffering from a shotgun fired from some distance."

"I don't hunt, sir," said James. He started to pull on the clean white dress shirt Benson had brought from the wardrobe.

"Just a minute," said Dr. Granger. "You don't want to get iodine stains all over your shirt sleeve and I don't want those wounds to get infected. Hold your arm steady . . . there . . . against the wash basin."

Granger removed a roll of bandage and some scissors from his bag and within a minute James's entire forearm had been carefully wrapped and taped.

"Feel any better?" asked Dr. Granger.

"I feel like a fool and" — he gestured with the right arm bandaged almost to his elbow — "like an Egyptian mummy."

"Wait, don't put on the shirt quite yet," said the doctor. He was filling a syringe with a dark fluid from a vial.

"Wait, I don't think . . ." began James but the doctor had already administered the injection in the author's upper arm. "What was that?"

"Just a little something to help with the pain and to cut down on the chance of tetanus," said the doctor as he closed the bag.

Damn, thought James. He'd recognized the morphine and should have spoken sooner. Both he and Katharine Loring had been trained in how to administer the liberal doses of morphine to his sister Alice in her last months of dying...she'd actually passed away while lost in her morphine dreams...and Henry James had vowed never to allow anyone to put the stuff in his own veins. Too late.

And the pain was less. *Much* less. James thought of Sherlock Holmes and his abominable injections and wondered if this light feeling...almost of happiness...might be the result of those illicit injections as well.

"If I babble like an idiot during dinner," said James, "I shall blame it on you and your needle, Dr. Granger."

"If we're not *all* babbling like idiots by the third course," said the doctor, "we shall have to blame it on Hay for not providing sufficient wine and liquor."

* * *

As the other guests were arriving and just before they repaired to the dining room, Hay saw that James was concerned about something. He gingerly took the author's left upper arm, led him to the hallway, and said, "What's wrong, Harry? Can I help?"

James realized that he was biting his lip. "Absurd as it sounds, John," he said softly, "I find that I simply must get in touch with Mr. Holmes. It's urgent."

"Sherlock Holmes?" said his host. "I thought he'd left town."

"Perhaps he has," said James, "but I really must communicate something to him. He did leave the address of a cigar store here in town so if perhaps your man could find a boy to carry a message..."

"We can do better than that, Harry. We can see if the cigar store has a telephone and contact them directly."

"Why on earth would a cigar store have a telephone?" said James. He fought down another uncharacteristic urge to giggle aloud.

Hay shrugged as he led the way to his private study. "Strange age we live in, Harry."

James had noticed the telephone in Hay's study before, but he'd never seen his host operate it. Now there were several minutes back and forth with someone James understood to be an "operator"—or perhaps general information person—and then Hay grinned, handed the apparatus to James, and said, "Mr. Twill is on the phone. He's the manager of the cigar store Holmes mentioned and he's there now." Hay left the room so that James could have privacy.

"Hello, hello, hello?" said James, feeling rather idiotic.

When he and Mr. Twill had both identified themselves again, James said, "I understand that someone at your store receives and conveys messages to Mr. Sherlock Holmes. It is absolutely imperative...urgently imperative...that I get in touch with him at once. Or speak to him telephonically if he is there now."

"Mr. Sherlock Holmes, sir?" squawked Twill's voice through the rumble and scratching of the phone lines.

"Yes."

"English gentleman, sir?"

"That's him!"

"No, he hasn't been around the store, sir, since the day he paid me for this little service of sending along messages. He has a boy come check two or three times a day."

James sighed. If he didn't feel so...light...at the moment, he realized that his chest would be aching with anxiety at giving Holmes the extraordinary news of what he had seen and heard that afternoon.

"All right," he said. "Could you please take down this message and get it to Mr. Holmes as quickly as possible?"

"As soon as his boy stops by, sir."

"All right. The message reads...have you paper and pen ready?"

"Pencil poised, sir."

"The message reads..." James had to pause a second to frame it. "'I followed Professor Moriarty to a meeting here in Washington today. I overheard'...yes, yes, I'll slow down."

"You can go ahead now, sir. You overheard..."

"'I overheard Moriarty sharing his plans about May first with several...groups. It's absolutely imperative that you contact me at once. I leave by train tomorrow...that's Sunday, nine April...afternoon. Absolutely *urgent* that we speak before then. Signed, James'. Can you read that back to me, please?"

Twill did so, James corrected a couple of minor infelicities in the cigar-store keeper's notes, and then the line was dead and the author was fumbling to hang the hearing apparatus onto the speaking stem and then to get the whole contraption back on its shelf.

* * *

Perhaps it was the morphine—if it had been morphine—but the evening's dinner party was one of the most enjoyable Henry James could ever recall. James could not stop laughing. The day's events should have been hanging over him like a black shroud, but instead the sharp memories of hiding on the high beam, of Moriarty, of the criminals and anarchists, and of the street confrontation with the ruffians (a bloody confrontation of which neither Teddy Roosevelt nor Clarence King showed the slightest signs either in manner or spatters of this or that on their formal clothing) seemed to buoy James up with a joy and energy he'd not felt for years. He was wearing a fresh shirt and dinner jacket.

Hay sat at one end of the table again, overseeing the conversation and stimulating it when it lagged—which it almost never did with this all-male group. James was given pride of place to the right of their host and to his right was his old acquaintance Rudyard Kipling. James had given away the bride, Miss Carrie Balestier, at Kipling's 1892 wedding in London and, to complete the bonds of affection, the two men were mutual literary admirers. Why Kipling—who represented so much about Britain, proud and shameful, in his writing—chose to live in America was beyond James's comprehension.

Henry Adams sat next to Kipling and beyond him was Teddy Roosevelt. This night, Augustus Saint-Gaudens took the chair at the opposite end of the table from John Hay. James admired Saint-Gaudens's sculpture almost beyond words with which to praise it—he thought the sculpture at Clover Adams's grave site showed not only consummate skill but tremendous courage, stirring as it did no sense of hope or an afterlife or surcease of sorrow, as James remembered that hack Poe had once phrased it, but only the infinite depths of sorrow and loss.

To Saint-Gaudens's right on the other side of the table were Clarence King, Dr. Granger, and Henry Cabot Lodge to Hay's left.

All the men at the table seemed extraordinarily witty this night, but Kipling and Roosevelt stole the show as far as James's adrenaline- and morphine-muddled perceptions could judge such things. The 27-year-old Kipling, who'd been wintering at their home in snowy Vermont and whose wife Carrie had just had a baby on December 29, was the object of much congratulating and back-slapping. James would someday write—"Kipling strikes me personally as the most complete man of genius (as distinct from fine intelligence) that I have ever known."

"It was very considerate of Josephine to choose twenty-nine December as her birth date," the young writer was saying, "since my birthday is on the thirtieth and Carrie's on the thirty-first. Keeps thing tidy, as it were."

Dr. Granger—his nose already reddening with drink but his enunciation still perfect—asked if the addition of the baby helped them stay warm up in what the Kiplings had named Bliss Cottage near Brattleboro.

"The dear babe is not big enough to offer much in the way of supportive body heat," laughed Kipling, "but the exercise of walking back and forth with her on the nights she cries has been very helpful in keeping warm."

The conversation kept shifting but James could not stop his mind from wandering back to the incredible events of the day and his still urgent need to get in touch with Sherlock Holmes.

Kipling and Roosevelt were queried about their beloved Cosmos Club that sat right across Lafayette Park from Hay's home, combining the Tayloe House with the Dolley Madison home. Both Kipling and Roosevelt were fanatical about the out-of-doors, and the Cosmos Club, besides being perhaps the most elite and influential men's club in America, reflected their passions.

"We did start this little organization called the National Geographic Society there five years ago," said Teddy Roosevelt.

Kipling began laughing himself and when queried, said, "Forgive me, but I remember when friend Theodore first presented himself to the Club with thoughts of joining. Twenty of the older members set out several hundred random fossil-bones on a table in the main dining room and asked Theodore to identify any of them if he could."

"Could he?" asked Clarence King, obviously very well knowing the answer and already grinning.

Kipling laughed again. James thought it was a pleasant laugh, manly and rich but never caustic at anyone else's expense. "For the next several hours, Theodore proceeded not only to identify the fossil bones but to separate them into the various living and extinct animals they each represented—he did everything but wire them together, gentlemen—all the while giving a running commentary on the eating, grazing, predatory, and breeding habits of each animal."

"Teedie's been a star member of the Cosmos Club ever since," said Hay, ignoring Roosevelt's scowl at the use of his childhood name.

Others offered various anecdotes on various topics, even James, but before they'd opened the fourth bottle for the table, Kipling was begging Roosevelt to tell his story about "the grizzly in the bushes out in Dakota."

Roosevelt grinned and did so. He kept the story short, with just the right amount of detail, but Henry James found it especially humorous. The huge grizzly, it seemed, was old and myopic—almost blind. Roosevelt had lost his glasses during a fast descent on a steep, wooded hillside, so he ended up almost as blind as the bear. His first shot missed. "I missed the heart but caught him in the backside," said Roosevelt, following the true raconteur's prime rule of never smiling or laughing at his own tale. "The bear went into a thick mass of high willow bushes, almost too close together for me to push into, and—especially without my glasses—I found myself none too eager to force my way into those bushes where Mr. Grizzly and I could have met up in an instant, long before I could raise my rifle. And the animal was not in the best of moods that morning..."

Eventually Roosevelt did get into the bushes to distract the animal. After an hour of trying to lure him out, he finally thwacked his way into the willows using the barrel of his Winchester to clear his way and with a huge Bowie knife in his teeth. That image alone made the others at the table laugh and James laughed along with them.

"The blind stalking the blind," said Roosevelt. "And in the end, so to speak, the bear was blinder. Or I was luckier."

James enjoyed the anecdote—and had no doubt that it was true—but it reminded him that none of them—King, Roosevelt, or him—had mentioned the street brawl with the would-be street thieves just forty minutes earlier. Henry James did not know the etiquette involved in discussing violent street fights—perhaps a gentleman was not supposed to mention it if he came out on the winning side—or perhaps King and Roosevelt wanted to save James from embarrassment the same way they had saved him from what certainly would have been a severe beating, if not stabbing, and violent robbery less than an hour earlier. James made a mental note to have his protagonist behave precisely this way if he went straight to a fine dinner with friends directly after such a violent altercation.

But, James admitted to himself, he doubted if any of his characters would ever *have* such a violent encounter.

The conversation was turning to current events but Henry James's thoughts kept orbiting his afternoon and what seemed the absolute imperative of telling someone in authority about Professor Moriarty's plans for presidential assassination, the uprising of the anarchists, and mob warfare.

The other men were discussing finances—specifically the much-ballyhooed but never-quite-arrived "Panic of '93"—and this gave James a perfect opportunity to become lost in his own thoughts without seeming rude. Everyone at the table, save perhaps for Teddy Roosevelt, knew that Henry James was a writer; he *had* no finances. One was delightfully liberated from endless male chatter about investments when one could not afford a single investment.

If I don't hear from Holmes, James was thinking, *perhaps I should go to Washington's major and superintendent of police. Or perhaps to President Cleveland himself.* That last thought made him cringe.

It would be possible. Several of his friends at this table—Hay, Cabot Lodge, perhaps young Roosevelt—had dined with the president several times, maybe even

Adams who frowned on knowing all recent presidents. James might have an emergency meeting arranged for as soon as tomorrow morning.

To say what? he thought. *To report that while I was hiding out in the rafters of a former chicken slaughterhouse, I happened to hear Professor James Moriarty—who is considered a fictional character by most people, even possibly, most probably, his nemesis Sherlock Holmes—planning to assassinate the President of the United States and ten or more other heads of states and perhaps scores of top government officials in America and almost a dozen European nations... and not only carry out these assassinations, but simultaneously instigate anarchist uprisings and gang riots in all these scores of cities here and abroad.*

"...it can be traced back to the failure of the wheat crop on the Buenos Aires exchange..." Cabot Lodge was saying.

Hay waved that supposition away. They were all smoking cigars now, save for Roosevelt, Dr. Granger, and James.

"It's the railroad speculation, pure and simple," said Hay.

"Whatever it is or was or will be, you business types were talking about the 'Panic of '93' as long ago as November of '92. Something had better arrive soon or a lot of speculators selling short will be very disappointed."

Was this the renowned Sherlock Holmes's plan? To grab President Grover Cleveland's massive arm and pull him away from the button that would start every machine at the Columbian Exposition a few seconds after noon on May 1, tugging down the huge president and crying "Get down, you fool!" the way that young Captain Oliver Wendell Holmes was supposed to have done with President Lincoln at Fort Stevens in 1864? James doubted that.

"There was a clear prelude to panic in February when the Philadelphia and Reading Railroad went bankrupt by overextending itself," said Cabot Lodge.

"I thought Cleveland handled the Treasury crisis rather handily," said Hay, "by convincing Congress to repeal the Sherman Silver Purchase Act just days after his inauguration."

"For a Democrat—the only one elected president in my living memory—Cleveland does seem to be a man of action," said Dr. Granger.

"He could have taken on my grizzly bare-handed," said Roosevelt. "They would have weighed in the same before the bout."

"Now Theodore," said Henry Adams.

I can't delay leaving tomorrow, thought James. *If I stay, I'll never see the end of these conspiracies or complications. There's simply no other choice but to get word of Professor Moriarty's meeting with the gangs and the anarchists and to repeat what the... what had* The Times *of London called him after Reichenbach Falls? ... the Napoleon of Crime had said about the planned assassinations, uprisings, and lootings.*

I've been caught up in one of the romance-adventure novels I so despise—something less even than H. Rider Haggard's overly violent, overly specific potboilers—and the only way I can escape is to walk away from everything I've seen and heard today... everything I've seen and heard the last few weeks since the Seine. That way lies reality. Or at least literature. Anything is better than this penny-dreadful tale I've found myself in.

"The Free Silver Movement is the wild card in this game," said Hay. "Especially with the American farmers supporting it."

"If people and failing banks start demanding gold for their notes..." Henry Adams said as if he were thinking aloud.

"In the West and Midwest, more than three hundred banks have already closed," said Roosevelt.

"In the West and Midwest," said Hay, gesturing to his servant to pass a new bottle of wine around, "anyone with two barrels, a plank, and a cigar box full of quarters can declare themselves a bank."

I have to leave tomorrow, thought James with a sudden pain in his chest and left arm. *I must leave tomorrow. Buy a garden trowel along the way so I can bury the snuffbox with Alice's ashes securely inside it. I was tempted to go to Newport where she and Miss Loring seemed so happy after Alice had the house on the point built for them, but I think Katharine Loring has had just about enough of Alice's company. No, my dear, darling, caustic, death-desiring Alice needs to lie in the same soil as our parents and Aunt Kate.*

And then I have to rush to make that noon train to New York. I can't miss that German steamship's—the Spree *wasn't it?—departure time on Tuesday morning. Once aboard I can relax, I can think, I can take the time and energy to sort out what has been reality and what illusion over these past weeks. Mr. Sherlock Holmes will simply have to fend for himself in this multifaceted mess of a mystery. One thing is certain—I'll never be his adoring Boswell the way Dr.*

Watson is, if he is a real person or even if he's a product of Conan Doyle's literary imagination, faithfully chronicling the detective's triumphs. It's a poverty of triumphs I've seen him produce.

A servant slipped in with a slip of paper on a silver tray. The young man whispered to Hay who nodded and gestured toward James.

It was a telegram. James could not wait until later to open it—it had to be Holmes's response to his news about Moriarty and his urgent plea—so he slit it open and read it as he held it below the plane of the table. The telegram was moderately succinct:

JAMES. IF IT IS CONVENIENT FOR YOU, PLEASE MEET ME ON MONDAY AT 3 P.M. AT FOUR THIRTY SIX AND A HALF REVERE STREET IN BEACON HILL, BOSTON STOP IF IT IS NOT CONVENIENT FOR YOU, STILL MEET ME THERE AT THAT TIME STOP

YOU MAY LEAVE YOUR LUGGAGE AT THE NEW NORTH UNION STATION ON CAUSEWAY STREET IN THE WEST END SINCE WE SHALL BE TAKING A NIGHT TRAIN WEST TO CHICAGO THAT SAME EVENING STOP

HOLMES

16

God Might Envy Him

Sherlock Holmes rang Henry Adams's new-fangled electrical doorbell button in late morning, about an hour after James's train had left for New York and then Boston. The tall head butler, Hobson, answered the door and seemed no happier to see Holmes than he'd been during their last encounter.

"Mr. Adams is still in his bath," said Hobson, making ready to close the door in Holmes's face.

"That's all right," said Holmes, handing his hat and stick to the tall man as he brushed past him, "I shall be happy to wait for Mr. Adams in his study."

While the flustered Hobson sought out his bathing master, Holmes stepped into the study, poured himself a healthy dose of Scotch with a whisper of water, and sprawled in the chair opposite the infinite expanse of Adams's green leather desktop.

He lined up two fingers in a straight line with the Executive Mansion window of what had once been the office of President Cleveland's sister—before she had been replaced by a 21-year-old bride, Miss Frances Folsom. Since Cleveland was 49 on the day of the marriage, the public might have been shocked by the more than 27-year age difference—or, failing that, disconcerted a bit by the fact that his marriage was unusual, since Cleveland had been the executor of his friend, and Frances's father, Oscar Folsom's estate, supervising Frances's upbringing after her father's death; he'd bought her yellow baby carriage when she was a few days old and he still seemed to be giving her bright things.

Holmes had met with the Steamboat Inspection Committee that Sunday morning—minus former Major and Superintendent of the Metropolitan Police William G. Brock though his place was filled by Chief Daniel O'Malley, head of the 27-man White House Police Force—and while Mr. Rockhill, the State Department Liaison, was complaining that he had to miss church, Holmes was asking Vice-President Adlai E. Stevenson where he planned to be on May *first,* around noon, just about the time President Cleveland was scheduled to push the button that started everything at the Chicago World's Columbian Exposition.

Vice-President Stevenson had to think a minute and then refer to a pocket record-keeper, but finally he said, "Oh, I'll be in the Executive Mansion from ten thirty a.m. until mid-afternoon. Meeting and lunching with delegates from the current regime in the Philippines and then taking part in a formal signing of a Letter of Agreement with them."

"Where will the meeting and signing take place, Mr. Vice-President?" asked Holmes.

Stevenson had to think about that for a minute but then remembered. "Oh, that will be in what we now call the Small Treaty Room."

"Would that happen to be the north-facing room whose window one can see directly across the park there? The one directly across from Mr. Henry Adams's home?" asked Holmes. "The room that was President Cleveland's sister's office and reception room during Mr. Cleveland's first term?"

"Why, yes, I believe that's the same room," said Vice-President Stevenson.

Holmes turned to Mr. Drummond, the highly intelligent Chief of the Secret Service branch of the Treasury Department and to Daniel O'Malley. O'Malley had not struck Holmes as especially bright during the short time he'd been conversing with him that morning. "We have reliable indications that an attempt will be made upon Vice-President Stevenson's life at or around the same time that the president is scheduled to be assassinated in Chicago. The Small Treaty Room is in a direct line to various windows in Mr. Henry Adams's home less than two hundred yards to the north."

"Shall we request permission for the event to be moved to another room?" asked Chief O'Malley.

"I would suggest that you keep the vice-president—and his guests—out of the White House for all of that day," said Holmes. "Perhaps choose an inside room at the State Department and make sure that the change of venue and location remains a tightly held secret."

Drummond of the Secret Service nodded and Holmes knew that it would be done.

"You see how someone could use a good rifle to make a clear shot into the Small Treaty Room from one of the windows on the Adamses' home?" asked Holmes, pointing.

"Mr. Adams would never allow that," said White House Police Chief O'Malley.

"Next to Adams's house is the home of Colonel John Hay," Washington P.D. Major and Superintendent Moore informed Holmes. "We can't be bothering such important people just because of their...proximity...to the Executive Mansion."

"Of course not," said Sherlock Holmes.

"I'll look into it and talk to you in the next week," said Andrew Drummond.

Holmes understood that to mean that the Adamses' house would be thoroughly searched, the best shooting angles analyzed by marksmen, and that the head of the Secret Service—a department with no constitutional responsibilities to protect the president—would have men there on May 1.

Chief O'Malley," said Holmes, "are you still detaching two of your White House Police to travel with the president as is sometimes the custom?"

"Ahhhh," said O'Malley and looked around the room as if someone could give him the correct answer. "I could send more men or less men."

"Fewer," corrected Holmes. He had the same reaction to hearing the English language abused as he did to watching horses or dogs beaten with no reason. And he was not especially a sentimentalist when it came to horses or dogs. But he had once told Watson that the "less or fewer" issue, along with the use of "I" in such sentences as "He gave the money to Sheila and I", inflicted on the public by people who considered themselves well-educated, could be drastically reduced in frequency—if not actually abolished—by a few well-aimed pistol shots and an explanatory note that would be pinned to the victims' chests.

"Think I should send less than the usual two?" asked Chief O'Malley.

Here Vice-President Stevenson stepped in with what might have been the briefest of winks at Holmes. "We know there's a threat against the White House, Chief O'Malley. And Colonel Sebastian Moran is a famed marksman and soldier of fortune as opposed to these . . . phantoms . . . that the others are looking for. It might be wisest to retain all twenty-seven of your excellent roster of White House police officers on that day. After all, you were trained to protect the Executive Mansion from intrusion, not follow the president around to protect him."

"True," said O'Malley. "And it's the Chicago Police Department's job to protect the president. The host city always assumes that responsibility."

"Only partially the responsibility of the Chicago P.D.," said the Secret Service chief.

Holmes looked at Drummond. No one else had brought this up at any of their meetings.

"What do you mean?" asked Washington's Major and Superintendent Moore.

In a private moment before the group assembled, Holmes had asked Drummond if he thought that Chicago had the honor of hosting the most corrupt police department in the country. Finally Chief Drummond had nodded. "Now that the last of the Tweed ring is out of New York and the new corrupters haven't yet taken their place, Chicago is the most corrupt. It runs in their veins like the booze they consume. But there are good men on the force there and very few out of the hundreds who'd aid and abet in the murder of a president."

Holmes had nodded.

Now Chief O'Malley said loudly, "What do you mean when you say that the Chicago Police Department won't be responsible for President Cleveland's safety?"

"From the door of the Lexington Hotel until he reaches the Exposition grounds—the so-called White City down in Jackson Park—the C.P.D. will be the responsible agency," said Holmes. "But once the procession enters the sacrosanct grounds of the World's Columbian Exposition, the group directly responsible for the safety of the President of the United States—not to mention the forty or fifty other dignitaries there that day, the President of Brazil, I'm told, being the people's favorite—shifts to the Columbian Guard."

"What the hell is the Columbian Guard?" asked O'Malley.

Drummond answered, "It's the private police force that Daniel Burnham put together just for the World's Fair."

"No Chicago police?" said Moore.

"None," said Secret Service Chief Drummond. "On the fairgrounds, the Columbian Guard have the power to detain, interrogate, and arrest—there's a nice little Columbian Guard jail just off the Midway Plaisance, but mostly of course they will be rounding up lost children, giving directions, intervening before private drunkenness becomes a public problem, and being courteous to hundreds of thousands of customers who've come to the Exposition to have a wonderful time."

"How many of these Columbian Guardsmen are there?" asked Vice-President Stevenson.

Holmes answered, "Just over two thousand, Mr. Vice-President."

"Two thousand!" exploded Washington P.D. Major and Superintendent Moore. "That's an army."

"That, I believe," said Holmes, "was Daniel Burnham's intention. The so-called White City will be electrified far beyond the current dreams of Chicago, New York, Washington, or any other major American city. Pleasant street lights and glowing electrical 'lanterns' and radiant store fronts and searchlights and lighting from huge windows and path lights illuminating more than six hundred acres of World's Fairgrounds—combined with the highest percentage of trained police officers, uniformed and plainclothes alike, to the number of citizens—will make the White City the safest urban environment in the world."

"As long as it's safe for President Cleveland during the hours he shall be there," said Vice-President Stevenson.

"What kind of weapons do these Columbian Guardsmen carry?" asked Moore.

Holmes smiled. "Most of them carry a whistle and a short sword in a scabbard."

* * *

Henry Adams came into his study wearing his dressing gown and slippers. He frowned at the detective, who remained seated. "I see you've made yourself comfortably at home, Mr. Holmes."

Holmes smiled and nodded.

"And no doubt taken the time to ransack my drawers and cabinets."

"Only to the extent of pouring myself a drink for the long wait, Mr. Adams. An excellent whiskey."

"I hadn't planned on ever seeing you again," said Adams.

Holmes nodded.

Adams went around to his side of the desk, hesitating as if debating whether he would acknowledge Holmes's presence more by sitting or by standing. He sat.

"I thought that I had made it abundantly clear at our last meeting, Mr. Holmes," said Adams, "that it *was* our last meeting. That we have nothing more to discuss, either in public or private."

Holmes removed one of the small She-was-murdered cards from his pocket and set it on Adams's green leather desk blotter.

"This has nothing to do with me," said Adams. He tore the card into shreds and dropped them into his wastebasket.

"Ned Hooper hired me to find out who was sending out these cards to you and survivors of the Five Hearts each year, and since he's now also dead, you were the closest relative, through your late wife, to whom I could report," said Holmes.

"By your own admission," said Adams, "you met my wife's late brother for less than an hour some two years ago. That hardly gives you the right, Mr. Holmes, to call Edward 'Ned' as his family and friends did. If you must refer to him, you may use 'Mr. Fowler.'"

Holmes nodded. "I was paid by Mr. Fowler to use my skills to discover who was sending these cards—and also, in his very words, 'To see if Clover actually died by her own hand or by some means more sinister'—so in Mr. Fowler's absence, I shall report to you."

Adams had turned his face toward the windows but now he shot a glance at Holmes. "You know who's been sending those cards the last seven years?"

"Yes."

A charred log collapsed in Adams's small fireplace. Even on warming spring days, he evidently kept a small fire burning in his study. Holmes wondered if the widower historian suffered from a permanent chill.

After a stretch of silence, Adams snapped, "Well, are you going to tell me or not?"

"No," said Holmes.

Henry Adams's face flushed even while his lips grew whiter. "You said that because your client, Ned, took his own life in December, you were duty bound to report to me. Now you say you won't tell me the identity of this person who has been hounding and harassing the four of us these past six years? Such insolence! If I were a few years younger, Mr. Holmes..."

Holmes nodded as if he could see such a prospect as scholarly Henry Adams giving the detective a beating. "I've deduced who the person is who typed and sent those cards," he said, "but I require a private, personal interview with that person. Such an interview isn't possible right now, but will be carried out by the first week in May."

"In other words," spat Adams, "you're guessing!"

"I never guess," said Sherlock Holmes. He'd steepled his long, pale fingers under his chin and his gaze seemed fixed on something very far away. His expression, which so often seemed impassive when not in the throes of excitement or strong intellectual emotion, now looked stern. That sternness was not directed at Henry Adams, but it still made the historian uneasy.

"I don't suppose you've discovered anything about the rest of this 'mystery' of my poor wife's death...which was never a mystery," said Adams. It had been a clumsy sentence and Adams, the constant writer and consummate editor, frowned at it.

Holmes seemed to return from wherever his thoughts had taken him. "Oh, yes," he said almost off-handedly, "I've confirmed beyond doubt that Clover...Mrs. Adams...*was* murdered."

Adams's bearded jaw dropped and, although he quickly shut his mouth and attempted to control his expression, it was thirty seconds or more before he could speak. "Murdered? How? By whom? And for what possible reason?"

"I expect to have the answer to all three of your new questions before the fortnight is out," said Holmes. "As to the 'how', there is no doubt that her death resulted from the administration of arsenic from her own photographic developing liquids. But the question stays on the list because we're not certain of how that poison was administered."

"So, in truth, you're still blindly guessing about everything," said Adams.

"I never guess, sir."

"Do you even have...what are they called in your cheap mystery tales?...suspects?"

"I know the murderer was one of three people," said Holmes, "with your name being the third on that list of possibilities."

"Me!" cried Adams, jumping to his feet. "You have the insulting, insufferable..." Words failed him and Adams reached for his walking stick propped behind him.

"You had the time, the knowledge of and access to the poison, and, as for motives, murders of a spouse always have the most complicated, personal, and opaque of motives," said Holmes. "In this case, everyone around you knows that your wife had always had a melancholy streak—she herself had written letters home during your long honeymoon in Egypt and elsewhere in which she admitted to her father that she'd been too...'overcome by my old nemesis of melancholy' was how she put it, I believe...even to speak to you, her new husband, or to anyone else for almost two weeks. Such melancholy, always hovering nearby over the years, grows wearing on a spouse and you yourself have described how more deeply lost in unhealthy sadness she'd been for much of that last year after the death of her father in March of eighteen eighty-five."

Henry Adams gritted his teeth so hard that the grinding of molars was louder than the cracklings of the fireplace. He lifted the heavy walking stick like a club, his knuckles white from the intensity of his grip.

Holmes did not stir or try to protect himself as Henry Adams leaned over the desktop toward him, the cane raised and shaking from the man's fury. Holmes's own stick was propped against another chair some six feet away. He made no motion toward it, but remained seated, his eyes on Adams's face, his hands calmly folded on his lap.

Adams dropped the cane onto the Persian carpet and collapsed into his chair, slumping down and shielding his eyes with one hand. After a moment, he said, "You must know that I did not...kill...my beloved Clover."

"Oh, I know you did not," said Holmes, now resting his chin on his folded fingers, propping his elbows on the polished wooden arms of his chair. "But any competent police officer, much less a competent and ambitious district attorney, could have—and probably should have, since you were investigated so shallowly primarily due to your station in society and your wealth—ended with you condemned to the gallows by a jury of your peers."

Adams's jaw dropped again and this time he did not soon think to close his mouth. He peered through his fingers at Holmes the way a child might peep through her fingers at a possible monster in a dark closet.

"You had the time, you knew where Mrs. Adams kept her deadly arsenic, and no servants on duty that morning saw you leave for this sudden Sunday-morning appointment with your dentist. Since you never saw your dentist that morning, you could have been waiting half a block down the street along the park's edge, waiting until you saw Rebecca Lorne come to your doorway. She was, in a sense, your alibi."

"If you think all this," rasped Adams, "then why do you *not* believe me to be guilty of this murder?"

Holmes walked over to the open secretary where the bottles were kept, replenished his Scotch whiskey, and poured a stiff drink of brandy for Adams, setting it in front of him on the desk rather than handing it to him.

"I know you are innocent not merely because of your obvious qualities," said Holmes, "but because you did not see Rebecca Lorne waiting at the front door of your home, pondering whether to knock and go up, as you testified to the police. Rather, you saw Miss Lorne come rushing out of your home, flinging the door wide, in a state of near-hysteria. It had been she, not you, who first discovered Mrs. Adams's body."

"How do you know that?" demanded Adams and took a long drink of brandy.

"You yourself ran two blocks to your doctor's home—and returned on the run with him—and Dr. Charles E. Hagner later reported to the press that the vial of potassium cyanide sat, still opened and venting its terrible fumes, on a table across the room from where Mrs. Adams's body had fallen to the floor in front of her favorite chair, and that an empty water glass lay on the carpet beside her," said Holmes. "Dr. Hagner also mentioned that Miss Rebecca Lorne was waiting in the room adjoining Mrs. Adams's bedroom when the two of you arrived and that Miss Lorne was so upset that he had to administer a tranquilizing drug to her. The police report, done under the investigation of Lieutenant Hammond—who arrived with two men some twenty minutes after you and Hagner did but who remained only a few minutes before you demanded absolute isolation with your wife's body—mentioned the position of the body and the vial of cyanide, now corked again, but made no mention of the water glass on the carpet."

"The scene is forever branded into my brain," said Adams, "but I remember no water glass on the floor."

"The bottle of poison was on a table some distance from where Mrs. Adams had lain on the carpet before you carried her body to the couch," said Holmes, tapping his lips with two steepled forefingers. "All agree on that. And yet there had been a spill of the chemical near where your wife's body had been lying. Your housekeeper commented that the lethal liquid had discolored the edge of the carpet and a bit of the polished floor. Her people had cut the carpet's nap and re-finished the floor-board to get rid of the stains, she said."

Adams's temples and cheeks grew flushed again. "My housekeeper had the temerity to talk to you about . . ."

Holmes held up both hands, palms outward. "There was not much of a police investigation, sir, but the servants did have to give statements to the police while you were in your darkest hours of mourning. I understand that you spent two days and nights alone with the body and did not later announce the time or fact of Mrs. Adams's funeral on December nine so your surviving Three Hearts friends could attend. At any rate, this information about the stained carpet and floorboard were in Lieutenant Hammond's notes."

"What's the importance of any of this?" shouted Adams.

"There was, lying near Mrs. Adams's body, a water glass that had obviously been the vessel from which she drank the poison, still lying there when Dr. Hagner arrived with you," said Holmes. "The stains on the carpet and floorboard must have come from the residue of the terrible liquid that remained in the glass when Mrs. Adams dropped it. Yet the glass was gone when Detective Hammond arrived about half an hour later."

Holmes leaned forward, his gray eyes as piercing as a predator's. "Someone removed that glass in that half-hour interim," he said softly. "Your housekeeper, Mrs. Soames, told the police three days after the death that there were only eleven small water glasses in the cupboard off the kitchen where they were usually kept. The glass had come from a set of twelve."

Adams finished the brandy. "Who? If not the servants, who would have removed the glass...the mythical glass I do not even remember seeing? The police?"

"They say they did not, sir."

"I don't...I don't understand the significance of a water glass or...or the vial of cyanide," managed Adams. "Why does it make any difference?"

"It would be easier to *make* someone drink from the glass than from a vial," Holmes said.

Adams's dark eyes seemed to recede in their sockets. "Make them drink? Someone might have forced Clover to drink that terrible, corrosive, painful, deadly poison?"

"Yes," said Holmes. "More than that, there is the time involved. Were there usually water glasses left in her bedroom?"

462 || Dan Simmons

"No," said Adams, his voice totally flat. "Clover hated rings on the furniture."

"In the adjoining bathroom?"

"No," repeated Adams. "There are glasses in our bathrooms, but not those small water glasses. And Clover's was...still there...when I looked in her bathroom some days later."

"From the time you left to see your dentist to the time you turned around and came back because of the commotion Miss Lorne was making as she came out of your front door"—began Holmes and noticed when Adams did not interrupt or contradict him—"it would have been very difficult for Mrs. Adams to go downstairs through the annex to the kitchen where the water glasses were stored...and to avoid being noticed by Mrs. Ryan, your chief cook, who was working in the kitchen at the time...and then to carry it upstairs and *then* to walk the length of the second floor to her darkroom and the special locked cupboard where she kept her photographic developing chemicals, then to return to her bedroom to take the poison."

Adams shook his head like a man in a bad dream. "You're suggesting that...someone else had carried up the glass and poison vial and was waiting somewhere upstairs, hiding nearby, listening, waiting for her to be alone even while I was talking to Clover before I left to see my dentist?"

"It is a distinct possibility," said Holmes.

"And it must have been Rebecca Lorne, whom Clover liked and trusted and who I also relied upon in the days after...after..." rasped Adams. "It would have to be Rebecca Lorne because she would have been the only one who could have taken the glass between the visits of the doctor and the police lieutenant."

"She almost certainly took the glass away with her," said Holmes, "but she is not the only suspect if it was murder rather than suicide. There is another."

Adams stared so hard at Holmes that the detective felt almost burned by the historian's gaze.

"Clifton Richards, Miss Lorne's...cousin...may have been involved," said Holmes. "He may have been in the house and gone down the back way, the servants' stairs, and out of the house even as Rebecca Lorne rushed up the main stairway to warn Mrs. Adams."

"To warn her," Adams repeated dully. He managed to focus his eyes on Holmes's face. "Who killed my wife, Mr. Holmes? I beg of you...if you know, tell me."

"I'll know for a certainty in the next few weeks, Mr. Adams. Which is why I need to ask a favor of you."

Adams may have nodded an infinitesimal bit.

"I've convinced John Hay and Cabot Lodge to move the visit to the Chicago World's Fair up a couple of weeks for the actual opening on May first, arriving in his private car perhaps a day or two early," said Holmes. "And Senator Cameron has his private yacht...the Great Lakes Yacht, I believe they call it...ready to anchor just off the pier of the Exposition."

"Going to the wretched Exposition will help reveal my Clover's murderer and bring him or her to justice?" said Adams.

"Yes."

"Then I'll go along with Cameron, Hay, the Lodges, and the rest. Although I saw the Philadelphia World's Fair and it was a monumental bore."

Holmes actually smiled.

As he prepared to leave, Adams gripped his arm and said, "But why would they kill Clover? Why would anyone want to harm that witty, sad, lonely, darling woman?"

Holmes settled back into his seat, sighed, and reached into his upper inside jacket pocket to pull out a small blue envelope still tied in pink ribbon. It had been opened. Holmes removed the handwritten letter and held it so that Adams could put on his glasses and read it across the wide desk.

Henry Adams read his own handwriting for half a moment and then let out an inarticulate noise and lunged for the letter.

"No," said Holmes, folding it, and putting it back into his jacket pocket. "I can't allow you to tear this up the way you did the card earlier."

"That's my property!" snarled the small historian.

Holmes nodded. "Legally it is, sir. Even though it was in the possession of another person."

"Why would Lizzie...how did you...why would she give you that most intimate of letters? My greatest folly?"

"She didn't give it to me," said Holmes. "She doesn't know I have it. I had to borrow it. When my investigations are done, I shall return it to where she kept it hidden."

"*Investigations...*" hissed Adams in contempt. "Reading other people's most private mail. Sneaking into boudoirs in the night. Stealing..."

"I assure you that I shall return it in the next few weeks," said Holmes. "Mrs. Cameron shall never know that I had taken the letter from its hiding place. I simply needed to know for sure what Rebecca Lorne and the so-called Clifton Richards were using to blackmail Mrs. Adams."

"Blackmail?" It sounded as if Henry Adams were going to start laughing wildly. "Then I did kill Clover Adams. I was the cause, alpha and omega, of my darling's death."

"No," said Holmes. "It was my duty in solving this case to find and read this letter, Mr. Adams, but I assure you that I took no pleasure in doing so. And I found no evil there. It was a note from a terribly sad man who had been essentially abandoned by a wife lost to melancholy not merely in the previous months but for years...a midnight love letter to another woman, one he knew well and admired much. It was folly, Mr. Adams, but exquisitely human and understandable folly."

"We went to the Camerons' house on the evening of December fourth," said Adams, speaking as if mesmerized, his eyes unfocused. "Two days before Clover...before her death. Lizzie Cameron had been ill and Clover had been unusually distraught about the illness. She knew...we all knew...that a major source of Lizzie's illness lay in the travesty of her marriage to Don. Clover felt bad about that as well. That night we took Rebecca Lorne with us...it was warm, I remember, not feeling like December at all.

"To cheer Lizzie up, Clover had brought along a large bouquet of yellow Marechal Niel roses—not easy to find in December in Washington—and she and Rebecca took the roses up to Lizzie's sickroom. Do you know the language of flowers, Mr. Holmes?"

"Only bits of it."

Adams smiled with no humor. "In the language of flowers so popular these days, the yellow roses signified 'I'm yours, heart and soul.' *This* is what she gave Lizzie Cameron less than forty-eight hours before her death."

"She was giving that message to you," Holmes said softly.

Adams shook his head. "If Clover knew about my...my mad, impulsive letter to Lizzie of the previous July...*that* letter..." He pointed at Holmes's breast pocket. "And begged to know if it was true...if Rebecca Lorne had tantalized her with the knowledge of that letter, or even of the possibility of its existence...and if Lizzie did not deny it..."

Holmes reached across the desk and touched Adams's forearm, squeezing it very softly. "Don't let your imagination run away with you, Adams. You know Clover's good heart. Her flower-language expressions to her sick friend were almost certainly just that—an act of love and generosity."

But Holmes knew that there had been a confrontation of sorts over the letter from Henry Adams that night. Clover had asked Lizzie Cameron if it was true...if such a letter from "my Henry" existed. Lizzie had been sick and in a foul mood and, while ridiculing the entire idea, had also gone out of her way not to deny. She even teased Clover and Rebecca Lorne for wanting to see "such a curious document". Holmes knew all this because, besides liberating that letter from Lizzie Cameron's hiding place of letters taped to the bottom of her dresser drawer, he'd also borrowed her private 1885 diary long enough to read entries from the first week of December. The diary had been put back in place—at some risk to Holmes's agent in these matters—but he would keep the July letter, and other letters taken from other homes by the same dirty means, until events of the next few weeks were settled.

Holmes could see and feel Adams approaching his personal breaking point. This was the man who, after his wife's death, had fled to the South Seas with an artist friend for three years and more than 30,000 miles of aimless wandering. This was the man who had sworn the great sculptor Saint-Gaudens to secrecy and then had him build that mausoleum for the living inside the extraordinary memorial not to his wife's memory—but to the memory of his own grief.

Standing, his hat and cane in hand, Holmes paused and removed another slip of paper from his jacket. "Hay gave me this, although all your friends know it, Adams. Clover...Mrs. Adams...began a letter to her sister Ellen shortly after you left that Sunday morning to visit your dentist. I know you remember the words but it might help find perspective to hear them again:

> *If I had one single point of character or goodness I would stand on that and grow back to life. Henry is more patient and loving than words can express. God might envy him—he bears and hopes and despairs hour after hour...Henry is beyond all words tenderer and better than all of you even.*

Holmes folded the note and set it away next to the blue-paper letter. "She wrote that note, Mr. Adams, *after* she had learned of the possible existence of your July letter to Lizzie Cameron. She had already forgiven you."

Adams stood and turned his unfathomable gaze toward the detective. "When must I see you next, Mr. Holmes? What new hell awaits me...all of us?"

"Chicago," said Holmes. He let himself out quietly without calling for Hobson the butler.

PART 3

ONE

Thursday, April 13, 10:00 a.m.

My plan for opening the Chicago World's Fair part of our tale was to explain why Henry James—against all his instincts and habits—would accompany Holmes on this part of the detective's adventure. But the odd truth is, I don't know why James did so.

We all know individuals who shield their thoughts better than others, but both Sherlock Holmes and Henry James have been the most difficult minds to penetrate in my long experience both of knowing people and of entering the thoughts of characters. Holmes's tight grip on his secrets and modes of thinking is understandable: the detective is a self-made gentleman with a base and secret history from the London streets and the majority of his life has been one long, dangerous high-wire act of exercising both his astounding intellect and indomitable will. Holmes's mind and heart—what there is of a heart—work in ways both too alien and difficult for most of us to understand. Or to bear if we *could* understand them.

But Henry James's thoughts and feelings are hidden behind an even thicker layer of psychic armor. Like Holmes, James has created himself—the artist Self, the Master Self, the married-only-to-his-art bachelor Self—out of whole cloth and through sheer effort of will, perhaps following John Keats's dictum of "That which is creative must create itself." But unlike the detective, James has attempted to hide the core of himself even from himself. Every word he has ever written—in letters, introductions, and fiction—threatens to reveal something, however ephemeral, that the writer does not want revealed. His self-discipline in avoiding such revelations has been painfully effective. His success in keeping his inner thoughts and his reasons for most of the decisions in his life secret has led us to this point where we can only stand outside that tightly banded and seemingly contradicted construct that is Henry James and wonder at his choices.

At any rate, James has chosen to follow Holmes to Chicago and I ask his pardon and yours for jumping ahead a couple of days in the strict chronology of the tale before doubling back to earlier events.

On their second day in Chicago, Sherlock Holmes insisted on taking Henry James on a brief morning excursion tour by boat of the new White City of the Columbian Exposition. The small steamship left from a pier in downtown Chicago not far from the hotel where they were staying. While never stopping at the Exposition and carefully avoiding the huge pier with its automated people-mover still under construction and extending far out into the lake from the World's Fair site, the tour gave gawkers a ninety minute glimpse of the Exposition structures from Lake Michigan.

"I'm not sure of the purpose of this outing," James said as he stood near Holmes at the starboard railing of the noisy little tour boat. The modern, three-decked steamship with rows of seats on each of its roofed levels could safely carry about 300 people—the ship was named *Columbus* and would be a ferry to the Exposition after the official opening on May 1, coming and going every hour to carry new revelers to the Exposition grounds and exhausted fairgoers back to their downtown hotels—but today there were about fifty people aboard to take the short scenic cruise down to Jackson Park, and with the exception of James and the almost always impassive Holmes, all aboard seemed profoundly excited about the simple act of glimpsing some unfinished buildings.

"I'm showing you the future," said Holmes.

There had been a haze along the lakeshore when the tour boat left the downtown Chicago pier but now, as they approached the Jackson Park area which held the Fair, the haze lifted and the sunlight took on an almost personal presence, warming the tourists and illuminating everything along the shoreline as if a huge searchlight had been trained on it. James knew that, technically, Jackson Park had been a southern extension of Chicago proper—away from the shore, 63rd Street had boasted a few shops and homes already—but this square mile of lake-front now housing the Exposition had been the worst sort of swampy, sandy, dead, and desiccated place, unwanted even by the land speculators who'd hurled the boundaries of Chicago further and further out onto the prairie following the deliberate extensions of the city's railroad system miles beyond the edges of the existing Chicago.

America's newspapers, for almost two years, had enjoyed telling the tale of how the famous eastern architects—the best in the nation—chosen by the Exposition czar Daniel Hudson Burnham, had been horrified to learn that under a foot of black soil all throughout the swampy islands of this Jackson Park site, construction diggers would encounter only more unsettling sand and super-saturated soil. Burnham had been asking these famous architects to design what would, for the duration of the Exposition, be the largest structures in North America (and, when Mr. Ferris's Wheel would be completed in June, the tallest) on mud—quicksand, really—rather than on the bedrock these architects were so used to in New York and elsewhere in the East.

It took about an hour for carriages to travel from downtown Chicago to the Fair site in Jackson Park, less time for the many yellow rail-cars—called "cattle cars" by the Exposition-savvy Chicagoans—that had been laid on to take the special spur line south straight to Jackson Park and the gates of the Fair. When speculators had refused to rent or sell airspace over the avenues leading south to the Fair for less than 100% profit for themselves, the railroad execs had designed the elevated special rail line to the Fair with its constant stream of yellow cars tailored to fit down the narrow north-south alleys where no air-space needed to be purchased.

It took the *Columbus* tour boat about twenty-five minutes to reach the Fair site in Jackson Park.

"Good heavens," said James.

In almost three decades of living and traveling abroad, James had seen enough architectural wonders that most of the new structures that Americans seemed so proud of seemed small or ugly or far too utilitarian in comparison to the millenniums of beauty he'd seen in Europe. But the White City was something totally new to him. For a moment he could only grip the rail and gawk.

"My heavens," he said again after a breathless moment.

What had been swampland had been transformed into more than a square mile of white stone walks, countless white buildings of immense and staggering size, soaring sculptures, giant domes, gracefully arching bridges, green lawns, a forested island, and fields of flowers.

The daylight on the white buildings seemed to make the White City incandescent. James found himself squinting. Downtown Chicago was a relatively new city—most of the buildings had been built since the terrible 1871 fire—but now the author realized that it was a dark, dirty, Black City compared to the vision before him. In Chicago itself, dark brick buildings grew ever taller to block the light from reaching the shorter buildings and sidewalks all around them. The cavernous streets were made even darker by the tracks for the elevated trains running overhead. Except for the rare buildings facing Lake Michigan, Chicago was a box-canyon city of darkness, dirt, noise, and grime. James knew that his beloved London was equally dirty—or more so—but at least it had the good grace to hide its filth in the thick, dangerous coal fogs a good part of the year.

Quiet until now, Holmes suddenly started playing the part of tour guide.

"There are fourteen of those so-called Great Buildings in the White City. The huge one we're approaching now is called the Manufactures and Liberal Arts Building and encloses one point three million square feet of space. The roof itself is a clear span some three hundred sixty-eight feet long and two hundred and six feet high. It alone had thirteen acres of surface to paint. Besides the Great Buildings, there are two hundred more buildings in the White City, including one representing each of the forty-seven states in the Union plus all territories."

James smiled, amused at having his own tour guide with a British accent. Some were edging closer along the railing to hear what Holmes was saying.

"When President Cleveland turns on the switch on the first of May," continued Holmes, either not noticing or simply ignoring the other listeners, "the White City's dynamos will provide three times the total amount of electric power available in Chicago and more than ten times that provided for the eighteen eighty-nine Paris Exposition. The White City has more than a hundred and twenty thousand incandescent lights, and seven thousand arc lights to illuminate its boulevards, grounds, pathways, and fountains. There will be very few if any dark corners in the White City and the designers have hired their own police force—the two thousand members of the Columbian Guards—not only to apprehend those who have committed crimes or disturbed the civic peace but to stop those crimes *before* they occur. No other city in Europe or America has what I consider so enlightened a law-enforcement policy."

"What's the huge but ugly and unfinished thing there, some distance north and a bit west of the big Manufactures Building?" asked James, gesturing with his walking stick. "It looks as if they are building the hull for Noah's Ark."

"That's to be the White City's answer to the Eiffel Tower that was such a hit at the Paris Exposition," said Holmes. "A certain Mr. Ferris is building a giant Wheel that theoretically will carry up to forty people in each of its thirty-six railcar-sized viewing cabins. The passengers will ascend some two hundred sixty-four feet into the air at the height of each revolution, giving—Mr. Ferris and the White City designers promise—an amazing view of Lake Michigan, the White City including the Midway Plaisance with all of its other diversions, and the Chicago skyline. What you see there is only the framework of the bottom half of the huge Wheel. They'll soon be bringing in and mounting an axle that I'm told is the heaviest piece of steel ever constructed on this continent. The axle shaft will be some forty-five feet long and will weigh forty-six tons and will have to be strong enough to bear a burden of the Wheel's own steel, carriages, and people that will amount to six times the weight of some cantilever bridge across the Ohio River at Cincinnati that you Americans seem so proud of. The White City people and Mr. Ferris keep promising that the great Wheel will be finished and carrying passengers by the middle of the summer, if not earlier."

"Where did you get all this information, Holmes?" said James. "All these facts and figures don't sound like you."

Holmes turned his back on the White City, leaned back against the railing, and smiled. "It's true that I'm often arithmetically challenged, as my brother Mycroft has pointed out on far too many occasions. But I had a private tour yesterday while you were in the hotel talking to the ailing Mr. Clemens and even a dullard can remember certain facts for a short period of time. It's how one passes through Cambridge or Oxford with Honors, as I'm sure you know."

James watched the White City as the *Columbus* made a wide, cautious arc around the 2,500-foot-long pier extending into Lake Michigan, its surface covered with workers and carts as the linear and then circular Movable Sidewalk took its final shape down the center of the wide pier.

"It will cost ten cents to ride on the Sidewalk the length of the pier where the steamers will drop you the half-mile to the entrance of the Exposition," said Holmes without turning around to look at it. "My guess is that most first-time visitors will try it just for the novelty."

James marveled at the tidy lagoons and carefully groomed streams that ran through the entire White City. Someone had turned a muck-ridden swamp into a cleaner, wider, airier version of James's beloved Venice.

"All in twenty-one months," said James as if reading the author's mind. "Where then will President Cleveland be doing his opening speech and switch-turning?"

Holmes turned and pointed with his own stick. "Do you see through the pillars or the Peristyle to that dome rising at the far end of the Lagoon—right in line with that canvas-shrouded tall pedestal that will be revealed as Saint-Gaudens's huge Statue of the Republic? Yes, the one with the four pavilions, one at each corner. That is the Administration Building where the president and other dignitaries will speak. They will be facing this way—east, toward the Lake and the statue—and one assumes that all the concourses will be flooded with excited American humanity, all the way back to the Peristyle gates."

Holmes handed James a small, folding telescope. The author put the object to his eye, brought the dome into focus, and said, "Are those angels on the upper promenade of that Administration Building...right below the dome?"

"Eight groupings of angels, actually," said Holmes. "All trumpeting the victory of Peace, although I fear they may be a bit overly optimistic about that reality. Besides hundreds of incandescent lights outlining the upper reaches and dome of the Administration Building at night, that upper promenade you're looking at is ringed with those huge gas torches designed to illuminate the golden dome."

"Good heavens," said James, turning his telescopic gaze on the myriad of what looked like huge marble palaces, each festooned with its own multitude of statuary, pinnacles, towers, arches, entablatures, and wildly decorated friezes. "I'm surprised that the denizens of Chicago won't wish to move into the White City once the Exposition is over," he said softly.

"They'd be out of a home after a winter or two, or even after a few months of strong Chicago rainstorms," said Holmes.

James lowered the telescope. "What do you mean?"

"While there's plenty of steel and iron—more than eighteen thousand tons of those metals in the Great Buildings alone, I'm told—not to mention wood, most of what looks like white marble to you is actually made of staff."

"Staff?"

"That's what it's called," said Holmes. "Evidently it's an exotic composition of plaster, cement, and hemp—or some similar fibrous material—that was sort of painted on or sprayed on to look like permanent stone. All of the Great Buildings, most of the State Buildings, and a vast majority of the statuary and bas relief you see is made of staff...in its semi-liquid form a very plastic material, I understand. And lighter than wood. Still, they used more than thirty thousand tons of the stuff to create most of the White City's structures."

"Not meant to be permanent?" asked James with a strange pang of disappointment. He found himself, against all reason and odds, taking pride in what his fellow Americans had created in so short a time.

"No," said Holmes, "although if painted regularly, it might last several years. Left to the elements, all those amazing structures you're admiring are going to melt and rot like Miss Havisham's wedding cake in a year or less."

James handed back the telescope, which Holmes folded and set in his large outer pocket. The *Columbus* made a wide easterly arc and headed back along the shoreline toward the Black City. He was thinking that no nation was better at creating metaphors for itself than America; in this case, the vision of a beautiful, sane, safe, marble future that is all dream and no marble to sustain it.

"Well," said James, still disappointed that his American Venice turned out to be so much marzipan, "I guess the future of the White City is not our problem."

"No," agreed Holmes. "One way or the other, all our problems will be over by the end of May first."

TWO

Monday, April 10, 11:20 a.m.

Three days before James's boat tour to the White City and the day after he'd left his friends in Washington, the author stood at the family cemetery plot in Cambridge. He'd last visited this spot a little more than a decade earlier when he'd rushed to America to be by his dying father's side only to learn when his feet touched the Boston pier that his father had died an hour earlier. On the day of New Year's Eve 1882, James had walked alone up the snowy hillside to his father's grave that had been filled in with the frozen earth only ten days earlier. William, unable to return from Europe in time, had sent a most personal letter to his father but the letter, like Henry, had arrived after the awful fact of death. It had been a very cold day—although with a clear Massachusetts winter sky—and James remembered both the ghost-smoke of his breath in the air as he read the long letter and the growing numbness in his freezing toes. William's long letter had begun "Darling old Father" and had passed through several pages of metaphysical speculation that seemed to Henry much like the continuation of debates and outright arguments William had been having with their father for decades. The letter had ended with "Good-night, my sacred old Father. If I don't see you again—Farewell!! a blessed farewell!" James was sure he had not wept that day a decade earlier because, if he had, the tears would have frozen to his cheeks.

This April day was the antithesis of the last time he was here. In the winter then he'd been able to see the whiteness of a distant field beyond the Charles River, but now leaves blocked most of that view and as they shifted in the warm April breeze, James caught glimpses of homes and shops that hadn't been there in 1882.

A year earlier, when William was in Italy, he'd had a marble urn engraved for sister Alice's ashes. Henry read the words that William had chosen:

*ed essa da martiro
e da essilio venne a questa pace*

James had recognized the passage at once—from the Tenth Book of the *Paradiso* in the *Divine Comedy*—and his translation from the Italian was roughly—"and from martyrdom and banishment it came unto this peace." It seemed appropriate for Alice's pain-filled and largely bedridden life. She had indeed embraced death as an escape for the final decades of her life, although James knew—better than anyone else in the family—that the pain and death-welcoming was, until very near the end, leavened by Alice's mischievous sense of humor and penchant for parody. When William had ordered her diary published, just for the family members, without asking Henry's opinion, Henry had been shocked by the names named and ridiculed. He would have edited the diary severely to avoid such insults to the living (and some recent dead), but perhaps older brother William was right... perhaps Alice defied editing.

In one hand James held the elegant snuffbox containing the small amount of his sister's ashes he'd pilfered after the cremation in England, while in the other hand he held the small gardening trowel he'd purchased in a hardware store not far from their old home on Bolton Street. But James had been as good as his vow not to go look at the now empty-of-family Bolton Street home, or to walk past the impressive home of William and *his* Alice—Alice the wife and mother—on the corner at 95 Irving Street here in Cambridge.

James felt like he'd failed his sister. His plan had been honorable enough—to have one of the brothers (himself, as it had to be) rather than Miss Katharine Loring help spread Alice's ashes, but spread them somewhere Alice had been truly happy. James had simply failed to find such a spot—at least one where the happiness hadn't been dependent upon his sister's Boston Marriage to Miss Loring, such as at the two's Newport home. James knew that he was being foolish and selfish with this after-the-fact jealousy of Katharine Loring. He'd never felt that way while Alice was alive—he'd simply been happy that someone could bring a smile to his sister's face or coax a laugh out of her—but since sister Alice's death and Miss Loring's monopoly in bringing the ashes back here to this sacred spot, the *Jameses'* burial ground, the jealousy and sense of stubbornness about finding a spot for *these* ashes had grown rather than diminished.

But in the end he had surrendered. There had always been a certain unique *oneness* about his sister Alice James, and her ashes should be to-gether...or at least in close proximity. James wasn't about to try to pry open the sealed marble urn.

Making certain that no one was watching him, James knelt and dug a small grave for the snuffbox. The jade and porcelain box had been given to James as a gift in the late 1870's by Richard Monckton Milnes, Lord Houghton, a friend of Henry James, Sr. His father had described Houghton as energetic and fun-filled—Henry Adams back then had told young James that Houghton was "the first wit of London and the maker of men...a great many men", but the lord was 68 or 69 when Henry, Jr., finally met him and was given to using elaborate breakfasts and dinners to "capture" famous artists and writers as if they were so many butterflies.

The ivory snuffbox, for which James had no use save to own it as an object of art, was of the finest Delft porcelain interset with tiny and del-icately carved androgynous human figures which, in their flowing and blowing robes, seemed to be saints or cherubs descended from some 17th Century painting. There was something spiritual in this little box and it was made infinitely more so now by holding his beloved sister's ashes.

As James set the little snuffbox into the small but deep little hole and began troweling dirt back into place, he recalled an early dinner he'd had with Lord Houghton where the fellow diners had included Tennyson, Gladstone, and Dr. Heinrich Schliemann, the fellow who had found and excavated Troy.

Finished with his own excavation and filling-in, Henry stood—feeling the sudden pang of pain in his always-aching back—and brushed off his trousers at the knees. He realized that he should say a little prayer, but there was no prayer in his heart or mind at the moment. He'd already said his good-byes to Alice—she was the only member of the family whose deathbed and long, difficult dying he'd actually attended. He took one last glance at the urn to fulfill any ceremony required.

ed essa da martiro
e da essilio venne a questa pace

* * *

In the hansom cab he'd kept waiting for him in the cemetery, James knew that he'd have to decide what he was going to do. There was only one sane and sensible course of action: the train for New York, for which he had a first class ticket, left from Boston's old central station in one hour. He'd made arrangements with the German steamship company to go aboard the *Spree* with all his baggage this very evening, as soon as he arrived in New York. He would have an excellent dinner and a good night's sleep in his first-class cabin aboard the elegant ocean liner and the *Spree* would depart for Southampton (then London by rail, then home!) in the morning. James would not even have to get dressed to go to the deck to watch the departure since no one was seeing him off; he'd simply sleep late and enjoy breakfasting in his cabin.

But there was the double issue of that damned telegram from Holmes—ordering him to meet the detective on Beacon Hill this afternoon, long after his train had departed, Holmes arrogantly moving him around as if he were a chess piece with no mind of his own—and, more importantly, James's news for Holmes about Professor Moriarty and the astounding meeting of thugs and anarchists that James had risked his life to witness. That was hardly something that James could put in a letter—even if he knew where in damnation Sherlock Holmes *was* at any given time—much less in a telegram.

Well, he'd have to decide soon. The hansom driver was showing signs of irritation and so was his horse.

Logically, there was only one choice he could make. He had to get out of this nightmare. He had to get to the train station, get on that train to New York, have his luggage and himself transferred to the ship, and settle into his stateroom on the *Spree.* Every bit of logic and reason screamed to James that it was time to return to his flat at De Vere Gardens and get back to work on the play that was going to make him a fortune.

"Driver," he called. "To the central railway station. And quickly."

THREE

Monday, April 10, 3:38 p.m.

Holmes ostentatiously checked his watch when the hansom—which had been moving almost at a gallop—came to a stop and a red-faced Henry James stepped out.

"You're almost eight minutes tardy, James," said Holmes. "I was about to give up on you and go on about my business."

James had paid the driver and now his face grew even redder. "Don't you *dare* chide me for being late for this rendezvous! First of all, you insult me in a public telegram telling me to come if it's convenient or *even if it is not convenient.* That may have been a misfired attempt at humor, Mr. Holmes, but it was not something a gentleman would do when communicating via public telegraphy with another gentleman. And as for the time . . . first of all, you very well remember that I lost my valuable watch when you were dragging me through Rock Creek Cemetery and less speakable places at midnight, so I've had to depend upon public timepieces, which are notoriously unreliable in America. And finally, I had to rush to the central Boston railway station to get my luggage and accompany it through heavy traffic to this new North Union Station which isn't *really* north at all, but far west of the city center. Then I had to store my luggage at the new station, which is deucedly crowded this time of day, and then fight Bostonians, who are only half a step up on the Darwinian scale from South Seas cannibals when it comes to refusing to learn how to queue, for a hansom cab to bring me back here. And I shan't bother to tell you what *important plans of my own* that this has ruined for me since . . ."

James stopped because Holmes was openly smiling at him, which made James all the more angry and red-faced.

"Such as missing the sailing of the *Spree* tomorrow evening?" said Holmes.

"How do you...how could you know...where did you..." spluttered James.

"Alas," said Holmes, "even our beloved telegraphy, whether sending communications between gentlemen or just to book a ship's passage, is not as private as it should be. There remain papers and copies of papers, easily accessible to the dedicated voyeur—especially if that dedicated voyeur enters the telegraph office only a moment after the cable-sender has departed. And it is helpful if one can read words upside down, a small trick which I mastered as a child."

James folded his arms across his chest above the curve of his significant belly while attempting to hold in the angry words and sentences that flowed into his mind.

The cab hadn't left and Holmes called to the driver, "Wait here another fifteen minutes or so, my dear man." He handed up some folded currency; the cabbie nodded, touched the brim of his hat, and pulled the hansom to the curb on the opposite side of the street.

"You think this business here will take only fifteen minutes?" hissed James in low tones so the driver would not hear. "I missed my train and ship to England for something that will take only *fifteen minutes?*"

"Of course not," said Holmes. "As promised, we leave for Chicago in"—he checked his watch again—"a little under ninety minutes. But our immediate problem, as you can see, is that there is no four hundred twenty-six and a half address here...the houses on this side of the street go straight from four-twenty-six to four-twenty-eight."

James sighed, obviously wondering at the denseness of a man whom too many people had called a "genius".

"The custom here on this part of Beacon Hill is to have a little room on the upper floor of a carriage house," said James. "Those are the 'halves' that the postal service delivers to."

"Aha!" said Holmes as if *he'd* been the one to come up with this widely known fact. "There's a carriage house or garage down this driveway at four-twenty-six," he said as he started walking down the paved lane.

James caught the tall detective by the sleeve. "The protocol is to approach the carriage-house apartments by walking down the alley. We'll need to go down this way and turn left to find the alley entrance."

"What an absurd protocol," said Holmes, following reluctantly. "The carriage house is visible *right there*." He flung out his left arm although they'd already lost sight of the carriage house at the end of the sloping driveway.

As they turned left on another street—all these streets and many of these homes were familiar to James from both his childhood and his visits home to Bolton Street as an adult—the writer grasped Holmes's upper arm and said, "I have urgent information for you, Holmes. Seriously urgent. Far more important than checking on this address, which shall almost certainly be a dead end. Let me tell you how two days ago I..."

Holmes gently removed the author's hand from his arm and said softly, "I have no doubt that you do have something important to tell me, James. But one thing at a time, old boy. We shall speak to whomever lives at this address and then be on our way to North Station and you may tell me whatever you have to say more at your...let's say...leisure."

James almost turned around and left then. His face grew as red as it had been when he'd arrived and he glared at the side of Holmes's head. He promised himself that he wouldn't say a single word about anything until Holmes asked him for it. So what if he, Henry James, knew the details for Professor Moriarty's plans for multiple assassinations and an anarchist and mob uprising set for May first? If Holmes was going to continue acting this way, Henry James would be damned if he'd share such vital intelligence with the detective.

"Who lives in these one-half numbered carriage-house apartments?" Holmes asked as if that were the most important thing for him to learn that day. "The servants?"

James considered not answering, but his cultivated nature demanded he answer a simple question. "No. Just as in England, if a family can afford servants, they live in the main house, up on the top floor under the eaves usually. These cottages have a tradition of being rented at very low prices to white people—cultivated people—whose jobs or vocations have steeped them in poverty. Local teachers, for instance, or the occasional college student, although the latter is often considered too volatile for these quiet neighborhoods... unless vouched for by multiple letters of reference, of course."

"Of course," said Holmes. He'd found the stairway up to the room or rooms over the still-active carriage house—active if the strong scent of manure from the barn level was any indicator—and took the steps upward two at a time in his eager anticipation.

After several knocks, giving James time to climb the steps more slowly and stand puffing a bit on the landing outside the door, a small, gray-haired lady with cataracts clouding her right eye cautiously opened the door.

Holmes removed his top hat. "Good afternoon, madam. My name is Sherlock Holmes and this is my associate Dr.... excuse me... Mr. James. We've come because I'm an old friend of Miss Irene Adler, the lady to whom you forward the letters sent here to a certain Miss Rebecca Lorne Baxter, and I wish to find her most recent address."

"What did you say your name was?" asked the old lady.

"Ah... Mr. Sherlock Holmes, madam," he said more slowly. "And whom do I have the pleasure of addressing?"

The woman with the white hair, pale white skin, and white cataract paused before saying, "Mrs. Gaddis."

"Were you, by any chance, a teacher for many years, Mrs. Gaddis?" asked Holmes. "Your diction suggests you were."

"I taught for twenty-eight years before retiring with commendations and honors and I don't receive a decent enough pension to afford these tiny two rooms over a smelly stable," said Mrs. Gaddis. "But your name was never mentioned to me by the lady who pays me five dollars a month to forward her mail, so I'm afraid I must close the door, Mr. Holmes."

As gently as he could, Holmes blocked the door from closing with his left foot and a seemingly casual hand set flat on the windowless door. "She must have left some instructions for my arrival," he said quickly. "I know how playful Miss Adler is. Some puzzle or question by which I could identify myself and receive her address from you."

Mrs. Gaddis squinted with her one good eye. "The lady who pays me for passing along her mail—and I shan't say where that final destination for her mail is nor even if it's under a different name than the Mrs. Lorne-Baxter you mentioned—did say that someday an Englishman with a Yorkshire accent might come knocking at my door, and if he did, I should put a question to him to verify his identity."

Holmes had been holding his silky top hat in his hand but now he almost set it atop his greased-back hair and tipped it symbolically. "*I* am that London gentleman she designated," he said happily, trying to jolly the dour Mrs. Gaddis into greater cooperation. "Perhaps you can tell by my English accent."

"Accents can be put on like hats or socks," said Mrs. Gaddis, still frowning. "But I shall ask you the question my benefactress told to me...*if* I can remember it properly."

James almost smiled as Holmes's face showed a quick glimpse of panic at this being a dead end in his quest to find Irene Adler, all because of an elderly former-teacher's faulty memory.

But age obviously hadn't clouded her mind as thoroughly as her vision. "Here's the question I'm to put to the Englishman caller," said Mrs. Gaddis, pulling it from her memory as if taking an aging sheet of parchment down from some high shelf. "What were my last words to him at our last brief meeting?"

Holmes laughed. "Her last words to me were—'Good-night, Mr. Sherlock Holmes',," he said. "But I didn't recognize her when she said it because my friend Dr. Watson and I were in the act of unlocking the door of our home on Baker Street when this thin young lad, short hair slicked back under a derby and wearing an oversized ulster with the collar turned up, said it in passing. Miss Adler was an actress and enjoys...or at least enjoyed...disguises almost as much as I do."

"The words were correct," said Mrs. Gaddis, still frowning. "You wait here and I'll find the copy I made out of her forwarded mail address."

Mrs. Gaddis was back in less than half a minute—James peered past Holmes into her small but tidy, almost cozy, apartment—and she handed Holmes the note card and said, "I believe that completes our conversation, Mr. Holmes."

The detective held up a finger in protest. "Not at all," he said happily. "Common decency, to say nothing of courtesy, compels me to pay you a very little something as mere metaphor for my sincere appreciation of the service you have been carrying out for my friend, Miss Adler, as well as for your help to me in finding that old friend."

Mrs. Gaddis shook her head, held up a blocking hand, and was about to say no when Holmes handed her a $20 bill and released it so she had to grasp it. Whatever she was going to say, she didn't.

"Teachers are the most underappreciated and least recompensed of all our esteemed professional classes," Holmes said quickly, ignoring Mrs. Gaddis's half-hearted attempts to hand the bill back to him. This time he did tip his hat and secure it firmly on his head before clattering down the steps. James nodded and smiled his own faux-appreciation before following Holmes.

*　*　*

While riding to North Station, James asked to see the address the retired teacher had given Holmes. It was, he recognized, very near if not quite on Dupont Circle in Washington.

"So she never left Washington after all," murmured the author. "I'm quite sure that Henry Adams and John Hay have believed her gone all these years."

"It's Adams that gave me this Beacon Hill mail address," said Holmes. "And she's been responding from there for years. Obviously Irene Adler posts the return letter from Washington with an envelope included with her handwriting and the Beacon Hill return address, and Mrs. Gaddis dutifully transfers the letter and posts it from Boston. For five dollars per month help on her rent."

"You're certain that Rebecca Lorne and Irene Adler are...were...the same person?" said James.

"Absolutely certain. If I hadn't been before, the 'identifying question' of her last words to me that night in London—I believe Watson wrote that case up under the title 'A Scandal in Bohemia', a nonsensical title because he felt that he had to hide the identity of the English Royal Personage."

"I'm only surprised that your friend Dr. Watson did not have the king exit, pursued by a bear," said James.

Holmes looked at James blankly for a few seconds and then exploded in that high, almost-cawing, full laughter that James had heard only a few times. Holmes's sharp barks of laughter always startled James.

"Anyway, it was, I believe, the first telling of my cases... *the first short story about the Sherlock Holmes character,* I should say... that appeared in *The Strand Magazine.*"

James had read that story the previous week. It had been in Clara Hay's collection of Holmes's stories. Or Arthur Conan Doyle stories... James was not sure which description applied to reality, if any reality there was.

"I always suspected that Irene Adler had remained in Washington," Holmes was saying.

"Why?"

Holmes reminded James of the bouquet of white violets that appeared as if by magic on Clover Adams's grave every December 6.

"But you're not rushing to Washington to confront her," said James. They were approaching Union Station here in the western reaches of Boston.

"No," said Holmes. "We have tickets for Chicago and much to do there. Besides, the mailing address near Dupont Circle will not be Irene Adler's address. Only another dead end... and this one quite deadly."

James nodded and made an almost swimming-motion in the air, moving that finished discussion aside.

"May I now tell you the details of what I discovered in Washington this past Saturday?" said James. "I assure you it's of the utmost importance."

"We're at the station already and we have to meet someone here," said Holmes. "Why don't you tell me when we get to our first-class carriage? It will just be the three of us."

"Three of us?" repeated James.

FOUR

Monday, April 10, 4:10 p.m.

To Henry James, the new North railway station was Boston's celebration of the modern age. The architecture was noble and the layout oozed common sense: rather than wait outside in the cold and damp under a gigantic open shed roof as in London's great and small stations, here one went down a ramp *inside* the sprawling structure, and the train came in to you on a warm and well-ventilated lower level.

When they'd arrived, James had said, "I'll have to go claim my bags for transfer," but Holmes had taken the handful of baggage check tickets and said, "I'll find some expert help in getting that done for us" and had disappeared for only a moment into the Grand Lobby crowd before returning.

"Are you sure..." began James. His continuing nightmare was having his steamer trunk or other pieces of his baggage, including the portmanteau filled with beginnings of his stories and the long, thrice-bescribbled scripts for his current and future plays, disappear during one of these American railway adventures. How much happier he would have been, he realized, if both he and his luggage were safely aboard the good ship *Spree* and safely out of sight of land by now.

Holmes led the way through the mob and down the graceful ramps to where signs announced that their train to Chicago would be leaving in fifteen minutes.

"'Ere you are, Mr. 'olmes, Mr. James, sir," piped up an unmistakably cockney voice.

James was startled at the sight of a short, rail-thin lad whose un-selfconscious grin showed where adult teeth had grown in only to be knocked out. The boy was obviously of that group known in London as "street Arabs" since before Charles Dickens's day. Yet he was dressed well in English spring tweed suit with tailored jacket and waistcoat, proper knicker trousers and quality wool knee socks, and well-polished quality London-made shoes. Even his cap, which he'd swept off when he'd presented Holmes and James with the baggage cart piled high with their luggage, was new and well-made, probably in Scotland.

"Give the tickets to that porter two coaches down and he'll arrange our luggage properly," directed Holmes. "Bring back to our compartment Mr. James's portmanteau—it has his initials on it—and my briefcase and small tan carrying case."

"Right you are, guv'ner," said the boy and disappeared in the gathering crowd, pulling the massive baggage cart behind him.

"You trust that strange child?" asked James.

Holmes gave him a strange half-smile. "More than you can know, James," he said softly. "More than you can know."

The detective went to a nearby stand to purchase some newspapers and magazines for the trip, so they hadn't yet boarded when the boy returned, handing James his portmanteau and Holmes two well-traveled pieces of personal luggage along with a new set of baggage-check slips. The boy stared straight at the author with a look that fell just short of insolence but certainly was not appropriately deferential.

"Nice to see you again, Mr. James," said the boy. James heard the "Misteh Jimes" and could almost name the streets within hearing distance of the bells of St. Mary-le-Bow Church where this young cockney had eked out his living in London.

James thought of all the porters and messengers they'd met or used on this trip, but none matched up with this strangely well-dressed lad—and he was sure he'd never seen the boy *before* this trip—so he said coolly, "I don't believe we've ever met, young man."

Again that too-wide, unselfconscious, missing-toothed smile. "But you saw me and I saw you a-seeing me, sir."

James smiled but shook his head. "I don't believe so."

The boarding area had emptied out as most of the rushing passengers up near the first-class cars had already gone aboard to claim their cabins. James and the boy were about ten or twelve feet apart when the youngster walked quickly toward the writer—so quickly and with such a sense of confidence bordering on aggression that James found himself gripping his walking stick with both hands—but the boy stopped only a pace or two in front of James, threw both arms in the air as if he were celebrating something, and, almost faster than the eye could follow, did two arching back handsprings—landing on his hands, flipping even higher to come down on his feet again, and not pausing even an instant there before performing a complete somersault in mid-air, his body descending parallel to the concrete boarding platform in the fraction of a second before Holmes grabbed the spread legs—now wrapped securely around Holmes's middle—and held the boy poised there horizontally with nothing but Holmes's powerful fingers and hands keeping him up.

Then Holmes gave a sort of juggler's cry, the boy put his palms together, arms straight above him as if he were diving into water rather than onto an unyielding concrete platform or iron tracks, and in a display of strength almost beyond James's comprehension, Holmes gripped the rigid boy's calves and extended the diver's form higher than the detective's or James's shoulders, then giving another cry—James realized dully that it was one acrobat's communication with another—he tossed the boy spinning out over the platform, caught him by the ankles, and held the lad there vertically, the boy's praying hands almost touching the platform.

Then Holmes went to one knee, the boy used that knee as a diving board, and leaped forward in a perfect head-first arc, hugging his knees as he turned in the air, to land lightly on his feet in front of James, arms still over his head.

The movements had jogged James's memory.

"Good God . . . the two of you . . . the chimney sweeps on the Camerons' rooftop . . ." gasped James.

Holmes gave one of his quick twitches of a smile.

"*You* had a Mohawk strip of orange hair," accused James, pointing at Holmes. "And you, *spikes* of green hair," he said to the boy.

"It's nice to be 'preciated, guv'ner," grinned the lad.

James was still blinking like a sun-blinded lizard. He turned toward Holmes again. "Why the 'Flying Vernettis'?"

"My grandmother on my mother's side was a Vernet," said Holmes, giving the name its proper French pronunciation. "The Vernets were artists. I felt that the Flying Vernettis sounded suitably acrobatic."

"To what *possible* purpose?" cried James. "All that week, Hay and others told me, the two acrobatic chimney sweeps had done the Cabot Lodges' home, Don Cameron's where I saw you perform, even Hay's house where you'd stayed..."

"I needed certain documents," Holmes said coolly. "Old letters, to be precise, although at least one lady's diary was included. It's so nice, after the sweeps have laid down newspapers on every surface in m'lady's boudoir to keep the soot from covering everything, they lock the door to the room and tell servants to stay clear."

"Those bedroom fireplaces are tiny things..." began James.

"Mr. Henry James," said Holmes stepping forward, "I take great pleasure in introducing you to Wiggins Two."

James remembered the telegram from Holmes's brother Mycroft he'd sneakily read — "Wiggins Two arrived safely in New York today."

"What happened to Wiggins One?" he heard himself asking.

"Oh, he grew up to where he was of no further use to me," said Holmes.

"Also," laughed Wiggins Two, "my brother's in the clink."

"For what crime?" asked James.

"Ah...the Holy Trinity, sir," said Wiggins Two. "Breakin', enterin', and resistin' arrest. 'E'll be there a few years, sir."

"Wiggins Two also answers to the name Moth," said Holmes. "Sometimes pronounced in the old English form that rhymes with 'mote'."

"Since a mere mote but a mighty mote I am indeed, Misteh Jimes," said the boy.

A conductor stepped down and spoke through a cloud of steam. "It is time to board, gentlemen."

* * *

It turned out that the Wiggins Two Moth had his own first-class bed-room right next to the one shared by Holmes and James, but the boy stayed in their compartment until the train had left the Boston suburbs behind and they were flashing past small white farms, stone walls, and green pastures.

"Well, I guess I'll go check on what the Yanks call a club car and round me up a pint," Wiggins Two said, sliding open the compartment door.

"They won't sell alcohol to a boy," said James.

"Oh, no, sir," agreed the Moth, clinking coins together in his pocket. "But they understand that I'm just fetchin' a couple of glasses for me two guardians, kindly gentlemen that they are."

Then they were alone and Holmes leaned forward and spoke to James where he sat dazed on the bench opposite. "You had something private and important to tell me, James."

Caught off guard, James needed a minute to arrange the events of the previous weekend in succinct but complete form, but then the words came rolling out of him.

"You actually saw Professor Moriarty on the street and followed him?" interrupted Holmes with a tone of amazement.

"Yes, that's what I've been telling you!"

"How did you know it was Moriarty?"

"Because I looked at his photograph in the mathematics-physics mag-azine at the Library of Congress," spluttered out James. "And he was photographed in Leipzig just last year, eighteen ninety-two, so I knew you'd lied twice—once to the world with your and Dr. Watson's tale of you and the Professor dying at Reichenbach Falls, and then you lying to me about having only made up Moriarty—created him as a figment of your imagination, were your exact words. Why did you lie to me, Holmes?"

The detective's cool, gray gaze met the author's angry, gray glare.

"Anything I've said that distorted the truth in some small way was done to protect you from harm, James," said Holmes.

"'Distorted the truth in some small way'," repeated James with a dramatic scoffing noise. "I'd say that denying the existence of Professor James

Moriarty and his plans for assassinations and widespread anarchy and riots is a bit more than *'some small way'!"*

Holmes only nodded slowly, as if not in full agreement yet on the seriousness of his infraction to honor, trust, friendship . . . and it just made Henry James all the more angry. "Professor Moriarty is a fiend in human form, Holmes! I *saw* him! I *heard* him! He was planning and coordinating the deaths of hundreds of people—the unwitting police in a dozen cities, the President and Vice-President of the United States, God knows how many innocent bystanders—as coolly as a businessman might announce a new sales campaign to his staff."

"That's rather well put, James," Holmes said with another twitch of an approving smile. "Well said, indeed."

James only grunted. He was in no mood to receive Mr. Sherlock Holmes's approval.

"Continue with your story of Saturday afternoon's encounter," said Holmes.

Later, James was surprised to see from Holmes's watch that it had taken him another half hour to tell the whole story. He was blushing slightly, since the part about concealing himself while the mob members took turns firing shotguns and rifles at the "rat" was more florid and less likely than any fiction he'd ever produced.

James readied himself for a long cross-examination, an interrogation, from the slightly frowning detective, but all Holmes said was, "How did you feel?"

"How did I *feel?*" James realized that he had almost shouted the words, glanced apprehensively toward the compartment's closed doors, and moderated his tone. "All that information for you—times of the assassination, plans for mob uprising and anarchists' murders across the United States, in London and in Europe, and you want to know how I *felt?*"

"Yes," said Holmes. "For instance, when you thought they were shooting at you and the shotgun blast shook the entire beam you were hiding on. How did you *feel,* James?"

The author had to pause a moment. He knew that the question really did not deserve an answer—there were far too many important questions he could and should have answered about the assembly of thugs and Professor Moriarty's plans—but he also realized that he'd quietly been asking himself the same question for the last two days. How had he felt during this, the most out-of-all-context almost absurdly unreal-feeling event of his lifetime. Frightened? Yes, but that was not the primary sensation.

"Alive," he said at last. "I felt very much...alive."

Holmes grinned his full grin, patted James's knee as if the master author were a retriever dog who'd brought back the pheasant unchewed, and said, "That being the case, I think you are going to enjoy the next couple of weeks."

FIVE

Wednesday, April 12, 8:05 a.m.

Holmes arrived in Haymarket Square and immediately spotted Inspector Bonfield standing across the street near the alley. Carriage and cargo traffic was heavy on Desplaines Street as was pedestrian traffic. Holmes waited for a break in the traffic and jogged across the street, accepting the inspector's eager handshake almost before Holmes had come to a stop.

"It's very good to see you again, Mr. Holmes," said Inspector Bonfield.

"And you, Inspector. Congratulations on your various promotions." Holmes had been here in May and June of 1886, gathering evidence for the trial of the anarchists who'd been behind the Haymarket riot where 8 policemen and 3 civilians had died. Bonfield had been a Captain then but the information he'd brought to the prosecution in the trial of the 8 anarchists had quickly earned him "Inspector" status and the supervision of the Chicago Police Department's Detective Bureau. Bonfield had also been detached to the Columbian Exposition to train and supervise the 200 or so plainclothes detectives who, among them, knew the face and modus operandi of every pickpocket, thief, and con artist in a seven-state region. The so-called "Columbian Guard", all decked out in baby-blue uniforms and, on occasion, their red and yellow capes, carried a cute little ornamental sword. Bonfield's plainclothes boys carried a heavy sap, a pair of brass knuckles, and a loaded pistol in their suit pockets.

"The promotions were aimed poorly," said Bonfield, who still seemed as quiet, reserved, and competent as Holmes had found him seven years earlier. "All accolades should have gone to you, Mr. Holmes."

The detective waved that away. "I see you have a statue commemorating that May fourth," said Holmes. "And a uniformed police officer to guard it."

Bonfield nodded. "That's a twenty-four-hour guard, Mr. Holmes. Vandals—either the anarchists or those countless thousands who've come to look at the anarchist-killers as social heroes—have beaten the statue apart with sledgehammers, scribbled obscene graffiti on it, painted it green—very disrespectful. So now we keep a man here all day and all night."

Holmes pulled out his pipe and began tamping in tobacco. Henry James had convinced him, for the sake of his American friends if for no other reason, to use a more expensive and less shockingly aromatic brand of tobacco while he was here in the States.

"You will never guess what is scheduled for Waldheim Cemetery for the day of May fourth," said Bonfield, showing more anger in his expression than Holmes had ever before seen in that stable younger man.

"Waldheim," repeated Holmes, puffing his pipe to life and setting away in his trouser pocket—next to the .38-caliber lemon-squeezer pistol—the unique lighter. "That's where the four hanged anarchists were buried, was it not?"

"It was," said Bonfield. "Now it's a shrine to the 'brave union organizers' who ambushed my men and me here seven years ago. They're unveiling a monument to the killers—or martyrs, to the popular press's point of view—and the monument is said to be taller than this twenty-foot statue memorializing the eight police who died that day. Early estimates suggest that there may be eight thousand or more people turning out in Waldheim Cemetery for the radical ceremony. We wouldn't get a dozen citizens if we held a memorial service here for the policemen who died."

"History is a perverse mechanism," said Holmes between puffs. "It demands the blood of martyrs—real or invented—the way a machine requires oil."

Inspector Bonfield grunted, checked the brief gap in the traffic, and stepped out onto the street, motioning for Holmes to follow. "This has been paved over by hot top since the riot and trial," said Bonfield, "but you'll remember that it was about here" — the Inspector's polished shoe came down on an unremarkable spot — "that you showed me the egg-shaped indentation in the cedar-block paving of that time, where the heavy bomb had first struck and..." Bonfield stepped further out into the street. "It was *here* where you noticed the smooth, oval crater where the bomb had actually exploded. By lining up the small impact dent with the actual crater — using red string in the model you provided us — we were able to show that the bomb had been thrown from the alley, not from somewhere south of the advancing police as the defense would have had the jury to believe."

Inspector Bonfield was so immersed in the memory that he failed to notice a large dray wagon with four huge horses bearing down on him. Holmes gathered the police detective by the elbow and moved him safely to the curb opposite the alley.

"The bomb went off right beneath Patrolman Mathias Degan," continued Bonfield, speaking as if from a mesmeric trance. "Degan was a friend of mine. The shrapnel that killed him was no bigger than your thumbnail, Mr. Holmes. The doctor gave it to me and I have it, in my bureau. But it severed Mathias's femoral artery and he bled to death, right there on where the cedar paving blocks used to be. And in my arms."

"We proved that six of the eight policemen who had been shot — rather than those wounded by bomb shrapnel — had been shot at a downward angle," said Holmes. "Someone firing a rifle from that window up there, next to the alley." He pointed at the window of the corner shop facing Desplaines Street.

"The prosecution made that case but the jury made nothing of it," said Inspector Bonfield. "But your evidence, Mr. Holmes, did prove that the carpenter Rudolph Schnaubelt was the man who threw the bomb from that alley right at the cluster of police."

"Showed it beyond a doubt," agreed Holmes. "But you've never apprehended or arrested him."

Inspector Bonfield held his hands out. "How can we arrest him if we can't find him, Mr. Holmes? We've tracked down leads saying

Schnaubelt was in Pittsburgh, in Santo Domingo, that he'd died in California, that he was begging in the streets of Honduras, that he was living in wealth in Mexico. That socialist rag—the *Arbeiter-Zeitung*—published a letter reportedly from Schnaubelt and the letter had been postmarked from Christiania, Norway. The man is a phantom, Mr. Holmes."

"The man—Schnaubelt—has been making a good living as a manufacturer of farm machinery in Buenos Aires," said Holmes. "He arrived in Argentina a month after the Haymarket Square riot and has lived and prospered there ever since."

"Why didn't you tell us this?"

"I cabled all the information—including Schnaubelt's work and living address—to your major and superintendent of police in early eighteen eighty-seven," said Holmes. "There was no reply. I sent a second cable with the same information, this time including various aliases Schnaubelt had used. Again...I received no response."

Bonfield had taken off his cap and looked as if he was preparing to rip clumps of his hair out by the roots.

Holmes glanced at his watch and removed his pipe. "It's getting late, Inspector. You're my liaison while we follow the carriage route that will carry President Cleveland to the Exposition grounds, and then I am scheduled to receive a quick tour of the White City itself. But we'll have to trot to get to the Lexington Hotel by their departure time."

"We'll let the horse do the trotting," said Inspector Bonfield. He whistled and a sleek black carriage, driven by a uniformed Chicago P.D. patrolman, glided up. The driver jumped down and opened the carriage door for them.

*   *   *

There were two carriages waiting for Bonfield and Holmes outside the Lexington Hotel at the intersection of 22nd Street and Michigan Avenue. The first was an oversized canopy-covered surrey with three bench-rows of seats facing forward rather than the usual two, plus a fourth bench seat looking backward. It was filled with uniformed police officers.

The second was an open carriage—much more comfortable look-ing—and the driver was a big man with bright blue eyes and a trim salt-and-pepper beard that looked a bit like that of former President Ulysses S. Grant. Holmes estimated from the man's hands that he might be around sixty, but there were no wrinkles, save for a few laugh-lines, on his face. He wore a working man's comfortable corduroy trousers and well-worn boots, but also a rather expensive-looking wool hacking jacket. Most noticeable was the black slouch hat set back on his head as if he wanted the April sun to turn his winter-pale forehead pink.

Inspector Bonfield said, "Mr. Sherlock Holmes, may I have the honor of introducing you to our mayor-elect, Mr. Carter Henry Harrison."

The handshake was firm without being bruising. "I'm delighted, ab-solutely delighted, to meet you, Mr. Holmes!" said Harrison.

"Mayor-elect?" asked Holmes.

"I was elected for a fifth term—not sequential, I'm ashamed to say—on April fourth," said Harrison. "But I don't officially take office until the twentieth. But Mayor Washburne was busy sulking and clean-ing out his office so I jumped at the chance to show you the route we'll be taking with President Cleveland."

One of the police officers was walking back to the mayor's carriage and the mayor said in a very soft voice to Bonfield, "Uh-oh, here comes McClaughry."

Holmes could see by the badges McClaughry was the Superintendent of the Chicago Police Force. Mayor Harrison introduced him as such and again there was a handshake, this one even more enthusiastic.

"Mr. Holmes, I have been so looking forward to meeting you!" said Chief McClaughry. "When I was warden of the Illinois State Prison at Joliet, I was responsible for creating America's first full system of *bertillonage.* You use that system, I believe."

"To be honest, I know and respect Monsieur Bertillon and have worked with him in Paris, but I've found that many of his categories of identifying criminals—bone length, centimeters of forehead, and all that—are rather unworkable. So these days I concentrate almost exclu-sively on fingerprints."

"Ahhh," said Superintendent McClaughry, seeming a bit cast down by

Holmes's lack of enthusiasm toward the full category of *bertillonage*. "Yes, well we have fingerprint cards, as well. More than five hundred at present. Do you keep your own cards, sir, or depend upon Scotland Yard's?"

"I'm sorry to say that Scotland Yard has not yet adopted fingerprinting as a universal practice," said Holmes. "But I have an assistant who visits the prisons and we make our own cards—photograph of the suspect on front, prints of all fingers and the palm on back. I believe I have about three thousand such cards on file."

Superintendent McClaughry was visibly startled at this information.

"Bob," said Mayor-elect Harrison, "it's time to move out. You're welcome to ride with us and Bonfield can ride with the patrolmen."

"No, I shall ride with my men," McClaughry said stiffly. "It was a great, great pleasure, Mr. Holmes, and I do hope we meet again when we have time to discuss Bertillon's methods and other forensic matters." A final handshake and the chief of police marched back to his crowded surrey.

"Hop on up here next to me, Mr. Holmes," said Harrison. "Bonnie, you get in back with Mr. Drummond. I believe you know Drummond, do you not, Mr. Holmes?"

Holmes nodded at the Secret Service director. "Yes. A pleasure to see you here, sir."

Drummond smiled and returned the nod.

"All right, it's time," said the mayor-elect and touched the two horses gently with his whip.

"I presume that President Cleveland will be staying there at the Lexington Hotel," said Holmes.

"Yep," said Harrison. "It's got the largest suite in town. But if it had been me choosing a hotel for the president, I would have picked one on a paved street."

Holmes had noticed that this stretch of Michigan Avenue was more yellow dirt than pavement.

"Just so it doesn't rain on Opening Day, we'll be okay," said Harrison. "This was the furthest-south high-quality hotel, built just last year, so I suppose it makes sense. It shouldn't take more than about twenty, twenty-five minutes to get to the Fair going down Michigan Avenue."

"Too bad Superintendent McClaughry didn't choose to ride with us," said Drummond from his place behind the mayor. "We need to discuss C.P.D. security arrangements as well as the Columbian Guard security."

Harrison chuckled and adjusted the brim of his black slouch hat to keep the sun out of his eyes. "Chief McClaughry is a good man. And a dedicated reformer. He sent me his letter of resignation on the day I was elected."

"Why?" said Holmes.

Harrison grinned. "All of the things Bob wants to reform—gambling, kickbacks to party officials, drinking, dallying with the ladies of the night—are more or less the things I most enjoy doing."

"Mayor Harrison has very strong support amongst the working class," said Inspector Bonfield from behind Sherlock. "Even among the colored folk."

Holmes decided that this was all the local politics he needed to hear. More than enough, actually. He said, "How many officers in Chicago's police force, mayor?"

"A little over three thousand," said Harrison. "We'll have mounted officers riding along and ahead when the actual procession from the Lexington gets going, but my guess is that a couple hundred thousand folks will be walking and riding behind us. Joining the parade, so to speak."

"And there are two thousand–some Columbian Guards *inside* the Fair," said Sherlock.

"That number of uniformed officers," said Bonfield. "Plus about two hundred plainclothes detectives under my supervision on the fairgrounds—both in the White City and along the Midway Plaisance where we expect the pickpockets and others to do most of their work."

"Hand-picked detectives?" asked Holmes.

"Handpicked not just from the C.P.D. but from all over the United States," said Inspector Bonfield.

"Mr. Drummond, what about your agents?" said Holmes.

Mayor Harrison broke in. "When Mr. Drummond showed up this morning and told me that he was from the Treasury Department, I was sure the jig was up. All my back taxes catching up to me."

"Someday, Mr. Mayor," Drummond said softly. "Someday." To Holmes he said, "I'll have fifty-five Secret Service agents in place when President Cleveland gets to the Exposition grounds. Eight of them are master marksmen and they've been checked out with the newest army sniper rifles. Six are on permanent detail with the president."

"Tall men, I hope," said Holmes.

"None under six foot three," said Drummond. "But, of course, no one can be standing in front of the president when he gives his opening address."

"How many carriages will be in this procession?" asked Holmes.

Harrison grinned again. "My guess is somewhere between twenty and twenty-five coaches. Mr. Cleveland and his immediate entourage will be in a landau. Very Important Chicagoans keep coming out of the woodwork like cockroaches and they all want to be in President Cleveland's procession to the Fair. All I know for sure is that I'll be in the last carriage, whatever number that will be."

"Why is that?" asked Holmes.

"Because I'm going to get the most applause and happy shouts from the crowd of anyone in the procession," said Harrison who was obviously just stating a fact rather than bragging. "I wouldn't want President Cleveland to hear that if I were ahead of him. It might hurt his feelings."

"Does the landau have a top?" asked Drummond.

"A foldable top," said Inspector Bonfield. "It'll be folded back so that everyone, even those in the higher buildings, can see the president. Unless it's raining, of course."

"Pray for rain," Drummond said softly, speaking to himself.

"Oh, Mr. Mayor," said Bonfield. "Mr. Holmes informed me that he knows the whereabouts of Rudolph Schnaubelt...the Haymarket Square bomb-thrower."

"You don't have to tell me who Rudolph Schnaubelt is, goddamnit," snarled Harrison. "I've had enough nightmares about the sonofabitch. Where do you think he is, Mr. Holmes?"

"I know exactly where he is," said Holmes and gave the mayor Schnaubelt's farm business and personal addresses in Buenos Aires.

"Well I'll be dipped in shit," said Harrison. "Bonnie, can't you send some of your boys down there to Buenos Aires to get that murdering reptile?"

"We have no extradition arrangements with Argentina, Mr. Mayor."

"God damn it, I know that," said Harrison. "I mean *get* him. A black bag job. Haul that goddamn anarchist back here to Chicago for a fair trial and very public hanging."

"If the Argentinian authorities were to discover a plot like that, it would mean war," Bonfield said softly.

"It'll be a sad day when the United States of America can't whip some pissant country like Argentina," said Harrison. "Okay, Bonnie, maybe we could just send someone down to shoot the sonofabitch. Bang! Take a picture of the corpse for the Chicago papers. No muss, no fuss."

"We should talk about this later," said Bonfield.

"You're right!" laughed Harrison. "I have my favorite literary hero of all time right here in my carriage to ask questions of. Tell me, Mr. Holmes, in 'The Sign of the Four', you were injecting a seven-percent solution of cocaine into your arm or wrist when you were bored. Was that accurate?"

"A habit I abandoned after my friend Dr. Watson convinced me that—how did the good doctor put it?—that the game was not worth the candle." Holmes saw no reason to mention his morning injection of this more powerful heroic drug or the fact that he planned to inject it twice more before this day was over.

"Ah, good," cried Harrison. "So tell me, if you are free to do so, in that same adventure, do you think the lovely Miss Mary Morstan had romantic designs on you? Did she just settle, as we say, by marrying Dr. Watson?"

Holmes looked up at the clear sky and sighed. This was going to be a long carriage ride.

SIX

Wednesday, April 12, 3:20 p.m.

Can I get you something to help you feel better?" asked James.

"A .40-caliber six-shooter so that I can blow my brains out," said Sam Clemens. "Or, since I am a devout coward, perhaps some painless poison that tastes like lemonade."

"Anything other than that?" asked James. He was sitting on a chair by the window a few feet from where Clemens, in his nightshirt, lay in bed. There were medicines and half-filled glasses on the bedside table and a pile of newspapers tossed on the only other chair.

"One doctor says this is just a bad case of the common grippe and he's predicted every day in the last eleven days that I'd be up and out of this bed on the next day," said Clemens between coughs. "The other doctor who's looked in on me says that it's pneumonia and that at my advanced age...fifty-eight...I should get my will in order and start getting measured for my coffin. I have the strongest urge to put these two medicos in a pit and see which one comes out alive."

James smiled at that.

"What brought you and Mr. Sherlock Holmes to the Great Northern Hotel anyway?" asked Clemens, setting down his awful-smelling cigar long enough to drink from a tall glass of colored fluid, grimace at its taste, and pick up the smoking cigar again.

"Holmes chose it," said James. Clemens had one of the corner rooms which included three tall windows in the curving bay, and James had all three open to the relatively fresh air of downtown Chicago. This hotel was at the corner of Jackson and Dearborn and this was about all that James knew of Chicago geography.

"He overheard a clerk telling a bellboy to take up a fresh pitcher of water with lemons to your room," added James. "That's how I knew you were here. I was surprised. When I was told you were ill, I thought I should check in on you."

"That's right neighborly," said Clemens and stopped to cough. It was a deep, phlegmy cough and James leaned back a little more into the fresh air. "I plan to leave for New York tomorrow, Mr. James, if I have to do so in a coffin with a chunk of aged Limburger cheese on my chest for verisimilitude. I may have to ask you to be my pallbearer."

Clemens coughed and drank from the glass again. He poured more colored liquid from a quart-size bottle into the glass.

"Is that cough syrup of some sort?" asked James.

"Of some sort," said Clemens and took another long drink. "It's laudanum. Liquid opium. A gift from the gods. My second doctor isn't shy about prescribing it by the hogshead barrel. So far it's the only thing that's smoothed this cough."

Wonderful, thought James. *Holmes is injecting himself with that new heroin drug every day and Clemens—Mark Twain!—is busy turning himself into a laudanum addict.*

"Did you get your business done here in Chicago?" asked James. "You told us in Hartford that you had people to see."

Clemens snorted. "I made the rounds of interested investors in Paige's typesetting machine, but they are small-minded, James. Small-minded. They insist on seeing a working example of the typesetter. They are prejudiced in favor of earning their money back with interest."

"And Paige doesn't have a working model?"

"He tells me almost every other week that he has a perfect working model," said Clemens. "But when I rush to see it and get within fifty miles of him, the machine either quits working or Paige decides to dismantle it and improve it in some arcane mechanical way. He's in Chicago to set up a second factory to produce the things while the first factory has yet to spit out a model that works for more than two minutes at a time."

"Did you see Mr. Paige while you were here?"

Clemens drank deeply from his glass of laudanum and refilled the glass from the bottle. "He's been wonderfully attentive, visited my sick-room at least six times, staying hours each time."

"And?" said James after a silence that had Clemens staring at nothing.

"And do you remember," said Clemens, glaring at James from under his bushy white eyebrows, "how I said that Paige could convince a fish to come out of the water and take a walk with him?"

"Yes."

"Well, this time he convinced this particular fish to come out, take a walk with him, climb a tree, and make noises like a parakeet."

James didn't know what to say to that so he remained silent, trying to breathe the fresh air from the open windows rather than the odious air from Clemens's cheap cigar.

"I came to demand—not request, not ask nicely for, but to *demand,*" continued Clemens, "that Paige immediately refund me the last thirty thousand dollars I'd put into this project. I need it. I'd borrowed from my little publishing venture to pay for the investment in the typesetter and now circumstances demand that I borrow from the typesetter invest-ment to keep my publishing house afloat. So I came to demand, in no uncertain terms, thirty thousand dollars of the hundred and ninety thou-sand dollars that I've poured into Paige's bottomless pit."

"And did he pay up?" asked Henry James.

"It ended with me writing him a check for fifty thousand more dol-lars," grumbled Clemens. "So that he can make those 'last few little improvements' before the automatic typesetting machine sets the pub-lishing world on its ear and I become a millionaire." Clemens coughed fiercely and, when he'd caught his breath and drunk some laudanum, said, "I finned myself far up and out of the crick this time. Livy will kill me."

"I hope it works out," said James who had never invested in anything save for his own talent.

"Say, where's your friend Sherlock Holmes these days?" asked Clemens.

"Today he went to meet various people at the White City," said James.

"Have you seen the Exposition yet, James?"

"Not yet."

"The White City is yet another thing in this life that I shall never see," sighed Clemens. Then, without any preamble, Clemens said, "Does Holmes still believe that he might be a fictional person rather than real?"

Taken back a bit, James finally said, "I believe he does."

"He may be right," said Clemens.

"Why do you say that, sir?"

"I've read the stories in *The Strand* and the novellas, and the Sherlock Holmes there strikes me as a particularly unrealistic fellow. His adventures sound contrived."

"You may remember Holmes saying in New York that he wasn't totally happy with Dr. Watson's representations of either him or his science of deduction," said James. "The tales may be true, but written by a mediocre mind."

"In the past weeks I've been thinking," said Clemens. "I doubt that there is any 'Dr. Watson'. It's all that Conan Doyle fellow creating a fictional narrator to relate the fictional tales of a fictional detective."

"Holmes says that Conan Doyle is his friend Watson's agent and editor," said James. "He says that Dr. John Watson shuns the spotlight and that he allows Doyle to represent him."

"But what if Holmes *is* a fictional character and this whole assassination plot is part of some melodramatic tale? All make-believe?" said Clemens, coughing more and drinking more of the laudanum mixture. "Where does that leave you and me, Mr. Henry James?"

"How do you mean?" said James, knowing full well what Clemens was leading up to.

"It would mean that *we* are fictional characters in this instance as well," said Clemens, staring balefully out from under his shaggy eyebrows. "You chosen as his Sancho Panza...or perhaps as his Boswell...and me as occasional comedy relief."

"I'll never be his Boswell," James said flatly.

"Have you ever thought, James, of the relationship between you and the characters you've created?"

"I'm not sure what you mean," James said, knowing full well what the humorist meant.

"I mean that you're God to them," said Clemens, "just as I am God to my small worlds of fictional people. You create them. You put them through their fictional paces. You decide their emotions and you decide when it's time for them to die. In other words, we're God to our characters."

James shook his head. "My characters have a certain life of their own," he said softly.

"Oh," said Clemens and surrendered to a spasm of phlegmy coughing. "Does that mean that Isabella Archer is having tea in England or Europe right now?"

"No," said James, "but it means there are depths to her...to Isabel's...character that I haven't explored."

"This is writers' doubletalk," said Clemens, drinking deeply from his glass. "We love to pretend that our characters have some lives of their own...but they don't, James. You know it and I know it. We move them around like puppets in a Punch and Judy show. Have you read any of my books, sir?"

"I've not yet had that pleasure," said James, surprised by the question. Writers didn't ask other writers for opinions of their work. It just wasn't done.

Clemens laughed. "Well, I've tried to read yours," said the white-haired author. "I declare, James, reading your prose is like translating medieval German. You have forty-two freight cars loaded with subordinate clauses being pushed along by a tiny cluster of underpowered engine-verbs tucked in at the end of the sentence. Reading your books is like listening to a man on a soapbox argue with himself, interrupting himself every few seconds."

James smiled thinly. "My brother William would agree with you."

"But still...with Isabella Archer and a few of your other characters..." Clemens's voice trailed off. He turned to stare fiercely at James again. "Do you know *why* Isabella Archer made that damned-fool self-destructive decision at the end of the book? Was that your plan all along or did the character take on some autonomy and make her life-ruining decision on her own?"

James lifted his hands, palms up. He was not going to discuss Isabella

Archer or any of his other books or characters with this laudanum-addled American.

"You hear your characters' voices in your head or you don't," said Clemens, speaking to himself. "Do you happen to remember that I published a book called *The Adventures of Huckleberry Finn* about five years ago?"

"I remember," said James.

Clemens looked at him again. "For months—years, really, since I'd set the book aside for a long time—I heard Huck's voice in my head as clearly as I heard my beloved Livy calling me to dinner. Huck was with me when I went to sleep at night and he was waiting for me when I woke up. And then...near what should have been the end of the story when they're off the raft for the last time and Huck's slave friend Jim has been captured...Huck just left me. He just lit out for the territory without me. I could no longer hear his voice, no longer look through his eyes. I was just a man putting words on paper."

"What did you do?" asked James, more interested in this topic and in the answer than he could show.

Clemens licked his lips. "I brought in Tom Sawyer from *his* book, turned Huck into the shallow supporting character he'd been in that Tom-Sawyer book, and essentially let the most important book I've ever written turn into another boy's book," said Clemens. "All games and coincidences and no-harm-done-to-anyone with Tom, a character whom I knew *shouldn't even be in this novel,* making the decisions."

"That sort of situation is unfortunate," James said softly. "And I am sure that it happens to all of us in writing one novel or the other."

Clemens shook his head. "Have you read the novel *Robert Elsmere?*"

"I've heard the title but haven't had the pleasure of reading it," said James.

"It created quite a sensation about five years ago and caused the rumpus," said Clemens. "It was written by Mrs. Humphry Ward. It advocated a Christianity based on social concerns and help for one's fellow man rather than on Scripture or theology. She made a lot of devout enemies."

James waited.

"Anyway," continued Clemens after some coughing and expectorating, "I copied a sentence from that long, sometimes dismal book because it relates to what we're discussing. Mrs. Ward wrote—and I remember it clearly—'I cannot conceive of God as the arch-plotter against His own creation'."

"That doesn't sound very radical," said James.

Clemens rounded on him again. "But *we're* God to the world and characters we create, James. And we plot against them all the time. We kill them off, maul and scar them, make them lose their hopes and dearest loves. We conspire against our characters daily. But in the Huck Finn book, I lost my nerve, James. I lost Huck's voice and then I lost my nerve. Or maybe—probably—it was the other way around. I so loved Huckleberry Finn that I failed to plot against him and the rest of my creation as I should have. If Huck's voice had stayed with me—if I'd had the courage to listen to it—I would have had nigger Jim captured and sold down the river to endless slavery in front of Huck's eyes and in spite of all of Huck's efforts—or at the very least had the decency and mercy to kill Jim and Huck—rather than bring Tom Sawyer into the tale to end it as a mere *boy's book*."

Clemens spat out the last two words.

"What has this to do with the question of whether Sherlock Holmes is fictional?" James asked bluntly. He hated writers' self-pity and detested watching it.

Clemens laughed until he began coughing again. "Don't you see, James?" he said at last. "You and I are only minor characters in this story about the Great Detective. Our little lives and endings mean nothing to the God-Writer, whoever the sonofabitch might be."

"Do you have any idea who that God-Writer might be?" asked James. "I've thought about this. Conan Doyle would never use living contemporaries in his tales...certainly not use their real names or make them so recognizable. Holmes said that Watson had to disguise the Prince of Wales as the King of Bohemia in one story."

"It doesn't have to be Conan Doyle," said Clemens, his chin almost on his chest as he poured the last of the laudanum from the bottle into the glass. "It's almost certainly some lesser mind, lesser talent, than you, perhaps even lesser than me, certainly lesser than Arthur Conan Doyle, which is saying a lot. And it might be written thirty years hence, or fifty, or a hundred."

"Well," said James, trying for a light tone despite the heaviness in his heart, "at least that would mean we're still being read thirty or a hundred years from now."

There was a long silence broken only by street sounds some fourteen floors below and the raspy, phlegm-filled effort of Samuel Clemens to breathe.

"If we *are* only fictional constructs, brought in to give the fictional-construct Sherlock Holmes company, what do we do next?" James finally asked.

Clemens laughed. "I'm going east to New York tomorrow, stopping at Elmira if I feel up to it. I'll probably be too sick to watch the procession of Great Ships scheduled for this weekend in New York Harbor, but I'd give two toes to see that. No sir, if the God-Writer of this tale . . . hack that he probably is — wants to kill this Sam Clemens off, he will have to do it offstage, the way Shakespeare killed Falstaff."

I need to leave, too, thought James. *Regain my autonomy. Regain myself.*

"What are you doing tomorrow?" asked Clemens.

"Holmes said that he wanted to take me on a boat tour of the White City."

"Well, enjoy what I'll never see," said Clemens.

"I'll look in on you tomorrow after my boat tour," said James. "See if there's anything you need."

"You could tell the porter — the little one with the hare lip — to tell the house doctor that I need a new jug of laudanum," said Clemens. "And a straw."

James nodded.

"As far as looking in on me tomorrow," said Sam Clemens, "there's no reason to. One way or the other, I'll be written out of this story by then."

SEVEN

Friday, April 14, 10:06 a.m.

Even though Friday morning was gray, chilly, and threatening rain, Holmes had hired an open landau for their carriage ride to the Exposition. James brought along his umbrella. Holmes was wearing the bright red scarf that he favored whenever the temperature dropped below 70 degrees. The driver was bundled in wool up on his perch.

Holmes was as taciturn this day as he had been voluble on their boat tour the day before. When James questioned him as to whether he'd driven to the Fair this way before, Holmes said that the mayor of Chicago had driven him this way on Wednesday.

"What is Mayor Harrison like?" asked James.

"Talkative," said Holmes. But then, after a moment of silence broken only by the sound of horses' hooves and passing carriages, he added, "And strangely likeable. Almost certainly corrupt, but loved by his constituencies, I think."

"What is the object of our outing today?" asked James.

"We're deciding where Lucan Adler will lurk to carry out his assassination," Holmes said so softly it was almost a whisper.

"I know nothing about the mental processes of assassins," hissed James.

"All right," Holmes said in a regular voice, "but I thought you might like to see the Exposition grounds before you leave Chicago tomorrow."

"We're leaving Chicago tomorrow?"

"*You* are," said Holmes and threw his red scarf over his shoulder.

*   *   *

The ride to the south side of the city seemed interminable, although James realized it took less than half an hour.

"This will be President Cleveland's route to the Fair?" whispered James. Holmes nodded.

James looked at all the buildings, rooftops, alleys. "It would seem that an assassin could secret himself anywhere along here."

"The Chicago Police Force will have more than a thousand men lining the route so no one can rush the carriage," Holmes said *sotto voce*. "Hundreds more behind the procession since Mayor Harrison predicts up to two hundred thousand people following the carriages for at least part of the way." Holmes leaned closer to James's ear. "But it won't matter. Lucan Adler is not going to come in close with a pistol. He will use a rifle. Probably at extreme range."

James was shocked at the thought. "The last two presidents assassinated in this century were shot at close range with a pistol," he all but whispered.

Holmes nodded. "Lucan Adler will use a rifle. And we don't have to worry about the procession route either here or once we're on the Exposition grounds."

"We don't?" said James. "Why on earth not?"

"Lucan Adler doesn't care a fig for the anarchists' cause," said Holmes. "He turns to them because they pay him well. He lives only to kill, preferably from long range. He's shot and killed eleven foreign leaders or dignitaries in the last two years."

"Certainly that cannot be the case!" cried James.

From his tweed jacket, Holmes pulled a small piece of paper showing a list of names and countries.

"Good God," said James.

"He and Sebastian Moran only barely missed assassinating Her Majesty Queen Elizabeth in eighteen eighty-eight," said Holmes. "And Lucan was still a boy at the time. He no longer works with Moran. All the assassinations on that list were his and his alone."

James was speechless.

* * *

They approached the Exposition from the northernmost western gate. Two members of the Columbian Guard, conspicuous in their uniforms of blue sackcloth, checked the special credentials that Holmes showed them, and two other guards swung the main gates wide.

Ahead of them, the Midway Plaisance stretched ahead for more than a mile. James saw signs saying that they were now on the Avenue of Nations. When James had heard of the Midway Plaisance, he'd imagined a slightly larger version of the carnivals and fairs he'd known. But ahead of him for thirteen city blocks were concessions and attractions the size of small towns.

They passed a rugged log cabin, which James thought was a strange attraction.

"That's the dreaded Sitting Bull's cabin," said Holmes. "Unfortunately, Mr. Burnham, the director for the whole Exposition, couldn't get Sitting Bull since the army killed him three years ago. So Chief Rain-in-the-Face occupies it now, when he's not performing for Buffalo Bill's Wild West Show just beyond the Exposition grounds. Rain-in-the-Face claims that he's the man who killed General Custer, and his fellow Sioux don't dispute it."

James looked at men wearing thick robes of hide and hair. They must have been insufferably hot even in this day's cool temperatures.

"Lapland Village," said Holmes. "God help them in July."

Some brown men wearing almost nothing at all except some leaves around their waists walked by.

"Cannibals," said Holmes. "From Dahomey."

"Of what benefit to the Columbian Exposition are cannibals?" asked James.

"It's a World Exhibition," answered the detective. "Daniel Burnham is trying to bring the world to a million Americans who could never afford to travel out to it."

"What kind of man is Burnham?" asked James.

"Handsome. Commanding. Busy. And driven. Very, very driven."

"I suppose one would have to be to build a complex like this in so short a time. But it looks far from finished."

"On May first it won't be quite finished," said Holmes, "but except for Ferris's Wheel that is still going up, it will be all tidied up and it will *look* finished. Burnham is working the crews day and night, quite literally."

A man with an ostrich on a short rein crossed in front of their carriage.

"California," said Holmes, which did not enlighten James.

"Good heavens," said James as they passed what looked to be an entire Austrian village, complete with stone buildings, towers, and inns.

"A good place to get a stein of beer and some schnitzel once the Fair opens," said Holmes.

James saw a large empty area boldly captioned CAPTIVE BALLOON PARK, but there was no balloon there yet. "What makes a balloon captive?" he asked.

"Ropes," said Holmes.

They'd come to the center of the Midway and now James saw how large Mr. Ferris's Wheel was going to be. Only half of the 264-foot-tall structure was completed but the axle near the top of the finished half-frame looked as huge as a horizontal redwood tree made of steel. There was a protective wooden wall around the work site, but suddenly one of the workmen on the upper tiers of steel beams and wooden frame shouted something and swung down from level to level like some arboreal creature. The workman jumped down to a lower level, used the top of the seven-foot safety fence as a jumping point, and landed right next to Holmes's halted landau.

With a shock, James recognized Wiggins Two—young Moth—dressed in the same workman's clothing as the other steelworkers and carpenters laboring on the Ferris Wheel site. The boy had slept on a cot in Holmes's room their first night in Chicago and James hadn't seen him—or really thought about him—since.

"Mornin' to you, gennelmen," said Wiggins.

"Greetings, Moth," said Holmes. "You appear to have found employment."

The boy grinned widely. "I 'ave at that, Mr. 'olmes. And at full work-man's wages. The supervisor, 'e says—'Moth 'ere, 'e's just a runt'—but Mr. Ferris, who was 'ere supervising the supervisor as it were, says 'I saw 'im climb, Baines. 'E's more monkey than runt and stronger than most of your men. Give 'im a job on both the framing and steel work. We need more monkeys,' 'e says. And so 'e did. Oh, and I ain't called Moth no more—they call me Monk now, short for 'monkey'."

"Do you mind that name?" asked James, leaning forward on his umbrella to see and speak beyond Holmes to his left.

The boy grinned again. "I love it, Mr. Jimes. You see, the tough blokes on London's streets they called me 'Moth' the old English way, what rhymes with 'mote', don't you see. And I was always bein' a mote in some fellow's eye and I didn't like that feelin'. Although I admit that I did like the way my Mote spoke, although maybe Monk shall speak the same."

"How did you speak when you were Mote?" asked James.

Again the gap-toothed grin. "So me supervisor, Mr. 'iggens, asks the lot of us at lunch—'How do I woo this Italian lady what lives in the tenement wi' me and never seems to notice me none?' And nobody speaks a word 'cause Mr. 'iggens has an 'orrible temper, he does, but I says to 'im, I says—'My complete master, Mr. 'iggens sir, you must jig off a tune at the tongue's end, canary to it with your feet, 'umor it with turning up your eyelids like, sigh a note and then sing a note, something through the throat, you see, as if you swallowed love with singing love, as it were, then sometime through the nose as if you snuffed up love by smelling love, all the time with your 'at penthouse-like all tilted o'er the shop of your eyes and with your arms crossed on your thin-belly paisley waistcoat like a rabbit on a spit, or mebbe your 'ands in your pockets, such as that French geezer in the old painting, and...this is important, sir...keep not too long in one tune, but a snip and away. These are compliments, y'see, these are humors as it were, these betray nice wenches nicely—mostly them what would be betrayed without these tricks, I fully admit—but doing as I say makes you a man of note—*do* you note, sir?—men that are most affected by these do these. And that concludes my penny of observation,' I says to 'im."

Holmes threw back his head and laughed that sharp, barking laugh of his. James could only stare.

"You'll go far Moth...I mean Monk," said Holmes and handed the boy a ten-dollar bill.

518 DAN SIMMONS

"Thankee, sir," said the boy, putting the bill in his cap, "and I 'ope it doesn't inconvenience you none that I h'ain't going back to England but will seek to find me fortune here by becomin' an American."

"Not at all," laughed Holmes. "You were a pleasure to work with when you were Wiggins Two of Baker Street but now is the time for you to show your true worth to the world."

"Mr. Ferris says this might not be the last Wheel 'e builds," said the boy. "Although the others most likely would be smaller, like. If I do well on the 'igh steel 'ere—I might travel with 'is workers to other states, even other countries."

"May it be so, Monk," said Holmes and told the coachman to drive on. He turned back to shout at the boy, "If you ever need anything—anything at all, Wiggins—you know where to find me."

The boy grinned and nodded. "I do," he said. "I will. And God bless you, Mr. Sherlock 'olmes."

When they'd traveled further, past what Holmes described as the Algerian Village where robed ladies watched them through their veils as they passed by, then an empty street that Holmes said would be bustling Cairo in a week, complete with real Egyptians, James said, "The lines from *Love's Labor's Lost*. Where on earth did Wiggins pick those up?"

"I take my favorite and most promising lads to the theater," said Holmes. "I'd say that if they were born into better circumstances many would have grown up to be MP's, but in truth most are too smart and too honest for Parliament."

James thought about that as they passed a gigantic zoo, complete with gigantic zoo smells. The author heard a lion roar and perhaps a hippopotamus making hippopotamus noises. He did not look up. Far to the west there came a roar of a happy crowd from Buffalo Bill's Wild West Show, which had been open for weeks and getting huge crowds.

Their carriage turned right into a dazzling array of gigantic buildings interspersed with canals, lagoons, bridges, and ponds. The largest lake was to their left—James could see the well-planned Wooded Island in its center—and the row of Great Buildings lined up to their right reminded James of the cliffs of Dover.

"We're officially in the White City now," said Holmes. "That's the Woman's Building we're just passing."

James could say nothing—he was surprised to find that he was physically stunned by the beauty, size, and layout of the White City, this "mere fairgrounds" as he'd thought of it in Washington. It felt to him like stepping into a clean, white, safe, sane future.

"It's a little less than a mile to the Administration Building outside of which your President Cleveland will be speaking," Holmes said softly so the driver could not hear. "Everything from this point forward is a potential assassin's roost."

Leaning on his umbrella, James turned to look at the man next to him. Holmes's eyes were bright with excitement.

"And I need your help, James, to find where Lucan Adler plans to do his deadly deed on the first of May."

EIGHT

Friday, April 14, 10:42 a.m.

The Administration Building where their voyage ended was essentially an 84-foot square supporting an oversized ribbed and octagonal dome. But it was beautifully made and held pride of place in the entire White City, centered as it was halfway between the main western entrance where the trains would dislodge their passengers and the eastern Peristyle entrance where those coming by boat would enter. There was an acre or more of paved open space around the Administration Building, but to the east was the Grand Basin that ran all the way to the Peristyle, to the north were the large Mines and Electricity buildings with glimpses of the Lagoon and Wooded Island down the narrow streets between them. To the southeast of it was a solid high wall of façades—the Annex, the Machinery Hall, and the Agriculture Building, broached only by the South Canal with its graceful bridges and lighted walkways.

Two men met them when Holmes and James alighted outside the east entrance to the Administration Building.

"Mr. Henry James," said Holmes, "may I have the honor of introducing you to Colonel Edmund Rice, Commandant of the Columbian Guard and chief of security at the Exposition."

James shook hands. Holmes had told him on the ride in that Edmund Rice had been awarded the Medal of Honor for the day at Gettysburg thirty years earlier when he'd not only helped stop the Confederate General Pickett's charge, but was gravely wounded in the counterattack.

Rice was a short, stocky man, balding, with a magnificent mustache. His natural expression seemed to be that of a scowl but James soon understood that was somewhat misleading. Colonel Rice was an intensely serious man who could, on occasion, be wittily humorous.

The other man, tall, thin, and immaculately tailored and turned out, was Mr. Andrew L. Drummond, head of the Secret Service.

"Good heavens!" said James. "I had no idea that the United States had a spy agency also called the Secret Service like the British."

Drummond smiled and explained that he was chief agent in the Treasury Department. "Many of our men are well trained in security measures," said Drummond, "including bodyguard protection, so we're helping out where we can with the president's visit to the Exposition."

"Shall we get started?" said Holmes.

"Started with what?" asked James. He felt that he was in the wrong place with the wrong people doing the wrong things.

"Looking over the grounds to find where Lucan Adler is going to place himself on May first to kill the President of the United States," said Holmes.

"You mean to guess where he might try such a thing," said James.

Holmes gave him a frigid look. "You should know by now, James," he said flatly. "I *never* guess."

On the steps up to the higher of the Administration Building's two promenades, Drummond touched James's forearm slightly and stopped. James stopped as well.

"I just wanted to tell you, Mr. James, in case I never get another chance," Drummond said softly, "that I believe that you're the most brilliant writer alive and that *The Portrait of a Lady* is the masterpiece of the Nineteenth Century."

James distantly heard his own voice muttering "Most kind...very kind of you..." and then they were climbing stairs again to the upper promenade. When they came out into the open air, James's morning surliness had disappeared.

The torches and angels that James had seen through Holmes's telescope were all too large and solid close up. The line of fluted pillars holding the gas jets which illuminated the dome at night must have been fifteen feet tall along the railing. In the angel tableaus, some of the angels' wings rose higher than that.

When Drummond made some polite comment about the statuary, Col. Edmund Rice removed the short, never-lit cigar from his mouth and said, "Those damned angels. Getting them up here was harder than reducing Vicksburg. The straps broke on one of them and the thing fell thirty feet, burying one wing four feet into the frozen ground while the rest of it flew all to pieces."

The four men gathered along the east railing of the upper promenade.

"Down there," said Colonel Rice, pointing and moving his finger in a square to show size, "will be the platform from which the president will speak. We won't let more than fifty people on that platform and...Drummond...Mr. Burnham has given permission for two of your agents to stand near and *behind* the president during the speech."

"Any shot wouldn't come from *behind*," Drummond said softly.

"For security reasons, we're closing off the two promenades here on the Administration Building and if you agree, Mr. Holmes—the wire to me and Mr. Burnham said that your advice was to be listened to and followed whenever possible, God knows why—but if you agree, we'll close off the promenades on all the high structures in line of sight and rifle range of where the president will be speaking."

"Which structures will that include, Colonel?" asked Holmes.

The Commandant of the Columbian Guards—out of uniform in shirt and suspenders as the clouds parted and the April day grew warmer—used the blunt cigar to point to their extreme right.

"The eastern parts of the big Machinery Building there."

The cigar shifted left, further east. "The Agriculture Building next to it."

Rice pointed straight ahead with his cigar. "The entrance Peristyle has its own promenade which we'll shut down during the ceremony."

The cigar moved left again. "The huge monstrosity of the Manufactures and Liberal Arts Building. Long, long promenade, almost as long as the Great Basin that runs down the middle here."

He pointed left to one of the Great Buildings they could see only part of. "The eastern part of the big Electricity Building there has a straight line to the speaker's stand. Most of the building doesn't."

"And then there are the avenues themselves," said Drummond.

"Yep," said Col. Rice. "Look out there now and enjoy the sight of the hundred or so workers you see, because on Opening Day there'll be at least a hundred thousand people crammed into these open spaces."

"No place for a sniper in a crowd," said Drummond. "Our last two presidential assassinations have been with a handgun and at very short range."

"That's very true," said Holmes. "Lincoln, with a small pistol shot from a distance of less than three feet, and President Garfield, shot in the back, point-blank range, by Guiteau."

"Who used a British-made Bull Dog revolver," said Drummond.

"Very true," said Holmes. "An excellent weapon. My particular friend Dr. John Watson owns a Bull Dog revolver."

"Assuming your theoretical assassin on May first..." began Col. Rice.

"There's nothing theoretical about Lucan Adler, Colonel," Holmes said briskly.

"All right, we'll assume that your would-be assassin will want to be somewhere high enough and stable enough and lonely enough that he can use a rifle. That could be from a window or from one of the promenades. Why don't we look at the four Great Buildings and Peristyle going counterclockwise, starting with the Machinery Building there to the right."

"Excellent idea, Colonel," said Holmes.

*   *   *

The roof of the Machinery Hall was all cupolas, arches, and Spanish-Renaissance-ornamented gewgaws to James's way of seeing things. In his opinion—neither asked for nor stated—any self-respecting sniper would die from the bad taste of all that ornamentation before being able to fire a shot. But Colonel Rice, Drummond, and Holmes focused on the high second-story loggia—an inset veranda that ran the entire eastern length of the building from the parade ground to the east of the Administration

Building, where the president and his party would be all too visible, back west to the larger open ground in front of the Terminal Station.

"You could get a thousand people on this veranda," said Drummond as if speaking to himself.

"More than that," said Colonel Rice. "Pack 'em ten or fifteen deep between these Corinthian columns and this grand loggia'll hold five thousand people, easy."

"Perhaps a bit crowded and joggly for rifle work," said Holmes.

"'Joggly'?" said James.

Holmes flashed one of those thin, fast, tight-lipped smiles.

* * *

Moving toward Lake Michigan, Colonel Rice led them to the Agriculture Building, a domed Roman-style structure encompassing half a million square feet of display space. Before they got too close, Col. Rice pointed out Augustus Saint-Gaudens's gold Statue of Diana, poised on one leg with her bow at full pull, that graced the top of the dome. "It was supposed to go on top of the new Madison Square Garden Building," grunted Rice, "but it was too damned big. It serves as a good weather vane here."

Before they entered the building, James gawked at the presence of dozens, perhaps scores, of whirling full-sized windmills, of all shapes and sizes and materials—wood, iron, steel—that filled an area near the Lagoon outside the Agriculture Building.

"That army would prove too much even for Don Quixote," said James.

The other three men looked at him and said nothing.

"If you're hungry, gentlemen," said Col. Rice as they climbed steps to the upper regions, "Canada sent a twenty-two-thousand-pound hunk of cheese to be exhibited down there. It's encased in iron and, the Canadians say, took sixteen hundred milkmaids to milk ten thousand cows to produce the twenty-seven thousand gallons of milk used to make the cheese."

"A fascinating bit of information," said Holmes who, unlike James, was not in the least winded by the endless flights of steps. "And now that I've learned it, I will eliminate it from my memory."

James thought it just a figure of speech, but Col. Rice stopped and faced Holmes. "You can do that, sir? Remove things from your memory?"

"I *have* to do that," Holmes said in a serious tone.

"Why?" said the Colonel.

"I was born with what some experts are now calling a 'photographic memory'," said Holmes. "It is my misfortune to remember everything. Give me a page of a magazine and, after glancing over it, I can recall every word, comma, and full stop on the page. But the mind is a little attic, as I once tried to explain to my associate Dr. Watson, and someone with a profession as defined as mine must be careful what to store there. If I know for certain that the information cannot help me in my detection—say the fact that the sun does not go around the Earth or the details of this great mass of Canadian cheese—I simply delete it from memory."

"Delete it?" said James with wonder and doubt in his voice.

"I imagine a red delete button, mentally push it, and the memory is gone," said Holmes. "Otherwise my brain would be a grab bag of odds and ends rather than a finely tuned engine for ratiocination."

"Delete button," said Colonel Rice and shook his head. "Now I've heard everything."

NINE

Friday, April 14, 2:45 p.m.

Mr. Drummond, Holmes, James, and the colonel had toured the upper regions of the Agriculture Building, the east-entrance Peristyle, the gigantic Manufactures and Liberal Arts Building, and the south side promenade of the Electricity Building, sharing a quick and late lunch with Colonel Rice in the canvas-covered temporary cantina set up for the workers.

It was at the northeast corner of the Agriculture Building that Holmes pointed to a post set at the end of the narrow promenade. A cable ran from the post down for several hundred feet to a 7- or 8-foot tall, lighted channel marker thirty feet or more from the seawall.

"Does this have a purpose?" asked Holmes. "Perhaps holding down the Agriculture Building in high winds?"

Colonel Rice clamped down on his cigar stub and grinned. "There's another one just like it at the southeast corner of the Manufactures and Liberal Arts Building across the way. Someone had the idea of dangling the flags of all the nations along the cables so that folks on the ships docking at the end of the pier would feel sort of welcomed with open arms."

"Is it still to come then?" asked Holmes.

Rice shook his head. "The halyards just wouldn't rig right, the wind was tearing the test flags all to hell, so the idea was abandoned. They just haven't got around to removing the cables yet."

"That cable is rather low to the beacons, light posts, whatever they are," said Drummond. "Isn't that a navigation hazard for small boats?"

Rice shook his head again. "Those beacons are there to warn away even the smallest crafts. All the area under water out to the beacons' tiny little concrete islands is filled with chunks of rock and concrete dumped when we built the sea wall. They'd rip the bottom out of a skiff."

James was deeply impressed by the Peristyle with its long row of Corinthian columns and great triumphal arch through which passengers arriving from the water would enter the Fair and see the grand view.

"The Peristyle connects the little casino building at the end of the main Casino Pier there to the south to the Music Hall there on the north end," said Col. Rice. "Forty-seven giant columns...one for each of the states and territories. This has a promenade up there, but just accessible by a stairway at the south end."

"By all means, let us enjoy the view," said Holmes.

Above the Columbian Arch at the center of the Peristyle Promenade—which did offer an amazing view both into the White City and out onto Lake Michigan—they were perfectly lined up with the front of the Administration Building where the president would be giving his talk.

"What is the distance, do you estimate, Colonel?" asked Holmes.

Rice squinted. "Five hundred thirty yards. No more than five-fifty."

"Certainly that is too far for someone with a mere rifle to aim and shoot with any certainty," said Henry James.

Rice, Drummond, and Holmes exchanged glances.

Rice spoke first. "The best of modern military rifles can give you five-inch groups at up to a thousand yards," he said softly, removing the cigar as if out of respect for such an achievement. Rice turned to Holmes. "Do you know what kind of weapon this Lucan Adler intends to use?"

"Yes," said Holmes, "we believe we do. He's assassinated four powerful figures in Europe since last autumn and in each case he's used a Model Eighteen Ninety-three Mauser rifle, most probably with a twenty-power telescopic sight attached. He doesn't leave casings behind, but each dead man seems to have been killed by seven-millimeter rimless bullets. The 'ninety-three Mauser—which was released early last autumn in major sales to Spain and the Spanish troops in Cuba—is a bolt-action with a five-round clip."

Colonel Rice seemed to grimace. "I don't know the Mausers—much less this new one. Do you know the muzzle velocity?"

"Twenty-three hundred feet per second," said Holmes.

"And actual operational range?"

"A little over two thousand yards. I believe twenty-one hundred and sixty is the precise number."

This meant nothing to James, but it seemed to affect Colonel Rice almost viscerally. For the first time, the stocky gentleman not only took the soggy stogie out of his mouth but removed his worn derby and rubbed his balding head. "My God," he whispered. "If we'd had that rifle at Gettysburg."

Holmes nodded. "You could have used aimed fire—individual targets—almost as soon as the Confederates came out of the trees a mile away across that wide, deadly space. With five rounds without reloading."

Rice let out a deep breath. "Well, it doesn't matter much. Your Lucan Adler fellow will want to get in as close as he can."

"Why is that?" asked James. "Especially if he can shoot a target a little more than a mile away?"

Rice smiled. "A man ain't a paper target," he said and James sensed that the failure in grammar was deliberate with this man who'd ended the war as a Brigadier General. "Walking at an average rate—two miles per hour—a man walks about two feet in the time it would take a bullet to reach him." He pointed at the Administration Building due west of them down the long Lagoon. "That would be a miss. Of course, President Cleveland will be standing still and facing this way, but the shooter has probably sighted in his rifle he'd have to hold over eighteen inches."

"I don't understand," said James.

Agent Drummond held out his hands as if framing the target area in front of the distant Administration Building. "That means, Mr. James," he said softly, "that to shoot accurately enough to hit the president in the chest—and we admit that it is a broad target—Lucan Adler would have to use his telescopic sight to aim about eighteen inches high—say at the top of the president's forehead."

"I would think that shooting for the head would be preferable," said James, appalled at hearing his own words.

Colonel Rice said, "Our heads move around a lot more than we think—especially when giving a speech. Center of the body's mass is the surest target."

They were all silent for a long, sickening moment. Finally Rice said, "Well, shall we tour the Manufactures and Electricity Buildings, have some lunch, and get this over with?"

Holmes, Drummond, and James followed him down from the Peristyle Promenade without speaking.

*　*　*

The Manufactures and Liberal Arts Building was by far the largest and most imposing structure they visited. The interior was chaos this day—a very controlled chaos once carefully observed—as thousands upon thousands of major displays were uncrated, assembled, and made ready. Far across the vast, cluttered floor, James caught a glimpse of an elegant telescope that must have been at least sixty feet tall.

"You should have seen this hall when it was empty," said Col. Rice as they waited for the Otis-Hale elevator to drop down in clear sight, the car now seeming to be suspended in mid-air among the iron beams some 200 feet above them.

"We had the Dedication Ceremony in late October last year," continued Rice. "This floor's thirty-two acres and it was filled that day with more than a hundred and forty-thousand Chicago folk. The carpenters had to build a platform that would hold five thousand grandees in their little yellow chairs. Ex-Mayor Harrison had a seat up on the platform, but he spent most of the time shaking hands with every one of the hundred forty-some thousand citizens standing. And it was a cold day...cold as a witch's tit. Men kept their overcoats and hats on and women tried to hide down in their fur collars and keep their hands in their mink muffs when they weren't waving white hankies to the music. And it was a bloody *long* ceremony, too. After an hour or so I heard a sound like a marching army approaching and realized it was all the men standing out there stamping their feet to stay warm. You could see your breath in front of you during the entire overblown ceremony and I swear that after the first half hour, little clouds formed under them iron trusses twenty stories up there, just from our breath."

"Could anyone *hear* any of the speeches?" asked James.

"About ten people up on that platform and closest to the podium," said Colonel Rice. "The place was so damned big and echoey that the organizers had to use ex-military fellows I provided to wave semaphore flags to cue the five-hundred-musician orchestra and five-thousand-voice choir when it was their time to play or sing."

"Did anything interesting come out of that day?" asked Drummond.

"Well," said Rice, "some fellow who edits some children's magazine wrote out a pledge that the Bureau of Education sent to every damned school in the country so that on that October twenty-one Dedication Day last year all the young brats in all the schools of the nation would be contributin' something to their nation."

"A pledge?" James said dubiously.

"I don't remember it but for the beginning," said Rice. "It goes 'I pledge allegiance to my Flag and to the Republic for which it stands...'"

"Forcing school children to recite a national pledge doesn't sound very American to me," said James.

"No," agreed Holmes. "It sounds German. Very German."

*   *   *

The elevator ride up to the promenade level was a surprise for Henry James. It literally took his breath away. The Otis-Hale Company had built a super high-speed elevator that was a simple cage, open on three sides, and it whisked upward so quickly through rings of electric lights and occasional high platforms that one felt both exposed to the height and heavier at the same moment. When it came to a stop at the top, the rear doors opening to the promenade, James thought for a moment that his feet had left the floor of the lift.

"That elevator should be a major attraction all on its own," said James when he could get his breath back.

"I'm sure it will be," said Colonel Rice.

"I'm not sure I would care to ride it more than once," said Drummond.

The promenade on the Manufactures and Liberal Arts Building was called the Observation Deck and it went all the way around the thirty-two-acre building. Instead of stone or plaster railings, the barrier was a simple metal chain link fence, which made the sense of height all the more palpable. The views were astonishing. James realized that if Mr. Ferris ever got his giant Wheel built, citizens on this Observation Deck would be looking at it almost at the height of its highest carriages as it revolved.

Naturally, Holmes, Drummond, and Rice were interested only in the parts of the Observation Deck that would allow a madman to murder a president from afar.

"Three corners of the Observation Deck have one of these huge searchlights," Holmes said as if to himself.

Rice answered anyway. "Yes, sir. They're German and terribly bright and focused. They will be used to illuminate buildings, fountains, the Wooded Island, and other things during the night. One of these lights could show us a rabbit a mile away."

Each German searchlight had a six-foot-square black base about two-and-a-half feet high. The steel was painted with black enamel.

They were at the southwest corner of the Observation Deck, the one that gave the best view of the Administration Building and area where President Cleveland would be standing in a little more than two weeks.

Holmes crouched, pointed to a lock along one side of the base of the searchlight, and said, "Would you happen to have a key for this compartment, Colonel Rice?"

Again Rice grinned around his cigar stub. "You've heard me clinking and clanking along the last two hours. I've got a key on this ring for everything in the fairgrounds."

In a moment he produced a small key that unlocked the compartment.

Holmes lay on his belly to look inside and Drummond joined him, but James refused to get his suit dirty doing so, and he crouched as best he could to look over the detective's shoulder. The dark space showed various thick insulated wires going through the floor and some iron support struts, but was mostly empty. The knee-high black steel square was obviously there primarily to be a base for the seven-foot-high heavy searchlight.

"Thank you, Colonel Rice," said Holmes, getting to his feet and brushing off his trousers and jacket. "Shall we stroll to the south*east* corner now?"

The last of the morning's threatening clouds had disappeared and now all four men leaned on the metal fence to enjoy the spring sunlight.

"Harder shot from here," said Mr. Drummond. "Adds almost another hundred yards to a shot from the southwest corner we were at."

"Quite true," said Holmes. "And it would be awkward steadying a rifle on that low steel fence. But a man standing on the searchlight stand..." He pointed his cane behind him without turning to look. "...would have the ridges on the searchlight itself to brace a rifle."

"How long is a Model Ninety-Three Mauser?" asked the colonel.

"Forty-eight inches," Holmes said at once, but then he smiled thinly. "Without its bayonet."

*　*　*

The Electricity Building pleased James the most of the four major buildings and Peristyle they'd inspected so far. It had a delightful curving promenade that looked down at the lagoons, bridges, and, for much of the southeast side, the front of the Administration Building. There was a large and elegant statue of Benjamin Franklin at the graceful entrance to the building with already the smell of ozone from the voluminous interior.

Holmes showed less interest in the promenade deck than he did in the eight high spires at various corners of the structure.

"Steps for the public up to them?" asked Mr. Drummond.

"Sure," said the colonel. "Those rooftop spires are a hundred and seventy feet in the air and the open arches at the top provide one of the best views in the entire grounds."

Looking out the broad opening from the spire closest to the Adminis-tration Building, Holmes sighted down the length of his cane. "A slight side shot, but the president standing alone to give his speech won't have Secret Service men or anyone else standing next to him then. The other notables will be seated, yes?"

"Yes," said Colonel Rice.

"Less than a hundred yards," said Holmes.

"Yes," said Colonel Rice.

And that was all for the Electricity Building. After a fast and late luncheon under sun-warmed canvas, Holmes said, "You'll pardon us a minute, I hope, Mr. James" and stepped to one side to talk with Colonel Rice and Mr. Drummond for about fifteen minutes while James drank another cup of coffee. When the conference was over, Drummond came over to James. "It's been a delight and deep honor to meet you, Mr. James. Should we cross paths again, I hope it will not be presumptuous of me to bring a few of your novels to sign for me. They would be the pride of my collection and a legacy to my children."

"Of course, of course," said James. Drummond shook hands with him, bowed slightly, and left the sun-warmed dining tent. James noted Holmes and Rice's discussion was over so he joined the two men.

As Holmes was shaking hands good-bye with Rice, the Colonel said, "There's one thing you haven't asked about or mentioned, Mr. Holmes."

"Yes?"

"Wherever your Lucan Adler sniper chooses to shoot from, there's go-ing to be the slight problem of him getting away after the fact. As we've discussed, upon such a terrible event as the shooting of the president, the Columbian Guard will close and lock all gates immediately. I have telephone lines to every exit. No boats will be allowed to leave from the pier. Is your man suicidal? Wanting to be martyr to anarchism?"

"Not in the least," said Holmes. "Lucan Adler has never carried out an assassination without having a brilliant escape plan in place."

Colonel Rice gestured to the boulevard along the Lagoon where they stood. "We can shut off access to the promenades and towers as you've asked, but that parade ground and all these side streets will be filled with more than a hundred thousand panicked people. And not one of them will get out without being checked out by police or my Columbian Guard."

"It is a bit of a challenge to think of a sensible escape route, is it not, Colonel?" said Holmes. The detective nodded, tipped his hat, and turned away.

Henry James said his own good-bye to Colonel Rice and followed Holmes through White City streets filled with great crates, rubble, straw, and thousands of workmen.

TEN

Saturday, April 15, 8:30 a.m.

Henry James's fiftieth birthday was as cold, lonely, and awful as he might have imagined it if he were writing a short story dipped deeply in pathos.

James had lain awake for much of the night, fighting a nausea that sent him rushing to the lavatory three times before a faint dawn began contouring the outlines of his hotel windows. As he checked out—he had tickets for a 9 a.m. train to New York—he knew that Sam Clemens had left two days earlier and the clerk, when queried, said that Mr. Holmes had checked out "very, very early".

The rain that had only threatened the previous morning was coming down now in a cold and unrelenting downpour. The chilly air felt more like November with winter beginning in earnest than mid-April. Even the fancily clad doormen were huddled under their umbrellas and looking sour this dark, freezing day.

The previous late afternoon when he and Holmes had returned to the Great Northern from their odd tour of an assassin's-eye view of the great Columbian Exposition and World's Fair, James had been surprised to find two telegrams waiting for him.

The first was from Henry Adams and read:

A SLIGHTLY PREMATURE HAPPY BIRTHDAY, HARRY STOP I KNOW YOU MUST BE EAGER TO RETURN TO LONDON AND YOUR MAGNIFICENT WORK, BUT I

SINCERELY HOPE THAT YOU RETURN TO
WASHINGTON TO STAY WITH ME AS MY GUEST WHEN
YOUR BUSINESS IS CONCLUDED STOP WE ARE OLD
FRIENDS, HARRY, AND IN A WAY I AM REQUESTING
THE PLEASURE OF YOUR COMPANY FOR THE NEXT
COUPLE OF WEEKS IN CLOVER'S BELOVED NAME STOP
HAPPY BIRTHDAY, MY DEAR FRIEND

James was stunned. He had no idea how Adams had found out that he
was in Chicago, much less *where* he was staying in Chicago, and he knew
it was highly unusual that Adams was inviting him as a house guest.
He'd rarely had guests stay in his huge home in the years since Clover
died.

The second telegram was from the Hays.

HAPPY, HAPPY BIRTHDAY, HARRY. STOP WE
UNDERSTAND YOU MAY BE CELEBRATING THIS
ESPECIALLY AUSPICIOUS DAY WHILE IN TRANSIT, BUT
CLARA AND I DEEPLY AND SINCERELY HOPE THAT YOU
WILL ACCEPT ADAMS'S OFFER AND RETURN TO
WASHINGTON FOR A WHILE BEFORE HEADING ACROSS
THE ATLANTIC STOP WE HAVE SO MUCH WE WANT TO
TALK TO YOU ABOUT—IN PERSON STOP CABOT LODGE
HAS LAID ON THE SPECIAL TRAIN TO THE CHICAGO
FAIR OPENING FOR APRIL 29, WITH SPECIAL ADMISSION
PASSES FOR ALL OF US, AND IT WOULD BE CLARA'S AND
MY DEEPEST WISH THAT YOU WILL JOIN US ON THAT
EXPEDITION STOP HAPPY BIRTHDAY

James had accosted Holmes in the lobby before the detective had
reached the elevator to go up to his room.

"Did you cable the Hays and Henry Adams that we were—that I
was—staying here in the Great Northern?" snapped James.

Holmes seemed a bit taken aback by the writer's ferocity. "Of course
I did, old fellow. I would have thought you'd want your whereabouts

known to some of your dearest friends. Especially right before your fiftieth birthday."

James felt even angrier at this comment but refused to satisfy
Holmes's sardonic sense of humor by asking how the detective knew that
the 15th was his birthday.

"Shall we dine together tonight at that interesting little Italian
restaurant just down Jackson Street?" asked Holmes. "The concierge
here strongly recommends it. And we may not be seeing each other again
for a while."

James started to say no—stopped—started to ask a question—and
stopped again. He just stood there with the telegrams about his dreaded
50th birthday crumpled in his hand and glared at Sherlock Holmes.

"Good then," said Holmes. "I shall meet you in the lobby promptly
at eight p.m."

* * *

During the night, between his bouts of nausea—an old foe of his along
with constipation and diarrhea—James had weighed his decision. He'd
studied the railway tables. A train leaving the new North Station at 9:45
a.m. went to Pittsburgh where he could transfer for a non-stop express to
Washington. The train to New York left from the old downtown station
at 9:00 and passed through Cleveland and Buffalo on its way to New
York, where he could immediately book passage to Portsmouth on the
highly praised new transatlantic steamer the S.S. *United States.*

In the end, it was the thought of the sunny warmth of his De Vere
Gardens rooms, his waiting writing desk, the salons he would be revis-
iting, the country houses of gentlefolk he'd be invited to . . . that and the
visceral sense of safe encirclement by all his books that made him decide
for New York and home.

He'd found a porter to carry his baggage piled high on a cart and
bought his ticket at the downtown station when, concealed as he was behind the high mound of his luggage and an iron post, he saw Professor
James Moriarty moving up and down the first-class coaches peering in
the windows.

He's hunting for me, was James's first gut-chilling thought. A thought that carried all the weight of certainty.

Two thuggish-looking men came up and reported quickly to Professor Moriarty, who dispatched them up and down the line of waiting cars. Moriarty stepped aboard and began striding through the first-class cars. James could watch his advance—like a high-domed scarecrow with white-straw hair, a mortician's overcoat, and long strangler's fingers—as Moriarty strode from carriage to carriage.

It made no sense that Moriarty would be looking for him, for Henry James. He was sure he'd not been seen on the evening he'd lain on that terrible beam high over the heads of Moriarty and his small army of anarchists and thieves. The only person he'd told was Sherlock Holmes.

But Holmes would have informed Drummond, the Washington and Chicago chiefs of police, and God knows how many other people here in the States and across Europe, to put them on their guard for the assassinations and uprisings of May 1.

Now it made perfect sense. James knew of Moriarty's vast crime networks across Europe and even in the United States. Someone in police enforcement—so many of them crooked in this Gilded Age—had told one of Moriarty's operatives.

It was possible, of course, that Moriarty and his thugs were checking the train for Sherlock Holmes and, for all James knew, Holmes might be on it and murdered at any moment, but down deep Henry James knew *Professor James Moriarty and his killers are looking for me this cold and rainy morning.*

As if confirming his intuition, Moriarty stepped out of the coaches and stood looking as three other thugs came up to him for orders. James stared at Moriarty's terribly long, long fingers with their long yellow nails, his hands on his hips now as he showed visible exasperation. The fingers were like great white spiders crawling up black velvet.

Moriarty dispatched the three thugs and then turned quickly to stare in James's direction, but not before James ducked down behind his piled-high mass of luggage. It took half a minute for James to work up the nerve to peek again and he let out a long breath when he saw that Moriarty was again walking the length of the train, looking in all uncurtained windows.

"Shall I load your luggage now, suh?" said the porter who'd been waiting patiently and showing no expression at James's sudden pallor or his absurd concealment.

"No, no," said James. "Find me a cab, any cab, as quickly as you can, and get these things loaded equally quickly. Here...for your trouble." He handed the porter some bill from his wallet, but it had been so long since he'd trafficked in American money it might have been a $50 bill or a $1 bill. Either way, the porter touched his cap and said, "At once, sir."

James kept the baggage between himself and Moriarty all the way out to the busy cab stand, nodded his head when the porter pointed to an expensive closed carriage cab, held his breath while the trunks were loaded with maddening slowness, and breathed again only when the cab started moving quickly away from the central station and Professor James Moriarty.

James, obviously still feeling edgy, almost jumped when the trap door opened above him for a second, just slitted to keep the pouring rain out, and the driver called down, "Where to, sir?"

"The new North Station," said James in a strangely high voice. "And quickly, please. I have to catch a 9:30 train. There's an extra quid in it if you get me there with time to spare."

"A *quid,* sir?" asked the driver out there in the downpour.

"Five *dollars* extra if you get me there at all possible speed and with time to spare before that nine-thirty train's departure," said James.

The driver used the whip. The carriage flew through traffic as though there were a derby stakes race in progress. James had to brace both hands against the seat cushions or be thrown left and right as the racing cab swerved around all slower traffic. Other drivers and pedestrians shouted profanities as James's carriage soaked them through with splashes.

The night before, at dinner, James had asked Holmes, "What are you doing next?"

Holmes, already smoking his cigarette after quickly finishing his dinner, touched a finger to his tongue to capture a mote of tobacco. "Oh, several things have to be looked into here and there. I should be busy until we meet again on Mr. Cabot Lodge's private train on the twenty-eighth."

James had to use all his control to avoid near-shouting—*"I won't be on Lodge's damned train!* And I won't be your Boswell. And I don't appreciate being abandoned like this in a city strange to me on the eve of my birthday. And I'm tired. And I'm going home."

He'd said none of that, of course. A graceful telegram—*two* graceful telegrams—sent from New York before his ship sailed would send his thanks and regrets to Henry Adams and the Hays.

Now, after his wildly whipping and racing cabbie had gotten him more or less in one piece to North Station with plenty of time to spare and he'd purchased his first-class tickets to Pittsburgh and then straight on to Washington, Henry James sat in his almost-empty and overheated compartment, rested his face against the cool glass of the window, and watched the black canyons of Chicago fall behind in the rain. He looked away as the train passed through a fringe industrial wasteland with slag heaps and squalid homes looking for all the world like a clumsy American imitation of a Dickensian nightmare landscape.

Happy Birthday, Henry James, he thought as they moved out into the country, and the rain, impossibly, pounded down even more heavily. *You're fifty years old.*

At that moment he found himself wishing that he'd done what he'd gone to the Seine that night to do, meant to do, had steeled himself to do at that dark river. It had been raining that night as well.

PART 4

1

On Monday, April 24, after a whirlwind visit to more than half a dozen large American cities, Sherlock Holmes returned to Washington and checked into the same Kirkwood House hotel at 12th St. N.W. and Pennsylvania Avenue where he'd stayed earlier. He knew it was dangerous to do so—if Lucan Adler had been searching him out, he would know about Holmes's earlier stay there and have someone keeping a lookout for him—but this part of Holmes's American visit *had* to be dangerous. If he could lure Lucan Adler to him before May 1, it would be the best for everyone—save perhaps for Sherlock Holmes.

Early that spring evening he went to the address near Dupont Circle that Mrs. Gaddis, the retired school teacher in her alley carriage-house apartment in Boston, had given him. This was also a calculated risk. Holmes did not believe that the odds favored Lucan Adler being there for long stretches of time, but there was no doubt that the assassin visited there.

It was a stately brick house on a quiet street just off the Circle. When Holmes knocked on the door, a tiny woman, barely four feet tall, dressed out in European livery of a maid, opened the door and squinted up at him.

"Is Mrs. Rebecca Lorne Baxter home?" asked Holmes, removing his hat.

"Nie, ona nie jest teraz w domu," said the tiny maid.

"Oh, a shame," said Holmes. "Would you please give her my card and this message?" He handed the dwarf-maid his business card and an envelope containing a short message:

*Irene—Would you be kind enough to meet me tomorrow evening (Tuesday)
between 7 and 8 p.m. at Clover Adams's Memorial?—S. Holmes*

The maid took the card and the envelope without saying a word—in Polish or any other language—and shut the door.

Holmes walked slowly away from the house and back to Dupont Circle, but all the time he was still in view of the house, the spiderwebs of scars on his back itched as if someone had painted a target on his back with turpentine.

2

Holmes arrived at Rock Creek Cemetery just before seven p.m. He told the cab driver not to wait. One way or the other, he would not need a cab home this night. The sun had just disappeared behind the forest to the west of the cemetery grounds but the soft spring twilight lingered and promised to light the sky for most of the next hour.

He walked directly to the Clover Adams memorial. He had his sword-cane in one hand and the little lemon-squeezer pistol in a jacket pocket, but he knew that neither would be of any use if Lucan Adler was lying in wait with his sniper rifle. He'd stipulated this night, Tuesday, to give Irene Adler a full day to contact Lucan with the information about this meeting.

He knew from his terrible experience in the Himalayas that it was true that one does not hear the rifle bullet—or in his case, three steel-cased bullets—that rips through your flesh since the bullet travels well above the speed of sound. In his instance, it had been three sharp sounds immediately following three unbelievable intense blows to his back and lower side. And, because of the mountains, those three sounds had echoed.

And the pain from those wounds still filled Holmes. He'd taken a second injection of the liquid heroin just before leaving the hotel.

And he knew there would be no echo of the shot here in the cemetery.

He reached the opening in the barrier of hedge and trees around the memorial without mishap, but paused just outside that entrance for a full minute so that his shadow from the lowering sun sending horizontal shafts of light through the trees should show his shape to maximum advantage. Then he entered.

He was the first one there. *Good,* he thought and crossed the triangular space to sit on the section of the three-sided concrete bench closest to Saint-Gaudens's statue. It was also the furthest from the opening in the hedge and would be invisible from anyone looking through any telescopic sight on the outside. If Lucan Adler wanted him tonight, he'd have to come within speaking range to have him.

At twenty-five past the hour, just as the dusk was settling gently, a dark form filled the opening. Then it approached him through the twilight scent of newly mown grass.

Holmes stood. Despite the years that had passed, Irene Adler looked no older to him than she had the last time he had seen her. Nor any less beautiful. Far more beautiful than the opera-ad image he'd shown other people. Contrary to style, she wore no gloves this evening and her sleeves were cut short enough to show her pale, bare forearms. She carried a small cloth handbag. *Large enough for a 2-shot Derringer pistol,* thought Holmes and immediately banished such thoughts from his mind. Now, later, much later—it no longer mattered to Sherlock Holmes. He only knew that the young man in black had spoken the truth when he said, "The readiness is all."

"Sherlock," she said and the sound of her voice moved something deep within him. She crossed the space, offered her hand in the American handshake mode, but he lifted it gently and kissed it.

"Hello, Irene." He pronounced her name the way she had taught him when they'd first met—*I-wren-ay.*

He realized he was holding her hand for too long a period of time and, suddenly embarrassed, he stepped back, gestured to the high-backed bench next to where he'd been seated closest to the sculpture, and said, "Will you sit with me?"

"By all means," she said.

They sat next to each other, silent, not quite touching, for what must have been a full three or four minutes. Holmes could sense that the leaves on the hedge behind them were moist with dew. The twilight deepened but the stars were not yet visible.

Finally Adler said, "Do we talk about us first, Sherlock? Or about this game we find ourselves in?"

"This is no game," said Holmes in a voice harder and sterner than he'd meant to use.

"Of course not," said Irene Adler and looked down at her hands folded on the small bag on her lap.

"Let us speak of personal things first," Holmes said in an infinitely softer tone.

"Very well. Which of us should start?"

"You should, Irene," said Holmes.

She turned a mock-stern face to him in the dim light. "Why did it take you almost two years to come to America to try to find me?" she demanded.

Holmes felt his face grow flushed. He looked down at her hands. "No one told me that you'd gone back to America. No one told me that you were pregnant. I worked for almost a full year in British theater troupes, looking for you."

"Idiot," said Irene Adler.

Holmes could only nod.

"And you practicing and preparing during your entire childhood to become the World's First and Foremost Consulting Detective," she said, but this time her tone was lighter, almost bantering.

Holmes nodded again but looked at her now. "I never found you in my time in America, either," he said, his voice sounding hollow even to his own ear.

She reached with her right hand and laid it on both of his. "That is because as soon as I heard—through the players' secret telegraph wires—that you had come to New York and Boston, I took the next ship to France."

"With the baby," said Holmes in something not quite a whisper.

"Yes." Her answer had been even quieter.

"When did Colonel Moran take him from you?" asked Holmes.

"When Lucan was four years old," said Irene Adler. "The day after his fourth birthday."

"How could you let that...that...brigand..." began Holmes and then fell silent.

"Because of the hold Colonel Moran had over me," said Adler. "The same hold that Lucan now uses."

Holmes, forgetting himself, took her by her upper arms, his strong hands then moving to her shoulders, as if he was about to draw her to him...or strangle her.

"Irene, you're the strongest, bravest woman I've ever met. How could a cad like Sebastian Moran have such a hold over you that you would surrender your child to him... *our* child?" The last two words had emerged as a sort of moan.

"Colonel Moran threatened to assassinate you if I did not do as he wished," she said tonelessly. "Just as Lucan does now."

Speechless, Holmes could communicate only by squeezing her arms more tightly. The pressure must have pained her, but she made no effort to pull away.

She turned to him, setting her own hands on his upper arms, until they must have looked to some stranger most like two people consoling one another. "You live a careless life, Sherlock Holmes," she said fiercely, no hint of apology in her voice. "You always have. That idiot doctor friend of yours—or Conan Doyle, I have no idea which—celebrates and publicizes your little front-parlor detection victories as if you were Achilles. But you sit at your window in plain view. You walk the streets lost in thought, oblivious to almost everything around you. You let the world know your street address and your daily habits. Colonel Moran—or others like him—have not long since murdered you because I've done what they want."

Holmes dropped his hands and sat brooding for a long moment. Finally, "But the child..."

"The child is evil," snapped Irene Adler. "The child was evil at birth."

Holmes's head snapped backward as if he'd been slapped. "No child can be evil from birth, for God's sake. It must take...years...parenting...evil influences..."

"You didn't hold this baby to your breast and watch its first actions," said Adler in a totally cold voice. "One of his first acts was to pluck the wings off a butterfly I was showing him. And he *enjoyed* it. It was as if I'd given birth to another Coriolanus."

"But even Coriolanus was shaped by..." he stopped.

"His mother," cried Irene Adler as if in physical pain. "Volumnia bragged to her hag friends about how her little boy Coriolanus loved to torture animals, give pain to any living thing. But never in the four years that I was with Lucan did I ever give him anything but love and training to love and respect others." She turned her face away and moved away from him on the bench.

He closed the distance again. "I was going to say that Coriolanus was shaped by warped Roman values," whispered Sherlock. "That's always been my understanding of what Shakespeare was trying to say."

Irene Adler laughed and it was a bitter, sad sound. "Don't you remember, Sherlock? We met in London during Henry Irving's troupe's presentation of *Coriolanus.* I a veteran of theater playing the old hag Volumnia at the advanced age of twenty-two and you an eighteen-year-old understudy, fleeing your first months of schooling in Cambridge, wet behind the ears and everywhere else."

"I've forgotten everything about the play," said Holmes. "But remembered every other second of our time together."

She touched his cheek with the backs of her fingers. "You were *so* young, my dear."

Holmes took her in his arms. She seemed to resist for a second or two and then melted into him. Then she set her hand on his chest and firmly pushed him away.

"Now," she said, "shall we discuss this not-a-game game we find ourselves in?"

Holmes couldn't speak for a moment and, when he did, his voice was ragged. "All right."

"What horrible thing first?" She'd obviously meant her tone to be light, but it came out as choked with emotion as Holmes's voice.

"The annual typed cards on December six," he said.

He could tell immediately that she had no idea what he was talking about. She was a consummate actress but Holmes now had decades of experience studying liars' faces and eyes when they lied. She was not faking her lack of understanding.

"What cards? I put flowers on Clover's grave every December six—white violets, she loved them—and I've sent a few flowers to Henry Adams on that date, but I've never included a card."

"Ned Hooper, Clover's brother, came to see me in London two years ago—he's dead now, by the way," said Holmes. "He offered me two thousand dollars and said he wanted me to solve the mystery of a card that each of the four surviving members of the Five of Hearts receives each December six—and has since December 'eighty-six. It's typed and always says the same thing... 'She was murdered'."

Irene Adler stared at him. "That's barbarous. I would never do that. There'd be no reason for Lucan to do that. No, he never would."

Holmes nodded. "I didn't think it was either of you but I owe it to Ned's memory—and the one-dollar retainer he paid me in eighteen ninety-one—to ask."

"That was the year that the papers said you died," Irene Adler said quietly. "In Switzerland, while fighting with some Professor Moriarty whom no one had ever heard of."

Holmes nodded again.

"I didn't believe it then," said Adler. "And I didn't believe it the next year when Lucan bragged that he'd killed you in Tibet."

Holmes smiled. "He nearly did. He put three rifle bullets through my back at a distance of almost a mile."

She seemed startled. "I'd always assumed he was lying. How could you survive three strikes like that from the kind of rifles Lucan uses?"

"I don't know," said Holmes. "But let's talk about Rebecca Lorne." The words clicked into place like the clack-clock of a bolt-action rifle bringing a live round into the chamber. "Was it for blackmail?"

"Of course," said Adler.

"Why Clover and Henry Adams?"

"They were rich. She was weak. At the time, in eighteen eighty-five, Lucan needed money for what he had to do in Europe. Blackmailing the

Adamses was an obvious way. Clover was so lonely and lost that I became her best friend in two days."

"But you continued the pretense for seven months," snapped Holmes.

"After the first days, it was no pretense," Irene Adler said softly. "I did like Clover. I admired her talent—as a person, as a photographer—far more than her arrogant, self-centered husband ever had. He used every possible chance to make her feel ... *less.* Less important. Less capable. Less than an equal human being. Have you read his novel *Esther* that came out not long before she died?"

"Yes," said Holmes.

"It's obviously a portrait of her ... of poor Clover ... and she's shown to be foolish and inept in her art, foolish in her life, and always dependent upon some merciful *man* for anything she might ever need or reach for in her life. If I'd had a husband who wrote a novel like that about *me,* I would have shot him twice ... the second bullet to the head to put him out of the misery of where I'd put the first round."

"Yes," said Holmes. And smiled this time.

"So you'd asked why I made her a victim," continued Irene.

Holmes nodded.

"I thought it was the fastest way to get Lucan out of her life," she said bitterly. "My dear Cousin Clifton. A mere boy." Her white hands became white fists in the dim light. "A mere boy who was a cancer ... a cancer which needed thousands of dollars to go back to Europe to murder someone alongside his hero, the great tiger-hunting Colonel Sebastian Moran."

"How did he ... Lucan ... find out about the romantic letter Henry Adams had sent Lizzie Cameron?" asked Holmes. "I presume that was the direction your blackmail took."

Irene Adler made a noise like a small dog choking. "Of course. That circle of friends was so small and so inbred that even young Lucan knew that there would be scandal just beneath the surface. After I'd become dear friends with Clover, and thus allowed into that tiny little circle of highest-society ladies, Lizzie Cameron herself bragged to me of Henry Adams's love letter to her. Lucan had said that there must be something, and in the end we didn't even have to dig. One of Clover's closest friends—quotation marks all around that phrase—gave us, gave *me,* the deadly dagger with a laugh."

"Why did you go with Clover to see Lizzie Cameron on her sickbed thirty-six hours before Clover's death?" asked Holmes.

"I wanted Lizzie to deny that any such letter existed," said Adler. "I'd asked her, Lizzie, just hours before, to deny it. She finally said she would."

"And did she?"

"She wouldn't. She was ill with the flu and all of her darker humours were in full control of her. She teased poor, silly Clover about the existence of the letter, playing dumb about it one minute, obviously acknowledging its existence the next. I almost strangled the woman in her four-posted silken-canopied bed. Clover went home that night certain that she'd so failed her husband Henry—at being his *real wife* as she always put it, she was terrified of sexual intercourse, you see, it was always strange and painful to her—that she decided that everything, including her husband's cheating attentions to Lizzie Cameron, was *her* fault."

"I can't see how driving Clover Adams to suicide could help Lucan or you in any way," said Holmes. "That's always been the sticking point of this conundrum."

"Not a very complicated one," said Adler. "Lucan had found other funding for his list of assassinations. Steady funding. Funding he has even today. He no longer had to wait for a neurotic woman to help us blackmail her husband."

"Did Lucan poison Clover Adams?" asked Holmes.

The long silence seemed to make the gathering darkness deeper.

"I don't know," said Irene Adler at last. "I know he brought the poison to her bedroom that Sunday morning . . . and the glass from downstairs. Suspecting that he would try something to get rid of her—she knew 'Cousin Clifton' too well to be on her guard—I rushed to her house that morning. But she was already dead on the floor. I heard footsteps on the servants' stairs—Lucan leaving, I believe—but somehow I don't think he forced the poison down her throat. Or even allowed her to see him, for that matter. It was just the bottle of potassium cyanide that had strangely moved from her photographic laboratory and the mysterious appearance of that single drinking glass that sent her off the edge. Per-haps she took it as a message from her husband . . . or God." After another silence, "But I was still as complicit in Clover Adams's death as Lucan was, whatever he did or didn't do. I even took the glass away in my hand-bag before I went down to meet Henry Adams returning from his walk."

"When you say he has steady funding, whom are you speaking of?" said Holmes. "The anarchists?"

Irene Adler laughed. It sounded almost authentic this time. Holmes remembered that she'd always had a beautiful laugh.

"The anarchists have no money to speak of, my darling," said Irene Adler. "They're *anarchists,* for God's sake. Most of them can't even find work in the factories where their fathers worked they're so drunk or crazy or lazy."

"Then who . . ." said Sherlock.

"I saw Lucan on Saturday," said Irene Adler. "He bragged about fol-lowing you and that writer you've been dragging around with you all through the Chicago World's Fairgrounds. You were within fifty yards of an entire building at the Fair dedicated to one of the primary companies funding Colonel Moran and Lucan Adler—they provide the list of tar-gets to be assassinated—and you didn't even peek into the building!"

"Krupp," Holmes said at last.

"Of *course.*"

Colonel Rice had gone on about how one of the great highlights of the World's Fair—at least for men and boys—was to be "Krupp's Baby", a 250,000-pound cannon so large that it needed its own building, tucked in between the Agriculture Building and the lake. The cannon, built by Fritz Krupp's Essen Works, was said to be capable of firing a one-ton shell twenty miles and still penetrate three feet of wrought-iron armor plating. Since the building hadn't been in a sniper's line of sight with the Administration Building, Holmes had had no interest in it.

"What do they want to come from these random assassinations?" asked Holmes and heard the one-syllable answer in his own mind a split second before Irene Adler spoke it aloud.

"War."

"Where?"

"Anywhere will suit them," she said. "As long as the major European powers are involved. From the list that Lucan has mentioned, I believe they place their fondest hopes for the fire starting in the Balkans."

"Then why on earth kill an American president?" said Holmes.

"A little test," said Adler. "And an easy one. American presidents are always so...accessible...aren't they?"

"Do you know where Lucan will be shooting from, Irene? His choice of a sniper's roost?"

"No."

He seized her upper arms again and squeezed hard enough to make a large man cry for mercy, but all the time he was looking into her eyes in the last of that April twilight. She was telling the truth. He let her go and said, "I'm sorry."

"I know that he expects you to figure out his shooting position," she said softly. Holmes noticed that she did not rub what must now be her bruised arms.

"Why?"

"Because he's already told me that he'll be killing you at almost the same time he will kill President Cleveland."

"Do you know *when* he'll kill the president?"

"He hasn't told me, but I know Lucan," said Irene Adler. "He'll shoot Cleveland during his short speech. When everyone is quiet and attentive. It will be the brightest spotlight on Lucan Adler's genius. He even described it in those terms."

"Do you know how he plans to escape?" asked Holmes.

"Not from wherever his sniper's roost might be," said Adler. "But I know the...vested interests who are paying him...have bought the swift-sailing ship the *Zephyr* and it will be waiting for Lucan in the lake just offshore. According to Lucan, the *Zephyr* with its sails, its German-trained racing crew, and new steam engine–driven propellers can outrun any police boat or yacht on the Great Lakes."

"Thank you for that," said Holmes. "Thank you for everything."

Irene Adler touched her locket, opened it, and held it up in the failing light, and for a second Holmes thought she might have a daguerreotype of him or some lock of his hair in there, but it was only a miniature watch.

She said softly, "Our hour is up, Mr. Sherlock Holmes."

"'Ill met by moonlight'?" he asked.

She smiled without effort, the way he remembered her smiling freely when he was not quite nineteen years old. "That's not the inconstant moon over the hedge tops, my lovelorn Romeo," she said. "It's one of the gaslights along the paved road in the cemetery."

He stood when she did. He made no move and neither did she. Then she turned toward the lighter opening in the monument's hedged-in space and he walked half a step behind her.

"I'll see you to your carriage," he said, taking her arm. They walked that way across the dew-wet grass where headstones were becoming vague and vaguely threatening inconstant outlines in the last of the twilight.

There were sidelights burning on her elegant enclosed coach. Holmes had an instant's perfect image of Lucan Adler thrusting his arm out the door of the coach and shooting him in the chest with a Colt .45 pistol.

He shook his head once, waving the eager driver/doorman aside, and helped Irene Adler step up into her empty coach.

"When shall we meet again?" asked Holmes, still holding the door as she settled into the cushioned bench.

"Oh, at your funeral or my hanging is most likely," said Irene Adler.

"NO!" said Sherlock Holmes in a voice so loud and so commanding that the horse twitched its tail in alarm and the driver turned around on his box.

She leaned forward and kissed him passionately on the lips. With her hands still on his cheeks she said softly,

> Now to scape the serpent's tongue,
> We will make amends ere long:
> Give me your hands, if we be friends...

Holmes immediately took both her hands in his and squeezed them.

And luck or Prov'dence shall restore amends.

She pulled the door shut and cried, "Drive on, driver."

Holmes stood there for a while in the dark. Then he walked back to Clover Adams's grave, stopped at the granite back of the monument, and pounded on it with his fist.

The stone door hinged open. Chief of the Treasury Department Andrew L. Drummond stepped out and pushed the granite shut behind him.

"Did you hear it all?" asked Holmes in a strained monotone.

"Yes, everything," said Drummond. "It shall be very helpful." He gripped Holmes's forearm in a man's more aggressive way than Irene had done just a few minutes earlier. "Holmes, the personal things . . . I swear to you upon my word of honor, upon my children's lives . . . that no one shall ever hear a word of them from me."

Holmes shrugged as if to say he'd known how naked and vulnerable he would be after this session.

"We'll find and start following the *Zephyr* immediately," said Drummond.

Holmes nodded tiredly. "But let it anchor there near the World's Fair," he said in the same monotone as before. "Nothing must let Lucan Adler know that we're on to his plan."

"We'll have to put Miss Adler under arrest," said Drummond.

"Not now, for Christ's sake!" exploded Holmes. "We'd just as well send Lucan Adler a telegram saying that we were on to him. Follow her if you can do so subtly—and I mean so totally subtly that a snake like Lucan Adler wouldn't spot the tail—but, better yet, leave her alone, unfollowed, and free until . . ." His voice trailed off.

"Until when?" asked Drummond.

"Until I tell you otherwise," said Holmes and turned to walk away.

Behind him, Agent Drummond blew a police whistle, and more than a dozen men—shadows among shadows—came from behind distant trees, boulders, headstones, and monuments to join their chief. Wagons were arriving at the park entrance. By their lamps, Holmes could see that most of the men were armed with pistols, as Drummond had been, but several carried long guns. None of them could have stopped Lucan Adler from shooting Sherlock Holmes—the sniper would have been too concealed for that—but the plan had been to capture Lucan after the fatal shot had revealed his position.

Holmes was waved into a comfortable open carriage that would carry just him and Drummond back into town.

Remembering the timbre of Irene Adler's voice, Holmes surprised Drummond by crying, "Drive on, driver!"

3

Early on the morning of Friday, the twenty-ninth of April, Henry Adams and Henry James rode together to the main railway station to meet the "special train" that Henry Cabot Lodge had laid on for them.

It was a short ride, but Adams used it for what he obviously thought was an important conversation. "Harry," he said, leaning forward toward the portly writer, "I need to tell you—before we meet up with all the others—how very important your visit has been to me the last two weeks."

James's gray eyes came alert. "And to me as well, Henry. I shall always treasure the hospitality and our nightly conversations."

"And you did get some work done on your play?"

James smiled ruefully. "Some. Then rewrote it. Then rewrote it again. Then I tossed it all out. But I did start to expand a short story I'd written—a slight thing about an impoverished tutor who loves the young child in his care more than do the child's careless parents."

"It sounds all too real," said Adams.

James made a slight gesture with his hand. "I shall see."

"Thank you for allowing me to speak freely about Clover—her life as well as her death—after my years of silence," said Adams. "I shall always be grateful to you for that."

James's eyes seemed to fill. "The honor and gratitude was all mine, my friend. I assure you."

Suddenly Adams grinned. "Do you remember what you said to Clover in eighteen eighty-two in what you said was your last letter, from the ship before it sailed? Why you had chosen her to receive what you called 'my last American letter'?"

"I said that I considered Clover the incarnation of her native land," said James.

"And do you remember her response to me when she read that? I shared it in a letter to you so many years ago."

Henry James said, "Clover told you that mine was, I believe her exact words were, 'a most equivocal compliment', and that it left her wondering, and I do remember her wording exactly—'Am I then vulgar, dreary, and impossible to live with?'"

Both men laughed heartily.

Adams held out his closed hand. Presuming his friend wanted to shake hands, James held out his hand, but Adams turned it over and dropped something cold and solid into it. James realized that it was his watch, the watch given to him by his father, the watch he'd lost that mad night he and Sherlock Holmes had been hiding in the Saint-Gaudens monument, Henry Adams's most cherished secret.

James blushed but, when he looked up, Adams was smiling.

"Clover and I will always love you, Harry."

James quickly lowered his face but could not hide the tears that dripped from his cheeks and chin onto his open hand holding the beloved watch.

4

Holmes appeared at the Washington railway station at the appointed time and was amazed at what Henry Cabot Lodge's casually offered "lay on some special private cars" amounted to. It was an entire private train unto itself. After the engine there was a car for servants' quarters. Then a lavish car just for dining. Then a comfortable car for smoking, conversation, and taking in the passing view. Then no fewer than four even-more-lavish private cars for Lodge and his guests.

Henry Cabot and his wife Nannie had the end suite, half a car at the end of the train. Senator Don Cameron and his beautiful wife Lizzie had an equally spacious suite—an entire suite, complete with water closet, on a railway carriage!—and the Hays had an elaborate compartment which adjoined a smaller one where their daughter Helen slept. Clarence King had chosen not to make the trip, claiming necessary meetings in the West concerning mining interests, but Augustus Saint-Gaudens had accepted Lodge's invitation. So the three bachelors—Saint-Gaudens, James, and Holmes—had smaller compartments, but each lavishly appointed and equipped with its own private toilet and sink. When told that the three gentlemen would have the constant services of only two valets—the servants' car was overcrowded as it was—James had sighed and said, "Well, we shall just have to rough it then all the way to Chicago."

James had received Holmes quite coolly when they'd met after two weeks of separation and silence, but the detective had seemed too distracted by some thought to notice James's carefully calculated snub. During the first hours of the voyage, James was irritated that he would be forced to break the mutual silence and talk with Holmes privately.

He found his chance after the elaborate dinner when the women went to the common social area on the first half of the fourth carriage and the men went into the smoking-room carriage with brandy and cigars. James pulled the detective into the dining room and told the servants to step out until he said they could enter again.

"What is it?" asked Holmes. The detective still seemed preoccupied with something and had barely spoken during dinner, even though Hay's daughter Helen had tried to draw him out with half a dozen questions.

"I saw Moriarty," whispered James. "I sent a note to that effect to your damned cigar store but they sent it back to me unopened with a scrawl saying that you were no longer picking up your mail there."

"That's true," said Holmes. He was applying his fancy modern lighter to a Meerschaum pipe and puffing offending aromatic fumes into the air that still smelled of beef and wine. "I've been traveling and wasn't checking for mail at that cigar store. Where and when did you see Moriarty?"

"On the day I was prepared to leave Chicago for New York," said James, his temper short. "On the fifteenth. The same day you left for heaven knows where."

"*Where* did you see him, James? And what was he up to?"

The writer thought that Holmes was being damnably offhanded about such a serious topic. "He was at the central Chicago railway station, looking through the carriages. Looking for *me*, Holmes. He had some thugs helping him search. I barely got away without him seeing me."

Holmes nodded and puffed. "Why do you think that Professor Moriarty was looking for *you*, James?"

"Well, *you* weren't taking the morning train from Chicago to New York that morning, *were* you?" demanded James.

Holmes shook his head without removing the stem of the pipe from between his teeth.

"Moriarty and his thugs were there with their eyes full of business," said James. "And that business was, I am certain, murder. And I was to

have been the victim. Somehow . . . from someone you told about my earlier eavesdropping on Moriarty and the anarchists and mobs . . . somehow
word got out. *He was stalking me, Holmes.* I am certain of it."

"Then it's a good thing you didn't get on that particular train," said
Holmes.

James's jaw dropped. "*That's* all you have to say about this? *That's* your
response to my news? Where have you been the last two weeks?"

"Oh, here and there," said Holmes, having to re-light his oversized
pipe.

"And what have you been doing about the threat that Moriarty and
his anarchists and his criminals pose to Washington, and New York, and
Philadelphia, and Chicago, and the other cities I heard him say would
suffer uprisings after President Cleveland is assassinated? Is the army involved? Have you spoken to all the mayors and chiefs of police of all
those cities? I can think of little else that could warrant your two-week
absence and your obvious . . . obvious . . . *insouciance* in the face of this imminent threat of what amounts to national revolution."

"I wouldn't worry about Moriarty," said Holmes, patting James on the
shoulder like a tutor reassuring a child. James was not fast enough to bat
away Holmes's hand, but he wished for hours later that he had been.

"*Not worry about Moriarty?*" cried James. "But certainly he must take
priority in your searches. Professor Moriarty is the . . . in your words, I believe . . . the mastermind behind all the murders and violent uprisings to
come. Surely you must seek out Moriarty as your primary duty and allow
others to take care of this . . . this . . . *boy* . . . Lucan Adler."

"No," Holmes said bluntly. "What we have to concentrate on first is
stopping Lucan Adler from killing the president. Then I shall deal with
Professor Moriarty. You need to trust me on this, James."

James could only shake his head in frustration and amazement. "And
do you know how to do that? Stop the assassination from happening?"
he asked at last. "Do you know where the assassin will be shooting from,
how he plans to escape, and . . . most of all . . . what on earth you could do
to stop him?"

"I believe so," said Holmes. "We shall find out in less than three days,
shan't we? Oh, and I shall expect you to help me when that time comes,

James." He had the effrontery to pat Henry James on the shoulder again before Holmes went to the connecting door, waved the waiting servants in, and said, "Shall we join the other gentlemen in the smoking car?"

Henry James had never in his life felt the urge to kill anyone—save for a few brief stabs of that emotion aimed at his older brother William—but now he felt he could take a carving knife to Mr. Sherlock Holmes. He went into the smoking room and found a seat as far from the detective as he could get in the long carriage.

5

Henry Cabot Lodge's special World's Fair Express train arrived in Chicago on the morning of April 29 with everyone well-rested and amused. Everyone, it seemed, save for Sherlock Holmes, who seemed further and further lost in his own thoughts.

Lodge had let everyone know that their special cars were going to be parked on a private siding less than fifty yards outside the Columbian Exposition's western gates where all the trains deposited visitors who went through the gates and onto the Parade Ground, flowing ahead to the Administration Building and the Court of Honor and then into the rest of the White City. All of his guests were free to come and rest or freshen up at any time of the days and nights they'd be there. The servants and cooks were on constant call.

But their first stop that morning was at a downtown-Chicago pier where everyone was ferried out to Don Cameron's "Great Lakes Yacht", the stately *Albatross,* where they were each shown slightly smaller but still luxurious rooms they could use whenever they wanted. The yacht was also heavily stocked with servants who would bring a cold drink or fix a full meal on a minute's notice. Cameron gathered everyone together before the expeditions to the Fair began and explained that messengers would run any notes from the *Albatross* to anyone who decided to stay at or visit the luxury train cars and that there would always be at least one, and usually two, steam-powered longboats to rush them to or from Casino Pier at any hour of the day or night.

And with that, the explorations began. John Hay and Cabot Lodge had made sure that everyone—even young Helen—had the all important SPECIAL VISITOR badges that allowed them the run of the White City and the newly vitalized Midway Plaisance at any time. Lodge explained that the director of the entire Columbian Exposition, Daniel Burnham, had said that there would be a lot of last-minute cleaning-up going on—rubble moved, temporary tracks being taken out, last-minute fields of flowers and even trees being planted, some of the huge buildings getting their last spray of white paint—but if they were careful, they shouldn't be in anyone's way.

Finally, Lodge warned them to be careful on the mile-long strip called the Midway Plaisance. Burnham had told Henry Cabot that everything and everyone was in place save for the...Lodge didn't use the word Burnham had...doggoned Ferris Wheel which should be completed in June. Meanwhile, the Midway offered complete Algerian and Tunisian Villages where they could sample the exotic food or watch even more exotic jugglers and dancing girls; the Barre Sliding Railway—a water-propelled ride that guaranteed screams and squeals of delight the whole length of the Midway; the Bernese Alps Electric Theatre where visitors in a hundred-seat diorama took a frigid (thanks to electrical refrigeration) trip over thirty simulated miles of Alpine peaks.

There was the captive balloon, which Lodge didn't recommend to the ladies, as well as the Chinese Village, Dahomey Village, Turkish Village, and German Village, all populated with hundreds of appropriately dressed natives. For those seeking out culture along the Midway Plaisance, there was Hagenbeck's Zoological Arena placed conveniently near the Hungarian Concert Pavilion where Gypsy bands would play and dance in native costume. Also nearby was the Vienna Concert Hall and Café.

There was a perfectly realized Street in Cairo—along with native Egyptians in their robes and with their dogs, snakes, and monkeys—as well as a huge building for the Kilauea Volcano for those who wanted a thrill. If they grew too warm in their weekend visit, there was the Natatorium indoor swimming pool. This Saturday night and Sunday night, the White City would be lighted only by its gaslights and the full moon, but Lodge promised that after President Cleveland turned the magic key on Monday, May first, the White City and its extended Midway Plaisance would become the most brightly and dramatically lighted place on the planet.

Everyone—wearing their darker suits and dresses for almost the last time before light summer linen clothing became appropriate on Monday—got onto the waiting power boats and went ashore. Sherlock Holmes left the others when he reached the pier; he had scheduled meetings with Colonel Rice, Agent Drummond, and the Chicago Chief of Police Robert McClaughry.

Henry James decided to stay aboard the *Albatross*—Lake Michigan was so calm at their anchorage that there was almost no discernible movement of the large yacht—and to take a nap in his mahogany lined, silk-and-velvet-cushioned stateroom.

He awoke sometime after dark to find the yacht empty save for crew members. Everyone must be partying somewhere ashore.

They'd left a power launch and boatman for him and, as James came to the boat ladder, the man at the helm said, "Take you into the White City dock, sir?"

"No," said James, his heart beating so quickly that he found it hard to take in a breath. "Take me to the main Chicago pier."

6

He had decided that he—Henry James—would track down the elusive Professor Moriarty. During the hours of his sleepless "nap" that afternoon aboard Don Cameron's yacht, James had convinced himself that Moriarty and his accomplices at the train station had not been searching for *him*. Searching for Holmes or someone else, perhaps, but not for him. What was he to Moriarty or Moriarty to him?

No, he'd assured himself, it had just been coincidence that he'd spotted the evil professor at the train station. James trusted again in his own anonymity—at least in terms of being a target for either the Adler boy or his dark master, Moriarty.

Telling the boatman to wait for him there at City Pier, no matter how late it might be, James took a trolley into the dark heart of Chicago and boarded one of the elevated trains there.

He had no real search plans and, of course, had not brought any weapon—the idea of searching night-time Chicago for Moriarty felt strangely thrilling. What reassured James was that the chance of him crossing Moriarty's path again by sheer accident was so small as to be something that could only occur in a poorly written popular novel.

Chicago's transit system of elevated trains—called the "L" even then—had only come into service the year before, in 1892. The first cars were wooden coaches open to the elements on either side, but now—as James rode through the night on the Lake Street Elevated Railroad—the carriages were enclosed. James had picked up a transit-system map at the first station he'd found and it clearly showed that, except for the Chicago and South Side Rapid Transit Railroad, which now extended south all the way to 63rd Street and Stony Island Avenue, the Transportation Building entrance to the Columbian Exposition, all the other terminals were, most inconveniently, James thought, at the periphery of Chicago's actual downtown.

On their first day in the city, Holmes had told him that this quirk was due to a state law requiring approval from the businesses and building owners along any downtown street before tracks could be built over that avenue.

James knew that he was headed south on this spur, but he had no intention of going all the way back to the Jackson Park stops at the World's Fair. Holmes and all of Cameron's other guests might still be there. Of course, so might Moriarty. But James chose to stay in Chicago proper—the Black City as he now thought of it—for his late-night search for the professor.

He stepped off the "L" train some blocks before the 63rd Street Station that would have brought him back to the Fair and began walking almost at random.

He'd gone several blocks in the poorly lighted section of the city before he realized three things: first, that there were no street lights in this part of town but many people on the sidewalks; second, that there seemed to be an ungodly number of bars and dance halls pounding the night with raucous music; and third, that his was the only white face present in the five- or six-block distance he'd walked from the "L" station.

Realizing (with some small flutter of alarm) that he'd mistakenly got off the elevated train in the south side Negro section of town—he'd heard Holmes refer to it once as "Ebonyville"—James whirled to walk briskly back to the elevated's platform and realized he'd taken several turns and not paid attention to which way he'd walked. No elevated tracks were visible down any of the cross-streets he was now coming to in a stride so urgent that it almost qualified as running.

Suddenly a Negro man in a rather showy pinstripe suit, amazingly bright tie, and quality straw hat came up to him and blocked his flight.

"Are you lost, sir?" asked the Negro. "Can I be of some help?"

James took three steps back but managed to say, "Would you be so kind as to tell me how to reach the 'L' platform that would put me back on the Lake Side train?"

The Negro smiled—perfectly white teeth against the darkest skin James had ever seen—and said, "Certainly, sir." He pointed the way from which James had just come. "Back three blocks along this street, then left at 48th Street, and it's just a block and a half to the 'L' station there."

"Thank you," said James, almost bowing in his relief. But as he headed back the way he had just come—the sidewalks and streets full of colored people who appeared to be celebrating something—he could not resist glancing back over his shoulder to see if his benefactor was following him for some dark reason.

The man in the straw hat was standing exactly where he'd spoken to James, half a block away now, and at James's glance, the tall Negro again showed that white grin and raised his hat in a friendly wave.

Had that wave been an act of insolence? wondered James. Immediately he was ashamed of himself.

But the truth was that although Henry James now considered himself to be one of the most cosmopolitan of men (especially of Americans), equally at home in the streets of London, Paris, Florence, Venice, Rome, Zurich, Lucerne, or Berlin, he simply hadn't had much contact with Negroes in anything but their occasional service capacities in American hotels.

But then he was on the "L" platform again, an enclosed-carriage train arrived within minutes, and he was riding north again.

* * *

For the next ninety minutes or so, James took the elevated lines as far as he could but then had to take the late-running trolley cars to areas such as Douglas Park, Garfield Park, Humboldt Park, and Logan Square (although the small print on his "L"-system map bragged of opening the West Side Elevated line within another year or two).

James didn't mind the transitions. The trolleys were more comfortable at any rate.

And in the few sections that had adequate street lighting—and white people on the sidewalks and in the carriages—James would stretch his legs for several blocks, always on the alert for Moriarty's gleaming bald dome and terrible gaze.

In one of these western, working-class sections of town, James realized that he'd not eaten anything since an early and light lunch that day. It was late enough now that some of the cafés were shutting down for the night, but others were open and several were crowded. Still, it was a working-man's clientele complete with cloth caps—kept in place even while dining—corduroy or moleskin trousers, and huge boots. There were a few women in these places but judging from the excess of rouge and other make-up, combined with their calculated dishabille, James supposed them to be women of the night.

He decided to eat when he finally returned to the yacht. For now he turned back to find the next trolley stop going west again.

*   *   *

James soon realized that there was a mystery to these trains and trolleys that had nothing to do with Sherlock Holmes or Lucan Adler or his prey for the night, Professor Moriarty. After sitting in more than two dozen mostly empty train carriages and trolleys, he had seen at least a dozen different men reading the same book.

All the men were dressed in poorly fitted wool suits and old but well-shined shoes and a few wore straw hats (but none as clean or well-blocked as that of his Negro interlocutor hours earlier) and each man held the book up close to his face as if he were near-sighted. But few of the men wore glasses. And, compounding the mystery for James, he would stay on for several stops and none of the reading men ever turned a page.

They simply seemed to be holding the book open in front of their bored (and sometimes closed) eyes. What bothered James most *was that it was the same book in each case.*

The title was *MAGGIE: A Girl of the Streets,* the volumes looked crude enough—to James's professional gaze—to be self-published, and the author's name was Johnston Smith.

Finally, near the southwestern end of the line on the trolley James was then on, he dared to sit in the empty seat in front of the "reading man", turned toward him, and cleared his throat loudly. The man did not lower the book.

"I beg your pardon," James said at last and the man started—he'd obviously been dozing—and lowered the book.

"I've noticed quite a few gentlemen on public transportation this evening reading precisely the volume you are," James said, "and I hope you don't think me impertinent if I ask why it's so popular in Chicago."

The man smiled broadly, showing nicotine-stained or missing teeth which suggested that the thick and uncomfortable-looking suit he had on was his *only* suit. "I've been waitin' for someone to ask," said the man. "Truth is, I haven't read a word of this idiotic book. A fellow pays me—and some twenty or so other lads—to just ride around on the trains and trolleys from seven a.m. 'til the transits close down at one a.m. I think the fellow thinks that if other folks see us readin' this book, they'll rush out an' buy one for their own selves. Problem is, the only other people I've seen readin' this here book are other coves like me who've been paid to do so. Or to pretend we are."

"How long have you and the other...ah...readers been so employed?" asked James.

"Three weeks now, with never so much as a question about the book. Until you come along, that is. I think our guy is runnin' out of cash though. I'm afraid that by this time next week, I'll have to find honest work."

"Is it the author, Mr. Johnston Smith, who is paying you for this...advertising effort?" asked James.

"It's the author all right, but his name ain't Johnston nor Smith. He's a young-lookin' cove, no more'n twenty-one or twenty-two at the oldest with shoes more worn than ours is...and his real name is Stephen Crane."

"Well, it's an interesting way to promote one's novel," said James, wondering if such a stunt might work for him in the more literary crowds of London. But, no...the literary crowds in London did not use transit designed for the masses save for railway carriages, and no British man or woman would start a conversation with a stranger in the carriage. It simply was not done.

"You know," said the man with the book now closed and on his lap, "I've read me a book or two in my day, and this *MAGGIE* thing ain't even a real book."

"How do you mean?"

"I mean," said the man, "that it's only about forty pages long, and that with wide white margins on each side and a bunch of empty white pages in front 'n' back."

"A short story bound as a book," mused James.

The man shrugged. "All I know is I got one more lousy hour to prop this thing up before the trolleys shut down and I can go home to sleep. My arms are killing me from holdin' this trash up to my nose all day and night, but this Crane fellow checks up on us almost every day. The lot of us've compared notes and, if the book ain't raised right or your eyes ain't open, you get canned on the spot. And there ain't many jobs these days where a man gets paid two dollars a day for just sitting on his ass."

James shook his head as if in sympathy.

The trolley came to a stop in a dark part of town and the driver and conductor got out to swing it around. The end of the line evidently.

James decided to stretch his legs for a moment.

"You're not getting out here, are you?" asked the paid book man.

"Just for a second," said James.

But as soon as he was out in the muggy air, he saw, half a block away, under the only street lamp working on that block, the flash of baldness, the glimpse of a frock coat and old-fashioned high collar, and the white-worm movement of the long strangler's fingers before the darkness swallowed the man up again.

Forgetting about the trolley, James began walking quickly after the apparition.

* * *

Beyond that last, weak street lamp, there was not only deep darkness but a sudden end to the tenements and shacks that had lined each side of the street. It was as if James had followed Professor Moriarty all the way out of Chicago and they were on the dark prairie together.

But then the smell struck James. The smell and the sense of hundreds if not thousands of massive but unseen animal hooves, the stench and the atavistic certainty that one is being stared at in the darkness by countless unseen eyes. The street ended in a T and straight ahead through the staggering stench James could make out a great, dark, occasionally moving mass of living, breathing, staring, and excreting organisms. Cattle.

He'd reached the Chicago stockyards. Not a single street light or building's lighted window pierced the darkness to either side. Far out in the filled corrals there was a gas lamp or two, but they were too far away to shed any light on his immediate surroundings. James saw the strangely dark glistening of horns far out there.

James chose to turn left and walked boldly into the breathing darkness in that direction.

* * *

It took a minute or two for him to realize that there was no sidewalk, no paved street under his shoes. Just gravel and dirt. At least it was not mud of the sort he was sure filled the cattle pens to his right. He could hear the squelching as sleeping cattle moved fitfully or others shoved their way through the mass to a feeding trough.

James also realized that he felt...different. The apathy and anger of the day had drained away with his bold searching out of Moriarty in the dangerous Chicago neighborhoods. He'd caught no more glimpse of the bald head and long, white fingers since he'd come to this black collision of crumbling city warehouses and the huge stockyards, but he hadn't really expected to find—much less confront—the mastermind of crime.

Henry James realized it was as if he was outside himself, above himself, watching himself (here where it was too dark even to read the hands of his watch without striking a match). Before this night, he'd been struggling to be a playwright; now he was both actor and audience, watching himself as he *acted*. Not "performed", but *acted*, as in carrying out a physical and purposeful (and somewhat daring) action. *If this is how a character in some lesser writer's novel feels...I like it,* thought James.

It was hard for him to believe at this moment that a little more than a month and a half ago, he'd been ready to drown himself in the Seine. For what? Sagging book sales?

James almost laughed aloud as he strode along in the night. As much as he still disliked Sherlock Holmes for a myriad of valid reasons, he now realized that the detective—whether real or fictional—had been Henry James, Jr.'s, savior. This strange night in this strange city, James felt younger, stronger—more alive—than any time he could remember, at least since his childhood. And he deeply suspected that the life and energy he'd felt as a boy was merely his lunar reflection of the sunlight of older brother William's wild energy and spirit.

Drastic engagement. These were the words that now echoed through James's mind. Not merely a reinvigorated engagement with the stuff of daily life, but an engagement with the dangers and dramas outside any life he'd ever allowed himself to imagine, much less live. For the first time he understood how his brother Wilkie could have suffered such terrible wounds, seen such horrible things—one of the two men carrying Wilkie along the dunes on a stretcher the day after the night battle at Fort Wagner had his head blown to pieces, the spatterings of brains and white bits of skull falling all over Wilkie as the stretcher fell to the ground—yet Wilkie, only partially recovered, had eventually gone back to the war. As had James's brother Bob after losing half his regiment in a different battle.

Drastic engagement. James suddenly understood why such moments *were* life to Sherlock Holmes and why the detective had to resort to injections of cocaine or morphine or heroin to get through the dull, backwater days of the quotidian between dangerous cases.

It might have been Moriarty he'd glimpsed from the trolley a half hour earlier, but probably not. It didn't matter that much to James at that moment.

And then he saw motion. Dark shapes moving toward him. Vertical forms outside the wooden fences of the corrals. Men.

James's eyes had adapted well enough to the dark—the backs of the warehouses to his left had no lit windows or outside lamps—that he could see that the forms were of four men and that all of them carried clubs, truncheons.

He stopped.

Lifting his gentleman's stick into both soft hands, James wished that it was Holmes's sword-cane.

Should he run? James realized that he had more dread of being dragged down from behind on the run, like one of these cattle at a rodeo, than of facing whoever or whatever was striding toward him so quickly in the darkness.

The four assailants—James had no delusions that they could be anything else and whether they worked for Moriarty or not was academic and irrelevant to everything now (he'd never know)—had fanned out and were less than ten feet from him when a voice boomed from a dark alley to his left.

"YOU THERE! STOP! DON'T MOVE!!"

The shield was raised on a powerful dark lantern and a beam of light stabbed out from the distant alley to illuminate Henry James—his cane held at port-arms across his chest—and four thugs in patched and filthy stockyard clothing. What James had imagined were truncheons *were* truncheons...knobbed, stained, deadly.

"FREEZE!" bellowed the God-voice again. James had already obeyed and did not move a muscle, while his four assailants exploded into motion, two vaulting over the corral fence to shove their way into the dark mass of cattle, the other two loping back along the fence into the darkness from whence they'd come.

The light shifted away from them to hold on the squinting James as the figure with the God-voice came closer. Then the beam lowered.

A Chicago policeman. Not one of Burnham's flashy Columbian Guardsmen for the Fair, but a real Chicago policeman. James took in the double row of brass buttons, the soft cap, the oversized star on the short but burly man's left chest, the narrowed eyes, and the luxurious mustache.

James felt some relief that the policeman had shown up when he did, but he'd not been frightened. *James had not been frightened,* even as the four thugs closed on him. He did not understand it. Nor did he under-stand himself at the moment.

No matter. He realized that he was giving the suspicious police officer a silly smile. James composed himself as best he could.

The now half-shielded beam from the dark lantern moved up and down James, from his soft, expensive black Italian-made shoes and dusty spats to his expensive jacket, waistcoat, collar, cravat, and stickpin.

"What are you doing out here at the stockyards, sir?" said the police-man in a human-leveled voice. "Those men would have robbed you of everything...most probably including your life, sir."

James fought down the strange impulse to grin at the wonderful policeman with his wonderful Irish accent and his wonderful waxed mustache and even at his wonderful short, black, heavy wooden trun-cheon, which Holmes had told him was called a "billy club" in America.

James tried to reply, but the master of the modern endless sentence could manage only ragged fragments. "I was...I wanted...to see Chicago...got off the elevated train...then the trolleys...got out to walk...suddenly it was all...darkness."

The police officer realized that he was dealing with an idiot and spoke now in a slow, reassuring, nursery-teacher's voice. "Yes, sir. But this...is no place...for you...sir."

James nodded his agreement and he realized, to his horror, that he *was* grinning now. *He'd not been afraid.*

"Where are you staying, sir?"

It took a few seconds for the meaning of the officer's question to sink in. "Oh, at the...no, not the Great Northern this time...no...on Cameron's...on Senator Don Cameron's...yacht."

The police officer squinted at him. James realized that the Irishman was handsome enough, save for a nose that looked like a squashed red potato. He bit the inside of his cheek to stop himself from laughing.

"Where is this yacht, sir?"

"Anchored off the Grand Pier of the White City," said James. He was in charge of his nouns, verbs, and syntax again. (In truth, he hadn't missed them much. He realized that he'd trade the whole lot for just more of what he was feeling right now.)

"May I ask your name, sir?

"Henry James, Jr.," James said at once. Then, wondering at his reply, he hurried to correct it. "Just Henry James now. My father—Henry James, Sr.—died about eleven years ago."

"How did you get ashore from this senator's yacht, Mr. James?"

"The City Pier. There's a boatman from the yacht in a steam launch. I told him to wait for me."

The policeman turned his lantern on an inexpensive watch in his palm. "It's after midnight, sir."

James did not know what to say to this revelation. He suddenly doubted if his boatman had waited all these hours. Perhaps all his friends presumed him lost. Or dead.

"Come, Mr. James," said the policeman, putting a gentle arm on James's shoulder and turning them back toward the dark alley from which he'd so magically emerged. "I'll see you back to the right trolley stop, sir. The trolleys and the new "L" quit running in less than an hour, now. Even on a Saturday night. You'll need to go straight back to the pier with no more sightseeing."

Not minding at all the friendly arm on his shoulders, James walked with the Irishman back toward the lighted parts of the city.

7

On the Sunday before Monday's May-first official Opening Day of the Fair, Henry Cabot Lodge's guests had broken into various groups to find their day's entertainment. During the time Henry James was with anyone exploring the quiescent but soon-to-erupt fairgrounds, he stayed with Henry Adams who was staying close to Lizzie and Don Cameron. But sometime in the afternoon, Adams had wandered off alone again. He'd spent most of the previous day alone as well. Everyone had agreed to meet back on the pier at seven to take the large motor launch back to the yacht. They were going up the lake to be guests at a gala given by the 68-year-old re-elected Mayor Carter Henry Harrison. Even young Helen Hay had been seduced by the old populist's energy, candor, and charm upon first meeting him earlier that day.

But when everyone gathered on the pier, Adams was missing.

"I believe I know where he is," said Holmes. "He tends to lose track of time there. You all go ahead but send the boat back...I shall be on the pier with Mr. Adams within twenty minutes."

Senator Don Cameron said, "Lizzie and I shall wait here for you and Adams and ride out to the yacht with you."

The rest of the happy party boarded and Holmes watched the powered boat churn out to where a cluster of yachts, including the noble *Albatross,* and even the iron warship U.S.S. *Michigan* were anchored.

Holmes had been with Adams when they discovered the Machinery Hall, and the older historian's fascination with the dynamos and other machines producing electricity suddenly became insatiable. Technically, none of the Columbian Exposition's thousands of electricity-driven machines were supposed to be turned on until noon the next day when President Cleveland would depress a solid gold telegraph key—set on a red velvet pillow—which would, besides causing a thousand flags and banners to unfurl, close a circuit that would start up the gigantic 3,000-horsepower Allis-made steam engine in the Machinery Building.

But Adams had poked around and inquired until he found the real dynamo that was already providing power to the White City's lights and the electrical railroad bringing yellow cars to the Fair. It was the world's greatest dynamo and it was all but hidden away in the Intramural Railroad Company building set at the far southern end of the grounds, sunken behind trees and grander buildings. Usually the building was empty save for the dynamo's constant attendants. The curved metal sheath of the actual dynamo was larger than the arched entrance to Henry Adams's mansion, but the various wheels—at least fifteen feet tall even with half of each wheel disappearing into its groove in the cement floor—dwarfed men and dynamo. Holmes had helped him search it out on Saturday, admired the machinery for a minute, listened long enough to hear one of the technicians shout to Henry Adams above the roar that even at that moment the dynamo was powering six and a half miles of railroad with sixteen cars in motion all at once, and then he left Adams alone in the noise and ozone. He knew that the historian was spending most of his hours on shore in this remote, almost windowless building staring at and experiencing the power of this new source of energy for the human race.

Now as Holmes came in through the shadows of girders and wheels, he saw that Adams kept removing his straw hat and mopping his brow with his linen handkerchief—the unshaded overhead work lamps gleamed on his bald head each time he removed the hat—and was busy talking to a tall young man dressed in a far-too-heavy wool suit who, because of the young man's long black hair, sharp beak of a nose, copper complexion, and black eyes, Holmes took to be a Red Indian. Adams was lecturing and looked as excited as a school boy.

"...But *this!* This, Mr. Slow Horse, the ancient Greeks would have delighted to see and the Venetians, at their height, would have envied. Chicago has turned on us with a sort of wonderful, defiant contempt, and shown us something far more powerful even than art, infinitely more important than mere business. This is, alas or hurrah, the *future,* Mr. Slow Horse! Yours and mine both, I fear...and yet hope at the same time. I can revel and write postcards about the fakes and frauds of the Midway Plaisance, but each day I pass through the Machinery Hall and each evening I return here, to this very chamber, to stare like an old owl at the dynamo of the future...".

Adams seemed to hear his own lecturing tone, took off his straw hat and mopped his scalp again, and said more softly to the young man as Holmes came up behind them—"I must apologize again, sir. I babble on as if you were an audience rather than an interlocutor. What do you think of this dynamo and the now-quiescent wonders of the Machinery Hall, where I've seen you staring each day even as I do, Mr. Slow Horse?"

The tall Indian paused before speaking and his voice shocked Holmes it was so resonant. "I think, Mr. Adams," said the tall, dark man, "that it is the true and revealed religion of your race."

Adams launched into another excited speech and Holmes made himself known to him—he knew that the Indian had noticed him enter and knew where he was the entire time he'd been in the vast space with them—and Adams was saying, "The Virgin Mary was to the men of the thirteenth century what this dynamo and its brother shall be to..."

He realized that Holmes was standing there and stammered to a stop. He removed his straw hat again and said, "Mr. Slow Horse, may I present my companion at the Fair today, the eminent Sher...that is...the eminent Norwegian explorer, Mr. Jan Sigerson."

Instead of offering his hand, Holmes stood straight, heels together, and bowed toward the man in an almost Germanic fashion. The Red Indian nodded back but also seemed as reluctant to touch bare hands as Holmes was. Without knowing how or why he knew, Holmes *knew* that this young man—not quite so young seen close up, Holmes realized, noting the creases around the eyes probably only a year or two short of Holmes's own 39 years—was not only a Lakota Sioux of the kind that Holmes had met more than 17 years ago, but was a *wičasa wakan*—a holy man of that tribe, a shaman, a man touched with the ability to see in more dimensions than most human beings.

"It is a true pleasure to meet you, Mr. Slow Horse," said Holmes. "We Europeans rarely get the opportunity to meet a practicing *wičasa wakan* from the Natural Free Human Beings."

The Indian, whose real name Holmes had known instantly and absolutely was not "Slow Horse", looked at Holmes in a way even more alert and startled than could be explained by this white man's use of the proper Lakota term.

Henry Adams, holding the brim of his straw hat in both hands, took two steps backwards from the two men. Adams felt he was looking at two huge eagles staring into one another's eyes.

Holmes broke the gaze first. He turned to Adams. "I apologize for interrupting, Henry, but Lizzie and the Senator are waiting at Franklin's steam launch at the main pier. Evidently we're running a little late for Mayor Harrison's dinner."

Adams said something to the Indian and turned to leave. Holmes bowed toward the tall man again—still afraid, for some reason, to touch his bare hand—and said, "It has been a pleasure meeting you, Mr. Slow Horse, and I can only hope that someday the *wasichu wanagi* will no longer be a problem for you."

Holmes realized that he'd said that he hoped "the Fat Taker's ghost, that is, the *white man's ghost,* would no longer be a problem for the man", but he had no idea why he'd said it. The Indian responded only by blinking rapidly.

Holmes turned in embarrassment and followed Henry Adams out of the roaring Intramural Railroad Building and had gone about a hundred yards before he stopped, touched the historian's arm, and said, "Please go out to the yacht with the Camerons. I just remembered one last thing I have to do."

"Well…" said Adams, seemingly shaken by something he'd seen or sensed. "If you must, but it would be a crime for you to miss Mayor Harrison's dinner…"

Holmes nodded even though he hadn't really heard Adams's words. He turned and jogged back to the railroad building.

The Indian was gone. Holmes jogged down actual dirt paths and then narrow lanes back to the Parade Ground near the railway entrances, thinking that if the Indian gentleman were there as part of Buffalo Bill's adjacent show, this would be the way he'd leave the fairgrounds.

It was. Holmes caught up to him just before the man went through the metal turning spokes of the exit.

"Mr. Slow Horse!"

The tall man turned slowly. He looked unsurprised to see Holmes again.

"I…there's something I must…if you could help me with…I'm sorry," stammered Sherlock Holmes. "Your name is not Slow Horse, is it?"

"No, it is Paha Sapa," said the other.

"Black Hills," whispered Holmes.

"And your real name is not Sigerson," said Paha Sapa. "You did not even try to hide your Oxbridge English accent."

"My name is Sherlock Holmes." He held out his hand and finally the Indian took it.

Holmes felt the greatest shock in his life, at least since the three bullets had struck him in the Himalayas. He saw and knew immediately that Paha Sapa had felt the same energy pass between them.

When their hands released, the energy was still there between them—far stronger than the ozone and charge in the dynamo room.

"I must ask you, Paha Sapa," said Holmes, "how can I tell if I am real or not?"

"Wicaśta ksapa kiŋ ia," said Paha Sapa.

Holmes somehow understood. *"The wise man speaks…"*

"But I do not yet know if I am a wise man," Paha Sapa finished in English.

"Tell me anyway," said Holmes. "I already know that *I* am not a wise enough man to answer this question."

Paha Sapa's eyes pierced him—it was a physical sensation of being pierced, as with arrows.

"All men born to women are real," said Paha Sapa. "But even some of them are…faint. Weak in reality. The strongest beings are those who sing themselves into existence."

"I don't understand," said Holmes.

"The Six Grandfathers were not born of women, but they are real," said Paha Sapa. "I and all my fathers and grandfathers before me have helped sing them into reality."

Holmes's expression asked the question—*How?*

"By telling their stories," said Paha Sapa and afterwards Holmes could not remember if it had been said in Lakota or English. "By telling their own stories. But mostly by having others tell their stories." Paha Sapa paused a second before saying almost fiercely, "Telling them and *believing* them!"

"Yes," said Holmes, not sure exactly what he was agreeing with but knowing that he agreed with all his heart and soul. *"Pilamayaye,"* said Holmes. "Thank you." It was not enough, but it was all he could get out.

He had nodded and started to turn away when Paha Sapa gripped him firmly by the upper arm. Again it was as if Holmes had walked into the spinning coil of the dynamo.

"Lucan, kte," said Paha Sapa. *Lucan, he kills thee.*

Holmes felt the cold fist of absolute fate start to close around his heart but pushed that away.

"Holmes, uŋktepi! Yakte!" It was said almost in a whisper but it struck Holmes like a shout, a wild war cry in the prairie wind. *Holmes,* you *kill* him. *Thou killest him!*

"Yes," whispered Sherlock Holmes.

Paha Sapa smiled. His deep voice came softly in normal tones as he said—*"Toksha ake čante ista wascinyanktin ktelo. Hecetu. Mitakuya oyasin!"*

Holmes understood it completely—*I shall see you again with the eye of my heart. So be it. All my relatives!*

" Mitakuya oyasin!" replied Holmes. *All my relatives!*

The two men walked away in opposite directions and it took Holmes almost two minutes before he remembered that he was supposed to go to the pier where the boat should be waiting.

8

The full moon was still in the paling western sky beyond the White City when Sherlock Holmes brought Henry James with him to the Manufactures and Liberal Arts Building before six a.m. on Monday.

"I don't understand why I have to be part of this...whatever this is," said the sleepy and irritated James.

"Because you do," said Holmes. "You have been from the beginning and today there must be an ending. You need to be there. Besides, I gave the lady your name for the key..."

"What lady? What key?" stammered James, but fell silent as he saw Colonel Rice, Agent Drummond, and Chicago Police Chief McClaughry waiting for them at the largest of the Great Buildings.

Rice unlocked the door, let them all in, and locked the door behind them. Holmes led the way to the Otis-Hale Company's exposed elevator. There was a metal gate surrounding the elevator area that stayed locked when the lift was closed to the public. Colonel Rice unlocked that outer gate now and handed the key to Holmes, who used it to unlock the actual gate to the elevator.

"You see, Mr. James," said Holmes, handing him the key, "the same key opens both gates. Use it only if a certain lady shows up and asks to go to the promenade roof level. She may be...persuasive."

"But I have no idea of how to handle...to control...to operate..." said James.

Drummond stepped into the elevator and showed a lever to the left of the doorway. "Pull to the left to go up. Further left you go, the faster you ascend. Don't forget to stop at the roof level or we'll have to look for you and your passenger on the moon."

"There's a mechanical sensor that slows it to a stop there no matter what the operator is doing," said Colonel Rice, obviously worried that James would take Drummond literally.

James still shook his head and tried to hand the key back to Holmes.

"Nonsense," said Holmes, refusing to take it. "You've been in a thousand lifts, Mr. James."

"Not so many," grumbled the writer. It was certainly true that London had little use for the modern elevator, any more than his beloved Rome or Florence.

As if the matter had been settled, Holmes turned to Drummond, the two standing within the cage of the elevator car. "How many marksmen did you decide on?"

"President Cleveland is adamant about refusing to have men with rifles visible on the rooftops," said Drummond. "He says that it would make this joyous day feel like Lincoln's Second Inaugural with soldiers stationed on every building."

"Fine, fine," said Holmes. "How many subtle, out-of-plain-view marksmen did you settle on?"

"Twelve," said Drummond. "Prone or otherwise hidden on the top levels of every other Great Building that visually aligns with the full south promenade of this building."

Holmes nodded. "Telescopic sights?"

"Twenty-power," said Drummond.

"Do not forget to remind them that they are not to shoot unless I either give the signal or have been shot down," said Holmes. "We don't want a gun battle raging above the heads of one hundred thousand people."

"How can you be so sure that Lucan Adler will choose the promenade of this building for his sniper's nest?" asked Colonel Rice.

"I just am," said Holmes. "He will be at the easternmost end of the promenade deck. Essentially beside or behind the giant German spotlight mounted there."

"A difficult target from all the angles the marksmen will have," said Chief McClaughry.

"Precisely," said Holmes.

"But we'll never let him get out of this building alive," said Rice.

Holmes smiled and turned to James. "People will be going up and down to the Observation Deck all morning until ten a.m., James," he said softly. "Then men from Colonel Rice's Columbian Guard will make a clean sweep of the entire rooftop area to make sure no one has stayed behind and after that, they will lock both the elevator door and the cage door. You will have the key."

"To give to what lady?" asked James. His voice was shaky.

"You will recognize her from the Irene Adler photograph I've shown you. Auburn hair. Strong chin. Amazing cheekbones. Eyes that are almost violet."

Holmes held out his hand. "Good-bye for now, old boy. Thank you for everything."

James shook the hand and gave one apprehensive glance up at the two hundred vertical feet through which he was supposed to guide that elevator. The four men left the building and Colonel Rice locked the outside door again.

"The Manufactures and Liberal Arts Building will open at its usual scheduled time," Rice said to Henry James. "At ten a.m., my men will make their sweep to empty the Observation Deck and rooftop level and then we'll put up the sign saying that the elevator attraction and promenade deck will be closed to the public between ten a.m. and two p.m. Many will want to get up to get a better view of the president, but all the high walkways will be closed through those hours. You need to be here at ten."

James looked at the large key and put it in his waistcoat pocket. "What should I do until then?" he asked somewhat plaintively.

"If I were you," said Agent Drummond, "I'd take that waiting power boat back to Senator Cameron's yacht and catch another couple of hours' sleep. Just make sure someone wakes you so that you can be here—with the key in your pocket—at ten a.m. You won't have to say anything to anyone—the sign will explain the closure, the outer cage door will be locked, and the disappointed public will go outside on the ground level to see the president."

Later, James didn't remember even nodding before he turned and walked back to the pier.

9

The morning grew chill and cloudy and was threatening rain until minutes before the President of the United States arrived, when the sun emerged on cue and bathed spectators and dignitaries with rich light.

Holmes heard the huge crowd gathered on the Parade Ground around the Administration Building cheer and clap the sun even before the president's procession of carriages came into sight. The detective peered out of the long, narrow slit he'd had Colonel Rice's crew cut out of the metal base below the giant searchlight on the southwest corner of the Observation Deck on the Manufactures and Liberal Arts Building. He could see the length of the walkway to the identical searchlight and metal base on the south*east* corner of the building. If Lucan Adler had chosen some other place for his sniper's roost, the world-famous detective Sherlock Holmes would be the fool lying, sweltering and sweating, in the tight airless box despite the cool morning, curled up like a useless fetus while the President of the United States was shot dead from some other sniper's roost.

Unless one of Colonel Rice's Guardsmen carrying handguns or Agent Drummond's marksmen with rifles saw and shot Lucan Adler before he struck.

Holmes knew they wouldn't.

His watch, which he had laid on the floor in the narrow strip of light coming in, said precisely eleven o'clock when the orchestra played "Hail to the Chief" as President Cleveland climbed the stairs to the speakers' platform. Curled and cramped because of the massive insulated wires filling so much of the space in the steel base, Holmes kept his vigil through the slit but saw no movement. The president was now an easy target for Lucan's '93 Mauser—if that's what he chose—from a hundred other places surrounding the open square massed with people. Holmes guessed correctly from the noise of the applause given the president's arrival and the first of the speakers—voices barely audible to Holmes—that the crowd must be lining both sides of the Lagoon all the way back to and possibly through the Peristyle, spilling out into every side street and out onto the pier itself.

Holmes knew the schedule to the second, so that he knew they'd already fallen at least three minutes behind schedule when the crowd quieted as a blind chaplain gave the Opening Day blessing.

After the debacle of the previous autumn's endless (and freezing) Dedication Day Ceremony, Daniel Burnham and the other Fair directors had decided to keep this opening ceremony as short as possible. But almost a full hour had passed between the president's arrival on the speakers' platform—Holmes heard faint echoes of badly written Odes to Columbus and other time wasters—and Director-General Davis rising to speak briefly and then introduce the president.

Through his east-facing slit, Holmes could see the supposedly locked door of the base of the searchlight at the far east end of the Observation Deck swing open silently. Lucan Adler uncurled himself from the dark space, reached in, and pulled out a long, cloth-covered object. He shook off the black cloth and, even from this distance, Holmes could see that it was indeed the '93 Mauser with the five-round clip and an attached 20X telescopic sight.

Holmes kicked his own door open, got to his feet, and began walking straight toward Lucan.

*　　*　　*

For two hours Henry James stood near the inoperative elevator and heard would-be president-seers express their anger and frustration at not being able to travel to the Observation Deck promenade. But now the president was about to be introduced—the huge hall had emptied out around him and James could faintly hear voices through the opened doors—and James stood alone near the elevator.

Until a few minutes before noon, that is, when a well-dressed woman perhaps in her early forties, a woman with auburn hair, a strong chin, high cheekbones, and violet eyes, came up to him and said, "Are you by any chance the writer Henry James?"

Blinking at being recognized in public, not something that happened to him in America, James said, "Why, yes, I am."

He was about to tip his hat to her when the woman took an ugly-looking and obviously heavy revolver pistol from her cloth handbag and aimed at James's belly.

"Take out the key," she said. "Open these two gates. And then take me up."

James hurried to comply although he almost fumbled and dropped the key at the outer gate and fussed too long with the elevator cage door as well. She all but pushed him into the lift cage and stepped in behind him, the pistol still trained on him.

"Take me up," she said. "Quickly."

James jerked the lever too far to the left, causing the car to lurch up like a rocket, and then he compensated too far to the right, causing it to slow to a near stop only forty feet above the floor.

"Oh, for heaven's sake," snapped the woman, moved James aside, and pushed the lever left so that the elevator hurtled upward.

* * *

Lucan Adler, even leaner and more aquiline in profile than his famous father, had settled in against and partially behind the large searchlight, the Mauser braced on one of the light's metal ridges. Squeezed in between the Observation Deck's fence and the searchlight as Lucan was, Holmes doubted whether he offered a clear target to any of Drummond's men, even if they'd caught his brief movement out and up.

Lucan finished adjusting the telescopic sight with a tiny screwdriver he set back into his shirt pocket—he was wearing no jacket of any kind—and held the Mauser aimed at the president who was in the process of being introduced. But Lucan was also watching Sherlock Holmes approach and was smiling.

When Holmes was about twenty-five long paces away, Lucan swung the rifle in his direction and said, "Stop."

Holmes stopped.

"I can get off three rounds in less than two seconds," said Lucan Adler and Holmes was surprised by the metallic sharpness of his voice. Nothing like his mother's voice. Perhaps more like his father's, Holmes could not be sure.

"Two into the fatboy president's chest and the third round into your belly before you get five feet closer," added Lucan. "If you move your hands toward your jacket or any pocket, I'll kill you first and put two or three rounds into the president before anyone looks up to see what the first noise was."

Holmes knew that he could and would do precisely that. He stood very still.

The president had not begun his short address, but Director-General Davis's introduction was winding down. Holmes knew, and Holmes knew that Lucan knew, that when Davis had introduced Cleveland and the oversized president actually stood at the podium, there'd be a full 90-seconds of "Hail, Columbia" being played and the added time and noise of the audience's loud approval.

The rifle shot killing Holmes during that time wouldn't be heard by anyone down there in the din and probably not by Drummond's sharpshooters either.

Holmes looked at the guy wire that ran from the post at the corner where Lucan hid himself and ran almost three hundred feet out to the warning beacon in the lake. He'd known that Lucan would rig some device there, but the simplicity of it was impressive: just a flywheel atop the wire within a welded unfinished square of metal to hold the wheel on the cable, with a modified bicycle handlebars, completely covered with rubber grips, hanging below it.

"Elegant," said Holmes, nodding toward the escape apparatus. He was sure that a fast powerboat was waiting at anchor next to that tiny beacon island of concrete. "But the police and Secret Service already know about the *Zephyr.*"

Lucan Adler shrugged and smirked. "The *Zephyr* was always meant to be a distraction."

Davis introduced the president and the band and chorus launched into "Hail, Columbia" as the president came up to the low podium. Holmes did not turn his head to look over his right shoulder to see it.

Lucan Adler raised the rifle higher, sighting it on Holmes's chest. "Use just your left hand," Lucan said, just loud enough to be heard over the roar of noise below, "and take off your jacket, waistcoat, and shirt. Quickly! If you don't have them all off in thirty seconds I'll shoot."

Holmes's left hand fumbled with buttons and clasps. But before thirty seconds were up—just a third of the scheduled time for the music and pre-presidential jubilation below—Holmes was standing naked from the waist up.

Lucan continued looking through the sight. "Two exit wounds. Nice cluster for the distance. Turn around. *Now.*"

Holmes turned and looked back toward the searchlight under which he'd hidden for the past six hours.

"Oh, that third entry scar looks very nasty, Mr. Holmes," hissed Lucan. "Is that bullet still in there? No, I think not. Did some humble Tibetan shepherd gouge around with a rusty spoon to dig it out? My, that must still be painful. Turn around and look at me! *Now.*"

Holmes turned to face the young man, hardly more than a boy but with the black-marbled stare of a cobra. Holmes's hands hung loosely by his sides. The sunshine felt good on his naked upper body.

"It makes more sense to kill you before I kill Cleveland," Lucan said, obviously enjoying himself. "But it might be more fun to allow you to watch the president being shot, and *then* dispatch you within those fast two seconds. What do you think, Mr. Detective?"

Holmes said nothing. Behind him, the elevator doors opened.

* * *

Henry James tried to remain in the elevator cage, but the woman—taller and stronger than he was—jerked him out by the arm and pulled him along as they walked east along the Observation Deck.

There was Sherlock Holmes facing the other way, his scars like rays radiating from the moon craters in the bright daylight, and Lucan Adler had swung the rifle in their direction.

"Why Mrs. Baxter," said Lucan with an audible sneer. "Stop there by dear old Dad and keep that goddamned Bull Dog revolver pointed downward."

Stepping beyond Holmes so he could see her, Irene Adler aimed the pistol at Holmes's chest and said, "I don't want to point it downward. I want to point it at his heart." She did just that.

Lucan laughed, a sound like steel rending steel. Above the music and noise below, he said, "And you are Mr. Henry James, the writer, whom Holmes has been dragging around behind him this month and more like a pet lamb on a string. Well, know that you will live out this day, Mr. James. I admire your writing. It is painful to read. I like pain. It should continue."

The music stopped. The crowd cheered and then, like a tide shushing out, fell as quiet as it could.

President Cleveland began to speak. He had a big, space-filling voice, said all the newspapers, but his words were inaudible at this distance. Mouse squeaks followed by wild applause.

"The target first," muttered Lucan and lifted and laid the Mauser along the flange of the searchlight, focusing on the president. Holmes knew that Cleveland's chest and belly would be filling Lucan's 'scope.

"No, Holmes first!" cried Irene Adler, aiming the pistol at Holmes from only seven or eight feet away and cocking the Bull Dog pistol.

At seeing her cock that hammer back, James reacted as he had never reacted before. He jumped at Irene Adler, managing to grab her wrist and force it down even as he realized, too late, that she had already swiveled the pistol away from Holmes and at her son.

The blast of the revolver deafened James.

Instead of hitting Lucan Adler in the chest, where she'd been aiming, the deflected shot struck the young man's right foot. Lucan lost his balance and fell to the deck, but rolled like some jungle cat and came to one knee with the Mauser shouldered, swinging it their way.

Holmes had begun sprinting toward Lucan before the pistol fired, but

James saw in an instant that he wouldn't be able to cover the distance in time.

Cursing in pain as he knelt there, but still holding the rifle with absolute confidence, Lucan Adler aimed and fired.

James felt the bullet buzz past his right ear and Irene Adler cried out and fell face forward. He had the presence of mind to look for the pistol, but she must have been lying on it.

The wounded, cursing Lucan started to swing the rifle barrel at Holmes but Holmes had closed the gap and kicked it aside. The heavy rifle went rattling across the paved promenade.

Lucan had time to crouch and suddenly there was a flat, deadly blade protruding from between the knuckles of his right hand. His right sleeve was torn and James could see the elegant mechanism that had thrust the blade forward. He swung at Holmes's bare belly and, although the detective arched his back like a bow, James could see blood fly.

Lucan Adler turned, leaped over the fence, grabbed the bicycle grips, cut the restraining string with one swing of his bladed hand, and began plummeting out of sight down the long guy wire.

Sherlock Holmes had not paused a second. With his blood still misting the air, he ran at the fence, jumped to its top, and leaped out into two hundred feet of open space.

1 0

The unseen crowd of a hundred thousand people roared as if applauding Sherlock Holmes's suicide. Running toward the south fence beside the searchlight, Henry James saw, in his peripheral vision, huge flags unfurling from the Agriculture and other giant buildings, the huge Statue of the Republic in the Lagoon directly south of him finally dropping its veil, fountains leaping into life. Part of him realized that President Cleveland had lived long enough to depress the gold telegraph key on its velvet pillow.

Later, James had the thought that any true gentleman would have first checked the condition of Mrs. Irene Adler Lorne Baxter, and helped her if he could. But at that moment Henry James didn't give the least goddamn about the condition of Lucan Adler's mother.

He reached the fence at the southeast corner of the building and gasped.

*   *   *

Holmes hadn't been able to leap far enough to get his hands on the rubber-tipped bicycle handlebar. Instead, one hand caught Lucan Adler's belt, the other hand gripped his shirt collar.

The collar came off and the shirt ripped down the seam, even as Lucan began to twist his body toward Holmes. With Lucan's sleeve torn open, James now saw the knife mechanism strapped on his forearm work again—slipping a wide, flat blade between the assassin's knuckles.

Holmes swung himself around the already turning killer and began clambering up Lucan's front like a monkey on a man-shaped climbing bar. His right hand now had a grip around Lucan's neck, pulling the younger man's head down like a lover enforcing a kiss, even while his left shifted quickly from Lucan's belt to grab his right wrist, arresting the blade. But not quickly enough to avoid another wound. James saw blood mist the air again... Holmes's blood.

Henry James looked around wildly. Part of his mind had recorded the sound of the elevator going down and now it was arriving at this level again, but that meant nothing to James. Irene Adler was still lying face-down, possibly dead.

James saw the Mauser rifle. He quickly picked it up—dear Christ it was heavy—and laid it across the top of the metal fence to steady himself while he tried to look through the telescopic sight.

Holding the wood under the barrel tightly, he worked the well-oiled and expertly assembled bolt. A complete bullet—James could see the lead points with little X's gouged into them—ejected and landed under the German searchlight.

For all James knew, that was the last live round in the rifle. He didn't have time to check. Nor did he wonder, as anyone who knew firearms would have, just how far off true the telescopic sight had been knocked in all its being thrown here and there.

For a moment nothing made sense and then, fuzzy but solid in the circle, there were Holmes and Lucan spinning as the single-wheeled mechanism flew down the cable. Lucan's white shirt was torn to tatters and covered with blood—Holmes's blood, James realized. Holmes's bare skin was as white, torn, and blood-spattered as his opponent's shirt.

The only reason they hadn't reached the bottom of this long guy-wired slide was that Lucan's wheel mechanism hadn't been designed for so much weight. It lurched along at high speed for thirty or forty feet, then caught, almost stopped, then lurched down and forward again.

The two men were fighting more like animals than men. When they were still moving quickly, Holmes grabbed Lucan's right wrist and forced the metal release for the knuckle knife up against the wire. Sparks flew. The blade mechanism bent into itself and was now of little use in the fighting.

Lucan switched his right hand to the handlebar and began to pound on Holmes's lower head and shoulders with his free hand, even as Holmes locked his legs around Lucan Adler and clambered up his bloody front. The two men butted heads, bit at each other. Lucan used the fingers of his left hand to claw at Holmes's eyes even as Holmes freed his left hand long enough to swing its wedge into Lucan's throat.

James realized that sweat had clouded his vision. He wiped at his right eye and found the two men in the circular scope again. Their pulley had slowed and they twisted while they fought, bit, kicked, and gouged, but then the wheel seemed to free itself and began falling again toward the still distant beacon island in Lake Michigan.

James saw whiteness fill the telescopic sight, thought that it was— might be—the back of Lucan Adler. He held his breath and squeezed the trigger. He'd not had the butt of the Mauser pressed solidly to his shoulder and now the recoil knocked him backwards from his half-crouch and firmly onto his rear end.

* * *

A hundred and thirty feet down the two-hundred-forty foot guy wire, Holmes had grasped the handlebar and pulled himself up to Lucan's level. The two men were now face to face, Lucan grinning wildly, as they fought with elbows, fists, head butts, and knees.

Lucan had been working on the knife mechanism and now he had the blade firmly between his knuckles again, his left hand locked firmly on the bicycle bar. Holmes's left-handed grip on the bar was more tenuous and left him unable to defend the bare left side of his upper body.

"Die, God damn you!" screamed Lucan Adler, bringing the blade around in a thrust that would reach Holmes's heart.

Holmes said something Lucan couldn't make out—it might have been "God forgive me" or "God forgive you"—but whatever the words were, they meant nothing now that the killing blow was already in motion.

Suddenly a bullet ripped through the narrow space between the two men, tore a furrow through Lucan's upper right arm and shirt, and ripped its way across the back of Holmes's dropping right hand.

The impact was just enough to turn Lucan's dagger thrust to Holmes's heart into a razor-sharp slashing motion that cut through flesh and skidded across a rib.

Holmes pulled the tiny lemon-squeezer cyclist's pistol from his right trouser pocket, pressed it hard into Lucan's belly—high, at the diaphragm just below where the assassin's heavily muscled flesh met bone—squeezed the pistol's handgrip tightly to release its silly lemon-squeezer safety, and fired twice into Lucan Adler's body.

*   *   *

James realized that Drummond and some of his gray-suited men had run up to him while two others were checking on the still unconscious Irene Adler. Drummond heard the two pistol shots, but was sure it was a double-echo of his own rifle shot.

Drummond helped him to his feet just as Lucan Adler, still seventy feet in the air, opened his arms and fell away. Holmes was clinging weakly to the pulley device's handlebars as it picked up speed toward the buoy post.

Lucan fell gracefully, his arms fully extended in what James could only see as a Christlike pose, his head arched back as if he were looking at the sky. James was sure that he would reach the water, but at the last instant, the back of Lucan Adler's head hit the concrete sea wall with a sound that could be heard all the way to where James and the other men stood numbly, dumbly.

Then James saw Holmes either let go or lose his grip and he dropped at least forty feet—but to the water just short of the concrete slabs that supported the beacon-light post. James, Drummond, and two of the agents leaned forward and strained to see if Holmes came to the surface. Drummond looked through his binoculars and then handed them to James.

Holmes hadn't come up. He hadn't come up. He still hadn't come up.

But suddenly Holmes could be seen weakly pulling himself up and over the gunwales of the power boat that Lucan Adler had anchored there. The bloodied Holmes lay on his back on the bottom of the boat and did not move again.

Drummond took back the binoculars and stared. "I think he's breathing. Here come the boats."

From behind the mass of the S.S. *Michigan* warship came roaring eight police boats—three belonging to the Chicago Police Force and five belonging to the Columbian Guard. They all slowed and centered on the boat where Holmes lay bleeding. James saw a man with a doctor's bag step into the blood-washed boat.

Then James had to sit down. On the pavement. Sit and try to breathe.

Drummond crouched next to him and lifted the Mauser with his left hand while patting James on the back with his right.

James shoved the rifle away from him. He knew he would never touch one again as long as he lived. Once again he thought of his brothers Wilkie and Bob, who had carried such death with them into the War and, even after their terrible wounds and pain and in the presence of real Death, eventually rose to carry and use their rifles again. He thought of his cousin Gus, so beautiful that day in the drawing class, whose pale and freckled body was now rotted in mold somewhere under Virginia dirt after a Confederate sniper had expertly done exactly what James had just tried to do. He shook his head.

The joy of *dramatic engagement* that had affected him like too much strong American whiskey at the Chicago stockyards had drained completely out of him now. It was not worth being a fictional character—or a real person, he realized—if ending someone's life through violence was part of the role. It was not civilized. It was not right. It was not Henry James. Nor was it honest to the hard-earned truth of his art.

"Lucan Adler's body hasn't come up yet," said one of the agents still standing at the railing.

Drummond crouched next to the seated writer and repeated that to James as if James had become hard of hearing.

"I...don't...*care*," said James and lowered his head to his raised knees.

11

Who knew that the World's Columbian Exposition of 1893 had its own infirmary? Actually, it was a well-stocked little hospital with squadrons of nurses and five full-time doctors on duty, one of them a woman.

Sherlock Holmes was the seventh person ever brought to the sparkling new infirmary—four women and two men had fainted during the crush and heat of the Opening Ceremony—and the two doctors checking him over (neither one a woman) decided to ask a surgeon more skilled in dealing with thoracic wounds to come down from Chicago General and give his opinion. He came—in a police wagon with a siren wailing and horses nearly out of control—and pronounced the wounds simple enough to deal with. No major organs had been punctured or slashed.

Holmes received stitches over his lower abdomen, his upper belly, his right ribs, his right wrist—which had a strange but shallow bullet-furrow in it—and on his scalp and back. He had a concussion, serious contusions around the head and shoulders, and it turned out that he'd also broken two fingers on his right hand and his right wrist in the "scuffling", as doctors who didn't know the details of the Opening Day's incident called it.

Few people ever did hear about this "incident". Neither Daniel Burnham, Director Davis, Mayor Harrison, nor President Cleveland wanted word of an assassin's presence or violent death on Opening Day known. Almost none of the crowd had seen the incident and most of those few who had thought that it had been a madcap part of the Opening Ceremony. The press was not told about it.

Henry Cabot Lodge's guests didn't mind staying two more days at the Fair until Mr. Holmes would be released; it turned out that the concussion was what kept him in bed the longest. On the third day he left with his torso tightly bound with bandages and his right arm in what he thought was an unnecessary sling, but movement without it hurt his wrist enough that he decided to keep it on for the time being.

Both Andrew L. Drummond and Henry James had visited Holmes in the infirmary, and James was there when Drummond told the detective that Irene Adler was in a room on the floor above him. A room guarded 24-hours a day by two armed Columbian Guardsmen.

"How is she?" asked James. He had been sure she'd been lying dead up there on the promenade deck.

"The slug passed through her shoulder without breaking her collarbone or hitting any major artery," said Drummond. "The lady is very lucky. One bone was nicked but she should heal quickly enough."

"Is she going to face charges?" asked Holmes from his hospital bed.

"Absolutely," said Drummond.

"Charges of what, exactly?" asked Holmes.

"Of...of...she was...of...God *damn* it!" said Drummond.

"Well, keep a good guard on her," said Holmes. "She's a dangerous woman."

* * *

Henry James had decided that he was sailing on the *United States* from New York to Europe, probably to England but possibly all the way to Genoa from whence he could travel to Florence and then north to join his brother William's family in Lucerne. Over James's loud and sincere objections, the Lodges and the Camerons decided that they would go home by way of New York, dropping Harry off—perhaps actually seeing him off at the pier—and staying a week or so to allow the wives and Helen to do some serious shopping while the men had some serious conversations with their Wall Street friends and brokers.

In Buffalo, New York, they had a three-hour layover as a new engine was attached to their private train, and that gave everyone time for luncheon at a decent restaurant there and to stretch their legs.

James returned early and alone to the personal carriage, and one of the valets who helped him said, "There is a gentleman waiting in your compartment to see you, Mr. James."

"What the devil is he doing *in* my compartment?" snapped James.

"He specifically asked to wait there, sir," said the valet, his face crimson with shame. "He said that he knew you, sir. He said that it was vitally important for him to talk to you as soon as you returned, sir. I apologize if I did wrong by allowing him in your private compartment."

James whisked that away with a movement of his hand, but he was not pleased. Not pleased at all.

James had stepped into his small but luxurious compartment and closed the door behind him before he realized that it was almost as dark as night in the room. Someone had pulled down both the lighter and darker shades over his compartment's windows. It took James a second to see the man sitting in the easy chair—the chair in the corner near the lamp sconce, the chair James used for reading—and another second to register just who the man was.

Professor James Moriarty. The dim light showed the overhang of that luminous, deathly brow, the thin white lips, the cadaverous cheeks and white sticks of hair sticking out over his vulpine ears. The tongue kept darting in its reptilian manner over the dried lips. The nails on the long, white fingers were inches long, curved, and yellowed with age and evil.

"We meet at lassst, Mr. Henry Jamesss," hissed Moriarty and stood up.

Lacking even his walking stick with which to fight, James flung open his compartment door when a too-familiar voice behind him said, "You're not leaving so quickly, are you James?"

James spun around.

Moriarty flung up the shades until the compartment was flooded with light. Then he carefully plucked off his long, yellow fingernails, one by one. Then he removed all his teeth, changing the shape of his face. Next the tall man clawed at his own face, pulling off pieces of forehead, cheekbone, nose and chin and dropping the fragments on a towel set out for the purpose. The rest of the forehead and bald pate came off in one piece, but with unpleasant ripping sounds.

Henry James stood there and watched silently while Holmes used some sort of cream and tweezers to remove the rest of "Professor Moriarty's" ears, face, chin, and neck. All the detritus piled up on the large towel atop James's dresser.

"You don't have anything to say about my greatest performance?" asked Holmes. He used James's mirror to brush his hair back into place and then he put his broken right wrist back into the black sling.

"Why?" asked James.

Holmes grinned and rubbed his hands together while ignoring the sling. "My brother Mycroft and I have been building this evil genius, Professor Moriarty, for almost five years now, James. First it was just the rumor of him in Dr. Watson's little fictions. Then actual appearances."

"What about *The Dynamics of an Asteroid*?" asked James. "It's real. I've seen the book."

"Very real," said Holmes. "And mathematically accurate . . . or so they tell me. My brother Mycroft and his old tutor at Christ Church, the don Charles Lutwidge Dodgson, did the maths for 'Professor Moriarty's' mathematical masterpiece."

"And Moriarty's presence at actual astrophysical conferences, as in Leipzig?" asked James.

"All unappreciated performances by yours truly," laughed Holmes. "But years ago I discovered something very interesting—if one takes extra efforts to look repulsive, to smell repulsive, and to behave in a repulsive manner, other people take far less close notice of you."

"Why?" asked James, his voice even more tired than before. "Why this elaborate play-acting?"

"As I said, more than five years of elaborate play-acting," Holmes said softly, sitting on the arm of James's reading chair. James crossed the compartment and sat on the bed. His face was expressionless. Outside, others were returning from their dining and excursions in Buffalo.

"Moriarty brought regular criminals into a true network of crime," said Holmes. "As Moriarty, I guided them into masterpieces of criminal endeavor—half a million pounds in scrip from the Second Reserve

Bank in London, *over* a million pounds in pure gold bullion from the Berne Gold Depository, hundreds of thousands of dollars from the Farmers' Trust Bank in Kansas City, five hundred million lire from Rome's Central..."

"All right, all right," interrupted James. "So I'm sitting and talking to a felon. Someone who's created successful criminal networks and robberies in America, England, and on the Continent for five years now. Why are you still free?"

"All the brilliant Moriarty triumphs were orchestrated through Mycroft and Whitehall, the local constabularies, and the local banks, depositories, whatever," said Holmes. "The stolen scrip turned out to be the highest quality Her Majesty's Government could counterfeit, and by tracking it we traced a diagram of more than a dozen criminal mobs in London, Liverpool, Birmingham, even Cambridge..."

"What about the gold?" said James.

"The criminals had their gold verified by experts," said Holmes. "But Mycroft and his friends took no chances. *We* provided the experts."

"What about the anarchists?" asked James. "Remember, I was at your Washington meeting of thugs and socialists."

Holmes shook his head in what seemed to be admiration. "And I shall forever admire your courage and initiative in doing so," said the detective. "I simply could not tell you about our plans when you shared this...vital information...with me."

"Plans?"

"On May first, in twenty-three cities in nine nations, the police and authorities have rounded up criminals and anarchists pledged to destroy their societies."

"And what will they be charged with?" asked James, putting only a fraction of the contempt he felt into the sarcasm in his tone. "Loitering as a group? Unseemly appearance in public?"

"Ninety-five percent of the criminals we've enlisted and who gathered for the Big Riots and Big Hauls on May first had warrants out for them already," said Sherlock Holmes. "Many in more than one country. For the anarchists, those who showed up at the designated places with bombs and guns will be charged immediately, the rest put on a watch list."

"So you…and your brilliant brother Mycroft…invented Professor James Moriarty, went to great pains to give him a believable mathematical background, turned him into the Napoleon of Crime, and then had the fictional villain kill you at Reichenbach Falls in Switzerland, to free you up, I presume, to spend three years running around in your little Moriarty disguise enlisting burglars and anarchists."

"Yes," said Holmes. "That is about it. I did ask for six months of my own time after my death at Reichenbach Falls so I could visit Tibet and ask some questions of the Dalai Lama. But that became a rather longer stay due to young Lucan's skill with a rifle."

"Three bullets through you," Henry James said softly. "I saw the size of those rounds…cartridges…bullets…whatever you call them, when I worked the bolt-action of that Mauser and one ejected. It was huge. How could you not have died?"

"Perhaps I did," said Holmes.

"To hell with this metaphysical tommyrot you've been shoveling onto me since we met," snapped James, standing suddenly. "You can go spend the rest of your life…if it is a life…asking yourself and everyone you meet if you're real. Sooner or later some drunk in some pub smelling of urine and sweat will give you a definitive answer."

"I've already received a good answer," Holmes said softly. "Just a few days ago."

James said nothing.

"Have you ever heard of singing yourself into existence?" asked Holmes. "Or others singing someone—perhaps you—into existence by telling stories about them? Passing the stories along? Is that what you're doing with your writing, Henry James…singing yourself into greater existence every day you work at your craft?"

James ignored all that twaddle. "Why," he said sharply, "were you and a bunch of thugs at the central Chicago railway station that Saturday morning when I was trying to get to New York?"

"Looking for you, James. And the 'thugs' were some of Colonel Rice's men he loaned me…there were too many carriages for me to check in the short time before your scheduled train left."

"Why were you, as Professor Moriarty, looking for me when I was trying to get out of all this . . . leave this fever dream . . . and go home to England?"

Holmes stood. "I was going to show you my Moriarty disguise that morning and ask you not to leave yet. To see our shared mystery through."

"Shared mystery," repeated James, pouring scorn into every syllable. "You never even solved poor dead Ned Hooper's question of who sends those typed cards every December six. 'She was murdered', remember?"

"The game's not over yet," said Holmes. His bandaged right hand and broken wrist obviously were hurting him and he shifted his arm in its black sling.

"Do you want to know what I think about your precious game?" asked Henry James.

"I do, very much, yes," said Holmes.

Henry James had never done this in his life, not even as a boy wrestling with William or Wilkie, not even at his angriest, but now he turned his right hand into the most solid fist he could and hit the Great Consulting Detective Sherlock Holmes on his pointed chin as hard as he could.

Holmes flew backward onto the bed, totally surprised. When he could sit up, he used his good left hand to rub his jaw. "I deserved that, I guess," he said softly. "I'm sorry, James. Especially since I've come to think of you as a friend and I really have no friends."

James turned and left his own compartment and walked forward through carriages until he reached the ladies' common area where he sat and listened to them for a while, pretending to be the tame cat that he often longed to be.

* * *

Holmes waited until a stop in Albany where John Hay and most of the others got out to stretch their legs before he approached Clara Hay, who had stayed behind with one of her headaches.

"May I speak to you privately, Mrs. Hay?"

She smiled wanly and touched her temple. "I have a bursting headache right now, Mr. Holmes. Perhaps later?"

"Now is a better time, Mrs. Hay," said Holmes and walked into her compartment and sat on a straight-backed chair.

"Well, I'll call for some tea," said Clara Hay. When the serving girl hurried in with a tray of hot tea and plates of scones and biscuits, Holmes said, "You may step out now and close the door behind you, Sally."

Shocked at the man in Mrs. Hay's compartment giving her orders, Sally looked to Clara Hay to see what to do. Mrs. Hay also looked shocked, or at least nonplussed, but she nodded for Sally to leave. Then she sat in her overcushioned embroidering chair, about as far away from Holmes as she could get in a train compartment. Even a luxury train compartment.

"What is it, Mr. Holmes?" she asked in a tiny voice. "Shouldn't John be here to be part of this discussion?"

"No," said Holmes. He picked up his cup of tea and saucer, added a bit of cream, and drank the steaming liquid. Clara Hay remained very, very still and watched him as if she had found herself in a room with a rattlesnake.

"I know that you typed and delivered all the 'She was murdered' cards, Clara," said Holmes. "You should probably stop doing that now."

"That is the most offensive and ridiculous thing that I have ever..." began Clara Hay, raising both hands to her cheeks.

"You and Mr. Hay stayed three days at Mr. Clemens's Hartford home in the year after Clover Adams died," said Holmes. "You were often alone and Clemens even remembered you asking how to operate his new typing gadget."

"Ridiculous..." managed Clara Hay, but could say no more than that.

"I tracked down two of Mr. Clemens's servants who remembered the sound of typing coming down from the billiards room when Clemens and Hay had gone out for a walk and you were alone in the house all afternoon, Clara," said Holmes. "But in the end it was the money, Mrs. Hay, that tipped me off to your involvement."

"Money?"

"In the spring of eighteen ninety-one, shortly before I had to leave for the Reichenbach Falls charade, Clover's brother Ned asked me to come to America to investigate the 'mystery cards' that appeared each year on the anniversary of Clover's death. I've told people the truth, that I took one dollar from him so that I would be on retainer and get to the puzzle when I could . . . too late for poor Ned, I'm sorry to say . . . *but he offered me three thousand dollars* to come to America right then and to solve this disturbing card case before I went on to anything else."

"Ned never had three thousand dollars in his life," whispered Clara Hay.

"Precisely what your husband and Henry Adams said when I mentioned the sum," said Holmes. "They insisted that Ned had fantasized that amount of money, Mrs. Hay. *But Ned showed me the three thousand dollars in my room at two-twenty-one-B Baker Street.* He begged me to take it and to follow him back to America immediately where, he said, there would be more money if I did my job correctly. I sensed even then that Ned Hooper had never even had the funds to travel to England alone. It was someone else's money. Someone else's need for a detective."

Clara Hay looked Holmes in the eye with a bold defiance that he never thought she could muster. "Are you asking for the three thousand dollars now, Mr. Holmes? Now that you have . . . how does Dr. Watson put it in the story magazines? . . . Now that you have 'cracked' this insoluble case? Or do you want more to keep your silence? My private checkbook is here." She actually removed it and a pen from a drawer in the nearby secretary.

"All I want to know is why, Mrs. Hay? Why seven years of making sure that all the four survivors of the Five of Hearts received that note every December sixth?"

"Because I knew something was *wrong,*" said Clara with a near growl of defiance. "I never even liked Clover Adams that much, Mr. Holmes. I thought she was arrogant and condescending and often acting above her real station. We had the Five of Hearts, Mr. Holmes, but in the five p.m. conversations and tea in front of the Adamses' fireplace every evening, Clover was always the First Heart . . . Henry Adams and my own John have referred to her that way ever since her suicide . . . and I wasn't even the Fifth Heart. The men used to joke with Clarence King that he needed to marry one of his swarthy South Seas women so that we could have a Sixth Heart, *but I was already the Sixth Heart.* Never fast enough with a witty rejoinder. Never witty enough when I did say something. Never knowledgeable enough about any of their fast-moving discussion topics at the right time..." She did not so much stop talking as she just ran down like a wind-up toy. She had been pointing the pen at Holmes like a stiletto or a pistol, but now she capped it and put it back on the secretary with her oversized checkbook. "I knew that when that Rebecca Lorne went out of her way to make friends with poor lonely, miserable Clover Adams that someone—most probably Rebecca or her hideous cousin Clifton—was up to something. Something harmful. Something that would be too much for Clover to handle. I still believe in my heart that this was the reason for Clover's suicide, if suicide it actually was."

The two sat in deep silence for several minutes.

Finally Holmes said softly, "But that's not the real reason you sent Ned Hooper over to London to hire me with that fortune to investigate things about the Five Hearts."

She jerked and then sat absolutely upright. She was almost unable to get her next words out through her tightened throat.

"What can...you...possibly...mean...Mr. Holmes?"

The detective reached into his jacket pocket and brought out four letters, each still in its mauve envelope and addressed in John Hay's bold, manly hand.

"I've seen you at dinners, Mrs. Hay," Holmes said softly. "I watch people and observe. While you were always the perfect hostess, you were also busy observing every word your husband said to the women at the table, every way he spoke to them, observing his every glance and move. Especially toward Nannie Lodge, who had these letters from Mr. Hay hidden in her bedroom."

Clara audibly gasped. "How could you possibly...stealing someone's private correspondence...breaking and entering..."

"Not at all," Holmes said with a smile. "I just had a small and wiry confederate with spiky green hair and instructions on where to look in the places where married women hide love letters from married men not their husbands. These letters—and others, but these were the important ones as I suspect you know—were taped to the bottom of Nannie Lodge's lingerie drawer."

The same place Lizzie Cameron's love letters from Henry Adams were hidden in her boudoir, thought Holmes. *Women are conniving, but I think too much like them to allow them to outsmart me.* Then he had to smile. *All save for Irene Adler.*

"Here," said Holmes and handed her the four letters. She accepted them as Cleopatra must have accepted the serpent that was going to nurse Death from her breast.

"If I read them..." she began hesitantly.

"You'll never forget some of the wording and images," said Holmes. "But you need to know that these are always the words and images that men suddenly encountering middle-age and their own mortality use in their foolish love letters. It is pure insanity. And purely *male* insanity."

Clara Hay spoke as if Holmes were not even there. "John used to send me love letters. And wonderful poetry I'd never heard of. And flowers. But then...as I got heavier after the children...I came home from church one Sunday and heard John laughing with that lout Samuel Clemens about how I...this is the way my darling husband put it...'Clara didn't get out of the hotel much during our Chicago visit but she certainly tucked into her victuals with enthusiasm.'"

She looked at Holmes as if first noticing his presence. "I love John more than life...I've given my life to John and the children...but at that minute I could have shot both him and that idiot Clemens dead on our parlor rug."

Holmes nodded and said nothing.

Clara kept staring at the letters, holding the envelopes away from her as if they could strike like serpents. "Won't Nannie Lodge notice that these are missing?" she whispered.

"Oh, yes," said Sherlock Holmes and allowed himself his rare grin. "She shall. I promise you she shall. And then...well, the concern about where those particular letters might have gone will be very great. I think you will see a change both in Nannie Lodge's behavior *and* in your husband's. Perhaps a permanent one."

"Then I don't really have to read these after all," she whispered.

"No," said Holmes and held out his hands, cupped slightly, palms up, as if he were ready to give or accept some Holy Communion.

He saw the recognition ignite in Clara Hay's eyes and, holding one envelope after another over his hands, she tore each into tiny shreds and had Holmes use his fancy cigarette lighter to burn each scrap above an oversized crystal ashtray. Soon Sherlock Holmes's hands were filled with tiny confetti—despite the bandage on his right hand, he'd not let one scrap of torn paper escape the flames—and now he used his good left hand to put that confetti into his jacket pocket.

"I'm going to go now, Mrs. Hay," he said, standing. "Go into the men's room in this station and flush some unwanted and useless scraps of paper down the toilet."

She stared at Holmes with luminous eyes, then touched her checkbook again. "The...money...?"

"I never came to America for money's sake," said Holmes. "I did so for Ned's sake. And, I think, for yours. Good afternoon, Mrs. Hay. We may not have the chance to talk again until I leave the train in New York."

* * *

The revelers gave Henry James a raucous bon voyage party, both at a fine restaurant on 32nd Street and then again at the wharf where the great S.S. *United States* was making final preparations to shove off. The tugs were already pushing their netted snouts into position.

"Funny that Holmes didn't come to dinner or stop to say good-bye," mused James when all the farewells fell silent for a moment.

"Perhaps he forgot the time," said Henry Cabot Lodge. "He's always struck me as a preoccupied fellow."

"Perhaps his injuries were bothering him," said young Helen.

"Or more likely he had another case to solve," said John Hay.

"Well," said Senator Don Cameron, his arm around his wife Lizzie who was smiling at Adams, "we had about enough of that man's company for one year. But you, Harry, you must hurry back to visit again."

James shook his head. "You need to come to London or Paris or Italy to see me."

Cameron and Lodge exchanged odd glances. "With the bank and Wall Street panic that we think is coming like a tsunami," said Henry Cabot

Lodge, "I suspect that most of New York's, Boston's, and Washington's better families will be living on the cheap in Europe by July or August, leaving their servants here to fend for themselves and their great houses shut up until this particular storm is past. Then they'll come wandering home in a year, or two, or three. Those that survive the storm, I mean."

"Now stop it, darling!" cried Lizzie Cameron, pretending to hit her husband on the shoulder. "No gloomy talk while we're wishing Harry bon voyage."

"It's not gloomy if it means you'll be in London to see me soon," said James and lifted his hat as he walked up the gangplank at the ship's final all-passengers-aboard, all-visitors-ashore whistle of steam. "Adieu!" he called over the scream of escaping steam.

Epilogue

Henry James hated epilogues and refused to use them in his fiction. He said that life granted us no "epilogues", so why should art or literature? Life, as he knew all too well, was just one damned thing after another. And there were no real summings up in life and definitely no curtain calls.

I feel much the same way about epilogues—as you may also—but this one is here and we have to deal with it.

*   *   *

By his last evening on the high seas—the steamer *United States* was scheduled to touch at Portsmouth but then go on to Genoa, where James had decided to start the last leg of his trip to see William and his wife Alice and their children in Lucerne—Henry James was bored.

The weather was perfect and the seas so calm that all the experienced travelers and even the crew kept commenting on it. James didn't care to play backgammon or the other silly games going in the common areas, so he read—either in his pleasant cabin or on his pleasant lounge chair, a blanket across his legs and lap, or while lunching alone. He'd been set at a table of important people for every evening's meal, but the men's "importance" was in business, and Henry James listened and nodded politely but had little if anything to say on the subject. He thought a lot about his play and about these days he was wasting when he should be writing.

It was sunset of that fourth evening when James was leaning on the mahogany railing in the first-class section, looking behind the ship at its wake and the beautiful sunset into the Atlantic, when he realized that another man had moved very close and was leaning on the rail next to him.

"Holmes!" he cried, then looked around to see if anyone had noticed his absurd shout. The detective was no longer wearing his sling but his right hand was still bandaged.

"Why are you here?" asked James. "Where are you going?"

"I believe the ship is headed to Portsmouth and then on to Genoa," Holmes said softly. He looked thinner and much more pale than he had in America.

"Why didn't you tell me..."

"That I'd booked passage on the same ship you were taking back to Europe?" said Holmes with that thin, fast flick of a smile. "I didn't think you'd be overjoyed to hear the news. I planned to make the entire crossing, no matter how far you were going, without letting you know I was aboard."

"But where have you been hiding yourself?" asked James.

Again that flicker that never quite resolved itself into an actual smile. "If you want the blunt truth, Harry, I've been in my cabin puking my kidneys out and trying not to scream like a gorilla on fire for more than four days and nights."

James took half a step back along the rail at the crude language. "But the crossing has been so *smooth.* The ocean's been a mill pond. Even the old ladies who get seasick looking at a large cup of tea have been healthy and busy on this crossing."

Holmes nodded and James could see that his forehead was beaded with sweat despite the pleasant coolness of the evening and the ship's movement through the fresh air.

"I decided that I had to go off that heroic medicine that I was injecting into myself several times a day there in America," Holmes said softly. "Did I mention that heroin substance by name?"

"No," said James. "I thought you... I wasn't sure what I thought..."

"Anyway," said Holmes with that smile, "even two months' use of that stuff makes stopping the use of it a terrible experience. I may see Dr. Watson in the coming months, and he would be most disappointed in me if I came back to England addicted to some new poison."

"So you've quit this heroic drug for good?"

"Oh, yes," said Holmes. "But that's not why I came up to find you, James."

"Why did you?"

"Because, after my four and a half days and nights of vomiting, my head was suddenly clear and I realized why you were so out of sorts and brooding those last days in America."

James looked away and felt the bile rise in his own throat. "It's what I did," he said at last. "I shall never truly get over it."

"And what do you think you *did?*" asked Holmes.

James rounded on Holmes with some of the old ferocity in his gray eyes. "I killed a man, Holmes. I shot and killed a human being. He was a villain and deserved to die . . . but not by my hand. I'm an artist, a creator, not . . ." He trailed off.

"That's what I thought you thought," said Holmes. "And you're crazy, Henry James. You should have been at the debriefings with Drummond and Colonel Rice and the others after the unpleasantness, rather than wandering away."

"What are you talking about, Holmes?"

Holmes held up his bandaged right hand and wrist. "Your rifle didn't kill anyone, James. It passed through Lucan Adler's shirt sleeve . . . and perhaps brushed him enough to make him flinch and save my life from that blade . . . then it burned its way across the back of my hand and went on its merry way into the lake. You . . . shot . . . and . . . *killed* . . . no . . . one."

James felt like crying from a sense of relief that almost made him sick, but instead gripped the wooden rail harder and stared into the disappearing sun behind the ship.

"Oh," said Holmes, "when I was finished with my little drug withdrawal adventure, I realized that I forgot to tell you about two relevant telegrams that I received in New York shortly before we sailed." Holmes took the flimsies from his breast pocket.

James, even though he felt that he could take his first deep breath in weeks, listened with some dread.

"The first one was from our friend Agent Drummond and is purely informational," said Holmes, unfurling the folded flimsy with some difficulty with his bandaged hand. "I quote:

PLEASE BE INFORMED THAT IRENE ADLER ESCAPED CUSTODY AT THE COLUMBIAN EXPOSITION INFIRMARY THE DAY AFTER YOU LEFT CHICAGO STOP GUARD MEMBERS FOUND THAT SHE HAD CUT HER HAIR OVER THE SINK QUITE SHORT WE BELIEVE, AND THAT ONE OF THEIR OWN GUARDSMEN HAD BEEN OVERPOWERED, STRIPPED OF HIS OUTER CLOTHING, TIED AND GAGGED, AND STUFFED IN A CLOSET STOP IRENE ADLER MAY HAVE ESCAPED IN A COLUMBIAN GUARDSMAN UNIFORM POSING AS A MAN STOP BE ON THE LOOKOUT FOR A WOMAN WITH HER LEFT ARM STILL IN A SLING STOP SHE MAY BE ARMED AND IS CONSIDERED EXTREMELY DANGEROUS STOP DRUMMOND"

James hadn't meant to but he started laughing and found it difficult to stop. Holmes joined in and it only made James laugh the harder. He really couldn't have said why he was laughing so hard. It's just that everything unreal finally felt . . . *over.*

"This telegram I received in New York right before we sailed will sober you up fast enough, James. I assure you." Holmes unfolded the flimsy and read carefully, in a slightly deeper voice than usual. "From my brother Mycroft, who never concerns himself about the cost of extra words in a telegram. Neither of us does. From Mycroft:

SHERLOCK IMPERATIVE THAT YOU CONTINUE ON TO GENOA ABOARD THE SHIP UNITED STATES AND THEN MAKE YOUR WAY NORTH TO LUCERNE SWITZERLAND AS QUICKLY AS YOU CAN STOP I WILL BE THERE IN TEN

DAYS STOP THIS IS A CONFERENCE OF INTERNATIONAL IMPORTANCE STOP YOUR PRESENCE IMPERATIVE STOP MYCROFT"

Holmes tucked away the telegram flimsies and the two men looked bleakly at each other.

"Your older brother and my older brother both in Lucerne," said Henry James in a disbelieving, stunned voice. "And us there with them? Inconceivable."

"I agree," Holmes said glumly.

Suddenly a young man with his heavy coat thrown over his shoulders and an oversized derby pulled down absurdly low walked past. The youthful voice said, "Good evening, Mr. Holmes."

James jerked his head around but caught only a glimpse of the young man's strong chin, high cheekbones, and dark hair clipped American military-short on the sides and in back.

"Friend of yours?" asked Henry James.

The sun had disappeared. All the ship's electric lights came on suddenly, brilliantly, the way they had at the Chicago World's Fair that Opening Night. Before the lights came on like fireworks, in the gloom and instant of the youth's passing them, Sherlock Holmes had seen the young man's left arm in a black sling under the open, caped overcoat.

Holmes passed his good arm through Henry James's and leaned with the older man over the railing. The sea air was so fresh as to be intoxicating.

"We'll deal with Lucerne and older brothers when we come to them," Holmes said, sounding happy for the first time since Henry James had first met him that rainy night along the Seine two months earlier.

"In the meantime, my friend," said Holmes, "this could turn out to be a very interesting journey after all."

June 2013–October 2014

ACKNOWLEDGMENTS

I wish to acknowledge the following people for their help in allowing me to write *The Fifth Heart*.

My wife, Karen.

My agent, Richard Curtis, to whom this book is dedicated. "I wish I had a better book for so good a man." (Robert Louis Stevenson's inscription to Henry James.)

My publishers, Reagan Arthur and Michel Pietsch, who encouraged me to go ahead with this rather odd pairing of Sherlock Holmes and Henry James.

My new editor, Joshua Kendall, whose understanding of the best complexities I can produce and whose suggestions were wonderfully helpful.

Also Gretchen Koss, chief of publicity; Catherine Cullen, senior publicist; Peggy Freudenthal, executive production editor.

To my much-needed and respected copy editor, Susan Brandanini Betz, whose self-proclaimed "obsessive compulsion disorder" (on getting words, facts, dates, names, and such right) served me and the novel wonderfully well.

Finally, thank you again to my good friend and excellent sociologist, Dr. Dan Peterson, who provided the many mixed CDs of "Music to Listen to While Writing Good Novels." The CDs were superb. Any failure to provide "good novels" is completely my own.

Thank you all.